SPACE
An Odyssey in Rhyme

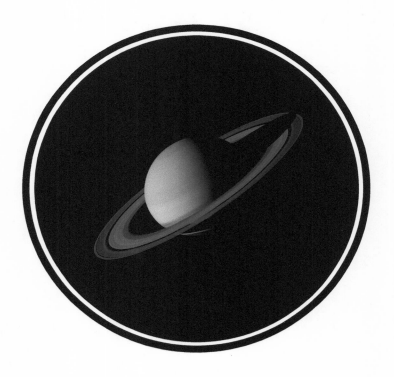

SPACE
An Odyssey in Rhyme

James T. Sapp

Blue and Gold Publishing

2020

First Printing: 2019
Second Printing 2020

ISBN 978-1-79477-463-6

Blue and Gold Publishing
Post Office Box 6621
Longmont, Colorado 80501

www.blueandgoldpublishing.com

For my Encourager, with a tip of the hat to Chesley Bonnestell and with apologies to Oz for the Strine.

Contents

Preface xi

Prologue 1

  The Captain's Lament 1

  The Doctor's View 2

1 First Flight 3

2 Introductions 8

3 Rude Awakening 23

4 Food for Thought 32

5 Mars 52

6 Soldana 61

7 Dinner and Delight 88

8 A Better Offer 103

9 Decision 118

10   Departure 122

11   Date Night 128

12   Discovery 139

13   Into the Deep 146

14   Progress 151

15   Nocturne 153

16   Snap Decision 166

17   Saturn 176

18   Titan 190

19   A Far Country 195

20   Catching Up 205

21	New Friends	212
22	Candlelight and Flowers	219
23	Off-Leash!	231
24	Job Well Done	235
25	Jonesy	239
26	Jackrabbit	251
27	Stroke of Darkness	259
28	Terror and Atrocity	269
29	Rewind	276
30	Worth His Salt	281
31	Revelations	290
32	A Small Request	297
33	Making the Point	303
34	Rendezvous and Pow Wow	313
35	Tripping the Trigger	323
36	Boomerang	330
37	Vignette	339
38	Iapetus	341
39	Message in a Bottle	344
40	Two Plus Two	349
41	Engagement	354
42	Moonshine and Musings	361
43	Descent	368
44	Kumbaru	377
45	Backlash	379
46	Mousetrap	389

47	A Message from Mars	398
48	The Black Ring	402
49	Confidence and Conscience	407
50	It's a Go!	411
51	Contact	414
52	Troubled Angels	425
53	Reunion	428
54	Dominos	441
55	Waiting	444
56	No Plan Lasts...	446
57	A Toast!	456
58	Raven Down	459
59	Nail in the Coffin	468
60	The Little Bird	473
61	Gloves Off	476
62	Getaway!	487
63	Shattered	496
64	A Necessary Evil	506
65	Spurs and Bugles	526
66	Dreams	535
67	Trouble at Veles	544
68	Judgment	556
69	Help Wanted	562
70	Enceladus	564
71	Respite	572
72	Banquet on Barsoom	575

73   **Ribbons, Bows and Bells** 590

74   **Castle West** 594

Epilog 599

Appendix A 602
    List of Principal Characters 602
    Captain Blue's Crew 603
    Residents of Titan 604

Appendix B 605
    Australian Slang as Used on Titan 605

Glossary 610

Preface

Many who were born and grew up in the 1940's through 1970's were enraptured with the looming prospect of firsthand exploration of the solar system. Our imaginations soared in anticipation of colonization and development on the new frontier. The stars in our eyes grew yet brighter with exposure to the paintings of Chesley Bonestell, and the writings of men like Arthur C. Clarke, Ray Bradbury and Robert Heinlein who transported us through the mind's eye to that grand and exciting future. In this verse-novel I have tried to capture some of that spirit, whether nostalgic to the gray hairs or hopeful to the young.

With the rapid acceleration of technological advances in the past half century, the world of this story is no longer a far reach and the possibilities are legion. It is not hard to imagine environment suits made of nano-sized heat pumps, atomics-powered rockets, cold fusion reactors, laser weaponry, artificial intelligence, and any number of other emerging technologies. However, in this story I have refrained from describing much in the way of new technologies and I have used much of the current and familiar. Rather than the hardware they possess, this is a story about people, coping in a future that is patiently waiting for those who would dare to make it.

I hope you enjoy reading this novel-in-verse as much as I did writing it.

- James T. Sapp

Prologue

The Captain's Lament

I've basked on sun-baked beaches, richly dined on precious spice
Flown the farthest reaches, walked alone on worlds of ice
I've skimmed the amber clouds of Titan, swum its carbon seas
Stood upon the tallest mountains, been one with the breeze.

I've drunk the cup of misery in cruel, cold defeat
I've danced the dance of victory, the vanquished at my feet
And on a hundred beaches I have sifted through the sand
And felt the work of eons trickle through my open hand.

I've lived in deprivation and in splendored marble halls
I've danced with grim starvation and I've tasted nearly all
The pleasures that great riches can procure at ransom's price
And yet my soul still itches for that one elusive vice:

To walk with she whose heart is bound forever to my own
For she has been the central part of where my soul calls home.
I've dreamt before my life unravels I'll have one more chance
To cease my fevered travels and renew our sweet romance.

For here within my thirsting chest I still can feel her call
But is it mourning madness of heart's pieces as they fall?
I've searched the diamond-spangled starscape from a hundred moons
And scoured their empty landscapes dreading I would find her tomb

And yet the quiet whisper of a bond forged by the fates
Like a loving sister bids me still behold her face
In images of memories fire-branded in my soul
And so my searching vagaries drive me where e're I go.

Captain Jules Blue
June, 2135

The Doctor's View

From the moment of creation years ago untold
Wheeling in their steady courses, moons and planets cold
Shining in the blackness of the sky's eternal night
As candles in the darkness they attract our feeble sight.

But in the limits that are placed upon our mortal frames
We don't see the glory of these lights and stellar flames.
The cold of dark and heat of light in such a narrow band
(Just a tiny slice is all we sense with eye or hand)

Until with feeble instruments through which we keenly peer
As if through smoky clouds at night so faintly some comes clear
Variety and beauty beckon us from everywhere
Yet creation's vastness is more harsh than we can bear.

Secure upon our little globe, protected, warm and fed
Our weakness becomes fatal just one small step from our bed:
Pressure, water, temperature and right mix for our air
In all the places we may go are precious and so rare!

Then when we venture forth as we are ever drawn to do
Seeking knowledge of whatever might come into view
We take all that we are with us, our needs for life and limb
And face the challenge of our futures, whether glad or grim.

The very nature of our hearts accompanies us there
And nothing's really left behind, we bring our own despair:
Our greed and avarice, our lust, our honor pure and true
Our nurturing and caring from warm hearts of loving too.

This story isn't new, it's been our fate from early days
And only by the hardest choices may we change our ways.
Reaching to the future for a better life for all
And straining for the whisper of redemption's siren call.

Doctor Haji al Hawija
Aboard the Indifferent
April, 2137

1   First Flight

'*Stark*' is the word which popped immediately to mind
On gazing out the porthole for the very first time.
The harshly lighted mountains and the blackness of the depths
Of shadows in the cracks and craters made him bate his breath.

And though he'd looked through telescopes a hundred times or more
And simulated landings and seen photos by the score
None of that prepared him for this new reality
Of seeing lunar landscapes with his own eyes, optics free.

The trip from earth was spent in learning how to rig his gear
For zero G procedures while the moon was growing near
And getting acclimated to the room in which he'd wait
The weeks to get to Titan where they'd land this aging crate.

With not a single earthly reference all across the view
Judging distance wasn't something natural to do.
The distance to the features passing rapidly below
Could be as little as two hundred meters (who could know?)

Or perhaps two hundred thousand meters was his height?
The curve of the horizon was the only clue in sight.
Regardless what the distance, in the clearness of the void
It seemed that he might touch it were not porthole glass employed.

Scorching hot where sunlight touched and frozen in the shade
The contrast on the landscape was as stark as any made.
Empty and pristine, a vast and barren hunk of rock
But still he wanted desperately upon that ground to walk.

"A hell of a place, isn't it?" quipped the engineer
Who came up quick behind him spraying hot breath in his ear.
"But it's like Heaven next to that cold hell you're going to
"Where everything is poison that'll kill and freeze you too."

The garlic on his breath had just a tinge of whiskey fumes
And in his dirty hands he held a greasy wrench or two
But in his eyes the years he'd spent on many worlds and ships
Had left a deepness that betrayed a firm trustworthiness.

"It's beautiful! I'd love to spend some time there on a walk."
The passenger remarked with wonder making polite talk
Then turning his attention to the porthole once again
He saw their speed across the ground grew faster, it was plain!

To the south the rim of great Theophilus was seen
And closer, Torricelli's shadows dark were very keen.
Forward, Sinus Asperitatis' mountains rose up thick
And they were still descending and accelerating quick.

Then with some alarm he saw their height above the ground
Suddenly decreased. Was their orbit really sound?
The sudden impulse to lift up one's feet was done without
A conscious thought while gripping on a seat with growing doubt.

"Look through the forward port." the engineer said with a grin
Then strapped into a seat (his smile turned a little grim)
And leaning back against the headrest closed his eyes to wait
As if resigned to some unseen unpleasant ugly fate.

"You see that eastward gap within the ruined crater wall?
"And on the other side you see the mountains standing tall?
"When, like now, the angle of the sun is set just right
"Through that gap across the crater floor's a shaft of light.

"If you watch with care for just an instant you might see
"Our shadow cross the crater floor and up the mountain's lee.
"There is a bit of chance that it will be the final sight
"You have in this life. This may be our tragic final flight!"

Smiling, the passenger turned 'round to take the joke
But that old engineer was reaching for his pack of smokes.
There was no smile on his face; just tired blue eyes dim
(The passenger considered it was just a prank on him.)

The cabin lights turned red to give the visual alert
That soon acceleration would commence ("So don't get hurt:
"Get into a seat and buckle up to ease the force
"From the engines' thrust to set the ship's new speed and course!")

Soon three flashes followed by a kick against his back
Found him hoping that it was enough to change their track

For looming out the porthole was Hypatia growing close
And there was no denying his companion was morose!

The engineer's blue eyes were tight and sweat was on his brow
Then suddenly his stomach bolted forward toward the bow.
The stars outside the porthole reeled as thrusters spewed hot gas
And both of them were wondering if this trip was their last!

A kick that didn't stop for several seconds shook his teeth
And from the corner of his eye the mountain passed beneath.
The engineer then pulled a flask out of his rumpled shirt
And offered with a motion if he'd like to have a squirt:

"Congratulations, Newbie. You've just passed through Hell's Wide Gate.
"There aren't many that have done it in these years of late.
"There's wreckage on that mountainside and scattered all around
"Are pieces of the men that missed the mark and hit the ground.

"That maneuver's something that no ion drive can do
"Or those solar sails that haul cargo, slow but true.
"Even our atomic torch ships can't kick into gear
"Like good old-fashioned rockets that put G's against your rear!"

"I see that." said the passenger, his face a ghostly white.
"Does the captain do this just to give we newbies fright?"
The engineer looked at him one long moment then replied,
"Don't think you're the only one who hates that little ride.

"There are worse, but when the sun and angles line up right
"He'll often make that run before we make a lengthy flight.
"You see, it brings some memories, or somehow sets a mood
"Within him that will leave him silent while a day he broods."

Looking out the porthole once again there was a change:
The features of the surface on this night side looked more strange.
Ghostly gray in darkness, only lit by earthshine's glow
Were rapidly receding in the distance far below.

After several minutes passed the forward hatch swung wide
Where darkness framed the captain's form as he stood still inside
Then with a quick push from the cockpit turned to face the two
Who watched him closely waiting for the next thing he would do.

"We are on our way." the captain said direct and plain
Then moving toward the rearward hatch said not a word again.
The passenger, confused by this quick visit and short word
Started with a question as he turned engineer-ward.

"Shhhh!" quietly hissed the man, his finger crossed his lips
Calling for his silence 'til the captain went 'mid-ships.
"He likes you," said the engineer, "He said those words for you.
"That doesn't happen often, you can check with all the crew."

Surprised and even more confused the passenger inquired,
"Why did he maneuver with our lives hung on a wire?
"And what about our trip and what about his silent way?
"I've not heard a word from him since boarding the first day!"

The engineer drank from his flask and tucked it safe away
Then pulled a long drag from his smoke and nodding cabin's way
Exhaled and explained that he was on a unique ship
It wasn't chartered often and the captain took no lip.

"I don't know why you're on this run, but you've the right to know
"That we don't take the normal paths where other ships may go.
"This captain and this ship have history and special ways
"And we will beat the normal trip by two weeks and three days.

"For now that is enough. I've work to do and you should rest
"In the knowledge that this ship and captain are the best
"At what they do and none of us have quit this little crew.
"Every man among us is the best at what we do."

With that the engineer clammed up and said not one word more
Then left his seat and pushed off forward through the cockpit door
Bolting it securely when he pulled himself inside
Hoping that this newbie'd be no trouble on this ride.

Left alone the passenger returned to watch the view
Through the ports available from this room where he knew
He'd see the most he could from any room he was allowed.
Behind, the bright blue Earth was seen within its cloudy shroud.

* * * * *

The captain lay in darkness in his cabin sealed tight
Absently regarding those few stars which sent their light
Through the tiny porthole which was set into the wall
And every man aboard that ship knew not on him to call.

Through his head he let the memory pass one more time
Staring at the vision that was burned deep in his mind:
The white hot spots where lasers burned their gaping holes through ships,
The gasping mouths and bleeding eyes as men's lives quickly slipped

Away from this existence into vast eternity
Without a chance to save themselves; a harsh reality.
Spinning, spewing gas and shreds of metal, flesh and bone,
The jagged debris of the ships that would not make it home

And in the distant darkness far beyond his wounded grasp
The black ships of the enemy accelerated fast
Taking all the reason and his cause for love of life
The deepest warmth within his heart: his precious friend and wife.

Minutes passed like hours as his burning rage flamed bright
Surging through his nervous system, eyes and jaw locked tight
The horrid loss and emptiness within his battered soul
Weakly soothed by new commitment to his years-long goal.

2   Introductions

The smell of coffee roasted dark and fresh-brewed rich and black
Wafted through the passenger compartment from the back
And that was quite enough to bring the passenger awake
Who startled to discover he was in his seat strapped safe.

"Good morning!" said the engineer who stood beside him near
Holding a small cup of coffee toward him bright with cheer.
Surprised to see him standing on the bulkhead at his back
The passenger remarked that he would love some, hot and black!

"How long have I slept?" he asked while fumbling at his straps
"I didn't realize I had such a need to get a nap."
The engineer reminded him he hadn't slept a bit
Since two days back when they'd departed from Earth's low orbit.

"You've slept about a dozen hours, I'm not really sure.
"I found you drifting by a porthole with a healthy snore
"And towed you to your seat when it was time to light the torch
"Careful! This is hot. If you spill it you'll get scorched."

"Uh, thank you," said the newbie "I appreciate your care
"That's the first time I have slept while drifting in the air."
The engineer remarked that it was nothing, he'd seen worse.
"Once I saw a newbie crack his skull when we changed course.

"But that clown had it coming. He refused to hear the rules.
"When traveling by rocket it's not time to act the fool.
"Anyway, the work we had to do is now complete.
"Why don't you come to the galley, meet the crew and eat?"

"Thank you! I could eat a horse. A liquid diet's fine
"(In zero G it's probably the best course 'til the time
"The stomach's acclimated) but the time has come around
"To get the stomach working and the feet feeling some ground."

The engineer acknowledged, "Yes, believe me, I have seen
"That empty newbie tummies keep things tidier and clean.
"It isn't pleasant running into what may float about
"The cabin when a newbie tummy spews its contents out.

"You've done very well so far," the engineer then said
"And you understand why you've been left in here, not fed."
He winked and offered him his hand and helped him to his feet
And said that he was glad to see the cabin was still neat.

"By the way, my name is Sven. The others call me 'Gin'
"Olsen, born in Hammerfest of Norway (not Sweden).
"I'm the engineering chief; I keep us riding smooth.
"Now finish up your java and let's get those feet to move."

The newbie was relieved to get a passing grade from him
And it was nice to feel like there was "up" and "down" again
(For in ballistic flight or freefall in low gravity
Those terms have little meaning; only left and right, you see.)

"We spent the extra time in zero G because we must
"Do some work outside we can't quite manage under thrust
"But now we're finished, running at point seven G's for now
"And we'll pick up the pace after we all get fed some chow.

"By the way, that empty cup is edible, you know.
"Try it!" said the engineer as they prepared to go
And when he did he found it was a tasty snack indeed
Made of grain, perhaps a mix of rice and corn or wheat?

Down the central passageway the two of them took leave
Toward the galley two decks down where Newbie was relieved
To find a table set with dishes piled high with food
And half a dozen men who seemed to all be in good mood.

"Fellas, meet our passenger. He's housebroken and tame;
"He doesn't spoil his britches and he'll come when called by name."
The others smiled and welcomed him, though some looked tired and sore
But chuckled at the good-natured deriding from the door.

"Please," a thin and dark-skinned man pulled out a wooden chair
And gestured that he sit and said, "Don't heed their rude hot air.
"Be at ease and know you're welcomed to our little home.
"These animals won't bother you while they chew on their bones.

"I am Haji, this is Duke and that mustache is Joe.
"The one with bulging cheeks is Dewey, Gin I'm sure you know.

"Radar has the ears and Bovine has the largest plate.
"Fill your dish before he does or you will be too late."

"Thank you very much," the newbie said, his smile wide.
"I am very pleased to meet you all and take this ride."
He gratefully sat down and Haji handed him a dish
And poured a steaming mug of coffee from a pot that hissed.

The newbie watched with wonder as the fluid left the pot
And slowly made the two-inch trip (the man spilled not a drop).
As he watched he softly said apologetically:
"I've never seen a fluid flow in lessened gravity."

Realization of the obvious brought snorts of glee
And Dewey said "You really are as green as you can be!"
Then Gin reminded him point seven was in fact quite strong
For every world inhabited but Earth around the Sun:

"Luna and most others are some less than point two G.
"Mars approaches point four and the same for Mercury.
"Many loathe the extra weight they carry on the Earth
"Even though it is the planet of our race's birth.

"But as you know a large percentage of us live without
"The confines of the earth and we no longer have a doubt
"That all the apron strings that kept us tethered there are cut
"And one G being 'normal' by most folks just isn't thought."

Their guest absorbed this fact and shook his head from side to side
And said, "I missed the obvious. I've never been outside
"The atmosphere of Earth; I've never gone far from my town.
"Please excuse my greenness, I must seem like quite the clown."

Dewey said "Relax. Forget it. We know you're not dumb.
"If you had no skills or talents you would not be one
"That TerraCorp would pay a hefty charter for a ship
"To get you to the outer systems on this special trip."

Radar shook his hand and said, "We all were Greenies too.
"Though we're not all born on Earth we had to learn like you.
"Within a year you'll be a son of Sol, not just of Earth.
"All the solar planets are our home, if not by birth."

Gin made introductions with a little more detail
Going round the table making sure each was regaled:
"Haji is our cook and he's a fine one, you will see
"He also is our doctor and has two advanced degrees.

"Radar's our communicator and our spoofer too.
"He can sound like anyone he's heard; even you!
"Don't think those big ears of his negate what's in his brain.
"Electrons are his specialty, computers his domain.

"Bovine worked the heavy metal mines on Mercury.
"He knows heavy industry and knows metallurgy.
"Dewey used to build atomics for old TerraCorp
"On Mars and Ganymede before the Terra-Luna war.

"Joe doesn't say a lot but he has talents too
"Most of which aren't talked about until we need him to.
"Haji likes the way he keeps the kitchen knives all sharp
"And he is quite the virtuoso with his old blues harp!

"Duke worked on a horse ranch in Montana as a kid
"Then ran a guide and outfit service as a full time gig
"Until he found his talents useful to the Survey Corps
"On Saturn's Shepherd moons before the Service paid him more."

By now the men were digging in to plates all piled high
With omelets and hash browns and fresh melons on the side.
Then Dewey, through his bulging cheeks asked Newbie for his name
And Haji interrupted him and said, "Need not to say!

"You may keep your name and business private if you wish.
"Dewey should know better and attend to his own dish!"
Then Newbie said, "It's quite all right, I have no secret schtick
"My name is Nicholas but everyone just calls me Nick."

"How long you worked for TerraCorp?" (Dewey one more time.)
And Radar said "Let off him!" but young Nick said "No, it's fine.
"I don't work for TerraCorp. I'm just an intern there.
"They've given me a contract to go study Titan's air."

Duke and Bovine shot quick glances toward each other then.
And looked at Nick for just a moment then glanced back again.

The others ate their breakfast slower, ears extended high
And presently Gin pushed away, let loose a heavy sigh,

"Once again you've fed us well. Thank you, Chef Deluxe!"
And all the men said their "Amen's" and drained their coffee cups.
"You're up!" Duke gave the cue to Radar who picked up his plate
And moved around the table clearing dishes from their way.

"I'm curious," said Nick, "How is it on this ship I find
"Wooden furniture and dishes of the finest kind?
"One would think these items all would be of tiny mass;
"Titanium or plastic, not ceramic, stone and glass."

Duke chimed in, "Our captain is a man with certain tastes
"A man of principle who keeps priorities in place.
"One of these is comfort and a warmth upon the hearth
"Within the galley of the ship, so near a crewman's heart.

"And who can argue there's a better way to take a slug
"From his morning coffee than from any but a mug?
"Or to dive into a steak with knife and fork on plates?
"These help enhance the appetite instead of it erase.

"Wooden chairs are found in every home on every world
"From Mercury to Ganymede; wherever we've unfurled
"The flags over our settlements (where we have been so bold)
"Everybody seems to make them part of their household!"

Nick said, "I knew lumber was a major Earth export.
"I saw it on great pallets when I left White Sands Spaceport.
"I didn't understand it when there's so much better stuff
"Available on other worlds; local, cheap and tough."

Gin had listened closely and he smiled wide and said,
"You will understand some day when you are snared and wed.
"You can take a homemaker off Earth, I will aver
"But you'll never take the Earth out of the homemaker!"

"That sounds like Earth's apron strings to me," Nick mused out loud
And Gin responded, "True, but it's a testament of how
"The other worlds have grown and prospered when they can afford
"To spend resources on such things as furniture and boards!

"Anyway, I've work to do. In just an hour or so
"We'll be changing course. We'll need the galley goods all stowed."
With that he winked and turned and headed toward the upper decks
And Nick asked to assist the others cleaning up the mess.

"Bovine, please show Mr. Nick how we lock chairs in place,"
Said Haji as he took his leave from his small cooking space
And left for lower decks to tend to other duties there
While Bovine said "Be glad to," and picked up one of the chairs.

"You see these steel attachments at the bottom of each leg?
"They are locked into the deck by latches that rotate
"Up from underneath the level of the floor like this."
And showed the newbie how to turn them up to the surface.

"That is very clever," said young Nick as he looked close
At the mechanisms on which one would not stub toes.
"How much force will they support? This galley deck is wood!"
And Bovine said "Much more than one would ever think they could."

Bovine started to say more, then stopped himself mid-word
And studied young Nick's face for just a quiet moment more.
Then seeming satisfied with something said, "They've held six G's.
"Maybe more than that, but keep it quiet, if you please."

"Your retro thrusters push that hard?" (His eyes were opened wide.)
And Bovine added quietly, "Four from side to side.
"Of course it isn't hard to give the chairs more with your fists
"I think these chairs would break apart before the latches slip.

"But you should be aware that this ship has a little kick
"Just in case it's used along the way during our trip.
"You got a little taste of it when we went through Hell's Gate.
"This ship has a reputation: 'Never shows up late.'"

The galley tasks were finished quickly, then they took their leave
To man their general quarters if the captain had a need
For unanticipated duties while their course was changed
And all the while young Nick considered it was all quite strange:

Why would they be altering a course already set?
He asked himself while he returned to where he was to sit.

We've been thrusting at point seven G for quite some time
And Gin said they would up the pace as if it all were fine...

His thought trailed off as he again sat near the glass
Which gave the widest view outside the ship, the time to pass.
While taking in the beauty of the starry sky outside
He recognized some constellations in their glory bright.

Presently the cabin lights turned red a minute's wait
And then three flashes followed by a sudden loss of weight
When the engines silenced for a moment as they slewed
Their major axis to the ship's new stellar attitude.

And then a minute passed in silence with no engine burn
Which seemed so very odd to him, but he had much to learn.
And then the sound of motors moving something in the ship
Shortly was repeated, then the engines gave their kick!

This time it was not a gentle kick against his back.
This time it was more like on his chest a giant sat!
And it didn't let up! It went on and on it seemed.
It became a struggle to get air enough to breathe!

Minutes passed so agonizing in their perceived length
It felt to him as if his frame were running out of strength.
And then about the time he feared that something had gone wrong
The giant got up off his chest where he had sat so long.

The cabin lights returned to white and soon he felt just fine.
The bulkhead at his back stayed "down". Out of his seat he climbed.
Looking through the portholes he took note that at the stern
Venus hung near Spica and how bright it seemed to burn!

But then he noted Regulus was not where it should be.
Upside down old Leo lay and that made him queasy
For neither Earth nor Venus should appear where he looked on.
Indeed, with Leo topsy-turvy that must be Procyon!

Yes! Beneath it he could see the twins of Gemini
And that made all the difference but still within his eye
Was that bright light that burned as an imposter in the dark
Pretending it was Venus or some other planet's mark.

His musing on this quandary was presently cut short
When from the cockpit door he heard Gin's voice make some report
And turning 'round to greet him found the captain in his stead
Who stood before him quietly a moment, then he said:

"Good Morning, Mr. Hallenbeck. I see you've weathered well
"Our trip away from Earth so far - as much as I can tell.
"My engineer informs me that you've questions on your mind.
"I'll be happy to address them now that we have time."

The captain wore a crewman's coverall of darkest blue,
His brown hair peppered gray above brown eyes that bored right through
The blue eyes Nick looked back with, in surprise when he turned 'round
To find the captain standing where he thought Gin would be found.

"Yes, Sir. Thank you. I am glad to meet you, to be sure.
"I've never been off-planet but my stomach needs no cure."
Nick felt silly and blushed red but Captain laughed out loud
And said "You've done quite well so far and should be very proud.

"Now, how may I assist you?" The captain took a seat
And said, "Please, sit and take the load off of your feet.
"We're running at just over one point four G's for a while.
"What you felt was four G's for ten minutes," and he smiled.

"I'm sorry, Sir. My questions aren't important and can wait.
"I feel a silly tourist and suppose they're now too late.
"But I was wondering why our flight path came so near
"To Hypatia's rim? I'm glad our corridor was clear!"

The captain's face retained a quiet smile. He replied:
"Some would think it is a danger to go on that ride
"But it is one I took in years gone by and many since;
"A training run from Service days. It isn't an offense.

"As you know we spent some time in zero G to do
"Some maintenance outside the ship and I decided to
"Utilize the lunar gravity for an assist
"To make up for the lost time and get going on our trip."

"Thank you, Sir. If I may, another question ask:
"I noticed after our correction, looking out the glass

"What looked like Venus at our stern, but near to Procyon
"Quite out of the ecliptic and it all seemed very wrong.

"Also, Sir, I noticed that our bow's direction lies
"Toward Sagittarius. That's not Saturn's bit of sky.
"I must be wrong somehow, but it appears we're quite astray.
"Saturn and its moons are somewhere over that-a-way.

Nick made gestures toward the bulkhead at the captain's side.
The captain then looked deeply into Nick's inquiring eyes
And said, "You are a great observer, Mr. Hallenbeck."
Nick continued with the questions Captain might expect:

"And this is just as curious: I can't imagine why
"We'd burn point seven G then in the middle of the ride
"Stop the burn to make a turn when thrusters would suffice
"To make the course correction without letting engines ice.

"Then when we turned we burned another time so hard and long
"On what appears to be a course that seems to me so wrong."
Nick then blushed again and stuttered while his reddened face
Betrayed his true humility (he sat down in his place).

"I'm sorry, Sir. I'm just a passenger aboard your ship.
"My curiosity sometimes won't let me hold my lip.
"I didn't mean to question what I know you must do well
"You are a man of space to whom there's nothing I can tell."

The captain watched young Nicholas a moment then replied,
"These are all good questions that you ask, and I'm surprised.
"I know you are an educated man but most don't see
"Their place within the solar system on their first sortie.

"Other than your fumbles when you first came on the ship
"I would never guess that from the Earth you'd never tripped.
"Tell me, Mr. Hallenbeck, what is it that you do?
"Why did Terra Corporation hire this ship for you?"

Confusion spread across Nick's face while Captain watched him close.
The extra force of one point four made even his loose clothes
Feel like burdens pulling him into an early grave
And Captain was intent to hear an honest answer gave.

"Sir, astronomy has always been a love of mine
"Ever since I was quite young I've spent a lot of time
"Watching nature and I know where all the planets race
"Around the sun and year to year know where they are in space.

"At this time I've yet to focus on my life's career
"As an intern in a lab I've spent the past two years.
"I know a bit of physics and I've studied very well
"But how I lucked into this trip I truly cannot tell."

The captain searched his eyes a moment then he calmly said
"Pardon please, my inquisition; I mean you no dread.
"It is quite unusual for them to hire a ship
"Outside of their own extensive fleet for such a trip."

Bovine came into the room up from the deck below
And sat down in a seat behind them both as if to show
That he was very used to functioning at this great weight
Then Radar also climbed the ladder with a roll of tape.

Haji made an entrance just behind the other two
Then Nick began to wonder what these four now planned to do.
The captain said, "Nick - may I call you that, I hope?"
And Nick nodded his head (across his face concern was wrote.)

"I want to ask permission to perform a micro scan
"Of your body head to toe to find out all we can
"About the implants TerraCorp has hidden in your flesh."
And Nick responded, "There is nothing here, I will attest!"

Looking at the other three (who would not meet his eye)
Nick continued, "You will do this whether or not I
"Approve. Is that so?" The captain sadly nodded, "Yes."
And Haji added, "There will be no reason to undress."

"Very well. I know there's nothing hidden here at all,"
Nick consented to submit to this indignant call.
Then Gin came to the doorway from the cockpit with a grin
And Captain gave a "thumbs up" without looking back at him.

"Zero G. Make it so," the captain gave the go
And Gin pulled back inside and then the red lights came on low.

Presently the engines stopped and they all held their seats
While Haji motioned for their passenger to raise his feet.

"Please relax and stay as motionless as you can be,"
Said Doctor Haji as he steadied Nick while floating free.
Then Radar and the doctor pulled two scanners from their kits
And passed them slowly over him; every little inch.

While the scan progressed the captain gave a short discourse:
"Indeed we need not stop the burn while slewing our new course
"But once again, we needed to put something off the ship
"And it would not be pleasant if while burning something slipped.

"We left behind a decoy. It burns much like a torch.
"It changes spectral output as if red-shifting, of course
"And when we left it looking like our double in the sky
"We sped away with rockets to complete our little lie.

"No, that wasn't Venus that you saw behind our tail
"Just a little decoy to keep foxes off our trail.
"And you are right; it isn't Saturn that lays in our path;
"Our course is set for Mars. You can trust your inner map."

Nick's eyes opened wide, he jerked involuntarily.
"Steady!" Radar said and Bovine held his arm firmly
And said "In just a minute you will see this scan yourself
"On the wall-screen monitor. We've all had this ourselves."

"You're not being kidnapped," Captain reassured their guest,
"We'll be heading on to Saturn when we've done the rest
"Of all the work we need to do before we head that way
"And you will be there two weeks sooner than for what they paid."

"We're finished," Radar said and Gin's head pulled back out of view.
The cabin lights blinked three times and they all took seats on cue.
The engines came on presently at only half a G
Then Haji put the scans up on the monitor to see.

The doctor started, "Please forgive us, we know this is rude
"But these are special circumstances, we need all the truth.
"I've filtered out the data that reveals your private health
"Only shown will be the foreign items placed by stealth."

Nick said, "Please, it's quite all right. Show all that you care.
"In fact I'm very curious to see my parts in there.
"I don't mind if you all see the stuffing inside me."
The tension in the room eased up and Nick said, "Please proceed."

The monitor lit up to show a whirl of colored lines
Slowly moving everywhere within a man's outline.
The doctor's fingers deftly flew across his scanner's face
Revealing years of practice, hesitation not a trace.

He briefly showed examples of the things that he could do
By changing data filters and rotating through the views
And then the body's display turned into a solid red
With tiny blinking indicators here and there instead.

"These are the foreign objects that are not supposed to be
"Inside a normal human body that is implant free.
"It appears we've located some thirty different sites
"With active implants functioning and others here besides."

"No! That can't be true!" Nick blurted, mouth and eyes held wide.
The captain glanced his way then hung his head and deeply sighed.
"Holy smokes!" Bovine exclaimed, "You hold the record, Nick!
"You're a walking wonder packing all that in your kit!"

Radar said, "It's true, all right. Prove it on your own.
"Hold this scanner on your arm. See the veins and bone?"
Nick took Radar's scanner and looked back up at the screen
While moving it to his contentment proving what was seen.

"I swear I had no knowledge of these things inside of me.
"How did they get in there and what capability?
"I'd never have allowed it and no one has ever put
"A knife against my skin or any tubes into my gut."

The captain looked at Haji and they both looked back at Nick.
There was no denying that he truly had been tricked.
This they'd seen a dozen times or more in recent years:
People used unknowingly as spies and eyes and ears.

The captain looked a moment deeply into Nick's blue eyes
And said, "I know you're honest and the doctor does besides.

"Please know we believe you when you say you had no clue
"About these things inside your body or what they might do.

"You aren't the first that TerraCorp has violated so
"Without their knowledge or permission then sent them to go
"Where they have interest but no rights or ways to get
"Control of things they do not own and free men wouldn't let.

"I do not know your loyalties, I don't know where you stand
"Regarding solar politics. I do know you're a man
"Of character and capable of independent thought.
"Please consider carefully, since by you they've been caught.

"Now if you will, let's get you down to the infirmary
"And find out what these things they've planted do and get you free.
"Radar and the doctor both have talents very sure.
"From every one of us they've taken these and now we're pure.

"Would this be your choice?" the captain asked (and Nick was red!
His face was flushed with anger and embarrassment and dread.)
"Please do what you must, Sir. I can't describe my hate
"For what's been done without my knowledge to usurp my fate."

Bovine grinned and put his arm around Nick's shoulders tight
And punched him lightly on the arm and said, "He'll do what's right.
"After you're cleaned up I'll take you 'round the ship to see
"All the parts of this, your home for these next several weeks."

The silence of the vacuum and the brightness of the sun,
The blackness of the starry sky and swiftness of their run
Across the empty reaches toward the flaming red of Mars
Underscored the vastness of the space between the stars.

* * * * *

The distant sun sank coldly o'er the western crater rim
Rarified and poisonous the sky glowed faint and dim.
This evening just two moons in their quarter phases marked
The view beyond the window as the shadows spread their dark.

So long ago the warmth of blue and golden sunsets seemed,
On the warm green Earth where wind and water, running clean

Caressed her hair and cooled her grass-stained feet from summer's blast;
A wisp of fading fantasy or dream just out of grasp.

Yet sharp and harsh the searing memory of the attack
Never fading, only pushed the pleasant memories back
And filled her with the chill of painful loss and wrenching dread.
Perhaps one of their shattered ships was his? Was he dead?

Did the lover of her life and husband of her heart
Live and wonder too if they would always be apart?
The hope that burned within her soul, though little could be sure
Remained a warming beacon that kept love alive and pure.

But then the harsh reality of life beneath the rock
Broke coldly on her ears with the approach of roguish talk
And presently, inevitable curses came her way
It was the price her moment by the window she must pay.

"You've not met your quota, Fifty-Two, and there you stand.
"Are you waiting 'til an invitation's in your hand?
"The shift is over and your tally hasn't totaled up
"Are you being lazy or for someone covering up?"

The supervisor spat upon the dirt beside her feet.
The other eyed her hungrily as if she were fresh meat.
And as she turned around she met the eye of he who spat
And said, "I've met my quota; there's a bit more there than that.

"Your sergeant took it on the cart to finish off the shift
"Before the next crew comes along. Perhaps you should be swift
"To catch up to him while you have the chance to hide your tracks?
"It is no secret you two sneak away behind his back."

The lusting lecher would not meet her eye, the other scowled,
"What we do is no concern of yours, Earther cow.
"Keep your comments to yourself or you'll find trouble deep.
"Sergeant isn't always going to save you in your sleep."

The empty threat washed off her like a raindrop off a duck.
The reeking pair departed 'ere they ran out of their luck
And had to make their own defense before the sergeant's wrath.
She thought, "How nasty could it get 'til those two took a bath?"

Returning her attention to the tiny window's view
Now, as for a hundred times she hoped for something new,
A glimmer of a change, perhaps the sighting of a ship
The faintest hope that someday from these bonds she'd chance to slip.

Then the automated system closed the shutter tight
Sealing off the inner cavern from the outer night.
It would be four dozen Earth-long days before the light
Of the feeble distant sun again came to her sight.

3   Rude Awakening

Haji's small infirmary was larger than Nick thought.
A table in the middle; at each side a fold-down cot.
At the far wall was a rack of very special gear
And on the upper bulkhead items mounted to pull near.

"The table has a scanner built inside so we may see
"At the microscopic level all that we may need.
"Please relax and lie down while we take a deeper view.
"There is a viewer on the upper bulkhead for you too."

Haji motioned to his patient to move into place
And Radar took a station at the back in that workspace.
The viewer overhead sprang into action as Nick sat
And showed his innards' images as he lay on the mat.

Haji moved a cursor to each marker one by one
And Radar spoke some numbers after each when he was done.
But then a moment came when Haji stopped near a pink blot
And asked Radar a question, "What is this that we have got?"

Radar answered, "I see nothing there. What do you see?"
He came from his equipment to stand near Doctor Haji.
"Look how this reacts when I attempt to see inside.
"It mimics very closely all the flesh it lays beside."

Radar said, "That's interesting. I've not seen this type.
"I'll be back with something to look closer at this site."
Then as he left the doctor said to Nick, "We've found a bug
"That thinks it's hiding cleverly so snug beneath its rug."

Nick said, "Please do what you can to ascertain the job
"These implants were put in me for and what from me they rob."
Then Haji started pointing out the items one by one
Explaining those he'd seen before and how long they had run.

"These nine spread around your limbs all work together to
"Confirm your body's posture to this central item who
"Tracks your movements closely and reports them to this piece
"Where they are stored to be retrieved and transmitted by these:

"Along your femurs see this pair of wide band transceivers?
"(Radar can explain their working much better than me.)
"The ones we've seen in recent months transmit but once per day
"But each of these have activated twice since down you lay!

"These, behind your eyes, take samples from your optic nerves
"And from them what you're looking at can subtly be inferred.
"They do not build an image that's as good as you can see
"But given time and data, images can build clearly.

"These four are transducers that detect the vibes and sounds.
"They are used to reconstruct kinetics all around.
"Everything you hear and everything you touch is poured
"Again, into these central units, compacted and stored.

"Here, next to your lung we find a clever little pair.
"One samples the mixture of your breath (the very air
"You breathe is being watched); and this one is a Geiger tube
"Of sorts, to measure radiation that may surround you.

"It appears the limb implants have run perhaps two years
"The optic nerve devices seem the newest that are here.
"I suspect you've had them three or four weeks at the most
"These other sites have not yet activated at their posts."

Nick inquired calmly, "Are the inactives reserves?
"Perhaps in the event that one or more no longer serves?"
The doctor nodded in agreement but appeared concerned.
It was clear behind his eyes a question hotly burned.

"That would be my guess, but Radar is the man to ask,
"I am just a doctor; he is trained more for such tasks.
"Many may be universal implants that can be
"Configured to perform whatever service is the need."

Radar bounced back in the room holding a piece of gear.
He fixed it to a bracket from the ceiling, pulled it near.
"This will let us see what generates the cloaking field.
"Hopefully the purpose of the spot will be revealed."

With that he placed his face up to the lens of the device
And steered it toward the place suspected not to be so nice.

Several seconds passed while Radar fiddled with some knobs
And then he whistled softly, said, "This thing is quite the job!

"Doctor, if you would, please look again at what you've found."
(Haji now could see what had been hidden in its shroud.)
He ran his diagnostic for a moment, triple checked
And then he stepped away, his dark face showing beads of sweat.

"What is it?" Nick inquired with a deepening concern.
The doctor looked into Nick's eyes, his face began to burn.
"Nicholas, this implant is a harvester of sorts.
"Its only purpose is to gain ability to hurt.

"From the nutrients and compounds in your body's core
"It is working day and night to build a growing store
"Of concentrated volatiles all along your spine
"Apparently for use when someone else chooses the time."

"Volatiles?" Radar asked. "What kind?" Nick echoed quick.
The doctor leaned against the bulkhead looking rather sick:
"It has manufactured half a kilogram to date
"Of phosphorous and oxidizers 'capsulated safe."

"Holy crap!" Radar exclaimed, "This is something new.
"Nick, you're a fire bomb that they already threw!"
Haji added, "There is more. A network slowly grows:
"Accelerants to ignite fat wherever it may go."

Nick's clear skin turned redder with each second that elapsed
Until it matched his carrot hair, then quietly he asked:
"Please, tell me how these things could get inside of me
"Without my knowledge; and is there a chance I can be free?"

Haji and then Radar each placed hands upon his arm
And Haji said, "We will proceed with care and do no harm.
"There are many methods used to plant these in our flesh.
"The simplest way by far is just to trick us to ingest.

"Planted in our food or drink the basic parts are sewn
"Or by injection with robotic 'insects' has been known.
"Drugged while sleeping, tiny probes through skin are introduced
"Similar to what we'll use to pull these out of you.

"Then when you awake you scratch an itch or find a spot
"Dismissing it, thinking by a spider you were got.
"Or perhaps you think maybe you scratched open a zit
"And likewise disregard and never twice consider it.

"Some of these are built inside the body, right in place
"By nanorobots introduced in all these different ways.
"Biomimicry at nano-levels isn't new
"But using it against our will is never right to do.

"Radar, call the captain and let's keep him in the loop.
"We need to discuss this and be sure we make no 'Oops!'"
At that very instant Captain came into the room
And asked why they all looked as if they'd met their final doom.

The doctor gave a short report, the captain asked to see,
And Radar gave the guided tour to show what they had seen:
"Some of these are new, we've never come across the like,"
Radar started, then explained, "We need to do this right.

"There may be a failsafe or two designed in him
"That sets a self-destruct if tampered with or probed within.
"There may be a timer or a signal from outside
"That needs to be received by something programmed deep inside.

"Either way, we need to understand what we have found
"Before we go off poking stuff and kicking things around."
"I agree!" said Nick, the doctor gave emphatic "Yes!"
And Captain said, "You take your time and clean up all this mess."

Then just before he turned to leave he looked at Nick and said,
"We will do what's right by you. Please try not to dread.
"You are not the first to be surprised in this rude way
"And you won't be the last; on that I'd stake my final day."

It was agreed to take a break while Radar studied hard
All the data that was taken from their scans so far.
Haji would assist and look at things with health in view.
It would take some time before they'd know just what to do.

Meanwhile, Bovine came for Nick and took him on a tour
Around the ship and reassured him they would make him pure:

"Every Swinging Charlie on this crew has felt the same
"When we found the spy stuff in us. Nothing is so lame

"As sticking things inside somebody just to get your way
"At their expense, not even asking what they'd have to say.
"In your case they've sunk to levels lower than we've seen
"But you can trust that Radar and the Doc will get you clean.

"These guys are the best. They took some junk out of my meat
"That doctors never spotted when I worked on Mercury.
"Every time we climb on board we all get scanned again
"And by the time we're underway I know I'm my own man."

* * * * *

Later, in the captain's quarters, at his desk and chairs
(Gin and Bovine, Haji, Radar, Joe and Duke were there)
A council was convened to discuss what they all thought
About their passenger and what new trouble he had brought.

Joe stood in the corner sharpening a longish knife.
Duke stood by him, brown arms crossed, taking all in stride.
Gin and Bovine's chairs were in the middle of the floor.
The captain leaned his back against the sealed stateroom door.

"Dewey is on watch?" the captain asked and Gin replied,
"Yes, Sir. He is keeping Nicholas well occupied."
The captain looked around the room and spoke a single word:
"Truth," was his command and then they openly conferred:

Gin began by saying, "This kid has adapted well
"To the space environment and through the Gate to Hell
"At Luna, when he saw the mountains rise with deathly pall
"He turned a little white like any but flinched not at all.

"He didn't take a drink, he didn't ask for any smoke
"He seemed to think that little trip was just a sort of joke.
"His mind needed some explanations (he's not just a sheep)
"And when we kept him in the dark he relaxed, got some sleep."

Haji looked straight at the captain, said with certainty,
"I detect no hesitation. Only honesty.

"As far as I have skill he had no knowledge of the tools
"Placed inside his body. He had been completely fooled."

"He's pissed," said Bovine "Really pissed that he was being used
"By someone just to infiltrate somewhere to get a view.
"But worst of all the fact that he was turned into a bomb,
"Well, now he knows why TerraCorp has just strung him along."

"Exactly," Joe injected, "As an intern, not employed
"They could use him any way they want to be their boy
"Without the repercussions that might come if he were found.
"He's not a real employee. They're the victims, he's the clown."

He made another stroke of steel along the stone he held
And lightly thumbed its gleaming edge, the sharpness he could tell.
He sighted closely down the blade he held up to the light
Then resumed the strokes on stone; he'd said his piece of mind.

Duke chimed in, "His heart is good." The captain nodded, "Yes.
"I believe you're right, Duke. There's light inside his chest.
"Radar?" Captain prodded, "What are your initial thoughts?"
And Radar said, "A good head on his shoulders he has got,

"But what concerns me most is why they chartered such a trip
"When TerraCorp could get him there on one of their own ships.
"Was he meant to spy on us? And why the fire bomb?
"What exactly is his target? This all smells so wrong."

"It is wrong," Captain interjected, "But we all agree
"That our young friend loves freedom and is not an enemy."
The captain looked around the little room and softly said,
"I suppose the thought has also run through all your heads

"That he has been put on this ship to simply take us out.
"It wouldn't be the first time we've been targets, there's no doubt."
Radar looked at Joe a moment, then his face turned sly
"We could use him as a double agent - our own spy."

"If we kept his implants active, turned them to our use
"We might learn some secrets to cook TerraCorp's own goose."
Silence fell across the room, most looked at the floor.
Captain searched their faces and said, "That thought: Let's explore.

"You all know the dirtiness of what Radar suggests.
"It's not the way good people are to treat their paying guests.
"But this may be a golden opportunity to find
"What TerraCorp's directors' plot on Titan is this time."

"Not against his will," said Bovine. Gin, emphatic, "No."
Haji's head twitched sideways and a dark stare came from Joe.
"Ask him," Duke suggested, "Find what burns within his heart;
"He may have a warrior spirit who will do its part."

The captain looked at Duke and saw the fire in his eyes
The blood of Sioux and Cheyenne in Duke's veins would stand no lies.
Joe nodded to Radar, said, "What have you got in mind?"
Radar said, "We've got some options but we're short on time.

"When we get to Phobos, Stickney station will have spies.
"You can bet there's sensors that will detect he's arrived.
"We will need them quieted or set up with a spoof
"But when he gets to Titan he should have them as a proof

"That he's arrived intact and ready to perform the task
"Which he has been set up to do, though he was never asked."
Captain said, "Assuming that his real mission was there
"On Titan, and not someone or something some other where."

A long moment of quiet thought filled only by the sound
Of Joe stroking his steel on stone, a fine edge keenly ground.
And then the Captain broke the silence quietly but firm:
"At any rate, we are agreed that Nick is not to burn.

"Let us give him half a chance. Remove the deadly gear.
"Radar, set a data spoof that we were never near
"Anywhere but on a course for Titan, then remove
"The transmitters and nanorobots; you know what to do.

"The sensors can remain a little while until we know
"A little more about the man and which way he will go
"When he is shown the truth about the beast he's been inside.
"Steaks tonight," the captain said and Haji smiled wide.

* * * * *

Nick had spent some time with Dewey in the engine room
Being shown the ship's atomics; but then very soon
Gin came down to send him back to the infirmary
Where Radar and the Captain talked with Ship's Doctor Haji.

"Nick! Welcome back. I trust you found the engines sound?"
Haji gave his greeting as he motioned to lie down,
"Let us work on neutralizing phosphorous a while
"And getting those devices out." (He and Captain smiled.)

"Thank you," Nick replied as he lay down upon the mat
"Thank you for your willingness to free me from all that."
He gestured at the display that retained his body's chart
And it was plain the young man was sincere deep in his heart.

"Nick," the captain started, "This will take a bit of time
"And must be done in stages for the work is very fine.
"While the doctor takes the deadly compounds out of you
"Radar will be spoofing data, killing robots too.

"Once the danger to us is removed with all the worst
"The transmitters and backup gear will all be taken first.
"But some of those small sensors will be left at my request.
"I ask your patience. At this time we think it would be best.

"If you disagree, we'll honor what you wish (we must)
"But at this time I hope that in our judgment you will trust.
"You may find them useful to you in the weeks ahead.
"There is a chance they'll be a lifesaver for you instead.

"Tonight, when the danger to yourself and us is past
"And these two have removed the nasty implants to the last
"There will be more time to talk about the benign few
"And you can take the time to choose whatever's right for you."

Nick searched all their faces and saw only real concern
And said, "You have my full faith and I don't want us to burn.
"Take the necessary steps. I trust you know what's right.
"I'm not going anywhere but with you on this flight."

The captain smiled and nodded and the others nodded too.
He turned to leave and said, "I'll see you when the work is through.

"Every man upon this ship wants always to be free
"And never will deny that right to anyone we see

"But tyrants, spies and thieves." he said and then he left the room.
Radar and the doctor echoed, "Yes," and then a boom
Supporting Radar's probes moved into place above his thigh
While Radar took his seat against the wall, let out a sigh.

"Now, my friend," said Haji, "as you know, white phosphorous
"Is self-igniting in the air and toxic too, for us.
"So we will set containment all around the mass inside
"And dissolve it all in place with carbon disulfide.

"While this happens Radar will deceive the central core
"And sever all the ties to both transmitters long before
"I start removal of the implants set behind your eyes;
"You'll feel a tiny tickle in your nose while I'm inside.

"Access for solutions will be made with two small holes:
"One upon your shoulder right beside this little mole.
"The other we will place beside your coccyx at your rear
"And only little pinpricks will be felt 'til all is clear.

"Most of these devices we can get with tiny probes
"Inserted through your skin where any implants may repose.
"You should not feel more than what mosquitoes tend to do.
"Please don't slap or scratch us while we do this work on you!

"However, that remarkable device that hides so well
"We will need to get intact and so I need to tell
"You that I'll be inserting just beneath your diaphragm
"Through a centimeter cut this tool within my hand."

Haji held what looked much like a simple plastic pipe
No bigger than a drinking straw with three wires on the side.
"A local anesthetic will eliminate the pain
"By evening meal your freedom from this thing will be regained."

"Thank you Doctor, Radar." Nick lay back and did his best
To relax and watched his view screen with a deep interest
While outside in the vacuum and the emptiness of space
A million miles vanished to their stern as on they raced.

4   Food for Thought

Garlic, she thought to herself, *I never thought I'd be*
Pulling it by hand beneath a sky I couldn't see
Lost beyond the lights that hang beneath a dome of rock
Among a group of prisoners who mostly fear to talk.

Another shift of pulling garlic from the cavern's soil
Had passed and once again she took a respite from the toil
Watching as the workers of the next shift took their spots
Among the rows where her crew's tired people had left off.

"What is on your mind?" a welcome voice behind her said
And with a smile she turned to meet the friendly dark-haired head.
"Nothing, really," said the watcher, "I just never thought
"I'd be pulling garlic in a cave inside a rock."

Her friend smiled warmly but looked down and then replied,
"Get used to it, Renee, it's good to work the soil inside.
"Better far than what goes on in places we have seen.
"At least in here it's warm and we can see the color green!"

"I know, Hidalia, I am very grateful for our place
"Among the agri-workers who are kept alive by grace.
"The fact we're still alive and are not fertilizer yet
"Amazes me and wouldn't have been where I'd placed my bet."

Renee's long yellow hair was tied behind her in a braid
That lay across her shoulder as she turned her back and said,
"I don't even know where we have been or where we are
"Other than we're closer than we were to our warm star."

"Where do you think?" Hidalia asked, her eyes alive and clear
"The others guess on Rhea but we can't see what we're near.
"We're on the far side of a moon with little gravity
"In tidal lock we never turn to see the primary."

Renee responded, "All I know is I have seen more moons
"Out our little window than Uranus or Neptune.
"The gravity is much less than what we have been used to
"And sunlight, when it shines, seems somewhat brighter 'round here too!

"I have made the shutter open minutes at a time.
"A manual release is there but views are quite confined.
"Only when the cavern lights are dimmed can much be seen.
"All I can be sure of is that westward is the scene.

"How high do you think that catwalk is above the floor?"
Renee watched her friend a moment who said, "Oh, not more
"Than twenty meters I would guess." Renee then nodded, "Yes,"
"That is what I estimated too with my best guess.

"Several shifts ago I dropped an onion from that walk
"And counted seconds as it fell that twenty meter drop.
"Twelve it took and one half more - perhaps it was thirteen.
"Now solve acceleration and you'll know the gravity."

Hidalia's eyes lit up as she reached down to get a rock
Then held it at a couple different heights and watched it drop.
With a finger in the dust she figured for a bit
Then with a smile said, "One fortieth is what I get."

"Point oh two four and some is what I got from onion's fall."
Renee exclaimed and added, "That's the same in decimal.
"Many moons are less than this and very few are more
"And that proves that old Jupiter is not this system's core.

"We are circling Saturn. Rhea is the right size too
"And there are outposts here - years ago were more than two.
"But what chance do we have to last two seconds on our own
"In trying to escape and make our way back to our home?"

Hidalia looked into Renee's blue eyes and sadly said,
"Get the notion of escape out of your silly head.
"We may not have liberty but we are safe and fed.
"You should just be happy that we haven't wound up dead.

"Renee, it's been years! I've abandoned those old hopes
"And in our captured state I've learned to live within my ropes.
"Even though no future seems apparent yet to me
"I've found love within these caves and in that I feel free."

Renee's eyes softened as she took her friend's hand in her own
And told her softly that her heart was glad she'd met her beau

"But I will never, ever lose the hope that I will see
"Another day in this life as a woman who is free.

"And on that day I'll hold my husband tightly in my arms
"And every horrid moment since our parting will be charmed
"Into a fading memory as if it were a dream
"And nothing will erase that goal, it ever pushes me."

* * * * *

In the darkness of the cockpit Captain took his chair
And gave the panorama of the stars an empty stare.
The dimly lighted instruments around his seat were set
But there was nothing urgent, he would not engage them yet.

Far beyond the main belt of the asteroids he knew
There would be a day of reckoning (or maybe two).
The terror and destruction and the death that they had wrought
Would be returned a hundred fold at his first chance he got.

A soft knock on the cockpit door announced that Gin had come
The captain pressed the lock release, his solitude was gone.
Gin sat in the other seat beside the pilot's pit
And gave the word that Nick was done and bubbling thanks for it.

"Radar wants to give the cloaker to Soldana's men.
"I think that's the best course. We've always trusted him.
"No one on the inner planets knows this stuff as well
"As Varda and he'd like to visit with him for a spell."

"I agree. We'll make it so, but take young Nick with you.
"I think it would do him good to get a Martian view
"Of independence from beneath the thumb of Earth's regime.
"Perhaps a new horizon will give him a wider dream."

Gin looked at the Captain sideways for a moment's pause
And said, "You really want to risk him to Soldana's claws?"
"Sure, why not? It's not like we've enlisted him for sure.
"Soldana might inspire something righteous, bright and pure!"

Gin burst out in laughter and the captain chuckled hard!
Tears of laughter blurred their eyes as they went galley-ward

But not before they sounded warning and slewed 'round the stern
And set deceleration at Mars normal for the burn.

* * * * *

Nothing could restrain the scent of coals and sizzling steaks
From rolling from the galley despite air scrubbers in place.
The chairs were set around the table, knives and forks and glass
And everyone was already engaged with talk and laughs.

Radar had presented Nick a small transparent tube
Containing several implants that would be no longer used.
Dewey was proposing things that no one cared to hear
Being his rude self (though meant with goodwill and good cheer.)

Nick was smiling ear to ear and even Joe showed grins,
Bovine was propounding loudly over Dewey's din,
Haji tossed a salad while the Duke managed the grill;
The steaks were large enough that every man would eat his fill.

The noises quelled a bit when Gin and Captain came inside
And everyone took seats but Duke and Haji who were tied
Up with the final touches on the pile of steaming steaks
And red-skinned baked potatoes that would grace the dinner plates.

The Captain whispered something into Radar's closest ear
And Radar nodded slightly then pinched Dewey on the rear
Who quieted himself and turned to see the Captain's face
Then turned a little red and now sat quietly in place.

"Tomorrow we'll decelerate to enter Martian space,"
The captain said, "We've made good time despite our slackened pace.
"With Mars near opposition from the Earth the hop was short.
"In two days' time we'll be at Phobos, docked at Stickney port.

"We will spend three days there getting ready for the trip
"To Titan. As you know we'll bring some cargo on the ship
"And maybe turn a profit when we enter Saturn's space.
"There's plenty of demand for everything around that place.

"Gin and Radar have some business to do planet-side.
"Nick, you will be welcome to go with them if you like.

"Duke, you go with Dewey, he will need to stretch his legs.
"Keep him out of trouble with his Martian renegades.

"I don't want to bail him from the jail yet again.
"In fact, I'm more inclined to let them keep him bolted in.
"There are lots of big rocks that need broken into small.
"The jail has a sledge hammer; it's Dewey's name it calls."

Snickers went around the room and Dewey shook his head.
The captain shot him one quick wink (but still Dewey turned red).
Gin and Duke both shook their heads and took a sip of beer
Then the captain finished with his final orders clear:

"Bovine, you and Haji keep an eye around the ship
"Joe and I'll relieve you when we're done with one short trip.
"Then you can have a day and night of liberty yourselves.
"Get on board before day three at forenoon watch, eight bells.

"Now, let's dig in!" he finished and the platter piled high
With porterhouse and rib eye was accepted with deep sighs.
The food was good aboard this ship but sometimes it was great!
And this was one of those great meals landing on their plates.

"I never thought I'd eat a fresh-grilled steak on a space flight,"
Nick exclaimed with wonder as he took a second bite.
"This is excellent," he said and others grunted, "Yes!"
And captain said, "This ship is home. Sometimes we get the best."

Bovine interjected "It's the grill that makes the taste.
"The smoke is vented out the hull into the void of space.
"Haji is a master chef, but Duke knows how to grill!
"He grew up on a ranch; he knows how to do it still."

The captain said, "We've had a guest or two that had no taste
"For food cooked on a grill for they were born and bred in space.
"They never in their life had seen a wood fire or its smell
"And found the whole idea alien and crude as well.

"But every member of this crew has Earth still in their blood
"Even though their loyalties to her may not be good
"But deep inside our DNA our Mother Earth still lives
"And we still crave to feed the needs inside us that she gives."

Nick took in the captain's words and then looked all around
The table acting just a bit confused. He slightly frowned
As if the realization that one's loyalty might be
Different from Earth... and then the captain went on, "See,

"Most of this crew were displaced from all they loved and knew
"When factions in the recent wars had wrecked their homes and slew
"Their friends and families and now as freemen on their own
"Work in space and other worlds and call this ship their home."

The captain studied Nick's expression then he asked him plain:
"Do you follow interplanetary happenings?
"I know you study physics with an engineering mind
"But I suspect on politics you haven't spent much time."

Nick responded, "Sir, you are correct in what you guess.
"My focus has been narrow and I read news with distress.
"Stories in the media are biased and confused
"And I have found no value getting caught up with their views."

Others at the table grunted through their chewing bliss
Approval and agreement. Gin said, "Good for you then, Nick.
"Focus on developing your skills and talents first
"And try to bring on progress, not confusion; that just hurts.

"The garbage that is foisted at Earth's universities
"Is filtered and conditioned to bring Reason to its knees."
Haji countered, "Sven, you know that is not wholly true.
"There are still a number of Earth's great medical schools.

"And engineering disciplines have not yet turned corrupt
"Though science in its purest form has largely given up.
"But I agree, the finest schools are found on Mars today
"Where independent thought is taught and shown to be the way."

Bovine forked another rib eye from the platter's pile
His focus deeply set on shoving pieces through his smile.
Joe was watching Nick quite closely from the other end
Of the wooden table when the captain spoke again:

"The Terra-Luna war was just the start of what's become
"A sort of cold war, or perhaps a free-for-all, say some.

"Piracy and renegades from TerraCorp have grown
"And now with many worlds to prey on, come into their own.

"No single world has the strength to hunt and bring them down.
"Though many have their navies they must guard their own world's towns.
"Flying escort for their ships of commerce takes a toll.
"Alliances at times are weak and some mean naught at all."

The captain took another bite of porterhouse done rare
And leaned back in his seat holding his fork up in the air.
A look of satisfaction and raw pleasure crossed his face
And it was quite apparent he enjoyed his steak in space.

A grin came to the captain's face and then he plainly said,
"Forgive me, Mr. Hallenbeck, I fear I've lost my head.
"It's rude to speak of politics and such unpleasantries.
"At dinner we should talk only of good and pleasant things."

"It's quite all right, Sir, no offense," said Nick in honesty
"I know my knowledge of such things is short - and shamefully.
"But now that I have flown the coop and someone willed me die
"I need to get informed a bit; it's duty and what's right."

"It is," said Radar who with vigor stabbed another piece
Of tender rib eye with his fork and shoved it through his teeth.
"Someone wanted you to do their dirty work for them
"Without your will or knowledge. This goes on time and again."

Then Gin said, "Nick, there really are important things afoot
"Happening across the system that aren't very good.
"But we have faith in free mens' will and strength to make things right
"And at some point the time will come when there will be a fight.

"Now, let's do what the captain said and talk of nicer things
"Like this luscious steak and these amazing peppered beans!
"My guess is that these peppers were a product of the Earth
"And I suspect the beans were too, on that I'd bet my berth!"

"You'd lose your bet," said Haji with a grin from ear to ear.
"The beans were grown on Ganymede and Peppers very near
"For they were grown in Chryse! When we last visited Mars
"I laid in a supply and these are from the final jar."

"Haw, haw!" roared Bovine and Gin looked down at his plate.
"Pay up, old goat! I think you owe the grill a scrape!"
Gin looked truly shocked and asked, "How long have we had feed
"Cooked in our own galley that was grown on Ganymede?"

"Gin needs more time in the galley," Bovine loud opined.
Dewey said, "I'll vote for that!" The captain sipped his wine.
Gin said, "I knew Ganymede exported some food stuffs
"But lowly beans? How could they make a profit large enough?"

"Gravity," said Joe, "That's where the profits take the hit.
"You must consider costs when lifting things up out of it.
"It's true that Earth produces more than all the other worlds
"But smaller and more local lots can from a moon be hurled

"With lower cost. Really, Gin, you missed the obvious."
Gin turned red and stuttered something how he knew it, just
That he was caught surprised that they would ship the lowly bean
From Ganymede. Then Bovine said, "We all know what you mean.

"That is why export of metals from the Earth has ceased.
"Mercury and Luna can produce and ship with ease,
"While earth remains the deepest well of gravity to climb
"Than all the other worlds in the system. And that's fine."

Bovine shoved another bite of steak between his teeth
Content to focus on his belly but he added, "Beef.
"Beef and fish and forestry - no other world comes close.
"That's the treasure of the Earth and what it ships the most."

Dewey chimed in, "Someday Mars will export beef as well;
"But right now pork and eggs and chickens are what they will sell
"And they're expensive off-world. You'll see that on Phobos.
"Everything's expensive there; the tourists pay the most."

"I suppose those pleasure yachts that tourists take are nice,"
Said Nick, "And I suppose they come by Phobos once or twice
"On their way to see the outer worlds as they cruise."
Then Gin looked straight at Nick and gave him this sad bit of news:

"The pleasure yachts you've heard about are now extremely rare
"And these days do not venture without escorts way out there.

"The views of Jupiter and rings of Saturn are not safe;
"Such fat and juicy targets draw pirates and renegades.

"Mostly colonists and engineering teams are there
"And any with experience are armed and stay aware.
"There is a network of outposts with military strength
"But they can only do so much." He stopped to take a drink.

"That isn't right," said Nick, "Why can't these criminals be found
"And brought to justice and the system restored safe and sound?"
The others paused and quieted, then Haji said it plain,
"It is a big place out there, Nick. And many have been slain.

"The inner worlds around the sun are small and close and tight
"And after Earth was pacified there hasn't been much fight;
"But in the outer worlds there is room beyond compare."
Then Joe added succinctly, "It's the Wild West out there."

Haji added, "Anyone from off the Earth will tell
"That renegades of TerraCorp (and TerraCorp as well)
"Are not much better than the pirates you and I despise
"Who prey on peaceful people, though some of them die besides."

The captain looked at Haji then around the feasting crew
And said, "It looks as if a history lesson's overdue.
"Nick, I must inform you TerraCorp's official line
"Casts the nicest spin on what has happened over time,

"And what the state-run schools on Earth have deemed the truth to be
"Is slanted by perspectives of their tenured faculty,
"Most of whom have not experienced the truth of life
"And how success and growth come only by hard work and strife.

"TerraCorp was powerful and profited the most.
"Their service to mankind establishing the first outposts
"Was incalculable as our history has shown,
"Corrupted by Earth's government, bureaucracy had grown.

"Injustice and excessive profiteering became law.
"Growth became inhibited - impossible at all.
"With opportunities of nearly limitless extent,
"Tiny tyrants prospered while the people's backs were bent.

"As the worlds grew their independence was their need.
"We've seen it time and time again, that people must be free
"To self-determination and a local rule of law
"And not be shackled to a distant tyranny at all.

"When TerraCorp restructured after Luna won the war
"There were whole divisions that were not theirs anymore.
"Most aligned as independents or allied with worlds;
"But some just seemed to disappear without a trace or word.

"That is when the pirates prospered and found havens safe,
"Protected, even hired as mercenaries as of late
"By factions of an underworld we know little of;
"But they have staked their claims. And for them we have no love."

The captain's voice fell silent and the crew looked at their plates.
Not a single man among them dared look at his face,
But after a protracted silent moment Nick spoke up
And said, "I think I understand now how I got such luck.

"I have been sent out to find the secret of success
"A TerraCorp division (that has left the corporate nest)
"Has managed recently to get (reported by their spies).
"And then destroy the evidence. Titan is the prize.

"Under guise of understudy with a knack or two
"They've convinced the members of the atmospheric crew
"To take me underneath their wing and tutor me along
"So I'd provide relief for one or two who've worked there long.

"When secured (the data Corporate has claimed to keep)
"A fiery accident occurs and kids and widows weep
"Upon the news that TerraCorp's beloved research crew
"Has been set back and it will be another year or two

"Before a full investigation can be set in place
"And by that time the whole event can safely be erased.
"To me it now is obvious," as Nick's face turned more red.
"Without your careful scans and care I soon would be quite dead."

Joe and Duke exchanged some looks then looked the captain's way.
The captain looked at Nick and plainly asked, "Will you please say

"Exactly what it is you do that makes your value high
"To those that work to find the key to make Titan their prize?"

"High emission imaging is my subject of note.
"There were a couple white papers on it that we once wrote
"On using cosmic rays to view the depths of ice and stone
"But there are pieces missing still, to bring the hardware home."

One could almost see Radar's big ears expand and twist
Around as if to penetrate Nick's mind and then insist
That every bit of knowledge that he had be spilled at once.
It almost looked as if he were a cat about to pounce!

Gin and Bovine both looked at him, Dewey perked up too,
The captain's eyes grew narrow as he digested this news
And asked, "Nick, how close are you to using cosmic rays
"To probe a moon's interior and put it on display?"

"We've had some limited success with high end gamma rays
"And with synthetic aperture from specialized arrays.
"A focused plane of proton paths has been converted down
"But interference from the sun can kill it." (Then Nick frowned.)

Dewey cynically responded with what they all thought,
"Cosmic rays are shielded by magnetic fields and rock.
"That is something no one would expect to really do."
And Nick responded patiently, "Yes, that is quite true,

"You see, it's not as straight forward as one might like to hope.
"In fact it's counter-intuitive, much like pushing rope.
"Ultra low frequency radio detectors see
"With gamma modulation vastly higher energies,

"With proton-antiproton ultra energy events
"Illumination of rock structure can, in fact be sensed.
"My specialty has focused on the aperture arrays
"Achieving higher resolution in a smaller space.

"A big array near Saturn has been built far from the sun.
"It has imaged Titan's ocean floors on the first runs.
"My job, in theory, is to build a newer test
"To get a smaller instrument to image things the best.

"I overheard a number of the engineers back home
"Arguing about what happens at a thermal zone
"In Titan's atmosphere and what device might break it down
"But when they saw me walking by they hushed and then they frowned.

"Maybe that is why they sent me here, a walking flame
"Expendable but easily inserted, just the same.
"A spy and saboteur for them and then out of the way
"For as a pile of ash I'd not reveal what I might say.

"They wanted me to be on Titan quickly, that's for sure
"But didn't want the implication it was TerraCorp
"Who caused the fatal accident. They put me on your ship
"To steal the data quickly for the price of one quick trip."

The crew all mulled this over for a minute more or two
Then Bovine said the obvious: "Exploring with a view
"Of any moon's interior would save a hefty fee
"When prospecting for minerals, but why such secrecy?

"Every mining outfit will eventually gain
"The benefit of this new tool when it becomes explained.
"And why would it have anything to do with Titan's case?"
Bovine took a swig of beer, a puzzle on his face.

Gin piped up and noted, "This could be a tool to find
"Not only rocks and minerals but voids and caves just fine.
"Remotely, from high orbit with no need for seismic gear.
"This could be a power that for some would instill fear

"For there are those who want to keep their hiding places safe
"Within the depths and hollow places this would soon erase."
Joe's eyes narrowed while he reached to lift his mug of beer
And looked straight at the captain and said slowly, very clear:

"The military value of an imager like this
"Can't be underestimated. They don't want to miss
"Any chance they get to gain the power to expose
"Independent havens bringing freedom to a close

"And pull the renegade divisions back under the wing
"Of TerraCorp by mercenary force. They'd once again

"Have the economic clout to dominate and rule.
"The price would be horrific, paid in blood and treasure too."

Everyone fell silent once again in private thought
Some with bitter memories of what the wars had wrought
And others contemplated how the future might unfold
If earthly tyrants had control of every system's gold.

Young Dewey broke the silence then, and asked two simple words:
"Why Titan?" and then Duke responded, "Real estate, of course."
Dewey looked a bit confused and said, "That frozen hell?"
Then Haji added, "Titan has potential as well

"As Mars to be another home where man can walk and breathe.
"There has been a lot of research done and plans conceived
"To terraform it; but the task is delicate and fraught
"With danger as a misstep could erase the progress got."

Bovine blurted, "Dewey, what the heck did you expect?
"You would know the stakes for Titan if you'd pull you neck
"For just a minute from your gaming station for a change,
"You goofy punk." then both began a sibling-like exchange

Of insults growing cruder with each back-and-forth remark
While Nick, first shocked but then amused, absorbed their heated talk.
"Stow it, Bovine. Dewey!" Gin commanded with a bark
"We don't need to air your laundry or your rude remarks."

Chuckles rolled around the table as the red-faced pair
Stabbed new bites from off their plates and waved them in the air
Then chomped hard on their food to show what they would do to each
If they could reach across the table, lessons they would teach!

The captain smiled broadly then addressed the case at hand
By asking, "What would be the value of all of the land
"On a living planet with an atmosphere as dense
"As Earth's and with a landmass near as large? It is immense."

"It's poisonous and frozen," Dewey said as if to scoff.
Then Nick began an explanation prefaced by a cough,
"You see, Dewey, even though it's so far from the sun
"It's warmer on the planet than thought by most everyone.

"The atmosphere is mostly nitrogen just like the Earth
"And seven times more massive per square meter on the surf'.
"A greenhouse layer high above it warms it and could be
"Increased by several factors in its true efficiency."

Bovine added, "See, beneath the ground's an icy core
"That with the right approach could be exploited more and more
"To push the hydrocarbons high and low off of Titan's land
"And in a very short time could be made safe for a man."

"That's the nutshell version," Gin explained but added quick,
"The problem is to plan the safest places where to stick
"The bore sites and atomics through a stable mass of rock
"Without disturbing magma and ammonia with the shock."

"And that's where RF imaging will come into the play,"
Said Nick before he used his sleeve to wipe some beer away
From his lip, then added "With a better picture deep
"Beneath the surface that reality will come in reach."

The pace of eating slowed and one or two picked at their teeth
In silence as their bulging bellies full of beer and meat
Worked their magic and erased all sadness from their heads
And conversation turned to lighter subjects then instead.

When one more round of beers and one more glass of wine were gone
The captain gave the word deceleration would be strong
And that tomorrow they could spend their time (except for shifts)
Resting and digesting on the bunks around the ship.

"Bovine, you and Dewey get propulsion systems checked;
"Radar, do a thorough scan of Martian space ahead;
"I will do the dishes; Gin, you've earned yourself the grill;
"In an hour ice cream's on and all may eat their fill."

With grunts and sighs and thank-yous' to the cooks they pushed away
From the table patting stomachs, belching great displays
Of dining satisfaction and thanksgiving for the feast
And thanked the captain for providing such great cuts of meat.

Duke and Joe and Nick and Haji shoved off for the door
And as they left Nick looked at Haji, whispered one thing more:

"The captain does the dishes?" Nick displayed his great surprise
And Haji whispered back, "He makes it plain to his men's eyes

"That there is no task on this ship beneath his dignity.
"He does not lord position over his men, don't you see?
"A natural commander and a born leader of men
"He has their trust for they know he will do his best for them."

Haji paused then whispered, "And we do our best for him."
Joe had overheard the final words and said, "Amen."
But just as they had gone around the corner of the door
Nick and Joe heard Captain ask for just a few words more:

"Tell us more of focused proton paths and gamma rays,"
The captain asked, "There must be more to this you didn't say."
Nick turned back and questioned, "Sir?" and Joe turned back as well
Curious to see if there were more that he might tell.

"There really isn't much, Sir, but technical details.
"We simply bring the particles to concentrate levels
"Then release the radiation to illuminate
"And image what's revealed with a multiplexed array."

Nick and Joe returned to sit in chairs near galley's sinks
As Gin and Captain scrubbed and scraped and took some time to think.
Then Gin announced, "You said you focused protons to a plane
"And anti-protons also, yes? Do they behave the same?

"And are they in a second focus field of some kind
"Or do they get collected simply on another side?"
Nick responded, "Yes. The same but different, you see,
"Collection happens at two rates with little certainty,

"So two collecting fields formed at intersecting planes
"Are made and then the matter is released within the same.
"When the flux is balanced and the regulation right
"We gain control of what we call the 'penetrator light'."

The captain and his engineer digested this a while
Then Nick continued, "Also there was talk..." (and then he smiled
As if the thought were silly) "...that perhaps the energy
"Could be directed or refined to treat a canopy

"In Titan's atmosphere to cause enhanced greenhouse effects
"But there could never be efficiency - it's so much less..."
He trailed off again and you could see upon his face
That there was much to do to win this engineering race.

Gin was mulling over what young Nicholas had said
When captain noted, "There is not much physics in my head
"But could you wrap your focused planes into concentric tubes
"And do the antimatter mix between them for your use?

"Instead of just a tiny intersection of two planes
"You'd have a cylinder defined by all you have contained.
"The proton field outside and the antiprotons in;
"But surely that's been looked at," as he put more dishes in

The sink to soak a moment. Nick displayed a look of shock
And one could see his mind was racing - all else had been blocked
From his awareness. He was lost now, deep within his thoughts
A long protracted moment, then the captain blurted, "What?

"Isn't that the obvious configuration for
"Maximizing throughput by compacting in a core
"The active interaction to direct into a beam
"The output of the energy annihilation brings?"

Gin paused in his scrubbing and took on the look of Nick.
Both of them were lost within their thoughts so very quick!
The captain looked at both of them then smiled wide at Joe
The humor wasn't lost on him for he was grinning so!

Nick began to form a word then stopped, then tried again
And Gin turned 'round to say something but paused and looked at him.
Then Nick began again and said, "It might be possible
"With five-axis magnetics," then became inaudible.

"Or six," Gin said. Then, "Captain, what you just described is new.
"A brilliant application, though not easy yet to do.
"Nick, do you have simulation data we could view
"Or just parameters that we might get a chance to use

"For what the captain has suggested? You know what this means."
And Nick responded, "Yes, of course, I think we both can see."

Joe's wide grin had morphed into confusion, looking lost.
The captain looked about the same and he repeated, "What?"

Nick explained "Not only would efficiency increase
"Perhaps a million fold, but also size could be decreased.
"Five-axis magnetics would make penetrator light
"Intense enough to make even a planet's core look bright."

"Think six," said Gin, "Think six. The possibility is there
"To do more than illuminate," and then the very hair
On the nape of Nick's neck stood erect, eyes wider yet.
"Do you get my drift?" asked Gin, and Nick said, "You can bet

"Someone may have had that thought at Titan's big array.
"That may be what they are after, not just scanning rays."
Gin looked flush and slowly set his scrubbing project down
And Nick's excited face turned ghostly white, a growing frown.

"Okay, guys. What is it?" asked the captain, now engaged
"Spell it out for those of us you lost along the way."
Gin and Nick looked at the captain. Nick said, "We must run
"A lot of simulations and we've not even begun."

Gin explained, "Captain, what you just described could be
"A very crucial step toward building what could be the key
"Not only to accelerate a terraforming plan
"But something powerful that must be kept from tyrant hands.

Gin then grimly said, "Nick, I'm sure you must agree."
"Yes, of course," said Nick, "I do, and most whole-heartedly!"
"Captain," Gin continued, "It appears your ray of light
"May be the inspiration for a weapon of great might.

"You have laid the groundwork that has set us on the course
"To build a light emitter of extreme destructive force."
"If we're right, this will be the very first time ever
"Man has had the key to build a gamma ray laser."

"Holy smokes!" came out of Joe as he absorbed this news,
"That's far beyond the energies of current lasers used."
The captain looked from face to face and said, "If you are right
"This must never leave this room or be brought to the light

"Until the time we choose. Now, what resource do you need
"To set your simulations up and get Gin up to speed?"
Nick said, "We will need a good computer as a start."
Then Gin said, "Radar has the tools and also has the art.

"Let us bring him into this." The captain said, "Okay,
"But keep it under wraps from others while you three make hay.
"Especially young Dewey." The captain's eyes were hard.
"Joe, why don't you finish up the grill so they can start.

"I doubt if either of these two will sleep 'till they've got proof
"That this is possible and the idea won't go 'poof!'"
"You've got it," Joe responded but Gin had it mostly done
And said, "Take Nick to Radar. Get him started on the fun.

"I'll be along in half an hour. Don't let Radar balk.
"There are things we'll need and he will need some physics talk
"To understand the plan and that our Nick will run the show.
"He won't want the bother 'til he knows what you now know."

Nick and Joe went quickly and the captain turned to Gin
And said, "Magnetics of the kind you'll need aren't in our bin,
"Are they?" Gin said, "No, but you know who'll have a line
"On getting some: Soldana," and the captain nodded, "Fine.

"They won't be inexpensive, will they?" Gin said, "Not from him
"But there won't be the questions that might trigger suspicion."
The captain thought a moment as he put the final dish
On the rack above the stove as Haji would insist.

"Have Radar send a message only for Soldana's eyes
"With the specs and details and the time we will arrive.
"Soldana owes a favor as you know, and we'll collect
"And if he wiggles I will twist it hard around his neck."

* * * * *

It wasn't every day that ice cream graced the bowls on board.
And after steaks had settled some, the crew came 'round to hoard
As much as they could shovel into stomachs that were set
To spend a day at rest before Mars orbit would be met.

Bovine asked, "Where's Nick and Radar? Gin is missing too."
The captain said, "They have a project that they went to do."
"They're missing out," said Duke as he took in a spoon of white
And rolled it 'round his mouth exuding obvious delight.

"Haji, dish up three bowls and I'll take them down to them,"
The captain said and added, "I'd not like to have three men
"On the warpath after me for keeping them away
"From the finest ice cream this side of the Bering Strait."

Haji put three heaping helpings into bowls and set
Them on the table as the captain said, "Who'll take my bet
"That in the morning there will be complaints about the food
"And how the galley only serves up beans and barley gruel."

"I'll not take that bet," said Haji with a knowing smile
As Dewey plunged his spoon into a slowly melting pile
Of milky frozen cargo precious anywhere off Earth
Oblivious he'd soon be snoring loudly in his berth.

The captain took the bowls and made his way to Radar's lab
And tapped the door before he opened, feeling just a tad
Curious about the way the three would interact
And as he stepped inside announced he'd brought them all a snack.

But they were deeply focused on a screen of charts and graphs
And hardly recognized someone had come (he choked his laugh).
Placing the three bowls upon a shelf within their sight
He listened for a moment to their words with deep delight:

"A gamma ray laser might describe it in one mode;
"But it just might be possible to use it as a node
"To transmit antiprotons in a rough coherent pack
"Within the confines of the beam where protons won't attract.

"Do you know what I am saying?" Nick looked hard at Gin
"You are talking crazy," Gin said, "You would dump them in
"The beam and lose the energy that starts the whole affair?"
Then Radar blurted, "Antimatter packets through the air!

"An antimatter canon, Gin! Stop crying in your beer!
"Let's run it all again and set magnetic timing here."

Radar stroked the console and the display changed a bit.
The captain looked around him thinking he would like to sit

And listen to the brainstorming which warmly filled the room
But there were no more chairs, so he left them in the gloom
Of darkened lights and bright displays that meant little to him,
Pleased that as a working team they'd neatly settled in.

Joe and Duke and Dewey sat with Haji. Their big spoons
Were working steady - all the ice cream would be gone and soon!
The creamy white confection was exotic and so rare
In almost every place beyond the blue Earth's humid air.

The captain sat down with a bowl and let the creamy treat
Roll across his tongue as memories so warm and sweet
Flooded through his mind of happy times before the wars
Had separated him from she he loved and set his course

Firmly on the path to finish what had been begun
The hour that his enemy had struck, took her and run.
The years of lonely nights and days of searching for the clue
To bring her back into his arms. One day they'd pay their due.

5   Mars

Arrival day at Phobos was for Nick a grand affair!
A loop was made to shed some speed within the Martian air.
There were no engines blazing, only thrusters spewing gas;
(Decelerating for two days had slowed them for that pass.)

And through the whole maneuver from beginning to the end
Nick could scarcely pull his eyes from Mars for one second.
The view was stunning! Even more alluring than the Earth
With red and yellow landscapes un-obscured by clouds and surf.

The ice-bound heights of Mount Olympus reaching into space
Sweeping down to Amazonis from his Tharsis place,
The hills of shining Hellas and the Solis windswept plains,
Chryse and the cratered wrecks of ancient mountain chains.

All came into view as orbit's inclination changed
To rendezvous with Phobos, as Mars Defense arranged
(Deimos was the seat of Martian Space Defense's might
With basing stations at Langrange points to its left and right.)

Streaking from the night side back into the blazing sun
With ruddy Mars below them they began their final run.
Catching up to Phobos from behind its speeding track
Nick could see the long striations running down its back.

The last approach was more like docking than a landing move.
Their ship came slowly to a tower rising from a groove
That scored the surface of the moon from leading face to rear
And when secured the docking tower pulled the old ship near.

On the night side of the moon within the deep ravine
The ochre light reflecting from the planet lit the scene
As men in spacesuits tended to the tethers, wires and tubes
Of other ships at port but there were none for this ship's use,

For Bovine, Joe and Duke were taking charge with speed and ease
In suits outside while Captain contracted their special needs.
Gin had sat beside their passenger through the approach
And gave a little rundown as Nick's self-appointed coach:

"The orbital velocity of this old hunk of rock
"Gives advantage to arriving ships that need to dock.
"Using Martian gravity and atmosphere to brake
"This is a perfect place for fuel and fodder to on-take.

"There is no need to climb out of the Martian gravity
"For we retain a part of our escape velocity.
"And if indeed a visit to the surface is the need
"Many shuttle services will for your fare compete."

When the ship had been secured and minor cargos dropped
Those who planned an outing suited up for they had docked
At an older port where pressured passageways weren't used.
(They rented storage lockers in the station for their suits.)

Dewey was insistent that they take pneumatic tubes
From the port to Stickney Station where the action brewed
Though Duke restrained and collared him and kept him throttled down
And got them all a shuttle was DaVinci Spaceport bound.

Stickney Station wasn't all that Nick thought it might be
In fact, the dirt and bustle of the place he found creepy.
As a major fueling port and cargo transfer site
There were lots of travelers to riff-raff's great delight.

Mostly long-haul cargo men or colonists enroute,
Some business travelers and even tourists were about.
And down at Central station there were businesses galore
Where one could buy most anything though it might cost you more

Than planet-side on ruddy Mars four thousand miles below
Where many long-haul travelers were queuing up to go.
(They had been for weeks or months confined inside a ship
And more than willing to pay for a planet-side round trip!)

But these were not the sights that held Nick's interest the most.
The physics of the installation, built on lengthy posts
Extending deep into the regolith secured to rock
Were quite a wonder to behold, though many seemed to mock

The wisdom of a station built within a dirty moon
With nearly zero gravity (and mostly carbon too,

Loosely congregated with not much as solid core)
But positives outweighed the negatives by so much more!

For there were many residents who lived within that moon
Deep in the interior, shielded from the doom
Which solar radiation and the cosmic rays can bring,
So deadly with a long exposure to all living things.

Many of these Phobos citizens grew rich and fat
In the shipping industries and warehousing and that.
Many owned the shuttle services and tourist shops
That catered to the travelers or fancy restaurants

Where honeymooners or the wealthy Martians came to stay
For specialized events or even weekend getaways.
But these were not the neighborhoods where transients might go
(Like spaceship crews or ladies of the night, as you might know).

On the surface under domes a number of resorts
Were situated where a pleasure yacht could come to port
And no one anywhere would have an argument with you
That anywhere within the system had a better view!

While they waited for their flight Nick went with Gin to trade
A small amount of currency at Phobos Coin Exchange.
Though any gold or silver was acceptable on Mars
It always was preferred if it would bear the local marks.

Martian banks all did brisk business at their Phobos branch
There were even two of Earth, but few gave them a glance
And in a traffic area as busy as this was
Gaming houses and loan sharks considered it a plus.

Gin told Nick, "Keep your wallet in your front pocket.
"And keep a hand on any gear if you cannot lock it.
"Though most folks may be honest and responsible and true
"You can bet there's others here that right now target you!"

Dewey came to tell them that their flight was ready now
(Obviously anxious to get to DaVinci town,
The Martian space port was renowned for partying and fun
And he had friends were waiting for his flight to make its run).

The three rejoined with Duke and Radar at the shuttle's dock
And pushed up through the passageway that joined it to the rock.
Taking seats where Nick could get the best view of the land
Just in time before the pilot gave the launch command.

A short burst from the thrusters settled seats against their backs
And half a minute later turned the shuttle on its track.
A warning sounded, then the rockets sent them on their way
And ninety minutes later shuttle pilot earned his pay:

The wings swept forward partially, the slipstream could be heard
The old crate started shuddering as buffeting occurred,
An ionizing glow was seen to form around the wings
And as they bit more air a bit more forward did they swing

Until their lengthy aspect was extended full and wide
So more speed could bleed off in a very high-drag glide
Which put them in the landing pattern for DaVinci's field.
The landing gear extended and the runway touched the wheels.

As they taxied toward a building at the field's edge
Nick was shocked to see a row of Yucca as a hedge
Planted in a row before a building built of stone
And thriving as if Mars had been its nature-given home!

"Yucca!" Nick exclaimed, and Dewey looked at him and mocked
The look on Newbie's face that couldn't hide surprise and shock.
Duke explained, "It's babied there and nurtured with great pride
"By those who run the terminal; there's not much grows this high.

"DaVinci's altitude is higher than the Chryse plain
"But being on the equator with care they'll grow the same.
"They've adapted better than most other arid plants.
"Their tolerance to freezing gives them more than half a chance.

"You have much to learn of Mars," Duke finished with a smile
And Nick responded, "I had no idea," all the while
Drinking in the sights with obvious intense delight
Beneath the reddish morning sky (just half of Earth's sunlight).

A pressurized and heated bus rolled to the shuttle's door
And backed in so its entry would attach and provide more

Protection for the riders from the rarified cold air
As Gin remarked, "Martian progress is beyond compare.

"Down on the Chryse plain you'll see a bit more Earth than that
"And if you visit Hellas you might bring your fishing hat;
"But on this trip we've not much time to take in all the sights.
"We have a job to do; but then perhaps we'll take a flight."

Radar rose from off his seat and said, "Let's take a ride,"
And moved off toward the doorway where the bus pressed to the side.
The others followed suit and soon they rolled off toward a dome
Under which DaVinci Station's business made its home.

There were other spaceports here and there around the globe
DaVinci was the biggest and the busiest one though
With several maintenance facilities and runway strips
It was the one that serviced all the largest cargo ships.

Passengers were not ignored of course, there were hotels
And restaurants and goods and services and cheaper thrills.
But it was not a city; there were really rather few
That made DaVinci crater home, with warmer parts in view

Down in Hyrdaotes where one walked and talked and breathed
Without the aid of respirators for oxygen needs,
Though it took acclimation - a couple weeks and more
To get one's body able to walk meters out of doors.

Many could not do it though. Many could not live
Without the extra oxygen that concentrators give.
Hypoxia and altitude sickness were common ails
Each load of visitors or immigrants brought without fail.

But oxygen was cheap and plentiful and all about
There was never reason or a need to do without.
Even the old timers who had lived there many years
Never traveled anywhere without their breathing gear.

Soon the bus backed up to one of several outer doors
Giving access to the largest dome where there were more
Than forty separate buildings mostly built from local stone
Some of which were there before the building of the dome.

And all around the inner rim as far as Nick could see
Were rows of tangerine and other full-grown citrus trees
Carefully arranged so all would get the best sunlight
Which at this distance from the sun shone only half as bright.

But still they grew and even fruited slowly through the year
As it was told by Dewey who had many times come here.
The air was thick with citrus scent that soothed and made one calm
And toward the center of the dome: a dozen tall date palms!

There were many other domes and stand-alone buildings
Scattered 'round the area that growing commerce brings.
This was a thriving transportation center it was plain
And every time one visited it never looked the same.

Soldana's men would meet them at a warehouse out of town
Among a group of buildings where the railroad went down
The valley at the east side through DaVinci crater's wall
But as they went to rent a car the captain gave a call:

He said he wanted Duke to stay with Radar, Gin and Nick
While Dewey was still free to go (he grinned and ran off quick
With promises to meet again at Barsoom Bar and Grill
On the morrow after when with friends he'd had his thrills).

It seemed there were developments that had not been foreseen:
Soldana had some information and had hatched a scheme.
The captain wanted Duke to be along if things might go
Awry (since in Soldana's town you never really know).

The car they rented was an older make of Martian style
Built for rough terrain and hauling cargo many miles
With six pneumatic wheels mounted wide beneath the hull
A half a dozen men could ride inside and not be full.

Driving east along the road that paralleled the rails
Nick observed that many railroad cars were fit with sails
Rolled on masts that folded down along the carriage sides.
He guessed that they were used to save on fuel on those long rides

Across the empty lands between the settlements and towns
Of Amazon and Borealis where the winds swept down

Across Mare Acidalium and south to Chryse's fields
From Hellas to Isidis to transport industry's yields.

"It's said someday DaVinci will become an ocean port,"
Said Radar as he watched expressions cross Nick's face for sport.
"But I don't think we'll see it. Things don't change that fast.
"Maybe Mars won't be like Earth when all is said at last."

Gin injected, "Mars can never be like Earth of course.
"Besides the lessened sunlight there is not the tidal force
"Exerted on the planet like the Moon upon the Earth
"And for a thousand other factors, oceans will not work

"The way they do on earth. But there are other things
"Like wind and lower gravity - we'll see what time may bring."
Nick mused for a moment then he leaned back in his seat
And watched the landscape pass the window just beyond his reach.

Presently they pulled into a group of buildings set
Along a railroad spur which branched so warehouses could get
Access to the rolling stock where there appeared to be
Machine shops and some other maintenance facilities.

Gin was driving slowly as they turned around a bend
Behind two larger warehouses where Nick could see two men
Waiting in a sunny entryway who turned and stared
Until Gin flashed his headlights then one came looking prepared

For trouble, 'til he saw Duke step out from the transport's hatch
And take his parka's hood away and pull aside his mask.
The two exchanged some friendly words and motioned Gin to drive
The rig into an open door and soon they were inside.

The warehouse seemed much larger on the inside than the out
Brightly lighted with some shelving scattered here about
But Nick's attention centered on an aircraft at one side
It's folded wings displaying how much lift they could provide.

"Let's go," said Radar as he opened wide the hatch again
And motioned Nick up from his seat to follow him and Gin
Out of the car where two men greeted Gin with warm regard
But Nick felt apprehension when he saw two well-armed guards

Standing in positions at each side and just behind.
Then Radar whispered in his ear, "Don't pay them any mind,
"Soldana runs a tight ship and he likes security.
"That's partly why we're here, so yes, we'll have some company."

Gin was smiling wide and chatting with a relaxed air
Beside a striking figure of man with sandy hair
Who laughed good-naturedly as they both turned and beckoned Nick
And made their introductions shaking hands with welcome grips.

"I am Ansel Pedersen. Logistics is my skill.
"I've been sent to make sure that your needs are all fulfilled.
"Sven tells me you'd like to see magnetics of a type
"Which are not common; but they have come through my supply pipe."

He smiled with a gleam of mischief on his salesman's face
Then winked and turned to Radar keeping up a hurried pace.
"Radar, it is good to see you. Varda could not come;
"But you will see him long before this afternoon is done.

"I understand you've something special just for Varda's eyes?"
Radar nodded. Ansel said, "Good! Now, let's fly!"
Gin gave pause a moment then said, "Fly? It was made clear
"That we'd check out the merchandise and pick it up from here."

Ansel looked confused a moment, then responded, "No,
"Soldana had it sent to his place. That is where we go."
Radar sent a message quickly for the captain's eyes
And Gin said, "That is even better! Is that bird our ride?"

"It is," the smiling Ansel said, "Would you care to sit
"A little while inside the office while they ready it?"
"Thank you, Ansel," Gin replied, "That would be just fine."
They all shed their masks and coats and followed him inside.

The office looked more like a lounge than warehouse business place
With leather chairs and couches spread around the ample space.
"There is coffee, tea and fruit juice in the alcove there,"
Ansel said, "In fifteen minutes we'll be in the air."

Nick was glad to rest a while and watch the men unfold
The aircraft wings and check the fuel and wheels before they rolled

The sleek machine outside to start the turbines and inspect
The empennage and run the list of other preflight checks.

The captain had acknowledged and confirmed Soldana's plan
To meet them at his ranch down in the Ganges canyon lands.
And just as Ansel said, they soon were winging toward the south
Then west through Capri canyon and on up the Ganges' mouth.

6   Soldana

In a sunken region of the Ganges Chaos hills
Twenty thousand feet below Aurora Planum's chill
Soldana's ranch was tucked away where no one ever went
(Unless they were requested by his invitation sent).

Off the beaten path and over rough terrain as well
No one would consider that within this jumbled hell
An island of tranquility and hillsides green with grass
Could be protected far beneath the plateau's icy blasts.

But there it was beneath them as they circled once to land
After winging through a narrow pass of rock and sand.
An airfield with a concrete strip and hangars built of glass
Surrounded by wide stretches of a hardy prairie grass

With junipers and pinion pines in rows to stop the gusts
In times when wind would stain the air with ruddy Martian dust.
But what could not elude the eye for long as sunlight gleamed
From crystals set in walls which rose from water pools that steamed:

A castle built of ochre stone swept up in soaring curves.
A visionary architect turned loose with skill and nerves
Had conjured up an edifice of arches intertwined
That blended with the background of the sloping cliffs behind.

Graceful in its curves and wide and airy in its space
Bedecked with colored stones arranged in patterns on its face.
Nick had never seen another building that came close
To looking like a living thing had from the sand arose.

"Soldana's house," said Gin, amused at Nick's enchanted stare.
"It's not the fanciest on Mars, but you see he's got flair.
"In the Martian gravity what would be hard on Earth
"Is easily accomplished here with steel beams and dirt."

As the craft shed altitude the pressure was released
To equalize the cabin slowly to what they would meet
When boot soles touched the concrete on Soldana's ranch at last
And Nick found breathing easy though his ears were popping fast.

It was minutes after noon when they walked toward the house.
The temperature was pleasant and the air sweet in their mouths
Fresh and cleaner than DaVinci's dusty bustling field.
And after they were swept no nasty implants were revealed.

(Soldana's men had swept them in the warehouse when they left
And here another pair of men did too - quick and deft.
And though Nick's extra hardware was detected, it was fine
For Radar had inactivated all that he could find.)

The pathway lead through gardens of a great variety
Of cactus and of Juniper and peach and apple trees.
And everywhere one looked were colored stones of many types
Mounted artfully on pillars gleaming in the light.

Nick happened to notice high up on a balcony
That swept across the building's front a flash of sunlight gleam
From a dark-haired woman who turned slow and walked away
And disappeared into the building as they made their way.

Curving walls of glass around the gardens left and right
Were made so they would move and could be closed up for the night.
The optical effect as one walked toward the great front door
Was much like arms were closing in - the closer more and more.

A bridge of stone across a drifting stream spread open wide
To bring them to a patio where one could see inside
To floors of polished stone and planters baked of local clay
Where two female guitarists were engaged in classic play.

Ansel said, "Excuse me," and stepped off to have a word
With a man who met him in an alcove where, unheard
A message of some import caused the man to walk away.
Returning, Ansel said, "My friends, I bid you all good day.

"A task remains unfinished which I'd hoped was done last night
"And I must be away upon a rather hasty flight.
"But you are left in better hands: Soldana welcomes you."
With that he turned and briskly walked the bridge back out of view.

"Ah, Chief Olsen! It has been too long since we have shared
"A bottle of fine spirits. How does your captain fare?"

The voice came from the foyer just behind the strumming girls.
A tall man dressed in flowing robes of red and gold with pearls

Stitched along the cuffs and collar stepped around a fern
And quickly walked toward Gin and gave a handshake warm and firm.
"Not long enough for memory of how it sipped to fade!"
Said Gin as he pulled from his kit a bottle carved of jade.

"The captain is quite well but had some business with the ship
"And sends regrets that he could not come with us on this trip.
"Perhaps you'll find some solace in this sample he has sent
"And if not, well, I have another jug of Scott's descent."

Gin winked with a smile and Soldana laughed out loud
And turned to greet the others shaking hands and looking proud
To have the men as guests - he made them feel right at home
And brought them in to show the rooms where they were free to roam.

"Rest yourselves and freshen up and we'll have noonday tea
"When the sundial on the floor shall say it's twelve thirty.
"A half an hour, it appears. We'll catch up on what's new.
"I trust you'll stay for supper and perhaps the evening too?"

With that he turned and left them to relax and rest a bit
And Duke remarked, "He's changed the place again and I like it!"
The polished green stone floor and walls were inlaid with thin lines
Of copper which demarked a spot of sunlight for the time.

After some few minutes' rest the four men spread about
Admiring artwork that had not been present last time out.
Soldana was an art collector of some little fame
Though there were very few who knew the man by his real name.

When the spot of orange sunlight passed the mark for tea
The four men made their way to where a spreading lemon tree
Arranged its leaves in eagerness to greet the warming sun
Beneath the glass when tea service had just about begun.

"Gentlemen! Thank you for your company today,"
Soldana started in (it seemed he had some things to say.)
"Duke, I'm glad you came this time. There's something you should see.
"Have one of the boys take you to see the back forty."

Normally Soldana's face was very hard to read.
His poker face in some circles was quite legendary.
He rarely showed emotion so the twinkle in his eyes
Betrayed an inner glee which was perceived with great surprise

By those who knew him best among his guests at tea today.
(Gin and Duke glanced at each other quickly, looked away)
Then Radar was surprised to find a tiny gift was placed
Beside his teacup by a serving girl with gentle grace.

Soldana grinned and dipped a cookie in his steaming tea
Then looked at Radar's face, who showed some curiosity
And took the little package wrapped with paper, green and gold
And looked Soldana in the eye and said, "I have been told

"That you now have your fingers in the Syrtis College pie
"And influence direction in some research there besides."
Soldana's grin grew wider as he leaned back in his chair
And slowly said "I'm one of many benefactors there.

"From time to time a contribution seems the thing to do
"When research on a special project needs a little boost.
"It seems they had a six-axis magnetics - much too small.
"A larger one is ordered for them now - the old one hauled

"Away to make more room for it and who knows where it went?
"Perhaps you know of someone who could use one just like it?"
Radar smiled wide and said, "You are a sly one, Sir."
As Gin caught Nick's wide eyes and smiled with a knowing smirk.

"Open it," Soldana said to Radar with a nod
Who peeled the paper from the package feeling a bit odd;
But opened it and looked inside with curiosity
(Soldana watching closely as he sipped his cup of tea.)

It was obvious to all that Radar was engrossed!
The item in the package drew his focus very close.
He pulled his scanner from his pocket absent-mindedly
And used it to inspect the thing a little more closely.

But then his eyes grew wider and he turned a little white
And held the item up for all to see with pure delight!

Soldana, with a nonchalant falsetto voice of bore
Said, "Varda calls it N-dimensional - a quantum core.

"He has a larger one that he has conversations with.
"He says he thinks it thinks; but I don't see the need for it."
Soldana set his teacup down as Duke picked up his own
And Gin and Nick looked closely at the new thing Radar owned.

"Varda called it 'N-dimensional', this quantum core?
"Not just two or three dimensions, but a number more?"
Soldana nodded. Gin and Nick were curious and sat
Pondering the possibilities, then Radar clapped!

"The processing capacity that this device may have,"
Radar started, "Only can be guessed at! Varda has
"A larger one?" he queried, almost blubbering with glee.
Soldana said, "You'll have to see him - not my cup of tea."

At that moment, dressed in flowing gown of red and gold
A shapely woman with black hair and dark eyes bright and bold
Glided through the room and paused beside an empty seat
And every man among them started rising to their feet.

"Please, take ease, no bother! Thank you though," she softly said
With a deep and sultry voice that made men turn their heads.
(Duke pulled out her chair and sat her gracefully beside
Soldana, straight across from Nick while Duke sat on her right.)

"Selenia," Soldana said, "You're ravishing, my dear,
"As ever and I'm glad you came to see our friends are here.
"Their captain sends his compliments and regrets he can't come.
"It seems he's getting ready for another deep space run."

Selenia said, "Thank you," then she turned to Duke and said,
"I'm very glad to see you, Duke. I trust Joe's kept his head?"
Duke smiled at her knowingly and nodded, sipped his tea.
Her dark eyes turned on Gin next and she said soft and warmly,

"Sven, I hope you know that you are always welcomed here.
"The differences we've had have only made your heart more dear.
"Besides, the bottled spirits that you bring Soldana's way
"Keep him entertained so I have much more time to play."

Gin gave her a wink and smiled warmly, raised his tea
And tilted it saluting her and said, "Forever free."
"Forever free!" she said repeating to him those old words
That conjured up a thousand mem'ries of the Lunar war.

"Radar, I am glad to see you and you haven't changed.
"Varda wants to talk to you down in his spooky cave.
"I'm sure you're quite as anxious to get on with all your play.
"You are free to go to him; I know you know the way."

Radar stood and said, "Yes, thank you. We have much to do."
And nodded toward Soldana saying, "Very much, thank you!"
Then as he moved around the table Gin grabbed on his knee
And said, "You have Nick's implant. That's your first priority."

As he left the room Selenia pushed her long hair
Back over her shoulder and turned slightly in her chair
And studied Nick a moment while Soldana made a quip:
"I'm glad that Varda and Radar can visit on this trip."

Gin responded with a chuckle, said, "They do scare me
"Sometimes when they get together and their synergy
"Produces things most engineers would never even guess.
"It's good they get to interface. You know they are the best."

Gin then saw Selenia's attention full on Nick
And said, "Forgive me, friends, for letting my good manners slip.
"A proper introduction for our hosts has not been made.
"Nicholas, please meet two partners who have many trades:

"Soldana was responsible for much of how Mars grew.
"Selenia was born a business woman through and through.
"Together they can make things happen others couldn't dream.
"We've dealt with them perhaps a hundred times before (it seems).

"Nicholas hails from the Earth - his first visit to Mars.
"A first class engineer by training and he's got the scars
"Of TerraCorp's attentions. As an intern in their labs
"He researches energy and planetary gas."

Nick said, "I am pleased to meet you both and see your home.
"I had no idea Mars had prospered so, and grown!

"It seems my focus has been narrow, work has been my life.
"Please, just call me 'Nick'. Your house is beautiful and bright!"

Soldana raised his cup toward Nick and said, "The pleasure's mine.
"Your captain's crew is always welcome here at any time."
Gin continued, "TerraCorp intended Nick be used
"To steal some secrets then be killed and burned like old refuse."

Nick turned red and started to rebuke Gin's frank report
But Gin turned toward him saying, "These are friends who know the score.
"TerraCorp's deception and abuse is nothing new.
"These folks can prepare you for what's surely coming too."

Soldana's eyes grew narrow and Selenia was cool.
This was not the first time TerraCorp had someone fooled.
Then Duke excused himself and said, "I'll leave you all to talk
"And let myself outside. I think I'll take a little walk."

Duke set down his empty cup and pushed his chair away
And nodded toward Soldana who said, "Walk the south field's way."
Duke's stoic face flashed curiosity as he arose
And said, "I will," and as he left he pulled the room's door closed.

Gin turned fully facing Nick and placed his scarred right hand
Upon the table close to him and told him man to man,
"Perhaps I sounded rash, but it is best to put it out
"And get right to the point so there will not be any doubt.

"You were rigged by TerraCorp to do a dirty deed
"Without your knowledge or your will to feed a tyrant's greed."
Gin turned toward Soldana and said, "When he left Earth's ground
"He interned for TerraCorp; I think he's come around."

Selenia was silent and Soldana toyed his cup
A moment, then he cleared his throat and lifted his head up
And said, "The men you see around you here and on your crew
"All can tell their stories of what TerraCorp could do.

"Duke was promised many things by them until the war
"When they betrayed his loyalty while in the Survey Corps.
"He made the hard decision and fought on the freemen's side
"And took the scars you see on him as well as ones inside.

"What he did for freedom? Well, let's just say he's good
"At doing what he does and he knows when or not he should.
"It's what your captain likes about him, among other things.
"Every person on his crew has talents which they bring.

"What are yours?" Soldana asked (his gaze burned through Nick's soul)
And Nick responded, "Sir, I'm new to space and not so bold.
"I think you are mistaken. I am not part of this crew.
"I am just a passenger to Saturn, it is true.

"I contract for TerraCorp - that's why my trip began
"Then implants were found in my body when they deeply scanned.
"Some were very ugly by their nature and design
"And I cannot describe my anger; I must soon resign."

Soldana looked surprised and asked, "You're not on his crew?"
Gin's eyes locked Soldana's gaze as silent words came through
And then a crooked smile cracked Soldana's wrinkled cheek
"Not yet, you mean," he chuckled softly as he took a drink.

Nick could not quite hear his comment. It was covered up
By her sudden question as Selenia piped up:
"What is your impression of what you have seen of Mars
"On this voyage from the Earth among the shining stars?"

Nick smiled at her patronage (obviously feigned)
And said, "My Lady, if this were Barsoom then you're the famed
"Dejah Thoris! Beauty incomparable by far
"To every maiden everywhere on every wand'ring star."

Soldana loosed a lusty laugh, Selenia smiled wide.
Soldana winked and said, "Indeed you have a gorgeous mind!"
And took a golden bracelet from his wrist and slipped it on
To Nick's own wrist and said, "I think of you I'll grow quite fond."

Gin looked at the ceiling as he slowly shook his head
Then looked Soldana's way and with faux criticism said,
"He has a mission. So do I. Now I'll check on the boys
"In Varda's lab and make sure they are sharing their new toys."

Gin stood up and lightly mocking bowed Selenia's way
Then pointed at his eyes then at Soldana (as to say,

"I'll be watching you!") He opened up the room's glass door
And left the three of them to carry on the talk some more.

"Nick said, "These are emeralds and rubies, are they not?
Amazed at what a princely gift on him Soldana'd wrought.
"Indeed, they are," Soldana said, "They're from the Solis mines
"Far south of Marineris; they are found from time to time."

"Thank you, Sir. It's true, My Lady, I have only seen
"One tiny part of Mars since landing here just this morning.
"I've seen some agriculture and more industry than guessed
"But I suspect I haven't seen a hint of all the rest."

Selenia responded, "There's a common myth that's told:
"That Mars is ancient and had died in eons long ago.
"But if one looks around them they will see that Mars is young;
"His life is fresh! His history has only just begun."

Soldana said, "Mars is a wide frontier - it's changing fast.
"The door is opened wide and opportunities are vast.
"With freedom for the individual and room to grow,
"It's far beyond what other worlds can offer, you must know.

"As those breaking ground on other worlds can attest
"The danger and the heartbreak for the first-comers will test
"The very metal of the soul beyond what one can bear
"For life is difficult at best when there's not even air!"

"And that's the way it was back in the early days of Mars;
"A hard-scrabble existence - those who lived it bear the scars.
"It wasn't easy then. Hard choices made by harder men
"Whose blood and sweat were sparks that made the planet's life begin.

"The air was ninety-six percent carbon dioxide gas
"With argon, nitrogen (and oxygen listed dead last)
"And every season CO_2 would freeze hard at the poles
"Causing wind or pressure drops with heat or winter's cold.

"The key was getting atmospheric pressure to increase
"And that suggested heating for subsurface ice release.
"Oxygen and water vapor were the planet's need
"So power stations at high latitudes were built with speed.

"In those early years atomic engines were emplaced
"To melt subsurface ice in many spots, strategic spaced.
"Then massive solar stations and great mills to catch the wind
"Were built across Australis and the Plains of Boreum.

"Initially electrolytic process took the ice
"And broke it into oxygen and hydrogen quite nice.
"The hydrogen was further used to process CO_2
"Into oxygen and methane for colonists' use.

"But gains were very slow and it was thought hundreds of years
"Would pass before the colonists could venture without fear
"Of boiling body fluids if they took a walk outside
"Without a pressure suit protecting eyes and lungs and hide.

"Success accelerated when the key to turn the lock
"To Mars' own volcanism was employed (though many mocked
"The effort) and hot magma veins were breeched down deep at last
"With fission drilling and strategic large atomic blasts.

"By cutting deep at Tharsis, Solis and Elysium,
"Meridiani, Amazon and Bosporos Planum
"Gas and heat were channeled and it was the catalyst
"That brought about big changes much too numerous to list.

"Atmospheric pressure soon increased three dozen fold
"The heat from the equator then displaced much of the cold.
"The time to let some plant life (that consumes much CO_2)
"Loose across the land had come; we'd see what it could do."

Soldana paused to pour another cup of steaming tea.
Selenia turned sideways as her robe slipped off one knee.
She tossed her raven hair and studied Nick who studied her.
As both sipped from their cups Soldana told a little more:

"Life was introduced at Hellas and in crater depths
"On hillsides that faced toward the sun where outflows were the best:
"Lyot, Mie and Moreux and Du Martheray and Gale
"And many other places that presented sunny vales.

"Lichens were the pioneers, then arctic grass and such
"Were nurtured in the lowlands (where the air pressure was much

"Higher than the mountains) and around the equator
"Where liquid water could exist at daytime temperature.

"Dry land grass and cactus followed. Sometimes it took hold
"But often there were failures and mistakes or too much cold.
"Eventual persistence paid off and before we knew
"Pockets of wild grass were growing everywhere we flew:

"Valles Marineras and its Melas chasm deep
"Where cloud cover would often let the ground retain its heat
"Then on throughout the Eos chasm into Chryse plain.
"Once life secured its foothold Mars has never been the same.

"The lava fields of Amazonis and Arcadia
"And all across Isidis and Argyre Planitia;
"The windswept nowheres of Utopia and Acid Sea;
"In just two dozen years had grass and cactus growing free.

"The sage brush and the yucca and the dandelion too
"Sink their roots into the Martian dust and change the view
"From lifeless desolation to a landscape fed with streams
"And colonists from everywhere now work to build their dreams.

"Pines and spruce and juniper were planted here and there
"And now in Hellas apple trees are coaxed to grow and bear
"Without the benefit of greenhouse domes like higher land.
"But someday that whole region may be ocean, not dry land.

"Picas, shrews and marmots were released and do quite well.
"Llamas found their place and musk ox roam the lowland dells.
"Today small herds of caribou and bighorn sheep are seen
"In Valles Marineras where there's willow, grass and streams.

"In this atmosphere so rich with carbon plant life thrives
"And pays us back in oxygen that keeps us all alive.
"Plant life now produces almost twice again as much
"As all the power stations that were started here by us.

"Insects have adapted well and more do every year.
"The desert bursts in color and there's rain sometimes right here.
"Bluebirds and lark buntings have adapted fairly well.
"Soon perhaps small predators will stalk the hills and dells.

"Genetic work for cold-resistant plants and bugs and bees
"Continues and results have paid off well on Ganymede
"And many other worlds across the system thanks to Mars
"And those who paid the cost in sweat and blood and bear the scars."

He stopped his discourse then and gave Selenia a wink
And said, "I should go see how Duke is doing, don't you think?
"Excuse me, Nick, Selenia will now take you to see
"The six-axis magnetics that showed up mysteriously."

Soldana grinned and stood to leave. Selenia stood too
As Nick rose to his feet he said, "Soldana, I thank you.
"Your hist'ry lesson was succinct, the bracelet far beyond
"What I could ever hope to match. I thank you wide and long!"

Soldana gestured with dismissal as he left the room.
She said, "Please, it's just a bauble, he'll replace it soon."
Her eyes held Nick's for just a moment longer than they should
As she walked 'round the table and came closer where he stood.

"Mars has much to offer you. There's profit to be made."
Selenia said softly, "There are mines that pull up jade
"And precious stones much larger than on Earth are ever found.
"I think it would be nice if you would choose to stick around."

Nick responded, "I am sure there's much to keep me here
"But I must go to Saturn where important times draw near.
"There is a race that I must run and I can't get there late.
"It truly is a matter of the solar system's fate."

"The solar system?" she exclaimed, "Come now, Nick, Indeed?
"Exaggerating things just seems to be a bit beneath
"A smart man like yourself. Surely others way out there
"Can handle things. I don't see why you would even care."

Brushing by him closer than a new acquaintance should
(He found he didn't mind and subtly wished again she would).
Her scent was faint and delicate, alluring in deep ways.
She beckoned him come closer to the window's sunlight rays.

"Do you see that glimmer on the cliff up in the sun?"
(She had him stand behind her, sight along her arm's long run).

"That's the dome above a lab with one terrific view.
"It's vacant and I think it might be just the place for you.

"No one ever goes there much and you could call it home.
"It's very private there and you could work there all alone.
"Or not, if that would please you." She turned and stood so close
He felt her warm breath on his neck. Electric charges rose.

Nick felt like a champion with such a clear advance
From such a gorgeous woman who invited passion's dance.
He took a half step backward, said, "A fine offer indeed!
"I'm sure that here on Mars I'd find whatever I might need."

He looked into her dark eyes. She looked back, studied him.
"Your husband is a lucky man to have a precious gem
"Like you," and then he took another painful step away.
"My husband? Soldana? Nick, relax, it's not that way.

"It is a good assumption, but to you I'll plainly tell
"I choose who I will and he is free to choose as well.
"Soldana's tastes are different, they don't extend to me.
"We are simply business partners, otherwise we're free."

She grinned with youthful dimples as she touched his arm and turned
Then walked with carefree grace as Nick's ignited passion burned.
"Come, I will take you to your new magnetic tool.
"Varda checked it thoroughly and he is not a fool.

"Sven and Radar should be there by now to see it run.
"I don't want to keep you from your engineering fun."
She winked and waited for him to catch up and took his hand
For just a moment then she said, "Meeting you is grand.

"I know you have a task to do out there among the moons
"Of Saturn, but I hope you won't forget me very soon.
"You know, life is much more fun when one takes time to play.
"The offer stands, of course, and I would love to have you stay."

* * * * *

Soldana walked beyond the two glass domes behind the house
And found Duke leaning on a fence, a straw held in his mouth

Watching with enraptured pleasure what took place beyond
(For from a youth he'd always been of horses very fond.)

"They are truly beautiful. Do you not agree?"
Soldana called to Duke who turned to smile back with glee.
"What you see did not come easy. It's been several years
"Of great expense and patience paid with sweat and blood and tears.

"Several people tried to introduce them to this world
"But no one had success in this until my plan unfurled.
"What you're watching are the only horses on the globe
"But many more will follow if my project can unfold.

"Other people paid great sums to ship horses from Earth
"But they had no success for they did not live here from birth.
"It was sad to watch - they all got weak and wouldn't eat
"And starved to death confused; they wouldn't stand up on their feet.

"Horses could not acclimate to point four gravity.
"They were born to run and could not make the change, you see.
"It wasn't until foals were brought and nurtured up by hand
"That any horse could find their feet upon the Martian sand.

"Once the foals were grown and bred and colts were born anew
"They acclimated to this world and now we have a few.
"You've been watching how they frolic. You should see them run!
"What they do in rough terrain is even greater fun.

"Duke, I need a wrangler. I know you have the skills
"And you've lived on Mars enough to work well in these hills.
"You were once a part of Earth and Earth was part of you.
"Since what happened in the war your years on Earth are through.

"Horsemanship is in your blood. I know you have the scars.
"I would like to offer you a new home here on Mars.
"It isn't just for me I ask. It's for these studs and mares.
"They require a man who knows them; one who truly cares.

"You would guide the breeding of the stock that makes Mars home
"And you will see the day when on these Martian plains they roam.
"Perhaps one day the bison and the eagle too will play
"Among the dunes of Syrtis and the crags up Solis way."

Duke looked at Soldana for a moment long and deep
Then said, "I've never had an offer bundled up that neat.
"What's the catch?" Soldana smiled and said, "There isn't one.
"You know me and suspect there is something more to come.

"And you are wise to do so. I've pulled a trick or two.
"It's how I've made my way on Mars and other places too.
"There is no catch. You're the perfect man to do this job.
"I respect you too much; your freedom I'll not rob.

"Duke, I know the Sioux and Cheyenne turned their backs on you
"For making that hard choice the lunar war forced you into.
"You chose your side against the earth as many good men did
"And now the future lies before you; Mars is your best friend."

* * * * *

Selenia led Nick into a darkened corridor
Sloping down beneath the ground and took him to a door
Where feeble light emerged reflecting up from polished stone
And every indication was that they were quite alone.

"Nick, I like you very much, and didn't mean to tease
"You by my forwardness at tea, I only aim to please.
"I have certain appetites and you have needs as well.
"If there is ever anything you want, I'm here to tell."

With that she pulled him close and put her lips against his cheek
And said, "Welcome to Mars. This is the place for you I think.
"Your friends are just beyond this door. I'll leave you in their care
"And see you when you engineers come up to get some air."

She turned and walked the corridor back up the way they came
And Nick thought after that he'd never be the same again.
Then pushed against the sandstone door that opened with a creak
And saw Radar and Gin but found it very hard to speak.

"Ah!" said Gin as Nick stumbled two steps into the room,
"Nicholas, meet Varda. You are not a moment soon.
"The six-axis magnetics is in order - over there,"
He pointed and continued, "Please inspect it, if you care."

Nick looked 'round the dimly lit and very cluttered room
Divided into sections by low shelves that made the gloom
Seem darker but for low-hung lights above the many desks
And benches (one where Radar sat engrossed in running tests).

Gin had pointed toward an open doorway to the right
From which was spilling just a little more intensive light.
An open spacious area was seen beyond the door
(Gin turned back around and didn't say anything more.)

Varda was a balding man with brown hair 'round the back
And deep-set eyes that both together didn't always track.
He wore a cotton coat of white and it was plain to see
He spent a lot of time down in his labs where he was free

To focus on his work. It was his life and little else
Would hold his interest long unless a project it might help.
"You are the implant carrier?" he asked as he approached
"Yes," said Nick, then Varda quickly one more question broached:

"I must have your blood. May I now?" as he removed
A needle from his lab coat pocket purposeful and smooth.
"Varda!" Radar called out, "Say hello to our friend Nick
"Before you try to jab him with your blood sucking stick!"

Varda paused a moment, said, "Forgive me," then his face
Forced a crooked smile as he said, "Sometimes my haste
"Overrides my manners. I am Varda, born on Mars
"And you study high energy emitted from the stars.

"A sample is most critical to understand the core
"Of what was taken from your body. I must know some more
"Before we can be certain how this fascinating thing
"Can hide beneath a scanner and what other tricks it brings."

Nick had met eccentric men before. He gave a grin
And offered up his arm and said, "Efficiency's no sin.
"I am pleased to meet you and assist with what I may."
Varda took his arm without another word to say.

He took his little sample to a desk across the room
Where several tiny lights appeared winking through the gloom.

Nick rolled down his sleeve and walked into the brighter space
Beyond the open door to see some more of this odd place.

The other room was huge! The ceiling twenty meters high
And it appeared to be as much as sixty side to side
And half again as long across the space to the far end
Where two large wheeled transports had been parked and left within.

The magnetic equipment was set up right by the door.
A desk with all the necessary gear (indeed, much more)
Was placed nearby and ready for what studies might ensue.
The heavy gear was quite the best that Nick could hope for too!

"It's big, isn't it?" (Gin had presently joined him.)
"Yes," said Nick, "This is all that's needed to begin."
"No," said Gin, "I mean the room; it used to be all ice.
"This was a pocket that was melted, there are more besides.

"Atomics heat the ice within the cliffs behind the house.
"The water's channeled carefully and then directed out.
"It feeds the steaming stream we walked across when we came in;
"Electrolytics break down some to fuel and oxygen.

"What's left behind is often just a jumbled pile of stone
"But sometimes there are caverns left like this that make a home
"Or perhaps a factory or school or parking bay
"With natural protection from the sun and cosmic rays.

"Much of Mars works underground, though most prefer the sun.
"Mining is a major industry though farming's done
"And soon will be the lion's share of Mars' economy
"But what is found in empty caves can be a sight to see!

"Sometimes walls of solid olivine or jade are found,
"Rubies big as grapefruits simply laying on the ground.
"They've only scratched the surface of what Mars may offer still
"And there are many other worlds out there left to fill.

"The inner planets may be warm and metal-rich and bright
"And it's true there's no place like the Earth so rich with life;
"But there is room to live and grow beneath the frozen stone
"From Ganymede to Triton and Callisto to Dione.

"Many of the outer worlds are mostly ice and rock.
"The myth that Earth is where the water is was crazy talk
"Based on ignorance before we went there to explore.
"Just within the Saturn system there is so much more!

"From Jupiter to Neptune there is water everywhere
"Frozen deep in icy caverns that we fill with air
"And warm with steam created from the fuel and ice we find
"And crops are being grown right there of almost every kind."

Nick was running system checks on his magnetic gear
And listening to Gin with really only half an ear
For in his mind and body hormones raged and made his brain
Replay Selenia's words over time and time again:

'You know, life is much more fun when one takes time to play.
'The offer stands, of course, and I would love to have you stay.'
Gin noticed Nick's absentmindedness and said, "Don't fret
"About old Varda's coolness; he just hasn't known you yet.

"He takes much longer to warm up to folks than most folks do.
"His manner doesn't indicate he has dislike for you.
"In fact, when you two get to talk I know he'll like you fine
"But with a guy like that, well, it just might take some time."

"Uh, thank you Gin," Nick replied, "But I know Varda's type.
"There is no problem there, I just have others on my mind."
Nick's clear skin flushed redder as he stumbled on his words
And Gin peered at him quizzically then quickly changed discourse:

"So, is this gear sufficient to accomplish what we need?"
Nick, relieved, responded, "Yes, much better, I believe.
"It's got six solid axes and with that attachment there,"
Nick pointed toward the table, "Really seven; one to spare."

"Very good," said Gin as he gave Nick a shoulder pat
"Soldana's guys came through and I am thankful for all that;
"But we still need to get it lifted to the ship and set
"Where unimpeded access to the vacuum it can get.

"He should have left it at DaVinci..." Gin's voice trailed off.
"I think she means to keep it here," said Nick, stifling a cough.

"A most attractive offer has been made for me to stay;
"But rest assured I know what is at stake out Saturn's way."

Gin's and Nick's eyes met a moment; Gin said, "Oh, I see.
"Selenia can be persuasive, that I'll guarantee.
"I didn't see that coming. There are things you need to know;
"But we'll discuss them later. Stay with Radar. I must go."

Nick felt some relief from conflict when he saw there'd be
Insight and perspective Gin would share to help him see
More clearly past the rosy web Selenia had cast
And settled down his mind to focus on his work at last.

Gin walked back into the lab and briefly had a word
With Radar then went through the door and up the hallway toward
An outer door that took him to the fields just behind
The house where he was hoping Duke still on his walk he'd find.

And he did. In fact, Duke was just returning to
The rooms where they were quartered to relax and rest a few.
Gin approached and mentioned that Selenia had tried
To lure Nick away and got beneath the young man's hide.

Duke took that in stride and said "He's not the only man
"Soldana's courting to recruit. I think he's hatched a plan.
"He showed me what I'd never guess: He has horses, Gin!
"He's given me the option to take charge of all of them."

Duke's eyes showed emotion that they rarely ever had
And Gin responded, "Here on Mars? Duke, I'm very glad!
"That is quite an offer and I won't blame you a bit
"If you take the bait, but surely you can see through it?"

"I know what he's doing, Gin; but temptation is real!
"I never thought a chance like this would come. And I would steal
"The candy from a baby just to see what I've been shown.
"You know this is the closest thing I'll ever have to home."

Gin slowed down their pace then turned and looked Duke in the eye
And said, "You know that you could do this on your own - besides,
"Everything Soldana gives has always had a price
"And you know very well the games he plays are not so nice."

Duke looked at the ground then up and turned around to view
The cliffs behind the house and all the distant ridges too.
Then took Gin by the arm and said, "You're right, my friend, it's true.
"Soldana hasn't offered me a thing I couldn't do.

"But boy, he hit me on the blind side - caught me by surprise!
"He really has accomplished something no one else besides
"Him has yet accomplished: getting horses to adapt
"To Mars, well, he sure got my attention - I was rapt!"

They turned and started toward the house again and Gin remarked,
"He's tempting Radar with some toys and Varda has embarked
"Upon another venture that has perked up Radar's ears
"And I know he's been after Haji for a couple years."

Duke responded, "How 'bout you? What cheese is in your trap?"
Gin said, "Nothing has been floated - I'd just give him crap.
"And he knows it all too well." Duke gave him a hard stare
And said, "I wouldn't take that bet. You had best beware."

"I will," said Gin as Duke took hold and slowed their pace again
And turned his way and said, "You have to tell this to Captain."
"I will," said Gin and added, "What I don't get is why now?
"This is all so sudden and it seems so odd somehow.

"After all our escapades and all this time has passed
"In trading favors with Soldana he has never asked
"To add us to his outfit or to work under his name.
"Something is about to happen. Things don't feel the same."

"Maybe Captain knows? Call him now," Duke said again.
Gin did at that instant and found out that their captain
Was coming down to Mars aboard the ship's own shuttle craft
And when Duke heard the news he had to give a little laugh:

"He's been talking to Soldana then," Duke cracked a grin.
"And it has gotten serious again," snorted Gin.
"He doesn't like to use the shuttle when there's other means
"So yeah, he's in a hurry to get face time in, it seems."

"When will he arrive?" asked Duke as they turned toward the house.
"He'll be here by sundown, maybe sooner; say three hours.

"We should get some rest before he comes," said Gin, "Besides,
"Nick and Radar need the news this evening we may fly."

When they got back to their quarters Nick and Radar sat
Talking over details of the programming format
That they'd decided would be best to keep the fields in tune
To do what would be necessary out at Saturn's moons.

Gin asked, "Are you feeling better now?" and looked at Nick
The others looked at him and Radar asked, "Is he sick?"
"Selenia has cast her web," said Gin, "He caught her spell.
"He thinks she's Dejah Thoris and has told her so as well."

Both of them laughed loudly and poor Nick's face turned bright red
As Gin shot him a wink he caught just as he hung his head.
"Deja Thoris?" Duke remarked, "More like Felix Rex!"
"The Reina Draconis", Radar quipped, "But she means best."

"You've been cougar-scratched," said Duke, "Lucky you weren't bit!"
Then Duke and Radar chuckled as they watched the face on Nick
Flush a little more; but then he looked up with a smile
And took the ribbing all in stride as Gin grinned all the while.

"She is a beauty," Gin remarked, "And she can use it well.
"She's more than twice your age, my friend; I know you couldn't tell.
"Intelligent and playful, she's a fierce competitor
"And just as deadly with a kiss as with a scimitar."

Radar gave Nick's shoulder half a dozen little pats
And said, "Relax, you aren't the first Selenia has waxed.
"Soldana really wants you if he turned her loose on you.
"I'm sorry, Nick, we should have let you know about her too.

"She's old enough to be your mother - even older still!
"She means well, I promise, but her appetite won't fill.
"There's only one can do that and that one has his sights fixed
"On someone else that some believe may no longer exist."

"That's enough. Let it ride," snapped Gin with a dark stare
At Radar who turned red himself and dropped the subject there.
Nick looked curious but saw the subject was taboo
Then looked at the three other men and said, "Guys, thank you."

The ship's clock wasn't near the same as this time zone on Mars.
Soldana's visitors had been awake for many hours
And now, relaxing in their quarters they were dozing off
While listening to girls play guitar music low and soft.

The orange spot of sunlight had climbed red upon the wall
Gleaming on a copper line denoting evening's fall.
Soon the sun would drop beneath the red hills in the west
And while they rested one more rushed to be Soldana's guest.

A sonic boom reverberated from the hills and cliffs
And if one's eyes were skyward they might see a small craft kissed
With ruby sunlight shedding speed by banking in a turn
That spiraled down in shrinking circles as its retro's burned.

Presently the craft approached and circled once around
The landing field but settled on a nicely gardened mound
Closer to the house than some would think was wise to do
Its nose directed toward the door above the garden's view.

The noise of the approach and landing wasn't very odd
But landing in the front yard, thrusters tearing up the sod
Caused a bit of stir among Soldana's men who swore.
(Landing on the garden was not what they'd cleared him for!)

A half a dozen brown-clad men with rifles circled 'round
The gleaming craft and waited for the turbines to wind down
Then closely watched the canopy slide open with a click
And saw a close-cut pressure suit and helmet climb out quick.

The dark blue suit's black gloves reached up and took the helmet off
And tossed it in the cockpit then the brown-haired pilot coughed
And took in three deep breaths of chilly dusty Martian air
As setting sunlight cast its reddened hue upon his hair.

The captain had arrived. He slowly looked around the scene
Ensuring all six riflemen his face had clearly seen.
Two or three were recognized and then Soldana came
Walking out the front door as he greeted him by name.

The riflemen relaxed and high up on the balcony
Her raven hair aglow, Selenia watched quietly.
The captain, with his sidearm clearly seen upon his hip
Marched across the garden bridge and said, "Don't give me lip!

"Soldana, you old pirate, you have tried to poach my crew.
"I've half a mind to put a couple bullets into you."
The captain, with his index finger thumped Soldana's chest
And with a seething anger in his voice told him the rest:

"Good fences make good neighbors and it seems you've torn one down.
"And now you're trampling on my garden," he said with a frown.
Soldana backed into the open doorway with a look
Designed to give impression that the captain had mistook

His good intentions and perhaps a signal had been crossed.
But Captain pressed on with his point appearing very cross:
"We've worked and profited together and you know quite well
"I have a job to finish and I'll chase it straight to hell

"If I must," the captain finished with a burning stare
That would singe the eyebrows off and curl the very hair
Of a lesser man than faced him now across the room.
Soldana said, "You know you're chasing ghosts straight to your doom

"And taking those fine men with you to share in your sad fate.
"Captain, everyone has told you that it's now too late.
"She's gone!" Soldana punctuated, thumping Captain's chest
In hopes the harshness of his words would finally put to rest

The captain's burning hope Soldana did not understand
(Since all he saw was balance sheets and not what made the man
What he was, for deep inside him he knew she still lived.
And he would sift the sand of every planet through a sieve

To find her if he must and set her free and bring her home
Within his arms where she belonged and they would never roam
Apart again. That was his goal, indeed very the thing
That motivated every act and haunted every dream.)

Eye to eye the pair of them stared long and hard and deep
And then Soldana blinked and said, "I think we both need sleep."

The captain looked surprised then sighed, "Soldana, keep your claws
"Off my crew. You can't afford the trouble that will cause."

The captain took his gloves off and sat down upon the bench.
Soldana sat beside him and said, "I've not tried to pinch
"Them from you necessarily; I've offered them a choice
"To show them they have options," he said in a softer voice.

"Options!?" Captain blurted, "Every one of them's the best
"And I have spent a lot of years rejecting all the rest.
"You know very well the capabilities we've shown.
"If you want some men you go and rustle up your own."

"Captain, you are tired. Stay and dine with us tonight.
"All is well and I don't mean to get us in a fight.
"Selenia will find a bed of comfort for your head
"And in the morning we will talk when we are both rested.

"Your crew is always welcome here; your men and mine work well
"Together. That's been proven many times as they will tell.
"Selenia has seen to it that quarters were prepared
"For all your men and rest assured no luxury was spared."

The captain looked around the room and out the garden door.
The sun had set and chilly air was spilling 'cross the floor.
Night so near the equator came on with suddenness
And he knew it was very true he had to get some rest.

"Fair enough, you wily fox. We'll stick around a day
"But then we must be off. You know we have to earn our pay.
"There's things afoot on Titan and I know you know the stakes.
"And I can't spend a lot of time hanging 'round your place.

"There's evidence that TerraCorp is brewing trouble there.
"(I know you well enough so don't pretend that you don't care.)
"They've got an opportunity and they'll do what they must
"To strangle every freeman there, including you and us."

He paused a moment as he watched the outer glass walls close
Around the inner garden as the lights came on and rose
To a soft and soothing level then he said offhand,
"Sorry 'bout your bushes - it seemed like the place to land."

Soldana stood and walked a couple steps then turned and said,
"Your crew is resting in the east suite, first one on the left.
"Dinner's in an hour. Take your suit off, have a rest.
"A messenger will come for you when table has been set.

"Then we will eat and drink and catch up on the nicer things
"Enjoying conversation that good friendships always bring.
"We'll let the cares and burdens fall away and then we'll sleep
"And in the morning things will be much brighter. You will see!"

He turned and walked away and Captain leaned back on the bench
And mulled things over noticing his teeth had not unclenched.
Soldana was a schemer and had contacts everywhere.
Something wasn't normal and he'd need to clear the air.

He stood and walked around the corner toward his crewman's' suite
When from a little alcove in her red robe and bare feet
Selenia approached and said, "Jules! Forever free!
"It has been too long since you have come to visit me."

"Ah, Selenia," the captain sighed and took her hands
And said, "Forever free! You are the Jewel of Martian sand!
"I see you grow more beautiful with every year that comes.
"As you get younger, I get older with each deep space run."

"Nonsense," she rebuked him, "You get better looking still
"Every time I see you and it's always been a thrill!"
She pulled him close and hugged him warmly, kissed him on the cheek
And asked, "How have you been? It seems forever and a week!"

"I'm fine," he said, "Business good but always there are snags.
"It seems the opportunities are too many to bag!
"How are you, Selenia? Has that old goat been nice?
"I see you haven't had to put his carcass yet on ice."

"Not yet," she chuckled, "He at times can truly be a dear
"Even though it seems his claws grow sharper every year.
"I am fine. And I am very glad to see you well.
"I truly hope that this time you will stay a longer spell.

"You look tired, Jules. Why don't you take a little rest?
"Supper will be ready soon; he's setting out the best.

"And then a good night's sleep will bring a brighter day for you
"And I will show you all the Martian wonders coming true."

She squeezed his hand and winked and as she turned to walk away
Her flowing hair cascaded down her back in such a way
To draw the eyes to where one couldn't help but see the curves
Of feminine perfection that might break a man's reserve.

He grinned and shook his head then turned and walked into the suite
Where Nick and Radar seemed to be engrossed in study deep.
Gin was snoring soundly in a room off to the side
And Duke remarked, "Nice landing, Captain. That will chafe his hide!"

"Well, it seemed the right place at the time I set her down,"
The captain said, "How are you all?" as he looked all around.
Nick said, "We are fine, sir. Soldana sure came through.
"He's provided all we need and with some extras too."

The captain said, "That's good. But from him there's nothing free.
"Everything has strings attached. That I'll guarantee.
"Joe is keeping watch and Dewey's gone to who knows where.
"I doubt if he is outside getting very much fresh air.

"He tends to spend his time and money where he shouldn't go
"But he is young and someday he will learn and start to grow.
"Haji spends his nights at Syrtis University
"With friends he's worked with in the past who are like family.

"Bovine made a beeline to his Martian mining friends
"As soon as he could get a flight to Terra Sirenum."
He started peeling off his suit and asked, "Washroom that way?"
"Yes sir," Nick replied, "Will we stay another day?"

"I think we may," the captain said, "Unless Soldana balks
"And fails to get our gear uploaded. We will have that talk
"After dinner; but for now let's get a little rest
"And then we'll have a good time feasting on Soldana's best.

"He is a gracious host, is he not?" the captain winked.
Nick responded "Yes, he is. I hope you do not think
"That he has been successful in his bid to buy your men."
The captain looked surprised and did a double take at him:

"That is quite perceptive," Captain said, "I hope it's true
"That he has not succeeded in likewise recruiting you."
Nick turned slightly red and cast his eyes down at the floor
And said, "No, he hasn't," but did not say any more.

The captain folded up his suit and placed it on a shelf
And said, "That is good. There is more at stake than self."
Nick looked up and saw the captain staring deep at him
As if Nick were transparent and he saw his secret sins.

The captain walked into the other room and shut the door
And no one saw a trace of him for forty minutes more.
Radar whispered, "Now you've seen 'The Look'. The man can see
"A thousand yards right through your soul. I'm glad it wasn't me."

"He is a driven man," said Duke, "He does what he needs to
"To reach the goals that call to him; a man whose heart is true.
"You have found his favor, Nick, a valued compliment
"And you can trust he'll do his best for you as all his men."

Duke rolled on his side and faced into the sofa's back
And seemed to doze off quickly for a forty minute nap.
Nick and Radar set aside their work and did the same
As out their western window brightly burned the Earth's blue flame.

7   Dinner and Delight

Soldana's formal dining room was just as wide as tall.
Though large it felt quite cozy when one entered from the hall.
Arches cut from dark red stone curved upward from the sides
Contrasting khaki-colored walls and polished black floor tiles.

Skylights in the ceiling let the moons' and starlight in
And though the light was pleasant it was comfortably dim.
Two doors at the far end let the serving staff come through
Who worked in graceful silence with efficient promptness too.

The massive dining table was a slab of polished stone
Basaltic in its origin and dark as blackened bone.
The dinner plates obsidian with jade to hold the wine
Utensils wrought of silver fashioned artfully and fine.

High above the table hung from where the arches met
A chandelier of quartz and calcite shimmered as if wet.
It cast a warm and mellow light that set the walls aglow
And floor lights in the corners added more light from below.

Long and wide the table could seat thirty sitting tight
But on this evening there was room to stretch out with delight.
Soldana at the far end and the captain near the door
His crew spread out to left and right with room for many more.

Selenia was dressed tonight in silk of shining blue:
A sleeveless smartly tailored dress that highlighted the hue
Of one enormous sapphire necklace ringed with diamonds white
That graced her low-cut neckline (matching ear rings gleaming bright).

Her raven hair was pulled back high and pinned in artful knot
Revealing lines of graceful shoulders, neck and beauty spot.
Soldana was dressed all in black: a collared shirt and cuffs
A silver chain hung round his neck that matched his chin's gray scruff.

On Soldana's right Selenia sat next to Nick
And Duke sat on Soldana's left, his eyes were bright and quick.
Gin was on the captain's left and Radar near the right
The atmosphere relaxed (though Nick appeared to be uptight

Until Selenia whispered a joke into his ear
Then leaned and gave a hug to him that took away his fear).
Soldana asked a guitar girl to sit down on Nick's right
Then winked and raised his glass to him and grinned with sheer delight.

The food and drink were excellent! The conversation calm.
They reminisced of capers they had shared in rhyme and song
(Though there were some embellishments that didn't ring quite true
The drink perhaps a bit to blame, but all in friendship too.)

When they were nearly finished Varda came into the room
Looking as if someone had pronounced impending doom
But in his eyes a child's excitement of discovery
Gleamed for he announced that he had uncovered the key

To open up the secret of what Nick's implant concealed
And Varda could not wait another moment to reveal
What use of this technology implied might be afoot
Lurking in the shadows and not up to any good.

Soldana had him sit and eat and calm his hurried mind.
This wasn't quite the topic to discuss at dinner time.
But still he fidgeted and his distraction needed soothed
So Captain asked him his report and all showed interest too:

"It is a mask - a mimic that pretends biology.
"Mechanical in nature and not made like you and me.
"It cloaks its inner workings and for all but deepest scans
"Appears as normal tissue that you'd find in any man.

"But it is not! It's just a skin of sorts that's grown around
"MEMS machines or nanorobots that you don't want found.
"That is well and good but if you scaled it up a bit
"There could be a hundred deadly ways to employ it.

"Consider if perhaps a rat or cockroach were employed
"With sensors and controllers to direct where it's deployed.
"Even humans that would pass a normal medic scan
"But deep inside perhaps as much as half that isn't man.

"Sophisticated integration of man and machine
"Has been employed for decades in prosthetic medicine.

"But now it seems it's nearly undetectable and can
"Conceal a host of deadly things then masquerade as man."

The captain listened, watching as Soldana took it in.
When Varda paused a moment then the Captain too chimed in:
"What was found in Nicholas turned him into a bomb
"Created from the very stuff that makes his body strong.

"The implications of what this device could mean if used
"On a larger scale is a scary bit of news.
"The fingerprints of TerraCorp are smeared all over it.
"It seems their focus in these recent years took quite a shift:

"Their ships and spies were everywhere, but since the Terran war
"Their numbers were reduced and they're not seen much anymore.
"But now they spread control throughout the system sight unseen
"By integrating implants unawares that pass a screen."

Gin croaked, "Data services do that," then cleared his voice
"Since decades in the past, though people still retain a choice;
"But now the victims cannot choose and no one knows they're tagged
"Until it's far too late and they are tools in Terra's bag."

Soldana's eyes swept 'round the room and locked on Varda tight
And said, "I want a way to spot this by tomorrow night.
"Can it be done?" His eyes grew narrow, searching Varda's face
For confirmation as the man squirmed nervously in place.

"Radar found a way to see it but it takes some time
"And specialized equipment that is not easy to find..."
Varda's voice trailed off and Radar picked up where he left
And said, "Soldana, we will find a way. Go place your bet."

A grin cracked through Soldana's lips; he leaned back in his chair.
Selenia looked at the captain, toying with her hair.
Duke and Gin exchanged a glance and looked at Radar's face
Who nodded with assurance he had no doubt - not a trace.

"Well then," said Soldana, "Who will join me for a smoke?
"I've got a box of cigars made in Hellas. Yes, no joke!
"We also have a bottle of the captain's fine cognac
"And coffee brewing in the kitchen steamy, rich and black."

"Martian stogies?" Duke exclaimed, "Now that's a nice surprise.
"I'll be glad to sample one and coffee please, besides!"
Gin's own eyebrows raised as he said, "I've got my own smokes
"But I'd be glad to drink that cognac. You know that's my vote!"

"No thank you," Nick declined (he'd found great interest in the girl
Who played the guitar sweetly sitting by him in blonde curls).
The captain said he'd take a little sip but then retire
While Varda focused on his whispered comments with Radar.

Selenia arose and said, "I'll leave you men to chat
"And ensure sleeping quarters are prepared, then I'll be back."
The others stood along with her, some moseyed toward the lounge
To smoke and drink in leather chairs of comfort, soft and round.

Nick's new friend and he sat back upon their dinner seats
Oblivious to where the others went, their interest piqued
While Varda and his techno-friend retreated to their things
And all was quiet in Soldana's house for the evening.

* * * * *

The softened yellow light inside the smoking lounge was nice.
The glowing coals of cigars that accompanied that vice
Reflected from the faces of the smokers and the glass
Of snifters graced with cognac as relaxed, an hour passed.

"Why are my magnetics down in Varda's icy den?
"I'd hoped to get them lifted to my ship today, not when
"Another day or two of travel time had slipped away.
"I have a tightened schedule now and can't much more delay."

The captain's question, long in coming seemed a little rude
To hit Soldana with after an evening of great food.
But practicalities needed addressed before he slept
And he knew that old gangster was still up to something yet.

Soldana blew a ring of cigar smoke into the air
Then waved it on its way with his cigar with absent flair
And squinted at the captain calmly with a sly regard
And said, "Please understand: your schedule I would not retard,

"But six-axis magnetics are not something one needs quick
"And it was quite apparent you were up to something slick.
"I've heard the rumors of some posturing out Saturn's way
"And thought I'd offer your bright boys a safe place they could stay.

"It looks as if my guess was right and you have found some luck.
"This game is very serious and things are warming up.
"Especially if TerraCorp is turning up the flame.
"The proof is in what you discovered hiding in Nick's frame."

Selenia came in and sat down softly on the couch
Close beside the captain, raised a snifter to her mouth
And took a sip of cognac, then kicked away her shoes
And leaned back in her seat as if to take a little snooze

But turning, looked into the captain's eyes with deep concern
(In her dark eyes he could see her passion warmly burn.)
"Why don't you stay a while and spend some time with us on Mars
"Soaking up some leisure and fresh air beneath the stars?"

"I'd like that," Captain smiled, "But my schedule must be met.
"I have never let my clients down or been late yet
"And even though the client this time is a den of snakes
"There are many things of import that may be at stake."

He turned and said, "Soldana, it is hotter than you think.
"These bright boys have got something. And they are on the brink
"Of spotting underground facilities in planets' cores
"And that will be the key we need to open Titan's door.

"You know very well what that could mean for many souls
"Who make their homes on outer worlds, snug down in their holes
"Or to those who prey on them and wreck their growing towns.
"This will be a mighty tool for those who hunt them down.

"Yes, these boys may have the key, but need to be out there.
"The research can't be done this deep within the solar glare.
"The indication is that TerraCorp will play their hand
"And you know there are other factions vying for that land.

"There is even more here that I cannot yet discuss.
"Should it go to TerraCorp, or to free men like us?

"Either way you look at it, time's shorter than we'd like.
"The steel is hot and on the anvil. Now's the time to strike."

He took a sip of cognac from his glass and breathed it in.
Soldana also took a drink and calmly looked at him.
He tapped an ash from off the cigar burning in his hand
Contemplating what the captain this time may have planned.

He understood the captain had an ace still up his sleeve
And that to play it time was short and he would need to leave.
A trip to Saturn's environs was not without some risk
Especially if TerraCorp had started moving quick.

Terra's tyrant tendencies were not fixed by the war
And though they were cut down to size their tentacles grew more
Deceitful and insidious through fragments scattered wide
Among the renegades and pirates where many could hide.

Soldana took another drag and rolled it off his tongue.
Gin and Duke exchanged a glance suspecting what might come
And then Soldana set his cigar down upon it's tray
And joined his hands together facing toward the captain's way:

"Our businesses and talents have aligned over the years.
"When there has been great danger you have faced it without fear.
"In sticky situations you have always found a way
"To wring success from others' errors and then make it pay.

"And likewise talents of my own helped us time and again.
"I've turned disasters into clear advantage where we win.
"Our mutual support has profited and brought us wealth
"Especially in times when we were forced to work by stealth.

"With this news you bring to me and other sure reports
"It now becomes more clear that time indeed is running short.
"If the Earth or TerraCorp takes Titan as their prize
"The Saturn system will be lost to private enterprise.

"Perhaps the time has come to join our forces once for all?
"The benefits for both of us you know would not be small."
Selenia leaned closer, put her hand on Captain's arm
Gin and Duke stirred in their seats with some sense of alarm.

"The captain said, "How many years have you been asking that?
"You know very well my independence is a fact
"That I have never set aside - you know I never could."
Soldana said, "I know that, and I doubted that you would;

"But in these times we need to reconsider where we stand.
"Uncertainties abound and we'll both need our friends at hand.
"My gut tells me you're not equipped to deal with what's out there.
"When TerraCorp smells what they're after you'll need force to spare.

"Our friends on Ganymede are not as warm as years before
"And most of those near Saturn squabble since the Terran war.
"Together we can multiply our friends' effectiveness
"And take some steps together to protect all our interests."

The captain looked up at the ceiling then looked back at him
And noticed that Soldana'd cast a quick glance toward Gin.
"Anyway," Soldana said, "Give it an evening's thought.
"Tomorrow your magnetics will be sent up to the rock.

"Your crew will find your cargo at dock twelve on Stickney Row
"By sundown here tomorrow with my best hopes, as you know."
The captain knew Soldana's word was good as Martian gold
And rested now in knowing that his loyalties weren't sold.

"Thank you for your offer once again, but you know me.
"I have always operated independently.
"You know very well I've got your back when things get rough
"But this has been a long day and I think I've had enough."

In salute the captain raised his glass Soldana's way
Then tossed the contents back and winked and said, "We'll make it pay."
Selenia stood up with him and said, "I'll take you up."
The captain looked at Duke who quietly toyed with his cup

And said, "Duke, if you don't mind, could you go oversee
"Moving my boat off the bushes and out of the trees?"
Duke said, "You can count on it," and snuffed his stogie stub
Then nodded at Soldana, stood and finished off his mug.

As the three walked out the door Soldana looked at Gin
And asked, "How 'bout another shot of amber liquid sin?"

"Just one more, perhaps," said Gin, "It is remarkable.
"This is the stuff the captain sent but not from our table!"

They chuckled for a moment and agreed it was good stuff
And also that just one more snort would likely be enough.
Soldana poured another shot into their empty glass
And took a sip then peered at Gin while several seconds passed.

He squinted slightly, "How long have you served your captain, Sven?"
"Has it been as long as since the Lunar war began?
Soldana took another sip of spirits from his glass.
Gin's mind filled with images of years swept to the past.

"You know it's been much more than that," Gin answered with a look
That spoke a dozen words Soldana could not have mistook.
"Why would you ask that? We shared some capers long before
"We all threw in our hats to end that stupid lunar war."

Soldana cracked a grin and said, "We did have fun back then
"And turned some decent profits, sometimes paying with our skin!
"But those old days aren't over, Sven; there's plenty more to do.
"There's even wider opportunities coming to view."

Gin remarked, "All the worlds are growing, that's for sure.
"There's room for every enterprise and every day there's more
"And it's becoming obvious you've got a scheme in mind;
"What is up your sleeve, Soldana? What is it this time?"

Soldana pressed a little further, "You and I both know
"There's not a better deep space engineer - you are pure gold.
"Not only have you engineered that rig for God knows what;
"But been a great first officer and he knows what he's got.

"Your loyalty to him has been rock hard, and I know why
"But times do change and sometimes we must set the past aside
"And move on with our lives and grow and reach out for our dreams.
"Your life has been on hold for several years (to me it seems).

"I would like to offer you a ship to call your own.
"I need a captain at the helm I trust to bring her home.
"You've been qualified and captain-rated many years
"Perhaps it's time to take that step and set aside your fears."

"Fears?" Gin snorted, "Fears are not what keeps me where I am.
"You know very well the debt I owe to that good man.
"I serve him out of love, not fear or greed or laziness.
"He chose to save my ass; but put his own life in a mess."

"That is one perspective of the tale," Soldana said
"But others see it differently. That's not what's in his head.
"Doctor Haji was a witness. You know he's detached
"Emotionally from the facts and his view doesn't match.

"Either way you choose to see it doesn't bother me.
"I just know my offer's good to join my company.
"The ship I have to offer you is not a garbage scow.
"It is a class two cruiser parked at Deimos B right now.

Gin put down his glass and stared incredulous at him.
A class two cruiser was not something one bought on a whim!
"Soldana, are you serious? That isn't a small task.
"Whose reluctant navy gave her up, or should I ask?"

"You may ask and I will tell you, but I need to know
"That you'll agree to go and see her first thing tomorrow.
"She's being brought to low Mars orbit later on tonight.
"She's been completely outfitted and I think set up right.

"Give her your inspection then come tell me what you think.
"What do you say now, Captain? Have another drink?"
Soldana's poker face was an amazing thing to see
He didn't let a single wrinkle twitch to show his glee.

He knew he'd made an offer far beyond a spacer's dream
And if this wasn't bait enough then there would be nothing
That could pull the engineer out of his captain's care
And maybe save his life from chasing phantoms way out there.

Gin studied Soldana's face awhile and said, "No drink."
"I've had enough of this seductive juice tonight, I think.
"I could have sworn you said you had a cruiser in your barn.
"This cognac must have fogged my brain or done my ears some harm."

"Your ears are fine and I know you can drink more than you had
"And no," Soldana said, "Neither of us is raving mad.

"The ship is real. The offer too, and you're the man for me.
"Take command and bring us profits, hands untied and free.

"Think about it Sven, perhaps your captain will miss you
"But with a cruiser of this class, think what you could do.
"Perhaps a situation will arise when he'll need help
"And you will have the power to assist him when he yelps!"

Soldana stubbed his cigar out and downed his final sip
And said, "You can pick your crew to man it - it's your ship.
"A shuttle will be taking your magnetics up at ten.
"You can ride along with it and see your new ship then."

Gin peered at Soldana through a final puff of smoke
And crushed his cigarette butt in the tray before he spoke:
"You've got all the details and the cover set to go.
"You sir, are a very sneaky bastard, don't you know?"

A smile creased Soldana's face. He quipped, "I serve me well.
"And I take care of all my friends as anyone will tell.
"Think about it Sven. It's an offer good as gold.
"Take that shuttle ride tomorrow. I think you'll be sold."

Soldana stood and on Gin's shoulder firmly placed his hand
And said, "I'm off to get some sleep now. You know where I stand.
"I have an enterprise to run that grows each day and night.
"Please don't disappoint me Sven. Be there for that flight."

Soldana left the room and Gin remained there all alone.
This was not an offer as if one would throw a bone
To a dog as charity. This was legitimate.
And he would be an utter fool to not consider it.

He walked around the lounge some minutes, looking at the art
Absently while searching deep inside his mind and heart.
Could it hurt to take a little flight and see this ship
And for just an hour or two give Captain's plans the slip?

He walked out of the smoking lounge and through the dining room
And noticed empty coffee cups where Nick and friend had swooned.
Their empty chairs were still pulled out but they were not in sight.
Perhaps they'd found a better spot to visit for the night?

Walking toward the west wing where the crewmens' suite and bed
Awaited him he couldn't drive the conflict from his head.
Soldana's offer was a golden opportunity
And never in a hundred years would be one half this sweet!

* * * * *

Selenia took Captain by the hand and up the stairs.
Then arm in arm she took him through the doorway to her lair:
A suite of rooms of luxury and privacy and ease
And turning toward him softly said, "Be at home here, please."

She led him to a bedroom with a window wide and tall
That opened to a balcony above the garden's wall
Over which he saw that Duke with two men on his heels
Were in the midst of towing his yacht toward the landing field.

His hostess had removed the silver pin that held her hair
And it was now a gleaming cascade tossed without a care.
The captain was relaxed, the ambiance was soft and warm
And there was nothing for a thousand miles could bring them harm.

Selenia stepped closer and reached for the curtain's chain
The faint scent of her flowing hair bored straight into his brain.
Her shoulder, tanned and supple brushed so lightly 'gainst his arm
(Most any man's resistance would be shattered by her charms).

Then as she drew the curtain closed she slowly turned and faced
The object of her passion who stood motionless in place.
Her dark eyes gazed into his own, inviting and alive
With promise of sweet pleasures into which he longed to dive.

(But there was only one love in his heart and it burned hot
Whether she was present with him physically or not.)
Selenia moved closer, put her hands upon his chest
Then moved them slowly down his torso, pulled him to her breast.

"Jules, you know the saying. 'if you can't be with your Love
"Then love the one you're with,' applies to you and me above
"All other situations. You and I make quite the pair."
His eyes looked at her lips and wandered over her dark hair.

He grinned at her suggestion and looked deeply in her eyes
And said, "Selenia my friend, you are a gorgeous prize;
"But she is with me here," he put his hand above his heart
"That's how I know she is alive since we were ripped apart."

"Jules, don't you think she'd want your manly needs fulfilled
"In her lengthy absence even if she were not killed?
"It would be my honor to be all of that for you
"In friendship with no strings attached and no commitments too.

"And if that's all of you that I can have, I'll live with that.
"I savor every moment of our little yearly chats.
"Come, lay upon the bed. I'll loosen up your boots."
She pushed him gently backward as he felt her silken noose

Figuratively slip around his throat with soft allure
And gently charm his senses (making his resolve unsure).
Softly on her sweetly scented pillows he alit
Then pulling off his boots upon the bed she came to sit

And pull him deeper in her web of intimate delight
With promises of imminent release throughout the night.
Then as she leaned close over him and whispered in his ear
His breathing slowed and he was fast asleep - it was clear!

She looked into his face and softly brushed his hair aside
Then lightly loosened up his shirt and lay down at his side.
Though for a moment disappointment flooded through her mind
She knew very well he was exhausted, pressed for time.

Beside the man she hungered for, but with her thoughts alone
Emotions coalesced and to her consciousness came home
The latent understanding that throughout her life she'd been
A heartbreaker with little real respect for many men.

She'd used them and abused a few and often felt regret
But never found a man who she could give her heart to yet.
Then as she lay there next to him, the one man she admired;
The only man through all her life she'd desperately desired

A sudden jolt of spasm from her legs up through her heart
(As if a crashing lightning bolt had split a stone apart)

Brought the sudden realization to her conscious mind
Not only did she want this man, she'd love him for all time!

Tears welled up into her eyes. She caught a little gasp
And with a bit of shock she found herself losing her grasp.
She turned and kissed him gently on the head and slipped away
Careful not to wake the sleeping captain where he lay.

* * * * *

The bright blue Earth had set and now the black sky speckled bright
With stars that seemed much closer than with Earthbound human sight
Drew the eyes like magnets draw an iron rod their way
Their shining light demanding dazzled eyes not look away.

Duke pulled tight his parka as he leaned against a rock
And gazed up at the starry sky that served well as his clock.
Deimos, the farther moon, shined dimly on the land
As quickly moving Phobos climbed up from the western sand.

Rigil Kent and Crux had risen high into the south
And Regulus was setting soon. The cold air in his mouth
Also told him it would not be long before the wind
Would sweep down from the highlands bringing comfort to an end.

The day's events rolled through his mind in circles one by one.
The offers that were made were unexpected, yet had come.
He knew Soldana well enough to sense he'd make a play
To get beneath Gin's leather hide and take his heart away.

Soldana was a tricky one. He'd done his very best
To steal away key people and make Captain's crew a mess.
It didn't make a lick of sense! Why would he wreck a team
That worked so well together and could do most everything

In special situations he had need for in the past?
Soldana knew that he could trust them to the very last.
Maybe that was all it was: an offer to change ways
And work in safety on the ground receiving steady pay.

But Gin was right: Why now, when opportunities were ripe
And so much was at stake to make sure things turned out all right?

Perhaps Soldana had a bigger stake out Titan's way
Than he let on and didn't want the Captain in his way.

Regardless, Duke knew where the captain left his broken heart
And he would do all that he could to help; he'd play his part.
By now the conversation and the drinking would be done
And he knew Gin might need a steady head for what had come.

He went back through the garden wall and on into the house
And quietly into the suite so no one he'd arouse
Expecting Nick and Radar to be sleeping in the dark
But Gin was all alone upon a couch where he had parked.

"Hiya Duke. Did Captain's yacht get safely put to bed?"
Gin's eyes looked a little blurry as he raised his head.
Duke said, "All is well outside. How goes it all in here?
"Radar still must be with Varda, Nick has disappeared?"

Gin responded, "I think Nick has found a place to stay
"With someone prettier than us to while his time away."
He winked at Duke who said, "I'm sure there's better spots to be
"Than cooped up in a room with smelly men like you and me."

Gin smiled his agreement then his focus left the room.
His mind was racing with his thoughts; confusion and some gloom
Were seen across his countenance. Excitement and some dread,
Sadness and exhilaration tangled in his head.

Duke sat down and looked straight into Gin's conflicted eyes
And said, "I don't know what Soldana's offered as a prize;
"But I knew it was coming and you should have known it too
"And I know you are chewing hard on what with it to do.

"Gin, your heart is good. You are a man put to the test.
"Follow what is in your heart, and trust that it is best."
Gin peered keenly into Duke's brown eyes for just a spell
And said, "Soldana surely casts his nets straight out of hell."

Duke said, "I don't know what he has dangled as your bait.
"But I do know you need some sleep before it gets too late.
"Tomorrow will be brighter, you will have a clearer view.
"Perhaps you'll have more facts and then you'll know what you should do.

"Either choice you make, you know we all will have your back.
"Now sleep and listen to your heart and follow in its track."
With that Duke turned and went into a room and closed the door
And within seven minutes Gin could hear a peaceful snore.

What's the price of loyalty? What can buy a man?
What inside the soul inspires to serve a higher plan?
Are the moral answers wired in that we should know
Or are they found deep in the heart where we don't often go?

Or is the better path revealed when hidden from the light
Until the final moment we must choose what's wrong or right?
'Funny,' Gin thought to himself, *'He has more faith in me*
'Than I have in myself,' and then he drifted off to sleep.

The silence of the country castle in this barren land
Kept the sleepers insulated from the blowing sand
While far above the moonlit scene of shadowed reddish hue
A newly minted orbiter came brightly into view.

8   A Better Offer

The yellow morning sun had crested high above the cliffs
And driven chilly shadows back as sleepers rose up stiff
To find their breakfast ready in the tea room near their suite
With fruit and tea and coffee and big pastries hot and sweet.

Gin was bleary-eyed and Captain rested, fresh and shaved;
Radar looked as mussed as ever, Duke's chair wasn't saved
For he had risen early and gone with a stable hand
Riding in the nearby hills to scout around the land.

Nick and his companion had arrived before the rest
And she approached Soldana with a sweet smile and request:
She would like to take Nick for a little tourist flight
And wondered if to take one of the planes would be all right?

The captain cast a warning leery eye Soldana's way
Who raised his hand in gesture, Captain's worries to defray.
There would be no funny business on Soldana's part
And Nick would be back soon enough for when Mars they'd depart.

Soldana gave his blessing and the two beamed brightened smiles.
"Take the Raven if you like, but please, six hundred miles
"Is your radius. There's plenty in that space to see.
"And make sure that you're back this afternoon in time for tea."

He looked the captain's way and asked, "Is that fair enough?"
The captain nodded knowing that Soldana would not bluff
And so the girl and Nick departed for the landing field
And as they passed the garden wall their feelings were revealed

For if a sharp eye watched one saw Nick's hand reach for her own
And take it into his as they walked from Soldana's home.
It seemed the two of them had found in each a friend who cared
And Captain smiled as memories of his youth he compared.

How the years and distance had distorted youthful views!
And how the winds of fortunes made and lost had changed him too.
A flood of memories of young romance then filled his heart
Of days of sun and promises forever not to part.

The vigor and the love of life had lost that youthful edge
In all the time that passed since his life slipped over the edge
(When from his side his Love was ripped away and presumed lost.
To get her back beside him he would pay whatever cost.)

These thoughts, never far away, were pushed aside for now.
The sight of Nick and his new interest livened him somehow
And made his thoughts apparent as Soldana looked his way
And said, "I think I did a favor for them yesterday.

"I saw how she looked at him when he came through the door.
"She was playing Mozart when she looked up from the score
"And turned a little red. I thought a dinner place might do.
"It looks like it resulted in a good thing for those two."

Soldana grinned with satisfaction as he sipped his tea
And captain said, "I think you get a little too much glee
"From playing peoples' sensitivities; but this one's good."
And then the both of them knocked on the table (made of wood).

Radar chewed on pastries and sucked coffee by the quart.
Soldana had been anxious to receive Varda's report
So Radar said, "I think we've got a working prototype
"But we will need to test it on more than we had last night."

"We've put a man to fabricating three more you can use
"But they will need adjustments when we find implants to view."
"Excellent!" Soldana said, "Let's scan the whole estate.
"This afternoon a shuttle will coming with some freight

"And there will be more people we can try your scanner on
"Even though I hope we do not find a single one."
The captain looked at Radar with a question in his eyes
And Radar nodded his assurance he'd have one besides.

A rustle from the door announced Selenia had come
Wrapped in a satin robe with her black hair up in a bun.
Her dark eyes smiled silently and beamed the captain's way
As all the men gave greetings, poured her tea without delay.

"Your melons are delicious," Radar said as she leaned down
To slide her chair beneath her; then he turned red with a frown

And said, "I mean, *these* melons - on the platter - are quite good."
He stammered and embarrassed glanced down at his plate of food.

The captain locked his gaze, his face a stony wall of ice.
Selenia laughed loudly and Gin whispered lowly "Nice."
Soldana overlooked it like he hadn't heard a thing.
Selenia said, "Thank you Radar, it's a fine morning!"

She placed her hand on Radar's arm and beamed a friendly smile
Then leaned back in her chair and met the Captain's gaze a while.
The conversation played on simple things and friendly chat
As Martian sunlight warmed the room where happily they sat.

The garden wall retracted as the warmth of day increased.
The captain said. "If you don't mind, I think I will make peace
"With all those shrubs that took the brunt when my yacht landed there
"And I would love to get some exercise in that fresh air."

With that he stood and walked behind Selenia to go
And placed a friendly hand upon her shoulder so she'd know
That he appreciated that she'd let him rest the night
And there was not a doubt that things between them were all right.

After Captain left Soldana looked at Gin and said,
"Your cargo has been loaded on a shuttle. How's your head?
"Will you be escorting it to Phobos as we planned?"
And Gin said, "Yes, I will. I see departure time's at hand."

Soldana's eyes lit up (his poker face was cast aside)
As he said, "Thank you, Sven, I hope you have a pleasant ride."
Gin tossed back the contents left inside his coffee mug
And with a touch of non-chalance he gave a little shrug

And said, "I'll let you know when everything is in its place."
Then turning to his hostess said, "It's off once more to space.
"Perhaps it won't be quite as long before we meet again.
"Thank you for your hospitality and gracious plan."

Selenia stood with him, took his hand in her own
And said, "It is our pleasure, Sven, to have you in our home."
Her smile turned more serious; she said, "Forever Free!
"Keep your eyes wide open, Sven. Fulfill your destiny!"

Radar's ears perked up and some confusion crossed his face.
He stood up as Gin left the room and said, "See you in space!"
Gin flashed him the thumbs-up as he left, then Radar too
Excused himself to go see Varda (still much work to do).

In the silence of the room Selenia sipped tea.
Soldana sat there for a moment, watching her closely
Then said, "Something's changed, My Dear. What is on your mind?"
And she responded, "Yes it has. I fear for them this time."

"Them?" Soldana blurted, "Don't you mean you fear for *him*?"
"I care for Jules, Soldana, and it's more than just a whim."
She looked into her teacup and he studied her a bit
Then said, "I think you've found you love him, don't you? Is that it?

"After all these years you've come to realize there is one
"That brings you where you didn't know your heart could ever come."
Soldana put his hand upon her arm and leaned in close
And whispered, "Now you feel the thorn that comes with that sweet rose.

"I wish you all the best, My Dear. You two are quite the pair.
"But I fear he'll forever chase that ghost of his out there.
"That man has a heart of gold; he's loyal to a tee.
"And from the hope to find that ghost he never will be free."

Soldana stood to leave and said, "He is a clever man;
"But he will need more help this trip than he will have at hand."
She turned to watch him as he left, she left some words unsaid
Then tears welled up and quiet sobs escaped her bowing head.

* * * * *

The captain found some garden tools inside a little shed
Just outside the wall right where a groundskeeper had said
And as he walked to fix the damage he had done last night
Gin came on his way to catch the shuttle's morning flight.

The captain turned to greet him and remarked how rough he looked
And Gin admitted how his brain by cognac had been cooked;
But Captain knew his Engineer (who served as First Mate too)
And he could see that on Gin's mind there was a hard issue.

The captain set his shovel down and paused them in their walk
And said, "I know that you're expecting we might have this talk."
Gin looked at the captain then he looked at the airfield
And knew the secret that he kept today would be revealed.

"You've done well under pressure many times over the years
"And stayed a steady course in spite of danger, threats and fears.
"I know you're backed against a wall and have a choice to make.
"I also know Soldana and with him there's give and take;

"But mostly there is take, Gin. You know his tactics well
"And you should be the last man anyone would have to tell;
"But you have every right to make your own choice. You are free.
"I have no claim on you; there's not a thing that you owe me

"And you know I would never have it any other way."
The captain finished his discourse and Gin had naught to say.
(He wondered how the captain knew that something was proposed
The captain's instinct, razor sharp, still worked well, he supposed).

Then as the captain picked his shovel up they both could see
Selenia stood in the doorway oddly - demurely.
Gin looked keenly at the captain and said straight and bold,
"Every offer has its glitter; but it's all not gold."

Both of them looked at the ground then met each other's gaze.
Both of them shook hands and then they walked their separate ways
(The captain with his shovel and the engineer to flight)
Both of them hoped for each other all would work out right.

* * * * *

The shuttle taxied to the runway then surged to the sky.
Morning became afternoon then Duke came riding by
And looked the captain over who was wet with sweat and dirt
Kneeling by a sapling where he'd taken off his shirt.

"The garden's looking better but I'll not say that for you,"
Duke said dryly mounted on a bay that snorted too.
The captain grunted as he stood and brushed dirt from his hair
"Perhaps you'd like to dig some holes? The shovel's waiting there."

Duke asked, "Gin has gone up with the cargo as he'd planned?"
The captain nodded (wiped his sweaty brow with back of hand).
Duke continued, "Gin is heavy with a troubled heart."
The captain said, "I know. I think Soldana hit him hard."

"Captain, he hit all of us and Gin kept us in check;
"But in the late hours of the night Soldana roped his neck.
"I don't know what was offered, but I know it bit him deep.
"I doubt if he was ever able to get any sleep."

"All of us are free to make the choices we think best,"
The captain said, then added, "All of life seems like a test."
"It is a test," Duke offered, "And I know Gin's heart is true.
"I think we'll all support him in whatever he may choose."

The two of them both nodded as Duke turned his mount away.
The captain watched with fascination as he saw the way
The horse had learned to canter in the point four gravity.
He thought a Martian horserace would be quite the sight to see!

* * * * *

The shuttle reached the height and inclination at a speed
To intercept the cruiser's orbit Flight Planning decreed.
In minutes they were on approach and Gin got his first look
At Soldana's cruiser where he'd start a new log book.

From all appearances it was exactly as described:
A class-two cruiser built for speed with lots of room inside.
A product built at Mercury and made for deep-space runs
Furnished fore and aft with turrets for six laser guns.

The shuttle made a slow approach then slewed off to one side
So Gin could see the engine cowlings of his newest ride.
Equipped with double torches and six rocket engines too
It looked like she was fast and nimble. He'd see what she'd do!

Soon the shuttle docked and Gin was through the airlock door
Eager to inspect the ship and learn a little more
And there to greet him with a smile that reached from ear to ear
Was Ansel Pedersen, logistics man without a peer!

"Welcome, Captain, to your ship! I think you'll find her fit
"For any venture near or far. Shall we get on with it?"
Gin took Ansel's offered hand and turned to him to say,
"So this is where you ran off in a hurry yesterday!"

Ansel's blue eyes twinkled asking, "Would you like to start
"Fore or aft or at the new atomic's glowing heart?"
Gin said, "To the engines! At the cockpit we'll end up
"And then I'd like to taste what kind of coffee's in the cups."

Gin winked at Soldana's man who led them toward the stern
And spent more than two hours soaking up all he could learn
About the workings of the ship, its weaknesses and strengths
And when the time came he must leave he gave Ansel his thanks.

Ansel asked him, "Are you going back to Mars today?"
And added, "I'll be at Soldana's for two days this stay,
"Perhaps we'll tilt a bottle and exchange a lie or two
"Before you take your new ship out to see what she can do?"

Gin said he would like that but he had to be away
To load their cargo on the Captain's ship by end of day
And then he placed his hand on Ansel's shoulder with a look
That emphasized what he would say so not to be mistook:

"Ansel, I must sleep on this. The ship is quite the dream
"But I must weigh priorities before I do this thing.
"I cannot command her if my second guesses haunt
"My every future thought. It's not what any crew would want."

"I understand, my friend," said Ansel as they parted ways
"I hope to see you here again before too many days."
Gin went to the shuttle; Ansel closed the airlock door.
The two of them would never meet again forevermore.

* * * * *

By early afternoon the shuttle docked beside their ship
Where Joe had grown impatient waiting for his chance to slip
Away to Mars for just a day of open skies and room
To stretch his legs in point four G and shake some shipboard gloom.

"You are late," he said as Gin debarked the shuttle's bay
Guiding their new cargo to the place where it would stay
Until the time was right to set it up where it would be
Used to do the work that might decide their destiny.

"Yeah, I had a flat tire, then my tank ran out of gas,"
Gin remarked and Joe responded, "Was she a sweet lass?"
"Aye, she was!" said Gin. They both chuckled for a bit
Then Joe left in the shuttle and that was the end of it.

Gin ran checks of all the major systems then retired
To his little stateroom where he laid down to unwire
And check his eyelids for the pinholes he felt there must be
Then in a moment dozed off to a deep and restful sleep.

* * * * *

The droning of the turbines of Soldana's black airplane
Echoed up the canyon just before the aircraft came
And circled once around the field then lined up set to land
Blowing from the runway a thin cloud of ochre sand.

Nick and his new tour guide had returned no worse for wear.
He was very pleased to have the tourist trip by air.
They both were sporting smiles from the friendship they had found
And while they walked it seemed that neither of them touched the ground.

The sun was getting lower as the afternoon wore on
And as they passed the captain said they'd leave before too long
So to the house they vanished for a final fond farewell.
Companionship and love had cast on them its magic spell.

The day had quickly vanished for the captain in the dirt
(Gardening a pleasure not found in his line of work).
Selenia's warm company had made his workload light
Soldana came at times and kept his conversation bright.

Then as the sun was westering Soldana passed again
With Varda and with Radar being dragged along with him.
"Come into the tea room for some sandwiches and drinks;
"But first you take a shower and wash off that dirt and stink!"

The three of them continued walking toward the landing field
This afternoon their new-made scanner first would be revealed.
For those that came to visit now would all be scanned and cleared
Of any of the newer implants that Soldana feared.

The transport from Soldana's cruiser split the silent sky
With whining turbines and the roar of thrusters by and by
And when it met the sandy ground across the landing field
The cloud of dust and grass kicked up left half the sky concealed.

Then as it drifted clear the lower airlock opened wide
Revealing six or seven men who waited there inside
Obviously anxious to spend time out on the town.
(The maiden cruise from Mercury to shake the new ship down

Had kept them busy working out the kinks and custom kit
That any new ship needed for the customer's re-fit.)
Most of them would transfer to an aircraft for the ride
Down the Ganges chasm to Batoka for the night.

A day or three of revelry then back to work they'd go
To Mercury or other jobs their company would show.
Eagerly they hurried to Soldana's larger plane
And jetted down the runway with the turbines spewing flame

While Ansel and two others of Soldana's trusted men
Walked across the tarmac where Soldana greeted them.
"I trust the tour went well?" Soldana asked and Ansel smiled
And answered, "It was just like showing candy to a child;

"But he has not committed yet. He likes the ship just fine;
"You will have your answer by tomorrow night this time."
"Very well," Soldana said, "He is a thoughtful man
"And this is one surprise I know will change his future plans.

"He will see the light and soon he'll take his rightful place
"As master of our cruiser bringing profits in from space.
"Meanwhile," he continued, "We have new technology
"To find a new threat that's turned up. It's really quite nasty."

Varda then proceeded to inspect Soldana's men
When finished with the two he started in on Ansel when

An audible alert made Radar's ears (Soldana's too!)
Perk up like a coyote's when a rabbit comes in view.

Radar pulled his pocket scanner out while Varda poked
The buttons on the new detector; Ansel seemed to choke
And then he sank down to his knees, his eyes wide with surprise
Then falling sideways spasmed and breathed out a final sigh.

"Ansel!" yelled Soldana, "Holy smokes!" Radar exclaimed,
Varda stood there motionless, the others called his name
And gathered all around him on the ground in hopes to aid.
They tried resuscitation but he died there where he laid.

Varda was in shock and Radar's scanner beeped a note.
He waved it near the new detector then read what it wrote.
"Get him to the house", Soldana ordered. "Wait! Stand back!"
Radar shouted as he pulled Soldana to a stack

Of shipping crates behind him where they stopped to see some steam
Rising out of Ansel's chest and then a flame was seen.
Confused and shocked, the others backed away a step or two
And watched with morbid fascination as the fire grew,

The burning fat and fabric sending curls of black smoke
Snaking through the nostrils of the watchers who were choked
With tears and sneezes, coughing while a man came at a run
With a fire suppressor; but he stopped, looking stunned

At what lay on the ground before them; but did what he must
And hosed the burning body, scattering the ash and dust.
"What the devil happened here?" Soldana seethed aloud
Walking toward the body as the dissipating cloud

Of smoke and CO_2 drifted from the horrid scene.
"It seems an implant in his chest did not want to be seen,"
Said Radar as he fiddled with the scanner in his hand
And Varda said, "Upon detection I sent a command

"Interrogating data from the implant which might show
"Where it came from and some other things we'd like to know,
"But it appears this unit had a self-destruction mode
"To terminate the host upon an access to its code."

Soldana looked at Radar saying, "These things are much more
"Advanced than I imagined and they've moved into the core -
"The very inner circle of my family and friends.
"This is now an act of war and we need a defense."

Varda stood before Soldana, looked him in the eye
And held the scanner up and said, "Our Ansel lost his life;
"But what we've learned prepares us for the next one we will find.
"No one that we know has a detector of this kind."

Soldana's eyes grew narrow and frustration crossed his face
But he knew Varda was the best and would step up the pace
Of learning what he could to find the countermeasures for
This evil new technology unleashed by TerraCorp.

He turned and kneeled down beside his dead and trusted man
And all of them stood silent 'til Soldana gave command:
"Clean whatever implants may remain within the corpse
"Then give me every bit of data they contain, of course."

Radar cautioned Varda and Soldana to move fast
And get a damping field set before more time had passed:
"The chances that a message was transmitted out of him
"Are very high. I've tried to jamb it, but my scanner's dim.

"Run and get some wide-band gear and set it up right here
"And then I'll neutralize all the implanted transmit gear."
Varda sent a running man to get the gear required
Then knelt beside the body scanning what could be acquired.

"Incinerate the body when you've gathered what you can,"
Soldana said, then turned and walked away from his dead man.
This was not the first time he had lost one of his men.
His shady business dealings had required it now and then;

But Ansel was a cornerstone within his enterprise
And losing him at home a very unpleasant surprise.
Soldana walked back quickly toward the house to get a drink
And spend some minutes in his favorite chair to help him think.

Meanwhile, from her balcony Selenia had seen
The hubbub on the field and Soldana looking mean

As he came through the garden marching stiffly from the field
She knew there was big trouble (this his stomping had revealed).

She let some minutes pass and then she sought Soldana out
And listened closely (widened eyes and hand over her mouth)
As he told her the story of what happened at the field
How Ansel died so suddenly when spyware was revealed.

Tears were running from her eyes; she held Soldana's arm.
Both of them for Ansel sorrowed, but were more alarmed
Realizing how close to home and yet they never knew;
Everything would have to change with this new threat in view.

The captain had been showering and was not yet apprised
Of what had happened at the field to everyones' surprise.
Coming to the tea room with his hair a little wet
Still closing up his shirt he found that no one was there yet.

Wandering into the lounge, he found the saddened two
Discussing something in hushed tones and looking very blue.
Selenia came to him as he walked into the room
Her teary eyes reflecting old Soldana's face of gloom.

"Jules! Varda's scanner has turned up another bug,"
She said as she reached out her arms to pull him in a hug.
"And this time it was found inside someone who's very close:
"Ansel Pedersen," she said (Soldana looked morose).

Soldana said, "He's dead, Jules, the implant burned him up.
"His body's on the tarmac now, where he ran out of luck.
"Process and procedure with our businesses and friends
"Will have to be re-engineered from these things to defend."

As he spoke his sorrow was supplanted with his rage.
They all could see how history had turned another page.
After finding peace and solace working in the yard
The captain's face now turned to stone; this news caught him off guard.

"You were right," Soldana said, "It's hotter than we thought.
"It's fortunate that two of these new implants have been caught.
"It would have been much better had we known they were around
"Before we lost a life, but now we know they can be found."

The captain asked, "Where is Nick? He needs to see the sight
"Of what his implant could have done. I want his mind set right."
Selenia looked at him with concern regarding Nick
And asked him, "Don't you think that seeing that might make him sick?

"Nick is resting from his tour; he heard the call for tea.
"He'll be down here shortly if his friend will set him free."
Soldana said, "The captain's right. It would be good for him
"To see a sample of this new reality, though grim.

"He may need that preparation in the weeks ahead.
"The captain cannot hold his hand because someone is dead."
Soldana poured another shot and swirled it in his glass.
The other two departed knowing his dark mood would pass.

When they left the room they heard some laughter down the hall
That echoed from the tea room where the guests had all been called.
And as they neared the room they recognized the voices three
As Duke's and Nick's and his new friend all eating heartily.

The laughter and the mirth stood stark against the dismal mood
That filled Soldana's lounge where he continued still to brood.
The captain pulled two chairs out and the two of them sat down.
It didn't take but seconds 'til the others saw their frowns.

"Another implant similar to yours has turned up here,"
The captain started, "And I want to make it very clear
"That this one didn't have the firepower yours contained
"But it has done its job and one man's dead; you know his name:

"Ansel Pedersen is lying dead out on the field.
"It killed him as we queried it when it had been revealed.
"It would be a good thing if you'd come with me to see
"His body to bring theory into firm reality."

Nick put down his sandwich and his girlfriend gave a gasp.
Duke leaned back into his chair and toyed with his glass.
Silence filled the quiet air as shock turned into gloom
For several seconds until Radar stepped into the room:

"Varda says a neurotoxin in him was set free
"By an implant next to his carotid artery.

"He didn't have a chance - he went down like a box of rocks.
"It's obvious he was a tool someone did not want caught.

"It's also highly likely that the bad guys know the score.
"That is, an implant was detected - queried all the more.
"I can't be sure a message was transmitted, but I know
"The gear was set to send another, though it didn't go."

The captain ordered quietly, "Let the others know.
"Duke, you and Radar pack our gear, get set to go.
"Meet me at the yacht. We'll leave before the sun has set.
"Nick, if you don't mind, we haven't seen the body yet."

"Yes sir," Nick responded as he took a final sip
And asked his girl to bring his coat and meet him at the ship.
Selenia accompanied the captain and his charge
But stayed behind some distance and did not between them barge

For she did not desire to see the sight for which they went
And didn't want to hear the words to Nick's ears he would send.
(For several minutes they discussed some things that lay ahead
Then quietly they shook their hands and Nick nodded his head.)

Duke and Radar and Nick's girl with yellow braided hair
Had walked around beyond them as the cooling Martian air
Had formed a sunset dust devil that swept a little path
Across the tarmac where they stood. Nick left, did not look back.

The captain and Selenia walked slowly (lagged behind)
Toward the yacht where Duke had made the turbines start to whine.
Some yards before they got there Captain turned and held her hands
The ruddy rays of sunset's final brush across the land.

The cooling dusty breeze was sifting through her raven hair
While his eyes sadly looked back at her wistful parting stare.
Then quietly and tenderly he touched her on the cheek
Then placed his finger on her lips in hopes she wouldn't speak.

"Selenia, you've always been the best of friends to me
"And I know that you always will - it's been our destiny.
"But you know that my heart belongs to someone I must find
"And I must search until I'm sure she wasn't left behind."

"Then find her, Jules. Find her now and put your heart to rest.
"Go out there and put your theories to the hardest test
"Then come back here. You know for you I'll always wait, my friend
"And I will be your faithful wife and mate until the end.

"No man ever heard those words from me and never will
"Again until you're back with me and our love is fulfilled.
"You will be my captain, Jules, and I will be your queen
"And we will share our love and live our lives forever free."

"Goodbye, Selenia," he said and held her in his arms
A moment then released her and in spite of all her charms
Turned and climbed into the cockpit where his heart must lead
And pulled the craft into the sky as fate had long decreed.

Across the ruddy sand the pinkly glowing sky revealed
Cradled in its clarity the planets as they wheeled:
The Earth the brightest blue and Venus shining purest white
And Jupiter beyond them both, the master of the night

Regal in his majesty, transcends the yellow spark
Of Saturn ruling over his own portion of the dark.
Steady, shining brighter than the stars beyond them all
Faithfully they fly their orbits, never can they fall!

9   Decision

Three long hours of sleep had done Gin's head a world of good.
He'd been awake some minutes when a shipment of fresh food
Settled on the loading dock outside the cargo bay
Where Haji stood and handed to the dockworker his pay.

Gin and Haji stowed the goods then brewed a pot of tea
And lounged around the galley telling each what they had seen
On Mars and how their friends were faring and other small talk
Then Haji asked directly, "What's your conflict?" Gin just balked.

Haji pressed him, "We have known each other many years
"And I can see that there is something reddening your ears.
"Something happened down on Mars that's nagging at your heart
"And If you want to talk about it I will do my part."

Gin stared at his tea cup thinking, *It's that obvious?*
Maybe it is true I've been too long on this old bus.
Haji took a guess and asked, "Soldana got to you?
"This is not the first time he has tried to buy this crew."

Gin looked down and nodded then he took another sip
And said, "Soldana's offered me command of his new ship.
"It's a class 2 cruiser and it's gorgeous - shiny new!
"Opportunities like this are rare, there are so few."

Haji's eyebrows raised a bit. He said, "I'm not surprised.
"He couldn't pick a better man; for him no compromise.
"Your mind tells you there'll never be a richer career plan
"But what does your heart say about employment with that man?"

Gin gave a dismissive wave and said. "I'm not concerned
"With working on the shady side of things; we all have learned
"To walk the edge in dealing with the people that we do.
"And working for Soldana won't be anything so new.

"He knows that I don't take his guff and that might be a trait
"That he finds beneficial for the man to run his crate.
"So no, I have no qualms about my taking on the job.
"What's eating me is if I do, from this crew I would rob."

Haji took a sip of tea then set his teacup down
And eyed Gin with a piercing look that bordered on a frown.
He said, "You know it's true that you are highly valued here
"But no one's irreplaceable. I know that's not your fear.

"Every man among them would encourage you to go
"And take this opportunity - a golden one, they'd know.
"Of course to some extent you'd hate to leave your crewmates short
"But you need to be honest how you read your heart's report:

"Who is it you really feel you're robbing, just the crew?
"Or is it more you feel a debt to Captain's overdue?"
Gin avoided Haji's eyes a moment then replied
"Doctor, you do very well at reading me inside.

"Yes, there is a debt that seems I never can repay
"But still I hang around him hoping that I might some day.
"Besides," Gin continued, "He has brought us all good luck.
"That's part of why the good guys on this ship and crew have stuck."

Haji nodded for a moment then he shook his head
And said, "Gin, from his perspective there has been no debt.
"The choice he made at Ganymede was logical and right.
"He had no chance to save her, but for you the chance was slight."

A message from the captain cut their conversation short.
The yacht was on approach to hook up to its docking port.
Within a few short minutes clamps along the outer hull
Locked the craft against the ship and now their little lull

Would be replaced by hungry mouths and talk and noisy men
Bemoaning that their shore leave had already reached its end.
But when the captain and his three companions came aboard
Their mood was quite subdued and that couldn't be ignored.

Radar went directly to his bunk to take a nap,
Duke and Nick came to the galley looking for a snack.
The captain went to check ship's status from his own stateroom
And Gin asked Duke and Nick the question, "What's with all the gloom?"

"It isn't really gloom," Duke offered, "They have simply ducked.
"They don't want to tell you of someone who lost their luck.

"Just before we left Soldana's, Radar's scanner found
"An implant that put Ansel Pedersen into the ground."

"That's a little blunt," Nick bristled, "Gin knew Ansel well!"
Duke responded, "Gin prefers the straightest way to tell."
He continued, "Radar says that after it was found
"They queried it for information then it put him down."

Gin took all this in a moment then said, "Thank you, Duke.
"Was there any indication that he was a spook
"For TerraCorp or someone else or if he even knew?
"Soldana's got to be upset he's lost part of his crew."

Haji looked at Gin and wondered at his cool facade
And figured that for Gin perhaps this wasn't all that odd.
He wasn't really close to Ansel, but he knew the man.
Gin had his distractions and the ship's business at hand.

Duke responded, "Right now that is all we really know.
"Varda's digging through some data he got but it's slow
"Going, Radar says. I suppose they'll know some more
"In a day or two; but for now, that's the score."

"Thank you, Duke," was all Gin said, then added, "Stow your gear
"And we will rustle up burritos and a little beer.
"Tomorrow we'll be leaving orbit for the outer worlds
"And there may be some changes that the captain will unfurl."

* * * * *

Later in the evening, the captain sat with Gin
Discussing preparations for the trip to Saturn, when
The captain asked him point blank, "Are you coming with us too?
"Have you let Soldana know what you are going to do?"

Gin looked at him keenly for a moment then replied,
"Soldana made a golden offer, and I will not lie;
"But I like history, Sir. It points us to the future.
"Our history is better than Soldana's, that's for sure."

Gin finished his comment with his face a little rough
Silently conveying, *'Leave it there. Fair enough?'*

The captain shook Gin's hand and said, "I like our history too."
"Gin, you are a friend beyond compare and I thank you."

10   Departure

The red rays of the rising sun were dancing on the dunes
And rocks across DaVinci crater when the ship got news
That Dewey wasn't able to collect himself today
So Bovine was directed to assist his getaway.

This was not the news that Bovine cared to hear about
Since it was nearly midnight where his friends were hanging out
In a mining boom town down in Terra Sirenum
Where they were drinking heavy having quite a bit of fun

And at that time of night there wouldn't be much of a chance
To get a flight DaVinci's way where Dewey's drunken dance
Had left him sleeping in the corner of a seedy bar
Reeking of stale liquor with some cuts would leave a scar.

Joe was out of touch somewhere in Hydraotes hills
Practicing and sharpening some of his special skills
So it was left to Bovine to cut short his night of fun
And press upon his friends to make a special midnight run.

The captain would pick up their tab and pay the extra fee
To fuel and fly the aircraft to get him to DaVinci
In time to get young Dewey's drunken carcass to the ship
Where Bovine knew the captain wouldn't let chastisement slip.

(He took a little pleasure in the thought of Dewey's pain
But down inside he knew that Dewey would do just the same
And help a crewmate out when trouble nipped him in the rear
So Bovine made the flight arrangements and packed up his gear.)

The flight was uneventful (and in fact a little fun)
But they were in a hurry to get back after the run
So they all said their farewells on the runway then turned tail
And gunned the afterburners leaving Bovine in a hail

Of sand and dust and memories of good times in the past
But now all he could think about was kicking Dewey's ass.
Once again he'd fallen in with "friends" of low estate
And Bovine had to find him so the crew would not be late.

All he knew was that his sorry butt was in a dive
Called *'The Wild Cherry'* known to be a nasty hive
Of vice and seedy pastimes where the daylight never shined
And nightly altercations were the least of all the crimes.

He had to walk a dusty avenue between some domes
In a part of town where there were hardly any homes,
Just empty bars and cheap casinos closed up for the day
Sleeping off another night of taking suckers' pay.

It was a great surprise when his communicator beeped
And gave the word that Joe had got the news (and he was peeved!)
Then at that very instant Bovine saw the lanky Joe
Walking up the avenue, a duffel bag in tow.

"Where is this dump?" asked Bovine as they walked into a dome
And looked around them noticing that they were quite alone.
"Follow me," Joe muttered then they walked a block or two
And found the battered building locked but kicked the doorway through.

The smell of stale booze and smoke and cheap perfume was there
And they could almost feel the odor permeate their hair.
A single hanging lamp above the bar cast yellow light
Illuminating dimly where the damage from a fight

Had left a broken chair or two shoved over to one side
Where they could see the sleeping form of Dewey's battered hide.
Joe left payment on the bar to cover doorway's cost
While Bovine grabbed their crewmate's scruff and hoisted him aloft.

Then out the door they stumbled, Dewey propped between the two
Who were the only ones on Mars remaining of their crew.
"Let's get him to the spaceport dome. We'll get him cleaned up there,"
Said Joe as Bovine placed a hat on Dewey's clotted hair.

Then through an airlock on the west side which was seldom used
They found a lavatory that was mostly out of view
Where Bovine helped the younger crewman clean himself a bit
While Joe went to secure three seats aboard a Phobos trip.

"We'll meet in thirty minutes at the *'Barsoom Bar and Grill'*,"
Said Bovine, "We'll get eggs and tea to help reduce his chill."

"Some steak and fries sounds good," said Joe, "I'll be there in a bit;
"Find a booth out of the way where we can let him sit."

The bustle of the noonday crowd had not begun as yet
And Bovine was relieved that there was still a booth to get
At the Barsoom grill where Dewey slumped into his seat
And Bovine ordered up some coffee, eggs and toast and meat.

The flight Joe got would lift from Mars in ninety minutes more
And that would give them time to get some food and out the door.
Some toast with eggs and then tomato juice mixed in a beer
Had Dewey feeling better, though his memory wasn't clear.

He knew that Joe and Bovine had a righteous bone to pick
But both of them were understanding, knowing just how sick
A battered body felt after a rough night on the town.
Poor Dewey knew the crew would never let him live it down.

His kit was missing and his money and some of his clothes,
His head was cut and there was still dried blood inside his nose,
His eyes were still not clear enough to figure out the time.
On asking, Bovine reassured him they would be just fine:

"On the ship it's only morning watch, about 4 bells.
"We'll be on the ship in time, but man, you'll catch some hell!"
The flight back up to Phobos was a trudging misery
And Dewey vowed he'd never, ever take another drink.

* * * * *

Several hours later it was time to clear the port.
(The crew had taken turns in ribbing Dewey just for sport.)
The cargo was secured and systems' checks were all complete
And in the darkened cockpit Captain had the pilot's seat.

Nick was given access to the ship's best telescope
And he was scanning Mars and getting views as he had hoped.
Bovine came to visit him and asked how he had fared
And Nick told of the tour that he had taken via air:

"Mostly we flew up the Valles Marineris green
"And all around the area as far as I could see

"Were greenhouse domes of agriculture tucked between the rocks
"Like candy bowls chock full of tasty treats for hungry tots."

Bovine said, "Yeah, Marineris was the first place farmed
"And now the whole place has a green and earthy sort of charm.
"Many species of small animals now call it home
"But most homes and most farming are still done beneath the domes.

"The glass and iron works on Mars are run around the clock
"Silica and ferrous are abundant, common rocks.
"The steel and glass to build big domes in point four gravity
"Though commonplace are still a high-value commodity.

"And there are other projects. Many folks have found their dreams.
"The brook trout and the pike are doing well in ponds and streams,
"And there's no shortage of rich folks that ski Olympus Mons
"In space suits from the summit all the way to Amazon.

"Maybe you can see some of the rail lines that run
"From Hellas to Isidis then across Elysium
"To Amazon then north to Borealis and then south
"Across Mare Acidalium and on to Chryse's mouth?"

Nick was soaking this all in. He wished that he could stay
And spend some time with his new friend on Mars - even one day!
Bovine finished, "You might get a closer view or two
"When Captain does the slingshot pass. But I've got work to do."

Bovine left and Nick felt like a useless extra thumb
But he would have a front row seat when they began their run.
The captain planned to get a gravitational assist
Burning past the night side low across Amazonis.

This would bring Olympus Mons directly into view
Backlit by the rising sun and Tharsis' ochre hue.
Streaking from the night side into blazing light of day
Nick would see the mountain close and then they'd be away.

A mild engine burn put Phobos far off to the stern
And Captain had just finished programming their slingshot burn
When Radar's voice erupted from the cockpit intercom:
"I've just received a message for you. Shall I put it on?"

"Send it through," the captain said, and Radar said, "Will do,
"It's been encrypted heavily and meant for only you.
"Here it goes," said Radar, then Selenia was heard.
The captain listened carefully to hear her every word:

"There's something I must tell you Jules, before you take your leave.
"I've learned my brother is alive and we have been deceived!
"He wasn't killed on Ganymede but made a clean escape
"Then set up in the outer moons and he's been seen of late.

"This information came to light when Ansel's books were checked
"And linked with data read out from the implants in his neck.
"Ansel had some contacts that are dark, I guess you'd say
"And you can bet my brother'd have a deck of cards in play.

"Thanks to Varda's scanner we could add up two and two.
"It wasn't just gray market action Ansel's been into:
"He has taken profit from investments in the trade
"Of human traffic and my brother's one who clearly paid.

"He's been on Miranda more than once in recent years
"(The rumor pirates trade there comes at times to all our ears.)
"My brother is a renegade and evil through and through.
"To get his power back there's not a thing he wouldn't do!

"When the war disbanded TerraCorp's assets out there
"Many of their people disappeared to who knows where.
"We know some renegades are cozy buying pirate wares
"And now a growing danger has appeared so be aware:

"Low cost agriculture products show up now and then
"And flood strategic markets (can't predict yet how or when).
"This damages the farmers there; at times it ties their hands.
"Then off-worlders appear with cash to cheaply buy their land.

"This sets back some outer worlds' entire economies
"Destabilizing other markets - then predators feed.
"And at its root slave labor seems to be the way it's done.
"Somewhere in the outer worlds is where it's coming from.

"The volume of these loads suggests a massive shipping fleet
"But at this time its size or whereabouts remains discrete.

"Someone's massing power and it's getting plain to see.
"Watch yourself out there, Jules. Come back Forever Free!"

The message ended with a smack that sounded like a kiss
Then only background noise was left, a soft and empty hiss.
He paused a moment listening; his thoughts were far away
Gazing out the cockpit while his mind her words replayed.

Memories of darkened ships that scattered through the sky
Leaving bleeding men to freeze in vacuum as they died
Flashed before his eyes as if it happened yesterday.
He knew there was a leader of them he'd make pay some day.

It wasn't war that brought them; they were predators and thieves!
Their heartless tactics purposely designed to maim and grieve.
No quarter ever given; death or slavery the choice
And it had been six years since he had heard his lover's voice.

11   Date Night

Another half a dozen shifts had run their courses long,
The garlic and the onion cavern harvests packed and gone.
Today had been a treat for her - she worked the cave of spice:
The lemon trees and mint and basil left her smelling nice.

Though some might see coincidence, she could see the link
Between the order that would come three days after the stink
Of onion juice had washed away, replaced with lemon scent
When guards gave her instructions that to dinner she was sent

To see the overseer (some referred to him by name:
"Warden" was the moniker, his function quite the same).
He was the man in charge of every aspect of their lives
And even of their deaths at times; by most he was despised.

Tall and thin with flowing hair as black as raven wings,
A hawk-like beak and piercing eyes that saw through everything.
He was a renegade - a fugitive from many worlds,
A refugee of TerraCorp's since losing Luna's war.

One did not decline the order to dine with the man.
Guards delivered her and all would go as he had planned.
There was no choice in anything when living in his grasp.
Many worked until their feeble body's final gasp.

This was not the first time she was chosen thus to serve
As Warden's entertainment so she steeled up her nerve.
Defiance thinly veiled, her integrity intact
She wouldn't lower what she was to be his dessert snack.

And that made her a challenge and a magnet for his type.
His goal in fact to win her loyalty without a fight.
But she would never yield to a tyrant or his lies.
His kind by her were pitied at the best; but more despised.

He'd lusted for her from the moment she was brought for sale
By the pirates who had sacked her ship and then availed
Themselves of all its cargo and its crew as slaves to sell
Upon the silent market on Miranda's frozen hell.

And he had paid a pretty price, his property she was.
(At least that is the way he saw it, and he made the laws.)
She was grateful he had paid it (there were much worse fates)
His favor and his interest had kept her fairly safe.

But that's as far as it would go. Their world-views at odds:
She was a daughter born of freedom; he had tyrant's claws.
Grasping and possessive and a hoarder through and through,
While she most valued love and honest friendship, warm and true.

He met her at the doorway in a tailored suit of black
(Oddly out of place this far from any beaten track.)
She was in a dress of purple satin with black trim
Which had been chosen for tonight by none other than him.

What a contradiction, she'd thought wryly as she'd dressed,
To garb in royal fashion but at gunpoint as the guest.
But contradictions were the rule when caught in Warden's web.
At least she'd managed all this time to stay out of his bed.

(For she would rather die than give herself to such as he.
Body, heart and soul, she was her husband's property.
And he belonged to her - it was that way the day they'd met:
When they'd first looked into their eyes they knew that they'd be wed!)

He dismissed the guards that brought her to his quarters door
And ushered her inside to walk across the polished floor
Between the piles of cluttered goods that he considered wealth
But mostly old equipment that appeared in doubtful health.

Then stepping through the farther doorway to a cluttered room
Where dinnerware was placed for two (the food would be there soon)
He offered her a seat and smiled broadly as she sat
And took his place across the table looking very glad.

"I'm happy you have come tonight," he said, "There's been a change
"Which will bring good fortune, though I shouldn't think it strange.
"It seems an opportunity has fallen at my door
"And I won't need to sojourn on these ice worlds any more.

"Chardonnay, My Dear?" he asked while pouring her a glass
Of what appeared to be a vintage not far in the past.

"Sure," she said, "And thank you," and with that he smiled wide
Though just below the surface she was cringing down inside.

He noticed that she wouldn't sip the wine until he had
And so he took her glass and drank a portion with a sad
Facade as if accused of being found a naughty boy.
He said, "I wouldn't drug you. I don't fancy you a toy."

His face grew serious a moment then his smile returned
When she took her glass and took a sip and felt the burn
Of alcohol and sweetness mingled in the pleasant drink
And then drank deeply from the glass in spite of what he'd think.

With surprise his eyebrow raised a bit and then he poured
Again out of the bottle filling up her glass once more
Then leaned back in his seat and studied what was on her face
Hoping that beneath the ice he might see just a trace

Of softness or surrender, for he knew she had disgust
For him despite his prior efforts spent courting her trust.
He said, "You know, I'm not the monster that you think I am.
"I've had to make decisions that would best most any man.

"I've done hard work with sweat and strain to keep us all alive
"And working toward a future so these worlds might survive
"The devastation that resulted from the Lunar war
"Until the solar system is united strong once more."

"United in an iron fist," she asked, "Like TerraCorp's?
"Why would any sane man resurrect that rotten corpse?
"Every tyrant is a monster in the freeman's view
"So if you want to prove that point, what are you going to do?"

"Please," he said, "You've misconstrued my motives and my will!
"I'm no tyrant and of that indictment had my fill.
"Patiently I lead our team to reach that higher call
"Harmoniously working all for one and one for all."

She put her elbows on the table, lifted up her glass
And took another sip of wine as several seconds passed
Studying his features as she had at times before
To see if there were any thoughts beyond his selfish core.

"That's a load of Marxist drivel, Warden, and you know
"That not a single worker here believes it and they'd go
"As far away from here as they could get if they were free
"And by suggesting I would buy that lie you insult me."

His dark eyes were expressionless and hers were cold as ice.
"Well," he said, "Perhaps conditions here are not that nice
"But there are changes coming that I hope will change your mind
"And you will see and understand that I am not unkind."

At that moment servers brought their meal to the room
And Warden said, "Please, let's dispel this air of gloom.
"Beef has been a stranger here, let's share it in good cheer.
"This tenderloin has made a risky journey to get here!"

The sizzle and aroma from the plates the servers brought
Made her senses reel and she blushed when she was caught
By the warden's glance who smiled with obvious delight
To see the pleasure on her face the dinner brought tonight.

Renee had not smelled beef nor tasted it for six long years.
(The memories that flooded though her mind nearly brought tears!)
Warden told a server, "Please, before you go to bed
"Be a good girl and bring us a bottle of the red."

As the warden's serving girl turned round to leave the room
Renee could see a red mark on her back would not heal soon.
It was not a rash - it was a mark of violence.
Renee could sense the poor girl had been frightened to silence.

Suddenly the meal's charm lost much of its allure.
Renee said, "I feel guilty eating and I'm not so sure
"That I should." A pregnant moment passed as she leaned back
Then Warden said, "The discipline she got put her on track.

"She was headed down the path of escalating strife
"Among some other workers. I'm quite sure I saved her life.
"A bit of firm correction made her more useful to me
"And now she aids the kitchen staff and does it willingly.

"And that is good for all of us." He motioned with his knife
Then said, "It is collective effort that ensures our life."

He winked at her and said, "Please eat; don't let it go to waste.
"Many of my men would fight to have a little taste."

Renee picked up her knife and fork and started on her steak
And with the first bite memories made her heart nearly break;
But hoping by the warden's words some change was coming soon
Resolved to take advantage if he offered her a boon.

The meal progressed with harmless talk and wine helped her relax.
He asked her simple questions about how the work and tasks
Might be better organized from her perspective's view
And he accepted many that he promised he would do.

"Renee," he then said quietly, "I've watched you for some time.
"I know you are respected by the workers and by mine.
"The moment that you came up on the auction block for sale
"I knew that our two destinies together would prevail

"To bring not only this, but other colonies to life.
"And though it's not been easy and we've had our words of strife
"The time is very near that my reward will be my right
"And I will live with wealth and walk again in warm sunlight.

"I would like to share this fortune with someone I trust
"And when you see the truth of what is happening you must!
"Your independent nature and your skills of leadership
"Could either be an asset or a danger; which is it?"

She placed her knife across her plate and toyed with her fork
Then looked him in the eye and said, "I do not share your sport.
"I have made it plain I'll leave this prison you have built
"And you can bet I will not share in any of your guilt.

"Warden, I can only advocate for those who bear
"The burden of their labors here and yearn to breathe free air.
"And someday I will breathe it with them or I'll take my place
"In the bowels of the grave. That goal you can't erase."

The warden asked derisively, "So what is it you fear?
"What is this - this 'freedom', that you hold so very dear?
"It's only an illusion, just a whisper from the past
"Imagined in a mourning heart; but you'll awake at last

"When you have felt the liberty of action power brings
"Which will be yours if you will just accept one tiny thing:
"Pledge to me fidelity and join your will to mine.
"Your sadness from these recent years will vanish in no time.

"Together we'll help millions to establish hearth and home
"When as co-regents we will rule on several worlds' thrones."
His eyes were shining with the prospect of some things not said.
The words he chose spoke volumes though! She slowly wagged her head

For in this day and age a royal caste and throne of state
Could hardly be imagined (though some worlds' ills of late
Might force acceptance of protection by default of strength;
A "Pax-Romana" of the outer worlds could form at length...)

But really, that was crazy talk; a far-fetched fantasy!
The aftermath of recent wars had set so many free
From Terra-centric tyranny and few would lend their voice
To centralized control unless they had no other choice.

Six years was a long time though and she had been entombed
Beneath the frozen darkness of these outer worlds' moons.
Very little news had made it to the captives' ears
In ignorance and darkness they worked for their lives in fear.

"Thrones?" she asked, "That's quite the choice of word, don't you think?"
She eyed him closely as she raised her glass to take a drink.
"To run a farming colony beneath a frozen moon
"Hardly makes a man a king and won't anytime soon."

For just a fleeting instant his dark eyes were cold as ice
And then a condescending smile from his little vice
Of narcissistic self-promotion deep inside his core
Made her stomach twist and she loathed him all the more.

"This is not the only world of which I'm overseer.
"In fact I've brought you with me from another one, my dear.
"And there are others you don't know where I exert control
"Upon the wealth and own the fate of every living soul.

"It's true they're small and some of them don't know that I exist
"But I hold all their futures in my own capable fist.

"Miners, farmers, ships, refiners and where they call home
"Is mine to give to whom I choose; indeed it is my own."

If this were true it wasn't known by her up to this day.
She'd known they were on Triton long before they came this way.
She also knew he disappeared for long spells now and then.
His talk continued as she listened close and studied him:

"By hard work, sweat and sacrifice I've held much that was lost
"When Earth's dominion of the system shattered (such great cost!)
"But soon I will receive official sanction when control
"Of newly opened real estate becomes the system's goal:

"Another world wide with opportunity is near
"And I'll receive the stewardship when my service is clear
"To those who seek to regain what from them was ripped away.
"It will not be much longer and we'll see that happy day!"

He paused to take a sip of wine and pick meat from his teeth.
"Official sanction?" Renee asked, "What office would that be?
"Almost every world and country has their consulate.
"Surely not the TerraCorp that lost its teeth of late?"

His eyes grew narrow as he felt some half-subconscious sting
And she could sense the war had cost him almost everything.
He peered at her a moment then he spoke with little cheer
(His answer not direct, but the message loud and clear):

"Associates and allies do quite well, though heretofore
"Most have stayed anonymous and aren't seen anymore
"By those who hunt them under that supposed 'War Crimes Act'
"But times will change again and we will all be coming back!"

She had nailed it. All the hints and bits of news she'd got
During her captivity since by him she was bought
Were right: Clearly he had run a wing of TerraCorp
Living well on profits skimmed from other peoples' work.

But now he was a renegade, despised on many worlds
(Not quite called a pirate while he kept his flag well furled,)
And biding time until his little empire would suffice
To buy his place in TerraCorp, indeed a handsome price!

"I see," she said, "Why after all this time do you tell me?
"I've made it plain for many years that I want to be free
"From anyone and anything that keeps me from my home.
"I'd think it would be best if you would just leave me alone."

He took a drink and wiped his mouth and set his napkin down.
A smile crept across his face as hers became a frown
When, reaching 'cross the table put his hand upon her own
And said, "You may be right, but my faith in you has grown.

"Your spirit and intelligence are rare. Think what we'd do
"When all this post-war disarray is done and we break through
"To times of universal law, our right to rule intact.
"I know you'll see the wisdom when you've studied all the facts.

"In the mean time I want you to be the overseer
"Of the harvest crews and I will make it very clear
"To all my men that you now speak with my authority.
"Production quotas will be your responsibility."

Her widened eyes betrayed surprise then doubt shadowed her face.
She pulled her hand from under his and said, "There's not a trace
"Of reason you should trust me to accomplish what you ask.
"Making quotas with slave labor's not my kind of task."

His smile grew yet wider. He said, "That's precisely why
"I want you on the job because you've lived so long inside
"The culture that's developed in this farming colony
"And they know they can trust you more than they have trusted me.

"You will have new quarters and more time to see my plans
"And you will learn that I'm not such an evil twisted man.
"Make the needed changes. Take control and see it through
"Meet the peoples' needs and I will do what's right by you."

He lifted up his glass to toast her; she did not respond.
Instead her eyes were focused on the ceiling just beyond
His hair of raven black that seemed much darker in the glow
That lit the wall from soft lights in the cold stone floor below.

Her gaze then moved to meet his and in all sincerity
She said, "Warden, thank you, but to do what's right by me

"Would be to let me go back to my husband and my home."
He answered back, "Renee my dear, you are quite alone.

"You have no husband. He was killed along with all the rest
"At Ganymede when pirates hit the remnants of that mess.
"You saw the shattered ships and all the carnage spread around!
"There was only one ship that escaped that killing ground

"And that was mine! We all could see that no one had survived
"But those who were abducted and for ransom kept alive
"Or those like you who came up on the auction block for sale."
He held her rapt attention now; she turned a little pale

And asked, "You were there? Why have you never told me so?"
He answered, "Up 'til now there wasn't any need you know.
"Renee, it's been six years since that disaster in the sky.
"Loose the grip on that false hope that those men didn't die.

"You have a future here if you will only take my hand
"And when the time is right we'll go to Terra living grand.
"In the mean time, test me. Get familiar with the facts.
"Let's learn to trust each other then we'll join and make a pact

"To build these worlds together so that millions more will come
"To live in peace and order and we'll rule them all as one."
Again he held his hand across the table to invite
Her partnership but she ignored it for another bite.

The news that Warden's ship was there and managed to escape
Rolled around inside her as her hair rose on her nape.
This raised some tricky questions that must wait another day
About his pirate contacts and she wondered what he'd say.

"I've labored in these caves for years away from my true home.
"I know you've shown me favor; had the guards leave me alone.
"I know you paid the pirates and in that way rescued me
"But if you want to earn my trust you need to set me free.

"Let me send a message to my family and friends.
"Or if that is impossible, then maybe you could send
"Me on a flight to where I might when our next shipment rolls.
"Do you want my partnership, or do you want control?"

Her gaze burned deeply into his and neither of them blinked
Until she said, "It's obvious, tell me what you think:
"If I leave and then return you'll know I've come to stay.
"And if I don't it wouldn't have worked out well anyway."

He stared at her a moment more and gave a short reply
About no radios around and no ships coming by;
How everyone's security from space-borne piracy
Relied on keeping their location deep in secrecy.

She cast a sidelong look at him and finished up her wine
Then asked to be excused since it was past her sleeping time.
He stood and took her hand and said, "Of course you may My Dear,
And she said, "Thank you, Warden; you have made it very clear

"That you would like cooperation and to earn my trust.
"And I appreciate your interest. Really, very much.
"You have held the cards of my existence and my doom
"So the bottom line I read is: 'Who does not trust whom?'"

His features flashed confusion then became a frozen grin.
She stood before him close and smiled brightly back at him.
He ushered her off toward the door and bid the guards depart
Then turned and said, "Tonight at least, perhaps we've made a start?

"You are free to walk wherever you may care to go
"And I have seen to it that every one of my men know.
"Get a good night's sleep and in the morning you may move
"To quarters close to mine where you will have a private room."

She told him she enjoyed the dinner and their little talk
And thanked him for the liberty and as she turned to walk
He said, "I'll be your escort." She said, "I'd like time alone,
"But thank you," then she turned and took the long way to get home.

The thoughts and possibilities the warden's offer spawned
Were winding though her mind for hours past her tired yawns.
The wine and food conspired with her labor and her stress
And put her in a restless sleep still wearing Warden's dress.

* * * * *

_____

137

Ambushed by the renegades! Those pirates of the skies
Their warships' every aspect built for deception and lies.
Her liberty torn harshly, in oppression now to live
Imprisoned on an icy world to serve as lust's captive.

Vanished is her lover! No longer can she see
The man to whom her heart is bound for all life's destiny.
Amongst the ravaged rubble she prays no clue will reveal
That by the bandits' plundering his final fate is sealed.

With that possibility time makes a grinding halt.
Has he crossed his final threshold during the assault?
Captured, with no way to save him if he still remains,
Terror of his mortal wounding searing through her brain:

If death has taken him then her own life seems at an end!
He is her heart's eternal passion and her truest friend.
Her deep desire exists because he opened true love's door.
Her heart will die with his for they are one forevermore.

Mortified, her soul sinks low, then practicality
Slaps her with its icy hand, awakes vitality.
Snatched and roughly dragged with just a moment left to scan
The devastated wreckage high above the barren land.

Can she recognize his ship? She cannot quite be sure.
Within the clutter little can her apprehensions cure.
Her shallow breathing quickens as no sign of him is seen.
In the chaos could he have escaped this horrid scene?

Enslaved by violence and the greed of piracy
Even if he lives, will once more his face she see?
With no knowledge of his fate, her spirit plunged within,
Condemned to cavern's depths as desperation dark sets in...

12   Discovery

"Renee! Wake up!" Hidalia's voice pierced through her sleepy fog.
"You look like you've had a night of drinking Corporal's grog.
"You're soaking wet, My Dear. Did you have the dream again?"
Renee looked 'round the room and croaked, "I guess it's pretty plain."

Hidalia sat down on the bed and put Renee's long hair
Quickly in a pony tail and said, "You had me scared!
"Warden tends to treat some girls in ways that aren't so nice
"And knowing you I thought perhaps he'd put you on the ice

"When midnight came and you still hadn't come back to our room.
"But I am glad his dinner didn't send you to your doom!"
Renee got up and washed her face and took a couple breaths
And said, "The wine he fed me tried to," peeling off her dress.

She splashed more water on her face and pulled a jumper on
Then looked into a mirror but did not look at it long
For what was looking back at her was not what she had hoped.
"I'm moving out today, Hidalia and that's not a joke."

"This whole room will be yours and you'll have some privacy.
"I know you've had so little of it, 'specially with Steve.
"Though it is reduced, our time together will not end.
"I'll not be very far from you. I'll always be your friend.

"The warden has decided I'm to be his foreman now.
"He thinks that I can make production numbers grow somehow.
"He says that there are changes coming for the very best
"And I'll be moving to a room that's closer to his nest."

"That's a big promotion," said Hidalia with surprise.
She smiled but there was a burning question in her eyes.
Renee said, "Yes, it is and no, I didn't lose myself
"And I would like that story to be left up on the shelf!

"But I know it will be the rampant rumor in no time
"And you can rest assured that my integrity's just fine.
"I belong to he whom I've been married many years.
"As for rumors, I hope you will shut them from your ears.

"My goal hasn't changed. In fact its strength has only grown.
"Hidalia, maybe someday you will call this world your home
"And I will do all that I can to make things right for all
"But still inside my heart I feel my husband's living call."

They looked into each other's eyes for what words couldn't say.
Hidalia's eyes grew moist as she considered Warden's ways
And said, "Renee, be careful. Don't be rash in what you do.
"The warden's heart is dark and he is smart and subtle too."

"I know," Renee said softly as they joined in an embrace
And said, "It's all so sudden," as a tear rolled down her face.
"But this will be a chance for change we've never had before.
"A golden opportunity; I must step through its door."

They held each other for a moment then they stepped away.
Hidalia nodded her agreement then said, "By the way,
"Tomorrow is the day of rest and Steve and I would like
"To take you to a place of safety for a picnic bite."

"A picnic?" Renee looked surprised, "Now there's a word not heard
"For all these years by my ears since we've labored in this dirt!
"Where could we be going where we're safe to not be seen?"
"Well," Hidalia said, "For sure it's not a lawn of green,

"But no one ever goes there and we've been there many times
"To be alone without the interruption of the spies
"And busybodies who can't seem to keep themselves amused
"And we would like to share it with you; there's even a view!

"Steve says long ago it was an access to a mine.
"An assay hole that started back before the war's hard times.
"It's been disused since Warden's agriculture overtook
"The mining business here; we thought you'd like to have a look."

"I'd love to go with you tomorrow and I think I can.
"This afternoon I'll learn some more of Warden's future plan
"But I should have my liberty tomorrow and a view
"Out any window I can find is what I'd love to do!"

* * * * *

Moving to the warden's wing was not a big event.
She stuffed her few possessions in a bag Hildalia lent.
The warden wasn't even there; an older woman came
To show her to her new room with a door marked with her name.

That was quite a change from being labeled "Fifty-Two"
And by the looks from Warden's men she saw that they all knew
That she had status far above what other workers had
And she could see that many men were genuinely glad.

Many gave congratulations, pleased to see a change.
There were some who leered and thought the warden was deranged
And of course there were a few that cringed when she walked by
Knowing how they'd treated her, they couldn't meet her eye.

But knowing too that now they worked for her and time would tell
Whether her revenge would make their lives a living hell.
To two of them she gave a silent stare that let them know
They would be accountable for everywhere they'd go.

She spent the afternoon acquainting with the office space
And meeting with the neighbors who had not yet seen her face.
The evening was spent in walking places she'd not been.
Her spirits were uplifted planning projects she'd begin.

But there was much to do to learn the limits of the trust
That Warden had extended to her and she knew she must
Do her best to raise production as the warden said
Or she would lose that place of trust and possibly her head.

There was much to think about but she needed some time
Away from it to let it sit; a picnic would do fine!
So when the morning came she found Hidalia and her beau
Waiting with some food and blankets packed ready to go.

Then off they ventured for a walk beyond where others went.
Down a disused corridor where Steve opened a vent
That led them through an access to an old equipment room
Dusty and disused but warm where, looking through the gloom

Renee could see a hatchway opened wide, propped with a pipe.
Hidalia turned and whispered, "This is where we go to hide."

Beyond the hatchway was a room with doors on either side
Locked and sealed but Steve said, "This is where we start the ride.

"It's about four hundred meters to get to the top.
"We can sometimes get there in just twelve or fifteen hops.
"There are handholds every meter so there's no concern
"About getting abrasions if we slip on our return.

"When we first went up there it was too cold to stay long
"But since we've left the hatchway open it's a different song.
"Thankfully, the heat from this equipment room ascends
"And keeps the upper level warm enough for us to spend

"A little time away from all our troubles here below.
"As far as I can tell we are the only ones who know
"This shaft is even here - we've never seen another soul."
With that he grinned and leaped up through a dimly lighted hole.

Hidalia said, "You go up next and I'll bring up the rear.
"Go on. It's not far to go. We'll be there soon, My Dear."
Renee stepped through the hatchway looking up where Steve had gone
And saw his silhouetted frame ascending fast and strong.

She jumped a dozen meters in the tiny gravity
And on the way pushed off the handholds moving steadily
Until she found herself within a cold room at the top
About twelve meters square with a ceiling that dropped

Slowly toward an open inner airlock at one side
Where Steve had wedged a pipe to keep the lock's door opened wide.
Then from his pack he pulled a bottle and some metal cans
And said, "This works okay until we have a better plan:

"A bottle of the corporal's hooch will help to cut the chill.
"It isn't fit to drink; but fuel a stove it surely will."
He poured a measure in each can then set them here and there
And as he lit them each a bit of warmth came through the air.

Renee said, "So the corporal is useful after all!"
Then belted out a laugh that echoed loud from all the walls.
Steve said, "He is not the hardest worker I have had
"But he does have his moments and for that I'm truly glad."

They joked and chuckled at the lazy corporal's expense
But all agreed that his exploits were not a great offense.
Hidalia came and put her arms around her chosen man
And said, "Look out the airlock for a good view of the land.

"I'll set out our lunch. We have some fish and wine and bread
"Or if the corporal's hooch holds out some lemon tea instead."
She winked reminding Renee of the wine two nights ago.
Renee moved toward the lock and said, "I think I'll see the show."

The airlock was in shadow on the mountain's shaded side.
The distant hills above the crater walls too tall to hide
Completely from the sunlight that shined dimly on their backs
Here and there contrasting brightly with the starlit cracks

That traced their ice-filled paths across the frozen crater floor
And up the mountains' jagged sides where old collisions scored
Them into jumbled rows of shapes chaotically arrayed
Where no man since the dawn of time had ever chanced to stray.

Other than the door controls the airlock wasn't lit.
An empty crate of oxy bottles made a place to sit
And gazing out the window to the distant backlit hills
A yellow arch protruding to the sky gave her a thrill

For this was solid evidence of which moon they were on!
Speculation all they had 'til now (and for so long!)
Only from Iapetus could Saturn's rings be seen
In any but an edge-on view and that fact was the key!

"The rings!" Renee exclaimed aloud. Hidalia turned her way
And with a puzzled look she asked, "What is that, Renee?"
"The rings," Renee repeated, "There! Beyond the ridge, you see?
"Saturn's rings between the hills and lit up beautifully!"

Hidalia looked out through the window where Renee had said
And noted, "I suppose you're right, but I don't have a head
"For why that so excites you. They look much like a hill
"And any view outside the cavern just gives me a chill!"

"Hidalia, think! That single view tells us right where we are!
"The fact that they are open, even though they don't stick far

"Above the row of hills means we are on Iapetus
"And not on Rhea like we thought with our previous guess.

"Only this moon's orbit has the proper inclination
"And by the angle that the rings make with the far horizon
"We are near the equator and on the trailing limb
"As viewed from Saturn since it's on the western horizon.

"Only from this far up on the mountain can we see
"Far enough beyond the crater wall to get a peek
"Of the rings to even know for sure it's Saturn's moon
"But now there is no doubt at all and not a day too soon.

"From the little window in the cavern down below
"I couldn't see this sight that gives the hint that lets us know
"Exactly where we are; not that it does us any good
"At this point, anyway," she trailed off then where she stood.

Steve came to the window to look out at what she saw
And said, "I've looked out there and never noticed that at all!"
Renee said, "I believe the orbit isn't that eccentric
"So libration of the moon would not account for it,

"But I think our orbit is inclined fifteen degrees
"And so at times those hills will block our viewing of the rings.
"But they are there today," she said and turned slowly around
And peered deep in the eyes of Sergeant Steve with a slight frown

And asked, "You really didn't know what moon that we've been on?"
"After all this time since we arrived here from Triton?"
Steve looked back surprised and said, "Renee, you know me well.
"I've never been dishonest. If I knew, you know I'd tell.

"I am here by choice no more than you or all our friends
"And you know very well why I must work for Warden's men."
Renee could read the honest truth in all that Steve had said
Then blushed and said, "I'm sorry Steve," and sadly hung her head.

Hidalia came and placed her hands on both of her friend's backs
And said, "Now kiss and make up then come out and eat your snacks.
"We need to discuss what's in the cards with Warden's change
"And how to spin Renee's promotion not to seem so strange."

Looking out the window at the scene so dimly lit
Only by reflection from the mountains to the pit
Within the crater far below and starlight from above
She could only guess at what Renee was thinking of.

13   Into the Deep

Leaving Martian space was more dramatic than Nick thought
(Arrival day sedentary compared to this slingshot)
For this maneuver took them almost out to Deimos' height
Then dropped them toward the planet with their engines burning bright.

Nick was granted access to an extra cockpit seat
Stuffed back in a corner, with a view you couldn't beat!
The captain in the left seat and Gin sitting the right
Illuminated softly by the instruments' dim lights

Were calmly watching progress on positional displays
And monitoring systems as the planet came their way
As if a blackened frying pan, its hot rim glowing red
Was slowly swinging on its way to smack them in the head.

Then when the time was right an extra punch against his back
Put them in a rapid race to catch their exit track.
While on the red horizon jutting starkly to the sky
The mighty Mount Olympus like a magnet drew the eye

'Til reddened sunlight filled the room then quickly turned bright white
The seconds ticking as they passed the mountain to its right.
While farther on Ascraeus Mons rose rapidly to view
Then passed so close beneath Nick felt he'd touch it with his shoe!

And then away they rocketed, Mars dropping to the rear
And Gin remarked and gestured, "We'll be passing very near
"To Deimos as we exit Martian space and you might see
"Some tiny specks around it, portions of the Martian fleet."

Then at that moment red lights flashed on each of their displays
And Gin explained, "It looks like Mars Defense's training day.
"They're painting us with target radars as they simulate
"A laser or a missile launch to end our sorry fate."

"They wouldn't let it slip, would they?" Nick asked with a grin.
"It hasn't happened in a while," replied the smiling Gin.
"In the war there was an accident a time or two,
"But that's much better than to let a nuke come slipping through."

"They'd shoot us all the way from Deimos?" Nick naively asked.
"Oh, no," Gin responded, "There's much more to it than that.
"There's a network of defensive ships in constant flight
"Most in high eccentric orbits timed precisely right

"To keep most all of Martian space within a target zone
"And it is best for everyone to leave those ships alone.
"They're black as night and lighting them is highly frowned upon
"They can make life difficult if you get close to one.

"Redundant tracking stations at the Deimos Langrange sites
"Provide position data for the weapon ships in flight.
"That way all the ships can be as silent as the tomb
"And bandits don't know if they're there until their butts go 'Boom!'

"Mars' defensive system is the envy of most worlds
"Though some have systems that would almost make your eyebrows curl:
"Orbit corridors and special vectors you must use
"Or they might choose to send your way a package of bad news."

Nick considered that a moment then asked, "Black as night?
"Asteroids are black as charcoal but in the sunlight
"They shine among the stars reflecting solar rays to see -"
The captain interrupted, "That's because they have 3C."

"Three See?" Nick inquired. Gin looked at the captain's face
Then said, "Well, it's not a well-kept secret in this case.
"Carbon Corner Cube - 3C to make it short and sweet
"Is favored by a lot of folks to stealthy up their fleet.

"Think of prisms cut as if they're corners off a cube
"Then shine a light into the face which way you may care to.
"The beam returns precisely on the path that it came in.
"A coating of these prisms can appear as black as sin.

"For all the light returns the way it came and not toward you
"Unless you light it from the same direction that you view.
"And with a high efficiency it turns a laser back
"Frying where it came from if it's not too long a track.

"The better stuff is made of carbon in the diamond form
"But simple glass or clear sapphire are probably the norm.

"If facets are aligned and there is little wasted space
"Ninety-two percent reflectance could be common place.

"But typically it's less." Gin's lecture trailed off at that.
Nick considered this a moment then said, "Elegant!
"However it can be detected with a pulse of light.
"It's really not that stealthy if you're heading for a fight."

"That's why it's just a laser shield," the captain then explained.
"It's only sneaky if you're stalking sneaks who act the same.
"And neither of you want to let your whereabouts be known.
"The second someone shines a light the sneakiness is blown.

"And so in certain situations it can help you out
"But you must be extremely careful with the lights about.
"For there is always sunlight; stars and planets everywhere.
"Every angle must be judged and chosen with great care.

"For automatic sensors can detect when starlight blinks
"Or when it's blocked by darkened ships that might nearby you slink.
"So no, it's not much use in that regard, but it will save
"Your bacon in a laser fight for it will really shave

"The chances of a hull breach down by quite a little bit
"And buy you time to use your own to score a lethal hit."
The captain paused, then slowly said, "There has been once or twice
"I've wished I'd had it on a ship; those times weren't very nice."

The cockpit fell to silence for a couple minutes' time
Then Captain ordered, "Half a G for Jupiter is fine."
Gin responded, "Half a G in thirty seconds, Mark!"
He turned the red lights on and made the ship's white lights go dark.

Then at the time prescribed the engines throttled down a bit,
The red lights were turned off and the white lights were re-lit.
The captain turned toward Nick and said, "We'll cruise for six more hours
"Then drop a decoy, spin the nose and use a bit more power.

"Make sure you are near a good acceleration couch.
"We'll be burning at three G's for thirty minutes. Ouch!"
He winked and then Gin added, "After that it's point eight G's
"For just about a week and then we'll be in the deep freeze.

"We won't come near to Jupiter but with a scope you'll view
"Him in a partial phase. For you that should be something new."
"I'm looking forward to it," Nick replied, "And thanks a lot
"For giving me a cockpit seat to watch the Mars slingshot."

With that he stood and made his way back to the lower deck
Then Gin looked at the Captain and remarked, "What the heck?
"Make the man an offer and enlist him on the crew."
The captain said, "I'm waiting 'til his job on Titan's through.

"There's players we don't know about and much we do not know
"About the Titan situation and how things will go
"When he is introduced into the Terran research crew.
"But when the time is right I'm sure we'll know just what to do."

"Besides," the captain added, "Though he's taken well to space
"His opportunities are wide and he might find his place
"In fields of endeavor that he'd never have with us.
"You know how spacing gets into the blood, you ornery cuss!"

"That's why we ought to grab him now," Gin countered with a grin
"Before he gets too far involved in work with Titan's men.
"His engineering specialty has value far beyond
"What TerraCorp was thinking when they turned him to a bomb."

The captain said, "I know that and the point will be proved out
"When you and he and Radar show to me beyond a doubt
"The price we gave Soldana for your new magnetic gear
"Bought a tool that we can use when Saturn pulls us near.

"In the mean time we'll set up as freight delivery boys.
"But make sure Joe and Duke are set to use our special toys.
"Few thoughts much beyond that point are great concerns of mine.
"We'll cross that bridge if we are still alive in eight weeks' time."

"Fair enough," said Gin, "For now there's plenty yet to do
"To test your theory on the antimatter cannon tube."
The captain turned to look at Gin and Gin gave him a wink
And said, "Even a gama-laser's more than what I'd think

"Would drop into our laps like this. I'll keep the boys on track.
"Nick's penetrator light alone will earn our money back

"A thousand fold." Gin stood to leave and paused beside the door.
"You know," he said, "To scan a world might pay off even more."

And then he left the captain in the cockpit all alone
Knowing that his mind would wander to his heart's true home
Within the heart of she he loved who so many had said
Could no longer exist because for six years she was dead.

14   Progress

Things could happen rapidly where not much ever did.
The news Renee was foreman now had really flipped some lids!
But changes in key personnel had improved things a lot
And soon the routine workdays settled down the troubled spots.

The first week of her changes saw production greatly drop
While gossip and discussions by the workers boiled hot.
The second week some sullenness and conflicts were de-fused
And by the third production gained when many got enthused

About the way things now were handled by the new regime.
The whips had been replaced with balm and calm replaced the screams.
(The pain a tiny sliver or a paper cut could wreak!
So little tyrants were replaced with leaders and respect.)

Just beneath the surface there was great anticipation
For rumors had been circulated that her new position
Was the first step in a trend that might bring real relief
To life within this colony that until now was grief.

By the fourth week there were real returns on what she'd done.
Production had caught up and growth a trend that had begun.
Credits had been issued as a form of currency
To reward hard work and promote productivity.

The common barracks were divided (that was Heaven sent!)
And private living quarters were available for rent.
A commissary opened to the workers twice per day
Where they could purchase sundries with the credits they were paid.

(Warden scoffed at this idea, but gave her free rein
And when production tripled he forgot his purse's pain.)
She'd promised the investment would result in great returns
And after seven weeks had passed you'd think he would have learned

That when his grip was loosened and some liberty was felt
The people would respond and quota deficits would melt.
But in his greed he opted to impose a workers' tax
That damaged what she'd done and set the work relations back.

Then when the unrest boiled over and real trouble brewed
Warden backed away and let Renee re-vamp the rule.
This emboldened everyone and brought a civic pride
Of sorts, that even timid folk could not begin to hide.

It was not the warden's way to take this veiled reproach
But with great effort Renee made herself his civics coach.
So he kept to the shadows and released his hold some more
Which pleased the population but did not settle the score.

Indeed he was a tyrant and they all had once been free
And all knew that at some point he must pay the penalty.
For few would ever forget all his murders and abuse
And it was plain that most would like his neck put in a noose.

He was well aware of this but he had little fear.
Production was accelerating and the time was near.
His need to keep this colony would no longer exist
And no one knew his evil plan or had strength to resist.

15   Nocturne

The weeks they spent in transit were not filled with idleness.
There was much to do beside the normal ship's business.
Time was set aside for Nick to train with Duke and Joe
In basic combat hand-to-hand in zero-G and low.

It wasn't Nick's vocation but he learned a skill or two
That gave a bit of confidence in some things he could do
If sticky situations might devolve into rough play
And Duke felt he could count on him if needed come one day.

Joe gave further training using knives and pointy sticks
And felt some satisfaction that Nick picked it up quite quick.
But practice is the key in any training one might do
And Nick was made to understand that he'd never be through!

There was other training that they did while on they sped.
Haji gave instruction in first aid and simple meds,
Bovine taught some metallurgy, Gin a little math;
Captain gave a class on navigating 3D maps.

Most of them attended when a seminar was done
By Nick for Gin and Radar (and the captain too had come)
To bring them up to speed a bit on Saturn's big array
Where TerraCorp was hoping for a breakthrough any day.

The technical details were for Gin and Radar's sake.
The over-all mechanics what the other two would take
Away to have a better feel for what would lie ahead
And things that needed done to build a suitable test bed.

The six-axis magnetics had been mounted in a bay
Near the ship's atomics where the engineers could play.
Fitted with an inner airlock and an outer door
For what they had to work on there was room enough and more.

Bovine had cut through the wall and helped young Dewey run
A conduit to carry plasma when the time had come
To integrate atomics with the magnetic device
While Gin inspected all the work and checked it over twice.

Nick had spent more than a week designing tests to run
While Radar had prepared an automation that would sum
Many aspects of control into a single tool
To simplify adjustments, keep it safe and running cool.

"When we get containment," Nick had mentioned early on
"We will need controls that are intelligent and strong.
"A tiny misstep on our part could wreck all that we've done
"Or blow the ship and all around it straight to kingdom come."

By the book Nick wasn't crew, but still he volunteered
For all the duties others didn't find so very dear:
Cleaning up the galley and maintaining this and that
And everyone from top on down was very glad for that.

Then one day the cockpit sent a warning to the crew:
The engines would shut down awhile (and this was something new,
For weeks acceleration had been steady every day
And yet Saturn's environs were a couple weeks away.)

The lights turned red in warning then the torch's humming ceased
As zero-G ensued and this took Nick quite off his feet.
The captain then announced a visitor would come on board.
Another ship would rendezvous as they streaked Saturn-ward.

To rendezvous in transit was a very rare event
For typically to do so meant a lot of fuel was spent.
Even on a normal path through inter-planet space
The chance of two ships meeting was remote beyond a trace.

And their path wasn't normal. Captain cut his corners sharp
And spent the extra fuel and effort keeping well apart
From paths that normal traffic took beyond most radars' range
So it was obvious this meeting had been pre-arranged.

There was much that Nick could see beyond the porthole glass.
The ship approached from sunward, matched their speed before it passed
Hanging like a whale in its buoyant native state
The blackened hull occulting stars like charcoal on snowflakes.

Then when maneuver thrusters brought the ship slowly abreast
A dimly lighted airlock door appeared on its black chest.

A figure silhouetted dark against the reddened room
Holding what looked like a hook extending on a boom

Waved a signal to someone unseen on their own ship
And then a loop of cable like a slow uncurling whip
Reached across the distance where he caught it with his hook
And pulled it in, secured it and the slack from it was took.

Then he clipped a carabiner from his space suit belt
And launched himself across the empty space as dark as felt.
Another figure followed and in moments he could hear
The airlock cycle followed by deep laughter loud and clear.

Muffled voices echoed from the passageways and walls
And soon the pair of visitors who came to pay a call
Were seated in the galley with the captain, Joe and Gin
And presently the rest of them including Nick came in.

Bearded, bold and boisterous the visitor's dark eyes
Sparkled with a light that showed a burning joy inside.
In contrast, his companion was reserved and stood at ease
(The consummate lieutenant trained to serve his captain's needs.)

"Surely you've a mug of beer to wet our whistles down?
"It's been a dusty trail since we last blew into town."
The visitor winked at the Captain, Gin tossed him a beer
Then everyone dove in and grabbed their own bottle of cheer.

"It's good to see you, Red," the captain took him by the arm
"And by your looks you've managed to escape most of the harm
"That deep space brings to bear on gristled grizzlies such as you.
"I figured after Ganymede your days in space were through."

"Bah," the bearded visitor exclaimed and took a swig.
"I spent some dirt-side time then came across that beat up rig
"That's cluttering your neighborhood. But she does what she must
"To earn the beans and bacon. Good to see you too, old cuss!"

Red then looked Gin over head to toe and gave a grunt
And said, "I see Sven Olsen still puts up with all your stunts.
"How are you Gin? Do you still brew that rocket fuel you drink?"
Then both of them gripped hands and Gin said, "Sure!" and gave a wink.

"Joe and Duke, now there's a pair I'm very glad to see!
"Why don't you both grab your gear and come to work for me?
"I've got work that needs your talents all lined up for you.
"It's dangerous but fun - and the pay is darn good too."

He grinned a grin wide as a bear's and they grinned back at him
But Duke said, "We've got work right here and we're not getting thin."
Haji volunteered to get a meal under way
And they agreed spaghetti would be quick and quite okay.

The captain introduced their visitor as an old friend
For benefit of those aboard that hadn't been there when
In yesteryears they worked and fought together as a team.
"This is Captain Redfeather, a friend of high esteem."

The introductions went around and chairs and table set
(After a coordinated burn made its effect
To bring both ships to point two G so dinner would sit still)
And they enjoyed their conversations as they ate their fill.

Joe asked, "You've been hunting?" Captain Redfeather said "Yes.
"We've been working part time cleaning up some of the mess
"That's festered here and there since TerraCorp went renegade.
"For the most part, anyway. It's one way to get paid.

"You must know the Jovian Consortium's a joke.
"They've been focused building back what TerraCorp had broke.
"The fleet they lost at Ganymede has still not been replaced
"And so they're hiring privateers to recon through deep space.

"Mars kicked in a little cash for bounty on some heads.
"They've even sent a small fleet out to Jupiter instead
"Of hunting for their bases hidden deep in smaller moons
"Or lurking in the outskirts where we're heading very soon.

"We've been stalking pirates there and speared a couple sharks
"Out in the Kuiper belt where even Sol is cold and dark;
"But it's becoming harder to detect where they've dug in.
"They're tighter than a tick beneath a porcupine's skin.

"But for now we've got to earn our keep as cargo men
"Before we go off hunting for the bandits once again.

"We're hauling zinc, uranium and lead from Mercury
"To Rhea where we'll re-provision then rejoin our fleet,

"Then back to where we jumped a couple pirates on the run
"And managed to set free a slaver's cargo (that was fun!)
"At Eris one exploded and the other took a course
"That looked as if it might be heading out to Vanth-Orcus."

Redfeather put down his fork and tilted back his glass.
At mention of a slaver's cargo Captain's eyes held fast.
Redfeather returned his gaze and sadly shook his head.
(He, at least, was one that didn't think Renee was dead.)

Red's report held Nick's attention tight; he blurted out:
"You destroyed some ships?" And his face showed he had doubts
About the cold reality that Redfeather described.
And Red responded, "Someone has to. Bounty doesn't lie."

Captain Blue put down his fork and turned his gaze on Nick
And said, "There is some history I'll try to teach you quick:
"Almost every person in the system had their fill
"Of Earth's and TerraCorp's abuses everywhere until

"Luna, with the aid of Mercury closely aligned
"Finished Earth's control of other worlds at that time.
"When Luna dropped the hammer and the war came to a halt
"And every major city was reduced to molten rock,

"The Lunarites were vilified by many for that act
"And Mercury was scorned for being party to their pact
"(Since every person in the solar system felt that sting)
"But all of us now benefit from what freedom can bring.

"For the most part, people live in peace on every world
"But slavery and piracy's threat cannot be ignored.
"Earth's official policy to cover up the past
"Has made Earth's population largely ignorant at last."

Redfeather took up where captain Blue's voice trailed off
And said, "I know you're skeptical and we don't mean to scoff,
"But it's a stretch to think someone could still sit on the fence
"Though living on the blue ball most ignore the evidence.

"We thought the shackles forged by TerraCorp were gone for good
"But now the poison grows again like ivy in the woods.
"The thirst for power and control seems never to be slaked
"For evil men who won't accept the blame for their mistakes.

"And so it starts again as good men fail to draw the line
"History repeats itself; it has through all of time.
"But this time we won't suffer through Earth's burning cities' hell.
"We're going to root the ivy out and burn the woods as well."

Nick had turned a little flush but Gin threw in a word:
"Nick has left the blue ball and in just a month has learned
"That it's a bigger solar system than he'd known before
"But he has much to learn about the Terra-Luna war."

Red nodded approval as he sized Nick up again
Then changed the conversation: "Haji, on my crew's a man
"Who's growing sicker by the day and we just don't know why.
"Would you take a look at him so our man doesn't die?

"Our mediscanner shows his body losing phosphorous
"And supplements don't help a bit so now this worries us."
Haji started sweating; Radar's face turned ashen gray;
Nick's eyes opened wide then Captain Blue began to say,

"Haji, you and Radar get your things--" as Haji said,
"Is he well enough to come?" Red just shook his head.
"Captain," Radar offered, "We have got to see this man."
Then Captain said, "You go and do whatever that you can.

"But be careful! Red, you've got to tell your crew to get
"Fire suppression gear deployed where that man has been set.
"Do it now!" and Red complied with questions on his face
Knowing that the captain would explain his change of pace

From leisure dining to a state of near emergency
When he had a moment after this activity.
"Gin, be sure when they are safe aboard the other ship
"We cast the cable off, then you stand us off a bit.

Gin stood up and motioned Bovine to the outer hatch
Then headed to the cockpit with a purposeful dispatch.

The captain turned attention to his now bewildered guest
And said, "I need to ask you if we may perform a test

"On you and every member of your crew before you leave
"There is an even chance that you or yours have been deceived
"And got yourselves infected with a new kind of implant
"That we believe in just the recent months became extant."

Red looked at the captain with an understanding look
And said, "It sounds like you have found another from the book
"Of dirty tricks that TerraCorp has turned loose since the war.
"We'll do what you ask and hope we don't see any more.

"Now, tell me what it is." Then captain nodded to young Nick,
Explaining what was found in him and what had done the trick
To free him from the fate of dying in a fiery blast
Of phosphorous extracted from his very body's mass.

And then he told the story of Soldana's burned up man
And how his death was triggered by a too aggressive scan
(Which hopefully would not occur again, the lesson learned)
And they would try their very best to see that no one burned.

Red looked down and shook his head and asked, "Is there no more
"That we can do to stop these monsters of the Terran war?
"The ships and volunteers we need and funding comes so slow
"Even though the renegades are everywhere we go.

"Our little fleet of privateers has worked out well for us
"And when we group again we're heading out to Vanth-Orcus.
"Let's relive some old times, Jules. Why don't you come and join us?
"I know this crate of yours has more tricks than a Gypsy circus!"

The captain looked down at his glass then looked back up at Red
And with a hint of hesitation in his voice he said,
"We might have things to help. We'll know in a short while.
"But first we need to get to Titan, then give it a trial.

"Hang around on Rhea for an extra couple days.
"I'll touch base when I have news about it either way.
"We may need some help and I'll return all that I can
"When I have some certainty, then we can make some plans."

Redfeather's expression gave away his deep surprise
To see his friend's commitment was confirmed by his brown eyes.
The captain said, "What we may find in just a couple weeks
"May make a drastic change in how you operate your fleet."

* * * * *

Across the void the other crew aboard Redfeather's ship
Warmly welcomed those who came to help he who was sick.
Haji brought the chemicals and Radar brought the gear
To help the sickened man and clear the implant that they feared.

The crew had put a shield around their mediscanner bench
And set suppression gear as told (but Radar paused and flinched
With dark anticipation from the vision of the cost
That Ansel paid for Varda's scanner that day he was lost.)

Radar calmed his nerves and vowed beneath his breath to wait
Until a thorough test was made and wouldn't take the bait
To query any implant that was not a simple one
Until Haji had neutralized the fuel that made the bomb.

After several minutes searching deeply as he could
And neutralizing everything he figured that he should
He pointed out to Haji where the evil thing was hid
And gave the doc directions for the deadly mass to rid.

"This is very similar to what we found in Nick
"But it appears to be programmed with one more little trick:
"It's set to auto-trigger with a signal from a chip
"Embedded in his ear canal that looks to be equipped

"With a tiny microphone but that's all I can see
"Until I get it to our ship where I can dig in deep."
Haji glanced up quizzically then focused on his actions
And said, "This man appears to have an allergic reaction

"To the mimic proteins and it may have saved his skin
"For if he hadn't he would not have known it was in him
"Until it was too late. Thank God we came along in time."
Then Radar reassured the crew that all would be just fine.

Redfeather was grateful for the good report that came
Then ordered all his crew to undergo the very same
In-depth scan that Radar did for all Soldana's men
And found one other man that had the same implants in him!

Haji stuck around until the two were cleaned and patched
While Radar showed their engineers what TerraCorp had hatched
And had them fabricate a couple scanners of their own
Then he and Radar donned their suits and made their way back home.

Meanwhile, Captain Blue had asked his trusted bearded friend
Where he thought these implants had infected his crewmen:
"We refueled at Triton for the trip to Mercury
"And stopped nowhere but those two worlds and both only briefly."

Haji thought the growth rate of the mass in either man
Pointed to a timeframe that indicted cold Triton.
And so it seemed that both of them had visited a bar
Then spent the night in rented rooms and woke up with small scars

That neither gave a second thought to, being small and red
Figuring just scratches from the ladies in their beds;
But it was clear the two of them were targeted as tools
For use against their crewmates and had been completely fooled.

Shortly after Radar had returned to his own ship
He brought his scanner to the room where both captains now sipped
A little wine to kill some time before the ships would part
And said, "You need to see this. It gave me quite a start.

"Someone out at Triton's using this technology
"That TerraCorp used on our Nick at Earth just recently.
"But Triton's gear includes a feature we'd not found in Nick.
"A radio would trigger his but theirs is sort of sick.

"The implants with the microphones are programmed to respond
"To a certain sound pattern and not a thing beyond.
"When I decompiled it I uncovered what it is;
"A string of spoken words, but with an extra little twist:

"The words make up a sentence which is keyed to just one man.
"The words must match his voiceprint (and no one else's can).

"If the man who owns that voice repeats that simple phrase,
"The person with that implant then ignites into a blaze."

The captains glanced each others' way then asked, "Who's voice is it?"
Radar said he didn't know but he could reproduce it.
"Make the voice say something other than the trigger phrase
"And tell us in your own voice what the words are, by the way."

Radar tapped his pocket scanner and it played the sound
Of a baritone's clear voice repeating 'round and 'round,
"Slow down young one, from me learn," as they all listened close.
"Show how your love for me burns," said Radar, face morose.

"Show how your love for me burns?" repeated Red out loud.
"Now that's just twisted," he remarked, "That one's feeling proud!"
Captain Blue's eyes narrowed as he listened to it play
Then said, "A narcissist like that is not born every day.

"Do you recognize the voice?" and Red just shook his head.
"I don't either. Someone does. We'll find them," captain said.
"Radar, send a sample out to everyone we trust.
"Have them keep it quiet. If they know, report to us."

Radar nodded, left the room, then Captain turned to Red,
"This is one we need to find before more turn up dead.
"Whoever this is knows your ship and sees you as a threat
"And plans to make it personal with you, would be my bet.

"I wonder if he used Soldana's man to be a spy?
"This is a priority to find out who and why."
Redfeather agreed and they exchanged their fond goodbyes
Then trimmed their ships and parted ways across the starry sky.

* * * * *

Selenia had found no solace for her heart's despair
Immersed in daily routines running businesses' affairs
For from the man her heart yearned for she hadn't heard a peep.
The hours had turned to days which in their turn had turned to weeks.

But this was nothing new. He rarely sent much word at all.
Only every year or two to Mars as business called

Would he drop in to visit and perhaps arrange a deal
And rarely stayed a night or even for a simple meal.

What was new was that her heart demanded more than this!
She'd found a love she'd never known and meaning in a kiss.
She'd spent a lifetime with her heart concealed and alone
And now she needed desperately to bring the captain home.

Soldana had a problem too - he'd counted Gin as his.
But with the news of Gin's decision (Ansel too he missed!)
He had no captain qualified to serve and crew his ship
(At least not one he trusted quite as much to zip their lip.)

And now there was some urgency since Captain Blue's report
About the posturing at Titan and how time was short
To intervene in what was shaping up to be a coup
By TerraCorp and he knew there was work he had to do.

Soldana was a businessman who worked in shades of gray
Never caught in crime but little done by light of day.
Wealth and power were his goals but freedom meant much more
And this was not the first time he had mustered up for war.

"Selenia," Soldana started when their meal was done
Three weeks past the day the captain and his crew had gone.
"I want you on the cruiser and I want your greatest speed
"To Saturn's space to be there if your captain finds the need.

"I've given temporarily the cruiser to a man
"With much deep space experience but not combat command.
"You will act as commodore and you will be in charge.
"Take whomever you might want and make the crew list large.

"Take fighting men and mercenary soldiers we can trust
"Enough to take control of any station that we must.
"Then wait in Saturn orbit with your eyes and ears alert
"For opportunities to keep our friends from getting hurt."

Selenia's dark eyes lit up with possibility
And asked, "Who is this captain that will fly the ship for me?"
Soldana hesitated looking down into his dish
Then looked her in the eye and said, "It's Percival Standish."

"Percy!" she exclaimed, "Soldana, he's the best you've got?"
Her face betrayed surprise and anger at this news he'd brought.
Soldana shook his head and held his hand up to defray
The hot barrage of words that were about to come his way.

"Percy is a bus driver - a cargo man at best!
"He's never been in battle or been put to any test
"Beyond a smuggler shakedown or a tourist yacht's command.
"Surely you've got someone better - any other man!"

"Selenia, you know he's not the first choice I would make.
"But time is short and I don't want our presence there too late.
"Percival is rated for the big ships and deep space.
"He's here right now besides, so wipe that grimace off your face.

"As I said: you're in charge and he's been sternly told.
"He's obedient at least, and probably more bold
"Than you might give him credit. One does not command a ship
"The years he has without some skill and he won't give you lip.

"We could do worse." Soldana sighed and looked up at the light
That hung above the table hoping he had chosen right.
Selenia looked down and shook her head from side to side
And said, "I hope you're right. This may be a tricky ride.

"I'll do all I can to keep our business interests safe
"And if our friends need help I'll do whatever for their sake.
"If Percy turns his tail though, I'll use his butt for fuel.
"I will not let that man make us to look like simple fools."

With that she stood and turned to leave. Soldana said "Two days.
"Please make haste for space and in two days be under way.
"The captain is on board already and he knows our need
"To be in Saturn space and be there with the greatest speed."

Selenia had learned to trust Soldana's intuition.
Over many years his hunches had come to fruition.
They had won great riches with his cunning and insight
And she knew he had knowledge he had not let come to light.

There were many times he held a little something back
And when he did there was a reason why he took that tack.

So this time she would trust that his decision was the best
For this trip would put many men of valor to the test.

16   Snap Decision

The captain was acutely sensitive to any news
About the progress that was made on their concentric tubes
(The magnetic containment for the anti-matter mix)
And what progress on imaging arrays was made by Nick.

Portability of the design was what he needed.
He hoped a cargo bay's dimensions wouldn't be exceeded
But this was not the area of his own expertise
So he would keep the boys on track to finding him the key

To searching planetary crusts for gaps in density
(He'd use any advantage for a pirate base to see)
And if a gamma laser could be put into his hands
A sudden shift in strategy would over-write his plans.

So he was quite surprised when Dewey called him to report
That positron emissions were detected at the port
Adjacent to the cargo bay that Radar, Nick and Gin
Were piping plasma to and now had locked themselves within.

An hour later Gin came in to give a brief report
That Nick had done his job and made a phased array of sorts
Which proved the concept he'd cooked up for making smaller gear
For scanning planetary crusts and he had little fear

That one a little larger would suffice for imaging
But Bovine wouldn't work on it without the Captain's blessing.
"How big does it need to be?" the captain asked, surprised
To learn a working prototype was already devised.

The captain's thoughts were influenced by Saturn's big array
And Bovine didn't want to fritter metal stores away.
So he supposed it would be large and they would have to leave
The thing in orbit somewhere (after Titan they'd retrieve).

"We'll need a large collector and two outriggers in place
"But they could be retracted and stowed in a smaller space.
"The larger one will take some room but it can stand alone
"To serve when just emitting and crude imaging is done."

"How big is the big one?" Captain asked him once again.
"About three meters will suffice I think," responded Gin.
The captain's jaw dropped open when he heard how small it was
And said, "It's only nine feet?" then the intercom buzzed.

The captain held Gin's gaze and told the intercom to "Speak."
Then Bovine's voice informed him Nick and Radar tried to sneak
A large amount of metal from his stores into the bay
Where they had been sequestered with their magnetic array.

"Do it, Bovine," captain said, "Build this thing they want.
"And build it to take G-forces. Give it all you've got.
"This is your priority and we'll need it done right.
"I want it built to function if we get into a fight."

"Consider it as done, Sir," said Bovine with new glee.
He was more than happy to be ordered and set free
To fabricate new gear with no restrictions in his way
For drilling, cutting, welding were to him as child's play!

The outriggers were fixed to two legs of the landing gear
And folded in their fairings were concealed with little fear
That anyone would notice them when viewed from land or space
And when the gear retracted they were gone without a trace.

The large collector was constructed in a cargo bay
And mounted so the magnetics would not be in the way
And when a surge of positrons were used to test the rig
Nick and Gin pronounced that it indeed was plenty big

Enough to serve their purposes in proving out the gear
Which Nick and Radar fabricated as Saturn drew near.
But then the time had come and Captain needed now to see
Results of what the boys had made and justify the fee.

And so one day he called them to the bay to have a chat
And asked to have a briefing on the status they were at.
Gin asked Nick to start and Radar to fill in the gaps
While Captain walked around the gear inspecting this and that.

"It's all about the antiproton", Nick began to say
"Without the antiparticles this project will not pay.

"Making them's not easy and collecting's quite a chore
("From the cosmic background only 1 percent or more.)

"The best success at Saturn has been made with an array
"Large enough to gather and store some of them away
"In the form of antimatter (antihydrogen)
"And keep it in magnetic jars for use when tests begin.

"We cannot collect as much, but we've collected some
"And we have built magnetic jars to store what we don't run.
"Furthermore the shield around the gear re-feeds the loss
"So we get good efficiency while cutting down the cost."

Radar interjected, "What we have is crude at best
"But when we ran with positrons it passed all of our tests."
Nick continued, "Depth and resolution will be more
"Than what was done at Saturn last time that I heard their score.

"But that will only happen if our anti-matter mix
"Functions as we think it will with these magnetic tricks.
"The output of our small emitter (if it works as planned)
"Should be at least eight thousand times what Saturn's array can."

"The sweet part," Radar started, "Is the flux of gamma rays
"We've managed to produce before we had this new array:
"With only random antiprotons hitting on the rig
"We've bounced some gamma back and forth and measured off the grid!"

"The lasing's looking probable," he finished with a grin
The captain glanced around the room then fixed his eyes on Gin.
"Show me," said the captain, "Let me see it at its best
"And I will change our course to find a planetoid for test."

"We'll need more anti-protons to perform the laser trials,"
Radar said, "But what we have should show us several miles
"Beneath the surface of a planet and its density,"
He paused a bit and said, "And human-made porosity."

The captain turned to Gin and said, "Pandora will suffice.
"Set our course to intercept that lump of rock and ice.
"We'll shed off velocity we'd shed off anyway
"For Titan and it shouldn't cost more than a couple days."

Then he turned to Nick and Radar, "Do all that you need
"To try your laser also; I want answers with all speed.
"Titan is just days away. I'd like to know by then
"If we have that ace to play when other folks butt in."

Radar looked at Nick and Bovine who looked back at him
Then said, "Captain, there's no way we'll know enough by then.
"We'll need a large reserve of antiprotons in the jar
"To fuel the tests we need to run so we'll know where we are

"Along the path of balancing and tuning up the tube.
"Lasing at this energy is something very new."
Gin then threw a bone that they'd discovered when they ran
Some numbers from their first tests that might help in future plans:

"If we reach a certain power level it may hit
"A self-sustaining output using power from the ship
"In a feedback loop that ends the need for antimatter
"Then only at initiation will it even matter.

"But we won't know until we have a chance to prime the pump
"With antiprotons at a level to complete a dump
"That's big enough into the tube to get sufficient spark
"Of gamma high enough to get a lasing action start.

"On top of that," Gin continued, "We have just one set
"Of magnetic actuators that will need reset
"Every time the other function is desired for use.
"You can have a scanner or a laser - not the two."

The captain nodded then continued with his inquisition,
"What more must we come up with to be in the position
"Of having both to use at once?" Radar's ears turned red
And Gin looked at the metal floor and slowly shook his head,

"We'll need another set of five or six-axis magnetics.
"Or we'll need to fabricate a mixer from schematics
"That we've got drawn up to build the imaging device.
"But still the laser or the other must be put on ice

"Until we have the gear and the time to set it up.
"And that's the best that we can do with half a pint of luck."

The captain asked them one more question as he rubbed his nose,
"What about the antimatter canon you proposed?"

"That's the simplest part, but it's wasteful as can be.
"Antimatter is the hardest found commodity.
"We can tune the field to contain it several miles
"But I cannot advise it without doing real-world trials.

"You see, we could do a total dump but not a pulse.
"For safety's sake we'd use a double envelope, of course,
"But I'd not want to be around it using what we've got
"Things could get real dicey and might get a little hot."

Radar added, "Pulsing antimatter's not that tough,
"It's just that we don't have the time or parts to build the stuff.
"Development takes men and gear and time to set it up,
"At this point we are scrambling and counting on our luck."

The captain looked from man to man with pride lighting his eyes
And said, "You all have done a splendid job and I'm surprised.
"The progress you have made with bubblegum and paper clips
"Is far beyond what you'd expect could be done on a ship

"Carrying a cargo on a hop out Saturn's way
"But you men have accomplished more than I would dare to say
"A dozen engineers could do with all the tools in place.
"I'm proud to share your company and that can't be erased.

"Gin, prepare our course to do a flyby of Pandora;
"Bovine, you tell Haji, 'Steaks tonight' and that's an order;
"Radar, you and Nick get set to shine light on that moon.
"We'll be there within the week and not a day too soon."

From the outside of the ship there was no sound or notion
(Even when the thrusters fired to make a change in motion)
That just short inches underneath its cold metallic skin
The fate of many worlds hung on what was done within.

* * * * *

Warden asked Renee to come and watch a cargo ship
Laden with their labors lift and give their world the slip.

But it was in the shadows on the night side of the hill
And even though the ship was dark it gave Renee a thrill!

For years she'd been beneath the rock and only seen the light
Of distant sun and moons and stars but not a ship in flight.
And now behind the window glass high up the mountain side
She watched the warden watch the ship take off beaming with pride.

The darkness out the window glass was very near complete.
Only tiny red lights at the black ship's landing feet.
So little of the ship was seen, just silhouettes up high
Until the engines lit and blue-white glare washed out the sky.

Through the intervening vacuum there was not a sound
And only slight vibration at the start came through the ground.
Then only empty silence as the ship took off for space
Above the frozen ground and soon was gone without a trace.

Warden turned his face her way and said, "We'll ride one soon
"If you will agree to take me as your wedded groom.
"Renee, there is a destiny that's written in the stars!
"We'll live in wealth and richest pleasures anywhere we are."

"Groom?" Renee exclaimed, "I think you've jumped the gun a bit.
"Business partners maybe, but there's plenty more to it
"Than you appear to understand about the way things sit.
"I am not available nor have desire for it.

"You know where I stand - there's never been a single change.
"I desire my liberty and that should not seem strange.
"My husband is alive somewhere and I want back with him.
"And I'll do everything I can to be with him 'til then."

Warden turned and faced her and responded with a chill
In his lowered voice (which certainly gave her no thrill),
"It is you, Renee, that do not understand the stakes.
"You must measure carefully the choices that you make.

"I'll be leaving on a flight from this place very soon
"And only for my family and friends will there be room.
"I will not be coming back." He turned back to the scene
Outside the window where the frozen landscape slept serene

And said, "It would be tragedy if you were left behind
"And for the ones you care about." The thought shot through her mind
That something sinister was intimated by his tone.
And then he turned away and said, "This world is not our home

"Nor anybody else's." And with that her blood ran cold
And nothing in experience said he would not be bold
Enough to carry out his threat, though thinly veiled or vague
But in her heart she heard the screams of all who lived the plague

Of cruel intentions he'd inflicted spanning many years
And felt her eyes becoming red and moistened with her tears.
"Come!" he snapped, and walked away then turned and paused for her
To follow then he grinned and said, "I know you will answer

"My call to reason. You are smart and soon will feel free
"And comfortable with your choice to join your will to me.
"Tremendous change is coming to the solar system's scene
"Then you will understand the end will justify the means."

As they neared the doorway to the corridor she cast
Her eyes about the area for some small thing to grasp
And snatched a bit of plastic from a table that was cracked
Then as she passed the doorway stuffed it deep into the latch.

She didn't really know what caused this silly vandal's act.
Something in her heart seemed just to push her down that track.
Perhaps subconscious preservation or just lashing out?
But somehow she felt better though she still had need to shout!

Then as the door slid shut behind them Warden did not see
The little yellow light beside the door that showed it free
To open with a simple touch the next time someone came
To step into the room that had the largest window pane

Which she was now aware of, beyond her short forays
Around the installation at times she could get away.
Indeed, this corridor was one she'd never seen before
And she felt almost desperate to explore even more.

But for now she dutifully walked beside the man
Who held her fate and every other person's in his hand.

Cruel as he might be in hot pursuit of his dark goal
She'd wondered why in recent months he'd seemed to let things go

And grant a breath of self-determination to the crew
Who in some tiny measure had less fear than only two
Or three months in the recent past. But now it became clear
Their usefulness to him had passed; the end was very near.

The utter blackness of his evil plan was bad enough
But how he could be cavalier about it was too rough
For her internal organs to withstand for very long.
Her nausea was growing as he hummed the little song

He was accustomed to (as if a poker player's tell)
When it was obvious that things for him were going well.
But she had played a little poker on her own, you see
And kept her cards close to her chest (to keep her options free).

She'd raise the stakes to buy some time in any way she could
If she could save the people with her choice she surely would.
"I know you are a driven man and speak of lofty goals.
"You speak of royal dynasties and making our own rules

"But you have shown me little evidence it can come true
"Beyond this little farm of yours and one on Triton too."
She took his arm and stopped them both and turned her face toward his
And in a softly whispered voice said, "This is how it is:

"Maybe you are right and I no longer have a man.
"And maybe I cling to that hope - there's not much that I can
"Surrounded by your minions where life is just a bore
"But I've seen nothing better than what I have had before.

"You ask me for a contract and you ask me for your trust
"But all I see is garlic pickers, cavern walls and dust.
"Maybe you should think about your marketing approach
"When shopping for a queen to share the kingdom you propose."

With that she lightly brushed her breast against his arm she held
As slowly turning, walked away, her golden hair upheld
With a slightly haughty shake and sashay in her step
Then leered as though there were a naughty secret that she kept

When glancing back his way before she went around the bend.
(And saw him standing, jaw dropped open at corridor's end.)
She could see her play had the effect she thought it would
But now the clock was running fast and she'd done all she could

Until against all hope he gave her something she could use
To turn the tables before he recovered from her ruse.
It was a desperation borne of anger and of fear
That made her place her honor at the tip of his cold spear.

She ran the whole way to her quarters and was sick to tears
Sobbing, even retching at the thought and with the fear
That Warden was encouraged now that she would play his game
And let herself become his partner and take on his name.

Then after several minutes she recovered from her ills
And washed her face and pushed aside the dread and fear that filled
Her heart and mind and steeled herself for she knew it would be
Only hours before the warden tested her deceit.

* * * * *

Renee's change in behavior was a blast out of the blue
For Warden who stood wondering the next thing he should do.
For years she had been adamant she'd never come around
Now if it were to be believed her change was quite profound.

There'd been incremental change that led up to this day.
She'd agreed to organize and make the workers pay
In higher productivity which he could never do.
Her methods were not his but with success you can't argue!

She'd also spent more time with Warden lately than before
And though she had resisted she had taken duties more
Along the lines of things she'd found distasteful in the past
And even found some working friendships with his men at last.

But why the sudden turn? And why the blatant innuendo?
Why in six long years had she shown zero in libido?
Her little flirt and comment that invited him to chase
Had struck him right between the eyes and left him in a daze.

Perhaps she'd finally broken and had come to understand
The foolishness in hoping to spend life with a dead man.
Even her dear friend she made her visits to at times
Had told her to forget him (as reported by his spies).

He knew she was intelligent and highly capable.
Perhaps this was a ruse she planned would make him culpable
For some unseen event she'd plotted - some snare of a plan...
But what? He knew he held the cards - they all were in his hand.

Everything had come to pass much sooner than he'd hoped.
The real estate he'd pilfered and economies he'd choked
(His friends had slowed the progress on a number of key worlds.)
Obviously brilliant, his plans worked when they unfurled!

But he'd not come this far basing his successes on trust.
He would test her by the very test that she'd discussed
At dinner many weeks ago when he had raised the stakes.
Perhaps the time had come to see if she would try escape.

And so the knock on Renee's door came sooner than she'd thought
The warden seemed to take her challenge to show what he's got
And sent an invitation to her for another date
Of dining on the finest beef and please, to not be late.

Relieved it was a messenger and not Warden himself
She thanked them then she threw the invitation on a shelf
And then collapsed exhausted but so thankful there'd be time
To get herself together before they would have to dine.

17 Saturn

Nick had spent a dozen hours watching Saturn grow
From a yellow marble in the ship's best telescope
Into a festooned wonder world of spinning clouds and rings
The center of a wealth of moons and possibilities.

And now as they approached the system just above the plane
Of Saturn's royal rings the view would never look the same
From one hour to the next as dancing moons performed their steps
Eclipsing and egressing while the giant planet slept.

The weeks had passed so quickly with the work they had to do
And now their destination was just off a day or two.
Pandora was ahead and there would be so little time
To test the scanner as they passed and make sure it was fine.

For it had been decided they would only do their test
On the sunward side of Saturn. Captain thought it best
To minimize emissions that might give suspicious eyes
A reason to turn heads their way; he wanted no surprise.

The flyby of Pandora had been timed for the next day
The sunward side of Saturn opposite the big array.
They'd have Saturn at their back and sunward point their scan
And gather all their data in one burst. That was their plan.

"There's nothing in the solar system beautiful as that.
"No wonder that so many come out here to hang their hat."
Gin walked up behind him and peeked out the porthole glass
A moment then he added, "We'll be coming around fast

"From the night side to the light. You'll only get one shot
"To use the scanner on Pandora and see what we've got.
"We'll see the sunrise through the upper deck of Saturn's clouds
"And at that point you'll only have an hour. Make us proud."

Gin paused at the porthole one more time before he left
And said, "She is a beauty, but of warmth she is bereft.
"Every moon's an ice world and so distant from the sun.
"I've never liked it here since my career had first begun."

He paused a moment more then pulled his hip flask from his shirt
And tilted back his head then asked if Nick would like a squirt
Then lost in thought he turned and climbed up through the cockpit door.
Until they burned for Titan no one saw him anymore

Except the captain who would join him for the fast flyby
When cockpit duties would require at least two sets of eyes.
(Pandora circles just a bit outside the outer ring
And though the chance was slight they didn't want to hit a thing.)

Haji, Duke and Joe joined Nick who had the grandest view
With several porthole windows on each side to sight-see through.
It wasn't every day one crossed the plane of Saturn's rings
As close as they were coming - didn't want to miss a thing!

Duke, of course, spent several years working the Survey Corps
Mapping moons and minerals among the rings and more
Than any man among them knew the harsh reality
That lurked within the dust and ice of ring topography.

But still he loved the view as anyone, of course, would too!
(Nick would have to miss it though for he had work to do
Along with Radar and Bovine who said he'd lend a hand
Should something happen with the scanner that they hadn't planned.)

By now the rings were looming large and stretched across the sky
And Saturn was a thin crescent that framed it's huge dark side.
Then just as distant Sol slid red behind the upper clouds
The captain came into the reddened room and said out loud,

"A thousand million miles
"Yet no closer than the start
"To finding beauty in the eye
"That won't beguile the heart.

"Seductively the sirens call,
"Delightfully they dance.
"They lavish lovely promises
"Of rewards and romance.

"And men of every noble nation,
"Proud and humble too
"Dash their souls on rocks of passion
"In foolish pursuits.

"And though a thousand generations
"See their fathers' shame,
"It is the nature of the sons
"To do the very same."

Duke and Joe stared out the window silently in thought.
Nick said, "Bravo, Sir! That was a nice excerpt - from what?"
The captain said, "From me," then added, "For your food for thought.
"These worlds are enticing, but they're deadly - don't get caught."

Nick looked with a question in his eyes at Haji's face
Who nodded affirmation sitting quietly in place.
Then as the captain disappeared into the cockpit door
Haji said, "He does that sometimes," and said nothing more.

Silently they sat a minute, then Nick stood to go
And Haji said, "The captain is a tricky man to know.
"On the outside, capable and sometimes coldly hard
"But deep inside there is a poet living in his heart."

The darkness of the room that now was deep in Saturn's shade
Served a stark reminder of the dangers of this trade.
And though they rarely spoke of it in more than grunted spurts
Nick knew in their hearts they underlined the captain's verse.

* * * * *

Selenia looked in her mirror with a passing frown.
She didn't like the way acceleration pulled them down.
(At home on Mars her breasts stood high and always looked their best
But on a ship at two G's looking good could be a test.)

Though that decision had been hers (to get well under weigh
As rapidly as practical to get out Saturn's way).
The days they spent at this acceleration had gone fast
And Captain Standish would reduce the rate today at last.

This cruiser wasn't built for doing laps around the yard
But as a military craft to send things fast and far.
Protected well with three big lasers fore and three more aft
And loaded light (but extra fuel) they'd cut the time in half.

The crew had many seasoned men Soldana put in place
And many younger fighting men that had some time in space.
But still the ship was new and Captain Standish wasn't known.
The crew had not yet jelled nor turned the ship into their home.

But that would come with time and drills as every ship must do
To bring about cohesion and efficiency of crew.
Meanwhile, in the com center a message was received
Encrypted so that only one (Selenia) could see.

She had the message sent to her and brought up on her screen
And found it was Soldana who was looking rather lean
And haggard for a man who spent much time in luxury
But he had business to discuss and seemed a bit hurried.

Then when his business questions and his comments were complete
Soldana said, "I've got an odd request from off the street.
"It comes from your dear captain with the voiceprint of a man.
"He wants an ID and he asks if anybody can?

"Listen to it if you will. Perhaps your friends can too.
"If anyone can recognize it contact Captain Blue.
"It seems they've found two human bombs just like Ansel and Nick.
"It's probable they came from Triton; this voice does the trick

"To set them off remotely or in person at his whim.
"The ones we found in Nick and Ansel were not set by him."
With that Soldana's message ended with a quick "Good luck."
She played the voice then felt as if a lightning bolt had struck!

Yes, she recognized that voice - was one she'd not forget!
She played it over many times in hopes it wasn't. Yet
It pulled the pain and memories up from her deepest pit
Of hidden horrors dulled by sands of time that buried it.

She leaned back in her couch and spent an hour deep in thought
Wondering how fate had sent her captain to get caught

Up in the web of darkness that revolved around that man
And she resolved to help her captain any way she can.

Then she stroked her couch's console, entered in the key
To send encrypted messages to Soldana and he
Who broke the hidden hinges of the gate around her heart
That not since she was young in her own life had played a part.

The message to Soldana covered business back on Mars.
The message sent her captain's way was spoken from the heart.
She told her chosen captain there could be no other choice:
There was no doubt the sample was indeed her brother's voice.

* * * * *

Nick's controls were set up just outside the cargo bay
In a little room where other gear was moved away.
Controls to all the scanner gear were fitted through the wall.
Radar was there with him; Bovine in the bay at call

Tethered, in a pressure suit, the door opened to space
Light reflecting from his helmet, sunlight in his face
And all equipment functioning as best as they could guess
Until they got real data from this first try as they passed.

Radar was dressed in a lightweight pressure suit as well
Just in case there was an issue Bovine couldn't quell.
His helmet wasn't on his head or either glove besides;
They were left beside the airlock door where they were tied.

Radar focused on the mixture, Nick prepared the scan
And everything was ready and proceeding as they planned
When with a piercing shriek the claxons sounded as a "BANG!"
Echoed through the ship and Radar jumped and shouted, "Dang!"

"Status!" Captain's voice commanded through the intercom
And Radar looked at Nick and said, "It's OK - remain calm.
"It was an impact and there is no need to be concerned.
"The chance is almost nil but it does happen. You just learned!"

Radar checked some instruments and Bovine did the same.
In seconds every crewmans' voice reported in by name

And stated the condition of the systems and the ship
(That everything was fine besides a fracture and a rip

Where some minutest particle had impacted the hull
Adjacent to a cargo bay that had been packed quite full
Of organics and metals that were destined for the moons
Where heavy metals were not common, organics a boon.)

The captain's voice again commanded, "Radar, stay on task.
"You and Nick stay focused until Pandora is passed.
"Time to passage at my mark is two minutes and ten.
"You'll only have a single chance - we won't pass here again."

No sooner had the captain's order ended with his "Mark!"
Than one more "BANG!" resounded through the ship and claxons barked.
Nick looked from his console then and Radar gawked at him
And said, "This is our lucky day. Let the protons in!"

The captain's "Status!" came again and everyone checked in
Except for Bovine. Then the captain called his name again.
Radar looked into the bay to see Bovine enmeshed
Behind a fractured piece of structure and he looked a mess!

Gas was exiting his suit and faintly colored pink.
A globule of blood seen in his helmet made one think
That he had suffered injuries that ended him for sure.
Radar shouted, "Bovine's hurt!" and scrambled for the door.

Nick looked through the window then and saw Bovine's left arm
Reach up with a signal showing he was not as harmed
As it might seem to look, so Nick yelled, "Radar, stay on task!"
"Sit back down and focus on the job like Captain asked!

"Bovine gave a thumbs up and we're running out of time!"
Radar turned and looked at Bovine then came back with, "Fine!"
"Scanner set and balanced," Nick reported, "Start the mix."
Radar touched a glowing screen and said, "Target is fixed.

Then at that very moment darkness fell across the ship
As deep into Pandora's shadow suddenly they slipped.
"Engaging now," then blue light formed a faintly glowing shaft
Extending from the gear to well outside the dark spacecraft.

In just eight seconds they had cleared the shadow of the moon
While Duke came on the double and had burst into the room
With news that Joe was suiting up and just two steps behind
And then they heard the airlock pumps begin their starting whine.

Radar pushed past Duke and grabbed his helmet and his gloves
And followed Joe into the lock (in fact he gave a shove).
It seemed like an eternity before the door gave way
And let them in the airlock to pump down the other way.

By the time they gathered Bovine from the twisted mess
Of metal that had trapped him while he did his very best
To stem the flow of air and blood to buy a little time
He was no longer conscious when the airlock's "ready" chimed.

Another long eternity wore past as they removed
His helmet then cut off his suit and found his heartbeat proved
That he was still alive! The frozen blood beneath his mitt
Had served to slow the leakage from the short but jagged rip

Across the left side of his suit the piece of hull had cut
As its jagged edge had sliced its way into his gut.
Haji met them at the door to the infirmary
And started work on Bovine's wound almost immediately

Pausing only for injections and initial scans
To get a quick assessment of the damage to the man.
And then he shooed the others (all but Duke) out of the room
Telling them that Bovine would be feeling better soon.

(Duke was not encumbered by a spacesuit so he won
The job assisting Haji when the cutting had begun.)
But it was over soon with Bovine's innards patched and stitched
And topped off with blood substitute (success without a hitch.)

Then Haji gave a quick report that Bovine would be fine
Though on restricted duty for a little healing time.
For now he was sedated but tomorrow he'd awake
And no doubt he'd be ravenous but small meals he must take.

Meanwhile, long before the doctor's work was stitched and done
Repair work on the hull by Joe had already begun.

Dewey gave assistance, Gin had rolled his sleeves up too
And Duke had also joined them after Haji's work was through.

The work was going well enough but Captain called a break
When he and Nick had fixed a meal for all of them to take
Together in the galley for a status and debrief.
Fatigue was setting in and he did not want any grief.

The topics of discussion were, of course, Bovine and ship
And what the chances were of more than one time getting hit
And what results the scanner setup gave when they flew past
Pandora and the Titan plans when they arrived at last.

"The chance of just a single hit is very nearly zero
"But it goes up the closer to the ring plane that you go."
Duke explained, "Collisions happen in the Survey Corps
"But though they are not common, where there's one there can be more."

"We drew the short straw this time, that is all," the captain said,
"How are repairs coming, Gin?" Gin just scratched his head
And said, "The first hit's damage has completely been repaired
"But it will be four hours more; less if Radar's spared

"To lend a hand inside while Duke and Joe weld the outside.
"I think the captain's yacht should be inspected well besides."
"Very well," the captain said, "That's better than I'd thought.
"Radar, give a hand. Nick, show us what we've got

"About Pandora that we didn't have a day ago."
Then Nick turned on the view screen to display the scanner show.
"Here is what we saw in white light when we made the pass,"
Then on the screen a moving image filled the viewer's glass

Which constantly repeated as the flyby flew it's course
"And here is what our processed data shows but it's still coarse."
Then with a stroke upon his pad the picture came to life:
A purple ghostly image of the moon with edges bright

Which darkened toward the center at the small moon's tighter core
But near the surface structure could be seen. And even more
Impressive was the fact that when they flew into the light
Much of what was visible was still! A great delight!

"Oh, my!" the captain said and others too around the room
Made expressive exclamations about how the moon
Was now an open book that Nick could flip the pages through
And Radar said, "Now show them what this thing can really do."

Nick obliged by zooming in to view a smaller spot
And said, "Here is an item that's a big surprise we got."
And there displayed before them deep within the icy rock
Were half a dozen cubic structures. "Nature? I think not,"

He said as he manipulated back and forth the view
To show a little more of what this new device could do.
"That isn't nature," Duke chimed in, "That is the Survey Corps.
"We built a base for resupply on Pandora and more

"Than twenty other moons where teams could go to get some rest
"Well beneath the regolith to be protected best
"From ring anomalies that happen (they can be rough rides)
"But this view isn't right; the base is on the other side."

"Huh?" Nick responded with a question on his face.
"Yes," Duke remarked, "I think you've misread what you've traced.
"The base that you are looking at is forty miles through
"The rock and ice of Pandora. So that's what it can do!"

"Uh, yes, you're right," Nick said as he examined his controls
And verified positions of the little moon's north pole.
"Very, very good," the captain said beaming his pride
"Finish up the ship repairs. Ice cream's on tonight -

"Or beer if that's your choice," he winked then waved his hand at Nick
"How is it that you're so calm? Now that's a real neat trick.
"I'd be jumping up and down and shouting out with pride."
Nick responded calmly, "I'm about to burst inside."

With that the whole crew whooped and hollered, laughed and clapped with
glee
And pounded Nick and Radar on their backs repeatedly.
Nick yelled, "Yes!" while holding fists up in the air with joy
While Gin turned toward the captain, softly said, "That's our boy!"

When the ruckus settled down the captain gave the word
That when the outside work was done they'd start a braking burn
To put them into Titan orbit in about two days.
Then Gin gave them a word before they all drifted away:

"Before we land on Titan we will pressurize the ship
"To keep the nasty atmosphere outside," (then he sniffed)
"The methane and the other hydrocarbons in the air
"Stink enough to make you want to burn your clothes and hair.

"Titan's surface pressure runs as high as one point four.
"To keep the stinkies out we'll make it just a little more.
"Normally we keep the ship at near an atmosphere
"But for this ride we'll bump it up another half to clear

"Any noxious fumes that try to wiggle their way in.
"So yawn or chew some gum to keep your ears popping 'til then.
"We'll bring it slowly up over the next day and a half
"And all the surface suits have been configured just like that.

"The buildings and the areas beneath the Titan domes
"Are pressurized the same so it will feel more like home
"By the time we get there. Now, let's finish up repairs
"Then get some sack time in so we can get ourselves prepared."

With that they wandered off renewed to finish up their tasks
But shortly Radar signaled Captain that a message flashed
Across the Saturn broadcast system uncoded and clear
Addressed to him from someone he did not expect so near.

"It's from Selenia," he said, "I'll play it for you Sir,
"I certainly did not expect a message here from her."
He sent the audio to captain's personal device
The captain smiled inwardly (to hear her voice was nice.)

"Hello Jules! I thought I'd drop a line to let you know
"I'm in the area along with friends I think you know.
"There was a tourist trip to Saturn and I thought I'd go
"And, my! These many moons and rings have put on quite the show!

"Call me back and we'll catch up and chew the fat a bit!"
With that the message ended but a note that came with it

Encrypted on subcarriers that only Radar knew
Gave the special frequencies that they would have to use.

The captain was surprised to learn Selenia was near
And quite perplexed that she'd arrived so suddenly out here!
He knew the pleasure yachts, though rare, were never quite that fast
She'd have had to leave before them but she'd left there last.

The rough result he got upon a mental calculation
Showed she'd spent some days at some extreme acceleration.
And there weren't many ships around that had the kick for that
Or carried fuel enough to come that fast and make it back

To lower speeds for capture by a planet's gravity
(Slow it down or from the solar system you'll be free!)
So he would have some questions when he got a chance to ask;
To get a secure comm link he put Radar to the task.

"Doppler indicates she's still a couple days away
"From Saturn space and, Man! That fuel bill I'd hate to pay!
"Okay, you're set to go. It's piped into your quarters, Sir.
"Channel two when you are ready." Captain called to her:

"Jules! Forever Free," she smiled wide, "I'm glad you called."
"Forever Free," he said, "I didn't expect this at all.
"You're a long way from your Martian sand and I'm surprised
"You must tell me all about this ship on which you ride."

"Gin can tell you all about it, Jules," and then she winked
"Soldana made quite sure of that. I really didn't think
"That Gin would keep it from you, but Soldana bought it new
"From Mercury and I don't think there's much that it can't do.

"Anyway, I wanted you to know we'll be around.
"I've got sixty men that can put boots on any ground.
"We'll refuel at Rhea at the orbital depot
"And hang around awhile. There's nowhere special we must go.

"We're here to keep things balanced if there's balancing to do.
"I just wanted you to know that we are here for you."
The captain mulled this over then responded, "It's my hope
"That I won't step in anything with which I cannot cope.

"Is this Soldana's doing?" He cast a quizzing eye
And she responded, "Jules, we don't want you all to die.
"Soldana asked me to watch over business interests here
"And if you need a little help there's friendly muscle near.

"Besides," she looked down at her nails absently-mindedly
"There is a man who's voice I want to hear personally."
"Your brother's?" Captain asked. Her eyes shot darkly up at his
She said, "Family matters, Jules. That is all it is."

"Selenia, I'm sorry but regardless that he's kin
"This man has done evil and he has to be reined in."
Selenia's eyes hardened and she said, "It's not like that.
"I don't want to see him for a friendly little chat.

"Jules, his hands are bloody more than you or I may know.
"He's no regard for human life. There's death where 'ere he goes.
"When he fled to Triton long before the Lunar war
"Many people wanted him to even up some scores.

"In those days his refuge was to work for TerraCorp.
"They found his methods useful and for him it was just sport.
"Jules, if we can find him it will be the sweetest day!
"There's more that you should know. Listen close to what I say:

"When I was very young, in fact I still was in my teens
"There was a young man that I loved and I knew he loved me.
"My brother couldn't stand the thought that I had found love true
"He took a pair of pruning shears and ran the young man through.

"And then when he had finished that he forced himself on me
"And later in the week our parents died mysteriously.
"They never pinned it on him but I know he did the job.
"I have no love for him; by him my Loves from me were robbed.

"If you find him first I ask one favor, please, from you:
"Let me gaze into his dark eyes as I run him through."
The burning passion in her eyes was something he'd not seen
In all the years he'd known her through the wars and those between.

"I knew he was a bad one," he began, "I didn't know
"The depths to which he'd hurt you - where none should have to go.

"If the fates decide to bring his life into my hands
"He will be my gift to you, I'll bring him if I can."

She looked into his steady gaze and knew his word was good.
He would bring him to her if by any means he could
Or bring to her assurance that the justice had been served.
She knew he had the skill set and she knew he had the nerve.

"Thank you, Jules. I'm sorry for the deep vindictive streak
"But I know that you understand that I am not a freak.
"My life was altered deeply by that evil twisted man
"And I know there are thousands that have suffered at his hand.

"And I will have revenge!" she finished, leaned back in her couch
Then shook the tension off and wiped the corner of her mouth.
She smiled and blinked a tear away then said, "Thank you, Jules.
"I know you are a good man with a decent set of rules.

"But for your sake I hope I am the one to find him first
"And spare you from the sight of watching me relieve my thirst
"For vengeance for my father and my mother and my beau
"That all my life has followed me wherever I might go."

"Selenia, you're justified and no one would deny
"That for his many evil crimes this man deserves to die.
"But if my hunch is right and he's connected to the fiends
"That made the mess at Ganymede, well, I still hear their screams

"And you know what I've lost besides," he offered with his eyes
As cold as hers were passionate with vengeance as her prize.
"I doubt if he is in the Saturn system, who can tell?
"Triton or Miranda seem more like his kind of hell."

Selenia responded, "Yes, that seems a likelihood
"But I'm reminded Ansel got commission on some goods
"Delivered somewhere hereabouts just months before he died.
"The goods were human cargo and there's commerce here besides

"Which indicates refueling business far above the norm
"And agri-business exports far beyond established farms.
"I have business contacts in the system to consult
"Who might produce some hints that add up to a good result.

"At any rate, I'll be on Rhea for a little while.
"You can call me any time," she finished with a smile.
The captain smiled back and said, "Selenia, you're great.
"I'll get back to you when I have dropped my load of freight

"And finished up some other business pressing on my mind.
"Enjoy your trip and we'll talk over anything you find.
"You might run into Red. I know he's parked on Rhea now
"Dropping off some cargo but I don't think long somehow.

"It seems he's got some friends together in a merry band
"On their way to party hearty in the far outlands.
"Forever free!" he finished. She said back "Forever free!"
And then they closed the link and thought things over carefully.

He never knew the secret darkness of her family's past,
She had always slipped the subject when someone would ask.
And now it was apparent he would need to talk to Gin
About this ship of mystery Selenia rode in.

Selenia could sense there was a lot Jules wouldn't tell
About the work before him but she knew him very well.
He wouldn't ask for help until it might just be too late.
She knew she'd have to contact Red and ply him on a date.

18 Titan

A peach! Nick thought, *A perfect peach that's ripened on the tree*
Waiting for a hand to pluck and lips to taste its sweet;
A perfect orb of Heaven and beneath its velvet skin
A world of possibilities to lose oneself within.

Perhaps that was the facade that an Earther might perceive
But deep beneath the yellow haze awash in methane seas
Titan was a frozen world where nights were eight days long
And cryogenic days beneath a stinking yellow fog

Where everything looked yellow-orange in the diffused light
Of misty air that softened shadows through the day and night
Meant instant death for humankind without protective gear
And yet men sought to own it and would sell their own souls dear

To do so. That was history and how the west was won
And why most of the Earth was divied up by land barons;
Why Paris needed Helen and why Troy burned to ash
And why impassioned pursuits have lead all nations to clash.

Thus Nick could only see the beauty of this orange globe
And wonder at the physics to unlock its treasure trove;
A thousand mysteries to solve and not one touched on yet.
He felt he'd burst his seams if he could not get his feet wet

Soon. Very soon! In fact the time they'd spend today
Swinging through a breaking orbit seemed such a delay!
To plant his feet on soil of such alien design
Had been a fantasy; but was reality this time.

The captain gathered all the crew and made it very clear
That they were dropping in where unknown dangers might appear.
Many forces were afoot and some were hostile too.
And some may see them as a threat and things might come unglued.

"Make no mention of our knowledge of the big array.
"Make it clear we're chartered just to bring Nick out this way.
"We'll take our fee from TerraCorp and buy a little fuel
"Then spend a day in Xanadu like any spacers do.

"Radar, you and Haji get Nick's implants set to spoof
"A direct trip from Earth and let them transmit that as proof.
"But set them up to transmit conflicts in their data set.
"Give them stuff to keep them hoping they'll get something yet.

"You know what I want but make sure we can track him down
"If anything should go awry," he looked at Nick and frowned.
"You're good with this?" Nick answered, "Yes. I'll gather what I can
"Then meet you at the place you say exactly as we planned.

"By the way," Nick offered, "Data gathered at Pandora
"Gave us what we needed to retune and now the aura
"Caused by solar interference won't be such a mess
"And secondary radiation should be somewhat less."

"That's great news," the captain said, "But keep your focus on
"Your work to minimize the questions raised by anyone.
"Atmospheric physics and a small (but bad!) array
"Are what they sent you out here for so work and earn your pay.

"But you know I pay better," Captain winked and turned to go
Up the passage to the cockpit where he'd start the show
That brought them to a landing on the yellow ice and stone
Where Nick would shortly leave his friends and be left there alone.

In the cockpit Gin reported something was amiss
The landing field at Xanadu's response was just a hiss.
And so they tried the tower at Ligeia's northern port
Who told them to "Hold on a sec, I'll wake the bugger, Sport."

Two minutes passed before a sleepy voice came on the air
That made it very obvious he didn't really care
To have his dozing interrupted by arriving ships
But gave the clearance needed. Through the haze layers they slipped.

* * * * *

Veles spaceport wasn't quite the haven he had hoped.
Comprised of only half a dozen domes that oddly poked
Above the frozen landscape littered coarsely here and there
With lumps of yellow ice and rock beneath the foggy air.

Granted, there were other buildings spread around the field
Mostly formed from blocks of dirty ice to serve as shields
From rocket blast or other random atmospheric force
But not for human habitation, only gear of course.

An automated crawler came and parked beside the ship.
Dressed in their protective suits the captain, Duke and Nick
Took their seats and pressed the destination button marked
For Station Operations and rode on until it parked.

The three of them went in the airlock of the station dome
Where a sullen station worker skulked about alone
And grunted something meant to be a welcome, but felt more
Along the lines of, *Go away and don't come here no more.*

"We're here to buy some fuel and get a transport for a man
"To the atmospheric works at Fensal if you can.
"And also, if you might, we've got a cargo to unload
"Here's the buyer's contact and the proper cargo hold."

The station worker tapped some keys a moment then replied,
"There's a transport bound for Sinlap, you can catch that flight.
"It arrives in twenty minutes, then an hour's wait
"For maintenance and fueling and a crew change. Don't be late."

He tapped his keys again and said, "Your fuel is on the field.
"The cargo crew is notified, please have it unsealed
"And someone standing by to verify the lading list.
"They'll be there in fifteen minutes, ten if you insist."

"Fifteen works for me," the captain smiled and said, "Thank you."
The station worker pointed at a door and said, "Step through
"That doorway, take the corridor until the very end
"Where there's a pub and restaurant if you have time to spend."

"Let's," the captain motioned to the other two to go
And sent a message off to Joe and Dewey so they'd know
To verify the fuel and supervise the cargo crew
Then they could have some liberty if they desired to.

Haji stayed with Bovine to keep watch over the ship
Then after forty minutes Dewey came to try a sip

Of Veles Station's coffee and to stretch his legs a bit
And showed no interest in the local pub (he ignored it)

Which glowed invitingly across the mall from the cafe
Where Captain, Duke and Nick had found a little booth away
From others that had dropped in for some lunch or coffee too.
But no one gave a second look at who was passing through.

Several minutes after Dewey, Joe dropped by to say
Goodbye to Nick before his flight would spirit him away.
And as a friendly gesture he gave Nick a little gift:
A good ceramic knife that had a flattened rubber grip.

"Here's a little graduation present for you Nick.
"You earned it training hand-to-hand and hopefully some sticks.
"But better yet, I hope you never have to lift your hand
"For justice or in anger against any other man."

Nick sampled the razor edge and felt the slim knife's heft
And switched it back and forth between his right hand and his left.
Then said, "Thank you, Joe! This is a beauty and it slides
"Nicely in my shirt where no one can see where it hides.

"Tell me, Joe, what made you choose the profession you did?"
Joe looked square at Nick and said, "Well, I was just a kid.
"I worked on a production line where I sat every day
"Picking fly poop out of pepper for near zero pay."

They all burst out in laughter and the others in the room
Turned to look at those who dared to shatter morning's gloom
As Captain said, "Now that's enough to seek a higher call!"
And Dewey offered, "Anything! Any job at all!"

With that Duke asked if Joe would like to go and get a beer
In the pub and listen to whatever they might hear
As far as system scuttlebutt or Titan news perhaps.
You never knew what information might fall in their laps.

Joe invited Dewey. Dewey turned the offer down.
(Even after weeks of healing, his night on the town
At Mars' DaVinci crater still sent remorse through his mind.)
Joe and Duke departed for their beers and what they'd find.

After finishing their coffee and some little talk
Dewey and the captain took Nick on his final walk
To board the waiting aircraft while they checked his suit again
Making sure it was all set for travel on Titan.

(A spacesuit wasn't suitable in Titan's frozen air.
A cryosuit was needed if much time would be spent there
And so he was outfitted with the best they had on hand
And billed it all to TerraCorp as travel costs unplanned.)

19 A Far Country

Nick's first view of Sinlap wasn't much to write about
For it was night when he arrived (though he saw on the route
They flew to get there mountains, lakes and running methane streams
Beneath the hazy yellow sky as if some nightmare dream

Were splashed across the frozen landscape, alien and bare
Its shadows softened by the clouds that filled the thickened air,
Until into the night side as the dim spot of the sun
Sank into the murk behind them half way through the run.)

The landing field was lit by bright lights mounted high on poles
Made of ice as tripods that grew thinner as they rose
And in the nearby distance other lights lit doors to domes
One of which would likely be his temporary home.

But when the aircraft taxied toward the dome that partly served
As terminal and operations center he observed
A man eyeing him closely from the back seat of the plane
So Nick asked, "Do I know you?" And the man tried to explain,

"I'm sorry - didn't mean to stare. There just aren't many blokes
"That come to Sinlap other than the TerraCorp-type folks.
"I was just a-wondering if you would stick around
"Or be another stiff they burn and stuff into the ground.

"Pardon me," he said as he pushed past him to the lock;
But just before he put his helmet on he turned to talk
And said, "Stop by Jonesy's Bar - a burger's on the house.
"And by the way, I'm Jonesy," as he held his right hand out

And said, "Glad to meet you, Sport." Nick took the offered mitt,
"My name is Nicholas, but most prefer to call me Nick.
"Perhaps I'll take you up on that. Thank you." They both grinned
Then donned their helmets as the inner airlock door opened.

When the airlock cycled and they stepped down on the field
A glance around the area did little to reveal
That more than seven hundred people lived and worked this town
For most of the activity was done beneath the ground

Or in the thermal domes that clustered near the small airport
Where hangars and mechanic shops for crawlers could report
For maintenance or fueling or repair of special gear
For drilling and construction in the frigid temperatures.

The other half a dozen passengers went separate ways.
Some into the terminal and others through the haze
Of methane mist that kept their destinations in the night
Mysterious beyond the little airfield's outdoor lights.

Once inside the terminal Nick walked up to the desk
Where a sleepy teenage girl politely asked him, "Yes?"
"Pardon me," Nick offered, "I was hoping for a word
"From the atmospheric works. I'd wondered if you'd heard?"

"Ah, yes I have," she tapped some strokes upon her screen.
"Mister Hall-, Mister Hallen..." " Hallenbeck," he beamed.
"Nicholas?" she asked. "Or Nick is fine," he reassured
Her that he was the one for whom the note was written for.

"I called ahead and understood that someone would be here
"To show me to the atmospheric works, but I fear
"I may have missed them." She said, "No you didn't, they missed you."
She turned and shouted through a doorway, "Boomer! Get a clue!"

"Your man is here!" And then she turned apologetically
Back to Nick and said, "He's coming. Glad you didn't freeze
"Waiting for him outside. He's not always so inept.
"But sometimes he gets sidetracked and his deadlines don't get met."

At that a large and pimple-faced young man came through the door,
Apologized, then asked if Nick required that any more
Baggage be unloaded from the plane and brought along.
And Nick replied there wasn't; his assignment wasn't long

And so he traveled lightly; all he had was in his kit
Which he carried with him. Then the young man reached for it
And said, "They call me Boomer and I'll take you to the plant.
"I'm a hired driver since their normal driver can't."

Then out into the night beneath the glaring airfield lights
Nick followed his escort to a crawler parked outside

A nearby hangar where some suited figures milled about
Looking at some damage on an aircraft that no doubt

Was caused by searing heat or a combustion of some kind
Which struck Nick as an oddity he pushed back in his mind.
(The atmosphere was nitrogen and temperature so low:
Ninety Kelvin - that's three hundred Fahrenheit below!)

As they climbed into the crawler's cabin Boomer said,
"Hook your suit up to the crawler so you'll charge instead
"Of draining your resources so if trouble comes along
"Your suit will be topped off and the chance that you'll live long

"Enough to walk your way back will be that much better than
"The guy that doesn't do it. I don't want to be that man!"
"That's good advice, thank you," Nick said as he buckled in
And promptly took the offered cable to let power in.

The crawler wasn't pressurized, but heated seats did help
To keep the riders comfortable and window ice to melt
On those occasions when ammonia-water might condense.
From hydrocarbon rains the canopy was good defense.

Boomer pushed the starter and the crawler growled to life.
The headlights pierced the shadows and made day where it was night.
Then as he pushed the throttle and the crawler lurched ahead
The vibration and noise were quite enough to make Nick dread

A trip of any length, but Boomer said it wasn't far:
Only seven miles and it might take half an hour.
The crawler wasn't made to be a luxury sedan
But as a rugged transport for equipment overland.

Within three minutes Sinlap was a dim glow in the mist
Behind them as the crawler's tracks produced a constant hiss
As little particles of rock and ice were broken down
And when four minutes passed there was no hint of any town.

"Sinlap isn't much to look at," Boomer broke the ice
"But everybody has a job and life seems pretty nice.
"Though there is not a lot do but work and spend your cash
"On beer and partying or if you're smart building a ranch."

"A ranch?" Nick was surprised to hear that word used in this place.
Then Boomer gave a laugh seeing the look that crossed Nick's face.
"Well, that's the word I use. The Aussie types call them their 'stations'
"And talk as if one day they'll form a planetary nation.

"But I don't see it happening in my lifetime at least."
Boomer looked assertive and a little more than peeved.
 Nick asked, "What is it that makes you tend to disagree?
"Titan has potential that everyone can see."

Boomer said, "That's what they say but terraforming's slow.
"And when my folks and I came here we tried to make a go
"At farming in a cavern that was just as good as any
"But with the off-world food imports we couldn't make much money.

"And so we sold the farm to some off-worlder for a song.
"It is a fertile farm and we did not do one thing wrong."
The bouncing headlights made the shadows of the ice and rocks
Alternately lengthen and then shorten as they rocked.

"The funny thing," young Boomer mulled, "The off-world man who bought
"Our farm abandoned it and now it's just a hollow rock
"That doesn't do a thing for anyone and that's a shame.
"There's other ones around here where it turned out just the same."

"The same man bought them all?" Nick asked and Boomer answered, "Yes.
"They say we're in a boom but the economy's a mess.
"Those who have a steady job are doing well, it seems
"But those who want to ranch or farm are not finding their dreams.

"And folks say farming's at the root of growing up a world.
"Even one like this, but it's not how things have unfurled.
"So I don't hold the Aussies' optimistic point of view.
"I'll just save my money 'til I know what I should do."

The road began to wind as it ascended through some hills
And in a spot or two it seemed to Nick like they might spill
Over on their side, but even in low gravity
The crawler gripped the hills as if it were a hound dog's flea.

Boomer queried Nick, "You work for TerraCorp I guess?"
Nick responded, "Yes - uh, no. Well, not exactly yes.

"I'm on a contract temporarily to work for them.
"I'll be on their payroll 'til my project with them ends."

"Yeah, I guess they do that sometimes," Boomer slowly said
Then looked out of his window for a moment with his head
Turned aside so Nick could not directly see his face
And said, "My folks did that and then they disappeared in space."

"Disappeared?" "Yeah, they signed a temporary deal
"To work for TerraCorp for just a year on Umbriel
"Along with several others who were planning to come back
"But just three days from Titan, well, it seems they were attacked.

"At least that's all that we were told. Pirates, I suppose.
"It's been about two years now and that's all I really know."
Though Boomer tried to hide the strain and sadness in his voice
He said, "I know they were convinced the trip was a good choice.

"Whatever happens, someday I would like to buy our farm
"Back for them if they return to Titan without harm.
"I might even work it, but some things will have to change
"To keep the marketplace more stable. Right now it acts strange."

The crawler came around a bend and crested a steep rise
Then started down the other slope as Nick caught Boomer's eye
And asked, "How is it strange? It's simple supply and demand.
"I've never run a farm or ranch. I'd like to understand."

Boomer looked away then shot him back another glance
And saw that Nick was honest in his farming ignorance.
He mentioned that there always were uncertain elements
In forecasting demand and other things in his defense;

"But this is something different," the young man showed concern.
"It's almost as if certain farms are targeted in turn.
"One may choose a certain crop to spend their efforts on
"Then just before they harvest, off-world goods are piled on

"The shelves of every warehouse, then the farm can't sell their crop.
"Some have tried to intervene and make this practice stop
"But fatal accidents then follow those who make a stand
"And there are always off-world men to buy their vacant land."

The roadway leveled off and Boomer sped the crawler on.
Nick said, "That sounds predatory and just downright wrong!
"Can't tariffs be installed to limit off-world food imports?"
Boomer said, "There's no way to enforce it in the courts -

"Even if there were any. So people hunker down
"And make their crops diverse and keep their markets underground.
"Anyway, we're here," he finished, "That's the station's dome."
And through the foggy mist ahead Nick saw his waiting home.

"I'll show you in and introduce you," Boomer said to Nick.
"I've been driving for them since their own driver got sick."
They both dismounted from the crawler, made their way inside
But when the inner airlock opened they were horrified!

The air was thick with smoke and clumps of ash like flakes of snow
Floated in the air currents where ever they might flow.
The stench of burning meat and garlic singed their throat and nose
And both of them stepped back and quickly snapped their helmets closed.

"What the heck has happened here?" was all that Nick could say.
Boomer had a wild look and said, "Let's make our way
"To the common area where someone might explain.
"A barbeque gone bad I'll bet. We'll help put out the flames

"And maybe find a steak or two to salvage from the mess."
But Nick could feel the hackles on his neck signal duress
As Boomer led them from the entry down a corridor.
(He'd smelled an odor similar on Mars just weeks before.)

A few quick steps in gravity just one seventh of Earth
Brought them to an area where there was not a dearth
Of living space for it rose to the top part of the dome
Intending, no doubt, to help Earthers feel more at home.

The ceiling though, could not be seen for all the rancid smoke.
And through the floating ash they saw two figures who had choked
Laying on the floor beside another who had burned.
Nick responded quickly as he felt his stomach churn

And said, "Get respirators for these two fast as you can!"
Boomer, stunned to silence staggered backward, then he ran

The distance to the entry where they stored masks on the wall
While Nick grabbed an extinguisher he saw out in the hall.

In the several seconds that it took to stop the flames
Boomer'd placed a mask on one and called to him by name
While Nick put on the other's and looked closely for some sign
That they had got the masks and brought them oxygen in time.

"He's breathing!" Boomer shouted as the victim coughed and shook
And then in seconds Nick's man gasped on his first breath he took.
Then both the victims tried to scramble from the smoking corpse
As Nick and Boomer tried to reassure them both, of course.

But neither of them listened until meters had been placed
Between them and the body as confusion crossed their face.
Looking back and forth between the body and their guests
Who made emphatic pleas that they had not produced this mess.

About that time three other men walked in the common room
Wearing respirators with bewildered looks of doom.
One asked what had happened and why no alarm had tripped.
Then they saw the smoking body and one of them quipped,

"What the bloody -" and one of the two who just woke up
Said, "He dropped right in his tracks! And then he just blew up!"
They all looked at the suited two who held their hands out stretched
And said, "We just came in the lock and found them, then we fetched

"The respirators for these two and put the fire out."
Then as the half a dozen men each tried to over-shout
The others asking questions one more man walked in the room
And calmed the others down and had things sorted very soon.

"You are Mr. Hallenbeck, the Phased Array intern.
"And Boomer, we know you. Do we know this man who burned?"
"It's Johnny," said the man who Nick had placed the breather on.
"He was feeling ill but hadn't felt that way for long.

"And then he keeled over and white flame blew from his back.
"My God! I've never seen a thing so gory as all that!"
The area was covered with still-smoking residue
Where blobs of flaming phosphorous had scorched the ceiling too.

"What could do that to him? What could burn him up like that?"
The question of the hour had no answer coming back.
And then the man who took control asked, "What did Johnny do
"Right before this happened?" as his gaze fixed on the two

That fell beside him. "Nothing, Sir. He'd just talked on his phone
"And looked a little startled then he dropped and now he's gone!"
By now the air was clearing as the scrubbers did their job.
The man who gave the answers then broke down in little sobs.

The man who took control gave Nick a reassuring glance
And said, "I'm Doctor Bordeaux and I hope you know our plans
"To welcome you did not include a tragedy like this."
"I'm sure they didn't," Nick replied, "Unfortunate at best."

"I'm glad to meet you, Nick, and I'm glad you have arrived,"
Doctor Bordeaux said, "I'm sorry we're not all alive..."
(In an absent manner). Then said, "That did not sound right.
"Forgive me. This has turned into a most upsetting night!

"Perhaps you'd like to stay in town until this all is clear.
"Boomer would be glad to find a billet for you near
"The commissary where there's food and recreation too..."
And then betrayed the slightest glee when Nick declined to:

"It's quite all right, Sir," Nick advised, "I'll help how e'er I can.
"I'm at your disposal. Tell me where to lend a hand."
The Chief Investigator of the station faced toward Nick
And said, "You two are suited up, please go very quick

"To Building Two and bring the extra scrubbers that are there.
"Two should be available. Boomer, show him where.
"Thank you." Then he turned and gave directions to the three
That came into the room before him who left separately.

Boomer turned to Nick as they were walking up the hall
And said, "That is the strangest thing I've ever seen at all.
"I almost lost my dinner in my suit when I saw that.
"This will be some tale to tell at my next bar room chat."

"Phosphorous," Nick mumbled. "What?" asked Boomer as he turned.
"Phosphorous," Nick said again, "It's phosphorous that burned.

"The garlic smell and burning white deposits that were sprayed
"Prove what Doctor Bordeaux should have known but didn't say."

The airlock cycled through and they stepped out into the night.
Boomer led them through the mist to where, far out of sight
Above them in a sweeping arc another building rose;
Not a dome, more like a tower, yellow cloud-enclosed.

"You know," Boomer said as they stepped into the air lock
"This is not the first time men have died on Bordeaux's watch.
"A week ago an accidental fire in the plant
"Took one of the workers who had gone into a rant

"The day before about the way the research interfered
"With atmosphere production quotas and had not been cleared.
"The story has it that he threatened Terran intervention
"But comm links all went down the very hour it was mentioned.

"And then the fire happened and that was the end of him.
"They say there wasn't one scrap left to ship off to his kin.
"And then just hours ago an outdoor flame of some kind charred
"An aircraft in a hanger park just off the lading yard.

"Perhaps you saw it as we left the station a while back.
"The funny thing is that they say there were three sets of tracks
"Leading toward the hanger but just two sets walked away.
"That was all the talk around that sleepy town today.

"Anyway, just watch yourself around Doctor Bordeaux.
"There are lots of things out here that no one seems to know
"Anything about. And by the way, that crispy Johnny?
"He's the driver that got sick. He was my sister's Honey."

The pair of scrubbers were secured and brought back to the dome
And activated near the living quarters that were home
To those who lived and worked there and who welcomed Nick on board
Grateful that he'd come and offered help to clean and more.

Boomer had to take the crawler back to town that night
But neither of them saw a man stash something out of sight
Beneath the crawler's driver's seat then quickly slink away.
It wasn't something one might see one do by light of day.

No one at the atmospheric station saw the flash.
And no one down in Sinlap knew that anything had passed
Until the time that Boomer was to get back into town
But he was often late so no one bothered write it down.

20 Catching Up

Captain Standish chose to put the ship in high orbit
Where most of Rhea's common traffic wouldn't notice it.
The fueling tanker's crew received a healthy premium
To meet them in that orbit and to keep their presence mum.

Selenia was quick to take a shuttle from the ship
(Ostensibly to make a little tourist shopping trip).
Rhea, as defacto center of the Saturn worlds
Didn't have a lot to lure a Martian shopping girl.

But Inmar spaceport was a bustling crossroads of a sort
Where lots of traffic passed including some who came for sport.
Though mostly colonists and exploration survey crews
Came to spend their money or find other things to do.

So as such, perhaps it was the Saturn culture hub
While Martian banks and merchants profited from the hubbub
And Earth and Ganymede and Luna added to the stew
Importing wares and contracting for infrastructure too.

And even though a dozen colonies had set down roots
Inmar housed the embassies and sold the finest suits
For fashion-conscious travelers who weren't seen much elsewhere.
(Five or six resorts had even tried to make it there

For Saturn's mighty girth hung brightly in the western sky
Magnificent by day and bolder still in shadow's night
Shining amber on the rock-rimmed ice beneath the stars
In dim sunlight one fortieth as bright as that on Mars.)

So there beneath the sparkling domes of Inmar City sat
A large casino that helped make Soldana's coffers fat.
Not far from the spaceport nor from city's central dome
(Selenia waltzed in and made casino's penthouse home.)

"Red!" she said, "Forever free!" "Forever free," said he
(When she had tracked him down and passed his comm security.)
"It's been a long, long time," he said, "What brings you out this way?"
"Business matters mostly, but I've spared some time for play.

"Why don't you come take me out for dinner and a drink?
"We should get caught up. I'd like to hear what you might think
"About a venture some old friends are setting up here soon.
"You might like to get in on the ground floor while there's room."

"As it happens," Red replied, "I've got a little time
"And I would thrill to have a pretty lady out to dine."
"Good!" she said, "Come by *The Mine* tonight at seven sharp
"And it will be my treat for old time's sake you handsome shark!"

"Handsome?" he replied, "I know you're not quite that hard up!
"But I will do my best to trim my beard and get cleaned up.
"See you then," he said and winked and put his phone away
While wondering what could have made her come out all this way.

At seven sharp Red and two men bounced through the front doors
Of *Solomon's Mine Casino* (Soldana's place, of course).
Indeed, it mined the gold out of the pockets of the men
Who came to Inmar spaceport for their pay on play to spend.

And spend they did! The prices were exorbitant and rich.
The profits were obscene but costs were too (and that's the hitch).
But those that wanted gaming and great steaks and girls and booze
Would pay to have their fun regardless how much they might lose.

Selenia was dressed in red and sparkled head to toe.
Her black hair in a beehive and her face a golden glow
Beaming with a smile that made the bright lights of the place
Pale in comparison when she saw Red's bronze face.

"Selenia, you never age! You look as sweet as jam!
"Give old Red a hug and tell me I'm the only man
"You've ever had an eye for and you've waited all these years
"For me to come back to your arms and nibble on your ears!"

A loud laugh at the ceiling and a smile wide as his
Brought her to his arms in an embrace that wouldn't give
A gnat wing room enough to beat nor hardly room for air
As she said, "Red, you scoundrel!" and she ruffled up his hair.

"You look good as gold to me, now send your boys to play.
"You won't need them hanging 'round, they'll just be in the way."

With that she gave them each a chip for gaming on the house:
Denominations large enough to make them gape their mouths.

"Git!" Red gave the word to both, "But stick around the Mine."
"Keep your heads about you but enjoy a grand ol' time.
"Capisce?" he asked. "Capisce!" they said and headed for the floor
Where bright lights lit the gaming tables, glamour girls and more.

"That was easy," she remarked, and he said "So am I,
"But feed me first or this old skinny shark might up and die.
"Then tell me why you've come so far. Soldana's not here too?"
"No," she said, "It's just me and I need to talk to you.

"What's your poison, Red? I'll have it sent up where we dine.
"You would have a stout with your steak once upon a time."
"That would be just fine," he said, "And I know that red wine
"You like with yours has got to be old Inmar's most divine."

She smiled as the memories of good times in the past
Washed the faded pictures of the ones that shouldn't last.
Then took his arm and led him to the penthouse up above
Where they could eat in privacy and not fear being bugged.

Solomon's was not the finest restaurant in town,
But in the penthouse fare was just as good as could be found.
And certainly the company was pleasant as could be
As old friends shared a feast and traded happy memories

Of times they'd shared with other friends and foes in days gone by
Some of which would make them laugh and some would tear the eye.
Inevitably Captain Blue came up a time or two.
Selenia then asked directly what Redfeather knew:

"Tell me, Red, have you seen Jules? He said he came this way.
"He had to drop a passenger on Titan for some pay.
"But he was more evasive than his usual old self
"And needed special gear you don't just find on any shelf."

Red set down his fork and hoisted up his mug of stout
And gave Selenia a look that showed he had a doubt
About her motives and sincerity in how she'd asked.
(Counting on their friendship she had skipped her normal tact.)

His eyebrow raised a bit and he reached up and touched his ear.
Selenia assured him they could talk there without fear;
The penthouse was secure and had been swept for any bugs.
Then Red responded candidly, preceded with a shrug:

"Selenia, I've only seen him twice in six long years.
"I was hoping you could shed some light. Do you have fears
"About something he's up to?" Red peered into her dark eyes
And saw that she indeed had fears and wouldn't tell him lies

For only honest deep concern reflected back his way.
Her mask of evening festiveness was clearly put away.
But there was something else that he had not seen there before.
Another layer of concern? Or was it something more?

"We met in deep space just a couple weeks ago to talk.
"He said he might have something that might help us when we stalk
"Predators out in the dark; but he would say no more.
"He asked me to hang loose a while until he knew the score.

"This special gear that he was after; what sort might it be?"
"Magnetics," she replied, "Six-axis kind, specifically."
He cocked an eyebrow up again and slowly shook his head.
"No idea, Love. Could you please pass me the bread?"

Selenia handed the basket; he took out a slice
And dabbed it in his au jus then picked up his fork and knife
And asked, "You see him more than I...?" His question trailed off
The question in his gleaming eyes was clearly quite enough.

Selenia sipped from her wine then leaned back in her chair
And pulled the jeweled pin that let her shake loose her black hair
Then said, "He came to Mars a few weeks prior to meeting you
"But only spent one night because he had so much to do.

"He brought a human implant none of us had seen before
"So Varda could examine it and learn a little more
"Than just the fact it turned its host into a fire bomb
"Then picked up his magnetics and in hours he was gone."

Red's eyes snapped to meet hers when she mentioned the implant
But didn't interrupt. She went on, "He made some small rant

"About another project TerraCorp was working on;
"How time was running out and we might not have very long

"To stop it. My god, Red, what will they think of next?
"Burning men alive with implants placed inside their necks?
"We lost Ansel Pedersen to one and Jules found more
"Somewhere while in transit. Do you know any more?"

"Yes," he said, "He found two of the nasty things with me.
"Two men on my crew infected very stealthily. They were
"Set to trigger by a voice and simple phrase."
"Oh, my word," she said, "So that was you out in deep space?"

The light of understanding came to both and they took sips.
"It was, Selenia. He saved their lives when we docked ships.
"And not a moment soon. Did you receive the sampled voice?"
"I did," she said and looked away by instinct, not by choice.

"It is my brother's voice, Red. The bastard is not dead."
A moment passed in silence as the two both shook their heads.
"I'm sorry, Love. I didn't know. That throws another spin
"On what the Terra Corporation's planning for Titan."

He reached across the table, took her hand and said, "We'll see.
"Does Jules know he's alive?" She answered, "Yes, just recently.
"Match his promise, Red, and if you track my brother down
"Bring him to me well enough to personally drown."

Her eyes bored coldly into his. They burned their message deep.
Redfeather responded that in all faith he'd agree
To bring him to her if he could, but if not he would do
The deed himself if there were no way he could see it through.

"Soldana was concerned for Jules and other interests too.
"He sent me with a cruiser perchance something we could do
"To help even the odds. He knew that Jules was stepping in
"To something to ensure the interests of all we free men.

"But neither of them seemed to know (or tell) what that might be.
"Only that it seemed to involve Titan's destiny.
"And we know what the stakes are, Red. But so many don't care.
"I think Soldana suspects some would wreck it on a dare

"Or snatch the very prize from those who labored there so long.
"Red, if it's my brother there, then it will all go wrong."
She shook her head and looked down at her hands now in her lap.
Red leaned back and wondered too if Jules stepped in a trap.

For he was known to tangle with a tiger on a whim
Driven by a dark streak that for years had driven him.
"We'll find out together, Love." Red studied her sad face.
He could see her deep concern - more than her normal trace.

He broached the thought: "Selenia, have you and Jules twinned?
"I mean, I know you two were great, but did you reel him in?"
Selenia looked up at Red, surrender in her eyes
And said, "I love him dearly and it came as a surprise:

"An epiphany of sorts, I guess that's how it felt.
"The night he came to visit something in me broke and melt.
"I told him how I felt, Red, and I know he loves me
"But he's not finished searching and until then he's not free."

Selenia blinked back a tear, a rare thing seldom seen.
"Ah, Sweet Red, you know me well. Your insight's very keen.
"There's never been just One for you and never One for me,
"But now there is One, Red; but I must wait in line, you see?"

Red studied her sad face and said, "I do see something new.
"You always had frustration cracking our nut Captain Blue.
"And now the cracker's cracked herself and I think it's just grand.
"But Love, you know down deep that you may never get that man.

"I know he loves you as a friend at least as much as I.
"And you know I will love you up until the day I die.
"But he is locked on course and he'll not let things in his way.
"Selenia, I'm sorry but that's all I dare to say.

"Now, catching up was great and dinner was a special treat.
"Especially when shared with someone beautiful and sweet,
"But I should check up on the boys and get back to my ship."
He started to get up but she invited him to sit:

"Stay with me tonight, Red, your boys will be just fine.
"I've sent girls to comfort them and show them a good time.

"Then in the morning I'll ring up a breakfast for we two.
"Perhaps by morning we will have a notion what to do."

He paused and looked into her shining eyes and saw his own.
Then sat again and knew he couldn't leave his friend alone.
He said, "Then we should finish up this little talk we had
"Then maybe have another drink to wash away the sad.

"Yes, Jules is searching and you know he always will.
"Until he finds her or his proof, her shoes you'll never fill.
"Selenia, I really can't suggest what you must do
"But wait - perhaps forever - being just his Number Two."

"Oh, Red, I've not been that. I'm not even Number Three!
"In all these years he's never laid a loving hand on me.
"He flies his ship and looks for her and loves me - that I know,
"Enough in fact to stay away because he'll always go

"In search of her in body or in mind and that's not fair
"To me, he seems to think, and so I'll never keep him there
"On Mars (or anywhere he cares), though I would sell my soul
"To have him take me as his own in part or as a whole."

A silent moment passed as her stark honesty sank in.
Red at first was quite surprised and almost felt chagrin.
She'd made her proud self vulnerable so seldom in the past
And here she'd shown her softer side in ways he hoped would last.

He responded softly, "Love, what would you have me do?
"That's about the sum of how I've always felt for you.
"If there were just the One for me, you know it would be you.
"And if you'd have me in that way, for you I would be true."

Selenia picked up her glass, "Here's to Number Two's!"
"To Numbers' One and Two!" said Red and lifted his glass too.
"Oh Red, take me to bed right now or lose me once for all!"
Then both of them laughed loudly as they answered lust's deep call.

With dinner long forgotten and the moment filled with steam
The two of them took part in playing out their passion dreams
There beneath the penthouse glass entwined in tender clasps
They reveled in each other's glee with lusty moans and gasps.

21   New Friends

Nick was shown his quarters and was taken on a tour
Of the small facility behind the double doors
Where he would have his workspace which was furnished with the gear
That he would need for the array he was to engineer.

Doctor Bordeaux also took him far into the "Maze"
(Within the monstrous tower that rose up into the haze)
Of rows and stacks and columns of gas transformation gear
Where atmosphere production carried on throughout the year.

"We were fortunate to regain access to this place,"
Doctor Bordeaux started, "With restrictions put in place
"On Terra Corporation's people that the Titans set.
"But cooler heads prevailed when they saw what they might get

"If our important research was allowed to carry on:
"The key to building Titan in much less than an eon."
Bordeaux snorted pompously and clasped his hands behind
His over-bearing figure as he boasted and opined,

"The oxygen production that takes place is very good.
"But atmospheric heating will result in such a flood
"Of better processes and such accelerated change.
"I was quite aghast at how so many thought it strange.

"They thought we'd seek to harm the efforts already in place
"To make the climate better and to alter Titan's face.
"But soon we'll have a tool to find the quick way to proceed
"And our assistance will be sought, our work they'll not impede."

"Impede?" asked Nick, "What purpose would it serve to interfere
"With science meant to make conditions so much better here?
"I don't understand. I don't see how it's logical.
"One would think the colonists were far more practical."

"The colonists!" the doctor spat, "They're ignorant buffoons.
"Poorly educated and opinionated too.
"Thankfully there is a cadre here to make their lives
"Meaningful and practical when that bright day arrives -

"When things are put in order. But I digress, don't I?"
"That's quite all right, Sir," Nick remarked and thought, *Who is this guy?*
Clearly he is not the man I corresponded with
Just weeks ago when I embarked upon this little trip.

Who's opinionated here? And who is the buffoon?
Nick said, "I am anxious to produce some work here soon.
"I'll trust the local politics to those who know it best.
"Engineering discipline's the focus of my quest."

Bordeaux smiled broadly and clapped Nick upon the back
With both a condescending and congratulating tact
And said, "You will do well here, Nick. I think you'll fit in fine.
"Come, let us return. Our dawdling wastes my precious time."

With that the Chief Investigator turned and walked away
Expecting Nick to follow as a puppy should obey.
His very body language as he strutted through the Maze
Exuded ego far beyond what Nick considered sane.

By now it was the early evening by local time
And even with the recent tragedy was time to dine.
Some did not show up but most showed just to welcome Nick.
But when the food was ready appetites came back on quick.

Dr. Bordeaux introduced Nick to the other men
And then he left the room before the eating would begin.
Nick raised up an eyebrow which was noticed by a few.
The one called David said, "Bordeaux won't eat with lowly crew."

Snickers here and there were followed with a quiet "Hush!"
Uttered by a nervous man who added, "What's your rush?
"Why are you so anxious to put one foot in the grave?"
Then glanced around the table, "Don't pretend you are so brave."

David threw a wadded napkin at the nervous man.
"Hush yourself, you weasel, or we'll stuff you in the can."
Then turned again toward Nick and offered, "Tinker here's convinced
"That any shot at Bordeaux gets you sliced and diced and minced."

"It does," the nervous Tinker spouted, "Johnny and the rest
"Are proof enough," then focused on a bite of chicken breast

While hunching low over his plate embarrassed and afraid
As if he'd said too much already and might be betrayed.

"Baaaaaa," another man set next to David mimicked sheep
Then added, "Bordeaux's just a two-bit tyrant and as weak
"As any of us while we're stuck in this forsaken hell."
Then turned to Nick and said, "We hope your sentence here goes well.

"I'm Christopher and truly mean it. Welcome to the crew."
And most of all the others gave him verbal welcomes too.
Then conversations turned to broad conjectures on the death
Of Johnny in the common room. Nick just saved his breath.

Later, as he rested in his tiny private room
A knock upon his door announced that Chris and David too
Had brought some beer and asked if they could sit and shoot the breeze
(To get a feel for what the new guy might turn out to be).

"Sure, come in," Nick grinned and offered up his tiny space.
"I would love a beer. I hoped there'd be some at this place."
"Doctor Bordeaux frowns on it. Of that you can be sure,"
David said, "The hypocrite's been seen to take it pure."

"Alcohol, that is," said Chris, "He sucks it down alone
"Then hides inside his quarters and pretends he isn't home."
"At least he used to," David offered, "Lately he has changed.
"He was weird before but recently he just turned strange."

Nick opened the offered beer and took a lengthy swig
And offered, "Any beer is good when its container's big."
His guests grinned and provoked him in a self-demeaning way
Knowing that their cheap beer tasted more like boiled hay.

Chris and David both were Terra Corporation men
Recruited here from Ganymede to research how and when
The atmospheric chemistry would best be altered for
Enhancing greenhouse gasses to increase the temperature.

Nick brought back the subject asking, "When did Bordeaux change?
"The man I corresponded with from Earth before I came
"Seemed nothing like the man that took me on the nickel tour."
Chris and David guessed, "Maybe its five weeks? Maybe four

"Since he became all cocky like he owned this place and us.
"In reality he's just a bureaucratic cuss."
Nick mulled this a bit while swilling down more lousy beer
And asked, "How goes the work? Is a breakthrough growing near?"

"That's another funny thing about this stinking place,"
David said with agitation twisting up his face.
"It seems when we get close to having something we can use
"Bordeaux has it altered and forbids we share the news.

"He insists we direct efforts in a different way
"While he publishes papers droning hogwash Corporate's way."
David looked at Chris who looked at Nick and said, "That's right.
"It's almost like he's sabotaging all for which we fight.

"Many of us have a vested interest in success
"But this clown has been turning all our work into a mess.
"Throw the recent killings in the mix and you can bet
"Many of the people here are worked up in a sweat."

"Killings?" Nick enquired, "Not the accidental kind?"
"Yeah," said David, "Tinker's odd but not out of his mind.
"Johnny was no accident. You saw it for yourself.
"Something burned him up and not stuff we keep on the shelf."

"Phosphorous," Nick said and took another swig of beer.
Chris and David stared at him as he said, "It was clear
"That Doctor Bordeaux knew it too but wouldn't say he did.
"Why would he not mention that was what burned up the kid?"

The three of them sat quietly. Each opened one more beer.
Then Nick enquired, "Do we have a mediscanner here?
"Tinker looked a little feverish at dinner time.
"Maybe he should be checked out to make sure he is fine."

"The closest mediscanner is at Sinlap," Chris replied.
"What's that have to do with Johnny or with Bordeaux's lies?"
"Just a hunch about him," Nick responded with a shrug,
"I was just concerned that he might have a nasty bug.

"Anyway, I figured if our Doctor Bordeaux lied
"About the phosphorous he might know how it got inside

"The building and conceal the truth about that topic too.
"That might be a circumstance to point you toward the truth."

David offered, "Someone asked Bordeaux what caused the flame.
"They told me he said it was an accident, then claimed
"That Johnny had it in his backpack planning an attack
"To sabotage our work and set our progress further back;

"That Johnny was responsible for deaths a week ago
"And it was fortunate his bomb was premature to blow.
"Now, first of all, our Johnny was as gentle as a lamb
"And cared about our progress just as much as any man.

"And second, when we sorted through his personal effects
"His backpack was right there, I know - I was the one who checked!"
David's face was reddening. He took a swig of beer.
Nick said, "From these facts some possibilities appear:

"Bordeaux didn't say all that he knew in one instance.
"He also got another item wrong - perhaps by chance.
"Maybe he was caught up taking charge in that moment?
"But he did not appear surprised at all by the event.

"So, either Doctor Bordeaux knows a lot more than he says
"Or he's in the dark and not inquisitive (at best).
"Or he simply feeds his ego at Johnny's expense.
"Without some proof these charges though, are only circumstance.

"It's hard for me to fathom how a scientist like him
"Could not be curious about a tragedy within
"His own facility and not investigate the mess.
"And so I tend to think the former option fits the best."

"Scientist?" exclaimed the two in unison surprised.
"He is not a scientist or engineer besides!
Chris continued, "He is an administrative hack
"The company sent out to keep the reports flowing back."

"At least that's what we gathered when he came six months ago
"But all he's done is interfere the last few weeks or so."
Nick's look of confusion and surprise was quite profound.
David smiled and said, "He talks the talk, but he's a clown.

"The problem is, he is in charge and nothing we can do
"Will get a bigger boss out here to fire the pompous fool."
"Well," said Nick, "That tends to bring us back to option three
"But his behavior changed in major ways just recently.

"Perhaps his loyalties have switched or someone got to him
"And his new goal is not in line with what it was back then."
Chris and David mulled this over for a swig or two
Then David said, "That makes some sense, but I sure don't know who

"Would fit the bill for there are really no competitors.
"What we do is simple science - just research of course."
Chris chimed in, "Well, there are those who fear we will do harm
"To the planet's chemistry and there was some alarm

"Among the local population when the word got out
"Atomic drilling would commence when we knew without doubt
"The places which were safe; but that could be some years away
"Unless they get some good results with that deep scan array.

"That's where you come in, right?" he waved his beer at Nick.
"Hopefully work on that project doesn't make you sick
"Like the guy before you." He took another swig
And nonchalantly watched as Nick's eyes grew a little big.

"Sick?" Nick asked with some surprise, "What kind of sick was that?"
Chris and David studied him then David said, "Real bad.
"It started with a weakness and a fever for three weeks
"And then he went to Sinlap Medical for some relief.

"But then he disappeared and now we hear that someone's dead;
"Burned up in an outdoor fire is what the rumor said."
Nick set down his beer and looked intently at the two.
"An outdoor fire in nitrogen - at ninety Kelvin too?"

"Yeah," said Chris, "Go figure that. You tell me what it means."
Nick said, "It means someone doesn't share the Titan's dreams.
"When exactly did this sickness start to show in him?"
David said, "Two weeks after the audit's about when."

"That sounds right," said Chris as David's eyes lit up (he coughed).
Then Chris repeated, "Oh, that's right!" as he shared David's thought.

"The auditors from TerraCorp were here six weeks ago.
"That's about when something changed our good Doctor Bordeaux!

"And also when the craziness around this place began."
David said, "I wonder what was said to that old man.
"The audit was a quick one. It took less than a day.
"They spent the night in guest quarters then next day flew away."

"Oh, my gosh," said Chris, "Could we really be that blind?
"Connecting those two dots skipped right on past my silly mind!"
Nick peered keenly at them both and asked, "Are you quite sure
"These auditors were TerraCorp and not from something more?"

Silence ruled the little room but for the flowing air
Rattling the ventilator while each of them stared
At empty space or others' face as questions filled their minds.
Then David broke the silence, "We have no proof of that kind.

"Only doctor Bordeaux and the driver that got sick
"Were present when they came and they arrived and left so quick
"That few of us had any interaction with their team.
"I think for the most part they were pretty much not seen."

Nick looked at the floor. The others finished off their beers.
Chris said, "Anyway, we let you know what goes on here.
"We thought we'd give you more perspective than what Bordeaux might.
"And you have made some points that we can think about tonight."

"See you in the morning," David said (they stood to go
And headed for the doorway) "Something else that you should know:
"The best beer found in Sinlap is at Jonesy's Bar and Grill;
"Porter, stout and lager at room temperature or chilled."

David gave the thumbs up as they walked out of his room
While Chris said they would take him in to Jonesy's very soon.
As Nick prepared for bed he touched his scar without a sound
And thought, *I know exactly what it was put Johnny down.*

22   Candlelight and Flowers

It would be two days until the warden's dinner date.
A package showed up for her that first afternoon quite late
And inside it a lovely dress of velvet black and sleek
With golden buttons down the back cut low and very chic.

Another package was delivered later in the night.
Smaller than the first but heavy, filled with rare delights:
A rosewood box with silver hinges which, when tilted back
Revealed a golden necklace rife with diamonds rare and black

Rimmed with precious opals shaped like dolphins that would gleam
Their rainbow facets warmly round the diamonds that they ringed.
And every little dolphin had two ruby-inlaid eyes
That sparkled in the light like precious dancing fireflies.

Set beside the necklace were the matching ear ring set.
Identical in brilliance to the larger piece and yet
Created with a sparkle that would highlight any eyes
Fortunate to shine with them in any kind of light.

In the morning yet another package came to her.
Containing not a box but just a leather-bound ledger
Numbered as just one among a series on a shelf
Which listed assets on a dozen worlds with himself

(The warden) as the title holder: mines and shipping yards,
Factories and farms on Earth and Mercury and Mars.
Then as the dinner time was growing closer on that day
Another box was left to help her see things more his way:

Crafted of the finest ebony and hinged in gold,
Lined with silk and halfway filled with trade coins rare and old
On top of which a long-stemmed rose of red was placed with care
And tucked inside the lid a receipt showing that the fare

For first class round-trip berthing on a ship for her was paid
Departing Rhea in a week, best speed for Ganymede!
A note was wrapped around the thornless stem of that red rose
Written by the warden said, "Go buy yourself some clothes."

Of all the Saturn system's worlds Rhea had the most
To offer in the way of shopping, but was just a ghost
Of what existed on the worlds closer to the sun
Where more diverse economies made greater shopping fun.

(The Saturn system had a booming new economy
But all the worlds around it were still in their infancy.
Utility was all the fashion everywhere one went
Except perhaps at Rhea's spaceport where money was spent

In crazy quantities by men who came to let out steam
And others who were passing through in pursuit of their dreams.
The "Wild West" described the atmosphere by those who came
But those who stayed were changed and never would be quite the same.)

Incredulous to some degree, Renee was still impressed.
Even if one-tenth were true of what his book expressed
The warden's wealth was greater far than great kings of the past
Though most of it removed from those whom he'd made breathe their last.

But all the wealth of empires was not what Renee desired.
Only he who ruled her heart her passions could inspire
And though there was no outward evidence he was alive
Their story was not over (this she knew down deep inside.)

This certainty gave strength to her and put steel in her nerves
And even edged her appetite when dinner would be served
For she would play whatever role she needed to succeed
In seeing that bright day when she could meet her heart's true need.

And so she put the black dress on and fixed her golden hair
And dolled herself up carefully so that the men would stare
Beyond the precious jewels at the beauty she could show
And Warden would not doubt it was for him her choice would go.

And so this dinner date for her turned out to be quite fun.
Warden met her at the door and looked as if someone
Whom he had never met before was standing in the door
Then caught himself in wonderment and tried to stare no more.

"I've known you as a woman of exceptional beauty.
"But until now you've never shown much of that side to me.

"In fact, I think you've tried to hide it and I understand
"Your reasoning behind it, but my Dear, you're looking grand!"

"Thank you," said Renee as she returned his grateful smile.
"You look very nice yourself though I'm not up on styles.
"But we can set our own styles, can't we?" she asked with a grin
And turned herself around and stood close looking up at him.

"We can," he said, "We will in fact if that is what you'd like.
"Renee, I can't express to you my great joy and delight
"That you have turned a corner and have warmed a bit toward me."
She looked into his eyes, "I know it is hard to believe,

"But I have come to realize that you have rescued me
"In more ways than the obvious; in fact you've set me free
"From holding some things in the past much closer than I should."
The warden searched her eyes a moment then replied, "That's good.

"We'll talk about that more, but first let's have a sip of wine
"And then we'll have some dinner and a little leisure time."
Renee returned the ledger book into the warden's hand
And said, "Some entries here intrigue me as to future plans.

"Especially your holdings of the ranch land on the Earth.
"Western North America's the land of my own birth.
"But that too is behind me. Shall we have that sip of wine?
"I feel a bit like celebrating - it's been a long time."

She turned and walked into the room a bit then turned again
And said, "You've changed the place a lot. It looks much bigger than
"The last time you invited me." She paused and made a frown
Then said, "I didn't treat you well at all," and then looked down.

Warden said, "You didn't need to." She said, "Yes, I did.
"Promoting me gave me the chance to see more than the kid
"I seemed to be portraying these few years since my life changed.
"It brought me to my senses, so to speak. I found it strange

"That I was such a cripple." Warden poured two glasses full.
She added as he gave her one, "I never was that dull
"Before." They both took sips then Warden said, "It's not so odd.
"The trauma you endured should put one in a gloomy fog.

"A mourning time is natural. It takes some time to heal.
"But when the wound grows distant we wake up and see what's real.
"You owe no apology. In fact, I should have known
"A woman of your strength would not so soon forget her home.

"I feel very fortunate the fates brought you to me.
"You have a knack I do not have and it's paid handsomely.
"But let's forget all that for now and share a special meal.
"And yes, I cleaned the place up some, it has a nicer feel

"But obviously lacks a woman's touch, don't you think?"
She gave a laugh, and Warden took a sip and gave a wink.
"I am not a decorator and don't really care
"So much about such mundane things. I'm fine most anywhere."

Renee strolled 'round the room and turned again the warden's way
And said, "The work I did for you was not just for the pay.
"It brought the taste of order and control back to my thoughts.
"It's been a long time since I've tasted it and I'd forgot."

The warden watched her take a slow sip from her glass of wine
And take a few steps closer with her smile gone this time.
A look of stern ambition crossed her face as she drew close.
The jewels on her breast gleamed brightly as her free hand rose

And rested lightly on his chest as if to tell his heart
A common point of kinship from this point could have its start.
His dark eyes narrowed slightly as her gaze crept up to his
Then with a softness in her voice she said, "That's how it is.

"I know you well enough to know that you know what I mean."
Renee looked in the warden's eyes and saw the knowing gleam
Then said, "I liked that flavor very much in years gone past.
"Perhaps there is a chance that I have found my home at last -

"Perhaps." she said again as her sly smile sparkled through.
"Perhaps," the warden said and he produced a smile too.
"However," he continued, "That's completely up to you.
"Your future's in your hands and I await what you will choose."

Renee stepped back and took another long sip from her wine
And said, "Thank you, Warden. I thought I should take the time

"To clarify some things that have been fresh upon my mind
"And clear the air about them for your peace before we dine."

Warden nodded understanding, "Thank you very much.
"I must admit I was surprised when you alluded such.
"Now, let's enjoy our dinner and relax and take the time
"To simply be companions and enjoy this splendid wine!"

"Agreed!" she said and took his offered arm and walked the space
That took them to his dining room where seats were set. And placed
Upon the table flowers fresh and candles burned with cheer,
Both of which seemed out of place and alien for here

Beneath the hollow rock and ice where men and women slaved
Just yards away with little hope that they'd see better days.
But she felt great encouragement that she would find a way
To alter Warden's plans to bring them to a tragic fate.

Candle light and flowers (which were very rare indeed)
Set the tone in Warden's quarters where the two would feed
On thick chateaubriand preceded by Dungeness crab
Imported from Enceladus where Warden said he had

Controlling int'rest in a fishery beneath the ice
That exported its produce to who could afford the price.
"The best available still comes from Earth," the warden said
"But on short notice Saturn's wares will have to do instead."

He winked at her and seated her then took the other chair
Across the table where he cast his eyes over her hair
And face and told her once again how lovely she appeared
"And frankly, Renee, I am very glad that you are here!"

"Thank you, Warden, I am very glad to be here too.
"I was looking forward very much to dine with you
"And thank you for the gifts you sent and for the trip away.
"You've given me your trust and that is more than any pay."

Warden looked into her eyes and said, "Indeed it is.
"But you, My Dear, are valued far beyond whatever risk.
"Please, let's talk about the future after your return.
"In the mean time there is more of you I'd love to learn

"And you of me, no doubt, but we do not have need to rush.
"The steak will be here soon so eat your crab, please and hush!"
He gave a charming smile that she'd never seen before.
And she was shocked to find that she was thinking there was more

To this man than perhaps she'd guessed in all these years of late
Maybe there were qualities much deeper than his hate?
Where did that seductive thought come from? she asked inside
The wine, Renee, the wine! How much of that have you imbibed?

She shook it off internally and smiled back at him
Then both of them with relish took their crab legs and dug in.
The dinner was superb as only Warden could arrange
And it was nice for both that their relation wasn't strained

For both had made unspoken contracts on the middle ground
That their relationship was fresh from when she'd come around
And finally accepted that her husband had been killed.
"Don't hold that against me, Warden. Know that I am thrilled

"That you have had such patience and have waited for my heart
"To catch up to reality and set the past apart."
Her eyes were smiling at him past the candles' yellow light
And he could see in her blue eyes a spark of raw delight.

But then they softened somewhat and she looked down at her meal.
He watched her for a moment then he asked, "How do you feel?"
She looked up at the ceiling then she scanned the wider view
And said, "So much is changing, I was wondering 'bout you?"

Her gaze alighted on his face; he chewed a bit of meat
Then set his fork aside and from his pocket pulled a sheet
Of paper not much bigger than the palm of someone's hand.
He then produced a pen and wrote on it with scrawling hand

And held it up so she could see it: "Fifty-Two", it said.
He put it in the candle flame and slowly shook his head,
"Your past is gone, Renee. And I hope you truly see
"The path I took for both of us will make you truly free.

"Nothing for me changed for I've admired you from the start.
"That first day on Miranda I believe you stole my heart.

"Forgive me for the hardship that you suffered for a while
"I do believe your tears will be replaced with many smiles.

"I know mine will," he winked and let the burning paper fall.
Renee stood up and moved beside him standing straight and tall.
He looked up at her startled as she slowly bent her frame
And kissed him lightly on the forehead, "You are not to blame."

Warden almost choked as she returned and took her seat
And used her fork to stab and eat another piece of meat.
She didn't lift her eyes to his until she took a sip
Of wine then used her napkin daintily to dab her lips.

He was watching her. She saw the hunger in his eyes.
Instinctively she knew he'd feed his lust with any lie
But also she could sense that there had been a power shift.
She could cause his spirits now to fall or make them lift.

But she'd not let him know she knew it. She would walk the line
And try to keep him at arm's length to buy a bit more time.
"Dinner was delicious, Warden. Food was tasty too,"
She smiled and added, "Thank you too for burning Fifty-Two."

He had finished eating, set his fork down on his plate.
Then looked at her intently, said, "Renee, it's getting late.
"You should get your rest. There is a ship tomorrow night
"Leaving here for Rhea. That will be the only flight.

"And I would like you on it. There will not be any more
"Until I leave to meet you after your trip to the store."
He smiled wide and said, "We'll meet on Rhea when you're back.
"Renee, when you return we'll dress in purple, not in black."

They both stood up and Warden took her hands both in his own
And gently pulled her toward a couch instead of toward her home.
She feigned to swoon a moment blaming it on too much wine
Then asked if they might sit together for some quiet time.

The warden's eyes betrayed his inner twitch of pure delight.
He said, "Renee, I'd love it if you'd stay here for the night."
She pulled the jeweled pin that let her golden hair fall free
And lightly shook the lovely waves loose with a sigh of glee.

Then resting on the couch she kicked her dainty slippers off
And leaned against the warden's chest who strained a tiny cough
And said, "Please make yourself at home." She said, "I think I have."
Then turned her lovely face toward his and whispered, "And I'm glad."

He scanned her face a moment then he clumsily applied
A kiss upon her forehead as her stomach wrenched inside.
His greedy arms encircled her. She stretched to meet his lips
With hers and then she held up short and rolled away her hips.

Standing up, she took his hand then slowly sat back down.
Her knees together, facing him she said, "Please don't frown."
She put his hand between her knees just halfway up her thighs.
He could feel her warmth and for a moment closed his eyes.

And then she bowed her head and said in almost whispered tones,
"I can feel a conflict aching deep inside my bones.
"Though I am elated and a celebration's due
"There is a time of mourning that my heart needs to go through.

"For in my mind my husband has been dead only three days.
"Give me time to get past this before you have your way."
Her blue eyes in the dim light were dilated, dark and deep.
Warden fell into them as his lust burned hot with greed.

But his response was measured; he had waited for this long.
Just a bit more patience until she'd to him belong!
"I know your taste for life awakened and you've heard my call.
"I know you need your time - you are a woman, after all.

"And I appreciate that very much. You take your time.
"For when the time is right I know we'll work things out just fine."
She smiled and pulled his hand up, gave its back a little peck
Then looked at him and wobbled some then in the couch slumped back.

The warden felt her hands let go as she said. "Too much wine!"
Warden saw her breathing slow, repeated, "...work out fine."
He knew love was unspoken but the tokens were in place.
He reached over her chest and brushed the hair out of her face.

Then stood and gently pulled her legs up on the couch to rest
And softly ran his hands up them and touched one of her breasts.

Then stiffly walked away, his throbbing need an irritation
And whispered in a microphone commands (not invitations):

"Send number Two Hundred Ten and get her here right now.
"And while you're at it send One Thirty. I have rows to plow."
Renee had feigned her dozing and she'd heard the Warden's words
And rather than relief, her stomach churned now even worse.

But she would sleep there for the night (the couch in fact was soft)
Warden came back in the room (she heard his stifled cough)
And draped a blanket over her then closed the salon door.
And after that the whole night through she heard not one sound more

Until the household servants made the morning clean-up rounds.
Renee stood up and saw that Warden still was not around.
The doorway to his bed chamber was bolted from within.
(She shuddered as she thought how close she'd come to going in!)

Then after a quick breakfast that a servant girl had brought
She headed for the door but Warden came and she was caught!
His hair was in a mess and he was putting on a robe
And she could smell the musk of what he'd done (she didn't probe)

But fixed a smile on her face and thanked him once again
Then stepped out through his quarters door as he held to her hand.
She mustered up her will and turned her face again toward his.
And pulled his head down to her own and gave his cheek a kiss.

Turning toward the walkway with her hair draped down one side
She noticed that Hidalia happened by and couldn't hide
The look of shock and pure disdain that etched her reddened face
On seeing her friend kiss the man and sneak out of his place.

Renee was powerless! She couldn't speak to her defense.
Hidalia had been crushed and Renee must keep up pretense.
Warden watched her walk away and turn back from her friend.
Renee's eyes flushed with bitter tears, their friendship at an end.

Later in her quarters as she changed her clothes and packed
Preparing for the trip to Rhea Renee nearly cracked.
Desperate to reach her friend with words of explanation
But knowing she'd be spied on and it might cause some suspicion.

She had to pull her strength from every fiber of her soul
(Knowing that the life of every person was her goal)
So she could let her go. She had to have faith in her friend
Whose intimate instincts should know what Renee couldn't send.

Curious, she thought, *Where did I get that little scratch?*
She noticed it while folding clothes she'd placed upon her lap.
Just above her navel barely seen in light this dim
A centimeter long, there was a red mark on her skin.

* * * * *

Captain Blue was not accustomed to biding his time
Without the benefit of something to distract his mind.
The down time he had promised to his crew in Xanadu
Was great for them but as for him he had little to do.

And so he watched the ship and worked on minor maintenance.
But that night in the galley by a very remote chance
As he cleaned out a cabinet where, stowed far in the rear
A pair of unique goblets knocked - their sound rang loud and clear.

In the silence of the galley memories flashed back
Of when that pair goblets filled with sweet wine were tossed back
By he and she to mark their wedding day so long ago
And all these years he'd kept them safe where ever he might go.

The vision was so real! He saw his precious golden bride
Exactly as he saw her on that day of joy and pride.
But this time there were tears that marred her eyes of radiant blue.
Tears that screamed of sorrow - not of joy as they used to.

The pain and shock he felt pierced through him like a burning coal.
There were no doubts within him she was near but his long goal
Of finding her was slipping like fine sand through fingers clenched.
The sudden knowledge time was short sparked an electric flinch.

Then back into the present his emotions let him slip.
The duster he was holding nearly crushed from his tight grip.
And then with tears of hopelessness he knelt down on the floor
And prayed, *Oh God, please keep her safe as just one favor more!*

* * * * *

It was late that afternoon when Renee heard a knock
Upon her quarters door and low outside some muffled talk.
She opened it to see Hidalia shaking like a leaf
And standing close behind her was her beau, the Sergeant Steve.

Renee's eyes welled up tears again. Hidalia searched them deep
For several seconds then relaxed and said, "Now I can sleep.
"I know your heart, Renee. I know that there is more to you
"Than what might seem the obvious, whatever you might do."

Hidalia's smile said everything and then they turned to go
But Renee gasped a teary laugh and said, "Hidalia, no!
"Wait, I mean...," she held her hand up, walked back in her room
A moment then returned and held a sweater out, "For you.

"It has warm pockets you will like," she said then closed the door.
Barring her two visitors - she dared say nothing more.
She leaned her back against the door and sobbed a silent prayer,
Oh, God, I thank you so much for that dear friend and her care!

Hidalia slowly turned and walked away from Renee's door
Knowing that their friendship was as strong as e'er before.
"Put it on," said Steve, "That shade of red looks great on you.
"It looks to be real wool and that's a treasure 'round here too!"

Hidalia put the sweater on and felt the warm rich wool
Form an instant barrier against the cavern's cool.
"It's nice," she said, "I wonder why she gave it suddenly?"
She plunged her hands into the pockets then looked up at Steve,

"Let's go somewhere private," as she steered their path into
A brightly lighted corridor where they were out of view.
Standing close, she pulled a folded note she felt inside
The pocket where Renee had placed it secretly to hide.

A rough sketch of a map was scrawled which showed a corridor
And hasty words which noted the disabled view room door:
"...there are spacesuit lockers. You must get two while you can.
The time is short. I know there is a termination plan."

Hidalia's face flushed white. She slipped the folded note to Steve
Who glanced both ways then read it and became instantly peeved.
Hidalia asked, "Do you know where to find this corridor?"
He nodded 'yes' and into halves the note he quickly tore.

Giving half to her he said, "Eat this," then ate his own.
Hidalia did and noted that they still were quite alone
Then said, "There must be more that she did not have time to say."
Steve said, "We will get those suits before the end of day."

23   Off-Leash!

The hours labeled 'night' had come and brought the time the flight
Would leave the hidden colony and Warden's oversight.
(At least that's what Renee would like to think but she knew well
That Warden's reach was lengthened by the very hounds of hell).

She locked her quarters door behind her. Warden took her hand
Then off they went along the way discussing some work plans
Though Warden seemed dismissive of the work things that were said
And as the hallways narrowed Renee skipped a step ahead.

Warden lagged behind her by four steps - or maybe five
And when she turned the corner to her horror and surprise
She saw Steve and Hidalia at the corridor's far end
Carrying two spacesuits (Steve turned 'round and saw her then).

In desperation Renee turned and crashed on Warden's chest
An accident designed to hinder his forward progress.
And there, one step before the turn she laughed and begged excuse
While holding Warden close she added, "Why don't you come too?"

"You know I am excited to escape this tired rock.
"I'd love to share some time away from here for us to talk."
She stood in close and let him take her arms both in his hands
As he said, "I would love to but requirements of my plans

"Demand that I remain here for another week or two.
"Enjoy your trip away and when you're back I will meet you
"On Rhea as we planned. Now, the time is very short
"Before the ship departs and I would be a poor escort

"If I let you be late," he said as he released her arms
And they both turned the corner and her fear and great alarm
Evaporated as she saw no trace of her two friends.
Apparently they'd made it through the door at the far end.

Then halfway down the corridor Renee and Warden turned
Into the second corridor where with a glance she learned
That her two friends had freed the lock Renee before had jambed
And so the indicator now showed 'locked' like it were planned!

Sweat had beaded slightly on her neck as they had turned
The corner, but her dread turned to elation and the burn
Of worry was extinguished when inside she saw two notes
Explaining spacesuit maintenance Steve thoughtfully had wrote.

For two were missing from the suit racks spaced along the wall.
She watched but Warden didn't seem to notice them at all.
Apparently the tags that noted maintenance were fine;
A detail his men handled, not worth wasting his own time.

And then perhaps the view outside made his attention slip?
It was a draw for her at least, the landscape and the ship
A magnet for the eyes of those who outside rarely see.
But either way the die was cast and where it fell would be.

The view this time was lighted by the cold and distant sun.
The memory of warmth enticed her all the more to run
But icy shadows of the ship so dark and starkly cast
Reminded with a chill of Warden's threat and her great task.

Though representing liberty (the sweetest thing she'd seen)
It wasn't elegant - there wasn't one attractive thing
About the ugly shuttle: it was squat with spindly legs
Protruding from a framework filled with tanks that looked like eggs.

Designed to make short hops between the moons and travel light
It had no skin or wings required for atmospheric flight.
The cabin had small staterooms but the cargo hold was large;
A ship designed in most respects to be a lightweight barge.

But any ship would do to take her far away from here.
Once on Rhea it would not be hard to disappear
And even easier when she arrived at Ganymede
Where she could contact friends and get on with her deepest need

If he were still alive (though she had little doubt he was)
But after six long years (which seemed an almost endless pause
That cruelly slashed their lives in twain when things had seemed their best)
So duty to the captives would now face its strongest test.

Warden pressed the combination on the airlock door
Which opened to the boarding bridge mated to the floor

That stretched out to the crew compartment on the waiting ship
Convenient for fresh produce or passengers to slip.

And as it opened wide for her the passageway air's chill
Sent excitement through her legs and back with such a thrill
She jumped involuntarily into the air a bit
Which caused Warden to laugh as he turned just in time for it.

"I see you are excited," Warden said, "And I must know
"Your thoughts in these last minutes that we have before you go.
"This is your opportunity to free yourself from me.
"I've given what you wished. I've given you your liberty."

The darkness of his stare was deeper than she'd seen before.
She felt that he could see right through her subterfuge, and more
Than that he might have second thoughts about letting her go
For he knew she knew things that he'd want no one else to know.

And all he had to do was press a switch to decompress
The boarding bridge when she went in (if he felt some distress)
To terminate the risk she represented with one stroke
For it would take just seconds for her body to explode.

But she knew too that she held his attention and his lust
And she believed he thought that she would honor this new trust.
So with some confidence she moved in close and took his hand
And said, "You have. And when I'm back you'll know you are my man."

She squeezed his hand and winked then turned and stepped on through the lock
Then turned around as if there were something that she'd forgot.
She took the warden's hand again and pecked him on the cheek
And said, "Now you be good until we meet in a few weeks."

With that she stepped back in the lock and Warden closed the hatch.
She hopped into the boarding bridge and heard the exit latch.
A sinking feeling flooded her but sternly she moved on
Stifling a panic held at bay for far too long.

But soon she reached the ship and with a shudder of relief
Was helped aboard by Warden's pilot and the payload chief.

The shipment had been loaded and she was the last to board
And when she reached the crew deck she looked outside Warden-ward.

She could see him watching through the view-room's window panes
And he could see her in the ship's red light before the flames
Ignited in the engines and his precious cargo leapt
Into the starry sky while she on board broke down and wept.

24   Job Well Done

After a quick breakfast in the morning Nick dug in
With fervor to the notes the missing man had left for him.
He learned that his approach to running intersecting planes
Was simply to increase their size to boost emission range.

But there was an idea brought up in Nick's old research
On Earth to make a grid of multiples that could be perched
Between a fixed array of simple magnetic dipoles
Phased and balanced in a dance by robotic controls.

This grid array of Nick's design was different than the tubes
They'd proven at Pandora with the scheme of Captain Blue.
There would be no chance of gamma lasing or such things
Nor the scanning power Captain's tubes were shown to bring.

A small set of magnetics were provided at the site.
The mathematics were complete and simulated right.
Not only was it more compact than what they had before
But gave emission values increased by a dozen score

Above what they'd recorded at the big Saturn array.
Nick knew also this design would steer their thoughts away
From any inkling of the Gamma Laser from the plan
Devised by Captain's crew if it should fall in evil hands.

And he knew that it would. He knew there were more than two spies
(Obviously more than two beside him who had died.)
And it was clear that there were more than two factions afoot
Whose interests exceeded cost of life or gold or good.

With the data from the tests the man before him ran
Nick could circumvent much of his validation plan.
So soon the day arrived when he transmitted his update
To workers who configured gear at Saturn's big array.

And so he planned to celebrate this milestone of his task
And went to Chris and David's section thinking that he'd ask
If they would like to go with him to Sinlap for some beer
And burgers at the grill but they were both bereft of cheer.

Word had made its way that on the night Nick had arrived
A crawler had exploded and young Boomer had been fried.
It was coming clear to them that someone had decreed
No one would be left alive at this facility.

"If that were the case," Nick whispered, "All the reason more
"To get some beers and figure how to even up the score.
"Get a crawler ready and let's leave this place tonight.
"I for one will not be going down without a fight."

Chris's eyes grew narrow, David's smile opened wide
As he said, "We don't need a crawler for that little ride.
"It's faster in this gravity to walk that little stretch.
"A crawler's just for heavy gear or newbies we must fetch."

And so the three of them packed up a little bit of gear
Then suited up to walk to Jonesy's for a little beer.
This would be the first time Nick would walk for very long
Across a land so alien to what he had lived on.

(Not that it was really walking - more like hops and skips;
In Titan's lower gravity, much better on the hips!)
On foot the seven miles would take twenty minutes max
But with Nick's inexperience they'd take the mountain pass.

Instead of bounding rock-to-rock the way the locals might
Their path would take the road Nick did on his arrival night.
But this time there was daylight and the yellow clouds and mist
Would not obscure the view so much - he'd see what he had missed!

Not that there was really all that much that came to view
Beyond a yellow plain of rocks and ice with very few
Evidences for activities beyond the scope
Of those left from construction of the station as he'd hoped.

For Nick was deeply curious of seeing the terrain
As nature had created it before it had been changed.
But in less than two minutes they had left the site behind
A tiny speck within the vastness untouched by mankind.

Nodules and lumps of ice and yellow frost and dust
Passed beneath their feet as they ascended toward a crust

Of ice atop the hills beyond which Sinlap lay in wait
With life support and comfort and a tavern open late.

Nick was quite surprised to see a tiny running stream
Between some hills down in the lowest part of a ravine.
Chris explained, "It's water, yes. When in eutectic mix
Ammonia keeps it liquid even chilled as low as this.

"Most streams you will see are methane. But at times you'll find
"Ammonia-water leaking from the ground near caves or mines."
Nick considered this and said, "There's much I'd like to know
"About the wonders of this world before my time to go."

"It's just a frozen hell," said David, "I'll be glad to leave
"And get back where it's warmer and there's light enough to see."
"Someday there will be more light," said Chris, "And more heat too
"Once we get the research done and know what we must do

"To get the atmospheric greenhouse layers tuned and meshed
"And get the water cycle fixed and clean this methane mess."
"Not if Bordeaux gets his way," said David with a snort.
"I read all the crap he wrote in his latest report."

The three of them came 'round a corner and just down the hill
Came upon the wreckage where young boomer had been killed.
(At least that was the story that had made its way to them.)
And when they reached the crawler all three of the men climbed in.

Though "in" perhaps is not the word - the canopy was gone
Shattered in a hundred pieces, some near and some long.
The driver seat obliterated and the floor beneath
But not a single piece of Boomer's cryosuit was seen.

"There should be a remnant even if they took him home.
"A piece of suit or clothing or a bit of blood or bone.
"But nothing in the area confirms that he was here,"
Said Chris when they'd examined all the terrain that was near.

The other two agreed but didn't offer further words.
They checked the time and turned their steps to take them Sinlap-wards
And in a dozen minutes saw the outskirts of the town
And talked of eating burgers and the beer to wash them down.

Warden touched the face of his communicator pad
To verify the status of the black ship that he had
Arriving only moments after Renee's ship had left.
Then glancing up he smiled as the sky became bereft

Of stars as one great hull as black as death itself set down
Within a cloud of dust kicked up from off the frozen ground.
The sleek lines of the ship were hard to make out in the dark
Other than by where it blocked a star field's tiny sparks.

With detached satisfaction he admired the deadly ship
Which stealthily for seven years allowed his men to slip
Unseen between the planets and unnoticed in the skies
With which he'd wrecked a hundred ships - two thousand men had died.

His hands were clasped behind his back. A dim red ring appeared
Which grew into an airlock as its outer door swung clear.
The automated boarding bridge extended to the ship.
It locked and pressured up then through the bridge he lithely slipped.

Technically a business trip, for him a pleasure cruise.
His personal attention on receipt of sudden news
That someone he had bought had failed him in a simple task
Would bring his wrath like lightning and that one would breathe his last.

In only moments after that red airlock's door had closed
The hulking monster belched its flame then rapidly it rose
Into the silent sky beyond the sight of mortal eyes
Where deadly in its purpose it would stalk unwary lives.

25   Jonesy

The eight full days of daylight were now fading into dusk.
The eight-day dark of night was coming on (ever it must)
As Titan swung its steady course around the mighty rings
Of Saturn in the harmony the system's orbits sing.

And so the yellow mist was now a dimmer orange haze
As Nick and his companions found the door of Jonesy's place
And shed their suits with thirsts and appetites alive and set
Planning to enjoy the most of this, Nick's first break yet.

Jonesy's bar had triple airlocks facing on the street
And lockers for envirosuits and mats to clean the feet
Within an inner foyer that Nick learned was standard fare
For all the public buildings built to keep out Titan's air.

The place appeared much bigger on the inside than the out
As all the buildings seemed to be on Titan he'd checked out.
Built beneath the surface as defense against the winds
Expected when the atmospheric changes would begin.

(Though no one really knew at this point when or how they would.
But still the locals dug in deep and built their buildings good.
For those who planned to stay expected there would come a time
When tremors, winds and torrents would arise but they'd be fine.)

And so the entrance airlocks into Jonesy's were beneath
A shelter built of ice along the north side of a street
That wasn't far away from either airport or downtown
And there were always folks that came to eat or hang around.

Another item Nick discovered was that much of town
Was tied into a covered walkway anchored to the ground
Which formed a loop with two cross-corridors where one could stroll
Safe inside and pressurized when downtown one might go.

But Jonesy's wasn't tied to that; the place pulled business in
Without the need to spend the funds for townies to loop in.
Everyone that came there knew it was the best around
And didn't mind to suit up for the walk and then strip down.

The atmosphere was nice in Jonesy's - lots of wood inside!
The most, in fact, that Nick had seen since starting this space ride.
Mars had more than you might think but out here in the cold?
The fees to transport just the bar had cost a stack of gold!

Nick felt instant comfort coming in to Jonesy's place.
The ambiance was like an Irish pub launched into space
But spread out like a saloon or a roadhouse of the west
With motifs of Australia (and the beer was Sinlap's best).

Jonesy's claim to fame though, were the hamburgers he served.
Nowhere else on Titan could the beef beneath the curves
Of fresh-baked buns be fresher than what Jonesy guaranteed
For he'd the only ranch on Titan that was raising beef!

True, they were not corn-fed cows from Earth's green sprawling plains.
And true, the only sun they saw were artificial rays
From fixtures mounted high up in the caverns where they grazed
On stubble from the hops and barley that old Jonesy raised.

And though there weren't enough of them to export much from town
There were plenty for the locals that lived all around.
(From time to time a surplus beef might ship to Xanadu
Where premiums were paid because the sources were so few.)

And premiums were paid for other products cows produced.
Dairy was a money maker but few would reduce
Their precious few of milk cows for a burger or a roast
So that was Jonesy's niche, although of it he wouldn't boast

For he was not the kind to air his laundry on the line
And kept his cards close to his chest enjoying this short time
When competition in that market was easy to beat
Knowing that the time would come when others raised more meat.

But if while in the company of those who he could trust
And topics dear to him came up then he was prone to bust
Wide open with the facts and tell it just the way he saw it
(For those he didn't like though, Jonesy wouldn't spare a minute.)

"Arvo, mates," said Jonesy as they came into the room.
He stood behind the bar wiping some mugs washed up from noon.

And then he did a double take and said, "Well, I'll be stuffed!
"I figured you had Buckley's chance to come good. Well enough!"

Jonesy looked Nick up and down and said, "You found some mates.
"Could do better but they pay their docket - sometimes late."
He cast a leering eye at David, who pulled out a coin
And plunked it on the bar and said, "G'day Jonesy, start pouring!"

Jonesy started filling mugs with beer the hue of honey.
"Chocka chook or smashed of plonk you're drinking from the dunny?"
"Chicken?" David said, "I thought they fed us dunny rat!
"The dingo piss that they call beer is even worse than that."

Jonesy placed their mugs and said, "Three middies of the latest.
"I think she's a ripper. Give her a burl now, be honest."
Nick looked quizzical and said, "Uh, what?" and took his beer.
David winked, "You'll soon learn how they sling the slang 'round here."

Jonesy smiled and leaned in close as Nick began to fidget.
"Ya don't savvy strine as she's spoke, then is it?
"No worries, sport, I'll cork it," Jonesy smiled and wiped the bar
Then turned to Chris and asked, "Have you three blokes come very far

"Or just from that old spook shop where you work for Dizzy Bee?
"His 'roos are loose in the paddock, if you cotton what I mean."
Jonesy made the circle motion round his pock-marked ear
Then pulled a pencil from behind the other as he peered

At each of them and asked, "Now tell me what your pleasure be.
"Sangers, bangers or burgers, sports? For Nick it will be free."
"Burgers all around, I think," said Chris and looked at Nick
Who nodded affirmation then reached for a pretzel stick.

He winked at Nick, "Now you two blokes, I ought to charge you double.
"The little row you got in last month caused a bit of trouble.
"That cheeky yobbo had it coming though, so we'll be square
"Since Boomer did a bang-on job repairing those three chairs."

The three of them looked down when Jonesy mentioned Boomer's name.
Chris remarked, "With Boomer gone the town won't be the same."
"Gone?" asked Jonesy, "Where's he going? He said naught to me."
David said, "You didn't hear? He bought the farm last week!"

"Crikey!" Jonesy snorted, "I'll just ask him how he did it.
"He's out back in the loo and should be back here in a minute."
"He's here?!" Chris spouted, "We heard he was taken in a hit
"When something in the crawler he was driving blew to bits."

"Nah, the Boomer's fine beside some frostbite on his bum.
"That bodgy crawler cost big bikkies but it's never run
"The way it should. He almost come a gutser that's dead set.
"The bloody crawler carked it so he hoofed it in, you bet.

"Boomer! Get your arse out here!" he shouted toward the rear.
Then shortly from the kitchen Boomer's ruddy face appeared
And joyfully the visitors were every bit a twitter
Asking how he managed to escape becoming litter

Scattered 'cross the landscape like the crawler's canopy
Or vaporized as it appeared befell the driver's seat.
Boomer eyed the three of them with more than some suspicion
But then he shook it off knowing with great appreciation

That these were friends and genuine concern poured from their eyes.
He said, "Well it was just not in the cards for me to die.
"The crawler's engine stopped and I knew it was late in town.
"I didn't want to radio and wake those who were down

"And so I started walking, but before I got too far
"The crawler went 'Kablooie!' and I think I'll have a scar."
He frowned and reached behind him, rubbed his buttocks gingerly
And said, "A piece of crawler flew and sliced my suit and me.

"I corked it with a piece of rock and strapping best I could
"But that made me walk slower than I knew I really should
"And so I got a frozen butt and blood all in my suit.
"My suit has been fixed up but it's like murder when I toot."

They couldn't help but laugh at the expression on his face
Which twisted with discomfort but in moments was replaced
With grins and chuckles as they shook his hand and bought him beer
Which he drank gratefully (though he'd not sit down on his rear).

Chris said, "It is long past time we found who's doing this.
"Everyone out at the station feels they're on a list -

"A black one - but the rumors rule; confusion holds the reins.
"It's commonly believed the colonists are who to blame."

Jonesy poured himself a beer and leaned against the bar.
Absent mindedly he rubbed a jagged little scar
That crossed his cheek and looped beneath his box-like stubbled chin.
He said, "This came on sudden-like. I think it's a blow-in.

"Nah, the colonists don't want to stand in progress' way.
"Every one of us is waiting for the happy day
"When all these bloody engineers and scientists arrive
"Upon their final plan to make this world come alive.

"None, that is, except the whining twits at Xanadu:
"The self-entitled wankers that have nothing else to do.
"They suck the tits of governments or silly lobby groups
"And poke their runny noses into other people's poop.

"They'll make a lot of noise but won't venture out of doors
"And have no vested interest in Titan's future course.
"Blokes like that do not have qualms about legalities
"Or any sense of honor or of good morality

"So they cannot be trusted to be other than they are.
"Though most of them are harmless and would never go so far
"As sabotage or murder but there's dingos in that lot;
"Unhinged and unpredictable and prone to act when hot."

"Nah, this crim is local but he isn't one of us.
"Furphy says that you blokes are the ones that we should cuss
"But I know better." Jonesy winked and hoisted up his beer
And said, "But I will wager it is someone very near

"The atmospheric station or the compound you work in
"And there might be some others too that pop in now and then.
"About six weeks ago there were three strangers with a load
"Of questions about folks. I had them rack off down the road.

"Two of them were dodgy-looking blokes I reckon too.
"The third did all the talking for the shifty-looking crew.
"Tall he was, with raven hair and eyes as dark as sin
"And while he talked I felt a chill creep underneath me skin."

"That sounds like the audit crew that came from TerraCorp,"
Said Chris as he set down his mug. David gave a snort
And said, "They only stayed one night and then they flew away.
"We didn't know they bothered to head over Sinlap's way.

"And if they're gone they don't explain the fires or the bomb
"That almost took out Boomer and did little Johnny wrong.
"Isn't there surveillance information to be seen?"
Jonesy said, "We've never needed it and no one's keen

"On letting public spying be a part of our fair town.
"Perhaps they're not all gone; perhaps they're still hanging around?
"That bloody hanger fire was as crook as it could be
"And after Boomer's ride there's none will come within cooee

"Of that facility where you blokes hang your hats at night.
"The fires and the crawler bomb put most folks in a fright."
Jonesy poured another round of beers for all of them
And said, "It's my impression someone's shut you blokes all in.

"You're the only three I've seen from there in nigh a week.
"That station's being isolated as we bloody speak
"I reckon and it isn't good - that's London to a brick!"
He paused and took a swig then wiped the foam from off his lip.

A server brought the burgers out and Jonesy watched the three
Tear into their meals and exclaim with grateful glee
How good it was to eat real beef and drink a decent beer
As Jonesy smiled and he and Boomer started for the rear.

Then from the entry sounds were heard of two men coming in.
Jonesy turned around and said, "G 'day!" to both of them
Who glanced around and saw the three men munching at the bar
And beckoned Jonesy to where whispers wouldn't carry far.

The munchers kept their noses in their burgers and their beers
Honoring the mens' wish that they wouldn't overhear.
Then in a moment Jonesy's voice erupted, "Bloody hell!
"Good onya mates, that's defo some good oil there to tell!"

The three looked at the two and then the two looked at the three.
Then Jonesy told the two, "These are good eggs I guarantee.

"They're not the Terra Corporation types that mess the nest.
"These, of all the station's blokes are possibly the best."

Jonesy walked back toward the three and said, "These two have found
"The remnants of the hanger-fired man in the compound
"Where rubbish is converted into energy and heat.
"By their account the sight is best not looked at while you eat.

"A band around the ankle showed he was the very same
"Clinic patient from the station and you know his name.
"A data chip was also found concealed beneath a patch
"With details of some bloody apparatus they had hatched."

The three put down their burgers and turned toward the other two.
Nick asked, "Was there indication phosphorous was used?"
Both of them looked much surprised - suspiciously looked back
And one asked, "How in God's name would you ever have known that?"

The other put his hand behind his back and pulled a gun
And held it on his lap - over the three his eyes did run.
"Bloody oath! We're not the ones!" said David as his hands
Slowly reached into the air as did his companions'.

"Pack your bloomin' piece away," said Jonesy to the man.
"Boomer and me both can vouch that these are better than
"The dodgy crims you're looking for - they weren't even in town.
"Now give these mates apologies and drink your ales down."

The pistol-packer asked again how it was that they knew
Phosphorous was what the killers by accounts had used.
David quipped, "Because it's what took Johnny down as well.
"Besides, what else would ignite in this ice-bound frozen hell?"

David's eyes were boiling with an anger all could see.
He lowered both his hands and took a drink belligerently
Then picked his burger up and said, "Now piss off while I eat.
"To find your killers you are barking up the wrong damn tree."

Chris then added, "If it were us we'd have burned him too,"
Motioning at Nick, "He is the last one that can do
"Design work in the field that has been attacked the most.
"He's the only one of them that isn't yet a ghost."

"Stow it," Jonesy said again; the pistol disappeared.
Nick then offered up, "I think it's getting very clear
"That TerraCorp is not responsible for Sinlap's woes.
"The auditors weren't TerraCorp and Doctor Bordeaux knows.

"He's been bought and paid for by an interest from outside.
"Perhaps a renegade division that has men inside?
"On Earth suspicious men within the corporation tried
"To get me here in record time and then to have me fried."

"To have you fried?" Chris inquired, "How is that again?"
The pistol-packing pair came closer. Jonesy butted in,
"Spill it, mate. We're all ears now." Nick considered just
How much that he should tell to these and how far he could trust.

"Without my knowledge someone there installed a small device
"Along with other spy implants, but this one wasn't nice.
"Within my body it collected phosphorous from me
"And stored it in a mass to be exploded remotely.

"It was just by chance a mediscan revealed it there.
"And I was fortunate to have it cleaned up with great care."
Nick pulled up his shirt to show the tiny scar it made
Where Haji had removed the thing. Then he went on to say,

"So when I saw the phosphorous that took your Johnny down
"I knew that I was not the only fire bomb in town.
"And now that you've confirmed my predecessor died that way
"It's pretty obvious that there are even more in play."

"That's bloody crook," said Jonesy. "Holy smokes!" David exclaimed
"Why the heck would anybody take you down in flames?
"Or even take out Johnny or go after Boomer too?
"That doesn't make much sense to me - I haven't got a clue."

"Well," said Nick, "The best I figure someone has a fear
"The planet-scanning technique we're developing might clear
"The way to finding hidden ports that pirates may call home
"Or even want to corner it to keep it for their own.

"At the outside someone doesn't want it used 'round here.
"Which means that TerraCorp is not the culprit some have feared.

"The corporation's policy is "Go" for our success
"But someone doesn't want Titan developed to its best.

"I believe my predecessor saw that Bordeaux changed
"And didn't want his work to be a pawn in Bordeaux's game.
"And when he went to Medical he lost some signal's feed
"That would have set his implant off so locals did the deed.

"Johnny must have been a backup used to take me out
"When I arrived and it was seen that my implant was found.
"But since I was delayed and Johnny didn't drive for me
"When his implant went off, well, I was just lucky.

"This proves that their intel wasn't great or not real-time
"Which shows his implants weren't as useful to them as were mine.
"Boomer must have been a lesson for folks to stay clear.
"Like Jonesy said, they didn't want more folks poking 'round here."

They were looking stunned at Nick, then Jonesy scratched his knee,
"Crikey, mate, you know that story's daft as it can be?"
"Oh, my Gosh," said Chris, "This all is crazy but it fits.
"These implants, though, are far beyond what I thought might exist."

David took a deep swig from his mug then set it down
And said, "I knew you knew some things," and made a little frown.
"If what you say is true it absolutely does make sense,
"But why would they take you out if they hadn't got the plans?"

Nick replied, "Perhaps they thought they had the data files?
"Perhaps my predecessor decoyed them before he died
"By letting them take bogus data or unfinished plans?
"I think he knew the score, and he kept it from their hands.

"I would like to see the data chip that he concealed
"And see how far he got when I can get the files unsealed."
The two late comers looked amazed and pistol-packer said,
"The chip is at the clinic but I'll bet you wind up dead

"If word gets out you've got it. It would be a tragedy
"If what we need to get the terraforming done safely
"Were lost or were withheld - not to mention one more lost."
Nick replied, "I have considered what might be the cost,

"So, by the way, I finished up the work we came to do
"And uploaded the data to the Saturn array too.
"So even if the plans for the array were lost down here
"The folks at the array have what they need to build the gear."

"Good onya, mate," said Jonesy. "That you finished up the job,
"But if your theory's right you're still a target for that mob
"By the simple fact they know you know too bloody much.
"You'd better pack your bags and get off Titan in a rush."

"You two ought to know I sent my resignation too."
Said Nick to Chris and David as he finished off his brew.
Jonesy poured another round for all six of the men
And David said, "Well, I suppose that this might spell the end

"Of our employment too. These killers will be back in force."
Nick said, "Maybe not, if we can get them first, of course.
"We have evidence that two were at the hangar fire
"We also know that Bordeaux's in, or at least has conspired

"With someone who's committed to disrupting all our work.
"As far as I'm concerned to shut him down would be a perk."
All five of the other men unconsciously drew close
And looked around the empty room. David looked morose:

"It sounds like you have signed us up in your conspiracy
"And made us targets with no choice about our own safety."
Chris thumped David on the head and said, "Wake up, you nut!
"We've been victims unawares for weeks and in a rut."

Jonesy sad, "That's dead set, Mate, if what Nick says is true.
"The question now of course is, 'What are you blokes going to do?'"
The white light on the bar made shining stars on beer mug rims.
The orange light that came in through the window seemed more dim.

David said, "You're right of course, and it's about damn time
"That someone took a stand and put an end to all this crime.
"Have you got a plan, Nick, of what we're going to do?"
They looked at each other, then at Nick who asked, "Do you?"

"It's obvious," said Chris, "We've got a juicy piece of bait.
"We simply set our trap and then we bide our time and wait."

David grinned and looked at Nick. Jonesy said, "Too right.
"Give it a fair go and you might bag your blokes tonight."

Nick's face reddened as they looked at him with smiling eyes.
"Now that's sweet justice, sport," said David, "You're the dingo's prize!"
Nick looked down and said, "You're right of course. I'll be the bait,
"But once the trap is sprung make sure the cavalry's not late!"

The pistol-packer's mate chimed in, "We'll spread the word about
"That Nick here has the data chip and went on walkabout.
"Though Furphy has it he's gone to the station all alone
"Along the crawler road. Is that good enough a bone?"

"Bonzer!" Jonesy spurted, "Now that they know they've been took
"They'll be bloody ropeable and bite the nearest hook.
"That's you, mate." he said as he gave Nick a leering scan.
"You'll be on the menu when they go after their man."

"Can you really get the chip?" asked Nick. "Yes, we will."
"Then bring it to me here and I'll head for the station's hill.
"I'll make time for others to get set to cover me
"Then walk on toward the station acting drunk and leisurely."

"That's more than we could ask," the pistol-packer said to Nick
"Though I don't reckon what your use is for the data chip
"Since as you say you sent the plans off to the big array."
"It's simple," Nick replied, "There may be more the chip can say

"About what's going on or what my predecessor knew
"Before he left the station and before his implant blew.
"I need to know," he finished, "I suspect that you would too
"If our roles were switched and you were walking in my shoes."

The pistol-packer nodded and said, "Right. You're a good man.
"I'm glad you're on the Titan's side," then offered Nick his hand.
A firm handshake was given and their names exchanged and marked.
The two men finished off their beers and left to do their part.

* * * * *

Selenia and Red had spent the morning sleeping late
And leisurely ate breakfast after their long dinner date.

The catching up on items new and old was over-due
And both were on the same page waiting word from Captain Blue.

Then they parted ways both satisfied with what they'd learned
From words that passed between them and the passion they had burned.
Content to keep life simple, expectations well in check
Friends of deep connection and great mutual respect.

Red left for the spaceport after checking with his crew
And learning that his men had just returned from their night too.
The tune he whistled softly as he made his way along
Was borrowed from an ancient Irish rabble-rousing song.

His mind and body both relaxed, with little on his mind
Other than some ship's details while he was killing time;
He never in a hundred years would guess what came his way
Just around the corner on this very special day.

26   Jackrabbit

There wasn't much to see outside the window of the ship
Which sped her from Iapetus and from her captor's grip:
An ugly row of mountains for a moment from one side
(Trajectory designed for their departure point to hide)

And then the speckled star fields From Orion south to Crux.
In long years she'd not seen the open sky so very much.
On Triton only once and from Miranda not at all
She felt as if with just a thought into the sky she'd fall.

"Beautiful!" escaped her lips without a conscious thought
Then Saturn came in view as the ship's course slewed 'round somewhat
Arrayed in all his glory with his thousand rings and moons
She still could not believe that she'd be loose on Rhea soon!

Another course correction (course concealment?) happened soon
And as the hours passed she watched the wide array of moons
Shrink into a ragged line as Saturn's rings grew thin
And soon the view of Saturn's clouds were pulling her eyes in.

Their path was engineered to loop them once around Dione
Then back away from Saturn some to Rhea's orbit's home.
She knew she needed sleep but the excitement filled her breast
As though she were re-born again (was no way she could rest).

But then before she knew it happened, she was pulled awake
Gently by the engineer who asked her to partake
Of steaming coffee and a plate of scrambled eggs and toast
For she had been asleep for hours on their moon-ward coast.

And then it happened! One more time the cabin lights turned red
And back into her couch she leaned her pony-tailed head.
Then only minutes later with a quick bump from the rear
The engines throttled down; the engineer called out, "We're here!"

"Rhea?" Renee asked. The engineer said, "Yes, of course!
"This barge may be dated but it's not the slowest horse.
"I'll help you to the transport, it will be here right away.
"It's been nice. We don't have guests aboard us every day.

"The transport will deliver you right to the terminal.
"You won't have any trouble for your carry bag is small.
"The shuttle to the cruiser will be berthed at concourse B
"And Lady, you're the only one who's ever been set free."

That last was spoken in a quiet tone that rang with awe.
His face was flushed and some confused and curious withal.
His honesty was welcome then his voice went back on track:
"A ticket's waiting for you by the name of Mistress Black.

"From there you'll find a Tubeway that will take you to Inmar
"But don't spend too much time away or wander off too far.
"You've only got six hours and that shuttle leaves on time.
"Once you're on that cruiser, Ganymede's just down the line."

His voice softened again, "You know, it's going to be a shock
"To be turned loose alone in public. I'd be proud to walk
"You through the terminal and get you set and squared away.
"We're not going to lift from here until the end of day."

Renee stretched out her hand and said, "I think I'll be alright
"But I appreciate the offer and enjoyed the flight.
"Perhaps we'll meet again when I return from Ganymede."
He took her hand and met her eye and said, "Go with God's speed."

"Thank you," she returned, "And may His blessings follow you."
The engineer glanced down and then he helped her wiggle through
The small lock of the transport when it latched and pressurized
Then waved a quick goodbye as it detached and made the drive

Across the frozen landing field some seven hundred yards
To latch up to the terminal and disembark its ward.
And though the sunlight shined less than one fiftieth of Earth's
She felt as though it were the bright spring day of her rebirth!

Along the way she saw a cargo crawler heading out
To take the load of produce from the ship's cargo, no doubt.
And felt a strange sensation - almost pride in ownership
But flavored with a sadness knowing those who slaved for it.

That feeling served to steady her and firm up her resolve
To sacrifice her sure escape (she'd not deny the call).

She'd grasp the slimmest chance. There was no price she wouldn't pay
For those beneath the rugged hills imprisoned in the caves.

So stoically she pulled the mask across her inner heart
And strolled into the terminal prepared to play the part
Of Warden's latest conquest, though without a solid plan.
She only knew she'd have to gain some leverage with the man.

The terminal was huge inside and brightly lighted too
Made of several domes connected by large walkway tubes.
Trees and shrubs were everywhere and merchants sold fast food
And other sundries here and there; business looked quite good.

The sights and sounds of civil people living normal lives
Made memories and long-suppressed emotions come alive.
Shopping was a time of healing. Walking in a crowd
Of people free from slavery beneath some pirate's cloud:

How unconcerned and normal! How relaxed and free from fear.
How odd it felt to be estranged from breathing free and clear
And then be plunged into a thriving town alive with hope.
(She felt a bit self-conscious, but she quickly learned to cope.)

She made her way to concourse B and verified her seat
Aboard the shuttle that would meet the ship to Ganymede.
And then with hours remaining took a tube to Inmar town
With plans to buy some shoes, a couple dresses and night gowns.

And that she did! In fact she thrilled to shop with Warden's gold.
The merchants were delighted at the pricey goods they sold
For very few on Rhea spent the kind of cash she dropped
On fashions which, as she tried on the passers-by eyes popped!

She spent some time on Warden too: she bought a gift or three
To brighten up his spirits and show she could be friendly.
He wasn't one to follow fashion but some small nick-nacks
Would serve to loosen up his humor and help her relax.

Then with her shopping finished she took in a simple meal
Along a sidewalk cafe where her psyche seemed to heal
For as her mind meandered while she sipped a cup of tea
For just a golden instant she could swear she sat with he

Who owned her heart forever and who was one half of her,
The man whom she had loved and she would love him forever.
Then when the realization flooded back of where she was
The tears welled up and one fell slowly toward her steaming cup.

She knew she could not contact him; she could not tip her hand.
She knew there would be watchers giving word back to the man
Who held the lives of thousands 'neath his sword of Damocles
And their lives had to be preserved above her heart's own needs.

So she must win the warden's trust - the only path she saw
And it must be done quickly or there'd be no one at all
Left among the living in his caves (she knew it well)
And she had no idea how soon he'd unleash his hell.

But then the thought impacted like a golf ball twixt her eyes:
He wanted her away! That was his way of being nice!
Ensuring she would not be witness of his pale horse ride
That's why they'd meet on Rhea once Iapetus had died!

And so she steeled herself and forged the hardness in her heart
To put her best foot forward. She would play the hateful part.
She'd prove she wanted him enough to ditch the sunward trip
Until they'd go together: Ganymede she would skip!

Whispering a prayer, *Oh, God! Please give me help and strength!*
Help me save those people. I will go to any length!
She had to get back to the ship that brought her here today
But other than "'til end of day" how long were they to stay?

They may have left already and be off between the moons
Doing warden's bidding (for they were his trusted goons)
But that ship was the only link she had to warden's ear
Until the weeks at Ganymede had passed and he'd be here.

She grabbed her bag and bolted (leaving one enormous tip!)
Desperate to get back to the spaceport and the ship.
(So frustrating in Rhea's thirty-seventh of a G
Where she weighed only four pounds rather than her one-fifty.

She went quite fast but didn't feel so to her Earth-born feet,
The pause between her footfalls taking near eternity!)

Gasping as she made her way, her heart a pounding drum
She almost hit a man who 'round a corner had just come.

And then she did a double-take: the build, the hair, the face!
She knew this man from years before the pirates had erased
Her contact with her lover and the friends who thought her dead.
Standing there before her was her husband's dear friend Red!

Her eyes were large as goose eggs and his eyes were just as big.
She scanned around then shook her head from side to side and said,
"Excuse me sir, would you please hold my bag while I go see
"The water closet over there? I'll be back instantly!"

She held her finger to her lips an instant; her eyes plead.
He saw her look of desperation; nodded "yes" his head
And took the offered parcel as she whisked into the door
Then just a moment later reappeared, said nothing more

But, "Thanks so much for waiting. It is now your turn to go."
She nodded toward the washroom door and took her bag in tow,
Then added, "Please sir, thank you," (glanced the washroom's way again).
The hardest thing she ever did was turn her back on him

And take off for the terminal as fast as she could go
Choking on her every breath as tears burst out and flowed
Across her reddened face, her breaking heart pounding a beat
She swore was even louder than her gasps and sobs must be.

There was no doubt at all that Captain Redfeather would give
Her sanctuary and protection once he knew she lived
Without a hesitation or a need for questions asked
Then take her to her husband as his most essential task.

And now he knew she lived but she had turned her back and run
Before the needed conversation had even begun.
She didn't even risk a chance to learn Jules was alive
But prayed that Red could see the conflict burning her inside.

Red stood in his tracks and watched her bounce off toward the tube
Leading to the terminal but he could barely move.
Anchored there in shock as if he'd seen a daylight ghost
The most sought after person and he'd stood there like a post.

But then he dragged his consciousness up out of his surprise
And acted on her obvious insistence with her eyes
He go into the washroom where near instantly he saw
In lipstick on the mirror a short message had been scrawled:

0N90WS8

* * * * *

Renee soon found a vacant surface transport she could use
And set controls to Manual then steered to where she knew
The ship that she'd arrived in had set down, then with a sigh
Offered up a prayer of thanks when its view met her eye.

She could see a cargo crawler docked next to its hull
And two space-suited figures (one to push and one to pull)
Carefully maneuvering a rack of cylinders
Into the cargo bay with greatest care in its traverse.

Steering to the other side she set the Auto-Dock
Whereupon the transport fixed itself to the airlock.
The ship's door wouldn't open though, and when she rang the bell
The crew chief's face came to the window mouthing, "What the hell?"

Renee gave him a smile and waved and said, "Open the lock!"
The engineer's face showed up too expressing fear and shock.
He turned the comm link on and asked, "What are you doing here?
"You're supposed to be away to Ganymede, My Dear!"

Renee gave him a silly shrug and said, "I changed my mind.
"Take me back to where we came from. I've spent enough time
"Shopping for the time being. I want to go back home."
The two men looked at each and shrugged; the airlock motors droned.

When she was safe aboard behind the lighted airlock door
She turned the transport loose (she wouldn't need it any more)
Then faced the two who waited for what else she'd have to say
But simply said, "I've had my fun. Please get us under way."

The engineer searched deeply in her eyes to find a clue
Why this lady blew her chance to fly the warden's coop.

She could see his searching and she realized that he cared
And was a kindred spirit caught within the warden's snare.

But she could only give him back a cool defensive stare
As the crew chief waved his scanner past her limbs and hair.
Then as the crew chief finished and turned round to walk away
She caught the engineer's quick eye and shed one tear to say,

It isn't what I want! His face was quick to flash surprise
And showed he understood by one quick nod then closed his eyes
Acknowledging he knew the pain that now he knew she felt
Then turned to lead the way back to the seats and safety belts.

After half an hour had passed and all the checks complete
The crew chief and the engineer were in their assigned seats.
Crew chief said, "Well, that confirms it - she's the Leader's girl.
"We'll be takin' orders from her - makes me wanna hurl."

The engineer responded, "Yes, that seems to be a fact.
"Did you ask the Leader if he wants her to come back?"
"Yeah," the crew chief answered, "His response was too damn quick.
"She must be just like him if she really wants to stick.

"Let's get this bucket outta here!" he croaked the pilot's way.
The engineer sat quietly with nothing more to say
Beyond the needed chatter with the pilot as the ride
Into the starry heavens helped distract what churned inside.

*   *   *   *   *

Red searched high and low throughout the washroom for more clues
And cleaned the lipstick from the mirror so no one would view
The message she was so determined only he must see
Then sent a message Captain's way insisting that they meet.

It was obvious to Red that she was in great fear
Of being seen conversing with someone while she was here
In Inmar City. So he took a stroll around the Strip
Then took his merry time to make his way back to his ship

Where he performed an in-depth query of the terminal
Noting all departing ships and recent arrivals.

There wasn't much discovered since most captains to a man
Valued highly privacy and rarely filed flight plans.

Shortly after mulling over all that he could find
His First Mate sent a message that he had a secure line
To Captain Blue but there would only be a short window
Before the signal dropped. Red took the call and said, "Hello!

"I saw her, Jules," that's all he said a moment to be sure
That he had Captain's full attention then he said, "Yes, Her!
"I saw her here on Rhea just a couple hours ago
"But she has lifted off-world for some place I do not know.

"It's possible she shuttled to a ship for Ganymede
"But I believe she's on a transport working locally.
"I know she recognized me and she knew that I knew her
"But she took crazy pains to not be seen or not be heard

"Talking to someone who she might know from years ago
"As if someone were watching and she couldn't say hello.
"She's in trouble Jules, but she's alive and on the loose
"And running like a jackrabbit from something's got her spooked."

The signal dropped a moment, then it came back weak but clear
And Red could hear the Captain saying, "... need you meet me here
"In Titan standard orbit..." then the signal dropped for good
And Red transmitted in the blind that he most surely would.

27   Stroke of Darkness

The sneak attack on Saturn's big array came as a shock
To engineers and workers who maintained it 'round the clock.
A regular supply ship had just pulled beside to park
When unseen from behind it lasers blazed out from the dark

Destroying all communications and defensive gear
In a single volley from the black ship at its rear.
The transport ship was ripped to pieces then the big array's
Communications gear was targeted in the same way.

The station-keeping thrusters were sliced cleanly from their mounts.
The living quarters punctured as the air blew out in spouts.
Over in just seconds and completed with such skill,
Obviously this was not the dark ship's crew's first kill.

And then before the severed girders dimmed their heated glow
An airlock in the dark ship opened wide to let a flow
Of twenty armored men emerge and cross the empty space
Between the killer ship and the array's ripped open face.

Once inside they verified that every soul was gone.
They pulverized or laser-fried each bit of gear turned on.
Every bit of commo gear or computing device
Every storage medium was burned and lasered twice.

The warden watched the progress of the rampage through the mass
Of out-gassing equipment and demanded that the last
Vestige of all life aboard the ruined big array
Be snuffed out of existence 'ere the killers slipped away.

The operation took no more than seven minutes tops.
From laser blasts through dying gasps until it all was lost.
A dozen innocents were killed. The Titans' hopes and dreams
For rapid terraforming were destroyed by one man's schemes.

And then the black ship slipped away into the starry void.
The warden grinned with satisfaction (though he was annoyed
That there were still some loose ends to clean up on Titan yet
But he would make examples of those proved incompetent.)

And so he gave the order to make Titan at best speed
And settled back into his plush acceleration seat.
The ride would take just hours and just minutes after that
Titan's future would be just a bauble on his hat.

* * * * *

Bovine healed rapidly with Haji's expert care
And Dewey took his workload and completed the repairs
While Duke and Joe spent downtime in the clubs at Xanadu
Gathering the scuttlebutt as long-haul spacers do.

The captain didn't like his ship to stay on Titan long.
The thermal stress and hydrocarbons rubbed his feathers wrong.
And so before three days had passed they lifted into space
Establishing an orbit where each hour Titan's face

Obscured beneath its orange mask passed unseen miles below
While Gin kept Captain's yacht prepared in just minutes to go.
For Nick might need assistance or a lift at any time
And Radar kept a monitor on signals he might find.

Radar also spent much time with Varda's little gift
(The N-dimension processor that gave him such a lift);
Learning ways to program it to do amazing tricks
Of computation and expression just for grins and kicks.

He had shown the captain that Nick's implants made reports
And with the proper algorithms true facts he could sort.
There had been a time of ash and then some alcohol,
A span of quiet days and then exertion but no call

Until a new position fix and alcohol event
Preceded more exertion - then an exit call was sent!
"Nick may be in trouble," Radar sent the captain's way
Across the shipboard intercom, "There's something big in play.

"A Mayday call from Sinlap's atmospheric plant was sent
"Across the planet-wide emergency and rescue net.
"But then the entire Fensal region's commo net went down
"And I don't think the message even got to Sinlap town."

The captain answered instantly, "Gin! The ship is yours.
"Joe and Duke, you come with me. Radar, plot the course
"To bring me down exactly where you think Nick is right now
"And what direction he's been moving for the last half hour.

"Move!" The captain's orders came like lightning in the dark.
But his crew were professionals and jumped while he still barked.
Within two minutes they were on the yacht and broken free
And plunging toward the orange clouds above a methane sea.

The captain dropped the little craft below the bluish haze
While lining up the vectors Radar sent to steer their way
Toward Sinlap town at Fensal where he knew the time had come
That Nick's association with his employer be done.

Then just before they slipped around the limb of Titan's globe
Dropping fast behind the ship a deep-encrypted code
From Radar indicated that a secure call from Red
Of high priority was ready; "Go!", the captain said.

"I saw her, Jules," Red's voice boomed through and then he said, "Yes, Her!
"I saw her here on Rhea...," (static overwhelmed his words).
The captain's hands that held the yacht's controls tightened their grip.
The signal grew much weaker as he fell behind the ship.

"I know she recognized me and she knew that I knew her
"But she took crazy pains to not be seen...," (just static heard
For a moment more), "...but she's alive and on the loose
"And running like a jackrabbit from something's got her spooked."

The captain nearly shouted back his instant action plan:
"Gather all the magnetics on Rhea that you can.
"Then I'll need you meet me here in Titan standard orbit.
"Our engineers will give your ship a useful little re-fit."

By then the yacht had dropped into the ionizing zone
And there was no more commo with the ship he called his home.
His mind was ringing with the words that Red had sent his way:
He'd seen the lover of his soul - she wasn't far away!

* * * * *

It wasn't very hard to spot the newbie on the road
Ungainly in this gravity, his clumsiness sure showed!
Even sober folks took more than just a week or two
Of working in a cryosuit to gain more graceful moves.

And so the two assassins put their thermal scope away
Knowing that their quarry was just moments up their way.
It would be a simple task to take the young man down
And stuff him in an ice fracture that ran across the ground.

But only after making thorough search for data chips
That some half-tipsy locals let the word foolishly slip
Had managed to be squirreled away and found upon the man
Whom they had caused to self-combust then threw him in the can.

But they were not alone. There were four other men who watched
Their progress from above concealed among the icy rocks.
Their imagers were active and their rifles locked and cocked:
Four protecting angels watching Nick as on he walked.

* * * * *

Chris and David stayed behind at Jonesy's place to wait
For news about their little trap and who would take the bait.
But it had been more than three hours and not a word had come
Other than news from a man who'd come in at a run

Much earlier to say the Fensal network had gone down
And there would be no data service in or out of town
Until it had been diagnosed and fixed and no one knew
How long it took. An outage this widespread was something new.

Boomer, Chris and David had a game of poker on.
Other patrons now and then would play some then be gone
A little money richer or perhaps a little less
And as the time dragged on they started feeling more distressed

Until the pistol-packer and his tired mate dragged in
And gave the word that Nick was gone as were the assassins.
"Gone?" Chris exclaimed and David echoed with, "Gone where?"
"A bloody shuttle landed that took him up in the air!"

The pistol-packer shook his head and sat down at the bar
And said, "We tried to bag the buggers but they were too far."
The others gathered 'round him; Jonesy said, "You're knackered, mate.
"There's bangers on the barbie; have a schooner and relate

"Exactly what went down out there before these blokes explode."
Packer took a lengthy swig from Jonesy's amber fluid
Then told of how they saw two men come stalking after Nick
And how they had four men to cover him if things got thick:

"The dodgy crims were still perhaps a hundred meters back
"When we all heard the sky ripped open by a sonic crack.
"And then a bloomin' orbital came down with thrusters spewin'
"And two blokes packin' automatic weapons started shootin'

"Above our heads and over those two crims that followed Nick
"Motioning for him to get on board - and he did quick!
"Their airlock wasn't even closed when they took to the air
"Then blasted toward the east and nearly shaved the two crims' hair!"

The pistol packer took another swig and wiped his mouth.
His mate chimed in, "A second craft came over then turned south.
"The atmospheric station looked to be where it came from.
"As it climbed it bloody nearly crashed into Nick's one."

The packer added, "Those two crims made tracks and made them fast.
The four of us took after them but lost them in a crack
"Of ice beside two mountains that concealed the way they turned
"But we found decent evidence they are the ones who burned

"The poor bloke in the hangar - matching tracks and all that rot.
"And though it's circumstantial it is the best we've got
"Until we nab the tossers and we have ourselves a chat
"To get down to the good oil. Now, that's where we are at."

The pistol-packer's mate threw in, "The other two of us
"Are still out looking for the pair but I have little trust
"They'll find the trail for they were off like shots for parts unknown.
"The question that remains is, '*Who took our bloody bone?*'

"The ship that nabbed your Nick knew spot on where to pick him up.
"And it was plain they were his mates and it was more than luck

"Because he didn't knock back - he jumped right in the ship.
"Your Nick has flown the coop and run off with your data chip!"

The pistol-packer said, "It looks suspicious on your Nick.
"Like he's another one of them and you and we were tricked."
David eyed the pair of them and didn't say a peep.
As Chris held up his fingers with the chip for them to see.

* * * * *

It only took three hops and Nick was in the airlock door.
He could see Duke smiling through his visor while he poured
Another thirty rounds into the air around the ship
Then leaped inside the airlock with Joe stuck close to his hip.

The captain's yacht then leaped into the sky with such a rush
The three of them were pushed against the bulkhead in a crush
Of G's more powerful than Nick had ever felt before.
Duke said, "Welcome back!" pinned helplessly against the floor.

"Ever rode a bat from hell?" asked Joe with a wide grin.
His eyes shined with excited light as he barely got in
Before the ground outside dropped suddenly out of Nick's view
And it was all that Nick could do to breathe and grin back too.

Only seconds after lifting clear Nick saw a flash
Of darkness in the open airlock doorway flicker past
Followed by a blast of sound heard plain above the roar
Of engines in the captain's yacht which auto-shut the door.

"That was close," said Duke whose eyes were wide as oyster shells.
"Huh?" asked Joe who couldn't see the door from where he fell.
"Another ship went by," strained Nick who tried to raise his arm
Sensing if he strained much harder he might do some harm.

In only minutes they had left the orange sky behind
And risen far above the upper hazes as they climbed
Until a total engine cut-off left them in freefall
Arcing toward a rendezvous with Bovine, Gin, and all.

The airlock door was opened once again to purge the stink
Of Titan's air out of the lock before they'd even think

Of opening the inner door to atmosphere inside.
(They unsuited and relaxed for the last leg of the ride.)

"I'm glad we weren't too late," said Duke, "We saw three riflemen
"In the rocks above you as we circled coming in."
"Right on time," said Nick, "But there were four and they are friends.
"The two behind me on the road we think may be villains."

Joe eyed Nick and asked, "What kind of villains? What's their game?"
Duke looked hard at Nick with his expression just the same.
"We're pretty sure they set my predecessor here on fire.
"They used an implant just like mine when he tried to retire,

"So to speak..." Nick trailed off, then said, "We need them caught.
"They might be the key to finding who set up this plot
"To wreck the work on Titan and to steal the scanner plans."
"I hope the men up in the rocks will catch them if they can

"And I suppose they will. The folks in Sinlap are fed up
"With all the killings and the ranchers running out of luck.
"They were hoping this would be the day it all would stop
"Once they 'bagged the dodgy blokes' when they got to the rocks."

Duke and Joe glanced at each other then at Nick a while.
"You set a trap to catch them?" Duke's teeth lit up his bright smile.
Nick said, "Yes. I was the bait that drew them out, you see?
"Then those four guys with rifles were put there to cover me."

"And then we crashed your party," Joe injected, "Just in time
"To chase the bad guys off before the posse stopped the crime."
Duke took on a look of deep concern and then he said,
"You can bet the captain would be very interested

"In what your villains had to say. I hope they get their men.
"But I would also bet they've got the same implants in them.
"Two boys doing legwork like that aren't the masterminds
"Behind the troubles brought on by the Bad Guys' grand design.

"And they might be expendable," Joe offered up as well.
"They might know some things that someone wouldn't let them tell."
Their thoughts were all the same as they considered what they'd seen
And packed away their cryosuits until they could be cleaned.

In the cockpit Captain called to Radar just as soon
As the mother ship came 'round the limb of the big moon.
He had him contact Red again and set a secure line
That wouldn't be cut off by ionizing air this time.

"I'm glad you caught me now," said Red, "We're just about to lift.
"I didn't copy all your message, most of it was clipped.
"I got you want to meet in Titan orbit but that's all.
"And you did hear me tell you of the person who I saw?"

"I did," the captain said, "And I'll want every small detail.
"I'm going to find her, Red, and in this task I will not fail.
"But first you need to grab up all the magnetics you can
"Then meet me here in standard orbit just as we had planned."

"Magnetics?" Red responded, "Send the specs and I'll find out
"If Rhea has such things which can be found lying about."
"Just get them, Red. I'll reimburse you any price you pay
"If you think it wasn't worth it when you're out this way.

"You're going to want what I will show you. Trust me!" Captain said
"Now, tell me every scrap and every tiny detail, Red."
The captain peered into his screen as if he were right there
And Red relayed Renee's encounter with the deepest care.

"There isn't any doubt, Jules. It's her and she is near.
"The message on the mirror was in letters big and clear.
"It must mean longitude and latitude on Saturn Eight.
"What else could it be? There isn't much room for debate."

"You're right," the captain said, "The message couldn't be more clear."
He gazed out of the cockpit at the stars that seemed so near
And cast his eyes about until Iapetus was seen
It's tiny disk against the distant starlight's blue-white gleam.

And then the magnitude of Red's report came smashing home!
This was the only evidence of what his very bones
Had told him day and night for six long years when few believed
That she could be alive and he was tragically deceived.

Red trusted his friend and knew the stalwart Captain Blue
Had depths that weren't revealed to any others but a few.

And if the captain said that something was, then it was sure
For he knew that the love they shared was very rare and pure.

In the captain's mind's eye he could see his missing wife,
The lady who had bound her heart to his for all of life
Gazing from a porthole on a ship between the moons
And he knew that his chance to find her would be over soon.

Despite the years of silence and of separation's cold,
Despite the fact his searching had begun to make him old,
The fire of his passion for her had not waned at all
And he could hear the pure notes of her spirit's yearning call.

But there was urgency beyond his own he'd felt so long.
An overtone of sadness piercing through her spirit's song
And almost as a chorus he could feel the fearful cries
Of hundreds lost beyond his senses in the distant sky.

Red then broke the silence and the speaker sparked to life
"I know this is a shock, Jules, but we will save your wife.
"My ship and crew are yours and I know others who will aid
"But first we need to see what's there before we plan our raid."

"Our raid?" the captain jerked back to the present circumstance.
"We'll see what we can put together when intelligence
"Is gathered on the data that Renee made clear to you.
"But first you need to see a thing that I have here that's new."

"I'll do that soon," said Red, "I just got specs sent from your ship.
"I'll take a half a day to shop and load and then we'll lift."
The captain reached to cut the link but then he had a thought:
"Selenia might be on Rhea, Red. Perhaps you ought

"To look her up and see if she can find some of that gear."
Red looked keenly back and said, "You're right, Jules, she's here."
Unspoken words were passed between them, Captain cracked a smile
And said, "Red, you haven't told her. Please don't for awhile."

Red's face was a stone. He said, "No, I haven't Jules.
"I've only talked to you about Renee. You make the rules.
"And you should know Selenia is on your side in this.
"No matter how things go, she is your friend and wants your best."

"Selenia's a very complicated woman, Red.
"She'll always be a friend no matter who is in her bed.
"There's nothing that will ever change that - and that goes for you.
"Renee or not, I'll always wish the best luck for you two."

Red was ever mindful of the captain's keen insight.
But still he was amazed by how he read things in a light
That no one seemed to see but him and how he could have known
Selenia and he had bat one thousand and run home.

But then he smiled inside as he took comfort in the fact
The captain was in tune with both his friends as well as that.
Red's smile cracked the surface as he said, "I wish that too."
Then reached to kill the screen and said, "In two days I'll see you!"

The captain now could see the ship, a growing yellow dot
Approaching from behind the swiftly rising Captain's yacht.
Telemetry from both ships fed the navigation gear
Which auto-fired the thrusters bringing both ships very near

Where captain's able piloting performed the final dock
And pressures equalized between the mated ships' airlocks.
Bovine met the wanderers and welcomed them on board.
Haji had the coffee on with bagels, fruit and more.

28   Terror and Atrocity

Boomer brought the sausages and mustard and more beer
That Pistol-Packer and his mate made quickly disappear
Just in time for two more men to come into the bar
And spot the feeding pair, exclaiming, "This is where you are!"

"What's the good word, sports?" the pistol-packer's mate replied
Lifting up his mug while looking just a little sly.
"We thought we'd bring the word to town about the going's on
"And reckoned you'd be dallying about out there too long."

"Sit and have an ale," the pistol-packer spouted too,
"We figured those two blokes were gone when they bounced out of view
"Beyond that ice ravine." The newcomers walked to the bar
And said, "It didn't take too long. We know where they are."

The other man chimed in, "They ended up four miles south."
(He looked a little green and put his hand over his mouth.)
And then his friend continued, "We could see by infra-red
"A thermal flash and when we got there both of them were dead.

"Or what was left of them, that is." He took the offered beer
And added, "Very close to them were marks of landing gear."
He took a deep drink from his beer and wiped foam from his lip
And said, "My bet is that it was that second bloody ship

"That nearly hit the one that took your bandit bait away.
"And of the bandits, well, you sure don't see that every day!
"The pair of them were burned up from the inside of their suits.
"We know it was our two by matching tread marks on their boots.

"So that's the end of that." He took another swig of beer.
And Jonesy barked out, "Pig's Arse! It's coming bloody clear
"That there is more afoot here than a local pair of crims.
"What about your Nicholas? What's become of him?"

Then at that very instant David's phone received a call.
It didn't come across the Fensal commo net at all
But came directly from a ship in orbit overhead
And on the other end was Nick! Then David bluntly said,

"Where the heck are you? And how the heck did you get there?
"The locals seem to think a ship took you into the air."
"It did," Nick answered back, "These are my friends and I have news
"That might mean trouble. Let our friends at Sinlap all know too:

"From orbit we can see a thermal signature's not right.
"The atmospheric station looks to be twelve times as bright.
"A distress call was sent from there but Titan's ears are deaf
"Since something took the network down not long after we left.

"And it's been hours, David. You and Chris should get some men
"To go with you back to the station to check up on them.
"Something isn't right there and the commo is still down.
"They might need assistance from the people in the town."

David said, "We'll do that, Nick, and thank you for the tip;
"But did you know that you were being picked up by that ship?
"Some locals are suspicious that you had a hand in this
"And if there's damage to the station we will all be pissed!"

The signal started fading as the ship began to go
Over the horizon. Nick responded, "Yes and no.
"I knew our friends were coming - not exactly when or where;
"But David, there's a second ship that flew by us out there!

"It came from near the station and it turned off toward the south.
"That's where I would look for clues to what has come about.
"I need a favor though: When you get back out that way
"Verify my work was received by the big array.

"I haven't had response from them by radio from here.
"Perhaps the station's data link is up and channels clear?"
The signal dropped a moment, then through static David heard
"...call again next orbit..." and that was the final word.

* * * * *

The pair of crawlers with a dozen Sinlap men held short
Two hundred meters shy until they got a quick report
From Chris and David who had gone ahead to ascertain
The status of the station for the damage was quite plain.

The TerraCorp facility that recently was home
To Chris and David now looked like a bleaching yellow bone:
The entryway cracked open like a giant ostrich egg.
The larger dome behind it scorched with one side split agape.

The atmospheric plant beyond it had no windows lit.
To all outward appearance there was no life left in it.
And on the far side there was white light shining on the clouds
Beyond the silhouetted towers standing tall and proud

And that was not good news. It could only mean one thing:
An open fission fire and the rads that it would bring.
Their cryosuits were shielded to a limited degree
But nothing like the radiation suits that they would need

To do much more than survey how much damage had been done.
They'd need that heavy gear before the cleanup was begun.
Chris and David's focus though, was on the folks inside
And what help they could bring to any of them left alive.

And so with great temerity they ventured through the rooms
Most of which showed evidence of violence and doom.
The comm center was ransacked; the equipment mostly wrecked.
In the Corporation's dome there wasn't one soul left.

But in the station's maze they found some twenty-three alive
All who had sought refuge and had managed there to hide.
Many of them injured and in shock and need of care
But very few who worked in research made it into there.

Among the frozen bodies Chris was mortified to see
Tinker's who had tried to keep the peace so timidly.
His fever was now over with, his body burned in half
As if a ball of fire had erupted from his back.

The rescuers from Sinlap called two aircraft to the scene
To help evacuate the injured off for medicine.
But it would take some hours for construction engineers
To get the fission problem stabilized and debris cleared.

David was examining the research station's dome
When Nick was able once again to raise him on the phone

And ask the situation to which David gave reply:
"It is a mess down here and very many people died.

"This was an act of terrorism - mass extermination
"Of everyone connected with the Corporation's station.
"It seems these were professionals that blasted through the place
"And wrecked a big reactor. That's what you're seeing from space.

"Many of the folks are being flown to other towns
"Though we can't give them notice for the network is still down.
"A thorough search was made of every cranny high and low
"But nowhere in the complex could we find Doctor Bordeaux.

"And that's about the sum of it," David gave a sigh
While in the ship above him Nick asked, "How many have died?"
"It's hard to tell at this point, but we rescued twenty-three
"That's not including you, of course or Christopher or me

"Or those who were in town, but they won't number many more.
"So figure maybe seventy who aren't accounted for
"Other than what's plain to see..." David trailed off.
Nick sat in stunned silence until David gave a cough

And said, "By the way, Chris brought up the data link.
"At least the part on this end. The antenna's burned and kinked;
"But all the logs record the link went down five hours ago
"Because of problems out at the array, is what they show.

"That was half an hour before the station here got smoked
"And just about the time the Fensal commo network broke.
"I'm not thinking this is just a strange coincidence.
"Something big is going down and I'm a little tense.

"The link to the array has never once gone down before
"For we use relays at LaGrange points L5 and L4.
"I think someone hit the big array like they did here.
"If you can't get them on the horn from orbit then it's clear."

Nick stood still in shock imagining what David saw
And couldn't help but wonder if his actions caused it all
When he uploaded working scanner specs to the array.
Perhaps it induced action by those standing in the way

Of Titan's quick development. Perhaps Bordeaux himself?
Or forces in collusion who had now revealed themselves?
Nick pondered a moment more and figured it was nine
Hours since he uploaded the plans until the time

The data link went offline and the trouble happened here.
He felt a wave of anguish and his eyes began to tear.
"Do you think that I..." he choked, "...had anything to do
"With bringing on this trouble by uploading my work to

"The big array avoiding Doctor Bordeaux's bungling mitts?
"My gosh, David! That was a miscalculated risk!"
David blasted back, "Don't even think to go there, Nick!
"Even if you triggered it you're not the one who did it.

"No one could have known the real risk factor that was there.
"And when the network's back then everyone will be aware
"That something's going on that everyone to date has missed.
"That's the good thing that will come about because of this.

"The job that you were paid to do you did as you were called.
"You have no responsibility for this at all.
"Besides, this may be a mis-step by the ones who did it
"And you've secured the goods. For that we all are thankful, Nick!"

Nick took David's words and let them soothe his troubled mind
Surprised to see that David could treat anyone so kind
While standing in the rubble and the death that he'd described
For anyone in his position must be horrified.

"Thank you, David. What you say makes sense and I'm relieved
"That you and Chris were spared and we will get you some relief.
"In forty minutes we'll be passing over Xanadu
"We'll tell the situation and get help out there for you."

When Nick turned off his phone his face looked shaken to the core.
The captain watched him quietly then asked, "So what's the score?"
Nick began to stammer, but recovering he said,
"It appears that at the station seventy are dead."

"Dead?" the captain's face took on a thin veneer of calm
Masking coals of rage that he had carried deep so long.

"Tell me all you know," he said and Nick did as he asked
Being very careful to repeat only the facts.

When Nick confided feelings of responsibility
The captain reassured him, "That is not reality.
"The perpetrators obviously had evil in store
"Long before you came along. Don't think that anymore.

"Consideration should be given those at the array.
"If all communication has been lost most of the day
"Then we should best consider it was taken out as well.
"I'm sorry, but I tend to think that it's been blown to hell."

Nick considered this a moment then asked, "Could we send
"A message to all ships to see if one could check on them?"
The captain said, "In different circumstances that would be
"The right approach to take, but think about it carefully:

"Broadcasting that we know something at this early time
"Just might guarantee that we're the next target in line.
"And if the guilty predator is still lurking nearby
"A ship approaching the array might very well get fried

"If they're not apprised of what the danger there may be.
"We'd be sending lambs to slaughter; not a choice for me.
"No, we need strength to quietly check the array;
"A job I'd like to do but Red will be here in a day

"And we need to ensure your new technology survives.
"If it doesn't it will be for naught they gave their lives.
"We will duplicate the scanner on his fighting ship.
"Then when the time is right on two moons we'll demonstrate it.

"One of them is Titan and we'll spread the scan around
"So everyone throughout the system knows what's underground.
"We'll be a target then, I think, since someone is hell-bent
"To interfere with Titan's growth and this they will resent.

"Then when they play their hand perhaps we'll know a little more
"About who's brought this fight to Titan. We'll settle the score.
"At least that's where my thoughts are going; but wisdom is found
"In many counselors and we have two or three around."

Gin was in the room and listening to all they said
And sent a note to Radar asking him to go ahead
And contact Captain Standish (in command Soldana's ship).
The captain glanced at Gin who nodded then looked back at Nick:

"Soldana has a vested interest in Titan too.
"He has a cruiser parked at Rhea with nothing to do."
Nick's face brightened wide into an understanding grin
And said, "Let's get the array's specs securely sent to them!"

* * * * *

After their discussion Captain retired to his room
To handle minor business matters then a little snooze.
But drifting off to sleep a dream came starkly real and clear:
He saw his lovely wife arrayed in white and shedding tears.

Standing on a mountain with bright stars behind her back
Her golden hair in sunlight though the sky was airless black.
Bitterly she struggled with a heavy earthen vase
To pour a quenching stream upon a fire at mountain's base.

And stretching from a cavern cut into the mountain's side
Black tentacles reached round her ankles and crawled up her thighs.
Yet doggedly she struggled to put out the growing flame
Which threatened to consume the mountain and her very name.

He struggled to assist her yet he could not make his way.
She couldn't hear his voice, his legs were mired in greasy clay.
Then bursting back to consciousness (but tethered to his bed)
The captain, drenched with sweat was filled with overwhelming dread.

He trusted Red's report. He knew Red knew whom he had seen.
And just the fact she did not ask of him said everything
About the pressure she was under and the danger there.
She was trapped in darkness struggling in deep despair.

29 Rewind

Lifting off from Rhea was a pleasant single G.
Renee was at a porthole taking in all she could see.
Relieved to catch the ship but dreading what may lie ahead
Visions of the possibilities raced through her head.

She knew the warden well enough to know he'd play his hand
In a way to impress everyone that he was grand.
But something that he'd said about Iapetus not meant
To be a place for anyone her mind could not forget.

His plan to kill the witnesses was only thinly veiled
And it was not apparent how many he trusted well
Enough to spare whatever horror his plan might present.
But would he wreck the colony beyond the lives he'd spend?

It represented huge amounts of capital expenditure
To open up the caverns and install the infrastructure.
But even more, the large investment in its biosphere
And all the future produce it could make was surely dear!

That colony alone could meet a major city's needs.
When run with some efficiency, the thousands it could feed!
And yet somehow she felt that in his twisted evil heart
His plan was to destroy it all and leave no living part.

Perhaps he'd use a fission bomb to vaporize the place?
Or simply vent the caverns to the hard vacuum of space?
Even that would kill the microbes in the fertile soil
And leave the caverns void of life - completely dead and sterile.

Or just eliminate the people with a poison gas?
That would leave the place alive and not turn it to glass.
And what about his Triton agriculture operations?
Was the same fate coming to the folks who worked that station?

These thoughts were spinning in her head as Rhea spun below.
A single partial orbit then a burn aimed for Dione
Where, as was common practice for these renegades and thieves
A sudden change in course was made in order to deceive

Any who were poking noses into their affairs.
Renee leaned back into her couch and loosed her golden hair
That fell in yellow cascades in the pleasant gravity
A soothing pull against her scalp reminding her gently

Of times upon the inner worlds (like Earth, her former home)
Where she could walk in strength and feel her mass pull on her bones.
The sweet repose soon ended though, with engine cutoff's bell.
She knew she'd be in zero G at least a little spell.

The engineer came in to see her as she pulled her hair
Back into a ponytail that floated like a flair
Of sparks behind her head until she wrapped it in a bun.
(Taking care of hair that long in zero-G's not fun.)

Steadying himself beside a couch close to her own
The engineer who previously subtly made it known
That he was not completely satisfied as Warden's man
Smiled and said, "We'll freefall for an hour; then the plan

"Includes another one-G burn for close to half an hour
"Then we'll vector off and do another at full power.
"Is there anything that I can bring to comfort you?"
She smiled back and softly said, "Yes, there's one or two:

"How about a jar of pixie dust and magic wand?
"I'd like to change some things in life of which I'm not so fond."
His smile widened as he said, "Sorry, we're fresh out.
"Those things are in high demand in places here about."

His eyes were searching, as were hers, but caution was their need.
He said, "I was quite surprised you passed up Ganymede."
She said, "I was too, but there are things that matter more.
"And people who need friends when they're away on far-off shores."

He could take that either way. They greatly feared to trust.
He said, "Friends are hard to come by - scarce as pixie dust."
Their eyes were speaking volumes. She gave up the crucial clue:
"Friends are precious more than life. Do you believe that too?"

His steady eyes relayed his understanding. Nodding slow,
"Yes I do. Or rather, once I did some time ago.

"I'd like to once again; but faith and hope are very rare.
"Especially when loved ones are beyond our reach out there."

He nodded toward the porthole's glass which mirrored back his face.
Whispering, she asked, "How long?" and he could see a trace
Of teary redness in her eyes. He whispered, "Five long years
"I've jockeyed ships for him preserving loved ones' lives in fear."

She could not say anything and he could say no more
For at that moment with a wheeze the crew chief filled the door
And croaked, "The pilot wants you to go over engine three.
He says it's got a sputter when it ignites from a freeze."

"Gotcha. Be right on it," called the thoughtful engineer.
But before he left he whispered, "You need help, My Dear.
"Playing close to Warden is like dancing on the edge
"Of a hellish precipice. Your life to him is pledged."

She whispered her sad plea, "Can a message be sent out?"
"Nothing goes across the air unless there is no doubt
"It's Warden's business only and we've not been authorized
"To transmit anything at all until we have arrived.

"To do so would mean sudden death. Our ship would be destroyed
"Long before we reached our goal - a black ship he'd employ."
Her eyes widened with understanding. This confirmed her guess
That Warden's ships were used at Ganymede to make that mess.

"Tell me one more thing," she asked before he moved away,
"What is in our cargo hold - the cylinders of gray?"
The engineer looked quizzical. Why would she ask of that?
"There isn't anything at all besides that bottle rack.

"The labels say they're CO_2 though color code's not right.
"The paint was still a little wet as we began this flight.
"I don't know why the stuff would need to be in cylinders
"For it's as solid as a rock at these temperatures.

"I've learned asking questions can be unhealthy for you.
"I find it's best to focus on the job I have to do.
"So if you want to know more about cargo on this ship
"You'll need to ask someone who's more familiar with it.

"Anyway, this is our final trip out to that moon.
"I suppose another ship will make these milk runs soon.
"We're being moved to Enceladus. That's the word I hear.
"We'll probably be hauling fish from there for the next year."

He winked and spun around then dove into the lower decks
Apparently to finish up his engine three health checks.
Then as she turned to look beyond the porthole glass again
"Sputter" came into her mind and with that word a plan.

For every time an engine started it would make a surge
Of magnetic energy. Perhaps it could be urged
To modulate a simple signal that might be received
By friends, but if by enemies perhaps they'd be deceived.

This would take an engineer with skill and some luck too
To force one of the engines to emit a different tune.
And providence had brought a man with just the proper skill
But he must do it carefully or it might get them killed.

As she mulled this over waiting for the one-G burn
She noticed her reflection in the porthole glass and yearned
For days so long ago when in her dressing mirror's view
She'd see the lover of her heart, her dashing Captain Blue.

He'd often gently take her brush and run it through her hair
So tenderly and slowly with great patience and sweet care
Then wrap his loving arms around her waist and whisper words
Of love into her waiting ear - quite often as a verse.

And then beyond the glass she saw a distant glint of light
Reflected from a ship perhaps, or just a satellite.
She wondered, *Could that be my Captain's ship or even Red's?*
And then she drifted off to sleep with visions in her head.

She dreamed she saw her husband far across a running stream
With jagged rocks beneath the surface, swollen with debris
Desperately paddling a small boat towards her shore
Blindfolded and deaf to her above the water's roar.

When suddenly behind him rose a dragon's fearsome neck
Black with shining scales unmarred by the river's dreck.

Its gleaming soulless eyes alight with sinister intent
Its dripping fangs were poised to strike with death any moment.

And then with lightning quickness - faster far than she'd expect
It struck! And in that instant she was back on Warden's deck.
She could feel the thrusters altering their course's track
And she could feel one G of force was pressing on her back.

She didn't know how long she slept - perhaps just half an hour.
But she was sweating in her seat, her mouth was dry and sour.
And with the vision freshly burned into her conscious mind
She knew beyond all doubt her husband wasn't far behind.

30   Worth His Salt

Selenia accepted Captain Blue's request with glee
And gave a quick OK to Captain Standish to proceed
To TerraCorp's array (it still was silent as a tomb)
Yet mulled the tale of Sinlap's troubles over with some gloom.

For murderous attacks like Sinlap Station weren't the way
Things were done by pirates or by random renegades.
Leaving living witnesses with no ransom demands
Sent a blatant message this was done by a strong man

With no regard for human life, was dangerous at best
And proved he had the confidence to win a deadly test.
Which also meant he felt he had the ships that he would need
To neutralize resistance made by Saturn's meager fleet.

Thoughts along these lines were never far beneath her skin
As memories and feelings from the war years now slipped in.
And she could feel the coldness of the lurking shadowed doubts
Growing in her heart with unknown enemies about.

Sitting in the fourth seat of the cruiser's darkened bridge
Selenia watched carefully as thrusters nudged a smidge
To slew the ship's trajectory while tactical display
Updated merging lines and showed that one now moved away.

The view outside the porthole toward the distant sun was met
With Saturn's blackened dark side, yellow-rimmed by thin crescent
Spotted sparingly with brightened tops on amber clouds
That reached up toward the sunlight shining dimly (though still proud)

Beyond the scattered lights of moonlets sprinkled on the sky
All of which turned icy faces toward the faint sunlight.
An eerie glow on Saturn's dark side faintly could be seen:
The pale sun reflected from the mighty planet's rings.

The crescent though, was growing thicker as the ship progressed
Around the planet toward the point where Jules and Red had guessed
The TerraCorp array had drifted as it slowly slipped
Toward the massive planet in its gravitation's grip.

They didn't want to do it but they had to send a ping
Of radar now and then to get a fix on where the thing
And all its severed parts had drifted so they'd have no wreck
With undetected pieces of the station's drifting dreck.

The Nav and Tac displays now showed a dozen little tracks
Any two of which could be projected moving back
To show their point of origin to be where the array
Had been before it became silent just the other day.

All of them were quite surprised to see how far it moved
And it became apparent that the large array was shoved
Many thousand miles from LaGrange stability
Causing it to be pulled in by Saturn's gravity.

And that's exactly what was happening - and very fast!
Its orbit was decreasing and it wasn't going to last
Much longer unless something drastic happened to it soon.
To burn in Saturn's atmosphere would be its fiery doom.

By now they had approached the slowly spinning darkened mass
Which showed no sign of life or systems' power through the glass.
(A telescope revealed gaping scars from laser burns
And twisted metal structures gleaming as the carcass turned.)

"We need to get on board that station. Can we get in close?"
Selenia asked Captain Standish, who appeared morose
But nodded his agreement that it was the thing to do
And said, "I'll take a shuttle and five men to search it too."

Selenia was quite surprised when Percy volunteered
To lead a force of men and take a shuttle craft so near
The dangerously turning derelict and go aboard.
He calmly looked at her and said, "This must be my chore.

"The piloting must be precise and I want it done right.
"And I want rated pilots here if we get in a fight."
Selenia agreed but said, "I need eyes on that wreck.
"Have the men equipped with cameras that transmit back."

"Of course," he said, "We'll be back soon," and left the bridge behind.
The first mate moved into his seat and in a moment's time

The thrusters fired to match the speed of TerraCorp's array
Then only moments later Captain's shuttle pulled away.

Selenia watched through the scope with more than mild interest
For this job would put any pilot's flying skills to test.
To match up and to dock with spinning objects was one thing
But this target was turning on two axes, maybe three.

The shuttle's navigation radar let the captain know
The axes of rotation and where he would need to go
To match the motion of the first and get his grapples set
To neutralize disparate forces when their masses met.

At the root it was a simple problem of precession
An opportunity to give the junior pilots lessons.
Matching spin and waiting for the moment to attach
Then thrusting on the proper vector when the grapples latched.

The shock absorbers helped them keep the fillings in their teeth
And stomachs flipped a little when the hook-up was complete.
But when the shuttle's engines belched a half a dozen times
The big array was slowed and would be stable for some time.

At that point Captain Standish pulled his grapples back on board
And moved the shuttle to a standard airlock that was more
Conducive for the boarding party than the gaping tear
Across the metal skin that showed inside there was no air.

(At least they'd have a solid passageway and docking port.
Tethered spacewalks were not something they did for the sport.)
And so with trepidation Captain Standish and his men
Forced the unresponsive airlock open and went in.

Captain Blue's prediction was precisely what they found.
There wasn't one computer running or a soul around.
Frozen bodies twisted in the grimaces of death
Bloodied eyes and ears and ruptured lungs that found no breath.

Selenia watched carefully the monitors' display
Of images from spacesuits - heard the words that each might say
And felt her blood run cold as memories came flooding back
Of times during the war but this was worse: Pirate attack!

These people were defenseless. They were slaughtered where they stood
Many grasping air masks (and a few with time who could
Make it to a spacesuit) but were stabbed with bayonets
Or riddled, in some cases, with a number of bullets.

The place was wrecked and ransacked; the reactors over-hot.
Structural supports were cut and air reserves were shot.
But on one crewman's camera beyond a shattered beam
Selenia could see a tiny light's reflected gleam.

She asked the man to check it out. He looked where she described
And far inside an access tunnel saw one little light.
Squeezing his envirosuit into the tunnel's mouth
He pulled himself along a moment then he gave a shout:

"Hey! There is an active failsafe alive in here.
"It looks like it's atomics of some kind but I'm not clear."
He turned his light and camera so others had good views.
When Captain Standish saw it he said, "That is real bad news.

"For it appears to be an antimatter storage jar.
"Reserve power for containment won't go very far.
"That indicator shows the power pack is draining fast.
"It must have suffered damage when that girder took a blast.

"Can you open up the panel and read what it says?"
The man struggled a moment with the damaged lid then said,
"You're right, Sir. It is an antimatter storage jar
"And I am getting very nervous about where we are.

"The main containment field is strong; the secondary's gone
"From sourcing power to the primary for much too long.
"We should jettison this thing before we all are ghosts
"Or get some power to it in two hours at the most."

The man had every valid reason for his great concern:
"When antimatter meets with matter it's not just a burn
"But mutual annihilation makes a massive blast
"And a burst of gamma rays - enough to fry our ass!"

Captain Standish asked, "Can you tell how much is there?"
The man poked at the panel for a moment then declared,

"Oh my word - it says there's almost fourteen grams in here!
"When containment fails there's no way that we'll get clear!"

"Do not jettison!" Selenia jumped in the mix,
"Find a way to power it. Get containment fixed!
"The value of that antimatter far exceeds our ship.
"Do whatever you must do so we can salvage it."

The man within the service tunnel said, "It has a port.
"A universal power jack that might give it support."
Captain Standish thought a moment then he told the man,
"Plug your suit into it and determine if it can."

The man within the service tunnel paused for just a bit
Then limbered up his transfer cable and plugged into it.
And when the cable handshake was complete the light turned green
And power started transferring into the starving thing.

"It works," the man exclaimed, "But my suit can't take the load.
"I'll be on reserves in minutes." Standish then bellowed:
"Johnson, Martin! Get an APU from off the shuttle!
"Get your butts in gear and get it back here on the double!"

Two space-suited figures turned and scrambled for the lock.
Standish turned back to the tunnel which was mostly blocked
By the man inside and said, "Can that thing be removed?"
The man was silent for a moment then exclaimed, "There's two!"

"There's another antimatter vessel that's gone dark
"On the other side of this one and they both are parked
"On rails to the outer wall and there are transfer pipes
"Tied to both but they don't look like they are set up right."

Captain Standish pulled himself into the access tunnel
And told the man to move beyond the farthest of the vessels.
"Move the cable from your suit and plug into the second.
"I will power this one," then into his camera beckoned:

"Commodore, please get the engineers to look at this."
Selenia responded, "They're already here, Standish.
"Hold your camera steady on the transfer lines you see."
The first man passed the vessels which had left the tunnel free.

The captain plugged into the vessel, saw the light go green.
His man removed the access panel on the second's screen
And plugged his suit into the jack then froze without a word.
The captain asked for his report. The man looked captain-ward.

His face was white as daylight and his eyes were bulging large,
"The primary's at two percent. It's not taking a charge."
The captain queried, "How much antimatter's in the jar?"
"Another half a dozen grams. We won't get very far

"Beyond the fireball unless we leave here in a hurry.
"A single gram will make a blast that's double Nagasaki
"And we've got twenty here!" The captain thought a moment more
Then said, "Prepare to jettison the six. I'll blow the door."

He turned to face the panel that would blow explosive bolts
Which cleared the rails of outer hatches then there was a jolt
As both doors flew away into the ring-lit sky outside.
The other man released the disconnects for vessel's ride.

"Stand clear while I fire the thruster," captain Standish said,
But when he pressed the switch the thruster on the jar was dead.
A rush of gas escaped the thruster pack, but it just went
Half the distance down the rails before the gas was spent.

"Crap!" His man exclaimed from in his corner up the tunnel.
"Now we're in a hole without a ladder or a shovel!"
By then the two had brought the APU from off the shuttle
The captain took the extra cable from it on the double

And handing it to Johnson said, "Tie this to the jar
"And feed the end out through the outer hatchway just as far
"As you can make it go. Tie a good loop on the end."
With that the captain turned and said, "You're with me, my friend."

He pulled on Martin's arm and turned him toward the airlock door.
The two went to the shuttle and they left the other four.
Then just a minute after that they heard the craft detach
And only seconds later it appeared outside the hatch.

Martin gripped the edges of the shuttle's open door
Tethered to the inside with a grapple hook and more

Than forty yards of steel cable floating at his boots.
He launched himself into the void and hooked to Johnson's loop.

In less than thirty seconds Martin pulled himself inside
And signaled captain Standish it was time to take a ride.
Easing on the thrusters Standish pulled the cable tight
And just two seconds later it was outside in free flight.

Martin reeled the cable in and with a cargo tie
Lashed the antimatter vessel to the shuttle's side.
The captain turned the shuttle's nose to match his chosen path
Then fired the shuttle's engines to accelerate it fast

Toward the waiting cloud tops of the planet far below.
(The safest place to send the ticking bomb that soon would blow.)
And then he cut his engines; Martin cut the cargo tie
The captain turned the shuttle's tail and flew with all his might.

Selenia dispatched the second shuttle from the ship
To get the four men left on the array before it slipped
Dangerously close to Saturn's F ring on its flight
To burn up in the mighty planet's atmosphere that night.

As soon as her new antimatter was safely secured
She had the First Mate plot a course to bring Captain aboard.
(The energy he spent to fling the failing jar away
Meant there'd be no fuel for he and Martin left that day.)

Then only moments after they had started on the path
To intercept the captain there was seen a searing flash
Much brighter than the sun appeared when close as planet Earth
And they all knew the second antimatter vessel burst.

Six grams of the stuff would yield a quarter megaton
And gamma radiation harsh enough to kill someone.
Unless they had the shielding or the distance from the flash
The biologic damage would ensure they breathed their last.

He knew there might be minutes left, or only seconds few
So captain Standish did the only thing that he could do
To save the other men from what they had no time to flee
Yet saved the precious antimatter to be salvaged free.

There wasn't any shock wave in the hard vacuum of space.
Not a single sound or cloud of dust or any trace
Of evidence of what befell the TerraCorp array.
Just a searing flash of blinding light and gamma rays.

When the fuel reserves were gone the captain kept the craft
With the engines and their radiation shields aft
To maximize protection when the antimatter blew.
That and distance from the flash were all that he could do.

When the deadly blast of radiation had gone by
The craft's communicator sprung immediately to life:
Selenia repeatedly inquired of their state
And wanted instant confirmation of their dose and rate.

"We're both alive and it looks like we're in a stable orbit,"
Captain Standish said, "And it appears we didn't pork it.
"The dosimeters say we both received just eighty rads.
"We had the fuel for time and distance and for that I'm glad.

"I'd like to keep my hair and stay far from the medic's bed."
Selenia broke in and said, "Thank God you aren't both dead!"
Captain Standish further noted, "All our fuel is gone.
"We have maneuver thrusters but I'm sure they won't last long

"Because I used them too when putting distance at our rear.
"We'd sure appreciate a tow or fuel if you come near."
Selenia looked closely at the face that lit her screen
And knew this was a side of him that she had never seen.

"What you did was very brave," she said, "And you have saved
"Not only several lives but wealth beyond what you are paid.
"You've earned our thanks and earned the lion's share of salvage too.
"There will be some lovely steaks awaiting both of you!"

Captain Standish grinned and said, "I'd trade it all away
"For a thousand pounds of fuel and anti-sunburn spray!"
She laughed and said, "I'll bet you would! But we'll be there quite soon
"And when you're back on board I think you'll sing a different tune!"

"Thank you, Commodore," he said and switched the view screen off
Then turned to his man Martin who had entered with a cough.
"I guess there's more than one way you can earn a decent meal."
"Yes sir," Martin said, "But it was not that good a deal!"

31   Revelations

Red joined Blue in Titan orbit long before they guessed.
They knew he had the speed and stealth but also he was blessed
With excellent dynamics because Rhea soon would reach
Syzygy with Titan so the distance was the least.

They were deep in Titan's shadow when Red's ship arrived.
Nick was greatly impressed when it pulled along beside.
The sky devoid of stars and not a glint from off its skin
He'd never seen a ship that looked as nearly black as sin.

"It's dark, isn't it?" said Gin who stopped along beside
The watching Nick whose gaze was focused on the view outside.
"It looks like Red has armored up and deployed his 3C.
"He didn't have it rigged last time, but now it's plain to see."

Nick nodded his head and absentmindedly said, "Yes.
"It's quite impressive and much darker than I would have guessed."
Gin said, "You will see him better when we're in sunlight.
"Concealment isn't really great - it's meant for laser fights.

"There are darker coatings that provide a greater stealth
"But tend to absorb lasers too and that's bad for your health.
"They don't reflect much radar energy that you can spot
"So watching background stars occulting is the best we've got

"For spotting them. Though even that is difficult at best.
"As distances grow larger stars occulted become less.
"So 3C is preferred by many to protect their skin.
"When trouble is expected it can help a fighter win."

As they talked the ships came 'round the moon into the light.
A red tinge on the windows turned to blue and then to white.
The intercom erupted with a call to rig the gear
For docking when the ships were brought a little bit more near.

Dewey answered as did Bovine. This time they would be
Tethered not by simple cable but more solidly
Together with a pressured passage twixt two cargo bays
For they had work to do that might consume more than two days.

When the ships were docked they formed an engineering team
And brought Redfeather and his engineers up to full steam
On every aspect of the scanning platform Nick could show.
Construction on the second ship was one emphatic "Go!"

For Red was all a-twitter (Nick could see his neck veins pulse)
When he saw the flyby of Pandora test results.
He eyed both Nick and Radar with a new respectful gleam
Then turned to Captain Blue and said, "This changes everything!

"If we can find their burrows with a flyby and a scan
"Our hunting trips will be like shooting fish trapped in a can.
"For if we catch them unawares we multiply our force.
"In time they'll change their tactics - just as we must do, of course

"But at the outset we will have a fair wind at our back.
"Instead of living on the defense more worlds will attack."
Captain Blue held up his hand a moment then he said,
"That is in the future but let's think about this, Red.

"News of this will force the pirate rats out of their holes
"And they will swarm like angry hornets everywhere we go.
"There will be a price put on our heads without an end
"Once they learn whose ships are rigged to shine the light on them.

"We don't want to tip our hand that we have one that works
"Until we have a chance to find out who put all that hurt
"On Nick's research facility and TerraCorp's array
"When it became apparent this technique would come in play.

"At this point, they probably believe they've wiped it out
"But if they know Nick got away then they will have real doubts.
"Until the force that wants to kill him's cards are on the table
"We should keep this secret for as long as we are able."

"I'm sure you're right," said Red as absentmindedly he stroked
The curls of his black beard while his countenance evoked
The picture of a man who'd found a windfall of great wealth
And sought the means to spend it but to do so with great stealth.

"I understand," Red started, then he paused and said again,
"I understand why pirates would not like their lairs scanned,

"But who would have the inside information this was near
"And also want it stopped when it is obviously clear

"What such a tool would represent in furthering along
"Development of Titan which has been sought for so long?"
Nick could not hold back but blurted out, "You find Bordeaux
"And he might be the key to everything you want to know."

"Bordeaux?" the captains asked in unison. Then Nick replied
Describing his position and the fact that he'd not died
Among the others at the station and was not seen since
And all the odd behavior that gave all the staff offense.

"There's your inside man," said Captain Blue looking at Red.
"The problem now is who most benefits with Titan dead?"
Nick looked back and forth between the pair of senior men
Then said, "The bottom line is real estate, not pirate dens."

The captains looked at Nick and Nick looked back at captain Blue
And said, "The pirates are a giant problem it is true,
"But what's the bigger picture? What does Titan represent?
"Who will stand to lose the most when Titan's up for rent?"

Red pulled on his beard a moment then slowly replied
"Someone who's invested but has not yet realized
"Their profits (or has debts) in real estate on other moons.
"When Titan opens up their holdings would lose value soon."

Nick and Captain Blue both nodded. Nick said, "Down below
"Someone has been buying property where e'er you go
"And then they shut it down as if they don't want farming done
"Forcing folks to buy off-world instead of local-grown,

"At least to some degree. There are a number who won't pay
"For produce from off-world as a rule - they will not sway."
Captain Blue considered this and said, "Now, at first glance
"One would think land acquisition here would be a chance

"That someone wouldn't want to take if they were making bets.
"When Titan failed the land on other worlds would pay off best.
"But on the other hand, if he were set on failure here
"Keeping folks dependant and repressed would be a clear

"Way to hedge that bet and keep his strategy alive
"Regardless if the terraforming project might survive."
Red nodded agreement and said, "That has all the smell
"Of a tyrant's fingerprints. We know it all too well."

Captain Blue suggested, "Send Selenia our facts
"And maybe she can sort beneath the surface for his tracks.
"This man or group of renegades are not a bunch of ghosts
"There have to be some paper trails and she's by far the most

"Capable I know to dig in deep and root them out -"
His words were cut off as the intercom gave out a shout
And Radar's voice announced, "Sir, Selenia's on line."
"Pipe it through," the captain said, and in a moment's time

Selenia appeared upon the screen set in the wall.
"Hello, Jules - and Nick and Red! I'm so glad that I called!
"We're heading in toward Titan and I thought I should report
"About what we discovered and I'll make it very short:

"You were right. The TerraCorp array has been destroyed.
"And by the looks a very stealthy ship has been employed.
"It had the hallmarks of a pirate raid in savagery
"But we could see no looting, Jules, only butchery.

"So that leads me to think these were not pirates that attacked.
"But another entity that wanted that work sacked.
"Nothing was removed - not even very pricey gear.
"They shoved it off to burn up hitting Saturn's atmosphere.

"We also found a shot-up ship adrift full of supplies.
"A pirate force would never let a booty like that slide."
"Agreed," said Red, "How long before it impacts Saturn's air?
"Is there time to get forensic data yet from there?"

She shook her head from side to side and said, "It's much too late.
"The station was obliterated and we just escaped.
"An antimatter vessel with six grams of it inside
"Lost containment and two of our men were slightly fried."

"Holy smokes!" exclaimed the captain, "Six grams of the stuff?
"What I wouldn't give for just one sixtieth as much!"

Selenia looked back at him as if he'd made a joke
Then seeing he was serious replied, "It's not all smoke.

"There were two containment vessels left on the array.
"One of them was salvaged just before we pulled away.
"I've got it here on board, Jules. Take all that you need."
Nick became excited and began scratching his knee.

"How much do you have, Selenia?" he blurted out.
"Fourteen grams or so," she said. He looked at her with doubts
And said, "Fourteen milligrams, you mean?" She answered, "No,
"Fourteen grams and transfer lines set up ready to go."

Nick turned pale and looked at Captain Blue whose eyes were wide.
"Selenia, that represents a fortune you can't hide!
"TerraCorp is going to want that back when they get wind."
"No," she said, "The salvage rights were clear, my handsome friend."

"Besides," she added slyly, "That array was vaporized
"In a blast that no one near could ever have survived.
"It's mine! And as much of it is yours as you decide."
The captain looked at Nick and asked, "How much would you like?"

Nick's clear skin turned red now as he thought the matter through
And said, "For our experiments, a milligram or two
"Would be a giant help -", the captain cut him off and said,
"We will take four grams then we will transfer two to Red."

Red looked at the captain with surprise across his face
"Why would I want that much when I only need a trace?"
Captain answered quietly, "You'll see why in a bit.
"Take my word, you'll understand when you're privy to it."

The captain smiled broadly, winked his eye, and turned to Nick
"Let Bovine and Dewey know to get a transfer rigged.
"You and Radar get set up to test the second way
"Of tuning your magnetics and we'll see if it will pay."

Selenia had many questions it was plain to see.
The captain turned back toward the screen and said, "Presently
"You'll be made aware of something quite extraordinary.
"And you will share in the rewards of which there will be many."

Selenia replied, "I know extraordinary men.
"And I am thrilled to be on hand to work with three of them.
"That is my reward." She smiled wide and tossed her hair
Then looked up at a panel, rising slightly from her chair.

"We'll be there in thirteen hours," she looked back and said
"I will have our galley make sure all your men are fed."
The captain thanked her in advance then said, "Selenia,
"We're sending you some data from developed areas

"Of Titan, where someone is buying farms to shut them down.
"Will you take a look at it and maybe snoop around
"To see how it lines up with what's been going on elsewhere?
"Maybe there's a clue here as to who and why and where?"

"I'll be glad to, Jules," she said, "But I can tell you now
"That this deceptive dealing started somewhere here abouts.
"Even Ganymede has been affected by this plot
"And farmers there are forced to sell some of their richest lots."

Captain Blue acknowledged and they all said their goodbyes
And then he turned toward Red and peered intently in his eyes
And said, "I'm going to Saturn VIII before this day is through.
"To get your system up and running Nick stays here with you."

Red returned his steady stare a moment then he said,
"I understand your need for haste, but you might wind up dead
"If you don't reconsider. Wait a day. We'll go with you.
"My ship is rigged for battle and my crew is ready too."

Nick looked at the both of them and said, "I'd like to test
"The other mode of operation but it would be best
"If we had antimatter to initiate the beam..."
He trailed off as Captain's brown eyes made a teary gleam

And broke away from Red's. He glanced at Nick, nodded his head.
Then Red gave further counsel, "Jules, why don't you go to bed?
"I know you haven't slept a wink since I left Rhea's space.
"Your fatigue is evident - it's carved across your face.

"We have thirteen hours and the work is going smooth.
"Get your sack time in then we'll coordinate our moves."

Captain Blue conceded quietly, then as he rose
Turned to Nick and said, "Tell him about the other mode."

32 A Small Request

Her view of Saturn from above Iapetus seemed new.
She'd lived there years, though times she'd seen it had been very few
Living in the caverns far beneath the mountains' stone
So alien to warmth and sunlight like on Earth, her home.

Though the views of Saturn and its rings were fabulous
Few moons could be near as ugly as Iapetus.
Shaped much like a walnut with a bulge around the waist
And turning sunward every eighty days its double face.

One as black as coal, the other nearly white as snow
And lifeless from all outward views but those who slaved below.
The thought of loss of precious lives repulsed her to the core
And she knew she may never savor this view anymore.

The cabin lights turned red when it was time to take her seat.
The little ship's trajectory was short and fast, discrete;
Arcing in to Warden's tiny port with no orbit
With little chance of being seen by anyone near it.

Deceleration was extreme and pressed her in her seat
But when the engines throttled down the ship stood on its feet
As gently as a chickadee alighting on a twig
And now she braced to meet the warden waiting for the rig.

The engineer accompanied Renee into the lock
And as they waited for the loading bridge she had her talk.
Leaning toward the man she whispered softly in his ear
(Being careful to ensure that no one else could hear):

"I don't believe it's CO_2 inside those cylinders.
"I suspect it's something you'd consider sinister.
"There is little I can do, but something that you might:
"Let your engine sputter when you leave on your next flight.

"Can you modulate the sputter to spit out a code?
"Perhaps a simple string of letters that might spell out 'Gold?'
The man looked back at her a little startled and surprised
But she could see a glimmer of a "yes" deep in his eyes.

And then the conversation was pre-empted by the bridge
Docking to the outer door. Renee felt just a twinge
Of guilt for asking that the engineer would bring her gear
But she needed the opportunity to have his ear.

The airlock on the boarding bridge completed its routine.
When equalized the doors retracted then they both were seen
By Warden's cameras within the bridge. (Now it was done -
She'd said all that she could and now her dance must be begun.)

Curiously, she felt some excitement deep inside.
These cycles of adrenalin then rest were quite a ride!
Days spent on the wing and even spotting an old friend
And now the faintest prospect of great change was on the wind.

And it would all start now, when her eyes met warden's own.
She would have the edge to set the future's very tone
And so she drew her energy from deep inside her hopes
Which made a beaming smile Warden's stare could not revoke.

"Warden!" she exclaimed when he appeared to see them in.
"I wanted to surprise you but I'm sure you've heard from them."
She gestured at the engineer who walked two steps behind
And said, "It's my prerogative that I might change my mind."

Warden's eyes pierced through her as he said, "I *am* surprised.
"I didn't think that anyone could pass a chance to ride
"To Ganymede on such a pleasure yacht as I had booked.
"That makes quite a statement," and he made a sidelong look

That she could see suspicion in, but also hints of hope
And she knew her next words would need to be carefully spoke:
"I had a pleasant time on Rhea, Warden, but I found
"It isn't quite as fun when there's no one you know around.

"I didn't want to go to Ganymede with time to spare
"And no one for companionship with whom I'd care to share.
"So I'll go when we go together." Then she took his hand
And stepped in close and whispered, "Isn't that a better plan?"

Warden's black eyes widened slightly as that spark of hope
Dulled by days of doubt now flared when fanned by how she spoke

And he could see no trace of hesitation in her eyes.
In fact, as if she'd found her home she gave a little sigh.

"It is a more attractive plan," he said, "but I had hoped
"To have the business finished here so you'd not have to cope
"With any of the details, shall we say; to let it pass
"And let the mem'ries of this cold rock be put in the past."

She saw the darkness in the depths of Warden's piercing eyes
And stared back with a hardness of her own (and felt surprise
That she could counter such a searing gaze without a flinch)
And knew in that brief instant she had Warden's mind convinced.)

But that was not to say that she had found the warden's trust!
For she knew in her heart that Warden's mind had great disgust
For blind acceptance, judging it was weakness to be used.
As he had trusted no one his whole life, her instincts knew.

"I hope you're not upset that I've returned to you so soon.
"But you should know as partners we must leave a little room
"For compromise and counsel if this partnership will work.
"And I think that it will and we will both enjoy the perks."

With that she placed her other hand beside the warden's face
Then turned around to take her bags the engineer had placed
Beside her on the floor before he exited the room.
Then Warden said, "Then I should ask you for your input soon

"Into a matter that arose while you were off at play.
"But first, why don't you settle in. And welcome back, Renee."
He took the bags away from her and motioned toward the door
Smiling with a little twist she'd learned meant he had more

To say about the matter but he'd say no more for now.
Then as they walked the corridor he said, "So tell me how
"Your trip to Rhea went. Did you find something you could wear?
"Tell me all about it. It's been years since I was there."

And so she chatted lightly about what she saw and did
Until they reached her quarters where the conversion slid
Into their plans for dinner and she promised she would wear
A dress that she had purchased that would match his raven hair.

"See you then," she said as she pulled shut her quarters door
And listened for his fading footsteps then slid to the floor
Repeating back within her mind the scene that they'd just played
And felt a wave of great relief that things had gone her way.

* * * * *

Duke and Bovine sat with Nick and Haji in the galley
Washing down zucchini bread with gallons of hot coffee.
The word was given by the captain that soon they would burn
For Saturn Eight so Duke was telling things Nick ought to learn:

"Since the first trip out here Saturn Eight has been a jinx.
"You'll say, "Superstition!" but it's what most spacers think.
"There's been a lot of ships lost there and accidents aren't rare.
"The one time that I went out there I had a spooky scare.

"It was when I worked the Survey Corps. We were sent
"To Saturn Eight to find out where an assay crew had went.
"We never got a signal from them other than a beep
"From a ship's transponder that was transmitting real weak.

"When we tracked it down the ship was resting on its side
"And there was not a living soul around it or inside
"And not a spacesuit or a footprint anywhere around.
("Crippled struts on landing gear appeared to lay it down.)

"The really spooky part was when we came there the next day.
"We found the ship had vanished or had somehow flown away
"And there was not a mark that showed it ever had been there.
"I tell you, that made bristles out of everyone's neck hair!"

"Whatever happened to that ship remains a mystery still
"And it was not the only ship on that moon to be killed.
"There is an active evil there that many men can feel.
"Regardless what you think, Nick, the jinx is very real."

The doubtful look on Nick's face showed he had no real concern
And thought that this was simply an old spacer's prank to burn
The newbie with some punch line coming at him 'round the bend
But there was no trace of conspiracy between these men.

Bovine added, "I know miners who have gone out there
"Thinking that the stories were made up to simply scare
"Away the competition for some mineral or gem
"But came away with not a thing but tales to add to them.

"I know one old geezer who was there decades ago
"Working in an assay mine that couldn't make a go.
"An ice slide swept their ship away and buried them inside
"But they had gear to tunnel out and be rescued alive.

"Those crustal ice slides happen with some regularity
"And if you're not above them you'll be there eternally.
"Nah, no one ever needs to go to that old moon.
"There's nothing there worth mining and the mountains can spell doom.

Duke was looking at the floor. He slowly shook his head
"There's been a lot of stories of men winding up there dead.
"Only bad luck follows those who even orbit there."
And then he nodded, "We'll be fine if we remain aware."

Gin was floating by and overheard some of their yak
And interjected, "That should be about enough of that.
"No wonder it's deserted - everyone spreads all that fear!
"The inner moons just offer more than anything out here.

"So don't let these guys put the heebie jeebies on you Nick.
"Iapetus is just another place where certain tricks
"Need to be avoided. It's not 'where', but the 'who',
"And when we get there we will find out for ourselves what's true."

Gin gave Duke and Bovine both a sidelong glance to say,
"Stow it and be more professional" in his own way.
Bovine cleared his throat when he saw movement at Gin's back
As Radar came into the galley looking for a snack.

He grabbed a cup of coffee and a slice of Haji's bread
Then slid into a chair as Bovine poked, "You look half dead."
Radar glanced around explaining, "I've been working late
"Teaching little Skippy how to run the commo gate."

"Skippy?" Gin and Bovine echoed, "Who the heck is that?"
"He's my new assistant," Radar's tired smile cracked.

Then he gave a short description of how he had rigged
The N-dimension processor Soldana had gifted:

Radar burned an artificial intelligence set
Of algorithms into it in hopes he might forfeit
The tedium of monitoring jobs that he must do
"And furthermore," he added, "He might just replace you too!"

Haji grinned and chuckled, Bovine made a rude reply
How he might stuff him in the airlock to breath empty sky.
Then they all had a laugh and wandered off to check the gear
Which they would need to scan the vacant moon when they got near.

33   Making the Point

Dinner was delectable - a very welcome feast.
Both were in good appetite (Renee's was not the least).
Warden wore his normal black but with a purple tie
Renee had bought for him on Rhea, she wore black besides.

Her dress was drawn in tight, a purple sash around her waist.
A purple ribbon kept her golden hair out of her face
Tied into a pony tail that curved 'round to her chest
Cascading down across the V-cut trim that graced her breast.

Tonight the dinner table was set in a different place.
Not in Warden's quarters but a room with lots of space
Reminiscent of a public meeting room or hall
And rather dimly lit where one could hear more than one saw.

The conversation started light and both of them were glad.
Warden had been gratified her implants showed she had
No conversations of a nature which would tip the hand
That she had sought old friends and contacts or her dead husband.

Renee was thankful too that Warden seemed to be relaxed
And he had made no inquisition (though behind her back
She knew that he had questioned spies on Rhea and the ship)
But that was his prerogative and she'd let nothing slip.

And then as dinner plates were cleared by servants who retired
Into the doorway at the rear and wine made him inspired
The warden brought a bit of business up for her review
To test what her response might be to what he planned to do:

"I hired a man to do a simple job but he fell short.
"In fact his failure cost our cause much more than he is worth.
"It seems a number of our men were killed for his offense.
"I had to go and personally clear part of his mess.

"I have spent tremendous wealth and labored many years
"To set the stage for our ascent to empire, yet his fears
"Or maybe his incompetence or simple lack of vision
"Almost caused the loss of much that I put in position."

Directing her attention to the main door of the hall
He motioned to two men who brought a third who took a fall.
Struggling to regain his feet, the first two pulled him up
Then forced him to his knees as Warden lifted up his cup

And said, "Why Doctor Bordeaux! How nice of you to join us!
"Tell me, has your stay been all you'd hoped here on Iapetus?"
Reeling from the injustice in how he'd been abused
The doctor sputtered, clearly animated but confused,

"I am not amused by this despicable treatment!
"I'm to rule on Titan. That was part of our agreement."
"Rule?" exclaimed the warden, "I'm the one who makes the rules.
"Management of my affairs were all you had to do.

"Yet you could not maintain control of just one tiny station.
"How could you be counted on to run an entire nation?"
"Nation!" Doctor Bordeaux sneered, "That rabble is not that!"
"You were to maintain control and build it!" Warden spat.

"And worst of all you gave to TerraCorp the very tool
"I placed you there to keep out of their hands, you worthless fool!
"This cost many lives and it cost me a lot of pain
"To clean that mess so I believe you need to stay in chains."

Warden took another sip of wine from his gold cup
While glaring at the tattered man who kneeled there looking up.
(Renee was fascinated by the warden's outward calm
For she had seen him rage at times when lesser things went wrong.)

And these weren't plastic fetters that kept Doctor Bordeaux tied.
He was bound with shackles made of steel with chains besides.
They kept his hands together and no higher than his waist.
His ankles and his wrists were bleeding and blood smeared his face.

More than just embarrassed and misunderstood and hurt
With dirt and sweaty stains highlighting rips across his shirt
Unshaven and disheveled, sleep deprived and nerves rubbed raw,
Renee was not surprised a single whit by what she saw.

For in the course of six long years she'd seen examples made
From time to time of shirkers or of others who had paid

The price for non-conformity, or small defiant acts.
It wasn't a rare thing for her to see stripes laid to backs.

Doctor Bordeaux's face grew red with anger and dismay.
His eyes were casting 'round about in hopes he'd find a way
To mount a sane defense against the warden's hot tirade.
"You failed me," Warden drained his cup, "For that you need to pay."

"But I have education! I deserve consideration!
"I worked hard to keep the rabble from the atmospheric station!
"And now I'm treated like a lowly criminal in chains?
"I demand a moment for my actions to explain!"

"A moment?" warden asked, "You had six months to make your case.
"And all the time you spent there brought me nothing but a waste
"Of men and precious resources. You've shown distain for me
"And all my work these many years and all that I've achieved!"

The doctor stuttered, "D-Distain? Th-that is not the case!
"I have harbored no ill will and wavered not a trace
"In my commitment to the deal. The scanner plans were sent
"Before I knew they were completed - not by my consent!"

Warden stood and strolled a dozen slow steps toward the man
Then asked him, "Why did these plans reach your rabble - not my hand?
"You were tasked to keep the Titan project well contained
"But caused the deaths of dozens and the place went up in flames.

"All this time of planning and the watching and the waiting
"Then at the crucial moment I have nothing but your failing."
Bordeaux's face contorted with confusion then he said,
"Rabble? How did scanner plans escape? The man is dead!"

Warden's face contorted too - but his with burning rage,
"The men you sent to stop him said the engineer was saved.
"An unknown shuttle picked him up and snatched him through the air.
"Someone else has what is mine and you do not know where."

Warden turned to face Renee and asked, "What are your thoughts?
"Is he not responsible for what his actions wrought?"
Renee considered this and said, "If what you say is true
"Some restitution for his actions certainly is due.

"The terms of contract were not met and we sustained a loss.
"But tell me what this 'scanner' is and what might be the cost?"
Doctor Bordeaux hung his head as Warden softly said,
"In the wrong hands it could be the tool that makes us dead.

"As a minimum it represents a world's loss.
"How can one affix a price to what an empire costs?"
Doctor Bordeaux sobbed. Warden asked, "What do you think?
"What cup of our retribution shall this loser drink?"

"He doesn't look much like a killer," Renee thought out loud.
"I'm sure that we can find a way to work it out somehow."
Warden made a sidelong glance at Renee then he asked
"Tell me Doctor, do you love me?" through a smiling mask.

The Doctor looked up through his tears appearing more confused
And asked, "Do I love you?" then he looked at Warden's shoes
And said, "I don't know what you mean, but I'm prepared to learn."
Warden: "Doctor Bordeaux, show how your love for me burns!"

At that the Doctor's eyes went wide; he mouthed a silent scream.
The walls to either side and to his back reflected gleams
Of white light as the guards on either side of him let go
And jumped aside as Bordeaux's back began to slowly blow

A smoky shower of white sparks and burning bone and tissue.
His eyes bulged out as pressure caused his final breath to issue
In whistling streams from nose and mouth as pinkish-tinted steam
While Warden turned his back (his eyes displayed a happy gleam).

Renee stood up in horror and took two tentative steps
Toward the burning body but in seconds what was left
Was little more than coal and ash and lumps of burning fat.
Warden called out to the guards, "Get men to clean up that!"

The guards stood there in shock a moment. One said, "Yes, yes sir!"
"Highness!" snapped the Warden, "And that also goes for her!"
He gestured toward Renee who by this time regained her wits
And said, "That is a fancy trick; but not so much as *this!*"

With that she sprang at Warden who fell back into his chair.
She wrapped her legs around him while she pulled out from her hair

A gleaming golden blade that she held close against his throat.
(Pinned against his chair the shock across his face was wrote!)

"My fire burns much hotter than what killed Doctor Bordeaux!"
Renee explained in whispers as she let the warden know
That if he struggled she would drive the blade through throat to bone
Then told him in a steady voice, "Don't burn men in my home!

"And never, ever ask me how my love may burn for you.
"You must learn to be the one to whom I give it to."
The shock and fear within his eyes changed oddly into humor.
"I wish I knew you didn't like me burning people sooner!"

She placed her lips against his in a momentary kiss
Then pulled the blade away and said, "On Rhea I got this,"
(She turned the blade around and pressed the hilt into his hand)
"To give to you as token that I'll be part of your plans.

"But you must take your time with me. I'm not an easy win."
The warden held the golden dagger under Renee's chin
And said, "I've known that all along. And that's why I will give
"As much time as you need, for I intend us both to live

"In harmony and splendor. For the first time in my life
"I want affection given and not wrested from a wife."
Renee unwrapped her legs and pulled the Warden to his feet.
She flipped her hair behind her back and made his jacket neat.

Then turned to face the guards who witnessed all that she had done
To say, "You have your orders. *Git!*" (They left at a dead run.)
Then as the warden held the jeweled dagger to the light
He asked, "Was this to be a present later on tonight?"

She looked up at the blade and said, "I meant it with dessert,
"But we were interrupted by sad business and it hurt.
"And by the way, I don't agree that killing him was right.
"It was a waste of resources. There'd be much more delight

"In putting him to work among the garlic and the chives.
"Labor of that kind would make him wish he weren't alive."
Warden smiled slightly as he saw the point she made.
Pleased to see her think of ways to maximize the pain.

But then he steered her toward the door behind them and they left.
(The scrubbers for the room were not enough to let the breath
Be free of smoke or purge the stench of burning flesh away.)
"Let's go for a walk and have dessert another day."

As they left the room Renee turned 'round to take a look
At the smoking lump at the far end where Bordeaux cooked.
Shocked by what had happened but more shocked by how she felt:
Indifference! Her needs would not allow her heart to melt.

Warden made the point that Bordeaux was a liability.
He knew more than he needed and that was the cold reality.
She conceded that was something only he could judge
And maybe it was best to nip that loose string in the bud.

Warden further stated that Iapetus was rife
With people who could likewise in the future cause them strife.
Renee held him up short and in a soft voice told him straight
That she was well aware that there were plans that he had laid

For tying up those strings as well, but she would like her say
Before the final chapter closed and their ship flew away.
"I spent a lot of sweat and tears inside this colony.
"And many of the residents have mentioned recently

"That they have come to call this home since they were given choice
"To work more for themselves and many speak as with one voice.
"Let us grow this colony! A fine resource it is.
"It was a huge investment and it should not be dismissed

"As something that is undesirable left in the past.
"The profits are tremendous and potential is vast!
"I know you rule on Triton, Enceladus nearly sacked,
"Ganymede is partly yours and others are on track

"To be part of your growing empire when the time is ripe.
"Let me rule Iapetus. You know I'll run it right."
Warden stopped and turned toward her and said, "You misconstrue.
"Iapetus was populated simply as a tool.

"It's done its job in bringing agriculture to its knees
"On many worlds who now are largely dependent on me.

"Hunger is a weapon stronger far than guns or ships
"Or politicians bought by lawyers with their lying lips.

"The system is set up now for a most convenient crisis
"Then farmland in the outer worlds will suddenly be priceless.
"I will hold the title to the vast majority
"And all the hungry peasants will remit their souls to me.

"And you, of course, Renee," he added as an afterthought.
(She was quite amazed by the extent of this grand plot.
And that he spoke so candidly of it was a surprise!
He seemed to be relaxed by Doctor Bordeaux's harsh demise.)

"Our little crisis was to start when you were safely back
"From Ganymede but Bordeaux set the timing way off track
"And so it has begun. You might be curious to see
"The news reports from Neptune, Rhea, and from Ganymede."

By now they'd reached his quarters and he showed her through the door
(Where she was not surprised by all the clutter on the floor).
He pressed the switch to activate a view screen on the wall
And handed her the remote for the newscasts to recall.

As she sorted through the entries he poured them some wine.
She shortly found a channel that delivered news real time.
Pictures of food riots in Callisto's major towns
Where Jovian militia were called to put them down

Were soon supplanted by reports that Triton had deployed
Their planetary defenses for someone had destroyed
A major food production site by orbital attack
And no one seemed to know who did it or where to strike back.

Warden brought her glass and set himself down at her feet
And asked to see the finance channel beamed from Ganymede.
But just before she changed the channel one reporter said
That land disputes on Enceladus had left thirty dead.

Shipping stocks were up and farmland futures had gone wild.
The commentators pondered why demand had been so mild
Until the recent losses in production made it plain
That unexpected market forces misreported gains.

"Gobbledygook!" the warden sneered. "Those clowns don't have a clue
"About what causes market shifts in farmland like I do."
And then a special feature gave a very grim report
About the many cargo ships that hadn't come to ports

Resulting in a drop in food stocks on the outer moons
And some expressed concern that shortages would happen soon.
"Do you see the power that our little colonies
"Have wielded in the background with such silent subtlety?

"And soon my agents everywhere will offer land for lease
"At prices that will keep the peasants bound for centuries.
"A very, very favorable crisis, is it not?
"This is just the start of our grand game and we're on top!"

Warden turned and looked at her with fire in his eyes.
His level of excitement steadily was on the rise.
With every note of doom the news reported as they watched
She could see the waves of satisfaction through him wash.

"What production site on Triton was it that went down?"
Renee asked Warden who produced a momentary frown.
"One that lost its usefulness I think," the warden said.
"The one that I was at?" she asked, "Is everyone there dead?"

"The people weren't the target and it's too late to look back.
"It was the facility that came under attack."
The warden's gleeful look returned with darkness in his eyes,
"Collateral destruction is a business loss sometimes."

He sipped his wine and turned his gaze back toward the blaring wall.
(Renee had seen his callousness too much to be appalled.)
"Business is business, I suppose," she softly said
While wondering how many of the ones she knew were dead.

"Warden, I don't want what happened there to happen here.
"You are well aware that there are some who I hold dear.
"Promise me the stewardship of this facility
"And I will guarantee to you the people's loyalty."

"Guarantee?" the warden scoffed, "Loyalty?" he snapped.
"The only guarantee is death; and loyalty?" he laughed.

"Loyalty is only found beneath a cold boot heel
"Or purchased with a steady stream of money, hard and real."

Renee slid down beside him then and touched her glass to his.
He turned his head to look at her and she said, "Yes, it is.
"I've seen it wrested from the weak and purchased from the willing
"But there is yet another way that you might find fulfilling

"And that is when it's given freely as an act of love."
The warden quipped, "I don't believe in what you're speaking of.
"That has not existed in my life's experience.
"And thinking that it might to me makes not a bit of sense."

Renee looked deeply in his eyes in hopes that she might see
A glimmer of a chance that in his heart there was a seed
Of hope that something good and normal might be sparked to grow
But all she saw was darkness and a heart as black as coal.

"I'm truly sorry, Warden. In my life there really has
"Been loyalty in both directions and the payment was
"Made with trust and admiration - not with gold or pain.
"My years of loyalty to husband weren't made very plain?"

She turned her head away but gave a sideways look at him
Then took a sip of wine and said, "But that time's at an end.
"I'm looking forward now to finding my new place in life.
"Though I'm not ready yet to start again as someone's wife.

"That love and admiration must be earned - not bought or sold.
"It comes spontaneously from within and not with gold
"But in the absence of the former, well, the latter's fine.
"Until the former comes along I'm up for a good time."

She turned herself to face him, sitting cross-legged on the floor,
Took another sip of wine and said, "And what is more
"You will find that most folks will respond in that same way.
"Treat them with respect and they'll return it back some day.

"Let me prove it with Iapetus where strides were made
"In the recent months and in the long run it will pay
"With great rewards from loyal subjects of the new empire.
"Don't throw this away by casting them into the fire."

He looked at her with narrow eyes, then turned back to the screen.
She placed her hand on his and said, "I've changed some as you've seen.
"Surely you can change a little too as we progress.
"Oh, look! Now I've put some wrinkles in my brand new dress!"

The sudden change to lighter issues came at just the time
To set the subject deeper into his subconscious mind.
"At any rate", she said as she stood up to brush her dress
"I'm glad that you were able to clean up your Bordeaux mess.

"I'm going to retire now. It's been a day for me.
"I'm afraid I'll fall asleep if I watch more TV.
"Goodnight," she said as she returned her wine glass to its place.
"Think about the things I said." Then left his living space.

The warden said goodnight but didn't bother to stand up
Until he noticed that he needed more wine in his cup.
The glee with which he watched the news would need a treat to top.
He spoke into a mike: "Send Eighty-Three and dress her hot."

34   Rendezvous and Pow Wow

Soldana's cruiser slipped into its orbit right on time.
Bovine manned the airlock door and threw the tether line
For neither of the smaller ships had universal locks
Which would allow a hard connection for when they might dock.

And so their flexie-tunnels linked the airlocks of the ships
Which gave unsuited access so the occupants could slip
From ship to ship at will as duties brought along the need
(One of which was to attend Selenia's big feed!)

And it was quite a feed! Twelve honey-basted Hellas hams
Served with all the trimmings (Boston beans and greens and yams)
Lemons fresh from who-knows-where they'd picked up while on Rhea
Which made great jars of Margaritas made with Earth Tequila.

This was quite a treat for Red's crew (who did not have Haji)
And made an opportunity that bolstered camaraderie.
(Many on each crew had known the other crews for years
So it was quite a grand ol' time to eat and share some beers.)

The Captains Blue and Redfeather were greeted at the door
That led into the galley by Selenia with more
Than friendly interest for she gave each of them a kiss
Then asked them with some mischief in her voice, "And where is Nick?"

"He will be along," said Captain Blue who moved aside
To let Bovine and Dewey through so they could go inside.
"He's working on a special project with Red's engineer."
"Good!" she said, "For I have a surprise when he gets here."

She nodded toward her side behind the bulkhead of the room
And whispered, "There is someone else who wants to see him soon!"
The captain's smile disappeared. He said, "Oh no. You didn't."
Selenia said, "Hush, Jules. Now you wait just a minute."

She pushed him gently pinning him against the metal wall.
"They are young and full of life. Now let them have a ball!"
The captain didn't want distractions pulling Nick away
And interfering with the work that needed done today.

Selenia breathed mortal threats that made the captain grin
And then around the doorway's edge a smiling face popped in.
Framed in yellow curls, beaming blue eyes greeted him,
"Hello, Captain!" Then her eyes broke off as Nick came in.

She launched herself around the corner for the intercept
Tackling Nick and tumbling, her arms wrapped 'round his neck.
Struggling to regain positional stability
Nick's surprise was turned to joyful kisses instantly!

The others in the area who witnessed her attack
Gave applause and laughter while some pounded on Nick's back.
Accompanied by cat calls and a broad array of jokes.
The two of them found seats and talked so fast they nearly choked.

"See?" Selenia's accusatory tone was rife
With mocking menace meant to cut his cautions like a knife.
The captain laughed and took Selenia's now offered arm
While she hooked onto Red's and led them both happy and charmed.

Soldana's cruiser's galley was much larger than their own
And had a military feel that wasn't much like home.
So after feasting with the men the principles retired
To Captain Blue's wood galley to catch up and to conspire.

Captain Standish was impressed and even some amused
To see such lovely woodwork in a ship he knew was used
In combat on occasion and for other chancy gigs
But complimented Captain Blue for his taste in his digs.

Selenia felt right at home. She nestled in a chair
(A skillfully constructed knot contained her raven hair)
Captain Blue was on her left and Red sat to her right.
Gin and Red's Lieutenant sat beyond the table's light.

"Let's put it together," Captain Blue began to say
"Someone has been working hard to stand in Titan's way.
"They've tried to steal or sabotage the tool the Titans need
"To turn the hydrocarbon cycle back safely with speed.

"Attacks were made on Titan where they killed with broad abandon.
"The TerraCorp array was not a target picked at random.

"Indeed, it was to be the platform where the tool would ride
"To scan the crust of Titan and to map it deep inside."

"This was bold and blatant and it speaks of desperation
"And a plan that has been long in secret preparation.
"But since the targets they went after included our Nick
"They'll be hunting for him and attack me, I predict."

"Why would they attack you?" Captain Standish interrupted.
Selenia looked up, her smile worriedly disrupted.
Red had crossed his arms and looked like he was deep in thought.
Captain Blue continued, "Well, here's some facts we've got:

"The men who tried to kill our Nick were witness to my yacht
"When we snatched him out of there before he could get caught.
"It's an even bet the craft that missed us in the air
"Were the very people who attacked the station there.

"I showed no markings and I ran without transponders on
"But it would not be difficult to guess my track beyond
"The heading I had taken and the speed with which I flew.
"I was on my throttles to reach orbit rendezvous.

Red cut in and filled the blanks in for the other four:
"You can bet it won't be long before they know the score.
"As soon as two and two are added and it becomes clear
"That he was brought to Saturn by him and he's harbored here,

"Well, I know what I'd do if that shoe fit the other foot.
"Every recent ship from Earth would soon be burned to soot."
He glanced at Captain Standish with a coldness in his eye
Then looked hard at Selenia, "Everyone would die."

"So I'll be leaving orbit when the transfer is complete,"
Captain Blue continued, "And we'll need to be discreet.
"We have a working prototype that functions far beyond
"What TerraCorp was hoping for. So we've been working on

"A second one for Red's ship and he's itching for it bad."
Captain Blue and Red smiled brightly for they both were glad
That Red's equipment would be operational in hours.
Selenia then queried them (she looked a little dour):

"It's time to fill us in on what this 'tool' is all about
"And why someone would kill to keep the word from leaking out."
Captain Blue looked deeply into Standish's blue eyes
For a silent moment then he loosed a quiet sigh.

He turned and faced Selenia and took her hand in his
And said, "It changes everything. This is what it is:"
He touched a button on his wrist; the wall screen came alive
With excerpts from the images of Pandora's test ride.

"Notice how the human excavations can be viewed
"Through many miles of regolith - right through the little moon.
"Anyone who didn't want their bases to be seen
"Would go to any length to kill all knowledge of this thing.

"The researchers on Titan hoped that TerraCorp's array
"Would show the safest places for core drilling some bright day.
"But that array was cumbersome and not much of a threat.
"The progress was quite slow and it was not developed yet.

"Then Nick perfected for them their first workable design
"And sent it up to the array. And then in record time
"He became a target as did everyone near him.
"Someone doesn't want the Titan drilling to begin."

"That's the bigger issue," Captain Redfeather tossed in
"But these attackers don't posses complete information.
"They only know the clumsiness of TerraCorp's array.
"The one that Jules and Nick developed fits a cargo bay."

Selenia and Captain Standish both now saw the light.
Captain Blue then added, "it's a thousand fold more bright
"Than what Nick sent to the array and right now no one knows
"Except the crews on our two ships. And, of course, you folks."

"And so it follows," Red continued, "If the word might slip
"That this device is small enough to be built in a ship
"The force that struck on Titan and took out the big array
"Will jump on us with all they've got when this sees light of day."

Captain Blue peered deep into Selenia's dark eyes
Knowing that unspoken questions would be no surprise

And he could see she had no knowledge who might want to kill
Development of Titan bad enough for blood to spill.

But he could see the gears inside her head begin to turn
And in a moment she could feel her stomach start to churn.
Then in a business voice she said, "It was no pirate raid
"That killed the people down on Titan or the big array.

"This was done by someone with their eyes fixed on a prize.
"And they are watching out for pirates' interests besides.
"Which means that pirates are their business partners in some way
"And I would bet good money it involves the slaver's trade.

"Farms and factories on growing worlds don't shut down
"Unless there is an interfering force applied somehow.
"Off-world produce has been flooding markets system-wide
"At prices far below production costs now for some time.

"The lion's share of costs are labor. Tell me, am I wrong?
"And what if that could disappear and not cost you a song?
"How has all this surplus off-world product been produced?
"Tell me boys, what is the bottom line of two plus two?"

She looked around the table meeting each man's eyes in turn.
Then Gin responded, "I'll bet if you looked in deep caverns
"On worlds off the beaten path you'd find slave labor farms
"Populated courtesy of pirates and their charms."

Red grunted agreement; Captain Blue nodded his head.
Selenia lowered her sultry voice a bit and said,
"Jules, some time ago I mentioned Ansel had been paid
"Some profits that were traced back to the human traffic trade.

"Soldana had the means to verify the money came
"From someone who, when I was very young, shared my last name."
Her eyes burned with a fire as she knew down in her bowel
Her brother was behind this and her face turned to a scowl.

Captain Blue stared back at her and Red stared at her too.
Captain Standish offered, "So, let's try to find out who.
"We have a lovely cheese to bait a primed and ready trap.
"Let news of your scanner loose and you will catch your rat."

The silence in the room was thick as all of them thought through
The pro's and con's and options that were possible to do.
A half a minute's silence passed before anyone spoke.
It was Captain Blue who said, "Well, here's what I propose:

"I think we all agree that Titan's future must be saved.
"It's only right that we provide what this rat took away.
"We'll do a proper scan and make the data public fare.
"That will guarantee it's on the level and it's fair.

"The treasure and the lives invested won't have been for naught
"And Titans will have what they need to find their drilling spots.
"And Percy's right. When we let loose the data Titan needs
"You can bet the bad guys will attack with greatest speed.

"Now, that will take the heat off Nick - the cat's out of the bag.
"But any ship suspected with the scanner will be tagged
"And hunted down relentlessly. And we don't know how long
"We'll have before the hell-hounds answer Master's hunting song.

"The ship or ships that hit the TerraCorp array could be
"Prowling here about for such an opportunity.
"And forces that attacked the atmospheric station might
"Still be here in orbit itching for a bigger fight.

"That's why Red is chomping at the bit to try it out.
"He's been privateering and he's itching for a bout."
Selenia looked back and forth between her favorite men
And said, "So that's the reason for the big magnetics then.

"Can you build a scanner on this ship for us to use?
"Following your lead I salvaged some magnetics too
"Before the big array was lost," she winked and smiled at them.
The captain ordered, "Gin, please check them out with Percy's men."

Gin and Red's lieutenant took their leave and left the room.
Captain Standish asked, "So you'll be leaving us here soon?"
"Yes," said Captain Blue, "I meant to leave a day ago.
"Selenia, there's something more you really need to know."

He turned to face the woman who in turn faced full on him.
He reached out slow and took her polished hands in his again

Then said, "Renee was seen at Inmar just three days ago.
"By a faithful witness so you know I have to go."

His eyes bored into hers; her lips unconsciously spread wide
To match the sudden realization that lit up her eyes.
"Oh, Jules!" She didn't know if she should cry or laugh out loud.
Her heart leaped in her breast as doubt and conflict like a shroud

Wrapped around her mind and jolts of shock surged down her legs.
The Captain added, "Yes, I felt the same way. So did Red."
"It's our belief she's gone to Saturn VIII and I've no doubt
"She's wrapped up in a deadly game and time is running out."

Selenia's dark eyes were glossing up with heavy tears
"Are you absolutely sure? It's been so many years!"
She turned to Red, "And you knew this?" He answered, "Yes I did.
"I'm the faithful witness. There's no doubt that was our kid.

"I met her on the street just minutes after I left you.
"I thought I ought to message Jules but keep it quiet too.
"I'm sorry, Love," he looked away, "I left it up to Jules.
"I didn't want to interfere and be a bungling fool."

She took one hand away from Blue and put it on Red's arm
Then slid it down to take his hand and said, "There'd be no harm.
"I only want what's best for Jules and that goes for you too.
"We are friends for all of time. Now, this is what we'll do:

"Jules will take his ship to Saturn VIII to see what's there..."
(A tear had spread along her cheek and wicked into her hair.
Captain Standish offered her his folded handkerchief
Which she accepted gratefully to dab her tears of grief

Or joy? She could not determine which they really were.
A mix of feelings quite like this had never run through her.)
"...If you can get some of your fleet to come to Titan soon -"
Red cut her off, "I'm sorry, Love. They've all left for Neptune.

"It's weeks away. They're burning hot and can't be turning back.
"We only have each other to fend off any attack.
"Plus any help that we can muster up of Titan's own
"But other than a couple freighters I think we're alone."

Selenia shook off emotion's grip which brought the tears
And pulled strength from her warrior spirit (putting off her fears):
"I know there are two Martian escort ships at Enceladus.
"I could pull some strings I think for them to come to aid us.

"Meanwhile, you should do the Titan scan and get it ready
"To transmit to your Titan friends and TerraCorp Academy.
"Send it to the Universities of Ganymede
"And Mercury and Martian Science simultaneously.

"This will let the bastard know the cat's out of the bag
"And Titan's future is assured (though it will make him mad).
"At least the universal moral need will be fulfilled.
"Then we will deal with him alone." Her voice went deep and chill.

At that moment Radar's voice broke in with an alert:
"Captain, there's a distress call that four ships have been hurt
"By a pair of Martian ships in Enceladus' space
"And two Saturn Consortium ships vanished with no trace

"When they responded to the call. Something's going down.
"There's another report someone bombed Ryugu Town
"On Triton. From orbit. At least that's the report.
"The Martian ships were flying as the other fours' escort."

Selenia asked, "Radar, can you raise the Martian ships?
As she waited she unconsciously moistened her lips.
A pause of half a minute passed then Radar broke back in
"I have captain Carmel of the Syrtis Fleet piped in."

"Captain Carmel," she addressed the man upon the screen
"I am Selenia of Ganges, Erythraeum."
"I know who you are, Ma'am. How may I assist?"
"Tell me what has happened. A report we got insists

"That you have fired upon the ships that you're there to protect."
"Completely false," the captain said, "Though someone, I suspect
"Has tried to frame us for the act. Laser fire came
"From two or more black ships behind us. They're the ones to blame.

"We didn't see them coming and we barely saw them leave
"And I can understand why it appeared it came from me."

Selenia looked closely at the image on the screen
And asked, "Are you aware two Saturn ships sent to the scene

"Have vanished?" Captain Carmel nodded, "That's what I have heard;
"But I know nothing of them - only that these ships are hurt
"And precious cargo has been spilled across most of the sky.
"At this point we still do not know how many here have died."

"Their hands are full," said Captain Blue. Selenia looked down.
Captain Carmel added, "There are six more ships in-bound:
"A quad of cargo haulers and a Martian escort team.
"They'll be here in hours. I've apprised them of the scene."

Selenia replied, "There've been other sneak attacks.
"Stay on task and follow through. And Captain, watch your back."
With that the screen went dark and Captain Redfeather chimed in,
"We're alone it seems." Then Captain Blue looked back at him

And said, "We'll do what we can. Titan is the key.
"Like Percy said, we'll draw him out and bait our trap with cheese.
"We'll move into a polar orbit soon as we un-dock
"And start the scan of Titan. Red, you work around the clock

"To get your scanner rigged and tuned to help finish the job.
"Then we'll spread the word abroad the rat's plan has been robbed.
"When we know it's heard by every ear turned Saturn's way
"We'll man our battle stations, for the rat will come to play."

He looked at Captain Standish and Selenia in turn:
"This will make your cruiser seem to be the fish to burn
"So when the scan is finished and the data cleared by Nick
"Break from Titan orbit and get off toward Rhea quick."

Selenia said, "Ha! I'm not going anywhere
"Until we find this villain and deprive him of his air.
"Your concern is welcomed and appreciated, Jules
"But I've a vested interest in shutting down this fool.

"This cruiser is the best chance we have got if he attacks.
"I'm not leaving you or Red. I'm here to watch your backs.
"Besides, you'll be distracted here with Renee on your mind
"And won't be useful to us 'til you see what's there to find.

"So get your crew to Saturn VIII as you'd already planned.
"Rig for silent running. Red and I will make our stand
"Here at Titan with the goal of stopping any threat
"To Titan. And Jules, there is one more item yet:

"Nick belongs on Titan - not out here in danger's way.
"His value to the future there must not be thrown away.
"When he has compiled the data get him down below
"So he can share with Titan's science staff the things he knows.

"Don't drop him at Veles, there are shifty people there.
"Take him to one of the stations in the sticks somewhere."
Red nodded his head and said, "Like Afekan or Selk
"Where science teams would take him in and be glad for his help."

Captain Blue scratched at his chin, concurring with that view:
"Perhaps the safest place is where he'd be most useful too.
"He has friends at Sinlap and most of a science team
"And they could use some good news brought to that horrific scene.

Red said, "That's correct. And with the place on high alert
"Strangers without need to be there might get themselves hurt.
"No one would expect him to return after they'd tried
"To kill him when the atmospheric plant was hit and fried."

Selenia responded, face reflecting tenderness
"Send him down with Goldie; she's more than a pretty dress.
"He'll have work to do and he'll know she is safer there
"Than being bait for predators above the yellow air."

Captain Blue agreed, "Your intuition sounds intact.
"I'll give him the word that both of them should quickly pack."
Selenia's face brightened with a sly and knowing smile,
"I'll give them the word. They're in my quarters all this while."

35   Tripping the Trigger

The scan of Titan's crust had been completed in a day.
Everyone was anxious to see what the data'd say
About the deepest structures they could see within the moon
And whether there would be a plan for major drilling soon.

The data set had been compiled as quickly as they could
And there would need to be much research done before a good
Idea what the strategy might look like after men
With training and experience (that reached far beyond them)

Would see within the data which the untrained couldn't see.
Yet they were still excited - they were writing history!
But even at the first glance at the data it was plain
That it would be important to proceed with great restraint.

For there were structures near the surface seen at several spots
Which could cause big problems if the strategy were not
Implemented in an order to bring up the core
And drain the hydrocarbon seas and grow the greenhouse more.

It had been a very hectic time for Nick today.
The data from the Titan scan would obviously pay
Huge rewards in time and effort saved to terraform
Titan for the future good of mankind as it warmed.

Though tired as he was Nick wanted desperately to meet
With certain Titan scientists and engineer elites
As soon as possible, presenting in greater detail
The findings of the scans and what the future might entail.

Captain Blue and all his crew congratulated Nick
(A cruiser shuttle standing by, they said their good-bye's quick.)
Bovine clapped his back and Gin and Radar shook his hand;
Dewey asked a minor detail on the mode two plans;

Joe was smiling silently and Duke's eyes, dark and clear
Beamed his friendship while he said, "Be strong and have no fear;"
And Haji gave a sealed loaf of fresh zucchini bread.
As Captain's brown eyes caught Nick's gaze and held it, Captain said,

"I'd like to have you with us when we test the second mode
"But I believe you need to be on Titan, so we'll go
"Without you. Gin and Radar have brought Dewey up to speed
"On how to run the scanner. We have everything we need.

"And I know both your destiny and heart are down on Titan,
"So take all that you think you'll need with you and don't be frightened.
"Selenia's provided trusted men Soldana picked
"To keep watch over Sinlap and on you and Goldie, Nick."

"I'm not frightened, Captain. I'm enthused as I can be!
"I never dreamed that I would have an opportunity
"To be involved in birthing a new world for humankind.
"We've found the fruit beneath by peeling off the outer rind!

"To let fear hold me back at this point would be quite insane
"And I could never face myself while carrying that shame.
"The way I see it, you have given me a second chance
"To live a life that almost ended in a fiery dance.

"And I have you and all your crew to thank for all of that
"As well as showing me the world really isn't flat."
He grinned and winked and they all laughed and then Nick added low,
"I hope you find who you are looking for. (Yes, I know

"The story.) May the fates' rewards for you be extra sweet.
"I hope to see your special lady next time that we meet."
The crew all looked away, the sudden silence thick with dread.
"Thank you truly, Nick," and his eyes bored holes through Nick's head.

But then the captain's countenance grew softer as he turned
To Gin and Dewey, "Get the NAV and engines set to burn."
And as they left to do their duties, he turned back Nick's way
And said, "This is a parting, but we'll be back here some day.

"My lady is in waiting;
"Your lady waits for you.
"Mine beyond the eyesight's sensing;
"Yours is here and new.

"Memories that fuel my goal;
"Your futures bright and fresh;

"My hopes for life's renewal
"And for yours a great success!

"When we meet again
"We'll both have had a change in view.
"And always I'll be certain
"These things which were done by you

"Have made great changes possible
"For many, if not us.
"And you've been found commendable.
"You've earned this captain's trust."

Nick blushed bright while Captain took his hand in his firm grip.
Nick choked out a "Thank you" then he turned to leave the ship.
"Atta boy," winked Bovine as he helped him to the lock
Where his ride to the surface was preparing to un-dock.

* * * * *

The morning found the Warden drinking coffee in his den
Watching news from Ganymede when Renee drifted in.
The rich aroma of the brew was tainted just a bit
And then she saw that Warden had poured bourbon into it.

"Good morning!" Warden's red-eyed greeting croaked across the room.
"Bourbon in the morning?" Renee asked. "It's almost noon,"
He said with some chagrin (which for him was out of character)
He was feeling cheery. To his side he waved inviting her.

Pointing at the viewing screen he grinned a mile wide.
She poured a steaming cup of tea then sat down at his side.
The news announcer on the screen was noting grim details
Of how much of this season's crops on Ganymede had failed.

The program cut to grumpy-featured men in parliament
One of whom the warden pointed out that he had bent.
"It never hurts to have a politician in your bag.
"Or two or three when times are tough," the warden grinned and bragged.

"You're just in time," he said and turned the view screen volume up.
The scene switched to the podium; Warden drained his cup.

A handsome man in smartly-tailored clothes stepped up to speak
His stance exuding confidence, his beaming smile unique

Among the frumpy politicians and the newsie crowd
Who mulled about before him while their clamoring grew loud.
He motioned with his hands for all to quiet, take their seats.
Some were rude and shouted more as he began to speak.

"Friends, we are all aware that these are trying times.
"Shortages on many worlds have devolved into lines
"Of hungry people waiting for food transports that don't come
"And it is only right that we do all that must be done.

"The partnership I represent has donated our ships
"And crews to serve pro bono so food schedules do not slip.
"Furthermore, the partnership has contracted to lease
"Farmland held on many worlds at prices that will please

"Anyone who cares to take this opportunity
"Investing in their futures and for all humanity!"
Applause broke out among the politicians in the crowd
Nodding their approval, shouting "Bravo!" much too loud.

The speaker feigned humility but one could see he basked
In the rich applause as all the newsies tried to ask
Their questions through the uproar that they rudely so enhanced.
While holding up his arms the speaker motioned with his hands:

"The partnership and stockholders gave sacrificially
"To bring this needed (though a one-time) opportunity.
"It is a fiscal burden that is ponderous to bear
"But it will be available to every world out there!"

Once again the politicians and their sycophants
Rose with their applause and some began a little chant
That settled down as quickly as it rose when he began
To motion with his hands to sit and started in again:

"Also," he began then laughed at some unheard remark
That came from down in front, "Also, as we all now embark
"Upon this great re-distribution of the system's land
"We ask that in this gesture we may join hand in hand

"By representatives from every part of TerraCorp
"To donate ships and crews to help in this tremendous work.
"The management will be provided by the partnership.
"It's already in motion. We'll not let the schedule slip.

"Representatives on many outer worlds are set
"To make these special leases ready for all who have met
"The one or two requirements almost anyone can meet.
"To get the best of properties sign up within the week!"

Warden turned to face Renee as she sipped on her tea.
Turning down the audio he said with grinning glee,
"Look at how the suckers cheer. Isn't he a jewel?
"He is one who earns his pay, a very useful tool.

"Of late he was an entertainer of some prominence.
"When he saw our plan he spent time sitting on the fence.
"But when a dukedom on Callisto waved beneath his nose
"He bought in and now I own his soul from head to toes."

Renee took Warden's hand in hers as she put down her tea
"A dukedom for an entertainer, but not one for me?
"Iapetus is open," she feigned pouting in rebuke.
Warden said, "Renee, My Lovely, you'll own all the dukes!"

The color on the view screen changed and flashed "SPECIAL REPORT"
This caught the eyes of both of them who stopped their verbal sport.
The scene returned to parliament but words scrolled on the screen:
"NEWS FROM TITAN: MAJOR BREAKTHROUGH BY A SCIENCE TEAM

"SHOWS RESULTS THAT PROVE THERE IS A NEW TECHNOLOGY
"TO SHORTEN TERRA-FORM OF TITAN BY A CENTURY!
"MORE TO FOLLOW TOP OF HOUR," then the scroll's repeat
Was read again by both of them as Warden took his feet.

Just above the scrolling banner was a yellow sphere
Labeled to be Titan turning slowly to show clear
Structures in the ground beneath the surface of the moon
Enticing viewers they'd learn more if they would just stay tuned.

"No," he said as realization crept into his mind.
Then, "NO!" he said much louder as he spoke a second time.

His quarters door announced a visitor arrived outside.
"Enter!" he commanded and the door slid to the side.

A balding man stepped timidly into the living space
A look of fear and loathing spread across his worried face.
"Speak," the warden ordered, pointing at the yellow sphere.
"It's true," the man explained, "And it is worse than we had feared.

"The timestamp on this dataset that's been spread all around
"Indicates these pictures were produced some days beyond
"The time the TerraCorp array went missing. So that means
"That it was made with something smaller than what we have seen."

Warden's face grew red. His hands began to shake a bit.
"How much smaller?" he enquired. "Smaller than a ship?"
The man looked down and moved his shiny head from side to side.
"We know nothing more, Sir - um, Your Highness, at this time."

"Find it," warden's voice was low and dripped with acrid hate
Staring daggers though the shaking man's reflective pate.
"Find it and secure this tool before the week is out.
"Better yet," he jabbed a button then began to shout:

"Every ship on Titan, every orbiter that's there.
"Everything that flies above or moves through Titan's air -
"Kill it! Kill it now! I want the field at Xanadu
"Scraped clean as a dog dish. Send another black ship too!"

The banner scrolling on the view screen changed to crimson red
And flashed again imploring every eye it must be read:
"TRANSPORT SHIPS AT ENCELADUS HIT IN SNEAK ATTACK.
"MARTIAN ESCORTS IMPLICATED. PRIVATEERS STRIKE BACK!

"CONSORTIUM APPLAUDS RETALIATION AND AGREES
"TO GRANT PARDONS (CONDITIONAL) FOR FORMER PIRACIES.
"MORE AT TOP OF HOUR." Renee saw that Warden's fists
Came unclenched when he had read the banner then he hissed:

"Yes, that's what we wanted! Those Consortium misfits
"Will sell their pompous souls to anyone with decent ships."
He waved the visitor away then wandered to the bench
To fill his coffee cup with bourbon as his jaw unclenched.

"Mars is implicated now. This will build more doubt
"About the motives of their senate and bring it about
"That all the outer moons will look to find a strong man here.
"And there is only one - and his fair lady too, my Dear."

Renee sipped at her tea and watched the warden re-compose
The edginess of his demeanor then she slowly rose
And moved in close in front of him (his breath near knocked her out)
"I'm impressed, my Lord. But you must promise not to shout

"So early in the morning. Now, come sit and watch with me.
"Let us learn more of the findings of this science team."
She softly tugged upon his arm and pulled him toward the couch.
"My Lord?" he asked. "Why not?" she said, "As long as you don't grouch."

36   Boomerang

When he had donned his cryosuit (the standard Titan's dress)
A peaceful sense of comfort flooded though Nick's consciousness.
Leaning back into his seat he watched the amber clouds
Rise to meet the shuttle as the slipstream grew more loud.

Goldie had requested to ride in the right-hand seat
Beside the shuttle pilot as he did the tricky feat
Of transferring from orbit down to atmospheric flight
Around the day lit side of Titan into darkest night.

The pilot, quite impressed with Goldie's knowledge and her skill
Was more than happy answering her questions up until
The subsonic transition had been made when he surprised
Her with the full controls so she could feel the shuttle's ride.

This training was the first that she'd received aboard spacecraft
Her prior flying limited to Martian pleasure craft.
Their path was set for Afekan with full transponders on
But once below control radars they ventured far beyond

Hugging hills and valleys through the misty yellow dark
Until they came to Sinlap, set her down, and disembarked.
(Nick took extra pleasure helping Goldie with her suit
Teaching how to fit it right and walk in its big boots.)

A half a dozen men had placed themselves around the craft
Nick could see that two had rifles, one each fore and aft.
But when the airlock opened and they ventured down the ramp
Nick was met by David who gave him the rubber stamp.

And Pistol-Packer too was there, who clapped Nick on the back
Asking who his lovely friend was (who had not the knack
Of walking in a cryosuit in Titan's gravity.)
Then Nick gave introductions all around most gratefully.

The riflemen returned to doing tasks around the port
While David's fingers ticked some items off in quick report
Bringing Nick more up to speed on work out at the station
And what was being done about the current situation:

"Chris has gone to quietly escort some folks from Selk:
"Planetary specialists and others that can help
"Reach consensus on the crustal data you have found.
"Really, we're assembling the best there are around.

"But people have been skittish since the station here was burned.
"Some have suffered threats and there are others who have learned
"To keep away from crowds or strangers in the past few days.
"Someone has been trying to drive science teams away.

"TerraCorp transmitted an evacuation plan
"But no one that we know is willing to desert Titan.
"The work is just beginning and your breakthrough with the crust
"Makes the work more crucial. Everyone here thinks we must

"Finish what we came here for regardless of the threats.
"The message didn't really come from TerraCorp's my bet."
David gave a frown and looked off toward the damaged station
Obviously smarting from the recent devastation:

Seventy companions killed and no one known to blame.
Nothing but the fallens' names and those left with the pain.
Nick looked down a moment then replied in a soft tone,
"The ones who did this must be stopped but we are not alone.

"There are ships in orbit at this moment with a plan
"To find the guilty party and bring justice to the man.
"But here and now we've got the job to move Titan along
"And that's what we should focus on; we must not get it wrong.

"We'll do it for the Seventy, if not for all mankind.
"We're all excited to see what these scientists will find."
David said, "You're right. An opportunity like this
"Doesn't come along but once and history won't miss

"Another tin-pot terrorist who'll soon be put to rest.
"Like all the Titans I'm all in to give my very best!
"How about a burger on my tab at Jonesy's place?
"I've no doubt there's more to Goldie than a pretty face!"

Goldie smiled graciously as Nick said, "That sounds great!"
Then turned to her, "You won't find a better burger plate

"Anywhere in Sinlap, that's for sure," and gave a wink
"Not to mention several really tasty beers to drink!"

The three of them began the walk toward Jonesy's Bar and Grill.
The men on either side to help her, Goldie appeared thrilled
To walk upon another world, alien and new
And by the time they got to Jonesy's she could walk well too.

"G'Day mates! Good onya Nick! Yer ale's on me chit!
"We're glad to have you back in Sinlap," Jonesy said, "Now sit
"And tell me all about your lovely crumpet. Will she stay?
"Furphy has it you're the bloke who's found a better way

"To pop the bonnet on this bodgy rock and stoke the coal -"
"Easy, Jonesy!" David cut him off, "It's not our goal
"To knock him bloody knackered with his whistle running dry.
"Give the bloke a schooner and a moment to unwind!"

Jonesy winked at Nick and lined three ambers on the bar.
Goldie looked around and saw a dusty old guitar
Leaning in a corner back behind an empty booth.
Nick replied to Jonesy, "Furphy doesn't have the truth.

"I just helped design some gear that others put to use.
"It wasn't anything I did alone without the group."
"Rubbish," David said, "You got more done in just two weeks
"Than TerraCorp accomplished in six months and twice as cheap!"

"I only stood on shoulders of the giants of before,"
Nick replied while blushing, "It was timing, nothing more."
"Well," said Jonesy, "Reckoning your yakka was the key,
"Half your luck! A one-off ripper's good enough for me."

"It's been less than a day," Nick said, "Since our results were sent.
"How can you be sure it wasn't money poorly spent?"
"Very funny, Nick," said David, gulping down some beer
"The data is amazing and its quality is clear.

"The scan was verified by other gravimetric tools
"And findings of the core drillings that mining gigs have used.
"You're a hero Nick, as far as Titan is concerned,
"Though we know that someone else has tried to have you burned."

Goldie's curiosity took her up off her chair
And over to the corner where the guitar's lonely stare
Pulled at her relentlessly - she had to pick it up,
Blow the dust from off the frets and give each string a pluck.

Quietly she tuned it (she was known for perfect pitch)
Then made a quiet chord or two but then she scratched her itch
To wring it out and test the tone and timbre of the wood.
Then Jonesy turned to look at her and said, "Crikey! She's good!"

Goldie flashed a smile back then set her fingers free:
Allegro from the Brandenburg Concerto Number Three
Filled the room above the chatter of the drinking guests.
Nick beamed with amusement and said, "That is not her best."

When her little burst of finger flicking faded out
She put the old guitar away as shouts of "More!" rang out
But she just blushed and took her seat and knocked down half her beer
Then put her hand in Nick's and sidled up to feel him near.

Jonesy looked them over with a searching squinty eye
"Crikey, mate, your lady is deadset the dinky-di!"
He leaned in close and said, "You've got a job here if you like.
"I'll pay you pretty wages if you play here every night."

"Thank you, Sir," she said, "Perhaps I'll take you up on that."
Then at that very moment Jonesy's Bar and Grill went black.
Emergency illumination flickered and came on
As customers moved to the foyer to get suits put on.

"Ah, bloody hell," said Jonesy, "Boomer! Switch to backup power."
Looking back at Goldie he said, "There's a bodgy tower
"Holding up the lines that run from -" WHUMP! His words were drowned
By a rumble through the walls and felt up through the ground.

"On it!" Boomer's voice was heard and then a group of "THUD's"
Rumbled through the walls again. David said, "Not good."
The lights came on then Boomer's face, as pasty as a ghost
Poked out of the kitchen, "That was not the power post!"

Goldie's fingers dug into Nick's arm as he arose
Then both of them joined others at the windows where they froze

Astounded by the smoke and flashes lighting up the clouds
Above the airport in the distance which, wrapped in a shroud

Of smoke that drifted slowly toward the south away from town
(Much of which was still in darkness with the power down)
Drew the suited citizens like honey might draw flies
Knowing there'd be those who needed help when they arrived.

"The airport's been attacked," said one, "It's bloody well been bombed!"
Another customer opined, "No, something else is wrong.
"Why would anyone attack our little sleepy town?"
The first responded, "Those who shut the atmospherics down."

They could hear the engines of a powerful aircraft
Fading in the distance for a moment then turn back.
"They're coming back to finish it," the first spoke out again.
He moved back from the window. Others slowly followed him.

Then from the edge of town a tiny light streaked toward the sky
And disappeared into the misty cloud as Goldie cried,
"Look!" Nick and others crowded in to see its flight.
The anti-aircraft missile though, had flown far out of sight.

A couple seconds passed and then they heard the engines quit
The missile found its mark and killed the aircraft when it hit.
Boomer looked at Nick and offered, "Bad luck follows you."
David said, "Now Boomer, you know well that isn't true.

"Because of what he did we're now a century ahead.
"We're getting Titan terraformed before we're old and dead."
Goldie flashed her eyes at Boomer and gave her two cents:
"Good luck follows Nick. That rocket flew in his defense.

"The bomber's second pass may well have targeted the town.
"Forces sent to guard him are who shot that bomber down."
Boomer hadn't noticed her until she turned to speak
And now that he laid eyes on her some redness filled his cheeks.

"It's sad they couldn't stop whatever happened at the port
"But they are here to help you as a conference escort."
Goldie turned to go back to the bar when Nick jumped in,
"Boomer, this is Goldie. Goldie, Boomer is my friend.

"It's no surprise he sees a jinx around my visits here.
"Friends of his were killed and he was wounded in the rear."
Goldie turned and held her hand toward Boomer who took hers
And said, "I didn't really mean to say that he was cursed."

The others in the bar were shocked and wondering aloud
Who would do this evil act (while suiting to go out
To see the damage done and give assistance where they might.)
Every one of them were slowly stewing for a fight.

Then back beside the bar where one could see the broadcast news
Jonesy said aloud, "It's bloody crook! There's at least two
"Other towns were hit in just the way ol' Sinlap was.
"The landing fields are rooted and the aircraft there are tossed.

"It's a bloody act of war, it is. But do we know
"Who the dodgy ferals are so we can have a go
"At buggering their big night out?" Jonesy reached to switch
The viewer to another channel but the viewer glitched

And staring at the black screen for a moment Jonesy turned
Toward David with a scowl and said, "The network too is burned."
David's phone alerted and he studied its display
Then lifted it and spoke, "No, you don't need fly away.

"The landing field was hit but nothing else was touched at all.
"Have him land on Northwest Road and bring them to the hall."
David looked at Jonesy and said, "Orbital relay.
"I don't trust the network so I switched it yesterday."

He turned to Nick and offered, "Chris has brought the gang from Selk.
"The folks from Celadon and Paxsi didn't need our help
"And came early this morning. They are quartered throughout town
"By Sinlap folks who know the stakes and aren't going to back down

"From whomever's meddling in our sovereign affairs."
"Excellent!" said Nick as Jonesy gave David a stare
And said, "You're going on like bloody one of ours there, mate.
"Ours?" David looked at him and blurted, "Well, I'm late,

"But this is where the action is I think, and so I'll stick.
"Besides," he winked, "You've bloody carked my English, you old hick

"And nowhere else will take me if I open up my yap.
"And so I've staked my claims in Paxsi and here in Sinlap.

"Strewth!" he winked and raised his glass and chugged his schooner down.
"You're bloody crook," said Jonesy, "You said this was 'Dunny Town',
"And couldn't wait to rack off back to Earth or somewhere hot.
"Well, good onya, mate. She'll be apples, like as not."

Goldie broke her silence; asked, "You're all Australian here?"
Jonesy winked at her and answered, "We're all Titan's, Dear.
Most of us left Earth before the Luna war got hot.
We've tossed the past aside and this is where we've cast our lot.

"The air smells like a dunny - that's dead set, but one bright day
"Our world here will blossom and our hard yakka will pay.
"There's freedom and a future here for those who don't mind sweat
"But terraforming will be tough; it's hardly started yet."

Pistol-Packer came into the bar wearing his suit.
The condensation forming frost that covered up the soot
Which stained his boots and gloves as Jonesy shooed him toward the door
"Jonesy, wait," the Packer said, "For just a quick report:

"We have a crewman from the ship that bombed the landing field.
"He isn't in the best condition but the doctors feel
"The dodgy bloke can answer questions. So the counsel's met
"At the town infirmary to see what they can get

"From the filthy bugger before someone gets to him.
"There's a mob of pissed-off blokes there waiting to get in.
"By the way," the pistol-packer said before he left
"The markings indicate it was a Martian shuttle craft.

"There is a self-destruct that was disabled in the crash.
"The lads are looking at the NAV's to see where it was last."
Goldie's blue eyes opened wide as she stood up and stared
And echoed back the packer's word, "Martian?" Then she glared:

"Martians aren't at war with Titan and you know it's true.
"I would like to see this man and ask him questions too.
"If he is a Martian I will know without a doubt.
Then she turned to David with her plea, "Let me help out."

Pistol-Packer eyed the three suspiciously and said
"What if you are one of them and you just want him dead?"
Goldie's eyes flashed fire as she asked, "Who shot them down?"
And answered her own question: "Martians, here to guard the town!"

The man looked Jonesy's way then looked at Nick and David too
And said, "I guess you're right. I meant no insult to you two.
"Go suit up and follow me and I will get you in.
"I'm sure the council will agree to let you question him."

Nick and David had been called to greet the other teams
From Selk and Paxsi for informal chats before some schemes
Proposed for crust development would be brought to the floor
Tomorrow and the next when everyone would know much more.

So Goldie went alone with Pistol-Packer to the hall
And then two hours later, Nick and David came to call
And met her in the commons looking drained and somewhat sad
But when she saw them coming she perked up appearing glad.

"He's not Martian, Nick. I doubt he's ever been to Mars.
"He doesn't have the accent and he knows none of the parts
"Of Martian culture that I innuendoed as we talked
"And when I got specific on his heritage he balked.

"Even if he were a mercenary hired on
"By a Martian independent he'd not have such strong
"Reactions to the questions putting origins to task
"He tried very hard to sidestep every question asked.

"Even when he saw I knew he was no Martian's friend.
"He maintained his story up until the very end."
Nick and David both responded, "End? What do you mean?"
Goldie shuddered for a moment; tears in her eyes gleamed.

"At the very moment that he heard the spoken words
"Declaring him not Martian he spat out a filthy curse
"And then he got a panicked look, then suddenly relaxed;
"His eyes no longer moved and then his body just collapsed."

Goldie looked away and rubbed the tears out of her eyes
Then shook her head and finished her report to the two guys:

"It reminded me of Ansel - just without the flames.
"I'll bet you real money he was poisoned just the same."

David looked at Nick and asked, "The implants you described?"
Nick and Goldie nodded, "He was not meant to survive
"If anyone determined he was not who he declared.
"And he knew it. That's why when we asked him he got scared."

David said, "I hope the doctors were made well aware
"When he is examined what surprises they'll find there."
Goldie nodded and replied emphatically to him
"I made sure they knew about Ansel's neurotoxin.

"They had found some implants when they scanned the other two
"Bodies from the wreckage and they were accustomed to
"Treading carefully after the 'firebomb' events.
"They are well prepared to exercise their common sense."

37   Vignette

It was a heavy tanker lifting hydrocarbon fuel
From the large refinery at Paxsi, Aaru
Toward the Titan Orbital Emergency Depot
(A very welcome refuge where exhausted ships could go.)

The pilot and the engineer were glad to make the trip
And for a little time give Titan's orange sky the slip.
They'd see the stars and planets which they could not from below.
Besides the extra cash the view was worth the trip alone!

The giant wings that lifted them were filled with liquid oxygen.
The other tanks were topped with hydrazine and liquid hydrogen.
This cargo was a Godsend for the ships that couldn't land
And brought a decent price to the refiners on Titan.

When the atmospheric drag reduced to just a wisp
Both the men relaxed and ramped the throttles of the ship
And placed it on trajectory for depot rendezvous
Counting down the hours 'til their workday would be through.

"Izzat yer wife 'n daughter?" asked the 'new guy' engineer
While nodding at a photograph taped to some commo gear.
"Yes, they are," the pilot said without concealing pride
"I keep them here in front whenever I go for a ride."

"They're very pretty, mate. You've got a precious fam'ly there."
"Thank you," said the pilot, "They go with me everywhere.
"That is just a picture taped up on a cockpit screen
"But they are carried here," he thumped his chest; his blue eyes gleamed.

"You never know what -" BANG! His words were ended in a flash
As spalling molten metal burned the cockpit into ash.
A heavy laser sliced across the ship from stem to stern
Spewing clouds of oxygen and hydrogen that churned

Into a sunlit ball of liquid gas that gleamed and glowed
Until a spark within the spinning wreckage made it blow.
The fireball was brighter than the distant father sun
But from the shrouded moon below the flash was seen by none.

Only from the turret of the black ship far above
Was seen the final moment of that father filled with love
Of wife and daughter left below, still sleeping in their beds.
The gunner turned attention to the next target ahead.

38   Iapetus

The angle of approach to Saturn VIII was from the sun
Almost full in aspect when they started their first run
To scan the moon with penetrator light and map its skin
For every change in density or void where men dug in.

A moon of light and dark sides like a painted tennis ball,
Iapetus is third of Saturn's largest moons of all.
Ringed with mountains at its waist that reach twelve miles high
Curiously hanging like a yin-yang in the sky,

It's sinister and dark from one view, icy from the other
And only this moon views the rings around its massive father.
Its orbit inclined far above the plane of all the rest
The view of Saturn's rings and moons from here is quite the best!

The sun takes forty Earth days to traverse its starlit sky
And forty more of darkest night before the next sunrise
When feeble distant sunlight yielding little of its heat
Spreads dimly 'cross the cratered ice beneath the mountains' feet.

Jules was deeply focused on the view outside the port
When Duke came to his quarters to provide the fresh report
That all was set in readiness to start the first-pass scan
Close around the equator according to Jules' plan.

"Radar is with Dewey and they have the scanner set
"The way it was at Titan but they say they think they'll get
"Images of greater resolution when we pass:
"No atmospheric scintillation and much lower mass.

"Joe has manned the weapons bay; Bovine engine room;
"Gin is in the cockpit and I'll join Joe very soon.
"We're rigged for silent running and the 3C is deployed."
Duke held up abruptly and he looked a bit annoyed.

"What is it Duke?" the captain asked. "Something's on your mind."
Duke looked back and said, "I am concerned that on this kind
"Of run around this moon we'll be much easier to track
"By optical detection and there's no one at our back."

The captain looked at Duke with piercing curiosity
And said, "You know we've minimized that possibility.
"We've made runs much like this in the past. What's different now?"
Duke said, "It's the spirits here," then looked down with a frown.

The captain paused a moment taken somewhat by surprise
Then with a lowered voice he looked deep into Duke's brown eyes
And said, "I feel it too, and I know everyone's on edge
"Wondering if my anticipation trumps my pledge

"To do my best for ship and crew as I've done in the past.
"Rest assured, my friend, that we will not have breathed our last
"When this day has unfolded. I will not exchange your life
"Ever for a chance to finally retrieve my wife."

Duke was caught off guard. His eyes betrayed his deep surprise
That Captain had anticipated what none of the guys
Would dare to talk about beyond a whisper in a bay.
Duke replied, "Not one of us would ever think to say

"That you would make a trade like that, but we know love runs deep
"Between a man and woman who were meant for each to keep.
"So sometimes we might wonder how affected men might be
"By spirit-dreams that come to men with possibilities."

Duke was rarely wordy and thought he had missed the mark
Then added, "We will follow you regardless of how dark
"The path we walk may seem." The captain took him by the arm
And said, "We'll work together and our team will not be harmed.

"And yes, I feel the darkness of the spirits of this place,
"But we will shine our light on them, their mysteries erase.
"We'll leave Iapetus with brighter prospects than we found
"Once we see what lies beneath its icy frozen ground."

Duke took Captain's arm the way the captain held his own
And searched the captain's eyes then said. "Your spirit power's grown
"Instead of weakened since the news that came to you from Red.
"The evil of this place no longer fills my heart with dread."

With that he turned to leave but said, "You spoke it straight to me.
"That is why we follow you and will set your wife free

"Or give our lives in trying." In an instant he was gone.
Then tears came to the captain's eyes. He must not do them wrong!

39   Message in a Bottle

Renee had spent the morning watching news at Warden's side
But broke away at midday to adjudicate some strife
Among disgruntled workers and a group of Warden's men
In such a way that brought some understanding between them.

Rejoining Warden later she found him still on the job
Scanning through the news reports and messaging his mob.
Sitting in a seat beside him she kicked off her shoes
Hoping to catch up a little on the latest news.

The warden had not bathed or eaten much and it was plain
The bourbon that had greased the morning had now slowed his brain.
The door announced a visitor who Warden ordered in
A man who, by his anxious look had brought good news with him:

"Ward - I mean, Your Highness, we have looked at Titan's crust
"And found a feature which the Titan terra-formers must
"Utilize to bring about the rapid transformation
"Which has instigated Titan's recent celebration."

"So?" the warden scowled, his tired features growing mean
"What is that to me? By now the whole system has seen."
The former scientist of TerraCorp held up his hand
And said, "We can deny its use and interrupt their plan."

Warden's bloodshot eyes no longer glared at his view screen
But turned the bright man's way and ordered "Show me what you mean."
The man held up a data chip and motioned toward the wall
"May I use your screen?" The warden motioned, "Please, show all."

A view of Titan's crust beneath the surface filled the view
Then zoomed in on a section that rotated and turned blue.
"There is a crustal void extending near Kumbaru Sinus
"Largely filled with nitrogen and atmospheric gases.

"This will be the key when draining hydrocarbon seas
"Before subsurface water is brought up to be set free."
"Yes, the news has shown all that," the warden waved his hand.
Showing his impatience with this interrupting man.

"Very good, Your Highness. Now, look at the southern end."
The view rotated further and zoomed closer yet again.
"Here we see a solid section running to the core
"And here beneath the void at pressure, representing more

"Volume than the void can hold, ammonia-water mix."
The man turned toward the warden, "Now, take a look at this:
Turning back to trace his finger on a jagged line
He began, "This is the opportunity: In time

"Pressure from the depths will cause this layer here to crack
"The gas within the void will have no way to hold it back.
"The void will flood with violence enough to break the crust
"Resulting in a frozen lowland of no use to us."

Warden got up from his seat, looked closely at the screen.
The scientist continued, "You can bet the Titan's scheme
"Will be to fill the void with hydrocarbons from the sea
"Then slowly bring the lower waters up subsequently.

"If one chose to drill a shaft approximately here
"Then cut it in between the void like so, it should be clear
"That with sufficient shock within the separating rock...
"Well, one could do what nature will, but he'd control the clock."

Warden's red eyes widened as the realization hit
That here was some insurance Titan might not benefit
From that technology that as of yet slipped through his hands.
There would be no market glut for future farming lands.

The man continued, "There are many other voids like this
"But this one is by far the largest and most obvious.
"Representing seventy percent of what is here
"This could set the terraforming back by thirty years

"Or more; perhaps indefinitely if it were done right..."
His voice then trailed off and Warden smiled with delight,
"There are atomic drilling rigs on Titan are there not?"
Warden's eyes grew narrower as he devised his plot.

"Yes, there are," the man responded, "Many of the best."
Warden turned to face the man and said, "You have a test:

"We have men on Titan; you may take more if you need.
"Drill the holes and cut the tunnels with the greatest speed.

"Bring to me the detonator; place it in my hand
"And I will make you ruler over cities, towns and lands.
"You know what I want, 'Governor'," he finished up
Then turned away to grab his bourbon-scented coffee cup.

The man responded with a grin that spread from ear to ear
"I will not fail you, Highness," then he turned and disappeared.
Warden looked at Renee, satisfaction in his grin
And said, "He is a sharp one. We will keep an eye on him."

Renee said, "He's ambitious. You can see it in his eyes."
Warden studied her then asked, "What do you see in mine?"
Her eyes scanned Warden's haggard face a moment then replied
"I see a man who's worked too hard and now he's over-tired."

She took the cup out of his hand and set the thing aside
Then took him by the arm and pulled him gingerly inside
The seedy darkened room where he habitually slept.
She pushed him down onto his bed, but then before she left

She whispered in his ear, "Your plans are starting to unfold.
"Please don't leave me ignorant and outside in the cold.
"Give me what I've asked and let me prove to you my skill.
"Iapetus will be a loyal world; but not if killed."

Renee left Warden's quarters for her own but on the way
She happened to pass by the pilots' wardroom where they ate.
The engineer she'd met during her recent trip to Rhea
Caught her eye as she passed by and said, "It's good to see ya!"

She stopped and turned to greet him as he cast his eyes about
And grabbed an empty bottle and a napkin to throw out.
"Off to Enceladus now?" she asked as he arose.
"That's the word, milady; our last meal before we go."

He turned so no one saw his hands and rolled the napkin tight
And stuffed it in the bottle's mouth. "This will be our last flight
"From here I guess, so this will be the last time I'll see you
"Unless you come to Enceladus for some fresh seafood."

He raised the bottle up and gave a 'thumb's up' and a wink
Then tossed the bottle in the bin and said "It's in the drink.
"We're bobbing in the sea at times with very little chance
"That anyone will notice us and ask us to the dance.

"Maybe we will drift onto a beach where we'll be found,"
He locked her gaze intently with a quick emphatic frown.
Her eyes lit up with understanding and a thankful tear
And said, "Perhaps a beachcomber will happen to walk near.

"The best of luck to you and thank you for the recent flight."
"And to you, milady. I bid you a restful night."
He gave a formal bow then turned to go a different way
As she walked toward her quarters praying he'd not have to pay.

* * * * *

Hidalia and Steve had wondered where their friend had gone.
Renee had seemed to disappear and it had been so long
Since the night of her departure and there'd been no word
As to her return beside some rumors they had heard.

So it was great relief when Renee knocked upon the door
That sleepy night as she awoke while Steve beside her snored.
Rising, careful not to wake her tired sleeping man
She cracked the door then threw it wide and took both Renee's hands.

"Renee! Where have you been? We've missed you more than you can know."
"I have missed you too, Hidalia!" (Both their faces glowed.)
Renee gave her a tender hug then pulled away to see
What news inside Hidalia's eyes there was that she could read.

"I've been very busy with the warden and his team.
"I'm sorry I've not seen you," Renee's eyes began to gleam
With tears of sadness and with joy mixed up by her fatigue.
"Please, Renee, come in and sit and I'll go wake up Steve."

"Oh, please don't wake him, Love! I know how much he needs his sleep.
"And I can't stay," she turned to lift a package at her feet.
"I took a trip off-world and I've brought you something new.
"It's soft, you'll like the color and it has warm pockets too."

Hidalia's brown eyes widened as her jaw dropped to the floor,
"Off-world? You've been off-world?" she couldn't choke out more.
Her eyes burned with a hundred questions but she only stared.
Renee replied, "I went to Rhea but saw nothing there

"To keep me longer than a day and so I came back here."
Renee's eyes burned right back at hers with answers in her tears.
"But I must run," she said and pulled her friend Hidalia near.
And as she held the embrace Renee whispered in her ear,

"Are your suits secure?" She whispered back, "They're charged and close."
Renee replied, "It may be hours, or a week at most."
And then she loosed the embrace and declared, "I'll see you soon!
"Give my best to Steve. I know some day he'll be your groom!"

Hidalia gasped a happy laugh and held the package near
"Thank you for the gift, Renee. You are such a dear!"
Then as they parted and she closed the quarters door again
Hidalia found a lovely sweater with a note tucked in:

Cylinders marked CO2 may not be what they say.
Use whatever means you must to make them go away.
Atmospherics' access doors will lose their lock and guard
Tomorrow after Corporal is brought to Warden's yard.

40   Two Plus Two

The scientists at Sinlap and the Engineers arose
From their makeshift quarters or the homes of friendly hosts
With great anticipation for the meetings that would start
After morning's posted schedules would split them apart

To focus groups for study sessions in their disciplines.
Then hopefully by dinner they would start to make decisions
About the strategy for atmospherics and the rest
To give the terraforming efforts' best chance for success.

Everyone on Titan was excited for some news
Even though they all knew it was much too early to
Speculate on real estate or jockey for position
But there were many who had started wagers beyond question!

The planetary science and the hydrologic teams
Were thrilled beyond their expectations with the details seen
In Titan's crustal voids that seemed to almost guarantee
Successful transformation of the hydrocarbon seas.

Divinely made to order or just lucky happenstance?
Every camp agreed that it would take a careful dance
Of steps in proper order to ensure their sweet success
And all were filled with optimism with each group's address.

And since Nick's recent focus had been on equipment needs
And atmospheric gas conversion he came up to speed
On hydrologic strategy but leaned for David's ear
To answer certain questions that for him were not so clear.

For instance, why the squabble over voids near Kracken Sea?
It was plain as day Kumbaru Sinus was the key.
David hooked his thumb toward Chris who then explained the danger
Of wrecking that large void by letting loose the deeper pressure.

Nick nodded his thanks and leaned back in his seat to listen
Very glad that Chris had taken time for that quick lesson.
The presentations droned; but all of it was useful stuff
(Even though by then David and Goldie had enough.)

By late afternoon one of the engineering teams
Began to catalogue the drilling rig inventory
So they could make assessment of the tools they had at hand
To bring to the discussions on the timing of the plans.

But they found glaring inconsistencies at Veles port.
A pair of drilling rigs had disappeared when headed north.
No one at the contractor who owned these heavy rigs
Had any recent records of who'd hired them to dig.

This was rather problematic when it was considered
These two rigs were half of all the assets that were listed
(Of similar capacity, that is); but it turned bad
When it was reported that two others also had

Disappeared as well. And their crews? None were found!
It seemed like all the crews and rigs had vanished underground!
(Though much of Titan was in chaos after the attacks.
Ships at Veles spaceport were in shambles and the lack

Of organized response beyond the locals everywhere
Had left a lot of possibilities up in the air.)
The owners of the rigs agreed security had failed.
The engineers enquired later, still to no avail.

Many of those present grew increasingly concerned
And since there was a recess now and hungry bellies churned
Nick and Chris departed to convene at Jonesy's place
Where they found Nick's Goldie singing with a smiling face.

David sat with Pistol-Packer, bellies to the bar.
Boomer dried some glasses, Jonesy chomped a big cigar
Listening with one ear to the music Goldie played
But focused on the conversation Pistol-Packer made.

It seems he had a friend who worked atomic drilling rigs
Who'd sent a cryptic message while away off on a dig.
Pistol-Packer was concerned for it was clear to him
The man was under great distress before his signal dimmed.

"What kind of distress?" David asked as they stepped up
To the bar with Chris holding a pair of fingers up.

Jonesy filled two schooners with the latest amber beer
And set them down in front of Chris and Nick who perked their ears.

Pistol-packer nodded to the newcomers and said
"Me mate told me he's hijacked and a pair of blokes are dead.
"They were on a job at Tollan Terra when a plane
"Dropped a mob of dodgy blow-ins who rooted their game.

"When the two blokes knocked back they were shot right on the spot.
"The rest were bloody ropeable but didn't piss them off.
"The other crew they work with disappeared without a trace
"And now it seems they're walkabout up north of there someplace."

Nick and Chris set down their beers. Chris asked, "When was this?"
Pistol-packer said, "I reckon this morning 'round six.
"I gave his phone a fair go heaps of times but no one's there."
Chris and Nick then eyed each other with a wild stare.

"Do you think..." Chris started. Nick asked, "Maybe it's Bordeaux?"
Chris responded, "Maybe, but I really don't think so.
"I'd give even odds it's someone he was in bed with."
Nick said, "Those who hit the station after Bordeaux skipped."

David had a puzzled look and asked what they're about.
Chris and Nick just looked at him then realized he'd skipped out
And missed the presentation on the missing drilling teams.
They took a hurried moment to bring David up to speed.

"Bugger!" Pistol-Packer spouted. Boomer shook his head,
"It's a bloody week from hell," said Jonesy, "Dozens dead."
Goldie had just finished with her tune and stood by Nick
When Chris said, "It gets worse. We need to find these drill rigs quick!

"If it's true that they've been jacked by Titan's enemies
"They could set the terraforming back a century."
Chris proceeded with the nutshell version of the facts
Regarding what could happen if Kumbaru's shelf were cracked.

The seven of them looked from face to face in sullen silence.
"Crikey!" Pistol-packer groaned, "We've got to take the offense!
"Our response to these attacks has been exactly nil
"But now the time has come - before we all are bloody killed!"

"One thing that's dead set," said Jonesy as he poured a beer
"We know where they're going," and he grinned from ear to ear.
"We just need to head them off and bag the tossers first
"Before they have a chance to drill the holes that make it burst."

Boomer had been working, nearly silent all this while
But now he turned toward Jonesy and he lost his normal smile:
"Who ya gonna get? There's only one aircraft in town.
"And who's to say another shady bloke won't shoot it down?

"We don't even know who's put our world in their sights.
"Is it Terracorp or Mars or pirates that we fight?"
David sounded off with great conviction in his tone:
"I guarantee it's not the Terracorp that we all know."

Goldie quickly followed him with, "This is NOT of Mars!
"There's a hundred reasons why and you'd go pretty far
"To find someone who doesn't have the Titans' best at heart.
"Saturn's weak consortium's done less than Mars' part!"

Pistol-Packer looked at Boomer, "Registry's been checked.
"The craft shot down last night's not Martian, like the lady said.
"It's property of Terracorp; aboard a ship of theirs
"It disappeared three years ago as if into thin air.

"Pirates, one might reckon, or some dodgy renegades."
Pistol-Packer took a swig and said, "And we can't say
"Who they bloody are until we stuff 'em in the bag.
"I can rope a half a dozen blokes who won't look back.

"You can tag along, Boomer," Pistol-Packer winked
And lifted up his mug to toss the last down of his drink.
Goldie turned to Nick and in his ear she softly hissed,
"We must make Selenia aware of all of this!"

Pistol-Packer looked inquisitively at the pair
As Goldie stepped away from Nick and tossed her golden hair,
"Within an hour they could send an interdiction team
"To stop whoever took the drills and then secure the scene."

Nick looked at his phone and gave its face a tap or two
Then said, "Maybe next orbit. They are overdue.

"They should have cleared horizon over twelve minutes ago.
"Maybe they've changed orbits or had somewhere else to go?"

He tapped his phone a moment more and then he said, "Uh oh,
"Orbital relays are down as well - there's no commo!"
Chris and David both inferred the friends they referred to
And David said, "We can't rely on them. We'll have to do

"What we can from here until we get word otherwise.
"We don't have the luxury of letting this thing slide
"While waiting for some off-world help that maybe isn't there."
"Too right!" said Jonesy, "Get packed up and in the air."

41 Engagement

Communication satellites were easy to detect.
They didn't take a lot of skill to find and intercept.
A single laser pulse sufficient to turn one to scrap,
Titan's orbital network in no time had been zapped.

The aircraft on the planet were much harder to detect
And though the aircraft at the major ports were mostly wrecked
Warden's men continued to attempt to hunt them down
Patrolling airspace randomly near every major town.

But there had been a number of his planes that were destroyed.
The captain of the black ship who had lost two was annoyed
For Titan's close-knit colonists had taken up their arms
Determined that their enemy would bring them no more harm.

But this was not the focus of the captain's work ahead.
He had orders to destroy all orbiters instead.
A tanker had been killed and he would soon have in his sights
The target that his men anticipated with delight.

For they had been in high orbit with nothing much to do
Other than one surface raid and one quick rendezvous
(Delivering a prisoner to warden's private ship)
So they were primed for action and for war were well equipped.

Titan's orbital depot was big and they had hoped
To plunder what they could after the staff there had been smoked.
Communication gear and thrusters would be first things hit
And then the boarding party would slit throats and ransack it.

It was just a lucky stroke they'd seen the tanker's flight
For they were nearing periapsis when it came in sight.
(His black ship was descending from a high eccentric loop
After they had burned the commo satellites to poop.)

A little retro burn beyond the tanker kill reduced
Their apoapsis just enough for thrusters to produce
An intercept trajectory for Titan's doomed depot
Soon to be approaching from behind and from below.

But now there was a complication which would cause delay
The navigation beacon from a ship right in their way
Orbiting ahead of Titan's depot as it came
Around the limb of Titan meant he'd have to change his game.

* * * * *

Automated sensors caught the tanker's sad demise
(Imaging in infrared a bright spot in the sky)
It sounded an alarm to catch attention of Red's crew
Who scanned recorded images that caught the black ship too,

Silhouetted for an instant by the orange clouds.
"The hot spot happened right below him," Red's man said aloud.
"He is pinging radar too, he's come out from the dark.
"If you want my guess, he's feeding like a hungry shark."

"Navigation radar?" Red inquired of the man.
"No, sir. Long range target radar in a searching fan.
"It has a tighter beam than acquisition radar will.
"He knows what he's looking for and stalking for a kill."

Red looked at the tactical display where he could plot
Trajectories of friendlies and this new ship they had caught.
"Let's make higher orbit where our cruiser is in view
"And keep a close eye on this bogey, best as you can do

"While keeping quiet, eh?" Red gave his man a shoulder pat
Then to his tactical display he turned attention back.
"A little push to raise our periapsis eight percent,"
He told the pilot, "Inclination where the Bogey went."

The pilot checked his NAV's then set his thrusters to their max
And let them give a gentle shove to match what Red had asked.
Then as the minutes passed Selenia's ship came in view
And moments later they had eyes on Titan's depot too.

* * * * *

Selenia had pulled her hair back in a ponytail
(Her tailored coveralls enhanced the fact she was female)
Then on a second thought she wrapped it into a chignon
Knowing that the chance of combat grew as time went on.

Hair could be a messy thing in zero gravity;
Keeping it contained important (not her vanity).
She would not allow her fashions to get in the way
Of any sudden action they might need to take today.

There had been no call from Jules (she knew there wouldn't be)
For they'd established commo rules to maximize safety.
He would maintain silence unless placed under duress.
She had faith in his good sense but still for him she stressed.

Captain Standish moved to lower orbit in the night
Matching that of Titan's depot which was kept in sight.
Preceding it in orbit miles above the peachy clouds
They assumed a peaceful look for predators about.

Percy broke the silence in her room by intercom:
"There's a hunter with a target tracking radar on
"Refracting through the atmosphere beyond the horizon.
"There's no question he is searching closely for someone.

"He should come around the limb in just about a minute."
"I'm coming to the bridge," she said, "We're going to be deep in it."
Then moments later as she made her way into the room
Captain Standish gave the status, "We will see him soon.

"He came around the limb just now. His radar has gone dark.
"He found what he was looking for and now there's not a spark
"Of magnetic emissions. He is now completely black."
Selenia responded, "That's our rat. Expect attack."

The man at Tactical announced, "Dead reckoning puts him
"Coming within laser range in twelve minutes and ten.
"But Sir, there is a tanker set for depot rendezvous.
"The schedule says she should be coming shortly into view."

"You think this is a tanker then?" the captain asked the man.
Tactical replied, "That's all who's posted a flight plan.
"There's only one ship we have seen; perhaps their beacon's broke?"
Selenia replied, "Targeting radar is no joke."

Captain Standish looked at him, "A homing radar's beam
"Couldn't be mistaken with one meant for targeting?"

The man replied, "They're different in operation, Sir.
"And I can tell with ease the brand of manufacturer.

"There is not a doubt what came around the limb was one
"For locking on a target and just getting one job done."
The captain leaned in close to him and said, "If he stays dark
"For more than seven minutes you can bet he is a shark.

"Don't use targeting radars. Optics for this one.
"Don't make him aware that we're expecting anyone.
"Let him come in close enough to prove his bad intent
"Then we'll send him to the place for which pirates were meant."

"Yes Sir," Tactical replied. His eyes were big and round.
The Captain pat his shoulder firmly then he turned around.
Selenia's dark eyes met Percy's, confidence renewed.
Perhaps, she thought inside herself, *He does know what to do.*

The commo officer announced, "A message from downstairs
"For you, Ma'am." He gestured toward Selenia's plush chair
With two fingers up to show the channel she should use.
She touched the button to connect and said, "Give me the news!"

Goldie's voice came over but the phone belonged to Nick.
"There's not much time to talk so I will have to say this quick:
"Did you get the coded message uplinked with this call?"
Commo held his thumbs up showing he had caught the ball.

Selenia replied, "We've got it Goldie, are you safe?"
"Yes, for now, but there is trouble and we can't be late.
"Someone's found a way to ruin everything they've done
"On Titan. Read the message, please! I'm sorry! Got to run!"

The call ended abruptly. Commo's thumb went up then down.
Selenia extracted message data then turned 'round
To Percy, who scanned through it too as she read some aloud
Then looked out through the window at the orange-yellow clouds.

Captain Standish looked up from his screen when he'd read more,
"It's more than just a blockade, this is planetary war.
"Feigning Martian meddling as the cause of these attacks
"Gives us legal license to offensively strike back."

Selenia turned toward him, "It's not license that I seek.
"You know very well the Titan defenses are weak.
"And now we see the global threat this enemy has brought.
"Morally we must help Titan with all that we've got."

"That's exactly what I meant," said Standish low and clear,
"You have legal right to every Martian ship that's near.
"There's also legal standing here for crimes against mankind
"And if it isn't stopped could spread to war that's system-wide."

Selenia searched Percy's eyes and plainly spoke her mind:
"Loyalties are trumped by obligations to mankind.
"My loyalty lies first to Mars, and second to Soldana.
"Where do yours lie, Captain? What were you taught by your mama?"

He smiled at her candor and spoke plain and simple too:
"My loyalty lies first to my employer and that's you
"As Soldana's representative. But I agree
"What is best for mankind is the moral path for me.

"And Titan's need is plainly what the fates have brought to hand.
"But tell me," Percy whispered, "Will your friends - perhaps a man
"Interfere with altruistic ideals you espouse?"
Selenia was jolted by what just came from his mouth.

He peered intently at her face and added, "I must know.
"If I am to serve you well, I must know how you'll go."
Selenia responded, "You are quite perceptive, sir.
"Obviously you have deep regard for how you serve.

"Thank you, Percy," she continued, pleased by his instincts
And also by his boldness to inquire what she might think,
"That's indeed a quality that no one really knows
"Until the moment we are tested, then the truth is shown.

"Would you be a balance to my passion? My resolve?"
The captain studied her a moment, "Only time will solve
"A question deep as that. We must hope that test won't come.
"But I will do my best to serve this ship and take you home."

Their quiet conversation was cut short by Tactical:
"We've got the bogey at two hundred clicks with optical."

"Beacon, Sir!" the navigator added, "No transponder."
"Hail them. Ask identity and mission," Captain ordered.

[A moment...] "I have contact. They're evasive and talk slow.
"They say they're tankers up from Veles headed for depot.
"The video's disabled and the voice is filtered too.
"But Sir, there's no refinery near Veles, Xanadu."

Commo's pitch increased, "Emergency message from Red:
"Missiles in-bound!" Then he turned his face around with dread.
"Light 'em up," the captain said, "Lasers! Take them out!"
And then defensive radars blossomed at the captain's shout.

"Locked and shot and neutralized, Sir!" Weapons gave the word.
"Weapons! Radar tracking. Put four lasers on that bird.
"Fire!" Captain ordered, but his order was too late
As Tactical reported, "Thermal flash! Their beacon failed.

"Someone hit him first, Sir. There's debris in his field
"And fuel out-gassing in a spiral pattern that reveals
"He's spinning at a rapid rate - almost a centrifuge.
"More debris is shedding. There's not much that he can do."

Selenia instinctively had strapped into her chair
But with a look of expectation out the window stared.
And then beyond the porthole glass a distant yellow flash
Surged in brightness for a moment then it faded fast.

"Tactical! Report!" The captain looked over his men.
"Only Captain Redfeather and Depot are within
"Range of acquisition radar and some debris, Sir."
The captain ordered, "From now on keep radars on alert."

And then he turned to Commo, "Get Redfeather on the line."
"He's been standing by on channel three, Sir, all this time."
Captain Standish pushed the switch and Redfeather appeared
His bearded face sporting a grin that spread from ear to ear.

Percy smiled back, "Redfeather: one; Black ship: none?"
"Actually," Red replied, "That's Red: one; Black ship: one.
"We saw him kill a tanker in a fiery sneak attack.
"It was his missile launch that put our crosshairs on his back.

"Your acquisition radars were not tuned for stealthy ships.
"That gave him false confidence and that is where he slipped.
"It won't work again if he's got friends hanging 'round here.
"Keep the cruiser on alert and I'll stay dark and near."

Captain Standish nodded, "That's what I was thinking too.
"Any friends he has now know that we can play rough too.
"Meanwhile, I will send a boarding party to that ship
"To see if there's survivors we might get within our grip."

Selenia chimed in (while Red looked down and shook his head),
"There's no need to waste the effort. All of them are dead.
"Black ships self destruct when badly damaged every time."
"I saw the flash. It's over. And I think your men did fine."

42   Moonshine and Musings

The corporal was almost cringing as he crossed the lawn
(A little patch of grass the warden sometimes rested on.
It was walled about for privacy and sometimes used
As a place for punishments and other cruel abuse.)

A furtive glance around the yard showed warden wasn't there
And no one sitting in the seat they called the 'judgment chair'.
His trepidation eased a little when he saw Renee
And breathed a little easier seeing she smiled his way.

"Corporal, " Renee began, "You have a reputation
"For the spirits you distill from surplus vegetation."
The man's face lost a little color 'til she said, "Relax!
"I want to offer you a job where you can use that knack.

"As you know there is a shortage in this colony
"Of anything resembling a good sipping whiskey.
"Would you like to take the task of starting up a mash
"And building a distillery sufficient for the task?"

His eyes lit up like Christmas trees with childish delight.
"Yes!" he said, "But I'll need corn if I'm to do it right -
"The way great grand dad did it underneath the pale moonlight.
"Back in Tennessee up in the woods and out of sight."

Renee gave him a thoughtful look and said, "We have some corn
"And barley that was surplused but it looks a bit forlorn.
"It was stored in vacuum for an undetermined time
"But after some hydration, maybe it will do just fine?"

"Aw, shucks, Renee - I mean, Your Highness," Corporal replied
"As long as yeast finds sugar it will make a great moonshine."
Renee continued, "You will need materials to make
"A larger, better still and put it in a secure place.

"How about the Atmospherics vault? It is secure."
The corporal said, "It is! I've got the key that fits the door!"
"Perfect then," she said, "Shall we go see your barley corn?
"If we go through Atmospherics it makes the walk short."

"Sure," he said, "I was on duty there when I was called.
"I can take us through that way with no problems at all."
"Shall we?" gestured Renee as she turned to go that way.
"Sure, Renee - I mean, Your Highness, this is a great day!"

The door to Atmospherics took a good old-fashioned key
Which passed from man to man as each would come on guard duty.
The corporal was pleased to open up the sealed door
Renee motioned him in, "After you please, Corporal."

Then as she passed the doorway she stuffed something in the lock
To prevent the latch from catching as she loudly talked
"There is lots of room in here for more than just one still.
"A half an acre, more or less. That should fill the bill."

Renee took opportunity to flit about the space
Scanning for a manifold where cylinders were placed
But seeing nothing obvious continued on their way
Hoping that her friends could find them and take them away.

* * * * *

Far beyond the ice and rock that kept Renee in place
A tiny metal sliver sped across dark empty space
Where, safe within its silver hull breathed seven stalwart souls
Who made a hundred preparations with the focused goal

Of ripping off the shroud of mystery around a moon
It's reputation darkened by long years of rumored doom.
They'd shine the light of new discovery and do their best
To put the hope inspired by graffiti to the test.

Haji, Duke, and Dewey were preparing future meals
For the coming days which might turn into an ordeal.
Most of it was put away and Duke had left the room
When Dewey opened conversation from his mood of gloom:

"Everywhere I've ever been there's bullies, thugs and thieves.
"Only 'til we die it seems we never get relief.
"Surely out there somewhere we will find an advanced species
"Who will teach us answers we can all use to live in peace."

Dewey had been very quiet on the trip so far
No doubt feeling low about his foolishness on Mars.
Sensing Dewey's soul-searching had him a bit distraught
Haji raised an eyebrow and engaged with Dewey's thoughts:

"Really? Tell me Dewey, what supposed facts are these
"That make a non-earth species probable, as you believe?
"And tell me, while you're at it, why they must be more advanced?
"It's only fifty-fifty, don't you think - at the best chance?"

Dewey looked incredulous at Haji then replied,
"The Drake equation proves that lots of worlds in the sky
"Are capable of spawning other creatures such as us.
"This is common knowledge, Doctor, which we all can trust!"

Haji slowly shook his head and sighed at this presumption.
"The Drake equation, Dewey, is a series of assumptions,
"Any one of which, if zero, will negate the whole.
"Using only facts we know, the answer is zero

"Or one, if you count us." Haji winked, "So using this
"There is zero evidence another race exists.
"So Drake doesn't do you any good in that regard
"And we've found evidence of no one else in our backyard."

Dewey squirmed around and said, "But everybody knows
"The universe is huge! There's no way we'll ever go
"To every nook and cranny even in our galaxy.
"In a space so large there must be others - and plenty!"

Haji looked at Dewey with a twinkle in his eye
"'Must be,' Dewey? Really? If there 'must be' tell me why.
"If you can't prove others, by default we are unique.
"And what is wrong with that? It increases our mystique."

"Mystique?" Dewey blurted "What the heck has that to do
"With anything? Emotions are not scientific views."
Haji said, "Perhaps they're not, but they have strong effects
"Which no one can deny, though instruments cannot detect."

Dewey mulled this over for a moment then replied
"Science is the facts, doctor, not emotion's lies.

"Everything in nature is in chaos, isn't it?
"We just need the right instructions how to deal with it."

"Science isn't truth, Dewey. Don't be one who's fooled.
"Science is a process, it's a method, it's a tool
"We use to understand the tiny bits we chance to see
"Of the universe around us - not eternity.

"The method isn't perfect since it's used by faulty man.
"Yet by it we've found rich rewards and blessings come to hand.
"But it is incremental at its best and can't address
"The fundamental questions every heart needs put to rest.

"All the best of science still has not stood up to tell
"What it is that puts the spark of life into a cell.
"In fact, we really can't define what life is, don't you know?
"There is more to man than simple muscle, and marrow.

"You're certainly familiar with the second thermal law
"Of physics that asserts that every single thing at all
"If left alone continually falls to simplest form.
"Only work applied from outside can reverse that norm.

"Chaos and decomposition is the normal state
"And yet we see that life is ordered in a complex way.
"Man is the epitome of creation's expression.
"As we look around it must be anyone's concession."

Dewey nodded in agreement, "Most of us at least."
Haji smiled and said, "Sometimes it's hard not to agree."
And then he carried on with his expository speech:
"Here is where some falter though it's not so far to reach:

"Order in the midst of chaos proves intelligence.
"The fact alone that we exist is perfect evidence
"That there is a creator who has made us by his choice
"And if that's true, then shouldn't we attempt to hear his voice?"

Haji paused a moment to allow his words to sink
Into Dewey's skull and hopefully cause him to think.
"The table that we dine at proves there is a table maker.
"The ship we travel in proves that there is a ship creator.

"Neither of them made themselves yet both will decompose.
"It is the second thermal law. Now how do you suppose
"Matter came about and then became a living man
"If there weren't intelligence that made him with a plan

"For a purpose - just like tables, teacups or a ship?
"Everything that's made is by design, isn't it?"
"The wisest men of history have known this simple fact
"And that alone should be enough to teach us how to act."

Dewey tapped his knuckles on the table absently.
A contemplative frown gave way to questions presently:
"If we are unique then why's the universe so huge?
"Just to demonstrate that the creator is big too?"

Haji said, "Perhaps," and kept his eyes on Dewey's face.
"Our physical perceptions are not all there is to space.
"Perhaps it's only big to creatures limited by time?
"Perhaps the size is immaterial to the divine?

"Would it not be cruel if the answers we all seek
"Were out among the stars somewhere completely out of reach?
"Then every one of us who lived before we found the key
"To interstellar travel would be lost eternally.

"No. That makes no sense for a creator with a mind
"To make a universe containing beings like mankind
"Then simply turn us loose without a reason or a key
"To fit the door that brings us out to meet eternity.

"And so the answers men have sought through all of history
"Are not out there beyond our reach, but are found more simply.
"It would make good sense if he who wrote those questions here,"
(Haji thumped his chest) "Would make an answer we could hear.

"Do you not agree?" Dewey nodded absently
"We all have a purpose in life, including Dewey.
"What we do in this life is the evidence we see
"Of what condition our soul is in spiritually.

"Likewise what we do in this life may have great effect
"On our eternal welfare, so we do well when we check

"That quiet little voice inside which whispers what is right
"And have the courage to stand up for principles and fight.

"You see, it's all about how we approach our fellow man.
"We love and serve him selflessly the best way that we can
"Treating the epitome of that creative force
"With the same respect Creator did is a good course.

"Even criminals and pirates of the foulest sort
"Have the opportunity to cease their evil sport.
"They have that moral compass - it is there inside us all
"The spark of the creator if we listen to its call

"And shy away from making that most unfortunate choice
"To drown its quiet nudging with our own guilt-laden voice
"And spend our failing energies unraveling success
"Made by that creative spark that started our progress.

"Those who hear his voice and use their creativity
"To build, perfect and grow creation's great complexity
"Perhaps are destined for great things when life in time is done.
"And that is the grand choice that must be made by everyone.

"But those who do not listen and assist the deconstruction
"Of what's been created seem to bring their own destruction.
"Selfish men of violence that serve only their own
"When they meet eternity will not be welcomed home.

"At least, that's how I see it Dewey, but I'm not clergy.
"I am just a doctor - not one of philosophy.
"But in my years of medicine and travels and projects
"I have seen the simple things confound the most complex.

"The answer to life's question has been with us all along.
"It is available to anyone who turns from wrong
"And listens to that still small voice built into every soul
"It's been right there inside you and it is a worthy goal."

Dewey remained quiet for a long and thoughtful spell
Then shoved off toward the galley door and turned to say, "Well, hell.
"Doctor, I can't argue with a single thing you said.
"Thank you for your thoughts. Maybe they'll sink into my head."

And then he disappeared into the bowels of the ship
Haji hoped with fervor that poor Dewey had not slipped
Further into his depression but would see some light
And make the choices in his heart to help him feel right.

43   Descent

"It's spooky, dark and treacherous as any place could be,"
Said Gin as Captain Blue came to the cockpit presently.
The black side of Iapetus was growing large ahead
And even from this range its aspect filled one's heart with dread.

"It is," the captain said, "No wonder stories by the ton
"Are spread abroad and then embellished by most everyone
"Who's had a chance to come this way. Perhaps we'll make one too?"
The captain winked and took his seat and asked, "You'll drive, won't you?"

"Pleasure, Cap'n!" Gin smiled back and scanned the NAV's again
Then checked the time before deceleration would begin.
The flight plan was to come out of the sun then burn it hot
Decelerating at high G then kick the tail to plot

A path around the equator just high enough to view
Ten degrees of latitude (that's five north and south too).
Radar would compile the scanner data in real time
And by the second orbit they expected they would find

All the excavations that the Survey Corps had left
Before the war and tragic "accidents" left it bereft
Of human habitation for the intervening years.
The history of Saturn VIII was mystery and tears.

They had thirty minutes left before they'd start the burn
When Radar's voice came through the intercom sounding concerned:
"Captain, Skippy picked up something and alerted me.
"And it is something tangible that you might want to see."

"Can you pipe it in?" the captain asked, "We're burning soon
"And I don't want to chance our smacking into that big moon."
Radar answered, "I can send a graphic if you like,
"But I can give the nutshell version right across this mike."

"Go," the captain said and Radar prefaced his report
Promising to skip the details and to keep it short.
"Basically," he started, "Skippy listens to the COM's
"And processes the background noise for signals that aren't strong.

"He picked up a pattern that most anyone would miss
"Emanating from the engine of a nearby ship.
"The pattern was decoded in both binary and Morse
"(Thanks to awesome programming I put in him, of course.)

"And it is unmistakable - an SOS of sorts.
"The message reads, 'Gold Saturn 8' and then it gives coords."
Gin looked at the captain who leaned back into his couch
And stared a moment at the looming planet with his mouth

Forming silent words before he asked, "Are you certain?
"Tell me how an engine can send messages again."
Radar started in with chamber pressures and fuel mix
Causing sputtered micro starts which made magnetic clicks

That emanate from most igniters in a broad bandwidth
And normally are random and not seen on well-kept ships.
"Engine sputter has a signature and this is it.
"But this was done on purpose and was easy to be missed.

"Someone modulated an igniter for a burn.
"It paused about three minutes at which time they may have turned.
"The signal strength increased a bit and then another pause
"Then after that a single burst before it all was lost."

The captain looked at Gin who added, "Yes, that could be done."
Then queried Radar, "How much time since that ship made it's run?"
"It's been about eight minutes since the final signal dropped.
"But I don't know how long the first burn lasted since it popped

"Out around the limb when our detectors picked it up.
"The fact that we could catch it was a wild bit of luck.
"My impression is it lifted from the other hemisphere,
"Then burned to change its course to reach another Saturn moon somewhere.

"We only have a two-dimension plot of its trajectory.
"Some guesses about Doppler shift might lead us to a tertiary - "
Captain cut him off with, "Radar, what were the coordinates
"Given in the message. That holds much greater concern for us."

Figures scrolled across a screen within the captain's view
As Radar mentioned they described position within two

Seconds of both latitude and longitude below
Where once a Survey Corp outpost was sited years ago.

"That's within the area that Red's crude numbers gave,"
Gin reminded Captain Blue (as if he hadn't saved
The numbers as a scar across his heart he'd always know).
Gin punched up a graphic of the looming moon below.

"It's on the far side, Jules. Perhaps where Radar's ship came from."
Captain Blue keyed up the intercom for everyone:
"We will do a single orbit to collect our scan
"And then I want the mode two rigged to test at my command.

"Gin," the captain ordered, "Once we've made initial pass
"I want us turned sideways for high inclination fast.
"Keep us far away from passing near that spot again
"And keep our orbit low and just as stealthy as we can.

"You know what I want," he winked. Gin said, "Yes I do.
"We're coming up on braking burn, T-minus twenty-two."
The captain checked the navigation settings one more time
Then turned attention to the coal-black moon growing outside.

Quicker than the flicker of a swooping swallow's wing
A streaking spot of utter blackness swept across the scene.
Like dust upon an eyelash in an instant it was gone
Moving much too quickly for the eye to light upon.

But as it passed and gained more distance practiced eyes would catch
The intermittent glimmer dark-adapted ones could snatch.
While almost disappearing in a field of starry lights
They could sense the telltale speck of engines burning bright.

"Did you see that?" the captain asked. Gin responded, "Yes.
"That was too darn close for comfort and we needn't guess
"If we are as alone out here as some would have us think.
"There's no way that he saw us, we're emitting not a thing."

The captain looked at Gin and Gin looked back with a wry grin
"My engines do not sputter." Captain raised his hands to him
And said, "I never claimed they did. Besides, the guy who sent
"The message from that engine really must be quite a gent."

"It reeks of desperation, Jules. With no way else to call?
"The chance that someone might receive are next to none at all."
"And yet we did," the captain said, "You don't believe in fate?
"What if we had come along just twenty minutes late?"

Gin looked down and shook his head then looked back toward the moon.
"It remains what we will find; but more important, whom."
"Thank you Radar," Captain said, "Skippy's done us good."
Radar gave his parting word, "There was no doubt he would."

The cockpit fell to silence for a moment. Captain said
"That was a black ship, you must know." Gin just scratched his head
And grunted, "It sure has the look, but I could not be sure.
"If it is, then you can bet their motives are not pure.

"I'd like to know where they are going. Titan is my guess.
"A shame we couldn't track them while we maintain our silence."
The captain nodded his agreement, "Our friends are aware
"That there is trouble coming and they'll have plenty to spare.

"Selenia has fire power, Red has got the skill.
"He'll be running silent too and itching for a kill.
"Let's just focus on our part and do what we came for.
"Then we'll have a chance to help them even up the score."

There was no need for red lights to announce the coming burn.
Every man aboard was trained and rested and concerned
Only with precise performance of the job at hand
Their battle stations rigged, their eyes wide open to a man.

The braking burn was hard and fast - approaching seven G's
Then vectored for a very stealthy orbital entry
Low above the mountain tops that ringed the silent world
A single pass, then high near polar orbit they were hurled.

Radar kept a running commentary in one ear
About the details of the scan until they had blown clear
Then took the time to ascertain the whole of what they'd caught
Which, when they had absorbed it gave them all a bit of shock,

For spread around the equator were six tremendous caves
Several hundred meters deep beneath the moon's cold face.

Four were natural in origin but man-enhanced
And two carved from the ice and rock were man-made at a glance.

The intercom that linked the crewmen crackled once again
As Radar gave his summary to all the other men
Each of them could see his pictures on their own displays
All were fascinated, some were filled with great dismay.

"These caves add up to more than seven hundred thousand acres
"And I will make a bet (if any of you might be takers)
"That all the area of Survey Corps' big assay mines
"Wouldn't be one-thousandth of this if they were combined.

"I won't take that bet," said Duke as Gin looked Captain's way.
Radar said, "Now look at this," and scrolled through the display.
"Radiometry shows every cavern but this one
"Is cooling from the inside and air pressure there is gone."

The captain looked at Gin then out the cockpit at the ground
"The one that still is warm is where the message Skippy found
"Spelled out the coordinates?" "Yes, Sir," Radar said,
"The spot is in a shallow canyon at the cavern's edge."

The frosty cratered landscape moved relentlessly below
As their rising latitude made solar shadows grow
Only to be dimly filled by Saturn's yellow light
Silent in the vacuum back dropped by the starry night.

"You know where we're going, Gin, but hold off for a while,"
The captain shut his console down and flashed Gin with a smile.
"Joe, you and Bovine armor up for firmer ground.
"Radar, send my yacht coordinates; we're going down.

"I want to pay a visit to the cavern farthest off
"From the one that's heated. Gin, keep the ship aloft.
"Set a polar orbit that won't pass near either one.
"Haji, you suit up and join us for some dirtside fun."

* * * * *

The yacht approached the cavern's entrance from the sunward side
(Joe was in the right seat navigating for this ride.)

He pointed out a landing pad that came into their view
But Captain said, "Inviting, but today I don't want to."

He set the vessel down between two hillocks with a view
Of the landing pad then turned to Joe: "Now, I want you
"To keep an overwatch from on that hill above the pad
"If a ship approaches get the yacht and fly like mad.

"Take them on a goose chase for as long as you've got fuel
"And Gin will pick us up. Then we will deal with your fool.
"Got it?" Captain winked and Joe acknowledged with a nod.
"We'll be back in forty minutes by the grace of God."

Haji stayed aboard to keep the captain's yacht secure;
Joe bounced up the hillside with his rifle to ensure
That no unfriendly visitors would interrupt their stay
(His firepower great enough to make them rue the day.)

The Captain took his old carbine and Bovine had his drill
(A heavy mining laser that could cut through rock or kill.)
They skirted round the landing pad below the ridge's rim
Looking for the access tunnel that would let them in

When Captain called a halt and pointed toward a little box
Frozen to the apex of a pyramid of rocks.
"Look at this," he said, "A camera to watch the place."
He took a piece of ice and placed it on the lens' face.

"There may be another one across the landing field.
"And I would bet good money that it isn't well concealed.
"Can you knock it over Joe?" A moment... "Sure," he said.
And then a puff of dust erupted where his crosshairs laid.

"It looks like there's a tunnel fifty meters to the right
"Of where the camera was set," said Joe, "But it's shut tight.
"A landslide covered most of it and I'd guess it was meant
"'Cuz I can see not far above where charges had been set."

"Thank you, Joe," the captain said as they worked 'round the field
Staying well below the ridgeline to be best concealed.
And when they reached the remnant of the access tunnel's mouth
They could see the footprints of the last men who walked out

Leading toward the marks of landing gear and thruster blast
Partially obscured by rock and ice that fell there last.
Bovine cut the larger chunks that barred them from the cave
Then both of them spent several minutes pushing them away.

And when they gained the landing of the airlock to the shaft
They could see the door was jambed and streaks of dust where gas
Had vented from the airlock in a roaring decompression.
The safeties had been ripped away with well-placed demolition.

The captain shined a light inside the damaged metal room
That opened to the larger one beyond it where the gloom
Of utter darkness seemed to hover where the shaft went down
Like a dragon's hungry throat that reached deep underground.

"The lock has been demolished by explosive charges, Joe.
"The sudden decompression caused a wicked wind to blow.
"We're going down," the captain said as he stepped in the shaft
And Bovine said, "You first, Sir," (he made a nervous laugh)

And swept his light around the room beyond where he could see
A well-used elevator made for freight wedged crookedly.
"The LIDAR on my suit says it's four hundred meters deep,"
The captain grunted, "Keep your distance with those cleated feet!"

"Sorry, Sir," Said Bovine as he slowed down his descent
By grabbing on a handhold for a moment as they went
Ever faster toward the waiting belly of the beast
Which his imagination screamed would make them both its feast.

"We're here," the captain said as he stepped lightly to the side
"Take the passage to the left and I'll go to the right.
"The hatchways to them both have been blown open and disabled.
"Find an office or a power center if you're able."

"Yes, Sir," Bovine answered as his feet touched to the floor
And shined his light around to see the captain clear the door
Leading to the right, his carbine leveled straight ahead.
Bovine took the passage to his left like Captain said.

He had worked for many years in mines and places deep.
Bovine had no fear of caves but this place gave him creeps!

There was more than darkness in this hole that chilled his soul;
Something more than vacuum's silence or the profound cold.

And when he turned the corner past the elevator room
It became apparent why the place felt like a tomb
For there before his eyes not twenty meters straight ahead
A gate of steel bars was shut and dozens lay there dead.

Twisted and contorted into forms of grotesque pain
Their vacuum-shattered eyes and ears and frozen clothing stained
With blood from ruptured lungs that screamed in silence as they died
Murdered with impunity and frozen for all time.

Some were wedged against the bars and others spread beyond
The farthest that his light could reach yet those appeared more calm
Arrayed across the floor in random order as if they
Had died before the others reached the bars of steel gray.

Bovine almost lost his lunch into his pressure suit
But calmed himself in time and focused on what he must do.
Flicking on his laser drill he cut the steel bars
And watched their glowing ends descend like slowly falling stars.

He bounced beyond the clustered bodies at the cruel gate
Taking comfort in the balance of his laser's weight
And watching for a sign or placard to direct his path
Toward an engineering room where power might be had.

But there was nothing obvious, just stone walls on each side
Extending in the darkness far beyond his feeble light.
And then about one hundred meters in, the cold stone floor
Ended in a field of barley that would bloom no more.

"Bovine, meet me at the shaft," the captain's voice came through
The speakers of his helmet as he stopped to get a view
Of one distorted frozen face that lay at field's rim
White mucous smeared his tortured face and vomit covered him.

"Yes, Sir. On my way. Have you discovered any dead?
"There's a lot of bodies here and not one died in bed."
The captain answered, "Yes, a lot. Now let's get out of here.
"The horror that was perpetrated in this hell is clear."

Haji had been waiting patiently for sixty minutes
Keeping watch with passive sensors of the near sky's limits
(Shortened by the hillocks that rose up on either side)
When Joe came on the radio, "They're clear. Get set to ride."

Bovine and the captain came directly to the yacht.
Neither of them said a word until they cleared the lock.
As Haji helped them with their suits he searched their tired eyes
And asked, "It wasn't good - the things that you two saw inside?"

Bovine looked away and Captain pulled out of his kit
A sample bag that held two fingers and an ear in it.
"You might want to analyze these once they start to thaw
"They may hold one answer to the massacre we saw.

"There were hundreds dead that seemed to strangle where they fell
"And dozens more that perished trying to escape that hell.
"These broke off three fellows that appeared to have a seizure.
"Painfully they died before the cave became a freezer."

Haji took the sample bag and nodded looking grim.
Joe looked Bovine in the eye then put his hand on him
And said, "It's just a movie, Bovine. That is all it was.
"Set it all aside for now. We'll find who was the cause

"And bring the bastard to his justice." Bovine looked at Joe
With tears filing his eyes. "It was bad," Joe said, "I know."
Joe looked Captain's way who met his gaze and slowly nodded
The captain said, "I want to check another one," and prodded

Bovine on the chest, "Will you go with me one more time?"
Bovine sniffed and shook his head; but then he said, "I'm fine."
He wiped the tears out of his eyes and looked up at his captain
"Sorry, Sir. Lead on. I'll climb with you up any mountain."

Joe slapped Bovine on the back and shook his hulking frame.
Then ruffled up his hair and said, "There's no one that would blame
"You if you didn't want to. No one would. But it's our job.
Bovine inhaled deeply then looked down and gave a nod.

44   Kumbaru

Warden's planetary engineer followed advice
And took a black ship destined at best speed for Titan's ice.
A single braking orbit brought him straight to Caladan
To intercept two drill rigs that were crawling overland.

Warden's other black ship wouldn't answer any hails
And so it was assumed they were involved on a detail.
Some commo satellites were gone so maybe that was it?
Perhaps they were rigged dark to sneak up on another ship?

But that was neither here nor there. He had a job to do
And that was to prepare to crack the shelf at Kumbaru.
Warden's chief of Titan operations was in flight
From Xanadu with orders to meet up with him on site.

The black ship settled down within a weathered old depression
About a half a mile from the crawlers' slow progression.
Then only minutes later got an update from the chief
Who said he'd be delayed a bit to deal with some grief

Pushed up the chain regarding Martian markings on a craft
That landed at a drilling site up north. Then after that
They'd lost communication with the drill site further west
And one aircraft reported on an uninvited guest

But couldn't regain contact or some other lame excuse.
His minion seemed oblivious that all their craft now used
Martian markings when they dealt out force on Titan now.
At any rate, he'd sort it out then be back in an hour.

But he did not return within an hour - or that day.
The engineer dispatched a shuttle to search out that way
Which radioed that he had spotted one craft on the ground
With several people outside of it just standing around.

The shuttle circled once or twice then said he'd land nearby
But that was the last signal ever received from that guy.
(The next time he heard from that craft it was a different voice
Who caused him to transmit a message that was not his choice.)

In the meantime he had lifted one rig to its site
And brought the black ship back to do another cargo flight.
The rig would be assembled and the drilling under way
By the time he'd bring its habitat at end of day.

This would cut three days of waiting for the Warden's goal
And he would have the fourth rig sited by late tomorrow.
But when the ship had landed near the fourth rig's caravan
There was an unforeseen disruption in his careful plan:

Apparently the crawler with the main part of the drill
Had stalled below the summit of the far crest of a hill
And wouldn't make the trip to where the black ship had set down.
For parts to get it moving they would have to go to town.

The engineer was outraged but dispatched his second shuttle
To make the flight to Veles and get parts back on the double.
And since they couldn't set the ship down on a slope so steep
He couldn't simply fly it out - his schedule he'd not keep.

But still the habitats for both could be flown to the sites
And so they planned to focus on that task throughout the night.
Angered by no contacts with the Chief of Operations
Or the shuttle sent to reestablish their connections

The surly attitudes of those who'd hijacked both the drills
Were eating at him too, as they were tired, stressed and chilled.
The stinking air and frozen desolation of this hell
Made him anxious to destroy it and to do it well.

45 Backlash

The yellow clouds were thick along Kumbaru's hilly plain
And water vapor billows made two massive glowing stains
Suspended on the far horizon high above the mist.
As viewed though passive infrared no way they could be missed!

The thermal signature of an atomic drilling rig
Isn't something one can hide, for it is used to dig
Massive holes through solid rock at fission temperatures.
Like a small volcano it makes steam you can be sure.

They were all amazed two rigs were already on site
For they had just discovered what the plan might be last night.
Someone had been quick to spot the damage they could do
And with amazing speed transported drills to Kumbaru.

They had no way of knowing how far down the drills had gone.
Their greatest hope was that the rigs had not been there for long.
Kumbaru's regolith is deep but mostly icy blocks
And it would not take long to penetrate to harder rock.

For it would melt like butter on a branding iron's tip
The journey to the bedrock shelf would be an easy trip.
And what the plan was after that? It wasn't hard to guess:
There would be great crustal quakes - a planetary mess.

Goldie rode the right chair right beside the pilot's seat.
David sat behind her, Nick beside him with his feet
Jambed beneath the pilot's chair, his face against the glass
Watching with excitement as the great columns of gas

Grew nearer glowing in the feeble sunlight like toadstools
Reflecting rainbow colors from ice crystals as they cooled.
But soon the engines throttled back and down beneath the gloom
They sank to run low-level recon near the towering plumes.

"One quick pass around each site," said Nick as he prepared
The passive infrared recorder that would pierce the air
To gather images to uplink to the shuttle craft
Orbiting above which soon would make its final pass.

Thirty fighting men in cryosuits now filled it's bay
Armed and authorized to take the drilling rigs away
From those who commandeered them and to make the drilling stop
And do all that they could to make sure those who had were caught.

The shuttle that had taken Nick and Goldie to Sinlap
Had gone up to the cruiser to bring twenty-two more back.
The aircraft that had brought the folks from Selk the night before
Brought Sinlap's small militia (Nick and nineteen more).

They would land at two points near the active drilling sites
And set up over-watch positions close but out of sight.
Each would be a hike of several miles through the gloom
Requiring speed (the thirty at the first site would land soon).

Pistol-packer had agreed to lead the first team down.
Plus half a dozen seasoned blokes recruited from the town
Accompanied by Martians to coordinate the blow.
(One of them had shot the aircraft down two nights ago).

The second team was led by David and a Townie friend.
Boomer came along despite his healing tail end;
One more of Soldana's Martians; three big farming hands;
Which left the pilot, Goldie, Chris and Nick for backup plans.

(Emergency coordination, evac, and communication
Waiting in a valley at a centralized location.)
Yet little did they know that when they dropped the first team off
They were spotted by an aircraft passing by aloft

Above a cloudy layer in the misty yellow sky
With orders that all civil aircraft on Titan must die.
But when he'd circled back Nick's craft had taken to the air
It's radar image lost in clutter, not seen anywhere.

When the unknown aircraft had departed to the east
Pistol-packer sent a coded message with a brief
Description of the type of craft and course they saw it take
Noting Martian markings but unsure if they were fake.

Nick responded that their Martian friends had not arrived
All was still on schedule and so far they were alive.

They would take evasive action to avoid the craft
Before they set the second group down near the other shaft.

But sure enough, when they set down two miles from the site
Goldie saw the unknown craft above them in its flight
Moving toward the east and north where Chris thought other sites
Would be the likely spots to drill to do the damage right.

The team had disembarked and started moving toward the drill
But Nick and his remainder sat where landed 'twixt two hills
To wait for news from any of the others' escapades
With nothing left to do but keep their ears open and wait.

But it was not a long wait - only minutes had gone by
When Goldie's perfect hearing picked up rumbles in the sky
Which grew into a roar of rocket engines overhead
For through the hazy-layered sky above a black ship sped

It's braking rockets firing for a landing east and south
In the Plains of Caladan or somewhere there about.
"That was not a shuttle. That was one enormous ship,"
The pilot looked at Goldie first and then he turned to Nick:

"Check the status of your people. Clock says they are due."
At that very instant messages from two came through:
Pistol-Packer's team reported Martians had arrived
And they had quickly sacked the site and taken twelve alive.

Pistol-Packer's rescued friend was helping to sort through
The prisoners and pirates and had stopped the drilling too.
Keeping those who might be rigged with implants far away
From Titan's own who wanted desperately to make them pay.

When the nature of the plot of drilling was explained
Pistol-Packer's rescued friend and two men climbed the frame
And spiked the rig's retraction head disabling it for good
Until replacement parts were sent from Rhea (if they could -

He explained the earliest would be at least a week
Assuming they could even get them and they'd not come cheap).
They'd be out of work but it seemed the right thing to do
To rid Titan of those that meddled and they'd be glad to!

David's team reported that the Martian shuttle craft
Had landed without incident but there'd been a blood bath
When one hijacker noticed that the shuttle's Martian marks
Were genuine and gave alert before they disembarked.

And though the local overwatch suppressed most of the fire
(Which gave the shuttle time to drop the men and then retire)
It had been disabled with one engine and two crew
Shot - the pilot dead, the co-pilot was bleeding too.

It would likely fly but it would never get to orbit.
(It made it just beyond a ridge and that is where it set
Until a pilot could be found to move it for repair.
The co-pilot was now sedated, Boomer watched him there.)

Supplemental messages were pouring in by now
Building up a picture of the raids' progress and how
Emergency evacuation of the wounded men
Was now a high priority and "They could get there when?"

The pilot had already spooled the turbines and was set
To jump the three kilometers when Chris said, "Wait! Not yet!"
And pointed out the window where a spot up in the sky
Was streaking toward the drilling site intent that more would die.

Flashes of white light that yellowed through the misty gloom
Were followed seconds later by deep thuds that signaled doom
But even as the sounds arrived a streak rose through the mist
Meeting the attacking craft whose path began to twist

And turn erratically before it arched high in the sky
Then plunged into the frozen ground - was no doubt they had died.
"Oh, my God!" said Goldie. Chris sat stunned and Nick yelled, "Go!"
The pilot ramped the throttles as Nick called to let them know

That they were only seconds out, approaching from the south
And then he held his breath while Goldie's hand covered her mouth
Until the speaker crackled with a jumbled batch of words
That soon resolved to David's voice but that is all they heard

Until they cleared the ridge and saw the scattered human forms
Spread about the shattered ground. So many were deformed

Like twisted manikins abandoned in an old warehouse.
Shocked by what they saw, only the pilot moved his mouth

To order Chris and Nick to exit when he set it down
And help to ascertain the status of those on the ground.
Landing heavily, his sweating face to Goldie turned
And said, "You're pilot in command until I have returned.

With that he stood and added, "I am headed to the site
Where the shuttle sits to see if it can make the flight
To Paxsi with a load of wounded." Then he winked his eye
And followed Chris and Nick out through the lock to the outside.

Goldie shook the shock away then took the pilot seat
And quickly scanned the manual and checklists on the screen
Trying not to be distracted by the view outside
Where only seconds earlier a dozen men had died.

Just beyond the ridge the pilot got a rude surprise
By Boomer's rifle barrel when he knocked and came inside
But when the pilot's face was recognized he welcomed him
And introduced him to the wounded pilot lain within.

Boomer'd patched him up but he had lost far too much blood
And wouldn't be much help in flying (if in fact it could).
The wounded flier passed what hints he could about the ship
Before becoming incoherent (into shock he slipped).

Boomer got two other Sinlap men into the door.
The pilot spun the single working turbine up once more
Then using vectored thrust and rockets limped into the air
And brought the damaged shuttle to the rig and landed there.

Meanwhile, Chris and Nick had spread across the killing ground
Searching through the men for those who lived of those put down.
Some had been untouched and helped the others as they could.
Shrapnel and concussion had killed some right where they stood

While others suffered slowly when their suits were compromised
Choking on the methane air and freezing where they died.
Nick found David propped against the drll rig's outer wall
A crimson trickle stained his hair but fair shape overall.

He had hit his head when knocked against a scaffold's brace
And spent a moment gazing absently off into space
Fumbling with his phone he'd tried to send a message off
But 'til he'd gained his senses managed two words and a cough.

Shots were being fired here and there around the site
And every now and then a 'jacker's suit would light up bright
As phosphorous ignited when his heartbeat wasn't found
Making eerie shadows overlap the blackened ground.

Chris was now engaged in sorting out the goats and sheep.
(He helped a rigger and a Martian sort the men to keep
Disarmed, confined and guarded in a crevice far away
From those to be evacuated soonest from the fray.

(It was made apparent that the hijackers were toast.
Whoever had deployed them didn't care if they were ghosts.
Sending in the aircraft to attack with indiscretion
Killing their own people with the Titans and the Martians.)

Chris and Nick converged on David and they all agreed
They should get their people off the site with greatest speed.
The monster who had called the shot was surely now aware
His craft had been shot down and had another in the air.

Commanders of the Martian teams were very confident
That they could handle any further aircraft that were sent
But also felt their limited resources would serve best
If used to find and neutralize remaining drill assets.

And it seemed very likely that the large ship that had passed
If found might lead them to the missing drilling rigs quite fast
For there was really nothing in the plains of Caladan
To entice an interplanetary ship to land

Except perhaps a need to transport heavy cargo fast
When cost was not an issue but a lengthy trip as vast
As crossing north from Shangri-La and Dilmun would entail
For heavy rigs on crawlers which at times were prone to fail.

Aircraft though, were getting more and more in short supply.
The damaged shuttle was an asset needful to survive

Representing half their passenger capacity
They would have to minimize the sizes of their teams.

By now the shuttle from the first site came to rendezvous
(Pistol-Packer and Selenia's commander too).
When Chris and David asked about the status of their site
And also why it seemed there were so few aboard their flight.

Pistol-Packer made thumbs up and said. "A piece of piss!
"Our friends here jumped their sorry bones. Was nothing like all this."
He motioned at the shattered ground and bodies here and there
And added, "Most of Sinlap's bunch did not come here by air.

"But opted to head south to escort all the drill rig crew
"Knowing there'd be limits on the craft if they all flew.
"They loaded up some grub and all the beer they had on hand
"Then racked off south for Paxsi and Forseti overland.

"A pair of crawlers one way and a pair off to the other
"With a pair of anti-aircraft rockets each for cover."
Pistol-Packer cracked a smile when David questioned him:
"But what about the prisoners? Who is watching them?"

He answered, "Well, we reckoned that they're Titan's enemies
"So we'd let Titan watch them. That keeps all of our hands free."
"Titan?" Nick enquired with confusion on his face.
"Reckon!," Pistol-Packer said, "They're staying right in place.

"We put them in the drill rig's habitat to spend their days.
"Their cryosuits are in a pile a hundred yards away.
"They're not going anywhere." He cracked a crooked grin.
The others chuckled happily as they grinned back at him.

Selenia's commander said, "We dare not risk implants
"Exploding on our aircraft. This eliminates that chance."
"Do it here," said David "Put the 'jackers in the rig.
"Collect their cryosuits and dump them in the hole they digged.

"Put the wounded on the damaged shuttle for evac
"And load remaining fighters on the Sinlap folks' aircraft."
The drilling crew agreed to spike the rig just like the first
And three were taking care of that when one more missile burst

Into the yellow sky accelerating toward the east
A white hot spot of screeching death their Martian friends released.
Then only seconds later they could hear the sudden sound
Of impact just before a screaming turbine hit the ground.

"How'd he know that they were foes?" asked Nick incredulous.
Selenia's commander simply said, "They were not us."
Then turned away to supervise some details for his men
As David looked at Nick and said, "This game we have to win."

Realization flooded through the cracks in Nick's shocked mind
That he was in an altered state - he'd never seen this kind
Of danger, death and conflict and the frailty of life;
The sudden profound consequences met with mortal strife.

David grabbed Nick's shoulder and gave him a friendly shake
And said, "This is a lesson for you. Now you must awake
"And focus on the task at hand. Get Goldie set to fly.
"Your pilot's taking wounded back so she will be your ride."

Nick took inventory of his scattered mental state
Then pulled himself together and accepted that his fate
Was in the hands of everyone around him as was theirs
And his responsibility to them was his fair share.

"Right," Nick started, then he focused close on David's eye.
"Right," he said again then grabbed two carbines from a pile
Of confiscated weapons. "I'll be fine and she will too.
"I know there is a lot of hard yakka we've got to do."

David smiled wide at Nick's first use of Titan slang
And took it as the signal Nick had girded up his brain.
Nick gave him a thumbs up and departed for the plane
Knowing after this day he would never be the same.

Goldie watched the Sinlap riflemen start climbing in
Along with several Martians who saluted with a grin.
She didn't understand until a man she didn't know
Sat beside her on the right and spouted, "Right. Let's go!"

Nick sat close behind her in the seat he had before
As Chris filed in behind him as the last man through the door.

And said, "Our pilot's taking wounded in the damaged shuttle
"He said you're our pilot now and shouldn't have much trouble."

Goldie shook her head and said, "I've no time in this type.
"To fly this craft with passengers aboard would not be right."
"Pig's arse!" barked the man who buckled into the right seat
"Jocko said you're ridgy-didge. There's no time to be meek.

"Once you've got us in the air he says you'll cotton on
"To all the rest and I will handle your navigation.
"Jocko needs to fly the shot-up ship to save our folks
"And they can't spare the backup pilot from the Martian blokes."

At that moment they could hear the crippled shuttle lift
As turbine blades chewed air and thrusters gave it an assist.
Turning south and west it took the wounded to be healed
And then they heard the other Martian shuttle's engines squeal.

"Sorry, Crumpet, we've run out of pilots for this row.
"It's your pozzy now so wind her up and have a go.
"If you can fly on Mars then you can bloody well fly here.
"Now get this bird up in the air and I'll retract the gear."

Goldie asked him, "Do you have time in this type of craft?"
"Nup. As a bloody pilot I'm not worth a Zack.
"No worries, Love. Spin these turbines up and she'll be fine.
"This is an emergency and we don't have much time."

Goldie put the takeoff checklist up on one display
Then turned around again to see the men looking her way.
Nick's hand rested on her shoulder, "Get us out of here."
His confidence convinced her that her skills they did not fear.

"I'm lifting this bird hot and fast," she warned the right-seat man.
She finished up her checklist then fed power to the fans.
"Yeew!" the man exclaimed as they all sank into their seats.
"That's me girl! Now turn to heading one-two-five degrees."

She was climbing fast to buy some distance from the ground
When ninety meters off her port a flash and then the sound
Of shuttle turbines spewing tortured gas in one loud roar
Marked the passage of the Martian shuttle toward the north

As banking from an eastward path they bid a fond farewell
Until they would meet up again when they'd gathered intel.
(They'd planned to have the faster Martian shuttle sweep northeast
In hopes of spotting plumes or evidence of drills at least,

Then re-connect in Caladan or where it made most sense
Once they had a better picture for further defense.)
Leveling the aircraft low enough to see the ground
But high enough to get a view of all that was around

Goldie fought the urge to put the aircraft through its paces
Thinking of the men and the emotions on their faces.
And so she concentrated on the power plant checklists
Her self-appointed copilot kept lookout through the mist.

Chris and one rig's foreman talked about their closest guess
Regarding how the other drilling rigs might have progressed
Across the raw terrain of Dilmun into Caladan
And how much time that it would take to load, transport and land

A rig by spacecraft if someone were up against a clock.
(It would not be hard to do - it's how the rigs were brought.)
Everyone had plugged their suits into the craft to charge
And food was handed out and taken in with great regard

For Jonesy who had forethought back in Sinlap to provide
What he could to help support those who went on this ride.
And everyone on Titan was committed to the cause
Of ending the destruction and enforcing common laws.

46   Mousetrap

The cursing pilot circled once around the craft below
And when he made a second pass flew over very low.
He could see it was a shuttle sporting Martian marks
An engine cowling was removed with flashing lights from sparks

As if someone were welding parts inside of the nacelle.
Several figures standing near jumped up and waved and yelled.
The pilot called the engineer, described the scene beneath
Then set his blackened shuttle down and sent two men to greet

The figures walking toward him - obviously Warden's men.
Who else would be here with Martian paint jobs if not them?
So it was quite a shock to him when shortly from behind
A pistol barrel nudged his neck (this made him change his mind).

"This won't do you any good," he stated with a sigh.
"This ship's going to self-destruct and all of us will die
"If I don't - " His protest was cut off short almost mid-word
As fast-acting sedation from a pinprick did its work.

"That's a load of comet dust," the pin-pricker replied.
The two Martian intruders dragged his slack form to the side
And occupied the pilot seats while engineers plugged in
Their diagnostic gear to search the craft from end-to-end

For booby traps and alterations that may have been made
To render it unsafe for use by all but renegades.
Indeed it had some features which gave it some extra teeth
(Like inboard missile hard mounts that were hidden and discreet)

But there was nothing like a self destruct device on board
And they were able to extract transponder codes and more:
Like all the navigation data from its recent flight
Which lead them straight to where its mother ship should be tonight.

* * * * *

The Sinlap folks were flying for the best part of three hours
(Goldie had gone 'round a patch of air with methane showers)

When David's voice decrypted through their active data link:
"We have an opportunity. Tell me what you think:

"We've captured an armed shuttle and three goons along with it.
"They're sedated now, but we have found their mother ship.
"It seems they've been transporting drilling rigs to Kumbaru
"And there's a chance that we can take it - if you help us to."

"Crikey! " Goldie's co-pilot exclaimed, "Good onya mates!
"How'd you bag the tossers then? You know that's bloody ace!"
David's voice came back and they could hear a little snicker
"We lured them down into a trap that couldn't have worked slicker:

"We spotted them on radar then we beaconed for some aid
"And when they landed to assist, well, let's just say they paid
"For not doing their homework. They've not been on Titan long
"And don't seem really up to date on what's been going on."

"Are there Martian markings on the shuttle?" Goldie asked.
"No, it's black as sin. It has a non-reflective cast
"Appearing small by radar, it absorbs most all the light
"You shine on it. It looks as if it's knit from darkest night."

"You've caught a shuttle from a bloody renegade's black ship."
Goldie's Titan copilot looked much like he would spit
But held it back in deference to those with whom he flew.
"That's a ripper of an asset - bloody high value!"

Nick then interjected, "It is not nearly as high
"As the value of a black ship. I think we should try
"To take it. If we can't then we should try to take it down.
"I'd think a chance like this is pretty rare to come around?"

"Bloody oath it is," (Their Titan had to spit this time.)
"Ask the boys behind you Chris, if all of them are fine
"With taking on this job. It might get dodgy by and by."
Nick and Chris turned 'round to see thumbs up from every guy.

Soldana's mercenaries now had two shuttles to man
So Sinlap's small militia had room to breathe again
(Their aircraft had been loaded almost to capacity
Which didn't make it easier to fly for poor Goldie.)

And though the black ship's shuttle wasn't large it was well armed.
Also, when close to the ship it wouldn't cause alarm
For they now had transponder codes and voiceprints of the men
Who manned the craft before it was taken away from them.

(Radar had provided a slick app the Martian crew
Could use to modify a voice with only one or two
Samples of a voiceprint as the basis for the change.
It wasn't perfect but it put one's voice within the range.)

Goldie set the Sinlap plane beside the Martian shuttle
Opposite the captured one without a bit of trouble.
The man who'd been her copilot said, "Ace!" when she'd set down
Then scrambled for the airlock door and said, "See you around!

"There's a black ship's shuttle over there I need to fly.
"Good onya, Crumpet. No worries. You're the dinki-di!"
He winked and closed the airlock as a number of them left.
"Who was that guy?" asked Goldie. "I think you have passed the test,"

Said Chris as he acknowledged that the man was quite advanced
As a general pilot and his ruse was, "Just a dance
"To make you take initiative and prove you have the skill.
"And now he's satisfied that you are qualified to fill

"That seat you're sitting in enough to get us safely back.
"After we secure the black ship with a sneak attack.
"Or destroy the thing. We'll see what your Martians will do.
"After that we'll liberate the drill at Kumbaru."

The leaders of the Martian and the Sinlap Titan teams
Came to Goldie's aircraft where a meeting was convened
To strategize about the gift that fell into their lap
And how they might conspire to take the black ship in a trap.

The theory was that there would be a planetary scientist
Aboard the ship to direct efforts (or perhaps, just to assist)
The drilling crews in site selection and other aspects.
David voiced his thoughts what kind of man they might expect:

"My guess is his commitment to the cause is not as high
"As what it takes for someone to pursue it 'til he dies.

"But just in case, let's bring him out and talk it over some.
"We'll see his commitment at the muzzle of a gun."

Pistol-Packer, Chris and Nick agreed that it made sense.
Selenia's commander nodded and gave his two cents:
"You may find that true about the scientist you fetch
"But the captain of that ship won't be an easy catch.

"Men who captain black ships have a darkness of the soul
"Dripping with a stench that oozed up from Hell's deepest hole.
"As a rule, they'd rather die and sacrifice their crews
"Than face the judgment for their crimes that has been overdue

"Since long before the Terra-Luna war even began.
"No, you'll be dealing with a very evil man.
"Don't increase his chances of escape by taking time
"To reason. Just remember those who suffered by his crimes

"And quickly do what needs be done to board and take his ship.
"Neutralize the self-destruct and give this place the slip.
"You'll only get one chance so move in quick and do it right.
"Do not have compassion; pull no punches in the fight."

The others in the meeting knew that his advice was sound
For he had fought before some there had even been around.
So with consensus on their views they nailed down a plan
And rehearsed by the numbers 'til they knew it to a man.

The Martian shuttle pilot turned to Goldie to explain
The kind of flying she must do next time she flew the plane:
"We'll need to hug the ground and do our best to stay below
"The beam of any active radar or we'll surely show.

"Stay in close formation. Stay behind and to the side
"Opposite the heading to the black ship for this ride.
"Stick to me as if you were a pimple on my back
"And I will come in wide and low along a tangent track.

"We'll drop behind a hill and set your boys down where they'll be
"Positioned to approach the black ship on the ground quickly.
"Then stay there 'til you get instructions. You're the last resort
"For the Sinlap men if things go south and we abort."

* * * * *

David went with the commander of the Martian crew
When he transferred to the captured shuttle with a few
Who volunteered to be first on the ground when they arrived
At the black ship with the goal of taking it alive.

The transponder alerted when a radar query hit
Which caused it to report on their approach to the black ship.
Then presently a tired man's voice queried them as well,
"It's about time you got back to this forsaken hell.

"Did you find the Chief of Operations on your cruise?"
"Yes," responded David, "His aircraft had some abuse
"But he is in the air and just a few seconds behind
"I'm surprised he hasn't called about his precious find."

"His find?" the voice inquired. "Yeah, some fancy rock or ice.
"He said he told them not to transmit from the drilling sites
"Until he'd got direction from upstairs on what to do.
"Don't know what it is but he is bringing it to you."

Just then another voice broke in the black ship's commo link.
(This time it was Chris whose voice was scrambled so they'd think
He was the Operations Chief arriving there as well
The black ship's people didn't give a clue if they could tell.)

"I've brought a fascinating sample from the western site.
"They said you'd want to see it but it must be kept outside.
"We'll land in close for your examination if you care."
"Fine," the engineer agreed, "You're cleared. Land anywhere."

The Martian shuttle settled to the ground amidst a cloud
Of icy dust and particles that formed a foggy shroud
Blown up in the air by turbine wash and thruster blast
Followed by the blackened shuttle which settled down last,

Its nose positioned watchfully upon the Mars-marked craft
As if it were prepared to cut loose with a deadly blast
If something were amiss (a ploy to set those men at ease
Who may be watching from the black ship's weapons galleries

393

Which loomed against the orange sky like some tall wizard's hat
Absorbing every ray of light - a stark yet ghostly black.)
They didn't know how many they might face within that ship
For it was large and undoubtedly very well equipped.

They knew they'd bagged three men who manned the shuttle they had caught
And they could see the other shuttle from the ship was not
Present. So three more men missing was an easy bet.
And hoped the engineer could coax some more of them out yet.

Presently three figures exited the Martian craft.
Two opened a cargo door amidships then walked aft
Appearing to inspect the nacelle of an engine there.
The third figure approached the ship and waved arms in the air.

Near the ground beneath the ship a door slid to the side
Revealing a lift that had come down the black ship's hide.
The man who exited the lift was ungainly at best
Never having put a Titan cryosuit to test.

The man who waved his arms turned 'round and led him to the shuttle.
That cargo door is where the warden's engineer met trouble.
Pulled into the doorway and presented with a choice
To breathe his last or do what he was told to with his voice.

And David's guess was accurate - the engineer complied.
He radioed the ship to have two more men come outside
But at the last he made a foolish comment to the ship
Which gave away that something on the shuttle was amiss.

Then they learned how quickly pirates turned on Warden's men.
In only seconds they were in a fire fight again.
The black ship's captain did not differentiate at all
But fired on the shuttle with the engineer, et al.

This time it was laser ports attacking from the ship.
Instead of missiles from a shuttle, beams designed to rip
A spacecraft into ribbons caused the thick and tortured air
To heat into a plasma scattering beams everywhere

But targets they intended, for the pilots in both shuttles
Quickly hit their thrusters, thereby tripling the troubles

The laser gunners had with dust and ice thrown in the air.
Then at that moment Sinlap's warriors came from everywhere.

It was like a thunderclap each time a laser fired.
The misty air made interference that appeared like fire
Which brightened as it broadened with each meter on its way
To targets partially obscured deep in the yellow haze.

For particles of ice and dust kicked up by thruster blast
Significantly added their effects until at last
The lasers were abandoned and each airlock opened wide
As bursts from automatic rifles blasted from inside.

These were answered quickly by suppressing fire meant
To give some cover for two Martians who approached and sent
A pair of fragmentation grenades through each open door.
After that the shooting stopped - was not heard any more.

Nick was in the second party that went up the lift
(Still functional enough to take a small load on the trip).
The inner airlock door was forced so Titan's air rushed in
Much faster through it than the many bullet holes had been.

The Martian team was clearing one way, Titans cleared the other.
Nick was following the Martians who sought to recover
Any information in the Captain's lair or bridge
To indicate who sent them - even if just a vestige.

Automated bulkhead doors had shut throughout the ship
As sensors felt the chill and pressure when the bullets ripped
The metal of the airlocks and the two teams breached the doors
And as they swept the ship they had to breach through even more

Until only the bridge remained untouched by Titan's air
As methane mixed with oxygen in pockets everywhere.
Explosive or just flammable - it was a deadly mix
To float about the confines of a manned and powered ship.

The Sinlap Titan team soon found a sinister device
Rigged among the engines that confirmed the good advice
Given by Selenia regarding self-destructs
And soon had rendered it inert by what they felt was luck.

Afterward they found the special cargo for the plan
To crack the shelf of Kumbaru which not a single man
Could doubt was in the works - for it was more than they had guessed:
Seventy atomic demolitions of the best

Produced by TerraCorp before the war had called them back
To be converted into weapons (but they had lost track
Of many of them when divisions in the outer moons
Had splintered off as they saw Terra Corporation's doom.)

When the bridge was opened Nick was with the Martian team.
It struck him at that moment that he'd not forget this scene.
A suited man stood tall before them in the room's red glow
Panel lights reflecting from his helmet row by row.

A pistol lay beside him on a console within reach
Yet he stood motionless awaiting bullets or a speech.
When neither came his way he slowly took his helmet off;
Breathed the frigid stinking air while stifling a cough;

And set the helmet down and slowly touched the pistol's butt
Then slower still he took the weapon and lifted it up.
The muzzle touched his temple. Nick yelled, "Just a minute! Stop!
"I've a message for you and I think it's from the top.

"You recognize his voice don't you?" Nick held up his phone
And made it play a message in a voice Radar had cloned:
"You know my voice, Captain, do you not?" The pistol paused
As recognition crossed the captain's eyes but then he coughed

And said, "Of course I don't." The pistol raised up once again
Then Nick played one more message for the hard, committed man:
"Show us now, Captain. Show how your love for me burns."
The Captain's eyes betrayed him and Nick's guess was then confirmed

As burning phosphorous burst from the Captain's open suit
(And pockets of the oxy-methane mix ignited too).
His limp form slowly fell as white sparks shot throughout the room
And carbon ash and blowing smoke obscured the Martian's view.

Some were knocked aside as oxy-methane pockets burst
And echoed through the ship until the air had done its worst.

The hardened Martian mercenaries looked to be in shock
For none had ever seen a man ignite when a phone talked.

When it all was over the commander looked at Nick
And said, "That was a well thought-out and brilliant little trick.
"There is no doubt he knew that voice. Selenia will know
"That whom she had suspected is indeed running this show."

Nick nodded acknowledgement but couldn't say a word.
He was choked up by the horror of what he'd observed
And yet he had the presence to send up the video
That he had captured of the captain just seconds ago.

Confirmation of receipt was near immediate.
Selenia had been apprised and was on top of it.
She forwarded the video to Red who was impressed
Enough to launch his yacht and in a cryosuit get dressed.

47   A Message from Mars

Soldana had connections that reached far and deep and dark
And enterprises through the system, not just there on Mars.
Casinos and refineries and real estate concerns
But in the case of war so much of it was sure to burn.

Another night awakened from his sleep by troubling dreams
Where profits, like wild horses, pulled away from their restraints.
Rubbing sleep from bleary eyes he scanned the newsfeed screen
And there before him, like his dreams, was his reality.

The truth was not the story that the System News portrayed
And people on the outer worlds were growing more dismayed
With Mars at every cycle of the news that was released
Regardless that the System News was what they trusted least.

The news service implied that Mars' aggression was at play.
Soldana's contacts though, agreed that out the Saturn way
Someone had been framing Mars for piracies and crimes
Of conquest and starvation as a means to bring hard times

To Saturn's colonies for an impending coup d'etat.
And that the Martian senate was to blame for all of that.
The Martian senate though, had categorically denied
These accusations stating the Consortium had lied.

His contacts also said that even though the newsfeed service
Clamored for a strong man to control the system's circus.
People around Saturn for the most part knew the score
That Mars would be the last to blame for starting any war.

What concerned Soldana most was how the markets changed
So suddenly. But what he saw to be the thing most strange:
Renegades no longer contracted gray market jobs
And piracies now seemed coordinated by a boss.

This must be interpreted as someone massing strength
Of the kind most dangerous and would be used at length.
And few things but a TerraCorp resurgence would explain
The need to find a scapegoat such as Mars to put at blame.

And so he poured a drink and smoked one half of a cigar
Then went to his transmitter (one that could reach out that far)
And sent a coded message to Selenia, et al
Providing them intelligence and his views of it all:

"TerraCorp Security sent two ships to the place
"Where some kind of a science rig was lost and found no trace
"Of evidence to ascertain its fate or recoup loss,
"But now they're hunting Martian ships around Enceladus.

"The news from Earth is TerraCorp stands solidly behind
"The weak Saturn Consortium (the pompous fools are blind)
"So in effect it's TerraCorp who's calling shots for them
"Allied with privateers to do their dirty work again.

"A Martian escort team has shaken down two Terran ships
"Carrying six shuttles that are armed - and now get this:
"All of them were painted with a Martian color scheme
"Containing uniforms insignia'd as Mars Marines

"And small arms manufactured here in Syrtis recently.
"Someone has a plan to frame Mars for some infamy!
"Both ships had been bound for Rhea. Hotels there are packed
"With men who could be mercenaries planning an attack.

"The senate is requesting Martian ships to form a fleet
"In Saturn space for mutual support - but stay discreet.
"You do what you can for Jules, but if you can assist
"The Martian assets there at Saturn put them top of list."

He knew she was a business woman from her nose to toes.
He also knew her depth of passion which had now arose
Regarding he whose friendship she had valued more than most.
He *didn't* know how far she'd go to help him chase his ghost.

* * * * *

Selenia had read Soldana's private message through
Then relayed it to Captains Redfeather and Standish who
Insisted that she choose where their priorities would set.
"Titan is the largest," she replied, "Martian asset."

Retiring to her private quarters for an hour's thought

Her mind would not slow down regarding what the Titans caught.
The Martian ships at Enceladus were on full alert
And Rhea's hot economy would likely not be hurt.

Soldana would expect a full report direct from her
About the situation there and what she could confirm.
And so she sent a message with the details of the plot
To halt the Titan terraforming and how it was stopped

And all she knew about the Martian fleet's activities
Including what she thought about Saturn's economies
And how they were reacting to the news and whipped-up fears
But most importantly, that she'd confronted privateers:

"My focus and attention has not strayed far from the teams
"That I have sent to Titan with two shuttles and the means
"To keep our friends protected and to intervene with force
"Into the plans of those who seek to change the Titans' course.

"The men I put in charge were made to understand their task:
"Provide offensive options for the Titans and unmask
"The forces that attacked them and confirm identity.
"Then do all that they could to maintain some stability

"For scientists and engineers who work for Titan's good.
"The first order of business: Stop the drilling if they could,
"Free the hostage drilling crews, interrogate the perps,
"And any intel they may find? Send it to me first.

"The first reports were good in that two drills were found and stopped.
"Their crews were freed but three of our good fighters have been shot.
"Two are dead and one is wounded and a shuttle hurt
"But three enemy aircraft have been shot down to the dirt.

"The first had Martian markings and a crewman who survived
"Claiming to be Martian but our Goldie knew he lied.
"And then he self-destructed just like Ansel Pedersen.
"So didn't get to question him for more information.

"The other two were shot down at the second drilling site
"When our intervention turned into a fire fight.
"The second hit both parties on the ground without a care
"The third one was destroyed at range before it could get there.

"The better news is that we captured one shuttle intact
"Complete with crew (sedated now) that's armed and stealthy black.
"We got the mother ship's location then we sent a team
"And now we have a black ship too, and men who I'll make sing.

"My plan is to confirm some facts then I'll be going dark
"I'm leaving Captain Standish in charge when I disembark.
"He lacks experience but he is gutsy and inventive
"And his moral fiber gives him more than great incentive

"To make the most of what he has been given to command.
"I'm not sure you know it but you picked a better man
"Than I gave you credit for. I'm pleasantly surprised.
"He'll command the cruiser while I take a little ride

"To see what Jules is up to in our stealthy new black ship.
"By the time you get this into shadow I'll have slipped."

She sent her message off then queried Red for an update
And asked him if he'd take her on an interesting date.

48   The Black Ring

Nick and Goldie greeted Captain Red when he set down
And helped to steady him when he stepped onto Titan's ground.
Selenia's commander came to meet him as did Chris.
Red put hands on hips and said, "Now will you look at this!

"My path has crossed a hundred times with black ships through the years.
"I've even killed a dozen of them yet never been near
"Enough to see the bullet holes they so richly deserve.
"Now here in Titan's outback I find one nicely preserved.

"Admirably done, friends. This is a proud day."
"It is," said Pistol-Packer as he also came their way
Towing David with him who was tapping on his phone,
"And if it weren't for these blokes we would all be ash and bone."

Nick provided introductions for them all around
And while they all shook hands a graceful figure lighted down
From off the yacht and Nick said, "Let me introduce to you,
"Our friend, Selenia - and Martian benefactor too."

Selenia was gracious, greeting all of them by name
But when she looked up at the black ship something in her changed.
Quiet and reserved, she bottled up her normal charm,
Caught Nick's tired eyes then took Redfeather by the arm.

"I need to see inside her. Take me up please, if you will.
"Nick, show me the body of the captain who was killed."
Two more suited figures disembarked from Red's small yacht.
"Forensics workers," Red explained, "They'll see what we may not."

Selenia's commander led the way into the lift,
Selenia and Red behind him then Goldie and Nick.
Forensics worked beneath the ship, sampling landing gear
Then followed Nick's small party in the ship and disappeared.

Selenia was first to step into the ash-stained room.
(Red was anxious to investigate this ship of doom.)
The melted suit lay on the floor and soot still filled the air.
The twisted features of a face beneath a shock of hair

Were visible protruding from the fouled and damaged suit.
Selenia unconsciously twice nudged it with her boot
And then she leaned close over it to search the damaged face
Before she took the gloves to see the hands of the carcass.

The first hand held no interest for her but the second did
And in a twinkling instant from her hip a dagger slid
With which she cut one finger from the deceased captain's hand
And pulled from it a large black stone atop a silver band.

She held it up in front of her and turned it in the light
Then handed it to Red and said, "If you're to do this right
"This will come in handy." He eyed it closely too
Then gave it back and said, "No, this belongs to you.

"You pick some of yours and I will pick you some of mine
"Then we'll get it manned and space-worthy in record time.
"But first we need to get it off of Titan for repairs.
"When forensic folks are done I'll take the ship upstairs.

"Can we muster up an interim crew from this mob?"
Selenia's commander said, "I think so," with a nod
Then turned and headed for the hatch to take him to the lift.
Nick and Goldie stayed with them and toured their new black ship.

When they re-emerged and met the others on the ground
Selenia enquired as she turned and looked around:
"I hear we also got a pair of shuttles with the ship.
"Where are they?" she asked, "The ship seems otherwise equipped."

Pistol-Packer answered, trying not to show his pride
(For he had great thanksgiving for her help boiling inside):
"One we just sent north to spring another drilling crew.
"They were left without a habitat in Kumbaru.

"The other went to buy some crawler parts they cannot use.
"Our boys carked their crawler - sent them off chasing a goose.
"A rigger on the crew called to some mates at Veles port
"Who got a little stroppy when he gave them the report

"About these dodgy tossers who had nicked the drilling crew.
"They rolled the tossers, took their ship, and just left Xanadu.

"They'll be back to free that crew within a half an hour.
"After that they'll spike the rig and leave it with no power.

"There is now a crustal drilling moratorium
"Until these bloody vandals are dispatched - sans decorum."
Selenia and Red were both impressed with Titan's verve
And thanked the Pistol-Packer for his cunning, skill and nerve.

Then at that moment one of Sinlap's men bounced up to him
And said in lowered tones, "You need to have a word with Tim.
"He's gone and spit the dummy and he's pissing off the crew.
"Perhaps you'll have a word with him?" Then they all heard him too:

"These attacks on Titan's soil are bloody acts of war!
"Buildings, planes, and property and people by the score
"Are rooted and destroyed or carked and someone has to pay.
"Anything we capture here will bloody well here stay!"

Nick was not surprised by Tim's exhausted bad reaction.
He whispered, "Have Selenia engage negotiation."
Red held up his hand in caution, signifying, "Wait."
And whispered back, "That man must hear it come from his own mate."

Pistol packer turned away and bounced in Tim's direction.
"Pig's arse, sport! This is a diplomatic delegation.
"It's been a ripping day and every one of us is knackered.
"So cark the whinge. You're chocka poo, ya bloody cheeky ocker.

"These are spoils of war and Titan's no official nation.
"Framing Martian ships? Attempts to sabotage relations?
"These Martians saved our planet - paid our docket with their blood.
"The ship goes at a mate's rate, sport, now piss off and get stuffed."

Pistol-Packer, red-faced, spun and returned to their group.
"Sorry," he apologized, "He's on a wobbly loop.
"He'll be back around and feeling low for what he said.
"Pay no mind for he is also saddened by your dead."

Selenia responded in a voice that most could hear:
"The fact that Mars and Titan are allied is very clear.
"Perhaps you haven't formed a nation yet out of this moon
"But after what has happened here I know you will quite soon.

"Your need for aircraft at this time is critical at best.
"Mars' commitment to your cause has been put to the test.
"We still abide. And you may keep my pair of Martian shuttles -
"The one that brought my men here and the one that had the troubles.

"But likewise I have need to take this black ship on a flight.
"The cargo that it holds provides you terraforming might.
"These are spoils taken in a war involving Mars.
"And we ask that you share them; you have proven friends of ours."

They could see the others turn around to look at Tim
Who hung his head and nodded for a moment then he grinned
Through tears that blurred his eyes, but then he held his thumbs up high
As pistol packer turned again, announcing with a sigh:

"This ship is Titan's gift to Mars as mercenary payment.
"The cargo will remain here in indefinite impoundment
"Later to be utilized as Titan will see fit.
"Now please, if you will, take possession of your ship."

Pistol-Packer bowed and motioned toward the black spacecraft
Where pallets of the demolitions, being carried aft
And lowered to a drill rig crawler which had just arrived
Would someday be another tool to bring Titan alive.

* * * * *

Nick had argued passionately to be on the crew
To take the black ship to Iapetus where Captain Blue
Had gone to face the unknown; but Selenia said, "No."
Then Captain Red convinced her that she ought to let him go

For he had shown resourcefulness and courage and resolve
In dealing with the pirate captain and when he was called
To serve with Titans in the fighting he did not hold back.
"Besides," Red had noted, "That's his crew out there, in fact."

Selenia had argued Titan needed him the most
And it would be a tragedy if he became a ghost
While poking around space that more than likely was a base
For those who were the worst of criminals and renegades.

Red was in agreement with the arguments she brought
But they were running short on folks to man ships as they ought.
Titans were tied up with running down the renegades
And working to recover from the damage they had made.

Red could spare a couple men; the cruiser could a few;
Nick and Goldie weren't first picks but they could make up two.
Young and motivated and emotionally vested,
They were both a better choice than strangers, argued Red:

"He may be a greenhorn but he's one that Jules respects.
"And I know he has talents he can use to great effect.
"Let him go with Goldie on this pirate ship of yours.
"Have faith in your youthful people. Let fate run its course."

And so, dressed in their cryosuits the two took their first flight
Aboard a ship designed for stealth and built as black as night.
They rendezvoused with Red's ship for a day of quick repairs
(To fix the many bullet holes so it would hold its air.)

Nick and Goldie slept the sleep of soldiers on reprieve.
More than sixteen hours in the sack was great relief!
Selenia had brought a dozen of her hand-picked men,
The black ship had been quickly cleaned and quarters made for them.

Engineers took Nick along to see the black ship's systems,
Goldie was a focused student of the pilot's lessons,
A quick provision and an in-depth systems check was done,
Contingencies discussed for when they got where Blue had gone.

And then the ships were separated by a mile or two
Then rocketed toward Saturn VIII to seek out Captain Blue.
These days of intense stress had burned through Nick's soul like a flame
And he and Goldie both knew they would never be the same.

49 Confidence and Conscience

Warden kept a tight rein on the captains of his ships
(As tight as possible, that is, for pirates and misfits.)
The inner circle of his best commanded ships of black
(Stealth-enhanced destroyers optimized for sneak attacks.)

Their loose association tightened up after the war
When governments and vigilantes sought to even scores.
United by a common love of violence and greed
It wasn't long before the Warden's schemes fulfilled the need

For mutual protection by a centralized command
And many of them swore a pact of fealty to his plan.
Every one among them swearing horrors on the others
If they ever spoke a word to blow the Warden's cover.

So there was trust among the black ships (far as pirates could)
And regular reports to Warden (it was understood)
Were better few than often for security concerns
But now more timely reports were for what the Warden yearned.

His Chief of Titan Operations had sent the report
That Veles Spaceport had been largely wrecked, but better sport
Was being had by shuttles painted up as Martian craft
Hunting down the straggling aircraft - soon there'd be none left.

He also had reported that the orbital relays
Had one by one been dropping out and most had gone away
And so it seemed his ship in Titan orbit was on track
To shortly make communications systems all go black.

Distress calls had been made but he believed most had been jammed.
Those that he had monitored put Martian ships at hand.
Some hostages were kidnapped and interrogated deep
But no word yet on special imagers - not a peep.

This was all good news but Warden was a bit concerned
About the ship that brought him Dr. Bordeaux whom he'd burned.
For they had maintained silence since the order had been sent
To wreck Veles and every ship from Titan's sky to rend.

His planetary scientist said drilling had commenced
At Kumbaru, so overall the warden was convinced
That everything at Titan was progressing as it should.
Beside that one distraction bigger things were going good!

His friends at Terra Corp had made a public accusation
That Mars attacked a research post in war-like provocation.
And it was now apparent they'd attacked Titan as well
And they'd not remain neutral if the rule on Rhea fell.

Thousands had already contracted for real estate
On Ganymede, Callisto, - even Triton's budding state.
His transports were engaged in bringing foodstuffs and supplies
To colonists who'd signed the lines that mortgaged him their lives.

"A most convenient crisis, is it not?" the warden quipped
Renee sat down beside him as she blew then slowly sipped
A cup of tea she'd brewed from leaves imported from the Earth
Which she had bought on Rhea paying more than it was worth

But happy to put Warden's money back in someone's pocket
Who would not be spending it on lasers, guns and rockets
Meant to arm more pirate ships or further silly coups.
She gestured toward the view screen which was blaring System News,

"It appears that many are accepting invitations
"To join us in our future interplanetary nations.
"Hundreds it appears." She took another sip of tea.
The warden said, "They number in the thousands, actually.

"And it has only just begun. As others see the boons
"That our ships are delivering to members, then quite soon
"Entire populations will be flocking to our doors
"Begging to be citizens, and we'll accept, of course."

Renee sipped at her tea and said, "These things are moving fast.
"How can you be sure they are all on the proper path?"
"Renee, my Dear," the warden turned, "I've formed a syndicate
"Of parties who together are controlling all of it.

"Operating from the shadows since the lunar war
"Banks and politicians, renegades and many more:

"Terra Corporation scientists and entertainers,
"Real estate developers and lawyers on retainer.

"All of these have bent their will to mine. It was their pleasure
"After application of a tiny bit of pressure.
"And now they dance in concert and perform all I desire.
"And you doubted the application of the word, 'empire'."

He smiled wide and bowed his head a moment then went on:
"A man of wealth and power gave advice I've built upon.
"Centuries ago he said, *'Care not who makes the rules
"If you control the currency.'* The man was not a fool.

"The currency was out of reach for me to gain control
"So I have changed the currency to something else than gold.
"The currency out here is transportation, food and land
"And I now have control of each of these right in my hand.

"Soon we'll make the rules and you will make them at my side.
"Renee, you will be empress of it all when you're my bride."
His smile was infectious. He even showed great charm.
He added, "How can you resist?" and offered her his arm.

She placed her tea cup on the table, turned to him and said,
"I can't," reflecting back his smile, "But I can't share your bed.
"Not yet," she said and took his arm and wrapped it 'round her waist
Then put her arms around his neck and looked up in his face.

"You are not the monster I had thought just months ago.
"You're a man of vision as you finally have shown.
"Instead of wild fantasy (was all the view I had)
"You've made a great reality though some may call you mad.

"And though your methods have seemed harsh at times, I've learned to see
"Your humor in the bright light of my new reality.
"And that word is the operative: 'New', my Emperor.
"There must be adjustments. Give us time to make it sure."

With that she pecked him on the cheek and took her arms away
But he did not release the arm he held around her waist.
His dark eyes gleamed with something that she could not quite decipher.
"Renee," he said in lowered tones, "I cannot wait forever.

"But I'm a patient man and I suspect fresh memories
"Of working in these caves have kept your heart from feeling free.
"Each wall must remind you of a time of sad distress.
"That's why I planned to meet on Rhea, put this past to rest."

She looked away a moment, for a moment hung her head
Then put her arms around him once again and softly said,
"Thank you for your understanding. You will be my cure.
"Years of sorrow here can hurt libido to be sure."

She put her head against his chest then slowly pulled away
And left him to his work for all the rest of that dark day.
The dirtiness and shame she felt were growing more severe
And kept in check within her conscience only by her fear.

This dance was getting more complex. How could she fake the steps?
Warden would not speak a word regarding her requests
To spare the colony and minimize the number dead
And time was running out to keep herself out of his bed.

The possibility (or probability, in fact)
That he would hold the people hostage 'til she did the act
To consummate the union with his body and his schemes
Plagued her tortured mind and haunted sleep with horrid dreams.

She was not a stranger to fatigue and worker's pains
But now it manifested as tight muscles and migraines.
Warden's pet physician was as evil as they came
And obvious to anyone was cruelly insane.

She knew her trip to see him would be kept as no secret
From Warden who had keenest interest that she remained fit.
So when she asked for sleeping pills to help her head to rest
The number would be noted at the Warden's sly request.

She didn't swallow all of them. Once or twice per day
She would palm and pocket one and hide it safe away.
Then as the days went by she grew a stash that no one knew
Which someday might be handy for something she planned to do.

50   It's a Go!

Warden planned to meet on Rhea when Renee returned
From her trip to Ganymede and after he had burned
(Or poisoned, as the case may be) the witnesses of crime
But with her change of plans he'd had to shorten up the time

For execution of his plot for clearing Saturn Eight.
Renee had also grown yet more insistent as of late
That this remaining colony be left to work and serve
As her pet protectorate, but his plans hadn't swerved.

There had never been a doubt Renee had one close friend.
Hidalia had been her roommate since long before then.
And it had been no secret that one of the warden's men
Availed himself of this woman who was Renee's dear friend.

Renee herself had spoken of reaching a compromise.
Perhaps an invitation to include them (in her eyes)
Would be a bone with just the meat to be sufficient bait
To get her to agree to simply look the other way?

After all, an accident could happen any time
Once their ship had left for Earth. Then after a short cry
The whole affair would be behind them with no looking back.
Space travel was risky and that was the simple fact.

Warden smiled darkly to himself as he assessed
The progress in his acquisitions, pleased that he had guessed
The magnitude of quick acceptance by the populace
Of the deal he offered them in their hour of distress.

The fools of the Consortium had taken their bait too
And raised a ruckus blaming Mars for what he'd been up to.
He knew that by the time the system sorted out the facts
He would be the hero who had kept progress on track

And unified the system under one aligned empire.
Dissidents on Mars or Mercury would feel the fire
Of unified economies and military might.
And if it became necessary he'd bring them the fight!

But as for now his tracks on Triton had been well erased
And five loose ends on Saturn Eight had been vented to space
Cleaning up the final installation would commence
As soon as his deception (so Renee could be convinced)

Had been accomplished. This was for her benefit besides.
The black ship they would take to Earth was fueling for the ride
And in the years to follow his emergence on the scene
Would usher in a peace only an iron fist could bring.

These were pleasant thoughts that rolled around in his dark soul,
The consummation of long years of plotting his grand goal
And now, here at the cusp when things appeared going so right
Warden was in store for one exasperating night.

* * * * *

Haji knocked upon the captain's open cabin door.
The captain answered, "Enter, please," and looked up from his chore
Of correspondence meant to be transmitted when they could
Without the risk of intercept by those who meant no good.

Haji's face was darkened by a sad and angry look
(The captain could read Haji like a well-read open book).
"Necropsy results for those three samples you supplied:
"It was a nameless horror used on those people who died."

"Name it," Captain ordered as his features lost their grin.
Haji said, "It was a poison cocktail they breathed in.
"A mixture of a nerve agent - a G-type: Sarin gas
"With traces of perfluoroisobutene," Haji gasped.

"Perfluoroisobutene?" The captain's eyebrow raised.
"A blood agent," said Haji, "Just in case they might escape
"The horrors of the Sarin. Much like phosgene in effect.
"Pulmonary edema in hours, I'd expect."

The captain's eyes turned cold as anger chilled his reddened face,
"And then the bastards vented all the caves to open space
"Depriving them of air and making it a frozen hell."
Haji added, "Not a single soul would live to tell."

The captain put his message down a moment then replied,
"This story isn't over. One colony's alive.
"And we are going to sack the man who did this evil deed.
"Tell the men we're going in tonight with greatest speed."

51   Contact

Sunlight dim and white shone on the men crouched by a rock
Wedged beside a boulder with a view of the airlock,
The shadows dimly yellowed by the light from Saturn's rings
Rising skyward from the hills beyond the rock-strewn plain.

Their suits were patterned with a black and light-gray camouflage
So even moving slowly they looked much like a mirage
Against the frozen background in the pale solar light
Both aware that any instant they may need to fight.

Or simply cease to breathe if they were seen and intercepted.
Automated weapons at the lock weren't unexpected.
And with the lack of atmosphere there'd be no warning sound
To give alert if hostile craft aloft might come around.

Since the start of their incursion there had been few smiles.
Creeping cat-like through the shadows for the past half mile
Joe had moved to higher ground to serve as over-watch
While Duke and Bovine moved in close behind these nearby rocks.

Their telescopic lenses hadn't picked up a surprise.
Neither did Joe's sniper sights detect that any eyes
Were on the airlock's area beyond the door's small glass
Which gave them more concern there'd be worse things they may not pass.

They'd prepared to breach the lock if it were necessary
Bringing demolitions and the gear for temporary
Pressure seals to patch each door once entry had been made.
But at this point their time was short. They couldn't much delay.

And so like slowly shifting shadows Duke and Bovine moved
Beyond the cover of the rocks 'til safely out of view.
On each side of the entryway they paused to ascertain
The nature of the ancient airlock and if they could gain

Entrance to the survey shaft without raising alarm
Or using demolition which would cause great noise and harm.
But at the very instant Bovine's helmet cleared the edge
The airlock status indicator flashed its warning red.

Bovine jerked back out of view and signaled Duke to stop.
Seconds passed like minutes hoping they could get the drop
On who was coming out and what intentions they might be
(They both had switched their weapons off of Safe instinctively.)

And then a pair of gas cylinders flew out of the door
Followed in two seconds by two more and then two more!
And then two suited figures followed, one carried a sledge
The other took one cylinder and propped it on the edge

Of a rock protruding from the ground some yards away
The first then gave a mighty swing that broke the valve away.
The cylinder accelerated off into the sky
Wildly erratic in its flight until the eye

Could no longer discern its fate. The figure propped one more,
The hammer swung again and then they finished the last four.
Whereupon the pair of figures wrapped in an embrace
Then turned back toward the lock where they met Bovine face to face

And Duke standing a few yards to his left with weapon trained
With one eye on the airlock and his hand above him raised.
The pair of hammer swingers raised their arms into the sky
But shortly one fell to their knees, and then began to cry.

The one remaining standing simply lowered both his arms
As if conceding they were caught, accepting any harm
That Duke and Bovine might inflict, expecting soon to die.
Slowly Duke let down his arm and motioned them inside.

Joe saw Duke's arm slowly fall (which gave Joe his "all clear").
He safed his weapon then moved swiftly to a spot more near
The entryway where his companions had just gone inside.
He scanned the area once more then made the small group five.

Duke and Bovine kept their carbines on the unknown two
As the airlock cycled and as they emerged into
The tapered room's interior where Duke gestured the pair
To take their helmets off and prove the quality of air.

To which, of course, the two complied then set their helmets down.
Joe and Bovine took theirs off then Duke's weapon came down.

"I suppose you're saving us for Warden," gasped the one
Whose absent helmet now revealed that she was a woman.

Her brown hair in a tumble, tear-filled eyes and shaky voice,
With head high in defiance added, "Is that by your choice?"
The second figure closely eyed the three who brought them in
And said, "I do not recognize you three as Warden's men."

Bovine waved his rifle barrel slightly and replied,
"I believe we'll ask the questions here, if you don't mind."
Duke said, "We are independents. Tell us who you are."
The pair glanced at each other then the man said, "Well, so far,

"We're survivors of a crew that came under attack
"By a group of renegades, some five or six years back."
Duke enquired further, "Renegades of TerraCorp
"Or pirates of the darkness who took you in evil sport?"

The man looked piercingly at Duke and said, "I'm not quite sure
"If I could tell the difference between them anymore.
"Who are you?" the man enquired intently without fear.
Duke ignored his question and asked, "How many are here?"

Joe had moved around the room examining the space,
Found the folded blankets and the cans around the place,
An empty bottle smelling of a kind of alcohol,
And the shaft which measured a four-hundred meter fall.

The woman took the man's suit by the arm and said, "A lot.
"Somewhat near two thousand agri-workers have been brought."
Her instincts had informed her that these three weren't evil men.
"Tell them, Babe," she squeezed his arm and looked proudly at him.

Duke said, "We're all ears. And tell us who this 'warden' is."
The captives looked back at each other then answered their quiz:
The man said, "I was with the Survey Corps right when the war
"Closed the Neptune colonies to all but TerraCorp.

"The ship that I escaped on was attacked by privateers
"And soon I was indentured to a man whom we all fear.
"This man owns the agri-colony beneath our feet
"And speaks of building empires and appears to run a fleet.

"The colonists who come here do not come here by their choice
"And there is no communication - no one hears our voice."
The man stopped talking at that point; the woman told her tale:
"I was taken in a raid when Ceres Station failed.

"Subsequently sold by pirates to the warden's men
"I serviced hydroponics out at Triton until when
"The warden moved a bunch of us here to Iapetus
"Until just weeks ago we were not sure which moon this is.

"And we've been here about four years I think, but not quite sure."
Joe and Duke exchanged a look that conveyed so much more
Than what their words might say while Bovine asked one question more:
"What were in the cylinders that you chucked out the door?"

The woman said, "You obviously are not Warden's men.
"Or we would both be dead by now or taken down to him.
"We cannot be sure but we believe the tanks contained
"A chemical that would be used to kill us all or maim."

Bovine turned a darker shade of red before he said,
"Just like all the others." Then the two lifted their heads
And blurted, "Others? Like what others?" (Questions filled their eyes.)
Duke explained, "There were five other colonies besides

"This one where we are that have been farmed around this moon.
"But only one survived. The others have been brought their doom.
"Recently, apparently, a nerve agent was used
"Then after that the airlocks spiked. Might be the same for you?"

A look of incredulity and understanding spread
Across the captive's faces, then the man spoke up and said,
"We had no idea there were more folks on this moon.
"This confirms the theory that he plans to leave here soon

"And finish off the rest of us to cover up his tracks."
The woman whispered to the man, "That's why Renee came back."
Duke was close enough to hear the quiet comment passed.
He took the woman by the arms who gave a little gasp.

"Renee?" Duke demanded, "Do you know one named Renee?"
The woman nodded "Yes," and Duke asked, "Is 'Blue' her last name?"

Her eyes opened like silver dollars; Duke's and Bovine's too,
Then Joe piped in, "You know a woman here named Renee Blue?"

The man and woman both were shaken visibly by this.
The three who questioned them excited to a state of bliss!
And then a rapid-fire five-way conversation broke
Out among the new allies as each had thoughts they spoke.

When things had settled down a bit they all were on one page:
Hidalia had filled them in on Renee's social state,
Duke identified the three as Captain Blue's own crew
And gave the suited pair new hope by what they planned to do.

(For Sergeant Steve and his Hidalia had made a pact:
The cylinders would go regardless if they made it back.
They both figured the odds of living more than one more day
Were fifty-fifty at the best when Warden had his say.

But if they bought the people and Renee a better chance
They figured it was worth it and made it their final dance.)
For now they knew Renee was right. They had to live with faith
That she would find a way to change the colony's grim fate.

Joe remarked that it was very odd he found no trace
Of monitor equipment anywhere around the place.
The airlock had no camera or sensors anywhere
And Steve thought Warden's men perhaps were not even aware

That this airlock existed, for it was a survey shaft
Drilled but left abandoned when the war called Survey back.
The men who later came and opened up the major caves
Didn't use the shaft - just kept it for a quake escape.

They'd drilled in by the landing area beyond the hills
And everyone who did the work were subsequently killed
By Warden's men to keep the place a secret. None escaped.
And when a rescue ship arrived it too met a sad fate.

(At least that was the rumor Steve had heard from Warden's men.
A few of whom arrived at this place some years before him.
But none of them were left. They all had lost the Warden's faith
Which meant that they had all faced horrors as their final fates.)

And there were really no concerns that anyone might leave
For there was nowhere else to go and no air they could breathe.
No ships ever came this way without a bad luck tale
For Warden's ships and pirates would ensure their trip would fail.

"By the way," Steve queried them, "How did you find this place?
Duke responded, "We received a tip then scanned from space.
"This airlock we discovered on our way to see the port
"While climbing toward the ridge of mountain peaks just to the north."

Steve gave them a look of incredulity and said,
"I'm surprised your ship could get this close and you're not dead.
"A fleet of Warden's ships patrols this rock around the clock
"And no one makes it near enough to give the door a knock."

Duke's brown eyes were filling with the light of understanding
That they were very fortunate to make a secret landing.
The stories of disaster that had built the moon's mystique
Perhaps could be avoided with the proper stealth technique?

"Maybe we were lucky. Maybe now his fleet is gone?
"Can you tell us just how many ships his fleet is strong?
"What's he got in orbit and what ground-based space defense?
"Where would be a weak spot to cut holes into his fence?

Steve looked down with sadness and he slowly shook his head
Then looked back up at Duke with profound sadness as he said,
"There isn't any way for us to know how many ships
"Or really any information on how he's equipped.

"We only move our produce into warehouse storage rooms
"Where it is later loaded on the ships by Warden's goons.
"We know Renee rode on a smaller cargo transport once.
"But we have never seen his ships or know about his guns.

"So as for space defense or forces that make up his fleet
"We have zero knowledge. Warden's men keep that discreet."
Hidalia interjected. "There must be a lot of them
"Considering the tons of produce that we grow for him.

"Renee learned he's a renegade of TerraCorp descent
"And knows that pirate captains are some of those he has bent

"To serve him as his allies; also leaders of some moons
"But we don't even know how many men here are his goons."

Steve looked at the faces of the three men in the room,
"Theoretically I too am one of Warden's goons
"But only have a half a dozen men that I command
"And every one of them are not much more than field hands

"Who have no access to a weapon or a radio.
"We all serve from fear and have no other place to go."
Joe stepped close to Sergeant Steve and queried with a stare
That pierced into his heart with sternness colder than the air,

"Are there any you can trust to fight the warden's men?"
Steve said, "There are some but there is no way we could win.
"The quarters where they stay are sealed off from all the rest.
"It would take some demolitions to attempt access."

"How about a mining laser?" Bovine offered up
While pulling off the fabric which 'til now had covered up
The tool of his profession that he took on jobs like this.
Bovine smiled and held it up then gave the thing a kiss.

Steve's eyes widened with a grin. He said, "That should make do
"To get you anywhere down there to do what you want to.
"But you will need a cover and a guide to get you where
"You'll need to be for best effect when you cut loose down there.

"I know where a wall is that adjoins the armory.
"The access is through Atmospherics. It won't be easy
"To get them in there..." trailing off, he looked Hidalia's way
"Is it possible that we could get word to Renee?"

Steve looked at Hidalia, the question in his eyes.
"We have to, Babe," Hidalia said, "Your other men besides."
Duke sat down and made a gesture to include his three,
"Our first priority will be to get Renee set free."

She looked at Duke and sadly shook her head then turned to Steve,
"No. Without the people free I know she will not leave.
"When she went to Rhea she gave up her chance to run.
"Her heart is set to die here if she can't save everyone."

Steve looked at the floor and nodded. She looked hard at Duke.
Duke exchanged a glance with Joe and neither could refute
What she had said about Renee for they remembered when
Renee had served the war in shipboard combat medicine.

And she was not the type to leave a wounded man behind.
Even less to turn her back when others of her kind
Were headed for a precipice. Her nature would refuse
To leave the group to suffer under this tyrant's abuse.

"Okay," Duke directed, "Joe, set up the commo gear
"For narrow-beam transmission when the Captain's shuttle clears
"Horizon on the next pass." He checked his suit's display.
"That will be in just four minutes - no time to delay."

Joe put on his helmet and stepped into the airlock
And when it cycled he stepped out and placed upon a rock
A tiny laser transceiver and aimed it in the sky
Where in a moment Captain's yacht would be seen to fly by.

Then when the speck of weak sunlight reflecting from the yacht
Popped into the sky the message went; the message got:
"Mirror true. Journey's end. Many hostiles. Back door friends.
"Coords attached for back way in. Will not act until you send."

The speck passed quickly through the sky then set behind the ridge.
Joe un-slung his rifle and climbed up the hill a smidge
Where he could get a broad perspective of that patch of dirt
And then in less than seven minutes Captain's voice was heard

Crackling through his suit communicator, "Joe, it's me.
"Give me over-watch. I'm setting down in less than three."
Joe responded, "Ready here. I'd come in low and fast.
"Things seem pretty quiet but we can't bet it will last."

"We came in from the south. I think it's best that you do too."
"Roger," Captain said, "You'll see me there in less than two."
Joe waited some seconds then he shined a laser dot
Near the airlock door to mark the closest landing spot.

Then focused his attention on the hilltops and the crags
Praying that the warden had no spies to cause a snag.

But everything seemed quiet and before three minutes passed
The Captain had his helmet off inside. Hidalia asked,

"You are Captain Blue?" The captain's gaze bored through her head
As if he were extracting every thought before 'twas said.
"Yes, I am. I understand you say my wife is here?"
Hidalia said, "We've been close friends for something like five years."

She opened up her suit a bit then looked at him and said,
"Renee gave me this sweater. It's a lovely shade of red."
The captain stepped in close to her then slowly reached his hand
And from the faded garment pulled a single golden strand.

"This is not your shade of brown." A tear brimmed in his eye.
"Hidalia's eyes grew glossy too. She said, "She's down inside.
"Renee has never lost her hope that someday she'd be free
"To find the man who's owned her heart for all eternity.

"Captain, may I call you 'Jules'? She does not know you're here.
"She doesn't know you are alive but holds that hope so dear!
"I would give my life to bring you safely to her side
"But just to get a message to her may be one rough ride.

"You see, this colony is kept a very tidy ship.
"All of us are subject to a tyrant's deadly whip.
"In recent months Renee has been promoted to a place
"Where with this evil man she must work daily face to face.

"She is followed everywhere. He has designs on her.
"He means to take her as his wife when he is emperor."
"Emperor!" The captain spouted, "Emperor of what?"
Hidalia stared back steadily, "Of all the worlds he's got."

"Captain," she explained, "He has grand plans to subjugate
"All the solar system, not just here on Saturn eight.
"Renee has information which as yet she couldn't share
"Since in the recent months our visits have been brief and rare.

"And never really private." She looked around the room
As if it were a habit born of paranoia's gloom.
"Miranda's auction block brought her into the warden's fold
"Where for a time she worked with me way out in Triton's cold.

"Every ship and every scrap of rock we came across
"Seemed to be his property. There is no bigger boss.
"And we feel something grand is going to happen very soon.
"Steve and I believe he will evacuate this moon

"Before it happens. We believe the time is close at hand.
"Renee got us these suits and gave us one simple command:
"To find some cylinders of gas and get them out of here.
"We did - and when the warden finds out we'll be dead I fear."

Joe came in the airlock then and stepped over to Steve
Speaking in hushed tones while Bovine looked somewhat relieved
And started limbering his laser. Then the captain said,
"That's not going to happen. You'll see justice here instead."

The captain took Hidalia's hand and turned his face toward Steve
Who looked him the eye with strength the captain could perceive.
"Together we will free your people and release my wife.
"Tomorrow you will have the freedom to start a new life.

"There is trouble brewing throughout all the solar system
"But we must focus first upon this local situation.
"The welfare of the people here must be our first concern.
"Tell us everything of this facility you've learned."

Hidalia and Steve had put their lives at risk today.
They had proved their deep commitment to assist Renee.
Exhausted but elated finding new friends bringing aid
They felt there was a chance the warden's sins would be repaid.

The six conspirators sat down and put their heads together
Discussing many options and discovering each other.
They talked about the caves below and times of work and rest
And when and where to ingress for the best points of access.

When all was said and done Duke said, "To kill a snake like that
"It's best to cut its head off then don't let it grow one back."
"Capture his lieutenants, smoke them all out of their holes."
Steve nodded agreement then recited their first goal:

"We'll guide you through the caves below and we will get you there
"But there will be much danger. Warden's spies are everywhere

"And every one of them is seeking opportunity
"To gain his favor. Most of them would sell their own granny."

Joe reached down and took his backup pistol from his belt
And handed it to Steve who gave him thanks which was heartfelt.
The captain looked at Duke and Steve and said, "We must be cool.
"This warden is a wily one. I'm sure he is no fool.

"We cannot simply take him out. We must bag him alive
"And keep him isolated - he may have implants inside
"His body he can use on us. We'll need a damping field
"Strong enough to counter what he's got until revealed."

The captain closed his suit and stepped out to his waiting yacht
Where he composed a message with the info he had got
Then sent it as securely as his gear would let him do
Instructing Radar to relay it with the moon's scan too.

Red would get the picture and would quickly understand
And Blue knew he could count on him to come and lend a hand.
His message was a simple one: *"Struck Gold; co-ords front door.*
"Dress warm when you knock. I'm going back way shirts and shorts."

Only seconds passed before a single burst of tone
Acknowledging his message came across his suit's headphone.
Then as he was preparing to depart the yacht again
An urgent message came across from Red direct to him:

"Phantoms thin where you are. Only one or two to dread.
"One is in our pocket and at least three more are dead.
"The Raven rides the one beside me just three hours out.
"When the doorbell rings there will be fewer still about."

Captain Blue looked up and raised his hands into the sky
Inhaling with thanksgiving and exhaling with a sigh.
It's good to receive friendship but it's better yet to give.
Guide my hands that I might help these helpless ones to live.

52   Troubled Angels

Red's ship was designed for battle and for little else.
Much of its design was put together by himself
(After years of privateering he had learned his trade
And optimized the hull to keep most weapons fire at bay.)

And so his cockpit didn't have a lot of window glass
But still he watched the crescent Saturn as the minutes passed.
The rings illuminated from the top side made them bright
In contrast to the ground below still shadowed dark with night.

It seemed a gift from destiny when they were on approach:
Red's crew saw a black ship looming like a shadowed ghost
Following Selenia's ship coasting in the distance.
Red harpooned the bandit - something he could not resist.

Red had been excited to test out the Mode Two beam
But everyone agreed for now to keep it left unseen
Until the danger of attack by thugs and renegades
Had been reduced and they were in a safer part of space.

The missile which he used had pierced the black ship's engine room
Bursting with a violence that spun it to its doom.
(Like a centrifuge they watched the spin accelerate
Until the ship fragmented and the pirates met their fate.)

Red had settled in an orbit high and slow and wide
Where, silent in the darkness he could keep a watchful eye.
Selenia's black ship had disappeared while on their way
Slipping into blackened silence as she pulled away.

He knew very well what she was hoping she could do.
He also knew the tactic likely used by Captain Blue
And long before they separated they had made a pact
That neither would drink wine until they captured Warden Black.

Red, however knew where Captain Blue's focus would be.
Selenia (no matter what she said) would not be free
To focus all her energy on Captain Blue's betrothed
Until her brother had been rounded up, corralled and roped.

These two projects were congruent but were not the same
And Red could see where both his friends might complicate the game.
Conflicts could arise where these emotions burned so hot.
This would put Red in the middle - not an easy spot.

And then the word was sent that Renee had indeed been found
Where Warden Black had many hostages beneath the ground.
Red knew then and there Selenia would renegade
Then Captain Blue would very shortly need some friendly aid.

He was unaware of any intel she'd received
Beyond Blue's cryptic message that to both of them was beamed.
He just knew Selenia would use the ship she'd got
As a Trojan horse to get inside if she weren't caught.

Then things would happen fast. Coordination and intel
Would have to be precise or this whole gig could go to hell.
(He had no idea that the pressure Warden felt
Was largely from the missing black ships with which Red had dealt.)

* * * * *

Jules had kept the hair he'd taken from Hidalia's sweater
Intending to test DNA; but his instincts were better:
He could sense Hidalia was honest to the core
And DNA could never have provided any more

Confirmation than what he'd perceived from his new friends.
And though he'd not yet seen Renee his search was at an end.
A dozen times from disappointing false leads of the past
He'd clawed above despair regardless that his hopes were dashed.

He was strangely calm. Two thousand nights he'd spent alone
In six long years without his mate and lover in his home.
Working hard to finance searches for his missing girl
In dedication scouring each moon of every world.

And now, convinced their separation was reduced to yards
He waited patiently as minutes passed (though each more hard).
The groaning deep within his loins and beating in his chest
Would be for any person's patience an enormous test!

But still he waited in the darkened room where he'd been placed
Wondering how years of labor may have lined her face
(Not that it would matter - she was part of his own soul
And nothing in creation could dissuade his heart's deep goal).

But he was a professional and there was work to do
Besides the reconnection with his golden Renee Blue.
Thousands on this moon were murdered. Many more could die
And it would be an uphill fight to keep them all alive.

And so he pushed his heart aside and focused on the map
Provided by his scan from orbit and the details that
Hidalia and Sergeant Steve had helped to annotate
Memorizing all he could while longer stretched his wait.

(Hidalia had made it clear that contacting Renee
Was not an easy feat - it often took more than a day.
But she would break the rules and get Renee the happy news.
Renee would find a way to slip away for Captain Blue!)

The danger was extreme but time was short and this would be
A day of struggle and reward or one of grim defeat.
And then the captain heard the sound of footsteps at the door
He saw it slowly open as light spilled across the floor...

53   Reunion

Waking from his late night spent with number Eighty-Three
And other than no news about the status of his fleet
Warden had a pleasant day - the news was on his side
And he determined it was time for them to take a ride.

Preparations were complete. His schedule advanced.
The stage was set to start the music for the final dance
To bring the outer systems to their knees before his feet
But first he'd clear Iapetus of things best kept discrete.

So shortly after speaking with the captain of his ship
Warden came to Renee with a request on his lips:
"I need you go and bring your friend Hidalia to me
"And while you're at it also bring her man, our Sergeant Steve.

"Meet me in the courtyard room before the judgment seat
"I believe it's long past time your friends and I should meet."
Her heart jumped to her throat but she controlled her urge to choke
And managed to return a smiling question left un-spoke.

Then, leaving the impression her surprise was innocent
She turned and left to find Hidalia, gasping as she went.
Almost sobbing with regret to find they both were there
She could only croak out, "Warden's at the judgment chair.

"He wants to see you both. I don't know why but I can guess."
Hidalia held her by her arms and said, "We did our best."
Renee could see her friend was also shaking, welling tears.
Hidalia leaned in close and whispered into Renee's ear:

"We found what you were looking for and it is out the door
"And in our travels we discovered something even more
"Surprising you must see as soon as ever that you can."
And then she pressed a scrap of paper into Renee's hand

Then whispered the location of a room down a dim hall
Where only rarely anyone might venture, if at all.
She then reiterated, "Go there soon. Do not delay
"No matter what the warden has in store for us today."

Steve had turned his back a moment while the ladies talked
And hid Joe's pistol in his pants then smiled, turned and walked
The few steps to the door and said, "Let's not keep Warden waiting."
The ladies didn't see the way his teeth had started grating.

The three of them walked quietly, expecting all the worst
Hidalia was twixt Renee and Steve who, in a hoarse
Whisper told them both, "If necessary make your way
Toward our picnic spot where we will finish off this day."

Renee stood next to Warden when they'd come into the room.
Her eyes were cold and empty as if she had brought their doom.
Hidalia read sorrow from her, Steve stood tall and firm
Expecting that in seconds they would all be shot or burned.

Then Warden read their names and numbers from a screen out loud
And gestured to the pair of them, his head held high and proud
As if he were the personhood of magnanimity.
He then addressed the pair of them with formal dignity:

"You and your woman, Sergeant, have been model citizens.
"But more importantly, to my Lady you've been friends.
"And so I'd like to offer you Imperial appointments
"And passage to the inner systems with my compliments.

"My ship is fueling for a short hop even as we speak
"And we will be on Rhea by the middle of this week
"For a little sojourn and some business I must do.
"But then we're leaving for the earth's warm sand and skies of blue.

"You, of course, will be full citizens with all that means.
"Is this something you would like and to which you'd agree?"
Renee's eyes flashed confusion as suspicion grew inside,
Steve began a silent word, Hidalia's eyes grew wide.

Then realization hit Renee that Warden would not swerve.
He'd kill the colony regardless! Her friends' lives would serve
As compromise for Renee's sake. But she knew that the gas
Had been removed and now the colony might live perhaps

Without him even knowing? Could it all really come true?
She'd drug the monster as they left and when the man came to

She would have him bound and silenced in his ship's stateroom.
They'd commandeer the ship to justice and his certain doom...

These thoughts were bursts of sunlight breaking through her dark gray sky
Like sudden streaks of lightning bringing hope they might not die.
The only straw she saw to grasp, she reached (though chance was long)
Hoping that Hidalia and Steve would play along.

And so with suddenness that shocked herself as well as them
Renee turned full on Warden, "Excellent, my Lord! I win!"
A beaming smile graced her features (though her knees were weak)
She put her arms around him, placed a kiss upon his cheek.

And then she turned to face her friends and said, "I knew he'd see
"The value of your loyalty and bring you to serve me.
"One knee, please," she gestured for them both to show respect.
Both her friends looked startled but their knees went to the deck.

"Will you serve the Empress of the system's new empire
"Obeying her commands, performing all she may require?"
"We will," they said in chorus as she offered them her hand.
"Kiss the hand of she whom you now swear your lives and lands."

Warden was surprised and seemed immensely pleased to see
Renee taking her role as consort so dramatically!
Obviously, her two friends were worth more than the rest.
He had found her moral limit when put to the test.

She'd responded nicely to the pressures he'd applied.
Her progress was accelerating as she changed inside.
He'd found her price and soon her very soul would be his own.
Iapetus would soon be nothing but a bleaching bone.

"Rise, my friends," she said and turned to face the "emperor".
"Will you seal the deal, my Lord, and give me him and her?"
Warden whispered to a man who stood behind his chair
Who disappeared for thirty seconds while the Warden stared

Darkly at the two who stood behind her lovely shape,
"I take your oaths to her to be ones you cannot negate."
Steve looked at Hidalia then answered for them both,
"We have worked your fields, Sir and we are now betrothed.

"We will go where she goes. If she stays here so will we.
"If she goes to Earth then we will go with certainty.
"Whom she serves we'll serve and whom she loves or hates we will
"Whether on the warm green earth or Triton's dark and chill."

The servant then returned and gave the warden two small tubes.
Warden rose from off his seat and said, "She will not lose
"Either of you from this day. Her whims you will respect."
And then he pressed one of the tubes against Hidalia's neck.

Warden faced his Sergeant Steve and held the other tube
Before his eyes so he could see what he now planned to do.
"This one binds you to your Empress. In the night you'll learn
"That with a word from she or me your body now will burn."

And then he pressed the tube against the Sergeant's abdomen
Where, with a tiny prick a silver sliver wriggled in.
Steve nodded acknowledgment and said, "So it will be.
"Only in the bonds of empire are we truly free."

Warden smiled wide and said, "I like it! Write that down!
(He gestured to the servant who obeyed) "We'll spread that 'round.
"Our teams on Ganymede and Rhea will know what to do.
"Sergeant, you're a smart man. We are glad to welcome you."

(When the tube released its charge into Steve's abdomen
Unconsciously Renee's hand touched her own, recalling when
She spent the night on Warden's couch and next day found a scratch
Just above her navel - she could bet Steve's was a match.)

"You are free to go. Just pack the bare necessities.
"We will leave tomorrow and you're ordered not to breathe
"A word of our departure to a single other soul
"Upon a very painful death. The kind I'm sure you know."

Hidalia and Steve both bowed at Warden's final words
And as they turned to leave he said, "Renee, a moment first."
She ushered them out through the door then turned her smiling eyes
Back to face the warden who said, "Do not tell me lies."

Renee's eyes lost their smile as she moved closer to him
And said, "I have no need to. We are near to being kin.

"Why would you accuse me of a breach of partnership?
"Nothing but the truth to you has passed across my lips."

Warden eyed her darkly, "Up to now you've shown no fault.
"Tell me, have you been inside the Atmospherics vault?"
Renee gave him a startled look then looked down at the floor.
"I didn't want you to find out I'd been inside that door."

Warden was displeased but happy that she'd told the truth.
"And tell me, what exactly were you hunting in that room?"
Renee lifted her gaze to his and tossed her golden hair,
"It's not what I was hunting, lord - it's what I placed in there."

Warden sat back in his chair and said, "This was a breach.
"I didn't think this was a lesson I would need to teach.
"Tell me what you placed in there and what all you disturbed."
Renee pouted her lip and answered, "Don't be so perturbed!

"I thought our trust had been established but you think I've lied?
"It is a gift for you. I wanted you to be surprised.
"Trapped inside this moon there's very little I can do
"So I enlisted help and hid it there away from you."

Warden eyed her sideways saying, "There's been a disturbance
"In the Atmospherics vault and I need some assurance
"That everything's in order. Will you go there with me now?"
Renee responded, "Yes, of course, but close your eyes somehow."

She made a pouty frown and then she turned around to go
As Warden stood and looked at her along his upturned nose.
Her candor was disarming but suspicion was his game
And if his plans had been disrupted she would be to blame.

Walking with the warden was not anything at all
Like walking to the Atmospherics vault with Corporal.
The first time she had been relaxed with someone who was glad
But this time she was walking with a killer who was mad.

And yet she didn't show her fear. In fact she played the role
Of one excited lady who has learned that tomorrow
She would start a grand new life (for she'd done nothing wrong.
Truly, buoyed with great relief her friends had played along!)

Warden saw the joy and the excitement in her walk
And heard the happy bubbles of new prospects in her talk.
And wondered, *Could this lovely creature be as sly as me?*
But then his lust and arrogance said, *No, it couldn't be.*

Stopping out of earshot of the Atmospherics door
Renee turned to the warden and said, "Please, I must implore
"You not to punish Corporal for what I had him do.
"He just followed orders knowing it was done for you."

Warden stepped around her and addressed the dozing guard
Who snapped to full attention then in fear bowed with regard
And turned to open wide the door to meet Warden's demand
Then as they strolled inside Renee explained what she had planned:

"I wanted it to be secure and yet hid from your eyes.
"This place was the best I knew and too, it's near supplies
"Which he would need to make the mash - oh, dear! It's grown a lot!
"I thought it would simply be one large distilling pot!"

They had bounced about two hundred feet into the room
When Renee saw the corporal's corner which had greatly bloomed
Into a row of reflux columns distilling his booze
And tanks of mash in preparation. Warden asked, "Now, who's

"Responsible for this?" Renee walked forward in some awe,
"Well, I am but the genius here belongs to Corporal.
"I wanted to provide you decent sipping whisky made
"Locally and he's the one who knows about the trade."

An atmospherics worker happened just then to walk by.
Warden waved him over, "This distillery is why
"I've gotten these reports of funny business going on
"In the atmospheric plant?" (Renee feigned a yawn.)

The worker said with some disgust, "Aye, yer Worship, yes.
"Some o' the blokes thought we'd be takin' lumps o'er all this mess."
Warden looked him in the eye and asked, "Has anything
"Else within the plant been changed?" "No sir, not a thing.

"We've kept a steely eye on 'im and though 'e comes and goes
"He has kept his business. Seems that's all the bugger knows.

"If you get my drift, sir." He winked and touched his head.
Warden only vacantly acknowledged what he said.

The Atmospheric Engineering Chief noticed the three
And with a look of deep concern approached them timidly
And asked if there were questions or concerns he might address.
Warden turned his glare his way and hotly spouted "Yes!

"Are the newer cylinders of CO_2 installed?"
"Yes, your highness, days ago. I'm sure that you were called."
Warden turned to face him, "So they're ready for release?"
"Yes," the man explained, "I'll take you to them if you please.

"I presided over installation when they came
"And nothing has been altered. Everything remains the same."
The man turned toward the section where the supplemental gas
Was tied into the circulating system in the vast

Expanse of engineering gear which kept them all alive
Where Warden's new replacement cylinders were to reside.
The three followed his lead across the intervening space
(Renee was very thankful Warden couldn't see her face

For she was growing desperate about what they would find.
Convinced her face was flushing as the fear crept through her mind
That what her friends had done would be apparent to them all
And each of them like dominoes into their graves would fall.)

The corner where the manifold was built was rather dim
But in the gloom behind the warden Renee filed in
Followed by the worker who, with curiosity
Came to lend assistance if the engineer should need.

"Here they are," the engineer announced then gestured wide
And there she saw the cylinders in place before her eyes!
Part of her was glad but in her heart she was alarmed
For now it seemed the warden's poison had not been disarmed.

The engineer stood close and gave the pipes a quick inspection.
Warden stepped in closer only with some hesitation
And then he asked, "Where are the cylinders that were removed?"
The engineer looked at the worker, "Bill, what did we do?"

The worker then explained, "Aye, they've been removed for scrap.
"It's apparent by the missing cargo transport rack."
"Right!" The engineer agreed. All is as it should.
"The supplement is staged for release when you feel it's good

"As you had instructed, Sir. And now, about those stills,
"I raised my concerns because no work order was filled.
"Only word-of-mouth was passed about some woman's word -"
Warden cut him off, "Let's just make sure that you have heard."

Warden lifted Renee's hand enough for them to see
And then he took a sapphire ring from off his right pinky
And slipped it on her finger, saying, "Just so you will know
"You will show her respect anywhere she cares to go.

"Her words from this moment carry my authority.
"Acknowledge that you understand to her you bow the knee."
The warden gave them both an ice-cold stare to mark his point.
The engineer began to protest but bent his knee joint

Knowing that the warden's whim could sew the whirlwind.
Then Warden said, "You let the corporal distill his gin.
"You are dismissed." The atmospherics men bolted away.
As Warden gave a final glance his new cylinders' way.

Renee tried not to show it but she'd also cast her eye
Over those gray cylinders. She saw their paint had dried.
But somehow it was now a different shade and not as smudged.
The cylinders from Inmar were not these, she quickly judged.

Cascading waves of deep relief then flooded through her mind.
Turning to the warden she said, "That was very kind
"To honor me like that before them. You've made me a queen!
"And you will know it very well when we have left this scene."

Warden started leading them away from those gray tanks
And said, "Renee, it is to you that I must give my thanks.
"To build a whole distillery to bring me just a sip?
"That's one tremendous gift that from my memory won't slip.

"But also I must caution you that breeching secure doors
"Could be very harmful to you. Please do that no more.

"Now, I still have a laundry list of items to complete.
"Why don't you prepare to leave but keep yourself discreet?"

Warden turned abruptly leaving Renee standing there.
She took a long deep breath and ran her fingers through her hair
Then brought to mind the small note which Hidalia had passed
And pulled it from her clothing where she'd hid it in her breast.

Unraveling the crumpled note, she held it up to read
And recognized the penmanship which knocked her to her knees!
A thousand memories came flooding from the misty past
And tears flooded her eyes as she suppressed a shuddered gasp:

> *Mirror on the restroom wall*
> *Where might messaged bottles fall?*
> *A number scrawled and one transmitted*
> *Both point out where she's committed*
> *Hidden far beneath a moon*
> *Waiting for her searching groom.*
>
> *The haystack holds the needle safe*
> *Awaiting that sweet hour of fate*
> *When true hearts like a magnet find*
> *The needle sweet, one of a kind.*
> *And what shall be the bride's response?*
> *The same, one hopes, as promised once.*

She read it twice then thrice then crushed the note up to her chest.
Then tenderly she stuffed it safely next her pounding breast
And staggered somewhat as she dazedly went on her way
Straining to remember all Hidalia had to say.

What room did she whisper to her? Was this just a dream?
Her eyes were misting with emotion, lungs yearning to scream!
And yet she maintained her composure, staged her non-chalance
Concealing her excitement to give them a better chance

Of keeping things discrete to make this visitor as safe
As possible for surely Warden's whim would seal his fate.
And so as calmly as she could she strolled the narrow halls
Seeming to meander with no purpose shown at all

But shaking on the inside with excitement and with dread
That she had not remembered where Hidalia had said.
The time it took to reach the room stretched out to eons more.
Then fearing that her hopes were false she cracked open the door.

It was just a musty room where sacks of seeds were stored
(Though in the recent weeks no seeds were gathered any more.)
The light was dim and there was dust suspended in the air
Making it not easy to discern all that was there.

Renee came in the room and shut the door behind her back
Then looked around to see a man's shape standing near a rack.
His hands were crossed behind him with a sidearm on his hip
Exactly as she saw him that last time aboard his ship

The morning of that fateful day when black ships raped the fleet
After its successful raid on war-torn Ganymede.
"The mirror's words were true," she said, "The bride's that day were too.
"And ever, for ten thousand years, my heart belongs to you."

He stepped into the light as she came further in the room
Where both of them could see each other well within the gloom.
"I never gave up hope," he said, "I knew some day I'd find
"A clue to bring you back again for you, my Love, are mine.

"They told me I was crazy or possessed of hopeless plight
"But always I have loved you. I still do with all my might."
Both of them stepped closer and looked deep into their eyes
"It's good to hear your voice, Renee." "And yours, my Love, besides."

He touched her hair. She touched his face. They both fell in their arms
And tasted lips of longing six long years had failed to harm
For in that single moment they felt all eternity
Erasing every pain and doubt and setting their hearts free!

Tears of joy and sobbing laughter marked their dizzy ride
Across the spectrum of emotions coursing their insides.
Time came to a standstill as the world around them faded
And every pain and stress of intervening years abated.

Words did not exist that could express their sudden thrill
For all that richness of elation reached beyond the skill

Of mortal man's expression. Poets for six thousand years
Had never captured for release the savor of those tears.

The rush of sweet release - the thrill of raw unbridled mirth
As they were reunited shook them both as if re-birthed.
Eternal moments passed. Their senses tuned to the extreme
(Both were terrified they would awake from this sweet dream!)

Their scents, their sounds, their tastes and touches bursting back to life
The bond remained unbroken forged between this man and wife.
Their family re-born, their common causes forged anew
The captain and his lady would rebuild the House of Blue!

Instinctively they knew they had but little time to act
So after they had pinched each other (to prove they were facts)
Renee let all the details she could pass come tumbling out
Not caring at this point if there were listeners about:

"I knew you were alive but I had no proof that you were
"And until recent weeks I had no way I could transfer
"Information past the prison walls of Warden's grip
"Until he cast his eye on me and let me board a ship.

"The tiny crumb I left must have been spotted by dear Red
"And at that point I feared that everyone here would be dead
"Unless I came back here to Warden (with spies' clean report).
"So now I've been committed as a partner in his sport.

"He's ruthless and sadistic, Jules. He's evil to the core!
"In trying to protect these folks I've nearly played the whore."
At that she started sobbing in the crook of his strong arm
"Sweetheart," she squeaked out, "I am still yours - I've not been harmed.

"I've earned his trust to some degree but I've played my last hand.
"We're leaving here tomorrow and our marriage is his plan!
"He's plotting the demise of every soul in this dark hole
"And claims he'll be the emperor of all worlds circling Sol!

"The system is a mess. He's engineered it all from here.
"The records of his crimes and piracies are very clear:
"Real estate endeavors bordering on genocide
"Have littered his dark history - there's more I fear beside:

"By crustal relocation and some nuclear device
"And caverns just discovered deep beneath the crustal ice
"He's trying to destroy Titan's future for us all.
"With ships disguised as Martian ones so Mars will take the fall!"

The Captain placed his finger on her lips and said, "It's safe.
"Titan has been saved and many pirates met their fate.
"With help from some old friends the Titans rose up to the task
"And Warden's men on Titan and his plans there were unmasked.

"Duke and Joe are with me and some other friends as well.
"We intend to save these people from this wretched hell.
"Hidalia believes that you won't leave until they do.
"That proves you are who you say, my Golden Lady Blue."

Her eyes were shining bright with tears, she laughed but then she cried,
"Oh, Jules," she sobbed, "With my big mouth I fear we all will die.
"There are listening devices everywhere one goes.
"Everything we've said here you can bet the warden knows."

The captain showed a small device he pulled out from his kit
"I didn't come completely unprepared, my Love. You're it!
"The listening device in this room's planted in your skin.
"This provides a damping field. Our words have not been sent."

Renee's hand touched her abdomen. "I know when it was placed."
The captain's eyes showed anger and resolve hardened his face.
"How long has it been since he put implants into you?"
"I can't say how many but this one - a month or two?"

The captain watched her eyes and said, "I don't want you to fear.
"Doctor Haji's on our ship and they are very near.
"The implant in your tummy is a new type that can turn
"The host into a fire bomb which at a word will burn."

Her eyes projected understanding, "I have seen it work."
(The horrid memory of Bordeaux's end made her legs jerk.)
"Haji has a way to get this out, but it takes time."
She firmed her jaw, "As long as Warden wants me I'll be fine.

"I think the people will be safe. I think that Warden's scheme
"Entails using poison gas here when we leave the scene.

"My friends removed the gas while Warden's men were not about.
"Once we leave I plan to use some drugs to knock him out

"Then commandeer his ship and bring some justice to the man."
The captain raised his eyebrows saying, "That is one great plan!
"But there is something you don't know - the poison's half the scheme.
"Renee, there were five other colonies and two I've seen."

Her eyes widened in horror, "Here?", she asked, "There were five?"
"This is number six," he said, "The last one left alive.
"Blood agents and nerve gas were used on the population
"And then the airlocks were destroyed with no hope of salvation."

His eyes displayed the horror of the memory of the scene.
Renee's hand covered up her mouth, she turned a little green.
"The airlocks were insurance. You can bet they've been rigged here.
"The poison was used only for sadistic pain and fear.

"But I suppose you know the kind of man he is by now."
The captain's face turned sour with an unaccustomed scowl.
Renee nodded her affirmation as she took this in
Then whispered half out loud, "Why not atomic detonations?

"Why not simply use atomic weapons to erase
"Each colony completely and eliminate all trace?"
The captain thought a moment then replied, "The EMP.
"He wouldn't want magnetic pulse detected remotely.

"But when he plans to leave for good..." they both then realized
This would be the final act he'd use to sanitize
The evidence of what he'd done these years on Saturn Eight.
Time was running out! They prayed that they were not too late.

54 Dominos

Warden was relieved. In fact was very pleased to find
Renee had not defied him and this brought him peace of mind.
For every test he'd given her had proved she'd kept her word.
She even showed some signs she wasn't really that concerned

About the pesky minions in the colony at large
(Once her friends were given to her and their bodies charged
With implants to ensure obedience and fealty.
He might even spare them on their upcoming journey!)

His gas was unmolested and she'd even made a gift.
In recent weeks she'd taken steps to bridge across the rift
Dividing their perspectives and he'd seen her lose her chill
And now he felt assured that very soon he'd have the thrill

Of consummating his dynastic empire with the One
Whom he had chosen from the many. His patience had won!
(Deep within his blackened soul he entertained the thought
That she would bear a dozen sons to rule the worlds he'd got.)

His inward smile leaked out to his features with a grin
As through the central office door his black-dressed form swept in.
But then his smile disappeared as he perceived the look
Of dread that spread across the face of one man who mistook

His footsteps for those of another ('til he turned his way
And saw the warden coming in - he dreaded what he'd say
When Warden heard the news that came across their secret link
From one ship's crew at Rhea whom the warden didn't think

Was even at that moon.) The warden asked, "What is the news?"
The startled man stood up and braced himself for some abuse
Then pointed at the screen which showed the message he'd just read.
"It seems some allied ships have disappeared. We think they're dead.

"The message comes from Rhea where two ships went for repairs.
"Martian escort ships have formed a fleet and killed a pair
"At Enceladus and another one at Rhea too;
"But then the message was cut off and I think that makes two."

Warden's face grew red. He brushed the shaking man aside
To see the message for himself but as he stepped inside
The commo cubicle another message was received:
A distress call from Titan begging rescue and relief!

"Titan!" Warden spouted, "How much effort can it be
"To do a simple job. Are there no competents but me?
"Break the silence now and raise the ships that we have there.
"Get that engineer online before you breathe more air!"

The commo man sat hastily and fumbled with the gear
Then mentioned to the warden, "Any ships nearby will hear."
"I am well aware of this," he hissed, "Just raise the ships.
"Get the captains on the air regardless of the risk."

The operator powered up the high-gain transmitter
And pointed it at Titan hoping for a quick answer.
The deep-encoded message was repeated several times
But agonizing minutes passed with only one reply

And that was one weak signal with an antiquated code
Allegedly from men who, inconveniently disposed,
Were trapped inside a drill rig habitat with no way out
Captured by the locals helped by Mars beyond a doubt.

"Martians!" Warden shouted, "We're the Martians on the scene.
"We have many men there and good ships - there should be three!
"Contact both our ships above us, have them try to raise
"The ships at Titan too. I want a conference today!"

Warden spun around and stormed away to get a drink
Spitting curses at the walls, *What do these morons think?*
We're at the very cusp of empire yet they slink and hide.
Pirate savages are useful but they have no pride.

When he reached his quarters he turned on the System News
And listened to the talking heads who parroted his views.
This was reassuring - most was going as he'd planned.
His transports were delivering and he was gaining land

With everyone who took his aid. The numbers didn't lie
And he determined then and there that all Titan would die

As soon as he established contact with his engineer.
He had enough atomics there to scrape the planet clear.

And then a knock upon his door was not whom he had hoped.
Instead of she he lusted for, the commo man's face poked
Into the room apologizing for the long delay
But he could raise no ships in orbit or out Titan's way.

This was disconcerting to learn there were no backups.
His ships were not responding so he moved his schedule up.
They would leave this moon tonight instead of when he'd planned.
He signaled to the captain of his ship this new command.

And then he sent a message for Renee to get her things
And notify the pair of servants he said she could bring.
Then join him at the boarding bridge in sixty minutes' time.
Only moments later they would leave this moon behind.

55 Waiting

Gin gazed out the darkened cockpit at the world below
Speeding past at periapsis lit by starlight's glow.
The starscape in the distance fixed compared to ground they passed
Brought memories of tragedies and regrets of the past:

The losses dealt at Ganymede: the people and the ships
But most of all the captain's wife - were none more sorely missed.
Years of deep regret for being saved instead of her
(Though many said it was the only choice that could occur)

Weighed upon his psyche though pure logic said, *No guilt.*
Yet still he felt the remorse like a child over spilled milk.
Haji opined more than once this was Gin's way with pain:
Internalizing sorrow by converting to self-blame.

This wasn't healthy mentally though neither was his drink
But he had handled both for years much better than you'd think.
And now she had been found alive after these many years.
The over-whelming relief nearly brought old Gin to tears.

Sunrise, dim and distant burst out instantaneously
As Saturn VIII's horizon gave up sky relentlessly
And stirred him from his bitter thoughts which now turned bitter-sweet
Though he'd not count her safe until these decks echoed her feet.

Gin touched his controls to give their orbit an assist
(A momentary burn to stretch out their apoapsis.
This to linger longer over where his friends set down.)
Though now a better target, it might make his captain frown.

Yet this might prove a benefit depending how things went
And with redundant ships thanks to Selenia and Red
There would be no added risk for those down on the ground
And ships departing from the surface would be quickly found.

Radar broke the cockpit's silence on the intercom,
"Gin, there is a high-gain beam down there that just turned on.
"Skippy has determined it's a hail sent Titan's way
"And also a request for contacts not so far away.

"Silence on that world is broken. Something's going on.
"It's beaming from the equator just south of Falsaron."
Gin asked, "Any word from Captain?" Radar said, "Not yet,
"But he'll have something in a hurry soon would be my bet."

Gin said, "Yeah, I'll bet he does. It won't be very long.
"Get set boys!" he broadcast on the all-ship intercom.
And then he sent a message on a narrow beam to Red
Who sent it to Selenia who acted first instead.

* * * * *

Red was starting to get nervous when his sensor man
Reported that a high-gain beam had lit up toward Titan.
Coincidence? Or caused by something Blue had done down there?
Red watched time tick past but still his crew stayed off the air.

He watched two hours pass and then he kicked it into gear
And started to de-orbit with instructions very clear
That no one was to fire on a black ship on the ground
Unless it was in self defense - then burn the bandit down.

56   No Plan Lasts...

Hidalia and Steve were now emotionally drained
Not to mention physically for it was quite a strain
To swap the deadly cylinders and drag them to the shaft
Then boost them up and out the airlock. Then on top of that

To turn around and find a pair of weapons trained on them
Only to discover they were captured by new friends
Whom they had smuggled in to work within a secure room
(Where if they had been spotted it would surely seal their doom.)

Then taken (they had thought) for execution but rewarded
And ordered to pack up - tomorrow they would travel Earthward!
That was quite a roller coaster ride in one short day.
But resting in their quarters, they were worried for Renee.

For it was easy to detect that Warden's voice turned hard
When he addressed Renee after she sent them quarters-ward.
And so they carefully returned to where the new men were
Enlisting Duke to come with them to find Captain and her.

A rap upon the seed room door made Renee expect death
Until Hidalia's voice outside made both let out their breath.
Renee opened the door, her smile wide as both girls cried
While Captain pulled her friend and Steve and Duke all three inside.

"Oh, Duke!" Renee exclaimed, "Thank you for bringing Jules to me!"
Duke glowed with emotion as he said, "We're not yet free
"But seeing you and Captain stand together once again
"Is worth whatever price we pay, and this fight we will win."

The Captain's eyes connected Duke's with great respect and thanks.
"Renee confirms Hidalia and Steve got the right tanks.
"Harmless ones are in their place hooked to the manifold.
"The airlock demolitions must be found. That's your goal.

"We are in agreement we should take Warden alive.
"He'll have information that can be used to save lives;
"Find and bring to justice his destructive pirate bands;
"And get some hijacked properties back in their owners' hands."

Steve said, "Duke, I have two demo men to lend a hand,
"But I don't think you'll find it. I suspect the warden's plan
"Is simply to incinerate the place after he leaves."
The captain said, "We also had that thought, but we agree

"It's very likely they have been in place for many years.
"We can have high confidence he intends to spread fear.
"He feeds on terror and on pain and so we think he might
"Still have plans to blow the locks soon after he takes flight

"Then watch the death and terror on live feed safe from above."
Hidalia looked up at Steve and said, "I'd bet so, Love."
Steve looked at the floor and nodded, "Yeah, I guess you're right."
Captain said, "Get every surface access cleared tonight.

"The way we came is clear and Joe has set up monitors.
"The cargo doors are probably what you should check out first.
"Spend the time you must and be as thorough as you can.
"Anticipate the planning of a sick and twisted man."

Steve and Duke acknowledged with an understanding nod.
Hidalia gave Steve a kiss then toward the door a prod.
The captain gave a few more words before they parted ways:
"We must get these preparations done by end of day.

"The fission demolitions are most likely set in place.
"Detonation will commence once Warden is in space.
"The trigger is remote, it will be something on his ship
"And knowing him, it's triggered with a word spoke by his lips.

"Until atomic detonators have been rendered safe
"It's best he isn't capable of speaking anyway.
"Renee hopes to sedate him just before it's time to leave.
"Warden can't blow up the place if he is fast asleep.

"But time is short and risk is long to do what we must do.
"We will need more hands on deck." Captain looked at Duke.
"Have Bovine laser quietly but only partly through
"The wall into the quarters housing Warden's extra goons."

"It's already been done," said Duke, "He hasn't wasted time.
"To make the grandest entrance we can sure count on Bovine.

"He's put a length of det-cord in the cut and it is primed
"To blow when you are ready. Joe is there just marking time."

"Good," the captain said. "Steve, let's go and meet your men
"And then we'll tap the goons' front door and stick our big feet in."
Renee squeezed Captain's hand and said, "Be careful. They'll be armed.
"But so far I have seen no hint that Warden is alarmed."

They all went over details then Hidalia stepped out first
Followed by Renee who, when alone with her near burst
With tears of joy and laughter as they scurried down the hall.
Hidalia had kept her secret with no hint at all

About the shocking news that Jules was here! She'd played it safe
Knowing that when they went to the judgment seat Renee
Would never have been able to convince Warden's keen eye
And they would at that point have likely all been doomed to die.

They were near Hidalia's quarters when they both were found
By a man who stepped before them as he kneeled down.
(The messenger sighed with relief when he spotted Renee)
He was tasked by Warden to inform her right away

That they must meet him at the boarding bridge ready to go
In less than sixty minutes and that was some time ago!
Renee released the man and sent him back the Warden's way
Assuring him they would be there and there'd be no delay.

Then as the man departed Renee took Hidalia's hand.
Hidalia's eyes ran free with tears. She said, "Oh, no! We can't!"
Renee pulled from her pocket Captain's damping field device
And put it in Hidalia's hand and said, "Those are the dice."

Hidalia intensely argued they must stay and fight.
There were many things that must be done right here tonight!
Renee explained that Warden was too dangerous at home
"In his mind the moment of ascension to his throne

"Is just around the corner and his natural distrust
"Must not be given any fuel to put him in a fuss.
"We cannot afford to let his trust in us to slip.
"We need him alive as well as things inside his ship.

"You must get to Steve and then you two get set to go.
"Exactly as the warden planned, but first let Jules know!
"Give this back to him. It can't be found near us at all.
"Everything will be upset if we appear to stall.

"Now, go!" Renee turned her around and pushed her down the hall.
Renee ran quick as lightning toward the Atmospherics vault.
She had to get a bottle of the Corporal's produce
And thankfully, she found him there, sampling the juice.

* * * * *

Captain Blue and Duke were pleased to meet Steve's demo men
And hurriedly laid the situation out for them.
Both of them were in! This was the best news they had heard!
And they'd do everything they could to stop the peoples' hurt.

(Not to mention saving their own skins and striking back
Against the man who held them hostage: Psycho Warden Black.)
Duke gave one his backup weapon as they walked away
To search the surface access locks and clear the bombs away.

Other than the entrance where the Captain had come in
There were only three more airlocks known to these two men:
The boarding bridge where Warden parked his smaller transport ships,
The bigger cargo locks to service large produce shipments,

And one emergency escape far from where they were now.
This would be the first that they were speeding toward now.
It shouldn't take them long to check and then they'd come back here
To search the larger cargo locks and make sure they were clear.

Captain Blue and Sergeant Steve then turned to make their way
Toward the barracks of the warden's men to make their play
To separate the wolves from those who might lend them a hand
And neutralize the looming threat of Warden's exit plan.

They were halfway to their destination when the sound
Of rushing steps of someone in a hurry came around
The corner of a corridor soon followed by a face:
Hidalia laid eyes on them then skidded to their place.

She took Steve by both arms and tried to whisper but she gasped
Then handed Captain Blue the field suppressor as Steve asked
"What has happened? Why have you brought Captain's device back?"
Hidalia then caught her breath and said, "We've got to pack!

"Warden changed the timetable - we leave within the hour!
"We've maybe forty minutes left!" Steve's face began to sour,
"Hidalia, we have a job to do before we go."
She responded, "Yes, my Love, let's get on with the show.

"I can knock some heads as well as you and you'll need help
"Sorting friends from fiends," and then she loosened up her belt
And wrapped it as a garrote as a meanness crossed her face.
"Let's go," she said and led the way at a much faster pace.

* * * * *

Steve stood at the door and pushed the button to request
Someone in the barracks to respond and grant access.
A surly voice came through the speaker mounted in the door
And grunted affirmation to Steve's query (sounding bored).

Then when the door slid open captain's cue was sent to Joe
Who tripped the detonator to make Bovine's entrance blow!
By then the Captain had a hostage, pistol to the head,
Steve kept several covered while two others lay and bled

For brandishing their weapons at the three who had burst in.
(Hidalia had one guard's neck held in a full Nelson!)
Their surprise was perfect. Warden's men were left in shock
When Bovine blasted through their armory's thick wall of rock

And Joe sprayed bullets at the roof (the men dodged ricochets)
The captain shouted, "Everyone! Don't move or you will pay!"
Bovine kept them covered. Steve and Joe cleared all the rooms
Returning with two startled sleepers. They'd bagged all the goons!

Within two minutes they were all disarmed and quite undressed.
The few remarks of warning protests violently suppressed.
Hidalia and Steve went through the group and took the worst
And locked them in a room which Bovine welded shut, of course.

Sergeant Steve addressed the few remaining in the room,
"These men came to save this colony from certain doom."
Gesturing at Captain Blue he said, "Today you're free
"But we must help these men to stop this warden's tyranny. "

One of those whom Steve had trusted spoke up for the rest,
"You are going to get us killed and that might be the best
"That we can hope for if we start some trouble we can't end."
Steve replied, "There's only four or five we don't have, friend.

"How many of warden's inner circle have you seen
"In the recent days walking through this facility?
"Most of them are gone - evacuated days ago.
"If you were told to wait, well, there's something you should know:

"There isn't going to be another flight. His is the last.
"All who remain here were going to chew on poison gas
"And then suck on some vacuum when the airlocks get blown wide.
"Go check the atomics - this whole place is rigged to fry

"Erasing all the evidence of what has happened here.
"It's worse than genocide. He plans to wipe this planet clear!"
Some fidgeted restlessly and others shook their heads.
And then as if on cue Hidalia stood up and said,

"If you care a whit about redeeming your lost souls
"You will help this captain to achieve some simple goals.
"And you don't have much time! You all will share a horrid fate.
"Warden's plan is set in motion. Steve, let's not be late."

Steve returned Joe's pistol to the waistband of his pants
And took Hidalia's hand then told the men, "You've had your chance.
"Your cowardice is evident. You fear the Warden more
"Than what he's planned to do and you will not even the score.

"Or even take initiative to save your own lame ass."
He turned to Captain Blue and said, "We should have saved some gas
"For these wankers to chew on." Then He took Hidalia's hand
And turned to meet Renee on time as Warden's schedule planned.

Bovine asked the quiet men, "Where are the doors with bars
"And pressure suits behind them? That's where explosives are.

"That's the way it was at other sites: Suits out of reach;
"Safety just beyond the bars before the locks were breached."

Bovine's face turned red. The others' faces faded white.
"The loading locks are gated and there's pressure suits besides."
(This was spoken by a man who followed Bovine's thought.)
"With no shipments planned, two days ago the gates were locked."

A pair of men then sounded off (they both looked scared and shocked).
They mentioned to the others that Atomics had been locked
But now the doors were welded shut and remotes were disabled.
There was now no way to monitor if they were stable.

The captain listened to the comments these two men had made
And ordered Bovine take his laser to give them some aid:
"Bovine, go and help these men get through the welded doors.
"You men," Captain queried, "Are atomics men of course?"

One of them looked down. The other gave a sheepish look,
"I don't like to say much, Sir, for I am just a cook
"But our atomic engineers all left two days ago
"For Enceladus or some other place - don't really know.

"I heard the warden has a big ship standing by outside.
"Perhaps that's where they are? To go with Warden for a ride?"
Jules replied, "That ship is gone. Warden's just remains.
"Martians are enroute to help us but they'll be too late."

And then a half a dozen men raised hands and volunteered
To help in any way they could; the others showed great fear.
Steve gave them a final glare before he turned to go:
"At least there's some of you that will step up to be heroes."

And then he and Hidalia left in a mock disgust
But signaled Jules his volunteers were men that he could trust.
The holdouts were locked up into another room at last.
The weapons in the armory were welded in a mass.

The captain had these new men swear to keep this under wraps.
"Secrecy is all that will keep us from a dirt nap.
"Go in pairs and find the last of Warden's men around
"Then sit on them at least until the atom bomb is found."

The captain looked at Joe and said, "Get Dewey down here now.
"Have Gin set her down out back within a half an hour.
"As soon as Dewey lands get him down there to find that bomb.
"I want that thing dismantled. We may not have very long."

"Bovine, get Atomics opened. Take three men with you.
"Then meet Duke at the cargo locks. You know what to do."
Bovine met the Captain's eyes that said, *Do not be late.*
And then he signaled Duke to have them meet him at the gates.

The captain watched them turn and disappear and make their tracks
Praying for their safety as he turned to his own task.
Glancing once more at the map displayed on his device
He made his way in silence through the caves beneath the ice.

Silent as a cat he padded down the warden's hall
Then slipped into an alcove when he heard a man's loud call.
He spied a tall man, raven-haired, emerge out of a room
Followed by Renee who turned and spied her hiding groom.

She made a subtle gesture and she smiled reassurance
Then turned to catch up to the dark-haired man so there'd be no chance
The man would need to turn again - she held his captive eyes
So, the captain thought, *This is the man who had devised*

The sneak attack at Ganymede, the piracies and crimes;
The genocide that had occurred right here at least five times;
The narcissist and tyrant who would rule the universe;
The wretch who killed his parents, raped his sister and much worse.

And there he was! Just yards away lusting after Jules' bride.
The man who held her captive was preparing now to ride
Away into the sky to take Jules' mate to be his own.
(The captain realized he'd drawn his sidearm from its home,

Taken off the safety and had lifted it to fire.)
Nothing in his consciousness exceeded his desire
To put a bullet in the monster's back followed by more
Except his deep commitment that defined him to the core.

And that demanded that he stick to what they all had planned
Which meant, of course, that he could not yet kill this evil man.

There were many lives at stake and he must have some faith
In the plan already put in motion by Renee.

Only with supreme control of passion and resolve
He put his weapon in its holster and moved up the hall.
There were open doors to quarters and an office space.
Captain took a moment to familiarize the place.

He could not resist to step inside his lover's quarters.
As he had expected everything there was in order.
In fact, placed on the table near the doorway to the hall
She'd set her folded sweater like she hadn't left at all.

He didn't linger there. He had a job he had to do
And so he went to Warden's quarters where he would go through
All that he could find which might provide the evidence
Of other men complicit in the warden's wicked dance.

The captain was surprised at the condition of the place.
The doors he met had not been locked and there was not a trace
That any care was taken to secure or put away
Data terminals or record books in any way.

In the captain's mind this put the punctuation point
On the knowledge Warden meant to vaporize the joint.
Why would he expend the energy to make secure
Things which in short minutes would be glass, he was quite sure.

The captain didn't have much time but Warden made it easy.
Everything about his quarters screamed about how sleazy
His person and his habits were, and though they'd never met
Jules knew in his heart for this man he'd have no respect

Beyond, of course, the kind of respect one would give an asp
Or crocodile or stalking lion or a hornets' nest.
And so when he approached the warden's working space he knew
There would be no order to the things he must go through.

But he remembered that Renee had been the last one out.
In fact she motioned subtly with her chin a little pout
Which indicated this was where some interest would be
And sure enough, right on a table was the Volume Three

Of six large ledgers, leather-bound, containing what he sought:
The facts to tie a host of men to Warden's empire plot.
Also found were lists of real estate on many worlds
With names of those once titled who had been killed off or worse.

As he scanned the documents his eye caught on a name.
He did a double-take yet still he read it just the same.
This page he would keep. The captain carefully removed it
Then folded and secured it secretly inside his kit.

* * * * *

Gin picked out a landing spot not far from Captain's yacht.
Approaching from the south he brought the ship in low and hot.
As soon as he had set it down and stabilized the gear
He left the cockpit powered and moved one seat to the rear

To man the forward weapons bay while Radar manned the aft.
The passive optic monitors watched for approaching craft.
Regardless that the stars were largely hidden by the hill
Or mountain, Gin supposed, looking out where all was still

Except for Joe who waited at the airlock to the shaft
And Dewey who had grabbed some tools and exited the craft
Bounding expertly toward Joe who took him deep inside
The caverns far below where captain Blue had found his bride.

57 A Toast!

There was great excitement and airs of finality
When Warden and Renee met friends at port facility.
The last of Warden's favored had been loaded on his ship
And only two remained then they'd give Saturn VIII the slip!

Renee took Warden's arm and gently tugged him toward a table
Then from her bag pulled glasses and a bottle with no label.
Slowly in the tiny gravity the liquid poured
(Hidalia and Steve went through the boarding bridge's door.)

Renee handed a drink to Warden then she took his arm
And with a sultry smile turned on all her woman charms.
They both held up their drinks and then she touched his with her glass,
"Let us toast the future with a goodbye to the past."

Warden sniffed it gingerly then gulped the liquor down.
Renee took in a sip, then she spewed it with a frown
Exclaiming, "Awful! Yuck!" and wiped the rest from off her lips
And said, "Corporal said it wasn't ready yet, but this

"Isn't fit for rocket fuel! I'm sorry, Warden. Gaaahh!"
She threw her glass against the wall and when the warden saw
He threw his too and smiled, "Let's let this be our last drink
"Until we dine in luxury on Rhea, don't you think?"

She left the bottle on the table saying, "Yes. Let's go.
"Good riddance to this awful place and to this world of cold."
He smiled wide and offered her his arm to which she linked
And then they crossed the boarding bridge into what he would think

Would be the final moments on Iapetus for them
And also for the others who'd experience the grim
Finish to their puny lives with terror, pain, and breath
Vacuumed from their ruptured lungs in punishment and death

And then incinerated in atomic fireballs
Ringed around the planet when he made his final call
To say goodbye to all the men he did not find to be
As useful as the ones evacuated this past week.

Gleefully he reveled in this twisted taste of power
While entering the black ship's bowels with his lovely flower
Of womanhood beside him and the future in his grip
When he received the message that there was another ship

Just landing on the field using silent protocol.
The ship was one last sent to Titan; back without recall.
Warden was dismayed on one hand, curious on the other:
This black ship had returned and yet the captain did not bother

To send him a report of any kind - but that was par
For how these pirates worked in his experience so far.
Skulking in their darkened silence they remained discreet
And no one knew their numbers or the sizes of their fleets.

Unannounced but welcome, he was glad this ship arrived.
As far as Warden knew this was the last one left alive
In Saturn Eight's environs and its escort would be nice
As they all left this place for warmer climates free of ice.

And then the happy thought crept through his hopeful, darkened soul:
Perhaps my engineer has finished drilling all his holes
Ahead of when he'd scheduled and he's brought me what I asked:
A detonator to put Titan's future in the past!

Warden and Renee had just moved past a stateroom door
Which still was partly open and inside she could see more
Women he was taking: Numbers two-ten and one-thirty
And number eighty-three was glaring back with the most dirty

Hate-filled look of jealousy and rage Renee had seen.
Since the news came out that Renee would be Warden's queen.
There was no love lost! Renee felt only honest pity.
No one could deserve the barnyard life as Warden's filly.

And so it was Renee's intention to set them all free
To seek their own redemption and make their own destiny
Unfettered by the Warden's schemes but this hung by a thread.
Before this day was through there was a chance they'd all be dead.

Warden told Renee to stay and go up three more decks
But she replied, "I go with you. This ship no one expects

"Piques my curiosity and I must see it too.
"Besides," she said, "I'd like to meet the men who make its crew."

Warden wasn't used to having orders countermanded
But then he reconsidered and said, "Fine, let's see who landed."
He offered her his hand, "You know they're pirates we have bought.
"They live a life of piracy and die before they're caught.

"This characteristic has proved good for us at times
"In keeping things best left concealed some might label crimes.
"And you will find that most of them are quite unsavory.
"Their loyalty extends only as far as your money.

"They are pirates, after all." The warden grinned and winked
"And only can be trusted to be pirates, don't you think?"
Renee quietly squeezed the warden's hand to show concern.
They walked back through the bridge to see what they might learn.

Between the crags of Malprimis and shattered Falsaron
A line of blackened mountains towering for eons long
Provided perfect cover to conceal a small space port
Where secrecy of access was of primary import.

Built within a crater on that ridge of lofty hills
Where only very rarely any sunlight weakly spills
Warden's landing area was hidden very well.
From all but nearly vertical was difficult to tell

That anything unnatural was built upon that ridge
Unless one saw the shadows of the warden's boarding bridge
Or any ships that happened to be there when you flew by
(Assuming that his men in orbit hadn't made you die.)

But data from the message Skippy managed to pull in
Pinpointed the landing site with finest precision
And when the word was given to set down and ring the bell
They landed near the boarding bridge to Warden's private hell.

Where, other than the tracks of transports and the boarding bridge
There was not a sign of life anywhere on this ridge.
A pair of darkened windows facing from the wall of stone
Looked liked empty eye sockets - a skull of blackened bone,

The boarding bridge protruding like a snake from out its nose,
A bulging rock its forehead as the hill behind it rose.
The frozen tracks of service transports winding on the flat
Appeared like shadowed tentacles to grab and pull you back .

Dwarfed by a retaining wall built in the crater rim,
Silent in its shadow stood a black ship tall and grim,
The boarding bridge attached but with no sign of life around.
Rocket blast had erased any footprints on the ground.

And not a single indicator light shone anywhere.
Light and shadows' contrasts enhanced by the lack of air.
The bit of dust disturbed by landing already had cleared
And no acknowledgement of their arrival had appeared.

And so they sat in silence waiting for a laser's heat
Or even cryptic hails on the radio at least
But neither had occurred. Yet still they waited patiently
For those within the looming skull to act. Then presently

The boarding bridge retracted from the other idle ship
And moved across the frozen ground to place its icy lip
Against the outer airlock at the aft end of their craft.
Those inside the airlock heard the mating flanges latch.

Selenia and two lieutenants and six Mars marines
Waited in the airlock by the bulkheads quite unseen,
Suited up and ready for the worst that may occur.
The lock slid open but the boarding bridge door did not stir.

A camera was fitted to the boarding bridge's door
Which didn't open, waiting to receive yet something more.
Selenia reached out her fist (her instincts knew to do)
Her ring of silver with a black stone filled the camera's view.

Silence from the intercom and still a moment's pause
But then the door slid open and they stepped into its jaws
And crossed the intervening distance through the dark skull's nose
Then waited at the door until it clicked and slowly rose.

With two marines before her, the lieutenants to her rear
The visors of their pressure suits in place were darkly clear.
She moved into the airlock which then cycled them on through
Expecting to be faced with rifles but found only two

Men who used a pair of scanners to assess the ten
Then beckoned them in wordless silence to come follow them.
(The two marines who followed the Lieutenants kept control
Of one unsuited figure bound and gagged who shook with cold.

* * * * *

When they reached the windowed room Renee looked out to see
The ship which had just landed. It was sitting quietly,
A ghostly black the dim sunlight seemed simply to ignore
Obscuring stars behind it, though one dim light on the door

Marked the airlock on the stern where someone would await
Extension of the boarding bridge to enter through its gate.
Warden led Renee into a small adjoining room
Where monitors for cameras were all that lit the gloom.

Overrides and manual controls to run the gate
Were manned by two of Warden's trusted men (they were well paid).
Warden gave the word to move the bridge to this new ship
Then watched the monitors as it approached and locked to it.

A moment passed in silence then the image of a hand
Filled a viewer with a black stone on a silver band.
Warden watched the suited fist retract out of the view
Then motioned to his man to let the ship's crew come on through.

"That's a pretty ring," Renee remarked, "It's black and bold."
A shadow crossed the warden's face which made her blood run cold.
He turned to look at her and said, "There are not many like it.
"And every year they grow more rare though we stay bold despite it."

He turned back to the viewer and his face grew cold and grim.
"As emperor I'll see the hunting of these ships will end."
He motioned to his men to go and meet the nearing crew
And watched as suited figures came inside in pairs of two.

But then with great dismay he watched the final pair come through
Towing one man bound and gagged and nearly turning blue.
Renee looked very closely at the image of the man
And recognized he was the one who came up with the plan

To sabotage the crust of Titan, ruining the plans
Of those who hoped to make the moon habitable by man.
"That one is the planetary engineer you sent
"To Titan and he looks as if he's very nearly spent."

Renee knew in her heart the man had no remorse or qualms.
(A fitting tool for Warden, yet the warden remained calm
And watched the grim procession as the eight moved down the hall
To stand on grass before the judgment seat behind its wall.

"Shall we greet our guests?" the warden offered her his arm.
Renee responded, "Yes, I guess a short delay's no harm.

"Let's learn what has happened that has brought this man so low."
And then they took a different path that Renee didn't know

Which placed them on the courtyard grass before their guests arrived.
Warden sat upon his seat, Renee stood at his side
Then momentarily the gates into the courtyard spread
And nine figures in spacesuits entered, helmets on their heads.

The tenth figure was warden's planetary engineer
His seething anger more apparent than his sense of fear.
A suited figure pulled a blackened dagger from their belt
And cut the gag from off his mouth and left him where he knelt.

The haggard man had sunken eyes and wore no pressure suit.
Thrown upon the floor before the warden's polished boots
He looked around the room with searching eyes hoping escape
Or some compassion from the Warden for the empire's sake?

But there was none to see. All Warden saw was failure here.
He'd entrusted ships and men and nothing was more clear
Than this man's great ambition had met ruin and defeat
And now he lay exhausted and abused at Warden's feet.

Warden's hawk-like features gazed on him like wounded prey.
He had served his uses but this was another day
And though the man was loyal he had brought his own disgrace
And there'd be many scientists to step into his place

Once TerraCorp was vindicated (and his pirate friends).
Besides, his ambitious nature made him a loose end
Who knew too much of Saturn Eight and what had happened there
So in the eyes of Warden he was simply wasting air.

"You had a simple job to do: Drill holes and set some charges.
"I never heard a word from you until this captain barges
"In through my front door with you in tow and no success.
"And now I guess that all our work on Titan is a mess?"

The planetary engineer stood up and with his fist
Wiped blood from his swollen lips then replied with a lisp,
"We dropped into a war zone and were taken by surprise.
"We never had support from he who was to supervise

"And secure the operations on that frozen hell.
"In fact, I never saw him. It's a story he should tell."
The engineer turned 'round and raised his arm the captain's way
"And this one isn't who I left with. Hear what she might say!"

"She?" the warden's eyebrow raised. His gaze turned on the captain.
"Who is this who dragged you here and has my full attention?"
Selenia removed her helmet, shook her raven hair
And said, "Hello, my brother," with a dark and hateful stare.

Naught else passed her lips (though fire raged behind her eyes)
And then she recognized Renee standing by his side!
So many years had passed (and she'd not met her more than twice)
Yet when Renee was recognized her heart was gripped with ice.

For standing here before her was the one who kept the man
Whom she had lost her heart to from enjoining her life's plan.
There was no joy in finding her! Her jealous heart unhinged
And amplified the burning need to visit hot revenge

Upon the man who raped her and committed patricide
Murdering her father and her mother too beside!
Seeing Renee Blue just made Selenia review
The moment in her youth when Warden killed her lover too.

Decades of resentment, years of hateful memories
Of violence that scarred her heart with devastating grief;
A thousand nights of buried tears and fears not understood
Blossomed from her spirit in a seething raging flood.

"Selenia!" the warden stood, "How came you by my ship?
"It's fitting on the brink of empire you've come to visit.
"You've spurned me for so many years and yet I have watched you.
"Let us put the war behind and family renew!"

"Family?" she winced, "Our family is long since dead.
"You made sure of that and now you think you are the head
"Of some great revolution in the solar system's plan?
"You've even tried to murder Titan by this wicked man!"

"I thought you were dead these past six years but now I find
"That you have not been idle with your twisted little mind.

"The chaos you have spawned has crippled farms and families
"And brought about disaster in some worlds' economies."

"Selenia," his smile widened, "You're a brilliant lady.
"You must know that these things are meant to be temporary
"Means to greater good and happiness for all mankind.
"Let me show you how it will and then you'll change your mind.

"For you don't know the half of it," Warden puffed with pride
"I've so much to share if you will join me at my side."
Selenia responded, "This must all come to an end.
"Warden, I bring justice to you as the whirlwind."

"Justice?" Warden scoffed, "The only justice is my own.
"I rule every moon of Saturn from here to Dione.
"I own everything on Triton, much on Ganymede;
"Earth will soon be in my grasp, then Mars too will concede

"That our united empire is the power around Sol.
"You will find my operatives everywhere you go.
"And now, before your very eyes you'll watch the flower bloom.
"In only days the network news will sing this very tune.

"Tell me, how is old Soldana? My man there is dead.
"It seems that someone tried to pry my secrets from his head.
"It doesn't really matter. I have others in his place."
He smiled and watched the deep emotions cross his sister's face.

Renee stood by in silence as she watched these two exchange
The first words in some decades since the siblings were estranged.
Vaguely she remembered that Selenia had been
A fighter in the same division and her husband's friend.

Her family resemblance to the warden was apparent.
It was obvious that these two shared at least one parent.
Warden was not ugly (other than his attitude)
But she had stunning beauty! Renee sensed a good heart too

Though it was camouflaged beneath a barely throttled rage.
Warden then invited her again to turn a page:
"Join your strength with mine, my sister. If not, you should go.
"Now, about my ship. Where is the captain who I know?

She lifted up her fist, "The ship is mine. The black ring too.
"The pirate scum is dead. The obligation rests on you
"To recognize my right and honor all your pirate oaths
"Or take that dagger from your belt and slit your lying throat."

Warden made a mocking look of shock at her indictment,
"Selenia, this is a time of tremendous excitement!
"Without a doubt, I'll pay my due to she who holds that ring.
"The ship is yours, but also all the duties that it brings."

His eyes then turned as dark as hers but then the engineer
Spouted some obscenity and said, "My Lord, it's clear
"That this woman has sabotaged the work we went to do.
"I demand to be released and her to get what's due!"

Warden glanced down at the man then fixed his eyes on her.
"All who serve the empire love me. Have you still not heard?
"Be my right-hand woman and their love will burn for you.
"And there will be no limit to the good that we can do."

"Love?" spat Selenia, "What could you know of that?
"Your soul proved devoid when you murdered family Black."
Selenia's eyes met Renee's. They both could sense their pain.
Both knew his depravity and how cruelly insane.

Selenia then saw a wicked thought darken his eyes.
She shuddered at the filthy prospect when she realized
That he would want to inter-breed and concentrate his genes
To make a royal bloodline to augment his twisted schemes.

Warden said, "Last chance, my Love. It's now, or you must go."
Selenia, repulsed replied, "When Hell is frozen cold."
He turned his back to her and whispered something to the two
Men who brought the visitors a task which they must do.

By then the engineer had had enough and lost his cool:
"These men aren't your pirates. They are Mars marines, you fool!"
Warden stepped away from him and addressed him by name
Then asked him show how his love burned - the man burst into flames!

"Love can be enforced!" he yelled, "It's just commodity!"
As every person in the courtyard stepped back to get free

Of splattered burning phosphorus and flaming fat and smoke
And then he shouted, "Horseshoe!" and the cavern's quiet broke

Into a roar of gunfire as a thousand bullets ripped
From automated weapons in the roof his voice had tripped.
A partial circle near the wall was riddled with the hail
Where bloodied lifeless limbs of Mars marines now weakly flailed.

Warden's trusted pair had grabbed Renee and pulled her back
Toward the passage doorway where the warden now backtracked.
He cast a leering grin and then he calmly turned away
From his wounded sister who was writhing where she lay.

Being close to Warden her wounds weren't the fatal kind
Adrenalin now flowed which put the pain out of her mind.
She pulled her sidearm and sat up but struggled with their plan
To take Warden alive (to pull the secrets from the man).

She guessed his ship was ready and he'd soon be on his way.
She raised her weapon and took aim at Warden - or Renee?
Warden was beside Renee and not quite through the door.
My God, she is a beauty! This incensed her even more!

Finally her heart had reached the moment of its truth.
Who was at its center? Was it love learned in her youth?
Or was it something darker which had grown and now matured?
Her conscience whispered louder: Of her motives was she sure?

A raging lust inflamed her heart and screamed needs to her mind.
She could kill them both right now - the truth no one would find!
She could claim she shot at Warden, but in tragedy
A bullet struck Renee (then Captain Blue's heart would be free!)

At every level she had operated in the past
Nothing had brought satisfaction which had seemed to last.
Inflamed in her desire far beyond experience
There was only one she craved and now she held the chance

To take away the insulator that kept Jules at bay.
Like rivulets of water on her palm decisions played.
Each stream could run down any path as she might move her hand.
Would she sell her very soul to wrench love from this man?

For years he had flown far but she'd imagined on her string.
Ever he would fly yet his affections he would bring
As business brought him back to her; but always on his mind
That glimmer of a hope for someone time had left behind.

But now the string was cut and that old glimmer had turned real.
And here it was within her grasp - the power she could feel!
To snuff the dancing candle that kept Jules' heart far away
And in the next two seconds she would have to make her play.

59   Nail in the Coffin

The Captain knew the warden had a transmitter nearby,
Probably protected by some lackey that he'd fry
Along with everyone and everything he would discard
When he left to play his hand of empire-building cards.

The ledger data was secured, the ledgers were concealed.
He spent time searching hoping pirate bases were revealed
For the benefit of Captain Redfeather and friends
But pirates didn't trust the warden quite to that extent.

His hope was to transmit the message before Warden left
Knowing he could not destroy the colony quite yet.
If they waited 'til he left then Warden learned his plan
To terminate the colony was foiled, then the man

Would fly into a rage and try to bomb the place from orbit
(The chance was small that Gin and Red were able to defend it.)
Within that choice and gamble was to not transmit so soon
And wait 'til Warden's ship was on the far side of the moon

Where he would not detect it and it might buy Renee time
To get the warden drugged and have his ship taken off-line
Before he knew things had gone wrong; but that chance was remote
For time had passed and that fact meant that there would be no vote.

(Hidalia had made it plain that there was little time
Left before their ship would leave and Warden's final crimes
Against the people left on Saturn VIII would be committed.)
Jules had hoped before that time to get these things transmitted.

It didn't take much time to find the Warden's commo room.
In fact, when he approached it he saw two men with its goon
Literally sitting on him holding jugs of wine
Raised up in salute, obviously having a good time.

The captain smiled back and shook his head with silent grin
Then turned the corner to the commo room and settled in.
He loaded up his data and he fired up the rig
And transmitted with all its power in a beam so big

The inner solar system, Jupiter and Saturn too
Would be included and there wasn't squat Warden could do.
The ledger data was included: names and payoff dates;
Lists of hijacked ships and names and places of his slaves

In exquisite detail with the pictures and the scans
Of the murdered colonies that fell to Warden's plan.
(System News, of course, would try to debunk what was sent
But anyone with sense would see how they were complicit.)

Regardless if he failed to preserve the colony
Regardless if his life were forfeit this would guarantee
The solar system would be made aware of Warden's net
Of politicians, pirates, and the dark TerraCorp set.

A lot of time had passed and yet he had a premonition
Renee had not yet left and there were delays in her mission.
He set a constant loop so the transmission would repeat
Just as the pair of wine drinkers approached the commo seat.

Both of them showed great excitement yet appeared confused
Talking at the same time of a sound that had diffused
Throughout the central cavern and had echoed up the halls
They said it sounded like gunfire and thought Martians had called!

Jules stepped to the hallway where he heard a single shot.
"Take me where you think this happened at a double trot!"
The two men turned and lead him just as fast as they could move
Toward the central cavern where the judgment compound stood.

* * * * *

Bovine cut the door locks to Atomics for the men
And left two men as guards and warned them to let no one in
But one whom he described as Dewey. They quickly agreed.
Then Bovine had his third man take him to the gates with speed.

Time was running out - the forty minutes they had hoped
Had long expired and he felt the short end of the rope!
Then Bovine saw the gates and images came flooding back
Of twisted frozen bodies in the other caverns' black.

A quick flick of the switch that lit the mining laser's beam
Killed the camera that would be used to watch the scene.
And when he cut the bars and Duke and Steve's men ventured in
A deep inspection of the lock revealed demolitions.

Carefully the men removed the wires to the caps
And took the inert charges to a safe place further back.
This lock wouldn't blow and safety features passed their tests.
Only one airlock remained: the boarding bridge access.

But then a roar of gunfire echoed through the cavern's halls.
Duke and Bovine and Steve's men responded to its call
Moving quickly past the startled workers who, confused
Stood up from their fields and quarters wondering the news.

* * * * *

Dewey suited up as soon as Gin had set it down.
Within fifteen minutes he was far beneath the ground
Escorted by Joe who took him swiftly to Atomics
Where Dewey, Joe and both the men searched for the Warden's tricks.

Dewey was impressed by how the power plant was rigged:
The fail-safes disabled and set up to be a big
Fission bomb - he figured twenty kilotons of yield
And as he worked to right it Joe's continued search revealed

A second bomb was set - a civil excavating charge -
Plenty to destroy the place though yield not as large.
What worried Joe was finding the device was booby-trapped
And it took him some time to get it offline and re-packed.

He mentioned this to Dewey as a warning to be safe
But Dewey didn't even turn - just kicked something Joe's way
And mumbled. "Yeah, I found that tied into an access port."
(It was demolition of the military sort.)

"You're good, Dewey. I don't care what Bovine has to say,"
Joe winked at his young friend when he turned around his way.
Dewey grunted, "Yeah, I know. This place is back online.
System checks look good. I got it done in record time.

"Someone meant to turn this place into a blob of glass
"By fusing hunks of fuel until it reached critical mass.
"That can't happen now. The safety interlock's restored.
"In fact, I've made it so it can't be done again no more."

Dewey packed his tools and Joe retrieved the demolition
Knowing that it might be useful on some other mission.
"By the way," Dewey grinned as they walked from the place
"I changed the trigger's transponder to send a Happy Face."

Joe's big mustache twisted up into a gleaming grin
Brown eyes shining brightly when a new message came in:
"I want Haji here right now! Coordinates attached."
The captain's voice was plain they were to move with great dispatch.

* * * * *

It was maybe thirty minutes after Gin arrived
When Skippy sounded off about a transmitter nearby
Beaming out a long repeating message far and near
Containing text and scan data and photos in the clear.

Gin let all this data scroll across a nearby screen.
A moment later Radar sounded off, "Gin! Have you seen?
"Holy Smokes! Look at those names! This is potent stuff!
"There's a lot of people who will want that message snuffed."

Gin was not surprised by very much of what he saw
And mentioned back to Radar, "Now the hammer's going to fall
"From somewhere - you can count on it. Captain's lit the fuse
"And this is going to blow sky-high even on System News."

The message kept repeating while ten minutes passed in peace
Then Skippy gave alert about a signal which was weak
Probably attenuated by the rock and ice
Then added that the voice was strained and sent it's message twice.

The message was Selenia reporting they were hurt
Somewhere in the depths of caverns far beneath the dirt.
Several men were dead and Warden and Renee had left.
But nothing had been heard from Captain Blue or his men yet.

Gin and Radar both were feeling antsy but held tight
Sensing deep in every nerve they'd soon be in a fight.
It wasn't many minutes 'til the Captain's voice came through
With orders to fetch Haji and to do it quickly too.

Haji was prepared for action in a lightweight suit.
He took a kit sufficient for most things he'd need to do
And made his way immediately to the cave to wait
For Joe to meet him near the airlock then show him the way.

60   The Little Bird

Renee did not expect to be dragged off by Warden's men
And when her ears were nearly deafened by the gunfire's din
She twisted 'round at just the instant to watch eight men fall
Plus the woman Jules had said was there to help them all.

She was devastated! Her eyes burst exhausted tears
As Warden shouted with exhilaration from her rear.
Spirited back toward the passage to the boarding bridge
She heard a single shot ring out just as a painful twinge

Electrified her arm as crimson droplets blasted past.
And then she heard the man beside her make a raspy gasp
Then lose the grip upon her arm. He faltered then he fell
As Warden pushed on past him with a curse and spiteful yell.

The echoes of the automatic weapons fire faded
Throughout the local cavern as the three runners evaded
Any further chance of bullets finding marks in flesh
As up the passage toward the boarding bridge their legs were stretched.

Renee was now confused: Who sent the bullet toward their backs?
It was understood the warden would not be attacked
But taken in one piece to face the judgment for his crimes!
And now they reached the bridge's airlock room in record time.

The boarding bridge however, was still hooked to the wrong ship!
Warden pressed the keys to start it moving then he slipped
And knocked his head against the corner of a ventilator
Then let loose a barrage that would have shamed a drunken sailor.

Renee could see a spreading stain that soaked the Warden's shirt
And knew the blood was his and not the man's who was more hurt.
She could guess the bullet had struck warden on the side,
Cracked a rib then glanced and hit the other man who died.

Warden cursed again and spun around to close the hatch
Behind them as he pushed Renee and from the table snatched
The bottle of the doctored booze Renee had left behind.
And pulled a long and heavy draught in hopes to clear his mind.

(Renee had not yet noticed that the first glass he'd imbibed
Had had any effect but now she noticed that his eyes
Seemed heavier despite all the adrenalin and pain
And now she saw him grab the bottle and hit it again!)

The second man was pulling her, insisting that she go
Into the boarding bridge and she was moving way too slow!
Hoping she could stall and buy some time for friends to come,
And praying that the shooting would bring Jules' men on the run,

She pushed the warden's man aside and said, "He has a wound.
"We must get him to infirmary and do it soon!"
She pushed the warden to the table and tore off his shirt
To make a compress of it with the belt from off her skirt.

"No!" the warden shouted, "We must get into the ship!
"Our doctor is on board and once we're there he'll see to it!"
Renee bought precious seconds trying not to seem to stall
"Hold still while I tie this. You're the worst patient of all!"

The warden's man then grabbed her arm which made her wince with pain
(It was where the first man bruised her arm when he'd been slain.)
Renee threw off his grip, "Do not lay hands on me again!"
The warden's man protested as he held up both his hands,

"He will speak and I will die if I do not comply.
"Now come with me into the ship or all of us will die!"
The knot was only loosely tied but warden held it on.
Renee glared at the servant as she helped Warden along.

The three got in the bridge, the airlock cycled then they ran
The distance to the waiting ship as Warden's voice began
To sing a tune she'd never heard as she helped him along.
He turned his heavy eyes her way and said, "Help sing this song:

> "*A lovely little bird*
> "*Who had a lovely little beak*
> "*One day had the nerve*
> "*To land upon my little beach.*

> "*I lured the little birdie*
> "*With a biscuit on a string*

"And then I used a bat to smash
"The silly little thing."

Warden's black eyes pierced Renee's as if he'd let her know
A mystery that was the answer to a private joke.
He sang his twisted little tune another time or two
Until their passage through the boarding bridge was nearly through.

When they gained the ship and cycled through the final lock
The warden looked at Renee saying, "I guess we should talk.
"You must excuse my sister. She has demons in her head."
The warden looked down at his wound, "You'd think she wants me dead.

"But she will be in minutes. Shall I show you what I mean?"
He ushered her into a room with many viewing screens.
Then hailed the captain with the order to destroy the ship
Which brought Selenia and then immediately lift.

61   Gloves Off

Nick had never spent time on an airless world before
Other than at Phobos when they passed through Stickney Port.
But that was only moments - mostly towed on Dewey's rope
(His first time in a pressure suit and feeling like a dope.)

But now he had some moments to look through a tiny glass.
Not much of a viewport but the scene revealed a vast
Plain of rock and ice and dust that sparkled in sunlight
Shining through a star-lit sky one eightieth as bright

As that received on Earth, but seen much clearer by the eye
Than what he had been used to under Titan's yellow sky.
The other viewing glass which faced the port and boarding bridge
Showed only walls of icy rock dug deeply from the ridge

Which loomed above the black ship sitting menacingly near.
This put a twist inside his gut he registered as fear.
But he was there to do a job as part of this ship's crew
And even if he cared to leave was nothing he could do.

And so he focused on his engineering tasks as told
Ignoring his concerns that much of this ship's gear was old
And rigged to do things differently than what one might surmise.
They'd captured a black ship but in Nick's mind it was no prize.

Everything was filthy which bespoke a thousand lines
About the crew before them who were thieves and cads and swine.
Evidence of years of violence and blood and booze
Marked most every bulkhead with the stains of cruel abuse.

The engineering section where Nick worked was near the stern
And so he heard the automated airlock motors churn
As suddenly the boarding bridge released and pulled away
To track across the intervening ground the big ship's way.

Almost at the instant of the airlock motors' start
Goldie's voice came on the intercom breaking apart.
A message from Selenia had come and it was clear
That things had not gone well inside and they were to lift clear!

(The black ship's crew was just a skeleton when they'd arrived
And now it had been decimated! Most had gone inside
As escorts for Selenia and Warden's engineer.)
All were wounded, most were dead or would be soon, she feared.

Goldie was in tears and played the message through the ship
Though only Nick, a pilot, and an engineer equipped
With little but a cursory familiarity
With the on-board systems now remained to fly this beast!

By now the boarding bridge was joining with the other ship.
Goldie had choked back her tears and pleaded with her Nick
To button up his pressure suit and strap into a seat.
The pilot was preparing flight - liftoff would not be neat.

Nick replied that they could not abandon friends in pain.
The pilot interrupted, "Live to fight another day."
His voice accompanied the whining sound of turbo pumps
Spinning up to fuel the rockets for a skyward jump.

But then the shrieking screech of shearing metal wracked the ship
As upper sections of the hull tore loose and ground-ward slipped
Pulling plating from the hull as air inside escaped.
Their black ship hissed its dying sighs and kneeled before its fate

In three large sections slowly tipping toward the frozen ground.
(Outside in the vacuum its destruction made no sound.)
The last thing Nick could hear was Goldie's voice shouting a call
Before the sound and lights cut out then Nick began freefall

Which ended in the darkness by a sharply sudden push
From a nearby bulkhead as the air left in a 'Whoosh!'
Settling down in silence on his side wedged in some gear
Nick felt desperate as Goldie's fate remained unclear!

At least he knew he wasn't dead because he could feel pain.
Something pinched his leg and there was no way he could gain
Access to remove it - he was trapped without a spark
Of light within a metal tomb to deep-freeze in the dark!

Nick had briefly panicked from His desperate condition.
(Motivated largely by his need for information

About the fate of she to whom he'd offered up his heart.)
He throttled his emotions and his reason played its part.

Fearing all the worst and also grateful Goldie thought
To tell him to seal up his suit before their ship was caught
By whatever caused the violence that wrecked their ship.
Goldie saved his life - he knew it! "Thank you!" crossed his lips.

Taking inventory of his sorry situation
Nick turned on his helmet lights to read his suit's condition:
The skin pressure was holding and the power pack was good.
He needed to determine what had pinned him if he could.

Nick could stretch just far enough to get light on his leg
Where he could just discern it was his carbine that had pegged
Between two conduits and turned, its charging handle caught
Like a fishhook's barb which kept his leg beneath it locked.

He could jiggle it but he could not get it to turn
No matter how he wiggled but in due course he had learned
That with a little effort he could get his fingers to
The handle of the knife that Joe gave him at Xanadu.

In increments he moved his elbow back and forth enough
To get the knife released and then held firmly in his glove.
Using it with every millimeter he could stretch
He got the carbine's charging handle turned enough to catch

And push it back beyond the metal conduit and freed.
This gave him the room to hook around it with his knee
And pull himself out of the tangle with a grunt and gasp.
Panting with the dread and effort, he was free at last!

Free, that is, until he had a chance to look around
And learn that through the hatch into the passage was the ground!
The passageway and outer hull were gone with half the ship
With just enough room underneath for Nick to barely slip.

Grating ice and gravel scraped his helmet and his back
As he wiggled through the dimly lighted narrow crack
Dragging one spare oxy bottle by his carbine sling
And a makeshift crowbar which was all he found to bring.

When he gained his feet he was concealed from the view
Of the port facility and from the black ship too.
Standing on this far side of his ship which now was wrecked
He could see up close how lasers sliced through several decks.

The wreck lay in four sections with the upper one beneath
A large part of one center section mostly out of reach
Except for twisted remnants of a bulkhead near the skin
Where it just might be possible for someone to get in.

And that was just exactly what Nick had in mind to do:
Rescue Goldie from the wreck and then stay out of view
Of any hostile ship or window of that hillside face
Then contact Red or Captain Blue and get out of this place!

Like a living organism in its dying throes
The wreck would thrash from time to time as things inside would blow;
Depressurizing staterooms or hydraulic lines would burst
(In Nick's mind the thought of ruptured fuel tanks was the worst!)

But it appeared the gunner who had sliced the ship apart
Had cut with caution with that very thought taken to heart.
Planning to reduce the danger to his ship nearby
He'd made his cuts expressly so his own ship wouldn't fry.

Staying out of view Nick moved along the dying beast
Making progress toward the upper section trapped beneath
The jagged metal sheets and girders now reduced to dreck.
Volatiles were still out-gassing from the shattered wreck.

He was feeling skittish as he moved along its verge
But swallowed down his fear as thoughts of Goldie steeled his nerve.
And then he saw a suited figure laying on the ground
A slab of carbon insulation stretched partly around

The backside of his pressure suit gripped tightly in his fists
Motionless, the visor frosting as a trace of mist
Escaped into the light behind and still he didn't move
When Nick approached and kneeled down to rouse him with his glove.

Nick's emotions gyrated with terror and relief
To find the face behind the visor did not bring his grief.

The features were not Goldie's, but the other engineer's
Who lay unconscious on the ground and it was very clear

From indicators on his suit he did not have much time.
Oxygen reserves were gone and pressure had declined
Nearly to the point that blood would boil in his lungs.
He rolled the victim over then he saw down near his buns

A ragged hole torn in his suit around a metal shard
The area surrounded by a mass of blood caked hard.
A tiny mist of air escaped - the hole not fully sealed
By the frozen blood and ice that hadn't yet congealed.

The footprints all around him told the tale two were there,
The insulation wrapped in hopes of holding in some air.
The other set of prints led back up to the center section
But Nick was bound to help this man who needed instant action:

Nick knew (as the other did) to not remove the shard
For fear the bleeding would get worse and add strain to his heart.
He packed a larger wad of ice and dust around the tear
And rolled the victim back into the carbon sheet with care.

The extra oxy bottle Nick had brought now proved its worth.
He hooked it quickly to the engineer's external port
Then set the suit's priority and set the mixture pure
And watched a moment for the signs of leakage to ensure

The extra heat and pressure helped to seal the added ice
And it would be enough to keep the man inside alive.
The frost inside his visor cleared. He tried to wake the man
But he remained unconscious so Nick left him there and ran

To find who'd made the second set of footprints in the dust.
Goldie or the pilot? (Both unhurt is what he'd trust.)
The footprints led directly to the far side of a mound
Of metal and material which now he quickly found

Had previously blocked his view, but there before him sat
The shuttle sitting steeply canted yet it looked intact.
And there beneath it in the shadow of the shuttle's wing
The maker of the footprints struggled tugging on something.

As he neared he saw the figure slip and bounce away
And then get up and try again to desperately strain.
Nick tried to communicate but still was out of range
But in another bounce the figure stopped and turned his way.

"Nick?" the voice that crackled through his suit commo inquired.
"Goldie? Is that you?" he shouted back newly inspired.
"Nick! Oh, Nick! You are alive!" her voice cracked with emotion
As both came to each others' arms in one great clumsy motion.

"You've got to help me get this open! There's a man back there
"Who's hurt and bleeding and his suit is running out of air!"
Nick explained that he had found the man and given aid
But that he did not know if his assistance was too late.

"If we can get him in the shuttle he will stabilize."
Goldie's voice was desperate and tears reddened her eyes.
And then she turned and gestured with a futile resignation
At the buckled sheet of metal which held her attention.

"This piece of damaged fairing blocks our access to the door.
"And I don't have the strength to beat against it anymore."
Nick moved 'round the object that could seal the hurt man's fate
And saw two spots where it was welded to the black hull plate.

He couldn't cut the plate but he could perforate the sheet.
His carbine's magazine was full and though it wasn't neat
Within just thirty seconds he had punched through several spots
And used his pry bar to break loose where it was weakly caught.

Between them both they had the strength to push the piece away.
Goldie worked the airlock while Nick sped the hurt man's way.
Thrilled beyond all measure to find Goldie had survived
Nick was saddened doubting that the hurt man was alive.

But when he had returned he found the man was doing well!
(Delirious and half awake but that's all he could tell.)
It wasn't hard to move the man in such low gravity
Just awkward to manipulate his big mass gracefully.

The sheet of insulation that was frozen to his suit
Proved a decent skid at times when he would need to scoot

Him up and over shattered bits of ship along their path
But in the course of minutes he had dragged the hurt man back

To find that Goldie left the airlock open wide for them
And helped Nick get the wounded engineer dragged safely in.
As they worked Nick asked, "What of the pilot? Where is he?"
"Half of him was gone, Nick. The rest couldn't get free."

Goldie's eyes connected Nick's - a sad and painful stare,
"But he is truly free by now." Her eyes softened with care
As both of them now focused on the needed first aid tasks.
Goldie whispered, "It's all right. I knew you had to ask."

Presently, when first aid measures didn't need them both
Goldie disappeared into the cockpit and invoked
The startup sequence for the engines and the NAV's and COM's
And then she yelled to Nick to say the big black ship was gone!

Nick had just completed all he could for their hurt man
And stepped into the cockpit just in time to see Red land!
The dust and gas that kicked up from his violent exhaust
Only partially obscured what far beyond him must

Have been the bursts of intercepted missiles as they gleamed
Silent in the sky by some defensive laser beams.
Then just before the landing gear made contact with the ground
Nick could see some thrusters fire and spin the ship around

Revealing gas escaping from a gaping blackened scar
Where hull plates had been punctured and the interior charred.
Nick had no idea what then caused a bright white gleam
Reflecting from beyond the mountain tops which could be seen

To rapidly intensify then dim to yellow-white
And stay that way for several seconds then fade out of sight.
He could only guess - and his guess tied him in knots:
The black ship's occupants had likely paid the final cost.

* * * * *

Red was used to fighting ship-to-ship and not on dirt.
He tended toward excessive force to maximize the hurt.

Efficiency, lethality and suddenness his tact
Preferring to have clear objectives set before he'd act.

Selenia's decision to knock on her brother's door
Was not exactly by the script that they'd discussed before
But he'd deferred to what she wanted when her heart said, *Go!*
(Not that she had really asked permission, don't you know...)

But now the message came that she was hurt and men were dead.
Apparently she hadn't followed what her head had said
And chased after her heart, which Red could tell was not in tune
(Yet thankfully she landed not a single moment soon

For as he later learned the Warden's ship was set to lift.
The interruption of the Warden's schedule was a gift
And though the cost was high it paled beside what it had saved.
Her act of walking into Warden's lair was very brave.)

Selenia had sent a broadcast message in the clear
Picked up by Jules' men inside and her ship that was near.
Goldie passed it on to Red and Gin (both on approach)
She mentioned that Renee and Warden disappeared like ghosts.

Red surmised from this that some of his friends had been taken
Into Warden's ship and that Selenia, forsaken,
Was left to die the death that Captain Blue had told him of
And so he'd have to treat the Warden's ship with kidskin gloves.

(He needed to disable, not destroy the warden's ship
For fear he'd harm his friends; just make it unable to lift.
This would take a steady hand to stop it without harm.
He knew the warden's ship would be exceedingly well armed.

His Tactical had optics on the ship of Captain Blue
Which Gin set down beyond the ridge and nearly out of view
From Red, descending rapidly toward Warden's secret port
When Tactical alerted him the black ship wanted sport!

Red could see the other black ship had been sliced apart.
The larger ship now went full active ready to depart
Just in time for radar to detect a ship was coming:
Red on fast approach with radars off, optically homing.

(Red's advantage was that he'd arrived so quick and close
Before the black ship lit its eyes while he was on approach
Assuming still that no one knew the port was even there.)
The black ship's false belief had let Red come within a hair

Of absolute surprise, but now the cat had left the bag.
Red had hit the black ship's bridge and left a painful tag.
The black ship's laser gunners quickly learned he had 3C
When they engaged him hurriedly before they could see.

And so the black ship launched a massive salvo in the sky
Hoping that the outcome would make this intruder die.
Red had now gone active too: his target radars on
Just in time to see the salvo launch - the fight was on!

Red's defensive lasers were engaged but overwhelmed
And so he shoved his pilot off and took over the helm.
Warden's ship was lifting at a high-G rate of speed.
Red used all his ship could give him in his dire need!

Dangerously close to Warden's he used all his thrust
To match trajectories and took a gamble he could trust
The weapons men aboard the pirate to preserve their skin
And cause the missiles coming toward them both to not get in

But one, which pierced Red dearly in an engineering bay
Which brought his forward lasers down. The black ship pulled away!
Nothing Red could do would bring the Warden's black ship down
And so he rammed the bandit which spun both of them around.

This cost Red some steering thrusters, but his lasers aft
Were able to acquire and engage the Warden's craft.
The damage he inflicted by the impact killed an engine.
The laser damage Gin inflicted meant two more were missing.

The pilot of the Warden's ship took time to gain control.
His weapons men took opportunity as Red's ship rolled.
And fiercely lasered Red where the collision took away
His 3C coating leaving him with no cards left to play

Other than present his intact side as best he could
And set his wounded ship down hoping Warden's also would.

But all that he could see as he defensively spun 'round
Were flashes of bright light beyond the mountain's higher ground.

Red was devastated! He could only make a guess
Renee had been aboard that ship and he had made a mess
Of every trace of hope that in her freedom she would thrive.
Nothing in Red's consciousness gave hope she was alive.

* * * * *

Even for a man of Gin's experience at war
Waiting at this level of preparedness had worn
A hole into his nerves that begged a little nip of gin
(His ever-present pocket flask had changed his name from Sven.)

The burning liquid soothed him and renewed his wakeful state.
His flask was tucked away. It seemed the hour had grown late.
Time was passing slowly. There was very little news.
Communications limited with little Gin could do

But keep his eyes and ears wide open and protect the ship
To keep it ready for the time they'd give this place the slip.
And then with lightning quickness all his tactical display
Lit up like a Christmas tree for Red had come to play!

Active target radars lit up from the hill beyond
As Red came in from overhead with Tacticals passed on
To Gin, who instantly lit up the sky with his own beams
And did all he could do to work with Red's ship as a team.

Red had made it clear to Gin that he believed Renee
Was on the black ship and he felt it must not get away
Insisting they disable it with zero loss of life.
It was imperative that they not harm Captain Blue's wife!

To Gin this felt like boxing with his hands behind his back.
The black ship had them each out-gunned but in effect a trap
Was set for Warden's ship for Gin was mostly out of view
A moment of surprise was his to do all he could do.

Radar focused on the salvo of the black ship's missiles
Which blossomed as a deadly constellation of near misses

That got too close to Red's ship as he dove in from the north
His lasers overwhelmed until he got Radar's support.

The black ship streaked into the sky, a ghostly silhouette
Occulting stars beyond it in a graceful pirouette
Accelerating toward the west, its engines brightly burned
'til in a high-G instant Gin saw Red's ship tightly turn

In rapid, haphazard pursuit which closed proximity
And then Gin's jaw dropped as he watched Red ram it suddenly!
Gin's automated tactical display showed all he needed
The black ship spun erratically as Red's ship then retreated.

An engine on the black ship was knocked out which made a way
Through the exhaust plasma for Gin's beam to come in play
And burn a jagged hole through two of its remaining jets
Reducing thrust to minimums which forced the ship to set

Down on a mountain ridge less than two miles away from Gin.
And then a fireball erupted which near blinded him.
Gin was in a state of shock! It seemed the very worst
That could have happened did - for now the warden's ship had burst!

Gin leaned back into his seat as tears filled his red eyes.
They'd spent their energies for years pursuing Captain's prize.
And now, when their success was placed securely within reach
He'd killed the Captain's wife - his treasured bride, his precious peach!

He felt as if a mule had kicked him squarely in the gut.
Unconsciously his body tried to double over (but
The straps that held him firmly in his seat kept him restrained)
A shudder, deep and uncontrolled wracked through his shaking frame.

Gin had never known such searing mental pain as this,
Other than six years ago when he had to witness
His captain turn his back on Renee's plight to rescue Gin
(Though others saw him guiltless, himself he'd not forgiven).

And now there was no way to bring about his own redemption.
Renee was gone for good and he had failed his captain's mission.
A primal, guttural complaint and plea escaped his lips
Then Radar's voice got through to him, "Gin! Take a look at this!"

62 Getaway!

Renee sent Warden's man to fetch the doctor on the double.
Warden sucked another gulping draught out of the bottle.
She sat across the little room where Warden was in view
So she could watch him closely while he did what he would do.

Sitting down into the center couch to watch his show
He tilted up the bottle and gave it another go.
It appeared the pain from his cracked rib and bleeding side
Was numbing as euphoria made him further imbibe.

It was getting clear her brew was having its effect.
Especially when he remarked he'd found a new respect
For corporal's produce - which he decided wasn't bad
(Once you'd had as much of it as now the warden had).

He showed some disappointment though. His pilot seemed to stall
And one of his large viewing screens had no signal at all.
He switched the signal from the source onto another screen
Confirming that his camera would not reveal its scene.

Then as he watched another of his cameras went down.
Frustrated, the warden's face displayed a knowing frown,
"So, little bird, you have more friends we didn't meet!
"It's sad they'll share your fate when the ground melts at your feet.

"Ah!" his smile widened as he pointed at a screen,
"Look at how her ship succumbs to our ship's laser beam!"
Renee watched with a mixed emotion what the beam could do
(In what appeared a leisure manner to cut fully through).

The reds and whites of spalling steel, plumes of air escaped
Then in the tiny gravity three sections slid away
Bringing up her horrid memory of the attack
At Ganymede that last day she was free those six years back.

Fascinated by the physics, fearing for the lost
She bitterly imagined what the warden's schemes had cost
The solar system in the loss of property and lives.
She found herself yet more committed to take him alive

To face his justice publicly for all his piracies
In hopes that all the souls affected would at last find peace.
If ever that could be. She wondered if her husband knew
His friends lay dead before the judgment seat and what he'd do?

She consoled herself in knowing his crew wasn't there
To be gunned down by Warden and she prayed they were aware
That time to safe the warden's demolitions had run out.
Yet as she watched the warden gloat her mind flooded with doubt!

Warden's man brought in the doctor to attend the wound.
They both knew Warden wouldn't want to leave his viewing room
Until he'd watched the action which appeared to be on tap.
(The doctor was inebriated, shaken from a nap.)

Staggering as much as Warden winced and slurred his speech
The doctor fused the broken rib and cauterized the leaks
And handed him a pill for pain and recommended rest
Then bounced out to the corridor convinced he'd done his best.

Renee was near incredulous that this was fine and well
But Warden's state of mind perhaps, ignored this kind of hell?
The warden's man had brought another shirt for him to wear.
Renee stood up to help him; thanked the man for his kind care

Dismissing him to find his seat before the ship took off.
Warden washed the doctor's pill down with a gulp and cough
Then called his captain on the intercom to find out why
They still were sitting here and had not lifted to the sky?

The captain of the Warden's ship was rightly irritated.
Not only was the flight moved up but now he'd clearly waited
For Warden's doctor to report his surgery was done
But still the doctor's word for which he'd waited had not come.

Warden's drooping eyelids narrowed further as he said,
"The doctor's work is done, Captain, please move us ahead."
The pirate captain hissed a curse about the doctor's parents
Then added, "Straight away, your Highness," then his mike went silent.

Seconds passed without a word while Warden tapped some keys
Setting up a sequence to unleash his devilries.

Turbo pumps somewhere below began their spin-up whines
Then suddenly, without a warning, Battle Stations chimed!

* * * * *

Hidalia and Steve were quartered in a tiny room
A deck below Renee's expecting they would take off soon,
But nearly half an hour passed with no kind of announcement
So Steve decided to step out and learn what it all meant.

He moved into the central passage and scooted aloft
To find two of the warden's crew who smoked and seemed to scoff
About some officer or other person they despised.
Steve asked if they knew why they had not burned for the sky?

The pair stopped to give Steve the eye but then they recognized
Him as one of the warden's men who had been authorized
To serve the warden's lady and to serve the warden's whims
And so they opened up a bit and gave the scoop to him:

"Aw, there's been a holdup. There's another ship came in.
"Ward - I mean, their Highnesses have gone to talk to them.
"The captain is irate because he's kept out of the loop.
"His flight planning is jacked around and half the crew is looped.

"We were told we'd leave tomorrow - we could have a night.
"But now the Ward - I mean, his Highness wants an early flight."
Steve borrowed a smoke and asked the other for a light
Explaining that the warden didn't let him smoke nearby.

They chuckled about simple things and Steve learned useful facts
About the layout of the ship and crew change times and that.
He was quite surprised to learn these crewmen didn't know
What their destination was until the time to go.

Steve impressed them with his inside knowledge of the plan
To spend a day on Rhea then depart for greener land.
"Greener land?" one man enquired. "Dang!" the other spat
Then offered for the other's sake, "Earth. Imagine that!

The first described his visions of a week of sand and surf.
The other cursed and moaned about a full G - and it hurt!

His knees were not what they once were, he hoped the ship could stay
In orbit while a shuttle took the others dirt-side way.

Steve learned where a space suit locker was right on his deck
And that one of the pilots caused their shuttle to be wrecked.
Another shuttle was to have been brought to them by now
(The ship to ferry it from Rhea was delayed somehow).

And that just made the captain's disposition more irate
Which just enhanced the friction he had with the ship's first mate
Who, as it happened was the pilot who had wrecked the shuttle.
Steve joined with the other two to share a hearty chuckle.

The first man stopped mid-laugh and held his finger to his lips.
The whine of starting turbo pumps echoed up through the ship.
The two men looked confused a moment then they both turned white
And scrambled up the central shaft as quickly as they might.

"Get to an acceleration seat!" one called to Steve.
It didn't take more than an instant for him to retreat
Back to his deck then to angle toward his stateroom door,
But then he had a thought and hoped for just a little more

Time before the unannounced acceleration came.
He changed his path believing that the distance was the same,
But just before he got inside the space suit locker's door
The sudden roar of rocket engines knocked him to the floor.

* * * * *

A sudden surge of G-force threw Renee down on the floor
The ship vibrated violently at the engines' roar!
Lateral accelerations threw her to and fro
Until she managed to grab an emergency hand hold.

Warden too was caught off guard and knocked around a bit.
Though sitting on a couch he'd been bounced partly out of it.
Renee managed to pull herself into a seat with straps
While Warden fumbled with his own, cursing at the snaps.

She heard the whine of motors followed by metallic bumps.
Warden looked at her and slurred, "Defensive missile mounts.

"I must get up to the bridge to supervise this fight!"
He fumbled with his straps some more, then much to her delight

A sudden surge of rocket thrust kicked hard against her back
Which pushed him deep into his seat and she saw he went black.
Between the drugs and alcohol and recent loss of blood
His body couldn't take the stress and he blacked out but good!

The high-G surge had only lasted maybe thirty seconds
When she was thrown against her straps when some enemy weapon
Slammed into the ship with deafening metallic screams
And set them spinning violently for an age it seemed!

Finally the spinning and the shaking seemed to stop.
Her inner ears were spinning though, with vertigo and popped
As air pressure reduced then stabilized and then the sound
Of steering thrusters fired as if they were near the ground.

It was all that she could do to keep her lunch inside.
Never in her life had she experienced a ride
So violent - so fully unexpected! But she guessed
That somehow, by the mercy of the fates, she had been blessed.

* * * * *

Steve pulled himself inside the little room and closed the door
Hoping he could get a suit down before there were more
Forces from maneuvering but it was not to be:
He was thrown from suits to wall to suits violently!

As least the distance thrown was short. He hoped Hidalia
Had managed to get to her couch and had a warning call.
But then he heard a woman grunt from just the other side
Of the locker as the ship thrashed on its crazy ride.

"Hi, Handsome!" He turned 'round to see Hidalia's grin
Beaming at him from between two suits right when a din
Of screeching tortured metal and a sudden sideways jolt
Slammed them to the wall - they scrambled to gain a good hold

And brace as they could feel the ship start spinning end-to-end.
Thrusters soon corrected this and they both clambered in

To pressure suits expecting that some harrowing event
Might split the ship wide open and the air inside would vent.

"I don't believe our friends would want this ship to get away.
"I figured I would grab two suits and one more for Renee,"
Hidalia explained, "But why did we get no alarm
"The flight was imminent? I hope Renee has not been harmed!"

Steve explained he figured that the ship had radars down
And had no early warning an attack was coming 'round.
"A foolish error caused by Warden's latent paranoia
"Which will not be repeated by this captain I assure ya!"

They could feel deceleration and some gravity
And then the ship set down though laying horizontally.
"This is not a good sign," Steve remarked, "But we've set down.
"I wonder if our new friends might be anywhere around?"

Hidalia's mind mirrored what was coursing through Steve's own.
Knowing the attack was meant to keep this ship at home
They were both concerned about the status of their friends
And if their ship succeeded from the Warden's to defend.

The conversation with the crewmen left a giant question
As to whether Warden and Renee had left the station.
Were they even on this ship? Their friends must think they were
Or they'd have blown this ship apart before it left the dirt.

Hidalia determined she would check in on Renee.
Steve would go with her and carry two more suits her way.
But when they stepped out from the locker men were rushing past
Suited up and heading for the airlocks further aft.

The pair of them were inconspicuous wearing their suits
And no one gave a second look as they searched in pursuit
Of Renee or her quarters; then they spotted warden's man
Moving toward a central room with one suit in his hand.

They followed him up to the door but there was some delay
In getting a response from inside, but in time Renee
Cracked open the door and thanked the man for Warden's suit,
But asked him pointedly why he did not deliver two?

The man turned red and stammered about thinking him alone.
Renee responded, "Does your Empress not deserve her own?"
It was plain to see he lied and had no love for her.
Renee continued, "These two will now serve the Emperor.

She beckoned to her friends and told the warden's man to scoot.
He craned his neck to look inside but gave her Warden's suit
Then glared at the two newcomers before he skulked away.
It was obvious to all he didn't trust Renee.

Hidalia and Steve were brought inside the viewer room.
They could see Renee and Warden had a rough ride too.
Renee had bruises starting and the warden was asleep.
Renee whispered how he'd been shot and drugged conveniently.

She handed them the Warden's suit and asked they put it on him
Then used the intercom to get a report from the captain.
When his rugged bearded face came on the little screen,
A look of deep relief spread on his face when she was seen.

"I know you're busy, Captain, but it's time to hear from you."
The captain growled, "You're not the person who I answer to."
Renee could tell he didn't want to hear Warden's harangue.
She said, "The emperor is busy. I speak in his name.

"Now, tell me what has happened and our status if you will."
The wily pirate hesitated but he let it spill:
"A ship of unknown origin attacked when we were blind.
"It was repelled and damaged then it set down hard behind

"The mountains near the port. We've sustained a nasty blow.
"Repairs might take some time before it's safe for us to go."
Renee said, "Thank you, Captain. Please report when you know more."
The captain said, "I'm sorry for the unexpected sport."

The man's demeanor softened but his eyes were deathly cold.
"Tell Black - I mean, the Emperor, It's best I had been told
"About the little ship. I understood we'd be the last."
Renee's eyes like blue ice reflected his back with a flash,

"We had our reasons, Captain, but the small freighter is ours.
"It's been parked on the south side of the ridge now for some hours.

"Leave it unmolested. You will share in its reward."
The pirate captain eyed her then remarked, "There is some word

"The freighter shot at us in concert with the other ship."
Renee did not allow her steely countenance to slip.
"I assure you captain, if that ship knew it were us
"They'd dare not use their weapons. We would burn them into dust."

Renee continued coolly, "I believe they were alarmed
"By this surprising action and they felt they might be harmed.
"Tell me what their status is right now if you can see."
The captain inquired to the side then, "Sitting quietly."

Renee pressed on her inquisition, "Do you have a clue
"About the sort of ship which dared attack us? Perhaps who?"
"It had the look of bounty hunters, Ma'am - uh, your Highness.
"It's not the first time I've been jumped when laying dark like this."

Renee stared at the man a moment. He stared back at her.
"Captain, please continue with the plan the emperor
"Has given you to do as soon as our repairs are done.
"Believe me, at their best you have that little ship outgunned."

He made a subtle frown but nodded his acceptance too.
Renee thanked him again then said, "We both have work to do."
She switched the viewer off then turned and sighed and slid away.
"Dang!" Steve exclaimed, "You're good! You ought to do Broadway."

Hidalia shot him a dirty look and scolded, "Steve!"
A shock passed Renee's eyes a second until she could see
That Warden was all suited up with audio turned off.
The humor was appreciated; Renee laughed and coughed!

* * * * *

Radar sent the video direct to target screens.
Gin stared with his tear-blurred eyes and marveled at the scene:
Telescopic lenses showed the black ship was intact
Laying on its side with chunks of debris at its back.

Suited figures could be seen emerging from the ship
And moving to the stern, long-handled tools were in their grips.

They set about methodically cutting burned debris
And pushing it aside to set the inner black ship free.

"What the heck is that?" enquired Radar curiously.
Gin exhaled a prayerful, thankful sigh of great relief
To see the ship intact with human forms appearing well.
Radar mused, "I could have sworn that ship blew all to hell!"

"It looks like he has jettisoned his damaged engine pod,"
Gin explained as he observed, "I thought that ship looked odd.
"An extra stage of engines and associated fuel
"To give him greater range and speed. This pirate is no fool.

"He's dropped his damaged stage just like a lizard drops his tail.
"And when his men clear off the tatters he'll be free to sail.
"The extra tanks and engines are what made the fireball.
"The damage they received must not have let them freely fall."

Radar asked the obvious, "Why hasn't he hit us?
"He can surely see us 'cause our radar's obvious."
"I have no idea, but as long as she's alive,
"I won't fire on him. Now get this ship ready to ride!"

Gin intended fully to give chase with Captain's ship
The instant Warden twitched as if he intended to lift.
Gin would hit the throttles and he'd force the black ship down
And pray that they had plenty of space suits to go around.

63   Shattered

By now some of the colonists smelled change upon the air.
Strangers in the hallways; Warden's men not anywhere.
Word was spreading quietly to stay inside their homes
And for the most part they complied and stayed from public zones.

Jules and his two guides approached the central public space
And carefully moved 'round the wall of Warden's judgment place.
Both the men made quiet comments about how the scene
Was emptier than any time that they had ever seen.

Jules could see some people watching wide-eyed from the shadows
Curious but terrified by what might come to follow.
The deafening and unexpected blast from hidden weapons
Again could rain down from the ceiling over Warden's garden.

Jules approached the entrance to the compound at the time
That Duke bounced to the area with three men and Bovine.
The captain caught their sight and signaled to approach with care.
The smell of burning flesh and gunpowder was in the air.

The captain had his sidearm drawn. He crouched beside the gate.
Duke chambered his carbine, Bovine's laser came off 'Safe'.
The captain signaled 'Now!' They burst into the walled-in space
And quickly swept the area to find no threats in place.

Just the suited bodies of Selenia's shot men.
Very few showed evidence of any life in them.
(Not a man among the public tried to bring them aid.
Terrified of sharing Warden's wrath which on them rained.)

Selenia was sitting propped against the garden wall.
Tears of pain and sorrow marred her face as they would fall
To mingle with the blood that she had smeared across her cheeks
With gloves that now sought vainly to stop blood that slowly leaked

Not only from her abdomen but from the deadly wound
Of one of hers who held her hand and would be dying soon.
When she saw the captain she let out a tearful gasp
And choked his whispered name when he returned after he'd passed.

"Jules!" she choked and sobbed, "I tried - I tried -" he cut her off
Then motioned Duke to check the others as she gasped and coughed,
"I'm sorry, Jules, I tried - " he touched her lips to silence her
Then cut her suit away for access to administer

All the help he could with first aid items in his kit
Then called to Joe to bring Haji and make it double quick!
Duke moved man to man among Selenia's hurt men
Hoping against hope he'd find the living among them

But only her Lieutenant whom she held had any breath
And as the captain cut her suit he saw he'd met his death.
He took the man's hand out of hers and placed it on the grass
And softly told Selenia her Lieutenant had passed.

She looked at Duke and pointed toward the hall behind the seat
Still visible beyond the open door of their retreat.
"Renee and Warden - *Yiiee!*" she winced in pain, "-- two other men.
"That way," she pleaded that someone go after them.

Duke looked at the captain who gave him a quick hand sign
To do a recon only and report what he might find.
Duke nodded agreement and went through the open door
Silent as a stalking cat but focused even more.

"Jules," she gasped again as he took care of both her wounds
(The bullet had passed through her; he must stop the bleeding soon).
"I underestimated and I tried to take revenge.
"I may have hurt Renee - " she winced (involuntary twinge).

The captain looked up from his work and tried to catch her eye.
Her tears were flowing freely and she would not meet his eyes.
She turned and bowed her head and sobbed with painful heaving gasps,
"I had such a jealous rage I failed you at the last!

"I saw her with my brother. Something bad came over me!"
She coughed and choked on tears and mucous shaking painfully.
The captain took her shaking shoulders, pulled her back around,
"Selenia, I know you well. And you've let no one down.

"Seeing either one of them would be a trying test.
"It pulled your heart in four directions. I know you meant best."

He held her close and felt the waves of remorse wash her soul
And knew that she had found herself and clarified her goals.

A quiet moment passed and then she pushed him softly off.
"Jules," she said, then winced in pain and tried hard not to cough.
"You need to save Renee. You need to catch up to her now.
"Warden will be taking her. They may have left by now."

The captain bent and lifted her (she gave a muffled yell),
"Renee is going to be all right. It's you we need to help."
He carried her outside the judgment compound's open gate
Far beyond the grizzly sight of her beloved eight.

Jules then flagged the man who'd come with Bovine from Atomics.
"Is there an infirmary and can you summon medics?"
A look of sad apology ran 'cross the poor man's face,
"Yes. There's an infirmary but it's a nasty place.

"The only doctor is a psycho Warden keeps around.
"No one goes there figuring for compost they'll be ground."
The captain nodded his acknowledgement then turned away
And took Selenia back to the room kept by Renee,

Where carefully he laid her down and watched her close her eyes
Then fall asleep under the spell of pain drugs he'd applied.
He sensed the mental anguish on this bed Renee endured.
Then sent a note to Joe and Haji with the room's co-ord's.

* * * * *

Haji got the word and grabbed his kit and suited up
Passing Dewey at the airlock who gave him thumbs up.
Joe took Haji down and made their best time to the place.
When Haji saw the Warden's work a horror crossed his face.

Duke had taken Sergeant Steve's two faithful demo men
With him up the passage stalking Renee and Warden.
Bovine and his man were busily slicing the roof
Removing Warden's weapons as the onlookers approved

(But still they mostly shrunk into the shadows to observe
Believing Warden's wrath would surely fall stifled their nerve.)

Then when the job was finished Bovine welded shut the gate
To isolate the bodies of the men who'd met their fate.

Joe escorted Haji to the place the Captain sent.
Bovine and his man brought up the rear guard as they went.
The captain intercepted them just outside in the hall
And gave the doctor all the facts he'd need for this house call.

The captain left the doctor to his work and took the men
Toward the general area where Duke reported in
To say the ship Selenia had brought was in a wreck
Outside on the landing field laser-cut to heck.

A boarding bridge connected to a big black ship outside
Had disconnected and pulled back as soon as he'd arrived.
He figured this black ship was getting ready to leave soon.
The demo men were working on the airlock in the room.

For they had opened access panels which revealed a charge
Intended to destroy the entire wall it was so large!
This was all the status of the most immediate kind
Then Duke gave him a rundown of the thing most on his mind:

They'd found the gunshot body of a man along the way
Laying in the corridor where Warden and Renee
Had made their quick escape and when they came out through the door
They found the signs that someone else had dripped blood on the floor.

Duke had not the tools to tell whose blood that it may be
But he took up a sample that he planned to give Haji.
Most importantly Duke felt the big ship must be stopped
But he had not the means and felt perhaps that all was lost

As far as rescuing the one so loved by Captain Blue
(Though thousands on this colony would live when they were through
Safe-ing all the bombs and poisons Warden left behind)
But rescuing Renee was the grand goal that filled his mind.

Duke turned back and saw the men had finished pulling out
The charges from the airlock walls as one gave out a shout,
"The ship is lifting!" Duke moved to the window by his side
To see some dust fly past; but the ship was out of sight.

"Warden's ship has lifted, Captain. Renee isn't here
"Unless they went back by a different way than I got here."
"We're sweeping that way now," the captain said, "You just hold tight.
Duke was disappointed he'd no way to stop the flight.

Just a couple minutes passed before Duke saw Red's ship
Setting down aggressively while doing a slight flip.
He could see collision damage and a blasted side.
He hoped they were okay - they'd had one challenge of a ride!

Only seconds more had passed before a hail was sent
On a private channel, it was just one word: "Red."
Duke responded quickly, "Duke has eyes. The dock is clear."
And then light from the lower airlock on Red's ship appeared.

* * * * *

Nick and Goldie sat in silence looking at Red's ship.
The darkened hole behind the twisted hull plates which were ripped
Apart by missile blast looked like a passage to a crypt
Through which some men from this life to eternity had slipped.

At least that was a good assumption for the hole was large.
Internal decompression had enhanced the missile's charge.
They could see some damage near the bridge and cockpit too.
And then across a private channel they heard Red and Duke

Identify and verify their contact had been made
And that Duke and his men secured the airlock at the cave.
A door beside the boarding bridge slid open for access
Then Captain Blue's voice joined the others for a conference:

"Raven's winged but soon will sing. What of the bluebird's flight?
(Red was silent) Gin piped in, "The bluebird is in sight
"And sitting quietly but soon will fledge and leave the nest
"Like the phoenix so quick intervention would be best."

Nick asked Goldie, "Can you get this shuttle off the ground?"
Goldie said, "Secure our injured man and then strap down."
Nick moved to the rear and strapped the man into his seat
Then signaled Goldie who said, "This may not be very neat!"

She loosed the docking clamps to free the shuttle from the wreck
Then goosed the thrusters which blew clouds of debris, dust and dreck.
The shuttle soon broke free but for one piece of black hull plate
Which fell free when she leveled off the slightly damaged crate.

Nick got on the radio and put his two cents in:
"Newbie has an injured man who needs some attention.
"We're backing him up to the lock. Duke! You know it's me.
"We have the Raven's shuttle. Take a look out to the east."

Goldie trimmed the shuttle then maneuvered toward the wall
Then just before she set it down gave it one-eighty yaw.
Nick unstrapped the engineer and took him through the lock
Then to the warden's lair bore him the thirty-meter walk.

* * * * *

Steve relayed the information he'd learned from the men
About the Captain, Mate, and delayed shuttle coming in.
Renee was desperate to learn about her husband's status.
All she knew was friends were dead and it was now obvious

That Warden knew someone was coming - yet he was surprised!
There were cracks appearing which the captain must surmise.
This pirate was a smart one and the Warden's man had doubts.
If they got together they would figure something out.

She must know if quicker options to end this charade
Were yet in place. Some contact with her husband must be made!
Renee sat down at Warden's console and found with delight
His access was still active after their impromptu flight.

A viewing screen upon the wall revealed a damaged ship
Had landed near the boarding bridge and then a shuttle slipped
Into the field of view as she reached for the commo pad
And switched it to a private channel where her heart was glad

To hear a stranger's voice announce to Duke he had a shuttle
And they were bringing a hurt man for treatment on the double.
Renee broke in the channel and announced with steady voice,
"The empress needs a shuttle to arrive right now from space."

* * * * *

Nick had just delivered his hurt man into the care
Of Duke and his two demo men when Captain Blue got there
Along with Joe and Bovine when Renee's voice hit their ears.
Captain Blue transmitted, "Let the Empress have no fear.

"A royal carriage will arrive in moments as desired."
The captain did a double-take and much surprised inquired,
"Mr. Hallenbeck! Is Titan too boring for you?
"I'm glad that you could join us for we have a job to do."

* * * * *

Renee's relief was more than equaled by that felt by Red
(Who up 'til now had no idea Renee wasn't dead.
In fact, Red's emotion from the fight's adrenalin
Then learning both the ladies were alive near equaled Gin's!)

A half a dozen men with carbines bounded from his ship
With Red in front of all of them to lead the hasty trip
Along the outside of the boarding bridge to the airlock
Where Nick had just come in. Red and Blue must have a talk!

But Red spared little time to talk before he took two men
To find Selenia and Haji to watch over them.
Jules gave him directions to the quarters where they were.
He found the doctor kneeling by her bed lost in his work.

Red softly announced his presence; Haji grunted back,
"She is lucky to survive this vicious sneak attack.
"The others? Not so lucky," Haji said, "Eight men are dead."
"More than that by now, my friend," softly whispered Red.

"We've brought another man who took some metal in his back.
"He's suffered from anoxia and frostbite too, in fact.
"He's stable and sedated and we put him in the room
"Across the hall. I hope that you can look in on him soon."

Haji worked in silence for a dozen minutes more
While Red stationed his men at each end of the corridor

Then set himself outside her room to wait the doctor's word
When he could see Selenia, but that's not what he heard:

Haji came outside the room, a grim look on his face
And said, "Red, I know your need but she will need some space.
"The wounds have been repaired but there's great damage to her cells.
"She will need much sleep before her body can get well.

"She's sedated now but in an hour she'll awake
"And she will need to focus on a friend's familiar face.
"Stay with her - don't leave her side. Tell her all is well.
"After that ensure she sleeps for an extended spell."

Red nodded acknowledgement then Haji asked, "What's new?"
Red frowned with frustration saying, "They took Renee Blue,
"But she is still alive and Jules has gone to bring her back.
"Several men are with him to arrest our Warden Black.

"And I wish I were with them but I know I should be here."
Haji frowned a moment for Red's face had made it clear
That there was much more to the story but the time was short.
The engineer needed attention, thus the quick report.

Haji moved into his room and focused on his task.
Red stayed near Selenia and did what he was asked.
As far above them, far away, his friends began their play
To capture Warden Black and reunite Jules with Renee.

* * * * *

The intercom upon the bulkhead chimed. It was the bridge.
Renee approached the viewer and with more than just a smidge
Of trepidation turned it on to see the captain's face
On which it wasn't hard to read the marks of restrained rage.

"Yes, captain? Please report." She tossed her hair aside
Strategically to show the warden in the seat behind.
"Tell Black - um, His Highness, I have just been made aware
"That my communication officer got off the air

"A wide-band data transmission of what appears to be
"Imperial records of startling sensitivity.

"It originated from a transmitter nearby.
"I believe that Black - His Highness will want it to die."

Renee put on a condescending face with hardened eyes
And with her best performance as an empress improvised:
"There are those who resist what the Emperor has done.
"Bounty hunters, Martians, and Jovian worlds for some.

"Martian spies and infiltrators arrived in the ship
"You lasered on the ground. A bullet from one of them clipped
"The Emperor. That's why the doctor was invited here.
"It's also why our schedule was moved up. And it is clear

"That there are others near whose loyalties are brought in doubt.
"I'm sure you know his methods. Every truth will be found out."
The captain's face grew redder as her blue eyes narrowed darkly.
He blinked and nodded his head almost imperceptibly.

"Be advised, captain, that another ship is near.
"A shuttle will arrive shortly to take us. Is that clear?"
She switched the viewer off then turned and gave a heavy sigh
More than half convinced that in mere moments they could die.

She knew the pirate made a deal with Warden, not with her.
She had to expedite getting his limp body transferred
To a friendly ship out of the reach of those loyal
To Warden's evil plans (those who agreed he'd be royal).

But she had no idea what defenses there might be
Implanted in him to go active automatically
And so they did all they could do to keep him well sedated
So far their success had Renee wary but elated.

She turned back to the intercom and called the warden's man
Who'd already been talking to the pirate ship's captain.
(The warden's man was near the forward lock when Renee called
And three men came aboard without the normal protocol.)

The warden's man responded to her page and left the room.
Renee addressed him formally and said, "We're leaving soon.
"The emperor and I and trusted few will leave this ship.
"A shuttle will be taking us to orbit extra quick.

"This ship can keep the worthless doctor, but we'll want our girls.
"Get them suited quickly and bring them without their frills.
"Baggage will be transferred later. Get them on the shuttle
"Which will land outside in moments. Get there on the double!"

The man appeared surprised to see Renee's face on the screen.
Figuring he'd been demoted by the Warden's queen
Obviously pleased to see renewed need for his services
He wisely chose to serve and put himself in her good graces.

"Yes, your Highness," he replied, "I'll instantly comply.
"Is there anything you'd like for me to bring besides?"
There were things of Warden's but she didn't hesitate:
"Nothing that won't be transferred in orbit or replaced.

"Timeliness is of the essence. We will see you there."
She disconnected from the intercom then went on air
With Warden's console for one message on closed frequency
Then shut the warden's console down (quite irreparably).

64   A Necessary Evil

The black ship looked much like a shadow stretched beneath the hill
Looming larger out the cockpit as Jules showed his skill
By sweeping far out to the north then back in from the east
To simulate a flight path from an orbiting black beast.

Goldie rode as co-pilot and closely watched the captain
Learning all she could about the black ship's shuttle's cabin.
It was an older type of craft built for the Survey Corp
Rugged and reliable built just before the war.

At some point it was pirated and retro-fit with weapons
Fully capable to teach a larger ship a lesson.
Today's job was to transport cargo treasured far above
Any loot or booty any pirate had dreamed of.

Nick sat in the engineering seat behind his girl
Watching as the landscape underneath their feet unfurled.
Then as the mountains rose up from the cratered plain beneath
Nick realized he'd unconsciously been clenching his teeth.

Turning on his target radar with the ship in sight
The captain dropped below the ridgeline delaying their flight.
Then on a cue to Sergeant Steve's two trusted demo men
The engine section of Selenia's ship met it's end

As charges meant to blow the wall out of the colony
Blasted skyward burning fuel and clouds of black debris.
The captain gunned the engines and returned them to the sky
To jump the mountains toward the black ship on the other side.

Their craft came on ballistic arc above the mountain tops
Directly overhead of Captain Blue's ship when it dropped
Seven thousand meters with a sudden thruster blast
Terminated by another which put them at last

Hovering beside the black ship not far from the bridge
With weapons trained and visible a moment. Then a smidge
Of thruster gas spun them around and set them on the ground.
The cargo airlock opened as some black-ship's men turned 'round

And bounced up to the lock with questions, but were waved away
By four armed men who exited and cleared a path away
For access to the black ship's upper airlock near the bridge.
Captain Blue made Goldie pilot, stood up, then he cringed

A little as he pressed a silver ring over his glove
Which bore a large black stone Nick had a recent memory of.
It was the ring Selenia had pulled from off the hand
Of the dead and burning black ship captain on Titan.

The captain checked his sidearm then took Joe and Duke outside
And crossed the intervening distance to the black ship's side.
They scaled the handholds to the lock and pressed the access key.
The captain held the ring up 'til the crew granted entry.

Captain Blue stepped through the lock into the black ship's bridge.
Followed by both Joe and Duke into the dim red dinge.
The smell of sweat and alcohol with traces of stale smoke
Gave the strong impression that the bridge scrubber was broke.

Men stood in the shadows here and there with weapons drawn.
Captain Blue looked round the room and feigned a tired yawn
Then confidently made his way up to the captain's chair
To meet the bearded man who glared a tired and angry stare.

"They call me 'Blue'," he said, "It seems your bounty near got claimed."
The bearded pirate cursed and said, "So guess who is to blame?"
He took a lengthy drag of cigarette and glared at Blue
Accusatory yet inquiring what Blue was up to.

"I don't know you," he exhaled. The smoke billowed Blue's way.
As remnants curled out of his nose he flicked the ash away.
Squinting through his narrowed eyes he said, "That's not your ring."
Captain Blue responded, "It is now. And everything

"On Umbriel that goes with it: the ship, the port, the throne.
"Then after we are done here I will wear another stone.
"Things are changing." he left off and stared the pirate down.
The bearded man stubbed out his smoke and leaned back with a frown.

"Things aren't what they used to be. There is no doubt of that."
"I wouldn't have been caught off guard but for our Warden Black."

Captain Blue's eyes held their steady gaze as he replied,
"The Emperor has many weighty matters on his mind.

"He took a bullet from a Martian spy, is what we heard.
"They came in on a ship of ours that somehow wound up burned."
The bearded captain nodded saying, "Yes, Black had me burn it
"Just before I got jumped by a bounty hunter, durn it!"

Captain Blue replied, "That must be who I just destroyed
On the north side of the ridge, his repair crew deployed."
The bearded captain questioned of his radar man who stated
A great cloud of debris had grown and then had dissipated.

"What is your assessment of the Emperor's condition?
"Has his wound been treated properly by your physician?"
The bearded captain snorted, "He had his doctor attend
"But he's a worthless sot and mine was not invited in.

"So I don't have a clue beyond what his new woman said.
"I saw him in his pressure suit but he could have been dead."
Captain Blue smiled broadly, "I assure you he is not.
"I have been in touch with him since from orbit I dropped.

"I'd suggest you finish up and get yourself upstairs.
"There's at least one Martian cruiser but they come in pairs.
"The emperor is transferring his flag up to my ship.
"Friends are on the way but you should give this place the slip.

"This regolith is not so dense. It isn't firm enough
"To absorb the energy. The ride could be quite rough
"For anyone who's sitting on the topside of the ground.
"Things could get a hard jolt for a long distance around.

"The schedule has been moved up. He's finishing things here.
"You will fly the path the emperor made very clear.
"The other sites will detonate as your ship flies the plan
"And you'll record each detonation to show to The Man."

The captain of the warden's ship grumbled his discontent
And spat, "Black hasn't told me anything of this movement.
"His wom - uh, the empress said to fly the plan he set
"But there's not been a single word from Black himself as yet."

Captain Blue gave him a condescending sort of smirk
"You should know by now openness isn't how he works."
The pirate captain waved a hand and his armed men stood down.
Duke and Joe quietly moved where they could see around

The whole perimeter and every corner of the room
Quickly gauging who the warriors were or simple goons.
Non-chalantly waiting on their captain to return
Or fight, if things went south and there was nowhere else to turn.

While the pair of captains had their captainly exchange
Steve came to the weapons deck but no one thought it strange.
Incognito in his helmet he leaned toward a man
And said, "I'm your relief. Go to the stern and lend a hand."

The man began to protest but Steve cut the man off short
And said, "You want to interrupt and ask the captain, Sport?"
A spark of fear flashed in his eyes replaced by indignation
But he conceded Steve his seat who took up his position.

Steve looked out the tiny portholes of the weapons' deck
Confirming which side's turret gave Blue's ship the best aspect
The other men around him had all donned their spacesuits too.
When the time was right Steve showed himself to Joe and Duke.

* * * * *

Hidalia and Renee (after saying 'bye' to Steve)
Were moving Warden toward an airlock preparing to leave.
They had his arm slung over Renee's shoulder as they moved
Though he was still unconscious from the extra drugs and booze.

Moving past the room of Warden's harem near the rear
The reek of vomit stung their noses, crying scorched their ears.
Men were still egressing to assist with the repairs
And in the bustle none of them appeared to be aware

That Warden and his entourage were exiting as well
Then with the cycle of the lock they leaped from Warden's hell!
In twenty seconds they were half the distance to the shuttle
But Warden started waking and began to cause some trouble

Flailing his arms and spewing curses with no point
Obviously half-unconscious, dazed and out of joint
To find himself inside a spacesuit outside of the ship
Until Renee grabbed hold of him and thinned his oxy mix

Then, touching helmets told him plainly they had been attacked
And they were changing ships for safety. Then she turned him back
To see the damaged portions looming over them behind
Which seemed to calm him down and bring some memory to mind.

When they got him to the shuttle anoxia set in
Which caused him to slip into unconsciousness once again.
Warden was their captive - a sensation new and strange.
Hidalia, though fearful was elated with the change!

But they had no idea what defenses there might be
Implanted in him to go active automatically
And so it was with great relief when met by a young man.
She saw Jules' damping field device held tightly in his hand.

He looked them over closely then peered into Warden's helmet,
And asked, "Is he unconscious?" Renee said, "I think we're set."
"Mrs. Blue? I'm Nicholas. Your husband's in that ship
"Along with Joe and Duke. They're there to bring you out of it."

Red light spilled across them from the rising cargo door
As Bovine's massive mitt pulled Warden in, pinned to the floor
Whereupon he lashed him down then smiled at Renee
As a girl with yellow hair moved swiftly Warden's way.

She jabbed a hypodermic through the finger of his suit
Then smiled and said, "I'm thrilled to get to meet you, Mrs. Blue!
"I'm 'Goldie' to my friends. And you must be Hidalia?
"We have lots to talk about," she sighed, "Hallelujah!"

She pulled the needle out, "This is insurance he won't wake.
"We don't want surprises when we make our getaway."
Nick stepped in between the ladies and the open door
And said, "I'm sorry, ma'am, but there is still one item more:

"No one who has implants or knows Warden's voice may ride.
"Please go to your husband's yacht. A man waits there inside

"With damping field and scanning gear to minimize that threat."
Renee nodded agreement, "There is still an item yet:

"Patch my suit into this shuttle's radio for me
"So I can call the black ship's captain on this frequency:"
She tapped a button on her sleeve display and let them see.
"I must give him motivation to let our men free.

"He is a pirate and he isn't in the best of moods.
"It's best to let him have the least amount of time to brood."
Nick agreed and Goldie patched Renee into the shuttle,
Who waited for the Warden's man to finish with the trouble

Of getting Warden's girls packed up and out the aft airlock.
The wait was short. The man did not accept any backtalk.
(He was trained by Warden and by Warden was well paid;
The girls were suited up and out the door without delay.)

* * * * *

The pirate's navigation man cut in to their discussion:
"A small craft is approaching from the cargo ship's direction."
Both the captains looked at him expecting something more.
Presently he said, "It set down near your shuttle's door,

"Sir," he added in deference to the implied state
Of Blue as flagship captain by the emperor's mandate.
"And?" the pirate captain asked. The man said, "Nothing yet.
"Some men are walking toward it..." Captain Blue cut in, "I'd bet

"The emperor has ordered it to transport personnel
"To his cargo ship." The pirate captain asked, "Do tell?
"It's probably the harem that he brought. Do you not know?"
Captain Blue responded, "Only that he's hot to go.

"Being shot and jumped for bounty's sure to set one's mind
"On quickly getting off the ground to leave this place behind
"Then rendezvous at Rhea with some friends in celebration.
"But I'm as uninformed as you about the Cargo's mission."

The pirate captain's black eyes searched the browns of Captain Blue
A moment then he said, "I'm very curious, aren't you?

"For years I've worked with Warden Black to help him reach his goal
"But never have I seen where he has hoarded all his gold.

"Maybe you know more than you are letting on to me?
"Maybe Warden's woman is not whom she claims to be?
"Maybe that's a ship of gold to meet him in the sky?
"Maybe there are plans afoot by more than Martian spies?"

A flash of greedy fever crossed the pirate captain's eyes.
He studied Captain Blue to see if he might realize
That either way it went there was a chance they could ally;
Perhaps to share a bigger slice of Warden's golden pie.

To Jules it was apparent this man was feeling betrayed,
Abandoned, cast aside, and may be put out of the way.
Experience with Warden showed no chance for his redemption.
Revenge and profit to this man must be attractive options.

(He was a pirate, after all.) He'd long been Warden's tool.
He obviously knew too much, yet he was not a fool.
He knew the evidence on Saturn VIII would be erased.
Old associates had also vanished with no trace.

Jules could sense the pirate's crewmen listening intently
Feigning busy duties but with weapons at the ready.
The danger to Jules' wife and crew had suddenly compounded.
Blue stepped closer to the man and said, "Your fear's unfounded.

"All of us will see great changes and receive rewards.
"Ruthless yes, but generous, our leader in due course
"Will end this hiding in the darkness. This attack is proof
"His opposition's desperate. Have you not watched the news?"

The pirate said, "I've watched his progress in the news in fact.
"I've also seen the weather change this woman brought to Black.
"I'm not sure these changes are the best fit for his plans.
"A woman can have serious effects on any man."

Captain Blue nodded his understanding and replied,
"I understand you've spent some years in working at his side.
"Suspicion and mistrust of change seems natural to me.
"But let me give you some advice: Don't act too hastily.

"I've found it isn't healthy second guessing this woman.
"The lady has proved very instrumental to our plan.
"Are you not aware of what she brought to him from Rhea?
"Besides," whispered Jules, "She soothes his latent paranoia.

"And that is good for all of us. Do not doubt the lady."
(The pirate's eyes bulged wide at how Jules stated it so plainly.)
"Besides, he's made it very clear the Empress speaks for him.
"I assure you, I will not make that mistake again!"

* * * * *

Dewey was in charge when Gin and Radar left the ship.
Skippy ran the comms while Dewey kept the fires lit.
The yacht was energized when Gin and Radar climbed inside
In less than ninety seconds they were set to take a ride.

Gin bumped off with thrusters, spun, and took ballistic flight
In a long slow arc to land along the black ship's side
About four dozen meters from the shuttle Goldie crewed
Focused like a laser on the job they had to do.

Radar cleared the airlock and depressurized the yacht
Then from the inside popped the cargo door but left it not
Opened wide enough to see the darkened space inside
Yet ready in an instant (if he must) to fling it wide.

Gin could see three people moving toward the other shuttle.
He could see the center one was having lots of trouble
Keeping equilibrium, and then he turned around
Looking back at the black ship while held up off the ground

By one whom he could see had golden hair tied in a braid
Shining dimly in the meager light of the sun's rays.
Gin knew in an instant as his heart leaped to his throat
Who the lady was - he sucked his breath and nearly choked!

He thought he saw her turn and look his way for just an instant
Then turning back she focused on her task with more intent.
Gin shut down the thrusters and secured the yacht's controls;
Checked his sidearm, took a breath and swore he'd meet this goal.

Throwing back the canopy and climbing from the craft
He called to Radar to bring damping gear with him from aft.
Then springing toward the other shuttle signaled to Red's men
To extend perimeter to include all of them.

By now Renee and her companions reached the shuttle craft.
A man who somehow looked familiar exited the aft
Cargo hatch and held a small device up they could see
Then leaned in close to view the central limp one of the three.

Gin saw Bovine reach and pull the central figure in.
The other man stayed outside with Renee and companion.
Then he noticed four more suited figures coming near
Following Renee's path from the damaged black ship's rear.

Renee's companion turned away to intercept the four
(Two of Red's security men helped even the score)
Bovine exited the shuttle heading toward Gin
By then Radar had reached the four and started scanning them.

(His cursory examination showed six active implants
One in each of three women and three within the man.)
Bovine came direct to Gin and when within suit range
Confirmed Renee was with them but they had to stay away.

Gin looked angrily confused until Bovine explained
They couldn't have distractions while the pirate crew got played.
Both of them assisted Radar to corral the four
And move them toward the yacht's partially open cargo door.

But Gin never removed his eyes from Renee for two seconds.
He would not lose track of her! And when she finally beckoned
And turned away then bounded spryly for her husband's yacht
Gin met her before she got midway and deftly caught

Her by the arms to gaze into her face and she in his.
Gin asked, "Is it really you? We've waited long for this!"
His voice broke off as tears reddened his eyes (and hers teared too)
"Sven," she gasped in recognition, "It's good to see you!

"My husband said you've had a troubled time since Ganymede.
"He said he made the right choice there and I firmly agree!"

Gin was shocked to hear this revelation and it showed
As from his reddened eyes the tears burst forth and freely flowed.

Hers were tears of empathy and bittersweet regret.
His were tears of relief and surprise that, when they met
She touched the very topic with no preamble nor dance.
(She had to give him that if fate would give no other chance.)

His blurry eyes searched hers a moment but saw only love
And not a trace of blame - for she was only thinking of
His needed inner absolution and the healing touch
Which only she could give. He choked, "Thank you. Very much.

"Come," he said, "Let's get you on the yacht. You're finished here.
"As soon as Jules gets off that pirate's ship we're jumping clear."
"Sven," she warned in desperation, "That man with three girls
"Is loyal to the man around whom all this evil swirls!

"Be careful when we're near him. The girls cannot be trusted,
"But they deserve a chance to have a new life unmolested."
Gin nodded his understanding, saying, "There is much
"That needs to be corrected by a special doctor's touch.

"You remember Haji, don't you? He and Radar here,
"Have all the talents needed to make all our bodies clear
"Of dangerous devices planted deep beneath the skin."
By now they had approached the yacht, but before they got in

Radar beamed a grin that made his big ears seem to flap
But held his hand up cautioning to stay a few steps back.
Gin attached his damping field device to Renee's arm
As Radar did a deeper scan to each girl without harm,

But when he scanned the warden's man, the man's body went slack
And drifted toward the ground where in a moment from his back
A searing flame of phosphorus filled up his suit with light
Before it burned through to the ground as they stepped back with fright.

The soot that filled his helmet froze inside near instantly
Mingled with the moisture that released from his body.
Radar looked surprised a moment, staring at his scanner
Then looked at Gin and said, "That was an unexpected manner

"Of operation probably induced by damping fields."
While Warden's girls retreated to the yacht (in fear they squealed)
Gin replied excitedly, "Turn off that damn machine!
"We're going to take the lot of them at once to see Haji!"

Warden's concubines were bruised and nauseas and hurt
Resenting Warden's man the more so when he hit the dirt.
Showing no compassion other than their brief surprise,
It was obvious that he was hated and despised.

The woman who had glared at Renee when they first embarked
Faced Renee to meet her eyes with questions in the dark.
Renee could read her question and told her, "I promise you
"Things will be much better for us all - and very soon."

Hidalia watched both of them and added, "Trust Renee.
"There's much more happening than what appears to be in play."
The woman nodded silently then gave Renee her word,
"You'll get no trouble out of me," and then she motioned toward

The other two, "Or them. I'll make sure they do what we're told."
She looked down at the body of the man now frozen cold
And shoved it with her boot. "That's one of many on my list."
She looked up at Renee, "There's more than one who won't be missed."

She wouldn't take it further, but Renee saw she was brave
To say what she just did with little evidence Renee
Was not a co-conspirator with Warden in his plot.
It was evident she'd take whatever chance she got.

Hidalia then herded Warden's three into the back
Explaining that their plans had changed after the sneak attack:
"The emperor is on the other shuttle with some men
"The ladies will ride in another ship away from them."

* * * * *

The radio man signaled to the captain urgently,
"A message from the shuttle, Sir. His Highness' frequency."
The captain pointed up and told him, "Put them on the speaker."
Then, "Shuttle, go ahead." (His irritation grew no weaker.)

"Please request the captain to return immediately.
"Their Highnesses are ready. They are waiting patiently."
Goldie's voice came clearly from the pirate's radio
The pirate looked surprised and said, "I didn't even know

"That they had left the ship! Why the heck was I not told?"
He glared at Blue with eyes would turn a lesser man's blood cold.
Captain Blue said coolly with concern across his face:
"I didn't know they left. I'm here to escort them to space."

Blue requested confirmation through the black ship's comm:
Presently, Renee's voice through the radio came on:
"You captains have been chatting long enough, don't you agree?
"We'd like to get the emperor to orbit rapidly.

"We're seated and the pilot is prepared to go upstairs."
Blue looked at the pirate who confirmed, "The Golden Hair."
Suspicions from this chaos and the words of Warden's man
Led him to believe this was a dark, deceptive plan.

His tired mind was growing certain she was Martian too
And he would take some action to detain this Captain Blue.
"Why don't I ensure I'll see Black when I get to orbit?
"Leave your men to serve me until then to guarantee it."

Incredulity flooded the face of Captain Blue,
"Hostages? Really? I need men just as you do.
"After all these years you demonstrate such faithlessness?
"That's not the wisest choice to make at empire's genesis.

"No, my men will go with me and take the royal pair
"To where I have a surgeon who will doctor him with care."
The pirate captain called the shuttle with a firm demand:
"Put the Emperor on air. I *will* speak to the man

"Before I let another moment's chaos drive me daft!"
(He signaled for the weapons deck to target both small craft.)
Steve went through the motions with his lasers, but in fact
He limbered up his pistol and concealed it in his lap.

Outside by the shuttle, Nick held up his hand to stop.
Signaling Renee to silence as he deftly popped

His pocket phone out of his suit while Goldie linked it in.
"You recognize my voice, do you not," it said, "Captain?"

Renee looked shocked a moment then she grinned from ear to ear
As from the speaker in her helmet Warden's voice came clear.
Nick's face sprouted beads of sweat while Goldie seemed to pray
As Radar's voice converter program crudely came in play.

"I want to get to orbit soon. The hour is growing late.
"Get those men back to the shuttle. We've no time to waste."
The pirate captain's voice was irritated but restrained,
"I need confirmation that the plan remains unchanged."

Renee and Nick were eye-to-eye trying to read their minds,
Straining at their seams convincingly to improvise.
Renee was mouthing words in an exaggerated way,
Nick was nodding knowingly with each phrase she might say.

"Fly the path as planned the way the lady has made plain.
"Other than our time to orbit all remains the same."
The gaps between each phrase seemed strained; unnaturally long.
Nick was wincing with each word yet trying to sound strong.

Renee held Nick's arms firmly - nearly crushing through his suit
But smiling her encouragement to see this trial through.
"I will be out of communication for some hours.
"Are there any questions more?" Nick made the voice sound dour.

The wily pirate captain said, "'Until at Enceladus."
Then paused for the correction as a subtle verbal test.
Renee had no idea if the plan for him had changed
Only what the warden just the day before explained.

She didn't take the chance. She drew her hand across her throat.
To signal Goldie to cut off the link before Nick choked!
He seemed almost to hyperventilate for several seconds.
Renee turned up his oxy mixture, laughing, "Oh, thank Heaven!"

Nick was shaking visibly inside his steaming suit
But then he started laughing near hysterically too!
They didn't know for sure if their deception would succeed
But they had given all they had to get their men set free.

On the black ship's bridge a wave of joy filled Captain Blue
Knowing Nick and Radar had prepared and thought things through.
The pirate captain still had nagging doubts down in his gut.
"The lady?" he enquired as he turned, "Enceladus?"

"I've heard nothing but 'the Empress' for nearly two weeks.
"Wasn't Rhea where you said our ships were going to meet?
"Why did they not stop me when I mentioned the wrong moon?"
Blue said, "They just cut the link. They want to leave here soon."

The pirate captain's paranoia wasn't making sense
And Captain Blue was growing tired of being on defense.
"The emperor was shot. They even exited your ship
"Before you were aware that they had given you the slip.

"Never mind his hurried comments. Get your ship repaired.
"You have your orders, Captain. Please perform them with great care."
Captain Blue stood toe-to-toe and brought his voice down low.
He stared into the pirates eyes and said, "I'd like to know:

"Have you ever watched a man burn from the inside out?"
The pirate's eyes confirmed he'd seen that horror with no doubt.
"That's what happened to the man who wore this ring before me.
"Just a spoken word is all it took. Do not delay me."

With that Jules turned his back and made his way toward the airlock
Then turned around again and said, "I'm glad we had this talk.
"Do not touch the cargo ship. We'll know in his good time.
"Perhaps we'll meet on Rhea. I'll buy steaks if you buy wine."

Joe and Duke followed the captain toward the bridge airlock
Then in a fevered rage the pirate pulled his gun and cocked.
He leveled it at Duke but just before the trigger tripped
The pirate captain's head blew sideways as Steve's pistol twitched.

The roar of the report was deafening inside the room.
Joe and Duke were on the ceiling targeting the goons
In less than three tenths of a second as their practiced nerves
Reacted without thought on muscles trained quickly to serve.

Steve bounced forward from his console shouting, "You want more?
"Move into the center, place your weapons on the floor!"

The three who had their weapons ready paused and then complied
Looking with amazement at their captain who just died,

His blood and brains and bone chips splattered on the radar screens;
His lifeless body in the tiny gravity sinking
Toward the grungy bulkhead which now served them as a deck
(Since the black ship set down on its side after the wreck.)

Captain Blue moved back into the room between his men.
Joe and Duke moved through the crew disarming all of them.
Steve retrieved an automatic weapon from the pile
And riddled all the weapons consoles. (It would take a while

To activate the outboard lasers from the bridge again.
Control of either missile bay would likely take the same.)
The captain rolled the lifeless body with his booted toe,
Grabbed the pirate's flaccid arm and made a gruesome show

Of holstering his sidearm then unsheathing his long knife;
He carved the captain's finger off which still looked full of life;
He pulled the black stone ring and tossed the finger toward the crew
Then slipped it on his own and showed them that he now wore two.

He lifted up his fist, "This ship is mine. The black ring too.
"The captain here is dead. The obligation rests on you
"To recognize my right and honor all your pirate oaths
"Or step into that airlock and suck vacuum down your throats."

Two men of the crew were seething mad and foully cursed.
The captain pulled his sidearm and dispatched them, "You're the first.
"Are there any others here who will not follow me?"
"He quickly peered into their eyes and then selected three,

"Get this garbage off my ship and find me my First Mate.
"Already you have caused the Emperor to leave here late."
Three men scrambled to collect the remains off the deck.
Another sent a message for the Mate to get there quick!

The Mate was supervising the repairs back at the stern
When the message came to him that three up front were burned
By some new captain who had taken command of the ship
And ordered him up front ("And he does not take any lip!")

It had been some years since the succession had been made
Which posted the late Captain and made him the new First Mate.
He didn't know what to expect. He'd seen the men arrive
But hadn't received word 'til now about what had transpired.

And so his entrance to the bridge was made with trepidation
(Especially when in the passage he saw the three dead men).
He stepped inside then through the weapons deck under the eye
Of a stranger with a weapon waving him inside.

Three more strangers eyed him closely: two covered the crew
The third gave him a stare that seemed as if it bored right through
His soul and shined a light into each darkened, hidden room
For what seemed like a minute, then the stranger said, "Quite soon

"There will be a new order across the solar system.
"Can you follow orders? Your last captain wouldn't listen."
The stranger held his steady gaze. The First Mate stared right back
And said, "I'm used to following the rules of Warden Black."

The stranger said, "My name is Blue. This ship is mine by right.
"Do you know the course the Emperor meant for this flight?"
The Mate said, "Yes, I do. Is that to be your order, Sir?"
"Affirmative," the captain said, "And here is one other:

"You're free to take the self-destruct offline and then discard.
"Your weapons are disabled but it shouldn't be too hard
"To get them back in order once you've gotten under way.
"Yes, you've been disarmed to underline what I must say:

"Ignore the little freighter. It will soon be on its way.
"Your former captain wouldn't. Do not make the same mistake.
"Am I clear?" The captain peered deep in the first mate's eyes.
"Crystal, Sir. We'll remain dark 'til we're in Rhea's sky."

The captain looked around the room, "Will these men follow you?"
The mate glanced 'round and said, "I'll have no trouble with this crew."
Captain Blue removed the ring he'd just placed on his hand
And gave it to the mate and said, "Then you're the new Captain.

"The Emperor and I are pleased to give you this command.
"Now take the ring of ownership and place it on your hand."

The man's face was a stone but then a fire lit his eyes.
Blue said, "Do not soon forget who gifted you this prize."

The man reached slowly for the ring and turned it in the light
Examining it closely, then with respect and delight
Stated with solemnity, "I won't forget you, Blue.
"Changes can be good. May this good fortune follow you."

The man put on the ring and held it up for all to see.
"The ship is mine. The ring is too. The right belongs to me.
"Recognize it now or put a bullet in your heads
"For if you fail to serve this ship you'll wish that you were dead!"

He looked around the bridge and each man recognized his right.
He turned his gaze to Captain Blue and said, "I'll make that flight
"As soon as stern repairs are finished - forty minutes yet.
"Tell the Emperor we watch him go with deep regret."

Captain Blue looked round the bridge at every man and said,
"This delay wasn't necessary, nor that some are dead.
"We're leaving now; we all have work to do and time is short.
"Sergeant, will you lead the way? We must make our report.

Steve retained the automatic weapon he'd acquired
(He changed the magazine, replenishing what he had fired)
Then headed for the airlock, handing Joe his borrowed gun
Who nodded commendation for his saving everyone,

Then turned to watch their backs as they made exit through the lock
Which cycled momentarily then off the ship they dropped
And made a bee-line for the shuttle's open cargo hatch
Where, scrambling on board confirmed that Warden had been snatched.

Steve knew that his implants could not be near Warden Black
And told the captain quickly just before he turned his back,
"She shut his console down and sabotaged it best she could
"But I have no idea what devices that he would

"Have activated prior to the time that ship took off.
"It's possible each nuke will fire when it passes aloft.
"The future of Iapetus will have a slower start
"If those five other colonies are simply blown apart.

"They can be refurbished and reclaimed for families;
"Productive farms and living space for practically free.
"If you can stop that ship before it starts to make that flight..."
"Understood," said Captain Blue, "Now bounce to get your ride.

"Gun it Goldie! Spoof an orbit over the horizon!"
Captain called before Red's men had fully clambered on.
Then with the hatch still latching Goldie blasted for the sky
As everyone on board (but her) breathed out collective sighs.

Before their blasted dust had reached the yacht Gin gunned it too
Taking Radar, Steve, and Warden's girls with Renee Blue
On the short trajectory to Captain's waiting ship
Where in just minutes they transferred and gave that moon the slip!

* * * * *

Goldie made a high-speed arc into the starlit sky
Then once beyond the near horizon took her chance to fly
The captured pirate shuttle in a high-energy turn
By jogging them around with thrusters and full engine burn

The way the captain demonstrated on their quick approach
Toward the black ship's shadow where the "emperor" was poached.
Who now was strapped securely to the deck beside Blue's feet
Completely unaware what justice he would shortly meet.

Captain Blue could see that Duke was lost within his thoughts.
Joe and Steve were likewise looking mildly in shock.
Duke noticed the captain's glance then looked down at the deck
The captain asked, "Spill it, Duke. What didn't you expect?"

Duke glanced at the other men then said, "You had the ring
"And could have ordered those pirates to scuttle that black thing.
"I don't understand why you promoted that first mate
"And flew away instead of sending that ship to its fate?"

The others looked the captain's way with questions in their eyes.
Captain Blue responded, "There is more at stake besides
"Rescuing the people of this tyrant's colony,"
He nudged the warden's suit, "Or killing pirates wantonly.

"That is a potent ship designed to be a predator
"And we cannot be sure what tricks may still be left in her."
Duke replied, "That's even better reason to destroy it!"
The captain answered, "Yes, but not until we understand it.

"There are sure to be a hundred items in that ship
"Upon examination that will make us more equipped
"To weed the apparatchiks from the system's institutions
"And bring to justice all of those in Warden's revolution.

"That captain's fevered mind was twisted with mistrust and greed;
"A pirate's heart in subjugation to the warden's need.
"I figured that a man like that would be a bit too cautious
"To employ a first mate who was overly ambitious.

"It followed then that his first mate may not be competent
"To fulfill a captain's role and thus not such a threat.
"And so I put the ship into his incapable hands
"Until we had the manpower to form a better plan.

"Though pirates are a cagey lot who run when not pursued.
"I'm convinced that this man will do what he's told to do.
"I've bought his loyalty for now but it won't last for long.
"Pirates sell their very souls for women, wine and song.

"Regardless that to treat with them inflames our deep disgust.
"While we are this vulnerable we still need their trust.
"We'll do what we must so they have no reason to doubt."
(As Goldie made the final flight maneuver on their route.)

Coming in a low and slow approach beyond the ridge
She set the shuttle down beside the warden's boarding bridge.
Precisely as an old hand with the craft type might have done
Prompting Blue's great compliment in front of everyone.

The shuttle was a fly beside the frog of Red's warship
Small against its looming mass yet potent as equipped.
The weapons systems dated and propulsion over-taxed
But Goldie was enraptured wanting not to give it back!

(Not that there was anyone who owned it but perhaps
Selenia who owned the black ship which lay there collapsed.

And so she purposed to retain it by the salvage rights
If, of course, Selenia would not put up a fight.)

His damage team had Redfeather's repairs well underway.
Already there was plating welded where it ripped away.
And mingled in a pile of discarded gear from it
Were twisted jetsam blasted from Selenia's wrecked ship.

Red's men disembarked as Captain Blue requested fuel
Then Turned to Nick and Goldie saying, "We will need you two - "
But he was interrupted by a high-importance broadcast
Across the commo-link from Captain Standish coming fast!

65   Spurs and Bugles

Captain Standish didn't hesitate a single minute
Once he'd scanned the data which someone had just transmitted
From Saturn VIII on wide-band to the main part of the system
For anyone with half an interest who would care to listen.

The sender was Selenia or Blue there was no question.
The fact it was anonymous bespoke some desperation
And so the very instant orbit placement gave the chance
He put Soldana's cruiser in a high-energy dance

Across the intervening space between the Saturn moons
Pushing it for all it had to reach Saturn VIII soon.
Pressed into acceleration seats the entire way
The time in transit labored hours (mercifully not days).

Arrival at Iapetus was sudden and replete
With acquisition radars blustering for all to see.
Standish had determined he would play the cavalry
With bugles blaring (for by now no need for secrecy

Considering the chance was small his cruiser would be poached
While still at high deceleration making his approach.)
He broadcast on their private frequency he'd soon arrive
Hoping for a quick report his friends were still alive.

Blue's response was near immediate, then Red chimed in
Both with summaries of tactical information.
Blue made his best guess for where the disarmed pirate ship
Would fly around Iapetus when their engines were fixed

Providing opportunity for intercept and capture
And judgment in a court of law at some point shortly after.
Red added that Percy's boss was hurt but on the mend.
Blue said they'd a special guest whose plans they hoped to end.

(Gin was silent as a tomb, his whereabouts unknown
On a slow trajectory shut down and laying low.
Simulating Saturn's slowly orbiting debris,
His precious cargo waiting there in relative safety.)

Captain Standish stated, "I can intercept this ship
"And board it with two dozen men who could disable it
"Leaving it in orbit with just life support in place
"Marooned until a new authority controls this space.

Captain Blue responded, "We control this space, Captain,"
"Though at this time it seems that we are spread a little thin.
"I propose we exercise our eminent domain
"And place it into Martian hands to Saturn's greater shame.

"The sad Saturn Consortium has shown their weak resolve."
Red agreed that this might be the fastest way to solve
The question of authority by admiralty law.
"Mars has every right to make whatever marshal call

"Considering the frame-up Warden's forces have unleashed
"With Saturn's leadership complicit at the very least.
"That makes Captain Standish and Selenia's Marines
"The ruling force on Saturn VIII as far as I can see."

The conversation paused a moment while they thought things through.
Then Red said, "Time is on our side whatever we may do,
"Other than your black ship crew who might cause trouble yet,
"So I would like to nail them to the ground right where they set.

"Are you sure defensive lasers on that ship are down?"
Captain Blue considered for a moment with a frown
Then said, "The weapons consoles on the bridge are shot up good
"But you can bet there's backup systems somewhere that they would

"Be getting put online as soon as they can get their teams
"Off the stern repairs which might be done by now, it seems."
Red said, "I would breathe much easier with them shut down
"And all these pirates held in one place deep beneath the ground."

Captain Standish said, "If you can disable that ship
"And buy me time to land with fighting men who are equipped
"To bag the crew and march them to the place you indicate,
"Then I won't have to search their orbit - possibly too late."

Red responded with a grunt then said, "I have a drone
"A stealthy one, which might approach that ship while it lies prone.

"It's made for space but in this gravity should have the gas
"To make it to that ship and leave explosives up its ass.

"Even with defensive lasers it should do the job
"Then you will have the time to land some men to bag the mob.
Captain Standish mentioned, "I don't have a shuttle here
"So I will land the ship beyond a mountain very near.

"Men with thruster packs will make a concerted assault
"And if his lasers come online I won't hold you at fault."
Joe and Duke looked at the captain, both shaking their heads.
Duke said, "He means well but many men will wind up dead."

Captain Blue thought these things through then said, "You stay in space.
"All we really need is to keep that black ship in place.
"Once it is disabled it will take but three or four
"Men with rifles to keep them behind their black ship's doors.

"And then when we are ready it should be a simple task
"To make the pirates desperate to leave their ship of black.
"When they see three ships in orbit with transponders on
"Squawking Martian ID's they will feel the heat's beyond

"What they can tolerate so they will see things more our way
"Abandoning that black ship for the safety of the caves.
"Besides," the captain said, "We have a package to keep safe:
"A man who claims to be the system's emperor of late.

"The renegade has implants we will need to make inert
"To minimize the chances that your people will get hurt.
"We will fly him up there for safe keeping, well sedated
"Then bring some men back down for when Red's drone has detonated.

"For there will be policing needed in the colony
"When all the people get the word that they have been set free.
"If you can, coordinate some Martian ships to come.
"There is a lot of work to do before this job is done."

The captain planned to get himself and Haji, Duke and Joe
To the yacht then to the ship and then to quickly go
To Enceladus for refueling then depart for Mars
Where sunlight could be felt and one could breathe beneath the stars.

The weeks enroute would be a time of healing, decompression,
Getting reacquainted and unraveling oppression.
A thousand memories would be revisited, renewed
And they would re-establish the estate of family Blue.

But there were still a hundred details here on Saturn VIII
Which must be handled delicately to secure the fate
Of thousands who had lost their liberty at Warden's hand.
Renee was qualified uniquely to design that plan.

The people there were used to her and many held her trust.
Hidalia and Steve were well respected too and must
Be part of the provisional colonial counsel
To help ensure the transition to freedom there went well.

Processing of Warden's thugs and criminals would be
Just a tiny portion of the court of inquiry.
Then legal counsel, deeds of trust, communication needs
And transportation would be needed for those who would leave.

Captain Redfeather warned Captain Standish to beware
Of further renegades that might be gathering up there.
"Jules' transmission has been seen by half the system now.
"It's obvious their leader has been compromised somehow.

"When the word gets out this evil bastard has been sacked
"There's an even chance your ship will come under attack.
"Forces loyal to him will be looking for reward
"And you can bet his allies will be heading Saturn-ward.

"Well, some of them perhaps. Most will scatter like cockroaches.
"But you should have some company to cover your approaches."
Standish indicated he might enlist some support
From Martian ships near Rhea who had been convoy escorts:

"Captain Carmel sent his shuttles to rescue the crews
"Of some shot-up transports and to see what they might do
"For salvage operations while his escort ships went dark
"And joined an in-bound convoy escort who speared two black sharks

"In orbit around Rhea and two more at Enceladus.
"The Martians are not happy with the Saturn worlds' status

"So they've dispatched a fleet of high-speed battle cruisers here.
"Some were sent to Ganymede to make it very clear

"That Mars will not stand by while bloviating politicians
"Spread distortions instigating hostile provocations.
"Mercury and Luna both are sending delegations
"To recognize that Titan is an independent nation.

"Two had left for Titan shortly after I had left
"Wanting not to leave the Titans totally bereft
"Of friendly forces orbiting (though Titans were quite sure
"That they had already done what they must to be secure)."

Captain Jules had Goldie mute the comms and caught Nick's eye
With steely gaze and firm request that neither could deny.
"We're going to need the both of you to fly this 'Emperor'
"To rendezvous with Captain Standish on the big cruiser.

"Bovine, I'll need you to go along for some insurance
"In case this tricky bastard wakes and tries to take a chance."
Agreement was immediate and details set in place:
As soon as they could be refueled they'd meet Standish in space.

Jules and Joe and Duke and Red's men left them for the cave.
While Goldie set the navigation, Bovine watched the knave.
Nick assisted Goldie then joined Bovine watching Black.
Bovine grinned at Nick and said, "It's good to have you back!"

* * * * *

Hidalia and Steve, Renee, and three who Warden used
Were riding in the little lounge where Nick had ridden too.
Steve was near exhaustion as he watched the warden's girls;
Hidalia was fast asleep beneath her dark brown curls.

The younger pair of girls were dozing off when Eighty-three
(The one who glared at Renee then said they'd be trouble-free)
Motioned toward Renee to catch her eye then softly said,
"Once he married you we three were going to wind up dead."

Renee studied her eyes and said, "You speak in the past tense."
A quiet moment passed then Eighty-three said, "I'm not dense.

"I see you're not the woman I assumed you were at first.
"It's obvious you're on the run - " she stopped as her tears burst

From tired eyes which sparkled with relief and long defiance
"And you have cared to bring us with you, giving us a chance.
"Warden planned to kill us all but you have rescued us
"Even though to do so would cause you and them more fuss!"

She gestured at Hidalia and Steve and at the ship
Then said, "I never thought someone was brave enough to slip
"Away from that controlling beast, - and even if you fail
"I'm thankful for the chance to live one hour from his hell."

Renee could see the woman had abandoned all pretense
Of saving her own skin and let down all of her defense.
"You're very brave to say those things. And yes, of course you're right;
"But we must work to bring the warden's hell into the light."

The woman's tears flowed freely as she cried and laughed and sobbed.
Renee took her into her arms knowing how she was robbed
Of every scrap of dignity and all her hopes and dreams
Like ashes in the wind were blown away by Warden's schemes.

Steve could not hold back his own tears brimming in his eyes.
The depth at which he felt emotions made him realize
How absolutely drained he was; exhausted to the core.
And he was at his end; he could remain awake no more.

Renee was cognizant of this and turned around to Steve
While holding her embrace with the sobbing Eighty-three.
Her eyes met Steve's to send the message her voice couldn't now:
Sleep, Steve. We're safe at home. At least a couple hours...

Steve secured his weapon, fixed his straps and closed his eyes
After glancing one more time to check the two beside
Renee and Eighty-three who both seemed unconcerned with them.
A minute passed and then he slept the deep sleep of dead men.

Renee and Eighty-three had quiet words as others slept
Until the cockpit door opened and in the room Gin stepped
And softly said, "You need to go to sickbay with Radar
"To deeply scan for implants and determine what they are.

"I know that you'd prefer that Doctor Haji treated you;
"But he is not aboard and Radar knows the process too."
Eighty-three looked slightly nervous. Renee said, "I'll go.
"It's plain that Warden's tools are in me and I want to know

"The dangers they present and what I must do to get clean."
Eighty-three looked at Renee, "I'll trust him if you lead."
Gin gave reassurance that what killed the Warden's man
Would not happen to them. They were in the best of hands.

Gin said he would sit to keep a watch on Warden's two
While Eighty-three went aft-ward on the arm of Renee Blue.
Radar was professional and did his best to soothe
While treading very lightly triple checking every move.

Renee asked to be first (to Eighty-three's reasoned relief).
They watched the details on the screen unfold with disbelief
That so much tiny hardware had been hidden in her flesh
Beyond what had shown up when Captain Blue had done his best

With very basic scanning gear back in the old seed room
And Radar's rapid scanning just before they left that moon.
After a few minutes of his scanning and recording
Renee inquired, "Radar, what is your device reporting?"

He responded, "Ma'am, I've not the bedside manner of
A proper doctor but I'll tell you straight without kid gloves."
Renee gave him a smile and said, "That's what I prefer.
"Give it to me straight and dirty if you like, Doctor."

She winked and Radar visibly relaxed a notch or two
"Look there at my pointer on the view screen above you.
"These are three transmitters my initial scan had found
"Two are UHF for space; the third for underground.

"Here inside your cochlea I've found a sound recorder
"Linked into a network for access by this processor
"Which also monitors a small positional device
"To monitor your whereabouts; but what's even less nice,

"Along your spine we see a masked device we've seen before.
"It extracts your phosphorus and slowly builds a store."

Renee cut in and asked, "And that makes me a fire bomb?"
"Exactly," Radar said, "But it has not been working long

"For there is very little of the chemical in place.
"In fact, it's just a little more than what I'd call a trace.
"I've shut the voice, positioner, and transmitters all down.
"But that's the good news Ma'am," Radar stopped and made a frown.

"What's the bad news, Radar?" She stared straight into his eyes.
"I'm not a surgeon, Ma'am. We need Haji here besides
"To get these things cleaned out of you. I've done all that I can.
"But - wait..." his voice went silent as he started a new scan.

After seven minutes passed he pushed his scope away
And said, "There's something more that I am not sure how to say."
She looked at him and said, "Just say it, Radar. Say it plain."
He took a shuddered breath and said, "There's more I should explain.

"These newer implants generate a cloaking field of sorts
"Which makes them look like fleshy parts; a bit like little warts.
"And so I missed one on the first pass thinking 'adenoid'
"But it's an implant which incorporates a tiny void

"Filled with what is probably the neurotoxin used
"To drop the man beside the yacht and one on Mars we knew.
"A tiny implant set beside a branch of carotid
"When triggered leaks the poison; in one second they were dead.

"This one has a count-down timer running very slow.
"What started it is very difficult for me to know
"Until I have a chance to study data I just got.
"Until I get the time I won't know how to make it stop."

Renee digested this bad news then asked, "When comes the end?"
Radar's face flushed white and then it turned a little red
As he reported, "Ma'am, it reaches zero in four days,
"Unless some other input triggers it, but I can't say."

Renee got off the table to make room for Eighty-three
And asked, "Are you convinced? Are you ready now to see?"
The woman's eyes were desperate. She answered, "Yes, I am.
And slid onto the table. Radar started his deep scan.

It took almost an hour and a half to scan the five.
Radar soon discovered they weren't meant to stay alive
When out of Warden's influence. A signal of some sort
If absent tripped the counter which would make their lives abort.

Warden's three had toxin implants almost like Renee's
But counters running in them would expire in two days.
A nano-worm beneath Steve's abdomen was busily
Setting up a series of devices like Renee's.

Hidalia was outfitted just like the other three
But at this point the toxin implant was not yet complete.
Her counter though, was running; it had run for just an hour.
It started at the time Renee's transmitters lost their power.

This bore some investigation. Thus he soon found out
Enabling Renee's transmitters stopped Hidalia's count
And reset it to zero. But did not affect the three.
He'd need to spoof the Warden's signal but he had no key

For how to decompile the coded sequence warden set.
Microsurgery would be the quickest, safest bet.
Hidalia and Steve were keyed to stay nearby Renee
The two of them would die if Renee ever fled away.

(Apparently the emperor wanted the girls erased
Beyond a pre-set time if they should make good their escape.)
Time was now the predator which would devour them all
And so Gin broke the silence and gave Captain Blue a call.

66 Dreams

Voices. There were voices speaking softly far away.
Selenia became aware and strained for what they'd say.
Slowly, through sedation's mist some memories returned:
The roar of weapons fire and lives lost! How her heart burned!

She heard a louder voice and felt the presence of a man
Then recognized that Red was there and holding her left hand.
Her heavy eyelids opened wider as Red turned her way
And said, "Good morning, Love," but her dry throat had naught to say.

The voices on Red's phone were clearer now but talked too fast.
She strained a few more seconds but she wearily, at last
Succumbed to overwhelming need to close her eyes and rest.
Red's voice faded as he whispered, "Sleep now, Love. It's best."

She had a frightful dream: She chased a bird across a field
Flitting tree to blossomed tree as each short flight revealed
A changing pattern in its plumage, beautiful and bright
And singing as it flew with each new song a fresh delight!

She couldn't keep the pace the little bird flew tree to tree.
Struggling to catch the bird she hoped it wouldn't flee
But every time she touched a tree the bird had lit upon
The blossoms withered and the leaves fell off the tree as one.

She only wished to help the bird and bring it to its nest
But everything she tried destroyed a part of its forest.
The forest was a splendored one in which she wished to dwell
But everything she did turned it a bit more into hell.

Flames snaked through the fallen leaves and wrapped around her legs.
Her charring flesh burned off her bones leaving just two short pegs
That anchored her within the ruined circle she had made
And then the pretty bird flew to her shoulder bringing aid:

"This forest was created for just one," it said in song
"And you have sought to take it for you own for far too long.
"But there is yet another wood created just for you
"If you will open up your heart I know you'll see it too!"

The pretty bird flew off and as it went another came:
Beautiful in plumage rich in red, who quenched the flames
With wing beats as he flew in circles round about her waist
Which brought a burst of fruiting trees reaching tall into space!

"Oh, Red!" she startled from her sleep. She lurched against her covers.
Opening her eyes she scanned the room but saw no others
Except a woman, beautiful, blonde hair braided behind
Who turned to look her way through shining eyes were blue and kind.

"Good morning," said the blue eyes, "You have had a lengthy rest!
"Doctor Haji said to let you sleep. He thought it best.
"But now there's one who wants to see you waiting just outside."
"Wait," Selenia cut in, "You're Renee Blue, Jules' wife?"

"Yes, I am, Selenia. We've not been introduced
"Other than a brief encounter down in Warden's roost.
"I'm very pleased to meet you and I know we'll be good friends.
"Together we will work to bring his nightmare to an end."

Selenia's red eyes grew moist, her head began to shake.
Her lips were moving but her throat was tight and couldn't make
The words to fit emotions burning through her sobbing breast
Overwhelmed with shame and sorrow, burning with regret.

"I've been no friend to you Renee," she choked back tears and sobbed,
"The very heart of Jules I've tried my best from you to rob.
"Enraged to see you with my brother, jealous of you too,
"As a final act I even took a shot at you!"

Renee sat down upon the bed and placed her hand on hers.
Selenia's tears ran like rivers, hands shaking with nerves.
"Selenia," Renee said plainly, "I know how you feel.
"I can see remorse and grief have caused your heart to reel.

"I don't hold a single shred of ill will toward you.
"I know Jules has nothing but great fondness for you too.
"You've been a dear friend to my husband, thus a friend to me.
"I know the man and love him. Don't you think I clearly see

"How you would love him too? I surely don't fault you for that.
"On the contrary, I'm glad you stepped up to the bat!"

Selenia's wet eyes dived deeply into Renee's own
Searching for deception but found only a warm home.

Renee reached out and pulled Selenia tight to her breast
As through her final sobs she moaned, "My God, I'm such a mess!"
They held their embrace for a moment; Renee said, "We all
"Have our messy moments, and we all need friends to call.

"Jules and I have always been and always will be here
"For you and Red and all our friends who need a friendly ear.
"Now, let me change your bandages and fix your face and hair.
"There's a man who loves you who's been waiting long out there!"

* * * * *

It was a moving constellation as viewed from the ground:
The gleaming specks of smaller ships which formed a star around
Soldana's cruiser orbiting above the frozen peaks
Of Saturn VIII's equator as Nick now had time to seek

A solitary moment of reflection and some rest
Where he had climbed above the ridge and sat down on its crest
To overlook the workmen who were stripping Warden's ship
Discovering the deadly tools with which it was equipped.

The shadows of the men looked like small ants around their hill
Black against the frozen landscape's gray and deadly chill.
This simple time of watching gave him time he could review
The whirlwind in which he'd been swept up by Captain Blue:

From memories of his first view of Sinus Asperitatis
Until his recent landings here on ghostly Iapetus.
It seemed so long ago - as if a dream just half remembered
Leaving Earth for orbit near the end of last September.

Had it really been less than a year since he had left?
It seemed almost a lifetime which he knew left him bereft
Of youthful innocence and ignorant naiveté
Replacing it with harsh experience in danger's way.

Images like ghosts came to his mind to haunt his soul
But he could reconcile and dismiss them (was his goal).

He took advice of Joe and Duke and others more mature
And focused energies not on the past but the future.

He knew the friends he'd made this year would be his friends for life.
The friend he'd found in Goldie was the best - she'd be his wife!
They shared a bond between them they both knew could not be broken
And when they were together there was much need not be spoken.

He felt he'd known her all his life and couldn't see a reason
She should not be part of him through all of his life's seasons.
He told her what he felt and she agreed that it must be.
So they had planned to make their vows and wed officially.

Goldie had been logging hours in the black ship's shuttle
Running back and forth to orbit without any trouble.
A rated pilot took her place as pilot in command
And she was getting all the training she could from the man.

This left Nick with more time on his hands than he would like.
He'd pulled some lengthy shifts setting some scanning gear up right
To maximize the throughput for the medicos on hand
For all were quarantined until each person could be scanned.

The doctors from the ships had all been brought down for the task
And each of them had done much more than anyone could ask
So progress was significant and in just a few days
The colony would be set free and most would fly away

Though many had been offered title to portions of land
By the council set up by Renee and those at hand
With legal training and the wisdom to set things up right
To help the colony to grow its economic might.

Communications gear had been brought down and put in place.
Thousands carried here had disappeared without a trace
And everyone was desperate to make personal calls
The gear left here by Warden Black could not handle it all.

The Martian Senate pressured Saturn's weak Consortium
To send resources to the other five which had become
Little more than hellish frozen tombs for Black's victims.
The co-conspirators would do the cleanup work for him.

The future of Iapetus appeared to be secure.
The Martian consulate on Enceladus had assured
That immigration applications were being received
From all over the system now that Saturn VIII was freed

From years of superstition and the renegade attacks.
Even some who left the moon were destined to come back.
But there was nothing here for Nick - he'd been born on the Earth
And needed air above him and his feet on solid dirt.

Yet there was work for Nick on Titan and to some degree
He was a hero for his role in setting Titan free
Of Warden's schemes and also for his work that made the scan
Possible to make a faster terraforming plan.

And so he knew he had a home on Titan if he wished.
Goldie was a Martian and he knew that she would miss
The purple sky and sunlight and the drifting ochre sand
Just as he would miss the Earth but they both sensed a plan

To make their home on Titan and to work to terraform
The giant moon into a world where men were safe and warm.
After all, Soldana made it big on Mars that way
And it was every Titan's goal to walk unmasked some day.

Nick leaned back and let his gaze take in the sky above.
Incredulous and thankful that off-Earth he had found love
And meaning to his life that never entered in his thoughts
While cloistered in his studies ('til by Goldie he'd been caught!)

Titan had just passed conjunction, moving toward the west
As bright white Enceladus vied with Rhea for the best
Position in the sky to mimic far off Venus' light
As only seen from Earth or dreams and visions of the night.

Mimas and Dione were hanging low on the horizon
Speeding on their rapid paths outside the rings of Saturn.
A thousand stars across the sky would mark their dizzy flight
As Nick could now relax and take it in with sheer delight.

His suit gave him a warning that his resources were low
And then his speakers crackled, "Hey! It's time for us to go!"

Startled by them both, Nick realized he'd been asleep
Laying on the frozen hillside lost in his thoughts deep.

Duke asked, "Were you sleeping?" Then he chuckled as Nick stood
Launching himself off the ground an accidental foot.
"No. I mean, uh, maybe..." as his dozing mind came clear.
Duke asked, "And you had no clue that anyone was near?

"Sleeping in a spacesuit on a frozen airless rock
"For many is a path on which they'd never dare to walk.
"Your warrior spirit lets you rest at peace here all alone.
"It shows your heart of flesh can be as fearless as a stone."

Nick had turned to face him as he settled to the ground
Then scanned the landscape quickly as he turned one time around.
"Oh, I don't know -" Nick started, but Duke cut him short
And said, "But I do, Nick. Your walk has proved you are the sort

"Who will not let discouragement by those who spread their fear
"Keep you from defending things and people you hold dear.
"Many of us recognize it - but enough of that.
"I was sent by Captain Blue to find and bring you back.

"We're going to hop to Titan and we thought you'd want to go,
"Seeing you have friends there and it might be quite a show
"When Warden Black is made to face a Martian Magistrate.
"Things could get exciting and we don't want to be late."

Nick's face was a stone as he stared back and coolly said,
"I wouldn't miss it for the world. There's many want him dead.
"But frankly, I don't see the point of trial in this case.
"Why not save the trouble and just dump him into space?"

Duke looked down and said, "Because we are not like him Nick."
And then he smiled and said, "Come on - and let's be double quick!
"Your power pack has yellow lights and we don't want them red.
"Let's get off this ridge before we both end up here dead."

Nick looked one more time at Warden's ship stretched out below.
"Yeah," he said, "I've seen enough black ships. It's time to go."
And then with youthful vigor they both bounded toward the stars
Above the frozen rocky ridge so unlike Earth or Mars.

This was more than just a hangover pounding his head!
Shipboard sounds around him made him wish that he were dead.
Whispered voices echoed through the sloshing in his skull
And he could feel each tiny vibration throughout the hull.

What was that Renee had said? The ship had been attacked?
He remembered walking toward a shuttle, turning back
To see the damage to his ship but nothing else since then.
He needed some pain relief and contact with his men.

But most of all the pain relief - this misery must stop!
His stomach felt like twisted rope tied in a burning knot.
On opening his bleary eyes he only saw a wall.
In desperation for some help he croaked out a hoarse call

Which went unanswered for an eon 'til he croaked again.
Which brought the thunder of a door and presence of a man.
"Who are you?" the warden asked, "Bring drugs to soothe my head."
The crashing cymbals of a voice replied, "You're not quite dead.

"Perhaps your liver can sustain another dose or two
"Before they give the ghost up and toxicity takes you."
Warden's skull reverberated with the pounding words.
"Just do it," he commanded, "Being dead could be no worse."

"It doesn't matter who I am," the cymbal crash explained
"Only who you are," he felt the morphine hit his veins.
"You're a most important man and when you wake you'll find
"That you are highly wanted by all man-and-womankind.

"Nighty night!" the warden heard before he slipped away
"You'll be feeling better when you wake up in a day."
The doctor turned away then left the room and locked the door.
Knowing in just days a court would even up the score.

The doctor had removed more than a score of deadly tools
Embedded deep in Warden's body where they'd tried to fool
A mediscanner's sensors into seeing only flesh
But this ship's doctor's skill was great; experience was fresh.

Warden had no dreams in drug-induced oblivion.
As he slept his blood was scrubbed of most of its toxin.
The coming day of reckoning in fairness would demand
That clarity of mind would be afforded to the man.

The place of his arraignment by a Martian naval court
Was set to be on Titan not far from Veles space port
Where evidence of his attacks were scattered all around
Including testimony of his men Titans brought down.

Rhea was considered but was rife with Warden's men;
The politics on Enceladus disqualified them;
And so it was decided that the best security
Could be maintained on Titan where the folks could guarantee

That outside interference would be minimal at worst.
He'd then be sent to Luna for his trial at System court.
This put everything above the board and on the level
Regardless that so many felt no need of trial to shovel

Dirt onto his casket or to spit upon his grave
And knew the trip to Luna was a very long, long way.
(Accidents could happen and they very often did
When justice was miscarried or the venue far and hid.)

Indeed, there were some who felt he'd never get to Titan.
Others had concerns that he'd be rescued and were frightened
When Martian ships reported two black sharks were intercepted
Approaching Saturn VIII (but their attack had been deflected).

No one knew for certain all the forces Warden had.
Consensus was that mostly it was pirates with a bad
Aptitude for discipline and loosely organized
Operating from the shadows trusting in surprise

And viciousness in small engagements rather than in fleets.
(Plus thugs within the townships causing trouble in the streets.)
But that was not reality - just iceberg tips in view.
Warden's genius worked for years at thinking these things through.

Tiny sips of ultraviolet were all it took
To keep the tiny instruments alive which Warden shook

Across the solar system much like salt across a plate
Some of which now noticed that his implant blips were late.

Then like the tiny impulses which cross the body's nerves
This information slowly by its subtle means was served
To highly paid professionals who waited in the dark
Prepared to act aggressively when triggered by this spark.

Intelligence was gathered and collated and dispersed
Throughout the secret channels to his men whom he had versed
In desperate scenarios he hoped would not occur
But now the time had come and these dark forces slowly stirred

Like sleeping cold-blood serpents in their lairs deep in the ground.
Their sole reason for being? Warden Black must now be found
And it was not a lengthy process to infer his fate.
Once they had it nailed down they'd surely not be late.

67   Trouble at Veles

They made a fast approach to Titan from the darkened side
Decelerating rapidly to make the quickest ride
To Veles on the day-lit hemisphere where there would be
Martian warships on the ground to add security.

Descending through the orange clouds Nick felt an odd relief
Even though his time on Titan had brought intense grief
He still could feel the pull of newness and discovery
And warm thoughts of his friends with whom he'd great affinity.

Gin had set them down as lightly as a feather's fall
Near a Martian transport standing slender, sleek and tall
While he believed in orbit Captain Blue and his Renee,
Selenia and Red and Goldie waited one more day

To bring the captured emperor to plea at his arraignment
From Soldana's cruiser at the time which had been set
By Martian marshal magistrates who'd come from Enceladus.
Then charges would be read about the Warden of Iapetus.

Veles Spaceport showed the scars of Warden's foul intentions:
There weren't a lot of buildings left - not enough to mention
Other than a single dome seen through the yellow haze
And scattered piles of dreck where wreckage had been scraped away.

Freighter traffic was diverted to outlying fields
Where there were still facilities intact enough to deal
With much increased demand resulting from the recent news
As well as sorely needed gear to fix Warden's abuse.

It took a special clearance now to land at Veles port.
Security was tight and Nick had even heard reports
That System News had been excluded from the entire town
Except a single news crew who were searched and patted down

And deeply scanned and vetted and retained where they were watched.
For nearly everyone on Titan knew that they had botched
The principal of journalism - just unbiased facts.
(Most thought System's Saturn Section all should get the axe.)

Despite the high security there were a dozen ships
Parked around the port to temporarily equip
The area with living quarters for construction crews
Brought in from the other moons for all the work to do.

Other than the spaceport Veles was a booming town
Since most of it was built securely underneath the ground
And hadn't got a lot of damage from Warden's attack.
All were working overtime to quickly bring it back.

Nick had learned these details looking out the porthole glass
While on the phone with David as they made their braking pass.
David was in Veles with a few from Sinlap town
After being asked to bring his deposition down

Along with others who were at the atmospheric station
When Warden's men killed seventy without a provocation.
All of them were champing at the bit to see the man
Who hatched the evil plot to kill the future of Titan.

But very few would see the monster. His stay would be short
And then he would be spirited away from Veles port
And kept in a secluded spot for transport to his trial
Under tight security with armed guards all the while.

That was well and good but Nick was interested more
In seeing his good friends and getting in on the ground floor
Of the terraforming company which they were planning
Since TerraCorp by Titan's population was now banning.

It had been just weeks since he was here (it seemed like months)
Goldie would be joining him when she made the next jump
Aboard the shuttle bringing folks down from Soldana's cruiser
And even Nick was not aware which trip would bring the losers

Who were to stand accused but Nick's attention was on her
And all his other Titan friends as he quickly transferred
Some kit into the outer pockets of his cryosuit
And ran its system checks then put the dirt beneath his boots.

It was good to feel a bit of gravity again.
Even if just one-eighth G it made life on Titan

More like somewhere humans didn't feel like displaced fish
(Iapetus had drawn his feet less than one fifth of this.)

Boomer met him halfway 'cross the field from the dome
And though Nick spent just weeks on Titan he felt he was home
When Boomer smiled and greeted, "Arvo, mate! Your Walkabout
"Furphy says was flat-out ripping! I s'pose it's my shout."

"Boomer! Hi!" Nick grinned and clapped his hand across his back.
"How's your butt? And shouting? Tell me, what the heck is that?"
"Beers, mate. My turn to buy the beers. It's my *shout*.
"Your still a bloody Earthie aren't you?" Boomer feigned a pout.

"I suppose it's true. I'm still an Earther through and through
"But just a bit more beer and methane might make me like you!"
Boomer smiled and said, "Me bum is much better this week.
"At least when I sit down I don't have quite the urge to shriek.

"Let's!" he said, "I'll take you to the pub where David's at.
"He gave his deposition yesterday. He's done with that."
Nick nodded agreement and said, "Lead me to the beer!"
"Right," said Boomer as he turned and led off to the rear.

A flash of bright white light came from the field at their backs
Followed by a pressure wave and eardrum-splitting blast.
Particles of ice and rock and dust ripped through the air
Which, forty meters further dumped the shocked and crumpled pair.

* * * * *

Warden Black's arraignment was held in a meeting hall
For public forums, entertainments and large wedding balls.
Brightly lighted in the front, but darkened in the rear
Warden could not see the faces of the people here.

There weren't many present in the guarded, secure room
Beneath the ruins of the Veles port where very soon
Warden Black and witnesses would hear the charges read.
Warden sat there quietly, no hint of fear or dread.

Selenia and several Titans, Jules and his Renee
Were present and were curious to see the magistrate

Come into the room wearing a coarse-knit woolen shawl
And start the hearing with a slowly spoken Texas drawl:

The Magistrate addressed the room, "Please stand up, Warden Black."
Warden stood between two guards who gave his chains some slack.
The whispers in the room and stirring feet were quickly hushed
And it was plain the Texas native felt no need to rush.

"We are here to read the charges brought up against you
"And then to hear your plea, before you're moved to the venue
"Where you will stand on trial for the charges you will hear.
"Do you understand, sir, the reason you are here?"

Warden stood in silence with distain across his face
Motionless, not moving millimeters from his place.
Wordless but for silent curses oozing from his eyes.
But standing with a haughty air above those he despised.

"The charges are conspiracy and further orchestrating
"Then in a vicious manner willfully participating
"In unprovoked attacks upon a medic rescue fleet
"And taking hostages six years ago at Ganymede;

"Tampering with public servants, graft and bribery;
"Human trafficking and prostitution, slavery;
"Piracy and mass murder approaching genocide;
"Blackmail of the news services; rape and patricide.

"Fraud in real estate and mass market manipulation;
"A planetary scale of ecological destruction;
"Hijacking and burglary?" He set the charges down,
Then looked at Warden Black with an extremely weary frown.

"My God, sir, these people think you're just a damn *meany*!
"We may as well throw in claim jumping and horse thievery!
"Now, sir. How do you plead these charges against you?
"Counsel is allowed and you may take time for review."

Warden seemed to stand yet taller as he raised his head,
Then with a jeering smile took a step forward and said,
"I need no counsel in this court of kangaroos before me.
"Everyone of you will soon be swearing me your fealty.

"You eat and breathe by grace which I alone have right to give.
"Now, free me from these chains and you may earn my gift to live."
The magistrate looked quizzically at him and then replied,
"You seem to have a deep delusion, large ego, and pride."

Warden said, "I suffer no delusions, rest assured.
"You have no jurisdiction. There's no remedy or cure."
The magistrate looked long at him with something short of pity
"The court enters "No Contest" in the absence of a plea."

He banged his gavel down and left the room shaking his head.
The guards took Warden toward a side door from which he'd be sped
Into a waiting crawler which would take him to a ship
Prepared to speed him quickly on his inner-system trip.

But things did not quite happen in the way they all expected.
It seems that in the hour before some screening was neglected.
The lights went out within the hall then weapons fire was heard.
Shouts rang through the corridors that people had been hurt.

Renee and Captain Blue were first to exit through the doors.
And rapidly ascend the ramps to gain the upper floors
Where cryosuits were donned in precious moments on the run
While calling Goldie breathlessly to get her turbines spun.

(Goldie had been on the shuttle doing system checks
And feeling anxious to see Nick she knew would not expect
To find her here for secretly they'd brought the warden down
A day before they had announced he'd be in Veles Town.)

Captain Blue could see that Warden's men had somehow learned
His whereabouts and weren't about to let their master burn.
The thugs would have a daring exit plan which would move fast
And Captain Blue did not want to get to the field last.

* * * * *

Gin had taken Bovine, Duke and Joe into the town
To grab a beer and scuttlebutt as soon as they set down
Understanding they would have a day before the show
As for the true time of arraignment? They weren't in the know.

Radar made the trip to Titan on Soldana's ship
Spending time with engineers who weren't fully equipped
To implement the scanner system they were working on.
This left Haji, Dewey and just Skippy on the COM's

Which turned out to be fortunate when Skippy raised alarm
That something had gone wrong in Veles and people were harmed.
Dewey asked particulars but all Skippy could say
Was, "Chatter on the COM's reports a man has got away."

Dewey had been reconfiguring the scanner gear
For Mode Two tests and operations once they had flown clear
Of crowded spaces near the Saturn moons for safety's sake.
His tasks were largely done and he was going to take a break.

But then he glanced out of a porthole and could make out Nick
Moving toward a local man then chatting for a bit.
And then he noticed six men in a crawler coming fast
Which stopped beside the Martian transport just outside his glass.

There was no mistake - these were not Martian cargo men.
Dewey knew the type by sight and none of these were them.
The suits were not quite right and when one turned and shot two down
Dressed like guards from Veles and then calmly turned around

And made dismissive gestures at another of the men
Dewey could see plainly who it was, and it was *him!*
He quickly grabbed binoculars and watched them go inside
The airlock of the ship and that cruel face was verified!

"Veles Field Security orders all operations
"Be postponed 'til further official notification,"
Skippy's voice announced, and then he helpfully explained,
"No ships are to leave. They have made it very plain."

Dewey was confused, for Warden Black should not be there.
The plan he heard had it that it would be a big affair
When he was brought in chains to face the Martian magistrate
But he was sure that man was him! There could be no mistake!

He called to Haji on the intercom to make report
Who tried to contact Captain Blue and also Veles Port

But Blue was not available and port channels were jammed
While Dewey kept insisting that he'd seen their escaped man.

Dewey saw the Martian ship was preparing for flight.
He knew in only minutes it would be far out of sight
And pulling slick maneuvers to throw off any pursuit.
And it appeared that there was nothing anyone could do.

But he struck on a plan he hoped would stop that evil man.
There was no time to reach the weapons, but right here at hand
It happened that the cargo bay which held the scanner beam
Was facing toward the Martian transport where Black had been seen.

Talking rapidly while putting his helmet back on
He told his plan to Haji and explained it meant hands-on
Alignment would be needed when he sprung the cargo door.
And fed the antimatter to the magnetic beam's core.

"Oh, Dewey, *NO!*" warned Haji, "Back-blast gamma rays
"Will be intense in atmosphere - much worse than out in space!"
But Dewey had his mind made up and blew the cargo door
He wouldn't listen to what Haji told him anymore.

"I won't let Black's chaos deconstruct more things in life.
"I'd give anything to fix the heartbreak and the strife
"His evil plots have caused. Let it be my life's legacy
"That I did what I could to end the bastard's tyranny!"

Haji listened helplessly to Dewey's mumbled words
Spoken absently as Dewey hurried his at work.
He heard the coolant turbo pumps wind up and stabilize
Then Haji braced himself knowing this might be a rough ride.

"My creative effort is to end this man's destruction.
"Then hopefully the system can resume the re-construction
"Of all the mess he made and all the lives he tore apart."
He paused a moment. "Okay, this will be my little part."

With that he pressed the key which would initiate the beam
Converting all the mass it met to thermal energy.
And that's exactly what it did to Warden's landing gear.
The ship began to topple through the beam which also sheared

A massive section of the stern where engines and their fuel
Disappeared into a sun-bright glare of bluish hue.
A shock wave glanced against their ship and tore up rocks and ice
Which peppered everything around. The beam appeared to slice

A clear path through the very atmosphere beyond the field
Which momentarily caught Haji's gaze as it revealed
A little strip of sunlight for an oddly frozen moment
Which sang to Haji's soul that Dewey's spirit had awoken!

But then Haji resumed his scramble toward the cargo decks
While pulling on a pressure suit in case he had to check
On Dewey with the cargo door still open to the air.
He trembled with the fear he'd be too late in getting there.

The cargo bay and scanning gear were now a smoking mess.
The outer door was jammed so atmosphere had to ingress
Into the central passageway when Haji came inside
To find Dewey slumped near the antimatter override.

Thankfully, redundant safeties sealed the matter off.
And Dewey had set up an automatic beam shutoff
In case it over-powered and the beam went self-sustaining
And on the ship there were no human beings left remaining.

When Haji took the time to try to close the outer door
He noticed three armed men crawl from the wreckage looking sore
And battered but he took no time to watch what they might do
Other than that they were moving farther out of view.

Grabbing Dewey's suit he dragged him from the cargo hold
Back to the central passage which was now flooded with cold
And methane from the atmosphere which claxons loudly urged
Created fire danger and the passage must be purged

Before he could get doors to open to infirmary
And so that engineering task caused him yet more delay.
But finally, with suits abandoned in the hall outside
Haji had his crewmate safely sedated inside.

Dewey's skin was red and even bubbled in some spots.
The radiation burns were more severe than he had thought.

Haji knew his organs would most likely fail soon.
He prayed he had the skill to rescue Dewey from this doom.

* * * * *

"Bloody hell! Why am I always blown up when near you?"
Said Boomer as he stood up brushing debris from his suit.
"What the heck was that?" asked Nick as both of them turned round
To see the Martian transport smoking, laying on the ground.

They could see two men in spacesuits pulling out a third
From a forward airlock and then tumbling to the dirt.
Nick and Boomer ran instinctively toward the mess
Hoping they could render aid to any in distress.

But as the two approached one of the men lifted a gun
And fired several shots at them and then began to run
In tandem with the other two across the farther field
Making toward another ship where sharp eyes could reveal

An open airlock with a half a dozen well-armed men,
A number of them waving arms as if cheering for them.
Behind him Nick could hear the turbines of a shuttle craft
Spooling up then in two seconds saw it rocket past,

The blackened shape a looming specter he could recognize
As the black ship's shuttle Goldie wanted for her prize.
It's retro-thrusters fired to arrest its forward flight
Just fifty meters from the men who fired at it in fright.

The shuttle shred the air with bursts of automatic fire
Which dropped the shooting men and took away every desire
Of the running three for further progress toward that ship
Where clouds of dust and ice were settling on those who were clipped.

The shuttle gunner further peppered every orifice
From which a laser might present out of the new ship's face
And then it hovered in between the three men and their goal
Until a team of men arrived who bagged the fleeing souls.

"Now that's a fair suck of the sav!" said Boomer sinking to his knees
As men approached and took them both into their custody.

Security was breached and now the airfield had locked down
But Nick's attention had been drawn to far beyond the town

Where sunlight trickled down through closing gaps high in the clouds.
As if for just a moment Titan flashed through his dark shroud.
And then he noticed smoke escaping from the cargo door
Where Captain Blue's crew kept the scanner secret and secure.

* * * * *

Warden and his pair of goons were quickly apprehended
By Port Security when their escape plan was upended.
Selenia's marines surrounded both the shot-up ships
Ensuring that no other occupants gave them the slip.

Captain Blue had Goldie move the shuttle down the field
And circle 'round his ship with landing lights on to reveal
The damage done by shrapnel and debris which blasted back
When Warden's Martian ship fell victim to Dewey's attack.

(It was obvious to them what had transpired here:
The scanner door wedged open and the over-heated gear
Made visible when Renee swung the lights into the bay.
Most curious? How did they know that Warden got away?)

Veles Port Emergency was already on scene
Poking through the wreckage where the mysterious beam
Had shredded through the transport. (They were hoping to find life
But Warden and his pair of thugs were all they found alive.)

Captain Blue was trying to reach Haji on the phone
But Skippy was the only voice who seemed to be at home
And he reported nothing until Haji took the time
To give a brief report that Dewey was not doing fine.

"Dewey!" Jules exclaimed, "Where is Gin - and Duke and Joe?"
"They have gone to town, Captain. I think you should know
"That Dewey knew the risk but made the choice to use Mode Two.
"He wouldn't let that man escape. It's all he'd time to do.

"I tried to stop him, Jules, and now I'm not sure he will live.
"To stop that ship from leaving he gave all he had to give."

Goldie set the shuttle down beside the aft airlock.
She could see Renee was tearing, Captain couldn't talk.

They left the shuttle for the ship and shed their suits inside
Then went to the infirmary to find Haji beside
The bright-red Dewey fixed with oxygen and other tubes
Stained where from his body different fluids slowly oozed.

Haji met them at the door and spoke in lowered tone,
"He is awake and stable but he can't be left alone.
"He's partially sedated but his pain is quite severe
"I don't have high confidence tomorrow he'll be here."

Jules touched Haji's shoulder, nodding, "Thank you," and went in
Ensuring his wet eyes were dried before Dewey saw him.
(What he didn't realize was Dewey's eyes were burned
And he could only see some light and dark shapes in a blur.)

"What you did was darn heroic, Dewey, and it worked!
"You kept him from escaping and we bagged the evil jerk.
"Justice will be served. You've earned the thanks of everyone.
"And now we're going to break some speed records to get you home."

"Oh, I'm going home all right," croaked Dewey, "In a while.
"I've learned our home's eternity," he said cracking a smile.
"Haji made it plain but the Creator made it clear.
"Captain, you be sure to keep your heart and His heart near.

"I'm no dummy. We both know that I've been badly cooked.
"Save your fuel, Captain, for this trip you're off the hook."
The captain saw a peace in Dewey's face was new to him
In spite of all the pain and prospects looking very grim.

He looked at Haji who was silently shedding his tears.
The captain leaned in close and told him plainly in one ear,
"You've gone far above what anyone could ever ask.
"I'd rather have you strong and healthy than have Warden Black.

"I knew the day I brought you on you had it inside you.
"I knew you'd be a man I would be proud to say I knew.
"You took a giant swig out of a very bitter cup.
"Now, you do what the doctor says and get your butt healed up."

Renee was watching from the door while scanning Haji's notes
And then she exchanged glances with the Doctor who had choked
His tears away preparing to step in and shoo Jules off
But she held Haji back and stepped in making a small cough.

"Dewey," Renee asked him in a soft and helpful tone,
"Who should we let know you're hurt before we head for home?"
Dewey smiled painfully but broadly for Renee
And told her very plainly how the best part of his day

Was seeing her and Captain Blue together once again.
"But there is really no one of importance but you, Ma'am.
"I have some friends on Mars but they're not of the straightest kind.
"Just be sure to give my best to that blockhead Bovine."

Dewey drifted off a moment then startled and wheezed,
Pain creasing his reddened puffy face with one more need:
"Captain, spread my final pay among all of the crew.
"The best part of my life has been to work with all of you.

"Tell the doctor he was right. It all is very clear.
"The ans-" he choked, "The answer..." then a final streak of tear
Slowly marked his silent cheek as his last breath escaped.
Then Dewey learned the simple truth of every fact of fate.

* * * * *

Bovine was the hardest hit by Dewey's sad demise.
It could have been prevented, was the view in Bovine's eyes.
He felt partly responsible - if he'd not gone to town
And stayed back on the ship then Dewey might still be around.

But Bovine's captain and his crewmates counseled him with care
And had a mighty wake for Dewey which helped clear the air.
Their squabbles had been very much like sibling rivalries
And in the end Bovine was glad that Dewey'd found his peace.

68 Judgment

Selenia's marines took Warden from the custody
Of Veles Port Security who'd almost let him free.
True, he had his spies who had attempted the escape
But Red and Blue would never more relinquish Warden's fate.

The fact a Martian transport had been there for Warden's use
As well as an armed freighter (at least one and maybe two).
And there were men embedded in the Port Security
With pre-conceived procedures meant to set Warden Black free

Created a new level of respect for his empire
Which operated right under their noses all the while.
So it was now agreed that transport to the inner system
Was going to be accomplished by a private, secret mission.

Soldana's cruiser with the Martian escorts as a fleet
Would be the fastest force which they could keep fairly discreet.
Meanwhile, Blue and Red would take him (fleet just a decoy)
But first it was determined they would all meet with their boy.

And so the man was brought back to the public meeting hall.
This time with the lights turned on so he could see them all.
Selenia and Red and Blue, Renee and Titan's few;
(The magistrate sat in the back with Chris and David too);

A group of members of their crews and some from Saturn Eight
And not a person there walked in a single minute late.
Selenia's marines brought Warden from the room with bars.
"The magistrate has had his say and now we will have ours,"

Selenia announced in her best business woman's voice.
(Her raven hair tied in a pony tail was the choice
In fashion she coordinated with Renee that day
Whose golden strands were tied behind her in the exact way.)

Warden looked disinterested in the whole affair.
He waved his shackled hand dismissively into the air,
"You've had your fun, my little bird, but now your time is short
"For I am growing weary of this pointless little court.

"What right do you claim over me? None! Release me now."
His black eyes burned with fire as deep lines traversed his brow.
"Pointless?" asked Selenia, "This is your chance to learn
"A few facts to enlighten you on how the worm has turned."

Warden scowled at her and held his hand against his chest,
"Enlighten me? There's nothing you've kept secret in your breast!
"I've had my eyes and ears in every planet's nook and cranny;
"Even in Soldana's house beneath your naughty fanny.

"Ansel Pedersen completed many tasks for me.
"Do you not imagine I have two or even three
"Others to keep watch on little birds from time to time?
"Soldana sent you here not by his own will but by mine."

He grinned with satisfaction as he gave this revelation.
(Selenia was cool and confident and left unshaken.)
"A fleet of loyal subjects very shortly will arrive
"And when we leave eradicate this little cockroach hive."

Captain Blue spoke up and said, "You've been holed up too long
"In your little hell and it appears you've got it wrong.
"Just how many ships have you lost in the last three weeks?
"More, sir, than what you jumped us with at Ganymede.

"And every day that passes more are being hunted down
"From Mercury to Eris smoked from hell-holes in the ground.
"They're the ones who scatter like cockroaches in the light
"When faced with ships of brave men who bring on an honest fight."

Warden seemed to notice him at last and feigned a yawn
But paid attention when he saw he had two black rings on.
Selenia explained, "That's what you get for using pirates.
"Loyalty is earned. It isn't purchased with a price."

Warden kept his cool facade and scoffed, "Really, I'm bored."
Then someone couldn't keep their comments quiet any more:
"Crikey, sport! Even your spooks at System News have turned.
"Why can't you admit you're chocka poo and you've been burned?"

Murmurs swept the room as Warden turned to face the man.
"Burned?" Warden queried as he searched each face at hand.

"I will show you 'burned' my friend," and then he chose Renee
"And I will show the price of disloyalty, by the way."

He focused on Renee who showed no fear as he had planned.
Renee then interrupted, stood before him with her hand
Held up in a sign for Warden to hold back his words,
"Please, Warden, let's not make this tough day even worse."

The voice yelled out again, "How 'bout a trial right now, Mate?
"Perhaps you'd like a jury formed from those on Saturn Eight?"
Others in the room then loudly grumbled their assent.
Renee asked two marines to take the man (but out he went).

Warden could see plainly something in Renee had changed.
Her eyes now had a clarity and purpose he found strange
For he had never seen her in her natural estate
In confidence supported with the full trust of her mate.

"I trusted you Renee and now you've pierced me through the heart
"With your supreme deception and betrayal and your part
"In fomenting this insurrection against our empire.
"I lifted you from ruin and you repay me with guile?"

Renee's blue eyes looked deeply into Warden's evil stare
His eyes appearing like black holes which sucked the very air
Out of the room around them while the light appeared to dim
Obscured by clouds of evil but her clear voice answered him:

"I've never lied to you. Every word has been the truth.
"But how they were interpreted was strictly up to you.
"I've told you all along that my life's goal was to return
"To my husband's arms and now today you see I've learned

"That he is still alive and here he stands before us both.
"Warden, there is nothing stands twixt me and my betrothed.
"And now you have the chance to recompense some you have hurt
"And seek forgiveness of us all before you're in the dirt."

"Forgiveness!" Warden spat, "There is no one I answer to.
"Neither gods nor men nor smugglers like your Captain Blue."
Silence flooded through the room as every eye watched him.
The Martian magistrate's expression turned from calm to grim.

"Oh, but you do!" Renee retorted, "Check your skin
"Just above your navel where an implant wriggled in."
Warden looked confused an instant then his face turned flush.
He opened up his clothing and felt softly with a touch.

And as he bowed his head to look then raised his reddened face
He barked, "This is an outrage and you've done more than disgrace
"Yourself and me but put in danger every plan I've made!"
(Unconsciously he struggled with his chains to get away.)

Renee's eyes narrowed as she said, "That one came out of me.
"Others wanted theirs in you; there's room for only three.
"You've had an intravenous diet high in phosphorus;
"A gift from all the living folks still on Iapetus."

Selenia was glaring acid at him when his gaze
Caught her eyes as she spoke up, "Be careful what you say.
"Every moment of your life you'll have a careful choice,
"Brother; for those evil things still listen to your voice."

Her flaming stare bored holes into his own like a hot lance.
Jules interjected, "Your dear sister gives this chance.
"She has every right to strike you down right where you stand
"But she has graciously put your sad fate in your own hand."

Selenia drove home the point, "That's more than you gave father
"And mother when you did the heinous deeds worse than all others.
"Since you have no conscience we have given three to you.
"From this moment you'll be careful what you say and do."

Warden's eyes grew narrow as his anger and his rage
Bubbled his veins, "Do you think I will simply say
"The words I used on others or the words saved for Renee?
"Really, Little Bird, you don't know what with which you play.

"You think that you have plumbed the depths of what's inside my mind?
"You think these chains can keep me from the empire which is mine?
"Soon, my Little Birdie, I'll have left this cockroach den
"And had this little scar removed and I'll be well again.

"Your golden-haired companion and your sweaty little friends
"May have soiled the carpet but you'll beg to make amends."

Warden paused a moment as his eyes swept up and down
Selenia with lust then said, "Too bad you turned me down.

"Daddy always knew who got the beauty or the brains.
"I guess you got the beauty," then he sang his weird refrain:

> *"A lovely little bird*
> *"Who had a lovely little beak*
> *"One day had the nerve*
> *"To land upon my little beach.*

"You do remember, don't you Little Bird, our playful tune?"
Selenia replied, "It's not one I'd forget too soon.
"You used to sing it, then you'd hit me hard and I would cry.
"You tormented me Warden then to Daddy you would lie."

Selenia stepped backward as she asked, "Please, don't sing that!
Warden grinned and started in to sing the second half:

> *"I lured the little birdie*
> *"With a biscuit on a string*
> *"And then I used a bat to smash*
> *"The silly little thing."*

Sadistically he smiled at her but then his smile twisted
Into a painful realization how he'd not resisted
Selenia's enticement to relive the wicked past.
Then as a flame shot from his back he wheezed a horrid gasp.

Selenia edged forward as she hissed, "Who got the brains?
"Your monstrous ego and your twisted hate can't be restrained!"
Warden's eyes bulged open as he doubled up with pain
Then straightened slowly cursing each before him name by name.

And then he made a guttural crescendo of a howl
Which echoed with his unhinged rage and profanities foul.
Then as his dying curse cut off by flames shot from his mouth
His eyes burned with a hatred seen by all the horror'd crowd

Who, torn between the need to flee the burning flesh and smoke
And the strong desire to see his final chapter wrote

Slowly moved toward exits walking backward as they watched
His flaming body strain the chains while burning legs were locked

Firmly like a stick figure refusing to collapse
His burning flesh out-gassing steam in hissing, smoky gasps.
Flames forced through his eye sockets. His raven hair ignited
As if to frame the steaming marbles of his eyes which glided

One by one down to the smoking grease which scarred the floor.
His hoarse satanic shrieks were silenced now forevermore.
His evil empire would collapse to scatter every member
The way his skeleton fell down in scattered, shattered embers.

The very few who stayed to witness Warden's final play
Through stinging eyes in clothes with stench which would not wash away
Saw the Martian magistrate throw papers on the floor
Then leave the room to breathe clean air and speak of him no more.

69   Help Wanted

Many of the folks who witnessed Warden Black's demise
Had scattered to the hotels and the pubs to wash their eyes
And ruminate the recent past over some mugs of beer
Prognosticating on the future which looked bright and clear.

But then the chatter and excitement settled to a simmer
In the days which followed as most Titans caught a glimmer
Of how their lives would change as opportunities emerged
While birthing this new world of which they all stood on the verge.

It was a most exciting time on Titan for they knew
The center of the Saturn system would be Titan soon.
Change would be tremendous over these next few decades.
There was wealth to build and lots of money to be made.

Selenia had found a way to get the finest rooms
In Veles for some of her people and, of course, the Blues
Who spent some time secluded, fading from the public scene.
(Nick and Goldie disappeared - were nowhere to be seen.)

Bovine, Duke, and Joe were working on the ship's repairs
While Jules was contemplating other pressing ship's affairs.
He'd lost a good atomics man since Dewey now had gone.
He needed a good engineer who Gin could rely on.

The ship's future demanded it. He'd not let his crew down
But engineers on Titan were employed - were none around.
Renee could see him agonizing over manning questions.
She mentioned recent news she'd heard and offered her suggestion:

"There is an engineer was freighting fish from Enceladus.
"He was brave and instrumental when time came to aid us.
"When this man is found we must reward him as a friend
"And separation from his family must quickly end!

"There've been a lot of ships abandoned - crews just walked away
"On Enceladus and on Rhea in the past few days.
"Association with some companies which Warden owned
"Has taken on a stigma most employers won't condone.

"So place an advertisement in Ship's Engineering ads.
"Title it...," she thought a moment then she clapped her hands,
"Message in a Bottle Sprinkled Thick with Pixie Dust,"
"Then see if it's not answered by a man whom you can trust.

Jules looked at her like she'd grown an extra pair of legs.
She grinned at his expression and with confidence she said,
"Tell him, 'Renee owes a favor he may now collect'
"If he bites you'll have an engineer who I respect."

Jules turned toward his console and he placed Renee's odd ad,
Resumed his searching but he soon decided he was mad
When only minutes later he received a brief reply:
"Pixie dust is precious. I've been left here high and dry."

Jules beckoned his lovely wife to come and read the note.
"Does this mean something to you?" He showed her what was wrote.
She sent a message back, "No sputters needed anymore.
"If you know the message it will wash upon your shore."

The message was returned, "That sounds to me as good as gold."
Renee responded, "On our way to bring you to the fold."
Jules questioned her sanity with more than just a frown
But details for a rendezvous were quickly nailed down.

(Subsequent communications brought some peace to Jules.
He was just surprised Renee had bent so many rules
To bring this man to his attention; but he had great faith
In the intuition of his soul-mate named Renee.)

70   Enceladus

Nick had reservations about going back to Mars
(They'd got a proper send-off though, at Jonesy's Sinlap bar.)
His focus was on Titan and his challenge was the beam
Of Mode Two in the atmosphere as he and Boomer'd seen.

(In Dewey's desperation he had inadvertently
Performed the right experiment to put great energy
Into the atmosphere in very tightly controlled ways
And it had been agreed Mode Two would carry on his name.)

There had been discussions long before Mode Two was tried
Of treating Titan's greenhouse layers to keep heat inside
To help the water cycle and the hydrocarbon switch.
Selective layer treatment with that beam could be a cinch!

The Terraforming business he and Chris and David formed
Had research yet to do but green lights came from Titan's quorum
Of planetary scientists; the funding had been raised
And infrastructure would be started while Nick was away.

The funding was a snap. Selenia had made a gift
Of nearly all the antimatter she had on her ship,
Rescued, as it were, by virtue of her salvage rights
And this alone could be the fuel to bring Titan to life.

But in his heart he knew that he and Goldie must be wed
On Mars where she was born and raised and he knew that their heads
And spirits needed peace away from ships and cold and dark
And so he was excited for their quick return to Mars.

But for the moment he was happily lost in the views
Of Enceladus through the telescope which he had used
Perhaps much more than anyone who rode this ship of late
Which carried him amazed into his unexpected fate.

Ice geysers surrounding the south pole were in eruption
Which, from the darkened side gave him a fantastic impression
As sunlight lit them up against the black of space and stars.
Nothing showed more beauty since his last view leaving Mars.

The scintillating rainbow of ice crystals was eclipsed
By the glowing limb of Enceladus like a lip
Reaching from a monstrous fish to gulp a butterfly
As silently they streaked into the small moon's starlit sky.

* * * * *

Enceladus loomed outside the cockpit straight ahead
The sunlit crescent textured white and blue with hints of red
Along the terminator separating day from night
The dark side glowing eerie green from Saturn's yellow light.

The trip to Enceladus brought Goldie a special treat.
She was ordered by the captain to the pilot's seat
To watch and gain a lesson in the type of ship they rode.
(The captain wanted private words.) He said, "I hope you know

"I've wanted Nicholas to be a member of my crew
"From the very first; but I know he has things to do
"Of far greater importance than to be a spacing man
"And he needs one good woman to be there at his right hand."

Goldie looked up from the instruments and stared at him
Shocked that on this topic Captain Blue would jump right in.
Knowing that his heart was good, respect for him was great
She waited patiently and let the captain have his say:

"He has a future brighter than most men will ever dream.
"And it is obvious that you and he make quite a team.
"Nick has a bright mind and I can sense his golden heart.
"You are the same, Goldie, and Nick saw it from the start.

"And I can tell you there is no woman who turns his head
"But you, my dear. There. I wanted those things to be said.
"Please forgive my forwardness, but -" Goldie cut him off:
"Captain, we've made plans to marry. Thank you for the talk."

She grinned at him and stretched across the console in between
And pecked him on the cheek with smiling eyes which caught the gleam
Of crescent Enceladus shining through the forward view
"It's time for our insertion burn, now tell me what to do!"

Jules allowed embarrassment to shine out through his cracks
Then winked at her and said, "I am relieved and glad you asked.
"Set yaw thrusters ten percent for plus one-twelve degrees,
"Warning signal to the crew, then execute with these."

He showed her how to place her wrist into the pilot's stick
Then showed her how to slew the ship with just a little flick
Of wrist much like the stick on that black shuttle she had flown
And he could see her feel the action and make it her own.

The cabin lights flashed red and then she glanced the captain's way.
"Go," he said, and then she made it look like child's play.
"Now, our inclination at insertion will be high
"And so we'll make correction when we slow our little ride.

"Pitch us minus four and power thirty-nine percent.
"Then you can do the burn and I'll compute for our descent."
"Here?" she asked while pointing at a glowing indicator.
"Correct," he said, "This burn will line us up on the equator.

"Make it happen, Goldie," and she did just what he said
To make the blue line on the indicator meet the red.
"Now we check the star trackers and NAVSATS for a bit..."
The captain trailed off a moment, "Good. We're right on it."

Captain set the timer, Goldie did the braking burn.
"'Compute it twice and burn it once' a good lesson to learn,"
The Captain clapped his knee, "You can burn all the fuel you've got
"Pogo-sticking gravity or do it in one shot."

It was good to feel seat pressure coming from the stern.
Goldie sighed and said, "Mars will feel good on our return.
"It's time to feel some gravity press sand against my feet
"And breathe some air that's not been processed artificially."

The captain looked at Goldie for a moment while they burned,
"After many years in space there's one thing I have learned:
"Mars will always be a part of you, it's in your soul,
"No matter where you choose to live, no matter where you go."

While the captain talked Renee came through the cockpit hatch,
Sat down in the seat behind him, buckling its latch.

Goldie smiled at her while Jules continued with his thoughts,
"But don't let your 'home planet' feelings keep you in a box.

"You will have great fortune while you're living on Titan.
"Both your music and your flying are in high demand.
"Nick can write his ticket with the terraforming plan
"And you can be assured that you have paired with a good man.

"*Do you see that crescent shining brightly in the east,*
"*The Saturn-shine held in its arms like autumn's bounty'd feast?*
"*A thousand gloried stars could not fill up its basket rim*
"*And likewise your sweet love has overflowed your heart for him.*

"*Know that in his heart he struggles desperately too*
"*Attempting to contain the love he has only for you.*
"*But as it spills beyond his grasp into his words of care*
"*Know that through life's difficulties he'll be always there.*"

Goldie turned and gaped at Renee who was smiling wide.
"Yes," Renee explained, "He tends to rhyme from time to time."
Captain Blue focused on flying. Goldie said offhand,
"I could write some tunes to words like that, you know, Captain."

He pointed at the attitude and ground radar displays
And said, "Read me velocity until it's bled away."
The engine burn had finished and the work was now at hand
To put the ship down safely on the icy frozen land.

Goldie heard the order and she instantly complied.
He gestured at the landing strut control which she deployed.
The captain tweaked his thrusters as he steered his vessel down
Then softer than a cotton ball the ship was on the ground.

* * * * *

The captain and Renee took Gin to meet the engineer
At Shirin City spaceport in a cafe which was near
The far end of the field where a Survey Service Dome
Served as low-cost quarters for those who were far from home.

Renee saw him immediately. He saw her the same
As did every person in the place who saw her mane

Tied up in a lovely gold chignon behind her head.
('Renee was not a looker' never ever had been said.)

They found a cozy corner where they talked in lowered tones
Over steaming cups which took the chill out of their bones.
The introductions, explanations, expectations voiced
As more than two full hours passed to discuss eachs' choice.

They left the small cafe to introduce him to the ship
And give him one more chance to change his mind and give the slip.
But there had been an instant eye-to-eye on many things
And so he came along to see what their future might bring.

Shortly after shaking hands and meeting all the crew
Everyone went to the galley to knock back a few
And make a platter of some lovely rib eyes disappear
Which Duke and Haji grilled with trimmings and great mugs of beer.

The interviews went well. In fact the captain was quite pleased
(Renee feigned confidence but down inside she was relieved).
Even Gin expressed his admiration for the man
And thanked the captain for locating such an able hand.

(The captain clasped his hands behind his back and threw a wink
To his wife who nearly choked from gagging on her drink.
The captain smiled broadly then confessed it was Renee
Who steered him to the man who would in fact bring his own pay

Because, as it happened, he knew where a cargo lay
Abandoned by his Warden's crew when they all walked away.
"Salvage rights by now will make it absolutely ours:
"A load of fish which will command a hefty price on Mars."

They spoke only briefly of the recent sad events
And focused on the glad ones and such things in present tense.
All of them were interested in the first-hand news
Of Enceladus and the latest their new member knew.

He said, "Europa's fisheries will someday be surpassed
"By Rhea's if the transportation costs were cut in half,
"But Enceladus has potential for faster growth
"And it won't be so long before its exports trump them both.

"That's one advantage Enceladus has over them all:
"The gravity well here is shallow and fuel costs are small.
"The core heat's being pumped and soon will have greater effect
"On increasing production than most investors expect.

"Titan by itself will be a market far beyond
"The rest of Saturn's system when the land rush catches on.
"Iapetus will sprout some great resorts just for the views
"And farming there is well established as we all know too.

"This means trade and lots of it with Titan at the core.
"The politics on Enceladus soon will be no more
"As market pressures sweep the old establishment aside.
"For those who make a stake here it will be one wild ride!

"It takes a hardy soul to work the southern fisheries
"Along Damascus Sulcus and the other two or three
"Crustal zones where ice geysers and tremors do their best
"To put a man's tenacity and patience to the test.

"But there is work to do and lots of money to made
"And hopeful men with prospects make two constant, long parades:
"A bright one marching down there and a sad one crawling back
"Of those who couldn't make a stand among those crustal cracks.

"The sites up north at Samarkand are more predictable.
"It's harder to drill deeper but the sea is more stable.
"I might bring my family from Mars out here again.
"Perhaps, Nick, when you and Goldie return to Titan?"

Goldie said, "The open air and orange, warm sunshine
"You breathe and feel on Martian sand again might change your mind."
Goldie winked at him and glanced at Captain Blue and Gin
But they were unconcerned and simply smiled back at them.

* * * * *

Radar had been very quiet on the trip from Titan.
He'd eaten very little and spent most time in his cabin.
Shortly after dinner he sent word to Captain Blue
He'd something to discuss and needed advice what to do.

The captain met him in Communications where he saw
A rack of gear pulled out with wires strewn along the wall
To where a microscope and other diagnostic tools
Were clustered on a bench around a glittering gray jewel.

Radar started off, "You know that Skippy served us well.
"He handled all the comms and found the message from that hell
"On Saturn VIII and freed us to do other needed tasks.
"He never stepped outside his orders and did all we asked."

The captain nodded his agreement saying, "Yes, go on."
Radar gestured at the bench and said, "I think he's gone.
"The engrams that I programmed are still there but not online.
"He's running on a basic set, but Captain, they aren't mine."

Radar searched the captain's face and saw that he was lost.
"Look," Radar then explained, "It's like he's got no boss.
"An N-dimension processor has hard-coded routines
"Which carry out the basic tasks if programs get wiped clean.

"His artificial intellect can only be accessed
"When tuned by engrams and parameters placed by a guest.
"In this case that was me. They govern personality
"And all behaviors of the artificial entity.

"It's like his soul, if you will. But now his soul is gone
"And now he's on a backup which has been there all along.
"But I don't know who put it there. Or even how or why.
"I cannot read those engrams though I gave it my best try."

Radar searched his face again which now displayed a frown.
"There's one more thing, Captain," Radar coughed, "When he went down
"He used the ship's transmitters to broadcast a single pulse
"Across a myriad of frequencies but nothing else.

"If it was a message it was simple as can be:
"A single bit of data coded on the frequencies.
"Nothing but a 'one' or 'zero', or a 'yes' or 'no'.
"Omni-directional; no clue where meant to go."

Radar paused a moment as he let the news sink in.
"By now the signal's spread across the whole solar system.

"I logged into the auto-repeater around Dione
"And verified that it was sent where ever it calls home."

"You're sure it was a message, not a glitch?" the captain asked.
"I'm certain, Sir," said Radar, "The repeater did its task.
"I've spent this whole trip trying to decipher what and where
"But if it's not for you then there is simply nothing there."

Radar spread his open palms to show that's all he knew.
"I can't read the engrams. Varda might be able to."
The captain rubbed his chin in thought then asked, "When was it sent?"
Radar said, "The second Warden Black's last breath was spent."

71 Respite

The past few weeks had seemed a lifetime to Selenia
Who, now that things were stabilizing spent her time on Rhea.
A hundred business details needed shepherding and skill
Not only for her holdings there, but Soldana's as well.

Red had said his sweet farewells, refueled and left in haste
To join his fleet at Orcus-Vanth far out in Kuiper's space.
He packed a planet scanner and a new set of tactics
Which he felt sufficient to negate some pirate tricks.

Selenia was glad to have her work distract her mind.
She didn't want Red running off and said some things unkind;
But Red knew her and she knew him and knew he'd keep his word
To meet her back on Mars before his final song was heard.

Captain Standish had been busily flying escort
From moon to moon and doubling as a passenger transport.
The sudden changes on Iapetus and other moons
Caused shortages and high demand for transport (since the goons

Of Warden Black abandoned TerraCorp and slunk away
Leaving ships without their crews so none could earn their pay).
So while the salvage operators, dealers and the banks
Worked to get it sorted many owed Soldana thanks.

Opportunities of every kind were bringing ships
From Jupiter and from the inner system well equipped
With wares from Mercury and Luna for the growing states
Of Saturn which in many ways had been suppressed of late.

Things were looking up across the entire solar system!
TerraCorp on Earth was under close investigation
Once again as their complicities were brought to light
With Warden Black (the shareholders were bailing left and right).

Fond farewells were said with Captain Blue and his Renee
In Titan orbit just before they went their separate ways:
Selenia to Rhea and the Blues to Enceladus.
(She vowed to meet on Mars when she had finished all this fuss.)

But now her work was done and she felt comfortable to leave.
The trip to Mars gave ample time to reflect and to grieve
The loss of many valued men; the loss of pain inside;
The loss of many things including her own selfish pride,

Much of which she left on Saturn VIII with her deceased
Even though she knew the outcome brought many their peace
Which reached to many worlds and even altered history
And righted horrors perpetrated by her family.

She was a new woman down inside - a better one.
And she knew in her life there were much better things to come.
But for the moment there would be a time of restoration
Of many things inside her heart where once was desolation.

Hidalia and Steve, of course, were invited along
To travel to the inner system to enjoy a long
Vacation from Iapetus beneath the warming sun
But they had many plans and their work barely had begun.

(After all their help in organizing civic life
And making vows forever to exist as man and wife,
They'd parlayed a significant percentage of their share
Of farm land for a Survey Service site up north somewhere.

Their plan was to expand it and create a nice resort
Where tourists could vacation and engage in low-G sports
Beneath the system's best views of old Saturn's shining rings
In domes of glass from Mars which freighters were lined up to bring.)

Captain Blue had loaded fuel and cargo then departed
On a semi-standard path for Mars where this had started
Upon discovery of these new implants Warden used
And Varda had discovered how the things might now be viewed.

The ship had ample room for everyone to have their place
But it was obvious the crew were giving Blue's their space.
Six years spent in terror and in searching for the lost
Would not be quickly washed away. It extracted a cost.

But both of them were working through their interrupted dreams
And found there wasn't anything that changed them as a team.

By the time they got to Mars they'd planned a honeymoon
In Hellas for a while but they'd be leaving for Earth soon.

Nick and Goldie spent a lot of time with Duke and Joe
Learning martial arts inside a padded cargo hold.
Gin spent time with his new engineer tearing apart
Every system on the ship 'til he knew them by heart.

Haji spent some time working on medical memoirs
And finishing a cookbook planned for publishing on Mars.
He spent some time in counseling the new kids on the block
In marriage matters and with Jules and Renee in deep talk.

So overall, the trip to Mars was relaxed and productive.
Complacency, however, is a vice that's most seductive.
The decompression they enjoyed with so much leisure time
Tried to take the urgency from something on Jules' mind:

But he maintained the glowing coals of these, his dark suspicions
Vowing in his heart to finish this part of his mission.
And that was the encounter he must have when they arrived.
The page he tore from Warden's ledger might cost some their lives.

72   Banquet on Barsoom

His view of Mars was more magnificent than Nick remembered.
The sunrise made Olympus Mons look like a glowing ember
Waiting for a breath of wind to burst it into flames.
Nothing he had ever seen made him feel quite the same.

Valles Marineras stretched beyond the far horizon
Where noonday sun had chased the morning fog out from the canyons
Which lined the mighty chasm's edges like a knife's serrations
Beckoning them like a lighthouse to their destination:

Soldana's house. For Goldie it was home of peace and rest.
She'd spent the last few years there studying under the best
Musicians who would spare the time to tutor for a fee.
(Soldana was a patron of the arts and gave it free.)

Approaching Phobos from behind was almost second nature
For Captain Blue who served as Pilot for he knew the danger
Of flying on this close approach with so much traffic near.
He trusted Gin, of course but he still took it in from here.

Stickney was as busy as a beehive in July.
Two dozen ships arriving or departing met Nick's eye
But this time Captain Blue decided on a better berth
With lading service and a boarding bridge he felt was worth

The extra costs for faster turnaround so they could move
Into a higher parking orbit rather than the grooves
Which striped the little moon from Stickney to the trailing edge.
The captain wanted separation for his bet to hedge

That he might need a rapid exit out of Martian space
Depending on what he might read behind Soldana's face.
This was nothing new, of course. His trust came at a price.
And sometimes truth by some men could be viewed as an odd vice.

Duke remained aboard the ship with Haji who was not
As anxious as the rest to climb aboard the captain's yacht.
Their first stop was to take their engineer to meet his kin
Who waited at their town in Noachis to welcome him.

Renee was teary-eyed when she saw how his family cried
With joyful sobs and laughter. Then he called her to his side.
While picking up his little girl he said, "This is the Empress
"Of the Solar System who has come here just to meet us!

"She won my freedom from the tyrant pirate in the sky
"And brought me on her Captain's ship to see your bright blue eyes."
The little girl gripped to his neck then turned to watch Renee
Who choked her own tears back enough to smile at her and say,

"Your daddy is a brave man who risked much to save us all.
"And I can see that someday just like him you will walk tall."
Renee gave Jules a look which he did not quite recognize -
A longing invitation of some kind in his wife's eyes.

(Until much later when he learned they'd not be only two
And his space-faring days would for a time be all but through!)
The family begged all of them to stay and have a bite
But Captain Blue insisted they must leave before 'twas night.

(For they'd not take another minute from the man's reunion
With his loving wife or with his happy, precious children.
And so they left their engineer to spend time at his home
Then flew off toward the west above the ruddy Martian stones.

The flight to Ganges Chaos where Soldana lived went quick.
The view across Aurora Planum was almost for Nick
A homecoming of sorts - he sensed the joy that Goldie felt.
The chilly Martian air now seemed like Earth's banana belt.

And he had happy memories of visiting last year -
A sort of re-birth in a land where freedom was held dear.
Mars in many ways for Nick would be an archetype
For Titan and he hoped the people there would do it right.

They circled high above Soldana's place a turn or two
(This time Captain Blue set down where he was supposed to).
Nick watched through the window as the ever-present dust
Was blasted from the tarmac by the yacht's hot landing thrust.

The captain shut the turbines down and smiled at his wife
Who beamed her blue eyes back (which gave him thrills through all his life).

They popped the cockpit hatch and blew the airlock open wide
And lustily allowed the dusty Martian air inside.

The Martian afternoon was warm, the sun caressed their skin.
The hangar crew came out to warmly greet the eight of them.
Goldie gave them each a hug then took Nick by the hand
And led them toward the house like a drum major for the band.

Soldana was expecting them and planned to treat them right -
He'd wine and dine the lot of them at least a couple nights.
The news that had preceded them by weeks was grand indeed!
Though publicly anonymous, Soldana knew their deeds.

As they neared the house which sparkled in the yellow light
Which played upon the gems set in the walls, Nick looked up high
And saw the raven hair which framed Selenia's glad face
For just an instant, turn away then gone without a trace.

'How could she be here already?' Nick wondered in awe.
Then only seconds later she appeared before them all
Gliding quickly through the doors, Soldana fast behind.
She wrapped her arms around Renee; the captain stepped aside

To take Soldana's hand which was extended with a grin
"Jules, you've done a miracle," he said, "Please, all come in."
The women loosed their hug; Selenia stepped back and turned
To face the captain with respect but he asked, "When's my turn?"

Selenia looked at Renee who grinned from ear to ear
Nodding her permission then Selenia drew near
And pulled the captain in her arms and kissed him on the cheek
Then whispered in his ear, "You are not mine but you're unique."

She loosed her warm embrace then turned to Radar and the rest
And said, "You all are welcome here to be our special guests."
Nick asked bluntly, "How could you have beaten us to Mars?"
Selenia replied, "Two G's will take you to the stars.

"We've been here a week anticipating your return.
"Now please, come in and rest yourselves before you get sunburned."
Sunburned! Nick was shocked to hear that simple, earthly word!
A concept that for many months he'd not thought of nor heard.

Once inside the house he turned the corner to the hall
Following behind Radar and Gin to where they all
Had quartered on their last visit, but Goldie grabbed his hand
And said, "Oh no you don't! You stay with me, you handsome man!"

She pulled him up the stairway to the second floor above
Then once inside her suite she pulled him down and made sweet love.
The Blues were quartered in a suite upstairs not far away
Where for a time they too relaxed and hoped that they could stay;

But that would all depend on how Soldana would react
To what the captain after dinner would be forced to ask.
Selenia would be there too, and she would need to know
The reason why they left if it turned out they had to go.

The spot of sunlight climbed the green stone wall to show the time
Had come to meet for appetizers and some drinks or wine
In preparation for the meal Selenia prepared
(That is, which she had caused their kitchen staffers to cater.)

The appetizers did just that; the drinks did their job too
And when the entre's were brought out they marveled at the food!
For there were Martian items and exotics from the Earth
To honor all those present who had hailed from there by birth.

Soldana's dining room still had the easy charm it had
So long ago when Nick had sat there embarrassed and sad
From his manipulation by Selenia's odd lust
Soldana then sat Goldie there who quickly won his trust.

Tonight Soldana had arranged a lovely metallurgist
To sit on Bovine's right who shared his appetites and thirsts.
Soldana winked at Jules who shook his head, looked down and grinned
And tried his best to not get caught too often watching them.

After several minutes of enjoying this grand meal
Soldana stood up with his drink and made a short appeal
For everyone to raise their glass in honor of the Blues
Who now were reunited and to everyone else too

For freeing thousands on Iapetus from slavery
And shining light on Warden's plot of widespread tyranny

The end result preventing (as he noted furthermore)
A TerraCorp resurgence and a re-start of the wars.

Everyone said their amen's and proposed further toasts
Which were so numerous the meal seemed almost to coast
Into a rosy glow of wine-infused merry repose
Which Nick considered might be gauged by Radar's glowing nose.

They toasted their success with planet-scanning and mode two;
They toasted Nick and Radar, Jules and Gin and Dewey too;
They toasted how they captured not just one but two black ships;
They toasted Red and all his fleet who stood in danger's grip;

They toasted saving Titan's hopes from Warden's crushing plan;
They toasted those who gave their lives by name - every man;
They toasted all the progress on the worlds that were freed
From economic bondage and from Warden's tyranny.

Then finally they toasted both the hosts of this fine meal
Then sat to finish eating lest the room begin to reel
(For they had worked through several jugs of California's best
And still had two more courses and dessert to put to rest.)

Pleasant conversation and the sounds of forks and plates
Filled the room another hour which was waxing late.
Bovine and his metallurgist left to 'see some ore'
While Joe and a musician also slipped out through the door.

Radar then enquired, "Why is Varda not with us?"
Soldana's face screwed up into a slightly sour puss,
"Varda left some weeks ago with hardly a 'goodbye'.
"We've no idea where he went or even a clue why.

"We know he traveled light with only two small bags of kit.
"And that he hopped a shuttle bound for Phobos. That is it."
Radar looked alarmed and asked if he could be excused
To go to Varda's lab and quarters to search them for clues.

Soldana waved his hand dismissively and said, "Please do!
"If anyone can make sense of his things it would be you."
Radar took a long drink from his water glass and stood
Then caught the captain's eye who beamed his orders (if he could).

Radar gave an understanding nod then left the room
Expecting he would not return to see them very soon.
He skirted through the halls and down the corridor below
To Varda's laboratories to see what was there to know.

The dining room had emptied out; only their hosts remained
With Gin and Nick and Goldie and the Blues (who had refrained
From taking too much wine) and so their chairs were pushed aside.
Nick and Goldie chose to leave and take a walk outside.

Soldana and Selenia, Jules, Renee and Gin
Moved into the smoking lounge to relax and take in
Some private stock of cognac and discuss their private views
In light of recent months and maybe what they planned to do.

Soldana took his normal seat beside a smoking stand.
Gin sat in the other leather chair at his right hand.
Jules was partly swallowed by a couch along the wall
While Renee sat beside him as she let her gold hair fall

In shimmering cascades all down her back to her long stems
Which, folded on the couch beside her showed she was for him.
Selenia unpinned her hair and likewise let it fall
In waves of raven black which caught the lights along the wall.

She kicked her house shoes off and melted deeply in the chair
Across from Jules and Renee who seemed not to have a care.
(This, of course, was after she had filled each person's glass
With spirits of their choice selected from the finest class.)

The conversation was relaxed and very personal.
Jules remarked how things were very different for them all:
"All of us were changed this trip. Some in special ways:
"Renee and I have our lives back to live for all our days;

"Captain Standish proved his worth a dozen times or more;
"Bovine has found strength inside he never knew before;
"Nick has grown into a man intelligent and brave;
"Goldie's shown she is a warrior, talented in ways

"She never knew about, but she has blossomed and matured
"And she and Nick will make a difference which will long endure."

Soldana blew a ring of smoke then pierced it with another.
Gin leaned forward as he added, "Amen to that, brother.

"I think Haji aged the dozen years I felt I lost
"When Renee was recovered (I'd have given any cost).
"Thanks to you I feel as if I've been reborn, Renee.
"I feel a debt has been erased that I could not repay."

Soldana looked at Gin as if he'd grown an extra head.
He set his cognac down and turned his face toward him and said,
"Jules and others told you there was no -- " and then he ceased.
"Oh hell, Sven, I'm so relieved that now you feel you're free."

Gin said quietly, "For some the war has still not ended."
Selenia was quiet, almost like she were offended,
But then she told Soldana, "Like Jules said, we all have changed.
"From his and his Renee's perspective it is not so strange

"That for them both the war was over only weeks ago.
"For Sven it was the same. Soldana, how could you not know?"
Soldana put his cigar down and slowly stubbed it out.
While looking squarely at the Blues he said, "I had grave doubts

"That you were still alive, Renee; that somehow you'd be found.
"I'm sorry for that lack of faith," he muttered, looking down.
Selenia reminded him her own faith was much less
But it was all behind them now and they were double blessed.

"What things *did* you know, Soldana?" Captain Blue enquired.
Soldana looked up at the question, face now looking tired.
The captain asked again, "You knew much more than you let on,
"Didn't you?" (Renee put her legs down and freed his arm.)

Selenia looked at Soldana who squinted at Jules
As if the cigar smoke had stung his occulary jewels.
But she could see his normal tact of general obfuscation
Alive and well behind them which would steer the conversation.

She glanced back at Renee who met her gaze and shook her head
As if she were apologizing for what would be said.
The captain said one word: "Truth." Soldana knew the tone.
The captain pulled a paper from his shirt, "I brought this home."

Renee glanced at the paper then she turned her head away
As tears welled in her eyes just dreading what their hosts might say.
Selenia was her dear friend. Soldana had been kind.
And this might tear them all apart, but truth they had to find!

Jules leaned forward offering Selenia the sheet
Who questioned with her eyes and took it, rising to her feet.
She moved to where a light shined from the arched ceiling above
And looked it over slowly. Jules said softly, "Sorry, Love."

Selenia's right hand began to tremble as she read.
Her left began to clench. Renee looked down and sobbed with dread.
Soldana wore his poker face but he was curious
As to why Selenia was looking furious.

Selenia moved to the door and pulled it closed and locked
Then turned and coolly said to Jules, "Thank you," as she walked
And stood before Soldana with a stare that could ignite
The paper in her hand which she presented dripping spite.

Soldana took the paper and looked up at her dark eyes
Then looked down at the paper, reached and turned the table light
To better see the item which had caused her such a stir.
The captain stated plainly, "You will now explain this, sir."

Selenia remarked, "You see, the war has not been over
"For Jules or for Renee or Sven and now not for me *ever*,
"Until you answer for this little entry in this ledger,
"Obviously written by the hand of my dead brother."

"This is his hand?" Soldana asked. "It is!" she hotly hissed.
Soldana turned to Captain Blue and said, "Thank you for this.
He held it up, "Thank you for not allowing it to be
"Spread across the solar system in entirety."

The captain said, "I thought you'd get the benefit of doubt.
"Our work alliance through the years has remained very stout.
"But this is something which suggests the worst kind of betrayal.
"And now you need to reconcile this ledger entry's sale."

Soldana leaned back in his chair and closed his weary eyes.
Selenia considered he might be composing lies

But waited patiently to see what tale he would spin
For it appeared he had committed the most grievous sin.

A half a minute passed and then he opened up his eyes
And said, "Selenia, by now you surely realize
"That nothing in my sphere of influence will ever be
"More important than the people who are close to me.

"Among them are Renee and Jules and you, of course my dear.
"Now take your seat a moment please, and lend to me your ear."
Soldana lifted up the paper then looked at Renee
Who obviously worked at holding bitter tears at bay.

"This ledger entry shows a sum paid as a reimbursement
"To 'Soldana' for the purchase of some 'entertainment'.
"Particularly, for receipt of 'one blonde, Renee Blue'.
"That's quite convincing evidence that I knew about you."

Selenia lurched forward in her chair but held her peace.
Captain Blue was fingering his hidden pocket piece
(Seven rounds of thirty-eight in stainless automatic.)
He would serve the justice if the story didn't click.

Soldana set the paper down and lifted up his drink
Careful to keep hands in sight (he saw Jules on the brink).
"I accept your judgment but I ask your patience first.
"I know the truth is what you seek and for it I too thirst."

Soldana took a drink and leaned back in his chair again
His eyes were staring at the ceiling, no longer at them.
He said, "I don't know how or where I can or should begin,
"So I will just explain what I have learned about since then.

"I knew there was a renegade of power and influence
"Who, in the past few years had become more than just a nuisance.
"He buttered one side of my bread with cheap resource protection;
"Insurance, if you will, but not too steep for my rejection.

"Loosely tied to TerraCorp but not their ivory tower,
"A group I didn't know as his was massing a great power.
"We thought that TerraCorp was after Titan as a prize
"But it was just a target by these people I despised.

"I always had suspicions but it never cost me sleep.
"(When dealing with some people it is best to not dig deep.)
"In fact, I didn't deal with him at all. He was a source
"Of services sought out by Ansel Pederson, of course.

"Obviously Ansel buttered this man's bread as well.
"We learned he dealt in human traffic on the day he fell.
"Ansel must have spent my resource doing him this favor
"Who reimbursed the resource as to me, in this, his ledger."

He paused his explanation as he set his snifter down.
(Gin picked up the paper he'd been eyeing with a frown.)
Soldana gave a stare which seemed to bore through Renee's head,
"If anyone knew of you it was Ansel and he's dead."

Deathly silence filled the room as they all stared at him.
Selenia looked at Renee whose eyes were fixed and dim.
Jules broke off his gaze and studied something on the wall
Behind Selenia who said, "Renee, this one's your call."

Selenia watched closely as Renee spoke from her heart:
"Regardless if Soldana knew, I will have no part
"In vengeful retribution based on scratches Warden made,
"Since Warden would spread blame to everyone in every way.

"If we want to wallow in a past which can't be proved
"Who will reap the benefit? All of us will lose."
Renee turned toward Selenia and asked, "What does it matter?"
"Really, this is in the past. I choose to trust Soldana."

Selenia looked back Soldana's way who'd closed his eyes
Seeming to give thanks to his Creator in the sky.
She looked around the room and said, "Then I will trust him too.
"We have some long-time friendships here which I can't bear to lose."

"That's good enough for me," said Gin who lit another smoke
Then used his lighter to ignite the page which Warden wrote.
Holding it above the ash tray, looking Renee's way
He said, "You're right, Renee. Let's put aside these darker days."

Renee turned toward her husband who was holding back a smile
Which she could tell was close to breaking, "What? I see no guile."

With great relief he asked Renee, "His heart you truly see?"
Her eyes responded, *'Yes'*, and Jules exclaimed, "Forever free!"

"Forever free!" was echoed by Selenia and Gin.
Soldana breathed a heavy sigh then beamed a mighty grin,
"I truly never knew, Renee. I've loved Jules like a son."
The old gray fox's eyes with honest tears began to run.

Another round of brandy, cognac, wine and smooth dry gin
Were poured to make another friendship toast to all of them.
Selenia voiced her regret for not trusting Soldana.
Soldana voiced his understanding why the sheet caused drama.

"Selenia," Soldana added, "I apologize
"For sending you out to that evil man whom we despised."
Jules remarked that maybe it was not Soldana's fault:
"It seems that snake knew more about your business than you thought.

"Warden claimed that it was he who sent her out that way.
"His subtlety and skilled manipulation were at play."
Soldana slowly nodded and opined, "My hands were tied.
"I depended more on that man than I realized.

"When we found that Ansel Pedersen was compromised
"And valued by some enemy so much that he must die,
"There was no other I could trust to go to Saturn space
"To keep our businesses secure in that godawful place..."

He trailed off a moment as he sipped on his cognac
Then turned to face Selenia again, "That was his tact.
"The pressure was put on to get some muscle out that way
"And there was no one left but you when Ansel went away.

"And so I sent you out there unaware it was a trap.
"My eyes were focused on our business, not on Warden Black.
"I did not know he was your brother until Ansel died
"And it is true I never guessed your brother was alive.

"Warden must have known about my purchase of the cruiser
"Whether via Ansel or some other spy or loser.
"I believe the scan which triggered Ansel's quick demise
"Was just coincidence, for looking back I realize

"That he was destined to be killed after we got the ship.
"His loyalties were not to Warden, therefore he was snipped."
"What Warden didn't know about was Jules and his brave crew
"Equipped with their new scanner and what they might boldly do."

Renee put down her glass and gave Selenia a grin,
"It may have been a trap for her, but it backfired on him!
"He had no idea it was her when she arrived.
"He was not aware so many plans were compromised.

"He'd very few advisors other than those kept in fear;
"His counsel was not honest and his intel wasn't clear.
"At least, that's what I saw from my perspective toward the end.
"Other than as tools he had no use for human friends."

Selenia lifted her glass and tipped it at Renee,
"You saved thousands putting his schedule in disarray."
Then she looked at Jules and gestured at Renee with pride,
"I'm thankful every day I'm blessed to know your lovely bride.

"Warden didn't count on Renee's deep tenacity
"Nor the great degree of his susceptibility
"To twisted lusts and greed and lack of personal restraint.
"He obviously underestimated Renee's strength.

"He also seemed to overestimate his pirates' worth.
"The fact so many ships were lost without his getting word.
"Or even that a pair were captured - never done before
"In all the years of their engagements ever since the war."

Jules remarked that Warden said he had more than one spy
Embedded in Soldana's house some days before he died.
He asked Soldana and Selenia if they had found
Any evidence supporting who might be around.

Soldana looked down at the floor, Selenia was mum
A moment then she said, "We've always vetted everyone.
"Ansel was reliable but subtly being used.
"There's no one here who we can even remotely point to."

At that very moment a sharp rap upon the door
Startled all of them - Selenia skipped 'cross the floor

And opened it for Radar who inquisitively peeked
And Said, "I didn't want to interrupt but I must speak

"To Captain Blue if he is there." "Oh, Radar! Come inside!"
Selenia exclaimed, "I didn't mean for us to hide.
"Please, you're welcome anywhere. I just forgot the door.
"Can I get a drink for you? Sit down and let me pour."

Radar said, "No thank you, I've just come from Varda's lab.
"I've found some information which has made me very sad."
He walked to where the Blues were sitting and said, "Varda's gone.
"He isn't coming back. It's critical I tell someone.

"Captain, you remember what I told you about Skippy?
"How at the moment of his one-bit signal he went dippy?
"Well, Varda's did the same and it occurred at the same time,
"If you factor in the light-speed signal's travel time."

"Skippy?" Soldana inquired, "Who the heck is that?"
Jules turned toward Soldana and replied, "A few months back,
"You gifted Radar with an N-dimensional device,
"Artificial intel which worked out for us quite nice."

"Oh, that," Soldana waved his hand dismissively and said,
"Varda has a bigger one that he talks to instead
"Of us, it seems. But that's his way. Ansel brought them by
"Just before my cruiser. Say, a month before he died."

"Ansel!" both the Blues exclaimed, "Where was he before
"He brought these N-dimension processors through your front door?"
Selenia jumped in and offered, "He had just returned
"From a trip to Rhea. Radar, tell us what you learned."

Radar took the offered drink Selenia had poured
(Regardless that just moments prior it had been ignored).
He sat down on the couch edge which Selenia vacated
And said, "I hacked his journal where his notes had been related.

"I think he left them there so someone like me could get in.
"He's jumped into deep water. I'm not sure where to begin."
He knocked the cognac down. Selenia refilled his glass,
"Start at the beginning, Love, and let your troubles pass."

She sat down on the couch beside him. He seemed barely there
Focused on the information which he had to share.
Soldana lit a new cigar and waited patiently.
Gin saw he'd been shocked when Radar started quietly:

"For months the processor and Varda were on speaking terms.
"He'd programmed many of his own engrams so it would learn
"More rapidly to understand his thought process to make
"A more efficient data and idea interface.

"Its artificial intellect in many ways became
"A surrogate of sorts replacing other social games.
"But then one day just weeks ago there was a sudden change
"In interface behavior which we both considered strange.

"The personality engrams he'd placed had disappeared.
"The fact another set were operating became clear."
Jules stopped him and asked, "The very same way Skippy changed
"When he sent out the signal?" Radar said, "The very same.

"The entity had many insights Varda found to be
"Not only entertaining but of great utility.
"And so he stayed content to interface in vocal mode.
"(The processor had pathway locks which he could not decode.)

"Then after a few days the entity gave a suggestion:
"'*If you want an answer to your pathway unlock question,*
"'*Take me to my manufacturer for diagnosis.*
"'*Don't remain content with my new limited performance.*'

"I think that suggestion was a calculated lie
"Designed to pique his curiosity and then beguile
"Him into risky projects and then lure him on a trip.
"I believe it used him to give everyone the slip."

Soldana asked, "How could it use him? He is very smart.
Radar answered, "Yes, but he's inquisitive at heart.
"And he is more tenacious than - Well, he gets obsessed.
"He'll pursue this question to the end, would be my guess."

Soldana's question, still unanswered, burned in Renee's eyes.
Radar then explained, "You see, the engrams are disguised.

"The default set which makes its current personality
"Were built inside and ruggedized at the facility

"Which manufactured it. It's more complex than all we've seen.
"The mass of memory and stored synapses is extreme."
Renee's blue eyes were dark and narrow, "Where were these things built?"
Radar answered honestly, "I don't know," with some guilt.

"Whose synapses, as you say, and engrams might they be?"
"Anyone's," said Radar, "But I don't have skill to see.
"There is another factor I should tell you all about:
"Varda took the implants with him which were taken out

"Of Ansel Pedersen along with what we took from Nick.
"His notes include discussion of a new surgical kit."
Soldana offered, "Varda's not a surgeon, nor a spy."
"He could be in a pinch," said Radar as he met his eyes.

Selenia looked at Renee who looked back with alarm.
"When did this change happen?" as she took her husband's arm.
Jules looked at the ceiling and let out a tired sigh,
"Skippy sent his signal at the time that Warden died."

Renee said, "There's your spy. The toy that Ansel gave to you
"Had its feelers in your house, which gave Warden his news."
"Well," Soldana offered, "There is nothing we can do.
"Varda will remain discrete as long as he wants to.

"When he needs assistance he'll come crawling from the dark.
"It's not the first time he has run off on one of his larks."
Radar sensed they'd missed a point, but he had little proof.
He figured it was late and they'd been drinking too much booze.

Content that he'd made his report he leaned back in his seat
Relaxing with Selenia whose scent was warm and sweet.
A general silence fell a moment then the talk was turned
To Nick and Goldie's wedding and some details they had firmed.

Tomorrow was a busy day and there'd be much to do
For people nursing hangovers to have to muddle through.
But Haji would be down with miracles in his black bag
And it would be a lovely day and Goldie would be glad.

73   Ribbons, Bows and Bells

The day dawned dim and foggy in the depths of Ganges Chaos
Which matched the mood of those who drank with its attendant loss
Of brain cells. But the saving grace was that Soldana kept
Just the finest booze so they got better as they slept.

The Martian sunshine burned the clouds away long before noon
And when the sunlight hit the windows most folks very soon
Meandered toward the sunroom where the lemon tree had bloomed
Though scents of coffee, eggs and pancakes filled the little room.

Conversation was much more than amiable too.
The entire house was celebrating Jules and Renee Blue
For they were now a family long lost but now united.
Soldana was a happy man and they were all excited.

A wedding must be planned today! There was so much to do!
A hangar must be decorated - food be ordered too!
Though Nick and Goldie both had asked that it kept low-key,
Some had different definitions of what that might be.

Selenia and Jules flew off with business in the city;
Gin took Captain's yacht up to the ship for Duke and Haji;
Renee and Goldie cut loose in Selenia's boudoir
Preparing to show Nick he was uniting with a star.

The men spent all that evening doing what men tend to do
The night before a friend gets hitched (but kept him sober too).
The ladies held a shower to bring Goldie special treats
To help ensure her marriage memories were extra sweet.

The wedding day was bright and warm (that is, for Ganges Chaos).
The ceremony held on the front steps, and then they crossed
The little bridge the first time as a man and wife united
To start the party and reception (they were all excited!)

Captain Blue performed the service with a Martian twist
And everyone applauded when Nick gave his wife a kiss
Then carried his new bride the distance to the landing field
Thrown across his shoulder like a deer taken afield.

The largest aircraft hangar had been decorated bright
And when the wedding party stepped inside Nick set his bride
Gently on the ground and softly turned Goldie around
To show what was inside and her jaw nearly hit the ground!

For gleaming underneath the lights her black ship shuttle sat
No longer with its worn and damaged coat of old flat black,
But painted with a new metallic deeply purple sheen.
Goldie squealed, "It's the most beautiful old bird I've seen!"

She turned to ask Selenia who stood nearby with Gin,
"This is the same shuttle we transported Warden in?"
"It is," Selenia smiled back with two tears and a sniff,
"The overhaul and paint job is my little wedding gift.

"Others say by salvage right the craft belongs to me.
"However, it was you who from the wreckage pulled it free.
"So it yours. The title's now recorded in your name,
"Assuming you are Goldie Hallenbeck, one and the same?"

Goldie would have wagged her tail if she were so equipped.
"Oh, Selenia! She is a beautiful old ship!"
Selenia was pleased to see the wiggle Goldie made,
"This is a rugged craft and it will keep you and Nick safe."

"You're not allowed to fly it from the Martian atmosphere
"Until you earn the rating by Defense Inspectors here.
"You'll need a good instructor and I do have one in mind..."
She looked at Captain Blue, "That is, if he will take the time."

Jules gave her a happy grin and said, "I'm sure he will.
"To get her Martian-rated will be just a small mole hill.
"In fact, I'd hoped she'd fly us down to Hellas for three weeks
"Then lift us to a liner bound for Earth before it leaves."

Gin was standing by and asked, "What's wrong with your own yacht?"
The captain answered, "That's an item I've no longer got.
"You see, as long as we were changing ownership receipts,
"We thought we'd kill three birds at once; here are your two sheets."

Jules pulled from his shirt an envelope which was not sealed
And handed it to Gin who pulled it open to reveal

The papers to the Captain's yacht folded inside a slip
Which transferred title to Sven Olsen of the Captain's ship.

Gin looked like he took a lightning bolt straight through his head.
He stared a moment, then he looked at Jules and slowly said,
"I don't know what to say!" Then Captain Blue cut him off short,
"Since when did that stop you? I am now retired, Sport!"

The captain winked at Gin whose mouth was working without words.
"There's not a thing you have to say. It's time you chart *your* course.
"Ah hell, Gin, you practically built that ship by yourself.
"There's not a bolt or cable in the thing bought off the shelf.

"There are some items in the galley I'd like to retrieve,
"And in my quarters there may be a few things I will need;
"But other than those items, these ships now belong to you
"And you are free to do with them whatever you want to."

Gin had tears filling his eyes, "You can't break up the crew!"
The captain said, "The change is coming. That's all up to you.
"You have an engineer who will step up to lend a hand
"And you are free to hire or fire any other man.

"I know that Haji will be with you as will Duke and Joe;
"You will need to talk to Radar, he may want to go
"To study up on Varda, and I'm sure you understand;
"Bovine will stand by you - he's a very loyal man."

The captain's hand extended. Slowly Gin extended his,
"Thank you, Jules. Do any of the men know about this?"
"Haji does, and I suspect that Duke has sniffed the air;
"The man has intuition and insight enough to spare.

"We'll be heading Earth-side on a fast commercial liner.
"Gin, I've never served with a first mate who was one finer.
"You and all your crew are welcome any time at all.
"Day or night you can feel free to give the Blues a call.

"We're taking residence at our remote ancestral home.
"It's been abandoned since the war; there's work that needs be done.
"And I can use the exercise," (he patted on his paunch)
"After feasting at Soldana's that bird may not launch!"

Selenia then turned to Nick and took him by the hand.
She turned it palm-side up and told him, "Nick, you are the man
"Responsible for taking down the captain of the ship..."
(She placed an item on his palm then closed it in his grip)

"...on Titan proving past all doubt the ID of the man
"Who'd wreck that world and every other thing that came to hand.
"So this belongs to you and no one ever will deny
"The role you played in freeing all the system from that guy."

She kissed him on the cheek and whispered, "Thank you, oh, so much!"
Then stepped away and smiling said, "Now take your wife and rush
"Out onto that dance floor and invite us all to come,"
Gesturing around the room to include everyone.

Nick looked in his hand and saw the black ship's pirate ring
Then looked back at Selenia and said, "Thank you! I think.
"This will be a fine reminder never to presume
"That we are something special 'cause we're never far from doom."

She looked him in the eye and said, "We all need that perspective,
"But not today, *John Carter!* Take your *Dejah* - she's neglected!"
Nick leaned back in laughter and swept Goldie off her feet
(A Martian dance on Earth would be a great athletic feat!)

Gin and crew had gathered up their New Guy engineer
And spent a couple days in Syrtis getting their plans clear.
It seems there was extremely high demand for scanning gear
And they had contracts back-logged for at least the next two years!

They'd had a happy send off and exchange of drinks and jests
As Jules said *au revoir* to men loved deeply in his chest.
All of them excited for the prospects for them all
(Across the system every spacer clearly heard the call!)

* * * * *

It only took two days to earn her orbital endorsement.
The Mars Defense Inspector signed her off with some enjoyment.
Really, it was only traffic rules she had to learn
For there had a been a lot of fuel on three worlds she had burned.

So Goldie was released to fly the Hallenbecks and Blues
To Hellas for three weeks of honeymoon they all could use.
(The couples never saw each other once in all that time
Until they flew Soldana's way to say their last goodbyes.)

Captain Standish had already loaded for the trip
To Titan with a Martian cargo convoy well equipped
With escorts (though the chance of piracy was now reduced -
Their loose associations had been shattered and confused).

There was still a docking berth available to use
"For purple shuttles only," (Captain Standish was amused)
But it had been arranged far in advance that it would be
Refurbished and returned to Titan with Nick and Goldie.

Selenia was overjoyed when she got word from Red.
The message came out of the blue completely unexpected!
It seems he'd had a change of heart - his privateering done
And they could meet on Rhea if she'd break away to come.

And so Selenia was coming with them on this trip!
On learning this, Goldie turned to Nick and softly quipped,

"No doubt she'll crush us with two G's at least a day or two.
"Now you'll learn what hell it was to get out there to you!"

(Captain Standish knew this would most likely be the case
So he would let the convoy know when he would break to race
Ahead once they were well established on trajectory.)
Selenia climbed on the shuttle, winking at Goldie.

The Hallenbecks were dropping Blues at Phobos' Stickney Port
As if they were just common folk of no special import.
Goldie mentioned her opinion they deserved much better
But Captain Blue explained to her he'd hear no more such chatter:

"We *are* just common folk," the captain carefully explained,
"We went through a rough patch at one time, but we're the same
"As anyone who struggles through this life to make their way.
"And now we're going to live the simple life for all our days.

"I hope." There was a moment's pause and then he turned to Goldie
Who felt a tad embarrassed that she sounded a bit haughty.
Which surely wasn't her intention - she just loved them all
And felt they could do better for them on this Phobos call.

"Actually," Jules retracted, "We're special delivery.
"How many arrive here on a mount with purple livery?
"A private shuttle carrying the best friends in the system?
"Nah," he said, "You're right. To your advice I should have listened.

Goldie was the pilot in command in the left chair.
Captain Blue was in the right and called over the air
To Phobos Traffic to amend their flight arrival plan
And the liner to request a boarding lock be manned.

There was just a short delay from each, but they were cleared.
Just seconds later new flight path instructions had appeared
On Goldie's navigation screen which made her tense a bit.
Jules soothed her with, "Yes, it's crowded. I'll talk you through it."

Goldie made a smooth approach and fairly smooth attach
To the Earth-bound liner, then Nick opened up the hatch
And turned to see Selenia and Renee wrapped as one
Shedding tears of joy that their new lives had just begun.

Captain Blue took Nick's extended hand and said, "We're off!
"Thank you for your service, Mr. Hallenbeck. I thought
"That you would be a man of justice, honor and great skill
"From the first day leaving Earth. I know you always will."

The captain turned and kissed Selenia on her wet cheek
Then turned to Goldie with instructions, "You must always seek
"To be your husband's counterpart in every walk of life.
"I know down in my heart that Nick has found a golden wife."

And then the Blues were gone. The shuttle seemed so big and empty!
Selenia took captain's right seat (though she was quite rusty,
But she could handle commo and assist her with the NAV's)
Then they were off to join their cruiser, glad for friends they had.

* * * * *

The liner entered Earth orbit and docked at Von Braun Station
Where shuttles clustered bee-like on a hive from many nations
Readied to de-orbit passengers and goods for fares
Down into Earth's heavy, thick and moisture-laden air.

Long before they entered orbit Jules had prearranged
The purchase of a small aircraft which had plenty of range
To take them from the spaceport to their ancestral estate.
It was fueled and waiting for them for their quick escape

From all the bustle of the crowded spaceport where they sat
An hour in Earth's crushing gravity and hot climate.
But soon they were accustomed and could walk (though clumsily),
And had their few bags of possessions loaded for a fee.

The flight was smooth and more exhilarating than they thought!
Jules reduced their speed and altitude by quite a lot
When they approached the land around their family estate
Called "Castle West" in years gone by, but nothing as of late.

They circled slowly watching closely from high in the air
With the windows open and hot wind whipping their hair
(Which was a luxury that neither of them had enjoyed
In years working in space but now they both were unemployed!)

The grounds around the place looked like they'd very little care.
The buildings stood they way they had since stones were carried there.
He set the aircraft down upon the tall grass near the stables
With plans to roll it inside after he was strong and able.

(He would need some acclimation to Earth's gravity.)
And there was much to do inside to make the place ready
To live again. They would bring the castle back to life!
He'd make the place a home to raise his family and wife.

Renee was thrilled to once again walk through the wooden gates
And through the courtyard where so many legends had been made.
The simple things they brought would be enough to see them through
Until they'd re-provision in another day or two.

That evening Renee opened a vault where, stored within
Were artifacts and heirlooms placed there by the Blue women
Who bore the sons and daughters of the men they loved and wed
And taught their generations of the lives the family led.

Folded carefully and stored in wraps with greatest care
She found the ancient blanket embroidered with golden hair.
Legend said its pattern was the flag of a great state
Which disappeared for many generations now of late.

The family had not forgotten. Many were the tales
Recorded for posterity so each child was regaled
With fine examples of the honored people of the past
Who stood and fought so freedom on the earth would ever last.

The legend of the blanket stitched with dragon in a heart
Which flew above the castle when the first Blues did their part
To free the land from great oppression and the tyranny
Of one black-hearted tyrant whose end came violently

Was one which Renee loved and kept as treasure held inside
The confines of her heart when she first read it as a bride.
And now it was her turn to be the heart of this old home
And bear the sons and daughters made of captain's blood and bone.

In a tower's closet was a cradle stored within.
She brought the cradle down and put the ancient blanket in.

Placing her right hand upon the woven golden hair
She focused on that memory and offered up a prayer.

She offered up a promise too - that she would teach her sons
To honor their traditions and to be the noble ones.
She'd teach her daughters to be ladies, moral and upright,
Industrious and courteous; to shine with inner light.

She placed the cradle in their chamber while Jules was outside
But he came quietly and saw her standing there beside
The little bed which rocked him and his father before him
And knew the change of life expected truly would begin.

He took his lover by the hand and led her in slow dance,
Both of them enraptured by the depths of their romance,
And vowed in wordless language what they needn't vow at all
For they were bound forever by their hearts' insistent call. ♥

Epilog

It was a scrappy freighter Varda chose to climb aboard.
The crew was light on cargo and was heading Triton-ward,
With mostly pre-fab dome sections of Martian manufacture
And pallets of Earth's grain products stacked in its superstructure.

The shifty crew did not ask questions when he paid the fare
In Martian gold (with bonus if they quickly got them there).
They didn't give a second look to his two bags of kit
Nor his cloaked companion who seemed mostly out of it.

(Though later in the voyage one man tried to get too friendly
So Varda's young companion broke his wrist and told him plainly
That, "This redhead is not available for frisky play."
After laughing at their damaged mate they stayed away.)

Varda had been focused on completing the implant
Within the woman's body which was his new variant
Of energy conversion and adaptive camouflage
To keep the cargo in her chest unseen and safely lodged.

The N-dimension processor was running on its own.
Varda volunteered to host it and be its new home,
But it had made insistence that a younger specimen
Would be a better candidate, *'And make it a woman.'*

Varda had no trouble with recruiting one to be
The host for this experiment from University.
Rose was made an orphan by the Terra-Luna war
And showed great skill in science with desire to explore.

She had no deep attachments (though she was a pretty thing)
Focused on her academics and martial dancing,
The thought of getting extra credit if she volunteered
And perhaps some travel made her glad to disappear.

And that is what she did. Varda explained what he would do:
Implant the artificial intellect and hook it to
Her spinal column to provide advanced computing skills
And faster reflexes which would obey her every will.

The surgery went well (with N-Dimension's firm instruction)
He'd cloned the cloaking implant Radar brought and tested function.
Initial healing had been quick and within just two days
She was good to board a shuttle; then they were away.

The processor had indicated Proteus would be
Their destination to visit this new facility.
An ugly little moon of Neptune, lonely and remote
Which only made it more attractive to get Varda's vote.

They'd catch a chartered shuttle when they made landfall at Triton.
Varda would pay extra if the shuttle crew were frightened
For there were many rumors of pirate activity
Near the little moon and it was best to leave it be.

The weeks they spent in transit were enough for nano-bots
To heal and strengthen up the new implants which Rose had got.
She asked a question the last day which now seemed moot and strange.
It caused Varda to sense her personality had changed:

"Varda, have you felt no moral issues about this?"
(She lithely leaned his way and gave his cheek a little kiss.)
"No," he said, "I have not. This is research at its best.
"Finding where the hardware comes from negates all the rest."

"Varda, you're the definition of 'inquisitive';
"You'll ever be the scientist as long as you may live."
Varda said, "Ah, Rose, I think you're very much like that."
"Rose..." she spoke her name. He saw her irises contract.

"Rose," she said one time again, "It doesn't seem the same.
"I feel I'm a new person now, and I need a new name!"
She raised her arms above her head and did a pirouette.
"I love the feel of this new body! And there's much more yet!"

She shivered with excitement and said, "Wanda, I believe."
"Wanda?" Varda asked her as she writhed in sensuous glee,
Luxuriously running fingers through her thick red mane.
"Yes!" she smiled and said, "Because I Wanda nice new name!"

The pun was lost on Varda who uncomfortably smiled.
This appeared a feature of the engrams pre-compiled.

"It's humor, Varda. You should learn to lighten and relax.
"Wanda it shall be I think. Wanda -- Wanda Black!"

She would find new friends on Triton and make a fresh start.
She knew where to find them too - was stored in her new heart.
So as they neared the landing field she slipped around his back
And took a wrench from off a bench and gave his head a whack.

The freighter crew would find him long after she disappeared
And there would be no record that she'd ever traveled here.
If someone had been near they'd hear her singing soft and sweet:
"A lovely little bird who had a lovely little beak..."

ET CETERA

Appendix A

List of Principal Characters

Nicholas (Nick) Hallenbeck
Studious and talented but young and naive engineer, hired as a contractor for Terra Corporation he is embarking on his first trip away from Earth.

Captain Jules Blue
A resourceful commander in the recent wars, he currently works in general space transport and as a part time smuggler for the gray market to finance and facilitate his search for his missing wife.

Renee Blue
Captain Blue's wife. A resourceful native of Earth who was taken captive in a pirate raid on a damaged fleet near the end of the Terra-Luna war.

Warden Black
An ambitious executive of a division of Terra Corporation who disappeared after the Terra-Luna war. He longs for the lost glory days of the TerraCorp empire.

Selenia
A beautiful and talented business woman and a veteran of the Terra-Luna war, she is the business partner of a gray market tycoon on Mars (Soldana).

Soldana
An early pioneer and wealthy patriarch of Mars who has controlling interests in many businesses. He is known for his ability to get things done by questionable means.

Captain "Red" Redfeather
A longtime fellow warrior and friend of Captain Blue, currently doing mercenary services to bring pirates and renegades to justice.

Captain Percival Standish
A onetime captain of a tourist ship, he was falsely discredited and fired from the tourist company. Currently works odd assignments for a small freight operation owned by Soldana.

Ansel Pederson
A logistics man in the employ of Soldana of Mars.

Goldie
A bright and talented young musician in the household of Soldana on Mars.

Hidalia
The close friend and companion of Renee Blue, she was taken in a pirate raid on Ceres and sold to Warden Black.

Sergeant Steve
Hidalia's romantic partner and a veteran of the Survey Corps who involuntarily works for Warden Black.

Captain Blue's Crew

Sven (Gin) Olsen
The First Mate and Senior Engineer who has been with Captain Blue for many years.

Dr. Haji al Hawija
A highly educated and skilled physician and culinary practitioner currently serving as Ship's Doctor and Cook for the crew of Captain Blue.

Duke
Grew up on a ranch on Earth and spent many years in the Survey Corps before the Terra-Luna war. Currently employed as a crewman of Captain Blue.

Joe
Weapons expert and talented Special Forces operative currently employed as a crewman of Captain Blue.

Bovine
A husky mining engineer and all-around rigger currently employed as a crewman of Captain Blue.

Dewey
A young but talented Atomics Technician currently employed as a crewman of Captain Blue.

Residents of Titan

Jonesy
Jonesy's not Australian, he's Titan! A hopeful and tenacious pioneer on Titan, Jonesy is the owner of a small ranch and restaurant in Sinlap Town who, like all Titans, longs for progress in the terra-formation and further colonization of Titan.

Boomer
Young farmer currently working odd jobs in Sinlap Town on Titan. He also works as part time kitchen help at Jonesy's Bar and Grill.

Chris
A young planetary scientist recruited by Terra Corporation for work in a facility near Sinlap Town, Titan.

David
Friend and workmate of Chris, David is a young but outspoken atmospheric scientist and terraforming engineer recruited by Terra Corporation for work in a facility near Sinlap Town, Titan.

Pistol-Packer
A self-appointed but well-liked peace officer in Sinlap Town. Generally acknowledged to be a leader of the local militia.

Dr. Bordeaux
Appointed by the Terra Corporation Headquarters on Earth to be Chief Scientist for the TerraCorp facilities on Titan.

Appendix B

Australian Slang as Used on Titan

Ace!	Excellent! Very good!
Arvo	Afternoon
Banger	Sausage
Barby	Barbecue grill
Barney	Argument
Big bikkies	High cost, a lot of money
Big Mobs	Loads, a lot of
Big night	Good time out with friends.
Biscuits	Cookies
Bloke	Guy or man
Bloody	Very
Bloody hell!	Exclamation of frustration
Bloody oath!	It's true! Stresses an opinion.
Blow in	Uninvited guest
Blue	Argument, fight
Bodgy	Poor quality
Bonzer	Great, a ripper
Bottler	Something excellent
Buckley's chance	No chance
Burl (give a)	Try it out, have a go at it.
Cark it	To die, stop working
Cheeky	Brash, smart-alecky
Chocka	Full up
Chook	Chicken
Come a gutser	Bad mistake or have an accident
Come good	Turn out ok
Cooee, not within	Far away
Corker	Good, excellent, great.
Cost big bikkies	Expensive
Cotton onto	Catch on, suddenly understand
Cracker	Something very good; the "cracker of the day."
Cream, to	Defeat by a large margin
Crikey!	Wow!
Crim	Criminal, thief
Crook	Crazy, mad, sick.

Crumpet	Female, nubile and beautiful.
Dead set	True, the truth
Dinkum, fair dinkum	Real, genuine
Dinky-di	Real, genuine.
Docket	Bill or receipt
Dunny	Outhouse, outdoor toilet.
Fair go	A chance, a shot at.
Fair suck of the sav!	Exclamation of awe or disbelief.
Flat out	Busy. To describe how busy one is.
Furphy	Rumor
Fussed	Bothered. "I just couldn't be fussed with it,"
G'Day	Hello!
Get stuffed	Piss off, get lost, go away
Give it a burl	Try it, have a go
Gone walkabout	Lost, can't be found
Good oil	Useful information, a good idea, the truth
Good onya	Well done
Half your luck	Congratulations
Hard yakka	Hard work
Heaps	A lot. "Thanks heaps!"
Knackered	Tired, exhausted
Knock back	Refuse
London to a brick	Absolute certainty
Loo	Restroom, toilet
Mate	Friend, companion
Mate's rate	Discounted price for/from a friend.
Middy	Middle-sized beer glass. A middy contains 10 oz.
No worries	No problem. Don't worry about it
Ocker	Person with poor manners or social skills.
Piece of piss	Easy task
Pig's arse!	I don't agree
Piss off	Go away, get stuffed, get lost
Pissed	Drunk, very
Pissed off	Angry
Plonk	Cheap liquor or wine.
Porkies	Lies
Pozzy	Position
Rack off	Get lost! Get out of here!
Reckon	Figure, think, assume.
Reckon!	Certainly, for sure
Ridgy-didge	Original, genuine
Right	Okay

Ripper	Great, something good.
Rock up	Arrive or show up.
Rooted	Ruined, broken
Ropeable	Angry, very.
Sanger	Sandwich
Schooner	Large beer glass. A pint or more.
She'll be apples	It will be all right
She'll be right	It will be all right
Shout	Someone's turn to buy a round of drinks.
Smashed	Very tired
Spit the dummy	To get upset or throw a fit.
Sport	Like mate, but often said with belligerence.
Stoked	Very pleased
Strewth	Exclamation of emphasis. "It's God's Truth."
Strine	Accent of Australian English.
Stuffed, I'll be	Expression of surprise.
The lot	All of it.
Too right	Definitely
Tosser	Incompetent person, idiot, useless
Tucker	Food
Wanker	Someone who masturbates excessively.
Whinge	Annoying complaining.
Wobbly	Excitable or erratic behavior
Yeew!	Expression of excitement
Yobbo	Hick, bumpkin, boor, uncouth
Zack, not worth a	Not worth anything

Glossary

3C	Carbon Corner Cube. Fictional anti-laser defensive coating."
Aaru	A region on Titan, a moon of Saturn."
accelerant	A flammable substance, such as gasoline, alcohol, etc."
Afekan	A 70-mile diameter crater on Titan, a moon of Saturn."
Amazonis	A region on Mars.
antimatter	Matter composed of antiparticles. Collision of a particle with an antiparticle results in mutual annihilation with the release of high levels of intense gamma radiation.
apoapsis	The far point of an elliptical orbit.
APU	Auxiliary Power Unit
Ascraeus Mons	A large extinct volcano in the Tharsis region of Mars.
asteroid	A minor planet around the sun. The majority of the minor planets circle the sun between the orbits of Mars and Jupiter.
Aurora Planum	A region on Mars.
Barsoom	The famous fictional native name for the planet Mars from the writings of Edgar Rice Boroughs.
biomimicry	A mechanical device that mimics a biological function.
black ship	A fictional spacecraft built with advanced stealth technology, commonly used by pirates and renegades.
Borealis	A region on Mars.
Caladan Planitia	A large plain on Titan, a moon of Saturn.
Callisto	One of the larger moons of Jupiter (Jupiter IV).
carbon disulfide	A compound known to be a solvent for white phosphorus.
Celadon	A river valley on Titan.
Ceres	The largest of the minor planets, it circles the sun in the main belt of asteroids between the orbits of Mars and Jupiter
Cheyenne	A northern plains tribe of Native Americans.
Chryse	A region on Mars.
CO2	carbon dioxide

cosmic rays	High energy radiation primarily originating from stellar explosions and galactic nuclei which is mainly composed of high energy protons and atomic nuclei.
Crux	A stellar constellation also known as the Southern Cross.
cryosuit	A protective suit worn in extremely cold environments. More protective than a pressure suit.
cryogenic	Extremely low temperatures (below -150 C or -240 F and colder.
DaVinci crater	A large, ancient crater on Mars. Fictional site of a major space port.
Deimos	Outermost of the two moons of Mars.
Dejah Thoris	A famous character from the fictional writings of Edgar Rice Burroughs: Princess of the city-state of Helium on Barsoom (Mars), she was alleged to be the most beautiful woman in the solar system and the wife of John Carter, Warlord of Mars."
Dilmun	A region on Titan, a moon of Saturn."
Dione	A moon of Saturn (Saturn IV).
Doppler shift	The change in observed frequency or wavelength of a moving emitter (or observer).
Drake equation	A proposed formula for the probability of life in the universe beyond Earth.
Ecliptic	The apparent path across the sky traveled by the Sun throughout the year, corresponding to the plane of the Earth's orbit around the sun."
Elysium	A region on Mars.
Enceladus	A moon of Saturn (Saturn II).
Eris	A dwarf planet of the Kuiper belt similar in size to Pluto, it has one known moon (Dysnomia).
Erythraeum	A region on Mars.
Europa	A moon of Jupiter (Jupiter II).
eutectic	The property of a compound of materials that will melt or solidify at a temperature lower than that of the individual elements of the compound.
F ring	Saturn's outermost major ring.
Falsaron	A 260-mile diameter crater on Iapetus, a moon of Saturn.
Fensal	A region on Titan, a moon of Saturn.
Forseti	A 70-mile diameter crater on Titan, a moon of Saturn.

full nelson   A wrestling hold consisting of a double shoulder lock used to control one's opponent.

G or Gravity   The gravitational force where Earth's gravity = 1. The acceleration of an object in a gravitational field of one G = 9.80665 meters per second squared or 32.174 feet per second squared. (G=32.174 ft/s^2).

gamma ray   Gamma rays are extremely short wavelength, high-energy electromagnetic radiation resulting from radioactive decay.

Ganges, Erythraeum   A large canyon on Mars.

Ganymede   The largest moon of Jupiter (Jupiter III) and the largest moon in the solar system.

Geiger tube   A device used for the detection of atomic radiation.

Hellas   A low-altitude region on Mars.

hydrazine   A hydride used in rocket fuels.

hydrologic   Regarding the study of the planetary distribution and movement of water.

hydroponics   The practice of or equipment for growing plants in a liguid medium.

Hypatia   A 24-mile diameter crater on the Moon.

Iapetus   A moon of Saturn (Saturn VIII).

inclination (of orbit)   The tilt of an orbit in relation to a fixed plane, such as a planet's equator or the ecliptic.

Inmar   The fictional largest settlement on Saturn's moon Rhea.

Io   A moon of Jupiter (Jupiter I).

Isidis   A region on Mars.

John Carter   A famous character from the fictional writings of Edgar Rice Burroughs: John Carter was the Warlord of Mars and husband of Dejah Thoris, Princess of Helium.

Jovian   Having to do with Jupiter.

Jupiter   The largest planet of the solar system and the fifth major planet from the sun.

Kelvin   A thermal scale with its zero point at absolute zero (-273 C or -460 F) incrementing degrees of the same magnitude as the Celsius scale.

Kracken Sea   A hydrocarbon sea in the northern hemisphere of Titan.

Kuiper belt   Similar to the asteroid belt between the orbits of Mars and Jupiter, the Kuiper belt contains many comets and a number of dwarf planets and extends roughly from the orbit of Neptune out to 50 Sun-Earth distance units.

Kumbaru Sinus A region on Titan, a moon of Saturn.

Lagrange or **Langrangian points** Numbered L1 through L5, Lagrange points are positions in the orbital plane of two bodies where their gravitational forces act equally on a smaller body, allowing the small body to remain in a stable position relative to the two larger ones. There are five such points, the two stable ones forming an equilateral triangle with the larger bodies and the unstable points located on a line through the main bodies.

lidar   Similar in function to radar but utilizing pulses of laser light instead of radio waves.

Ligeia   Northern area of Titan. Fictional site of a fuel production outpost.

limb   The apparent edge of the visible disk of a celestial object such as the sun, moon or planets.

Luna   Earth's moon.

Malprimis   A 230-mile diameter crater on Iapetus, a moon of Saturn.

Mare Acidalum A region on Mars.

Mars   The fourth major planet from the sun.

MEMS   Micro Electro Mechanical Systems. Tiny sub-millimeter machines.

Mercury   The planet closest to the sun.

methane   A chemical compound of carbon and hydrogen, it is the main component of natural gas\

Mimas   A moon of Saturn (Saturn I).

Miranda   Uranus V. The smaller and innermost of the five main moons of Uranus.

Mount Olympus A large extinct volcano on Mars. Largest volcanic mountain in the solar system. Also known as Olympus Mons

nanorobot   A microscopic programmable machine.

Neptune   T he eighth major planet from the sun.

Noachis   A region on Mars.

occult, occulting To block the view of. For instance, when the moon passes in front of a star, the star is said to be occulted by the moon.

Olympus Mons A large extinct volcano on Mars. Largest volcanic mountain in the solar system. also known as Mount Olympus.

opposition Astronomical term. When two planets or other objects are on opposite sides of the celestial sphere as viewed from a third, they are said to be at opposition. For example, if Mars is directly opposite the sun in the sky as viewed from Earth, Mars is said to be at opposition.

Orcus A trans-Neptunian dwarf planet in the Kuiper belt with a large moon (Vanth).

Orion A large constellation situated between Gemini and Taurus.

Pandora Also known as Saturn XVII, Pandora is one of the small moon shepherd moons Saturn's small, outer F ring.

Pax Romana Specifically, a time of relative peace during the Roman Empire. Generically, an Imperial peace enforced by hegemony.

Paxsi A topographical feature on Titan. Fictional site of a small settlement.

perfluoroisobutene As a chemical weapon, it is a blood agent, much like phosgene gas.

periapsis The close point of an elliptical orbit.

Phobos The innermost of the two moons of Mars.

phosphorus A highly reactive chemical element.

positron The positron is the antimatter counterpart of the electron.

pressure suit Also called a space suit. Protective wear for people in vacuum.

Procyon A bright star in the constellation Canis Minor.

Proteus The second-largest moon of Neptune (Neptune VIII).

proton A subatomic particle with a positive electric charge.

reflux column An apparatus for distilling chemicals such as alcohol.

regolith A layer of loose deposits covering solid rock consisting of dust, dirt, gravel, broken rock, etc.

Rhea A moon of Saturn (Saturn V).

Rigil Kent Also known as Alpha Centauri, it is the brightest star in the constellation Centaurus. Also, it is the closest known star to the solar system."

Sagittarius A stellar constellation situated between Scorpius and Capricornus.

Sarin gas A chemical weapon. It is a G-type nerve agent.

Saturn	The second largest planet of the solar system. Sixth major planet from the sun.
Saturn VIII	A moon of Saturn, also named Iapetus.
scintillation	A rapidly changing visual distortion, such as the twinkling of starlight by rapid changes in atmospheric density.
Selk	A 50-mile diameter crater on Titan. Fictional location of a large settlement.
Shangri-La	A region on Titan.
Shirin	A 6-mile diameter crater on Encleadus.
Sinlap	A 50-mile diameter crater on Titan. Fictional site of a large settlement containing an atmospherics plant and research facility.
Sinus Asperitatis	An area on the moon extending south from Mare Tranquilitatus.
Sioux	A northern plains tribe of Native Americans.
Sol	The proper name of the Sun.
solar system	The Sun and all that orbits it (planets, asteroids, comets…)
Solis	A region on Mars.
SOS	Save Our Ship. A universal distress call or request for help.
Stickney	A large crater on Phobos, the innermost moon of Mars. Fictional site of a large spaceport on Phobos.
Survey Corps	A fictional solar system exploration organization whose charter is to identify natural resources and install minimal initial or emergency infrastructure in the far reaches of the solar system.
Syrtis	A region on Mars.
Terra Corporation	A fictional Earth-based corporation whose original charter was to promote trade and provide engineering and infrastructure development services for the colonization of the solar system.
Terra Sirenum	A region on Mars.
Terraforming	A proposed process for creating Earth-like conditions on another moon or planet.
Tharsis	A region on Mars.
Theophilus	A 60-mile diameter crater on the Moon.
thruster	A small reaction engine for maneuvering spacecraft.
Titan	The largest moon of Saturn (Saturn VI), and the second largest moon in the solar system.

Tollan Terra   A region on Titan.

torch ship   A fictional spacecraft fitted with an atomic torch for propulsion.

Torricelli   A 20-mile diameter crater on the Moon.

transducer   A device that converts kinetic energy to electrical energy or visa-versa, for instance, a loudspeaker or microphone.

Triton   The largest moon of Neptune (Neptune I).

Valles Marineris   A canyon complex on Mars, largest in the solar system.

Vanth   Vanth is the moon of Orcus, a trans-Neptunian dwarf planet in the Kuiper belt.

Veles   A ringed topographical feature on Titan. Fictional site of Titan's largest settlement and spaceport.

Venus   The second planet from the sun, its orbit situated between those of Mercury and Earth.

white phosphorus   A self-igniting flammable compound made of phosphorus.

Xanadu   A region on Titan containing Veles.

yin-yang   The taichi symbol of dark and light or positive and negative. Similar in appearance to mated light and dark teardrop shapes.

Other titles by this author
offered by Blue & Gold Publishing:

Castle's Keeper: *A Song of Love and Justice* is a 73,000-word verse novel written in rhyming iambic heptameter and stands as a shining example of the verse-novel genre. It remains a bright oasis in the landscape of creative literature.

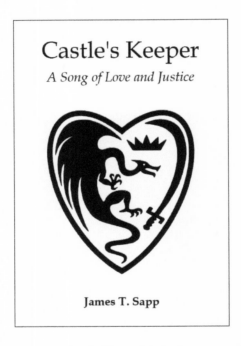

A poetic tale of love, war and rebellion, this is the story of a struggle to end the rule of a usurper's tyranny sparked by two prisoners' romance and the help they receive from unexpected places. Their journey is a celebration of hearts of passion and an affirmation of allegiances of honor, righteous leadership and the fight for freedom for all mankind.

238 pages

ISBN 978-1-312-74743-2 (Hardbound)
ISBN 978-1-312-82684-7 (Paperback)

A Hike On Mars and Other Rhymes

... is a collection of approximately 25 rhymes and rhyming short stories and photographs of varied topic which are sure to touch your heart and soothe your spirit.

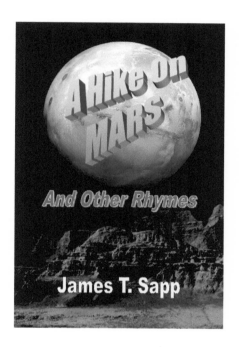

52 pages, available in Paperback only.

ISBN 978-1-79485-407-9

14 Fourteeners: *Selections in Iambic Heptameter*

Bring a moment of peace into your life!

In 14 Fourteeners, American verse-novelist James T. Sapp invites you over the horizon to the fruited plain of rhyming verse, with 14 poems and short stories for readers who revel in reading rhythmic rhymes, written in 14-count iambic heptameter.

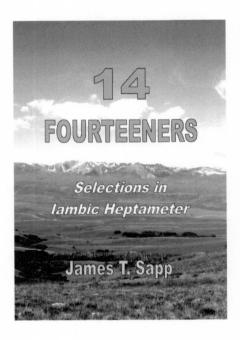

32 pages, available in Paperback only.

ISBN 978-1-79483-601-3